COMPLETE STORIES

VOLUME ONE

1976 - 2004

RUDY RUCKER

TRANSREAL BOOKS
LOS GATOS, CALIFORNIA

1st edition 2012. 2nd edition 2016. 3rd edition 2017.
4th edition 2018, 5th edition 2019, 6th edition 2020
Transreal Books, Los Gatos, California

Published in two print volumes, and as a single ebook.

The introduction and the notes on the individual stories
describe the previous publications. Later editions of
Complete Stories may expand to include later stories.

The cover painting for the print Volume One is *My Life
In A Nutshell*. The cover painting for the ebook and for
the print Volume Two is *Topology of the Afterworld*. Both
paintings are by Rudy Rucker.

Volume One Print: ISBN13: 9780984758562
Volume Two Print: ISBN13: 9780984758579
Ebook Edition: ISBN13: 9780984758517

www.transrealbooks.com

CONTENTS

INTRODUCTION

I've arranged my stories in the order in which they were composed. The later stories are more skillfully crafted, but the earlier ones have youth's reckless passion. Writing is something you learn on the job.

Over the years I've published five print anthologies of my stories:

The 57th Franz Kafka (Ace Books, 1983)
Transreal! (WCS Books, 1991)
Gnarl! (Four Walls Eight Windows, 2000)
Mad Professor (Thunder's Mouth Press, 2007)
Transreal Cyberpunk. with Bruce Sterling (Transreal Books, 2016)

All the stories from those books appear in my *Complete Stories*, along with about thirty new and previously uncollected tales. I'm publishing *Complete Stories* as an ebook, and as a two-volume print book.

But is this really the *Complete* collection of my stories? After all, with any luck, I'll go on to write a few more stories in the coming years. Well, as time rolls on, I'll simply make new editions of *Complete Stories*. This particular edition is the third, updated in 2017. Walt Whitman spent his whole life revising and expanding one single book of poetry: *Leaves of Grass*. *Complete Stories* can be my final anthology.

Flipping through my tales, I feel a mixture of nostalgia, pride, and embarrassment. I used to write as if women were wonderful, fascinating aliens—over the years I've gotten a little better at depicting them as people. Intoxication has remained a years-long literary obsession. My politics remain those of the hippies, punks, and grungers. But always the stories have their own wild humor and logic.

I can characterize my fiction with in terms of six concepts: (1) Thought experiments, (2) Power-chords, (3) Gnarliness, (4) Wit, (5) Transrealism, and (6) Collaboration.(1)

The notion of fictional *thought experiments* was made popular by Albert Einstein, who fueled his science speculations with so-called

Gedankenexperimenten. Thought experiments are a very powerful technique of philosophical investigation. In practice, it's intractably difficult to visualize the side effects of new technological developments. In order to tease out the subtler consequences of current trends, a complex fictional simulation is necessary. Inspired narration is a more powerful tool than logical analysis.

If I want to imagine, for instance, what our world would be like if ordinary objects were conscious, then the best way to make progress is to fictionally simulate a person discovering this.

The kinds of thought experiments I enjoy are different in intent and in execution from merely futurological investigations. My primary goal is not to make useful predictions that businessmen can use.

(2) I'm interested in exploring the human condition, with literary *power chords* standing in for archetypal psychic forces. When I speak of power chords in the context of fantastic literature, I'm talking about certain classic tropes that have the visceral punch of heavy musical riffs: blaster guns, spaceships, time machines, aliens, telepathy, flying saucers, warped space, faster-than-light travel, immersive virtual reality, clones, robots, teleportation, alien-controlled pod people, endless shrinking, the shattering of planet Earth, intelligent goo, antigravity, starships, ecodisaster, pleasure-center zappers, alternate universes, nanomachines, mind viruses, higher dimensions, cosmic computations that generate our reality, and, of course, the attack of the giant ants.

When I use a power chord, I try to do something fresh with the trope, perhaps placing it into an unfamiliar context, perhaps describing it more intensely than usual, or perhaps using it for an unheard-of thought experiment. I like it when my material takes on a life of its own. This leads to what I call the gnarly zone.

(3) In short, a *gnarly* process is complex and unpredictable without being random. If a story hews to some very familiar pattern, it feels stale. At the other extreme if absolutely anything can happen, a story becomes as unengaging as someone else's dream. The gnarly zone lies at the interface between logic and fantasy.

I see my tales as simulated worlds in which the characters and tropes and social situations bounce off each other like eddies in a turbulent wake, like gliders in a cellular automaton graphic, like vines twisting together in a jungle. When I write, I like to be surprised.

(4) My early mentor Robert Sheckley was a supremely *witty* writer. Over the years I got to spend a few golden hours in Sheckley's presence. And I think it's safe to say that wit, rather than mere humor, was his primary goal.

Wit involves describing the world as it actually is. You experience a release of tension when you notice a glitch. Something was off-kilter, and now you see what it was. The elephant in the living room has been named. The evil spirit has been incanted. Perceiving an incongruity in our supposedly smooth-running society provokes a shock of recognition and a concomitant burst of laughter.

Wit is a critical-satirical process that can be more serious than the "humorous" label suggests.

(5) *Transrealism* is a word that I coined in 1983. Early in my career, I found that using myself and my friends as characters in my science-fiction tales appeals to me. My actual life is the *real* part, and the *trans* part are the cool things that happen to the characters in my science-fiction stories.

In other words, I found that I could use the special effects and power chords of SF as a way to thicken and intensify my realistic material. The tools of science fiction can be a way to add a more artistic shape to the suppressed fears and desires that you inevitably incorporate into your fiction. To my way of thinking, not only is transrealism a good way to describe daily reality, transrealism is a path to understanding the higher reality which lies beyond.

(6) Regarding *collaboration*, note that nearly a third of the pieces in *Complete Stories* were written with other authors. As a practical matter, I get lonely working always on my own, and I welcome the chance to get into a collaborative exchange with another writer.

One of the remarkable things about science-fiction writing is the level of literary collaboration that it supports. In this respect, we're like scientists—and like musicians. Science fiction is a shared enterprise. And I'm grateful to be part of it.

Rudy Rucker,
Los Gatos, California
April 12, 2020

Jumpin' Jack Flash

It was a hell of a lecture. "Out of Your Mindscape," Jack had called it on the posters he'd put up all over town. The posters had a picture of a guy thinking a thought balloon of himself thinking a thought balloon of himself thinking etcetera and ad infinitum. Jack Flash was wild about infinite regresses that term.

I never could see the use of them myself. So my mind has an image of my mind which has an image of my mind and so on. So what. To me the fact that my mind is infinite is about as significant as the fact that human bodies have ten toes. Big Mind doesn't have anything to do with the finite-infinite distinction. And in terms of my immediate life, what counts in the Pure Land is having two minds instead of one mind…and who cares if they're infinite.

At the time I'm talking about, I was an English instructor at the same upstate New York college where Jack taught. People don't take to me, and I always have trouble keeping jobs on Earth. They were going to terminate my contract even though I'd just had a paper on *Invasion of the Body Snatchers* accepted by the *Journal of Popular Culture*.

I had just gotten the bad news from my chairman at lunch time, and I'd spent the afternoon going through my second to last spore of geezel. That's a pretty hefty dose for one sitting, so I was kind of lit when I walked into Jack's lecture.

Jack had drawn a big crowd, but they were pretty stiff. I was feeling reckless, and decided to loosen things up by laughing and stamping my feet every time Jack said, "infinity." Before long the place was rocking.

Jack likes to work a crowd; and once I'd gotten them started he kept bringing them higher…changing the subject, making slips of the tongue, and mixing in side-raps, one-liners, and level changes. It was a pleasure to watch him.

He was wearing light tan corduroys and a blue flannel Bean's shirt. He never stopped moving except when he wanted to say something heavy. For that he would lean forward on the desk and manage to look every one of us in the eye. But mostly he'd be writing things on the board, wiping chalk dust off on his corduroys, pushing his long brown hair back from his forehead, or taking his ratty black sweater on and off.

I couldn't really tell you what the talk was about. After all, I *was* pretty high, and I've never bothered to master a lot of the standard human concepts. Roughly speaking, it seemed like Jack thought he could prove that every possible universe exists. Considering my background, you'd think I'd be interested in what he might have to say on this topic…but you'd be wrong. I just wanted to lesnerize a couple of people and get the hell back to the Pure Land.

Without thinking about it too hard, I suspected that most of what Jack said was wrong anyway…but it was fun listening to him rave. Quite a few people came up to him afterwards, and I stuck around.

After a while it was down to just one chick talking to Jack. I walked up to join their conversation. "That was splendid, Jack," I said.

"Thanks, Simon," he answered. He turned to the girl, "What do you say the three of us go get a beer?" He had already put on his brown leather jacket.

"All right," the girl said, and we started out. I'd never seen her before. She reminded me of a Mercedes-Benz…classic features, and a flawless exterior, gliding along on smoothly meshing joints.

"I'm Si Bork," I said to her, hoping for a handshake.

"Helen," she said nodding, and then picked up the thread of her conversation with Jack. "I mean, how can you be sure that those parallel universe you were talking about really exist? Can you leave your body?"

Jack hated to answer no to a question like that, so he just shrugged. "How could I ever tell?" And then he was back on his favorite subject, his own ideas. "I've got a whole new thing I'm working on now. Did it ever occur to you that black holes and white holes really exist in your Mindscape?"

Actually he wasn't far off, but I wasn't going to start blabbing everything I knew. Not yet anyway. If I played it right Jack would probably go along with me…maybe…and if I could just find someone else…

Helen was talking quietly to Jack as we went into the bar. I was sure she was already wondering how to get rid of this obvious loser, Simon Bork, so that she and Jack could really rap. But I knew Jack wanted me to stick around, and I started trying to make friends with Helen while Jack got us a pitcher.

We exchanged a few listless facts about what we did for a living… she was in medical school…and then a silence fell. I had to say something interesting.

"You remind me of a Mercedes," I blurted out finally, unable to come up with anything more abstract. She gave me her full attention for a few seconds…sizing me up.

I know what I look like…hell, I build this body from scratch every morning, including the glasses. Gold-rimmed glasses, set deep into eye sockets with colorless eyes. Prematurely bald, with a few lank strands across the top. Twitchy face with a rabbity mouth. The kind of guy who eats Oreos for dessert after every one of the crummy little meals he cooks in his rented room.

Helen shook her head, "You look like a Studebaker yourself." But as she said it she patted my arm, and I could feel a tingle…almost a shock…pass up the arm and into my bodymass.

She was so beautiful. Teeth, mouth, swelling breasts, her voice. This was as close to a girl this beautiful as I had ever been. If only I could get closer…I closed my eyes to skren her better. It was so relaxing to be near this woman. She seemed so kind…perhaps I could tell her…

"I have this problem…" I started to say, but a gassy wet vibrato had crept into my voice. I was starting to flow! Beneath my shirt the stiff orange buds were already forming on the transparent hide covering my swirling green bodymass. Helen's eyes widened as my face sagged.

I couldn't stop myself from shlubbering out, "I want to lesnerize you." Why did I have to go and tip my hand like that, a part of my mind wondered bleakly. Helen had jumped to her feet, and when I slid to the floor I could see her shiny black underwear. It took the full force of my will to keep from beginning to rave in the mother tongue.

Not that she could have any doubts about what I was. In seconds she would begin to scream, and things would get worse until finally I would have to chirp again. I couldn't figure out how I could have let myself go like this. For two years I had held human shape except when I got into my werble…disguised as the bed in my cheap, but well-locked, boarding-house room.

But now sitting here with this woman my control had suddenly snapped…and I was flopping around under the table like a sun-ripened manta ray. This would make the third mission in a row I had blown. Any second she would scream.

I tensed myself and prepared to chirp. When the humans discover a "Venusian," we always take one of them with us. When forced out of my body, I convert its mass into a single pulse of electromagnetic energy…a chirp…which eventually reaches the Pure Land and is reconstructed there. They've got a radio-telescope hooked up to a vat of undifferentiated tissue.

Just so that the few humans in the know will think twice before attacking a "Venusian," we always make it a point to beam the chirp through someone's head on the way out. The energy density hard-boils their brain like an egg in a microwave oven.

But still no one came…and there was no scream. Something brushed against me. Something soft…it was the girl! Helen had sat down, taken off her shoes, and was gently kneading my bodymass. I grew bristles which slipped between her toes, and she clenched and gently tugged at them. Unmistakable pheromones were drifting down. I couldn't believe my good fortune. Helen was a V-sexual.

There was still time to save this mission. I forced myself back into human form and crawled out from under the table. Just as I stood up, Jack Flash came back with a pitcher of beer. "Was just talking to a friend," he explained, jerking his head towards a group of backs at the bar. "And what have you been doing down there, Simon…checking Helen's oil?"

I got back in my chair. "Just dropped some change," I said with a synthetic chuckle. My feet hadn't gelled yet, and Helen continued her gentle treading and plucking.

"Si spent the whole time you were gone under the table, Jack," Helen said, withdrawing her feet. "He was really behaving strangely." Her eyes bored into me with the twisted hunger of a V-sexual. I loved every minute of it. If I had to, I'd chirp and the hell with it. If not…

Jack looked at me with respect. "Didn't know you had it in you, Si." We all drank in silence for a minute. Finally Helen broke the relaxed silence.

"I don't see how it would make sense, really, to talk about moving from one parallel world to another, Jack. If you were in both of them already, then what would there be to move?"

Jack ran his hand back along the central part of his straight hair. "I am in many of the different parallel Earths…and in each of them I think that's the only one I'm really in. But there should be some sort of higher consciousness which could…" His voice trailed off. I liked that about Jack, that he couldn't figure this one out. I knew the answer to Helen's question. After all, I come from a parallel universe.

A "Venusian's" mission on Earth is to reproduce by lesnerization, and then return to the Pure Land. Once enough of us have done this, there will be a web of consciousness connecting our universe and yours, and we will be able to draw the two closer together so that even the weak and diseased members of our race can move freely between "Venus" and the Earth. Several members of my swarm have completed successful missions, and they have described to me in detail what it is like to have the sort of multiple trans-universal consciousness which Jack and Helen were puzzling out.

Suddenly I spoke up, "Jack, I know a lot about parallel universes." Helen gave me a cautioning glance, but I continued, "I have certain connections…"

Jack was laughing. "Connections with who, Si? Galaxy X?"

"Why don't we go back to my room and talk it over. The three of us."

Jack still didn't get it. He thought I wanted to turn them on to some dope. So of course he came along. And Helen…she and I dropped a little behind and she slipped her hand into my shirt. No human had ever touched me there before.

If a "Venusian" is exposed he chirps, and no evidence of his existence is left…save for the mysterious death of one of the people who discovered him. There are thousands of us on Earth now, but few of us are ever detected…and the establishment chooses to ignore whatever fragmentary proofs of our existence arise. But there are rumors and, more important, there is subconscious knowledge. V-sexuals are people who have fallen in love with this subconsciously-sensed other presence in the world. V-sexuality is, for obvious reasons, primarily a latent perversion…but as a few lucky "Venusians" know, a V-sexual can move to intense overtness in the space of a few minutes. I could hardly wait. And if we could get Jack to join in…

It takes a minute to get my door open. I have three locks. Jack began kidding me about it. "What have you got in there Simon, a suitcase of gold?"

"You'll see," I said as the door finally opened. Jack went in first, and Helen came in after me, her hand resting lightly on my back. I wanted to triple lock the door behind me, but I feared this might alarm them.

The door opens into the kitchenette end of the room. You can tell it's the kitchenette because that part of the room has a linoleum floor. Sometimes when I am too tired to cook, I just break some eggs on the floor, pour oil and ketchup on top of them, and then flow around on the linoleum until I have ingested everything.

But now I had company. "Beer?" I inquired. They were sitting on my werble at the other end of the room. The only other place to sit was the chair by the kitchenette table.

"Sure," Jack said, "But we really can't stay too long, Simon." He thought he was going somewhere alone with Helen. Couldn't he tell that now she only had eyes for me?

I got out three beers and glided over to the werble…my body movements suggestively fluid. Helen couldn't take her eyes off me. "Tell Jack, Helen," I said. "Tell him, and then I'll let you undress me."

With a visible effort Jack maintained his cool. "What makes you think Helen would want to undress you, Si? And what's she supposed to tell me?"

"Si is a 'Venusian,'" Helen said huskily. "I never knew if they were real or not. I've always...I've always..." her face was working, and she couldn't get the rest of the sentence out. She slid a hand back under my shirt and fingered a stiff orange bud. Her hand was damp.

Jack jumped up off the bed and began moving towards the door. "You go out that door, and I'll fry your brain," I said evenly. Helen was moaning now, running her moist, trembling fingers over my face.

"Flow now while I'm touching you, darling," she breathed.

I let my head go slack, and it began sinking down through the collar of my shirt. Helen was fumbling frantically at our clothes. I couldn't see Jack anymore since I'd let my head merge into my bodymass, but I could still skren him. He had stopped near the door and was hesitating... his emotions a mixture of fear and curiosity. Finally curiosity won out.

"I can't believe this," Jack said desperately. He ripped the top off another beer from the icebox. He'd left his first one by the werble, and he was scared to get close to me. He sat down on the kitchen chair. "I'll watch," he said shakily, "But I'm not going to let you lesnerize us."

That's what he thought. I didn't bother answering...it would have been too much trouble to form a mouth. It didn't seem like Helen was ever going to get my clothes off, so I reduced viscosity and flowed out of my left pant leg and onto the floor. She had gotten her shirt and bra off, and she lay down to rub her stiff-nippled breasts across me. It felt nice.

For the next half hour or so she sat there kneading and molding me...like a three-year-old girl at the nursery school play-dough table. Only they don't moan as much in nursery school. Somewhere along the line she got her pants off too, and I grew a few suitable protuberances. I liked that Jack was watching us. He might be smarter than me, he might be human...but I had the girl.

I guess Helen and I made something like the ultimate donkey show. When she finally got off me and lay panting on my werble, Jack was so hot that he pulled down his pants and jumped her. I flowed closer and laid a gentle pseudopod across the back of his thighs.

He twisted away, screaming, "No, Simon, not yet, don't lesnerize us! Please not yet! I've just got to...get to..." He was thrusting in and out frantically, and in a few seconds it was all over.

I should have taken them then and there...but lesnerization goes a lot smoother if the human hosts are completely willing. It's a simple operation. You just run a pseudopod up the person's nose, suck out their brain, and fill their head up with part of your bodymass. Over the next year, your offspring slowly absorbs all of the host body, learning how to model it in the process. It's the way we've always reproduced on Earth. When we fission like this, we have to split off two buds...baby "Venusians"...so we always have to lesnerize two people at once.

If I could only get those buds into Jack and Helen's skulls I'd be free to chirp back to the Pure Land. My mind drifted pleasantly as I thought of rejoining my swarm...a respected and successful colonizer... possessor of trans-universal consciousness.

I formed Si Bork's body again and lay down next to Jack and Helen. "How would you like to come forever?" I said softly. "That's what lesnerization feels like...an orgasm that never stops. All I have to do is reach up through your nose and gently touch your brain," no point telling them about what I'd do next, "and, wham, you're as enlightened as Gautama Buddha." Sex and enlightenment. It makes a nice package.

But they both looked a little doubtful. "What do you mean when you say 'wham,' hon?" Helen asked.

And then Jack chimed in, "Don't you think it might be risky to fool around with a person's brain like that?" He covered his nose defensively.

"Look," I said, readjusting my features to look fatherly, "No 'Venusian' would ever dream of doing anything which might harm a human. We want to be your allies...your partners in a new trans-universal culture. Now I know you've heard the rumors about lesnerization. Take it from me, they're all lies put out by chauvinist reactionaries. Lesnerization is just a way of getting to know each other better. Jack," I patted his shoulder, "Once you've lesnerized with me, you'll have more new stuff in that skull of yours than you can possible imagine. Lesnerization is simply a way for me to take things that I know and put them into your head."

They shifted uneasily and looked at each other. Finally Jack spoke. "What do you say we get dressed and go talk about it over a pizza. I can dig where you're coming from. Brain-to-brain communication. But I've got to have some food first." He pulled his pants back up.

"That's a good idea," Helen said, fastening her bra. "I'm famished." She began buttoning up her blouse. "Where is 'Venus' anyway, Si? And why are you all so secretive?"

I couldn't believe how distant she suddenly seemed. First she's all over me, and then I ask one little favor, and she starts asking questions like a hick at the freak show. I felt like just chirping the hell out of there and blowing one of them away. But if I went back to the Pure Land without lesnerizing anyone they'd just stuff me in a ship back to Earth...or worse. So I politely answered her question as I dressed.

"Actually, Helen, what you call 'Venus' is in one of those parallel universes Jack likes to talk about. In a way it's in the same place where your Venus is, only 'Venus' is a different superspace location. We don't call it 'Venus' though. We call it the Pure Land."

"But how can the Pure Land be where Venus is without really being there?" Helen responded. Jack interrupted impatiently before I could answer.

"It has a different fourth-dimensional location is all, Helen. You can read about it in that *Geometry and Relativity* book I wrote." We were all dressed and on our way out of the apartment. Jack turned to me. "What I want to hear is your answer to her other question, Simon. If you 'Venusians' are just here to make friends, then why do you sneak around so that only the nuts believe in you?"

I cleared my throat nervously. "We're scared, Jack. Scared of small-minded xenophobic bigots. We're really a very weak race. If we tried to land a ship openly, the pigs would blast us out of the sky. We want to come out in the open, but it's not time yet. We need to know more about human psychology first, and we need time to spread the right kind of rumors about us." I smiled self-deprecatingly.

But Jack seemed to be becoming more hostile. He was probably just jealous that I'd gotten more off Helen than him. "You say you're weak, Simon, but didn't you threaten to fry my brain just a little while ago?"

I generated a chuckle. "Oh that. Well, I *could* fry your brain...hard-boil it really...but only by converting my body into pure energy. That's how we get back to the Pure Land. We call it chirping." I explained the process to them, meanwhile trying to put my arm around Helen, but she shrugged it off.

Although it was supper time, the restaurant was almost empty. I'd never been there before, but Jack seemed to be a regular. He stopped to chat with the guy making pizzas in the front window.

I steered Helen to a table in the rear...I was hoping to lesnerize them after they'd had a good meal and a few beers. I was prepared to act forcibly if necessary...at the worst I'd lose a pseudopod. I smiled moistly at Helen. "Did you have a nice time in my room?"

"You know I did," she said haltingly, "But I'm scared of what I could become if I keep seeing you. And I don't know how I'll be able to stay away." She began crying, and reached out to touch my face. "One part of me already wants to do it again...especially with a man watching and thinking I'm the lowest kind of slut..." She hesitated, then resumed in a strained voice, "But if I kept doing that, what would happen to the rest of me...to *Helen*?" She covered her face with her hands.

Someone had turned the jukebox on, and over a background of moans and abrupt guitar chords a voice crooned, "Well it's all right now, in fact it's a gas…" Helen was slipping away from me…but where was Jack? Surely he would listen to reason. I skrenned him walking across the room. I started to turn, but then he was already upon me, and he sank an eight-inch knife into my neck.

That did it. No more Mr. Nice Guy. Jack Flash was going to get it. I relaxed my hold on the knotted spacetime which made up my body and put everything I had into my chirp…carefully beaming it at the spot behind me where he crouched.

But I should have looked first. The bastard had an aluminum pizza pan in front of his face…and I bounced off it and out through the ceiling.

It doesn't take long to get to the Pure Land from Earth. You get a faster-than-light phase-shift going in your pulse, lock it real, tear loose, and jump spacetime sheets. Once you're back in the home space, it's just a matter of a little simple tube-surfing. The only hard thing about it is that the whole trip seems to happen at once…so you have to know just what you're going to do before you start.

I didn't get much of a welcome at home when they found out I'd screwed up another mission. They said I could either go back to Earth or spend fifteen years in the tissue fields. I was frantic to revenge myself on Jack, and even more frantic to get back between Helen's legs, so I would have been perfectly willing to go back to Earth…except that the trip back takes so long.

You can't chirp from the Pure Land to Earth, since there's no one waiting on Earth to reconstitute you. You have to go the long way… around the Horn, as it were. That is, you have to take a spaceship out the collapsed star Gouda X-1, fly in, bounce off the ring singularity into a new universe, and fly back to Earth. It's dangerous and the whole trip takes about ten years proper-time. So the tissue fields didn't necessarily sound that bad.

I asked for a week to think it over. They gave me two days, and I went out into the plaza promising to be back.

It felt good to be flowing across the intricately grooved stones again with the swarm. We aren't very big on individual personalities, and before long I'd almost forgotten I'd ever left. A warm hydro-carbon rain drizzled down, and I circled around the plaza in the figures of the swarm's never-ending dance.

The pimpled hides of my fellow "Venusians" felt familiar and comforting…but still I couldn't put the feel of Helen's breasts and thighs out of my mind…she was so smooth…so slippery.

I realized I was horny, and found a willing fellow-citizen…whom you might as well think of as a girl. We flowed away from the plaza together, and our individual consciousness returned. She told me her name was Pasmit.

As we passed through a grove of geezel fungi I paused to pry loose one of the immature spores. I threw it to Pasmit, she digested a little of it and threw it back to me.

We went on for several versts this way, finally stopping when the singing in our tissues could no longer be ignored. We pressed our vents together, guided by the sensitive bristles surrounding them; and then we let our bodymasses mingle for a timeless interval. The hydro-carbon drizzle increased, and the geezel spore rolled stealthily back towards its mother fungus. Finally we stopped pulsing and slid apart. The gamma-radiation is much stronger out in the country, and every-thing was suffused with a kindly glow.

I must have been mad to want to go back to Earth, I thought. Pas-mit and I could build a burrow near the tissue fields. I'd get strong and green working in the fields, and every night we'd go dance with the swarm. It had been good enough for my ancestors; why shouldn't it be good enough for me? There was just one thing…

"Pasmit," I vibrated, "Could you do something for me…some-thing special?"

She snuggled closer to me. "What is it, Sibork?"

"Could you form your bodymass like this, and this, and this…" I gestured rapidly, "And then could you rub on me? I'll show you how I mean."

She burbled, and started to do it. I sighed and went limp, images of Helen filling my mind. Pasmit leaned over me and began to knead my bodymass with her hands. Quaveringly I pulsed my next request, and extruded the appropriate protuberances. She started to do it…

But abruptly she stopped, and her pulsations became harsh. "But this is *human* shape! You want me to be like a *human*, Sibork!" She recoiled and rapidly re-assumed "Venusian" shape. "You're a filthy H-sexual!" she shrilled, "Don't come *near* me!"

Pasmit delivered her parting shot as she began flowing back towards the swarm. "You're not fit to live in the Pure Land anymore, Sibork. You're tainted. You'll have to go back to Earth tomorrow."

I knew she was right. I couldn't even blame her for feeling the way she did…I used to feel the same way about H-sexuals.

I spent an uneasy night sleeping under a rock, and the next morning I shipped out for Earth again. Despite what I'd told Jack, we "Venusians" are virtually indestructible. So our spaceships do not need any very complex life-support systems.

My ship consisted, basically, of one hundred kilos of geezel and the shell of a nauton, a sort of gigantic fungus-snail common in the Pure Land. I packed the geezel into the front of the cone-shaped spiral shell, crawled in after, and sealed the back off with a specially thickened section of my hide.

During the trip I would feed off the geezel, and propel the ship by converting some of the food energy into a stream of ions, to be blown out of an aperture in my hide door. In effect, I fart myself through space. Given the steady force and the small mass of my ship, I can reach relativistic velocities rather easily...and once one travels close enough to the speed of light, time dilation sets in. As far as my body's aging processes are concerned, the one hundred light-year trip to Gouda X-1 takes only five years.

Even five years might seem like a long time to be wadded up inside a nauton shell, but I have the ability to let my individual consciousness go totally dormant...turning the control of my body over to what we call "Big Mind" in the Pure Land.

I spent five years in a trance, pooting along towards Gouda X-1. When I was not too far from it, the intense gravitational radiation jolted me back into existence.

For a few moments I was totally disoriented. I had no idea where I was...for a second I didn't even know if I was "Venusian" or human. Ahead of me I skrenned a hot bluish star with a huge tufty horn of flame growing out of it. The name Beetroot 322 popped into my mind. The horn fed an immense spiral of brightly glowing gas which was twisted around a region of what seemed to be absolute blackness.

I was falling...at almost the speed of light...down towards the collapsed star which nestled in the center of the spiral of gas it had pulled out of its companion star. The collapsed star was Gouda X-1, and at its very center was the gate which led out of the Pure Land universe.

As I drew closer I could see the ring singularity that lay at the heart of this whirlpool of space and time. If a star such as Gouda X-1 is rotating fast enough when it collapses to form a black hole, then the singularity at its center takes the shape of a ring. Space is infinitely curved at each point of this ring, and to venture too close to it is to be torn apart atom from atom. But if you manage to go *through* the ring, something quite different happens.

Think of the many parallel universes as being a stack of so many pieces of cloth. Now imagine punching a circular hole through this stack of fabrics, and then sewing all of these spacetime sheets together along the edges of the circles you punched out. That's what a ring singularity is like…almost.

But I left out what's *inside* the ring. Well, when you go through the ring you enter an antimatter, anti-gravity anti-universe…which repels you, spits you back like a squeezed watermelon seed.

When you come back through the ring, you go onto one of those many sheets of spacetime which are sewed together along the ring singularity…and if you're lucky you come out where and when you wanted to.

Actually it's not really luck that determines in which universe and at what time in that universe you come out. It's more like you come out where you *expect* to come out.

Causality takes a beating when minds and singularities interact. But Big Mind doesn't need causality anyway…every instant of every universe springs into existence together, and synchronicity is the natural order of things.

Anyway, there I was in a flexible nauton shell being sucked down into the heart of Gouda X-1 at something like the speed of light. And Jack Flash thought *he'd* been far out. I had to laugh thinking of that jerk sneaking up behind me like that with his knife and pizza pan. When I got to Earth this time things were going to be different. Because I was planning to get back there before I'd left.

The singularity was dead ahead now, a bright ring a few kilometers in diameter. Bright isn't the word for it, really. You know how a mirror looks when it bounces sun into your eyes?

All of Gouda X-1's mass had gone into that circle of light and, friend, it was a *perfect* circle. It was like looking at the ultimate platonic circle in Big Mind, the circle from which all other circles derive their feeble and reflected reality.

As you can imagine, the gravitational force coming off that ring was incredible. I was thin as a needle and I whisked through without even slowing down. But as soon as I'd gone through I was in an anti-universe, and every particle of that universe wanted me out of there. This was the most dangerous part of the trip. If some piece of anti-matter happened by and brushed into me I'd be annihilated. If I didn't steer just right the anti-universe would throw me against the ring and I'd be annihilated. If I panicked and chirped, my energy pulse would be trapped in an endless pendulum orbit around the ring and, for all practical purposes, I'd be annihilated.

There was also the matter of bouncing out into the right space and time. I could already see myself looking in through the pizza-parlor window at Jack Flash getting a knife and pan from his friend behind the counter. Jack looked scared and I felt a little sorry for him. Maybe

I shouldn't suck his brain out after all…but how else could I establish a trans-universal consciousness?

My attention snapped back to the situation at hand. The repulsive force from the anti-universe counterpart of Gouda X-1's mate, Beet-root 322, had decelerated me from the speed of light to rest, and had already started forcing me back towards the ring singularity. This was the roughest part of the ride. One second you're going 99.999 percent the speed of light one way, and the next instant you're going 99.999 per-cent the speed of light the other way. There weren't many "Venusians" who could handle the ring singularity bounce-trip. I'd been trained for it from budhood, and even so it must have taken five years off my life every time I did it.

As I zoomed back through the ring, I struggled to keep from blacking out, and I kept my mind fixed on frightened Jack Flash in the pizza-parlor window…and on Helen, across the table from me with her face in her hands…I'm sorry Jack…I love you Helen…

I burst out of the ergosphere of Gouda X-1 traveling so fast that it would have taken a photon a year to gain five meters on me. I had some slowing down to do before I got to Earth…if there was an Earth in this space.

The ship was traveling rear-end first now, and I began absorbing geezel and shooting out the ion-steam again. Five years of this and I would have decelerated back to rest. I had started out with revenge and lust in my mind, but for some reason I was now suffused with thoughts of peace and love. Good old Jack. Dear sweet Helen. Even my depart-ment chairman seemed almost "Venusian." I drifted into a trance and let Big Mind take over.

I was so anxious about missing Earth that I woke up a few months early. Those were peaceful months, hurtling towards the Sun with a speed that I steadily diminished. There was plenty of time to think about what I would do on Earth.

I began to wonder about the wisdom of reproducing by lesneriza-tion. The whole idea of reproducing ourselves on Earth by planting the buds inside people's skulls went back to Brow, the first "Venusian" who ever survived the ring singularity bounce-trip to any of the inhab-ited versions of Earth. Disguised as a Dutch mathematician, Brow had advanced the destructive mathematical philosophy called intuitionism, and he had lesnerized dozens, perhaps hundreds of people before chirp-ing back to the Pure Land. Many of the "Venusians" now on Earth are Brow's descendants, although every year a few new colonizers, such as myself, make the ring singularity bounce-trip to one of the Earths.

But what had made Brow feel that the only safe place to grow a bud was inside a human skull? At home we grow buds in nautons, in geezel plants…sometimes even in the ground. What gave Brow, and the rest of us, our conviction that on Earth we should only reproduce by the murder of innocent human beings?

The power of suggestion, that's what. A solitary "Venusian" on an alien Earth behaves as humans consciously or subconsciously expect a blob from outer space to behave. As I explain in my article on *Invasion of the Body Snatchers*, blobs from outer space symbolize the unchecked id. With their natural fear that their lower, more bestial desires will take over their minds, what could be more natural than for people to expect the "Venusians" to reproduce by lesnerization. Nobody had told Jack what lesnerization was…in his guts he *knew* I wanted to eat his brain… so he'd come after me with the knife.

Why couldn't I break this cycle? Why couldn't humans and "Venusians" *really* be trans-universal allies? But a less idealistic part of me was still wondering how to safely reproduce myself on Earth if not by lesnerizing. Would not the humans hunt out and destroy a bud which was hidden anywhere other than inside a human skull? And if I failed to achieve trans-universal consciousness this time I could never return to the Pure Land.

The topography of the Earth below me looked familiar, so I knew I'd bounced into a universe pretty much like the one where Jack had knifed me. I splashed down in one of the Finger Lakes, formed Si Bork's body again, and swam ashore. I didn't feel any special need to rush or to stall. If I was going to show up at the right time, I would.

It was around dusk when I reached the highway and stuck out my thumb. I'd grown my own clothes this time, and I looked like any other hitchhiker. After awhile a pickup truck stopped. The driver was an old farmer, bound for Livingston, my destination.

I told him I was an English prof at the college there, and we talked a little about monster movies. He had a strange way of putting his fingers under his nose and sniffing them when he talked about creatures from outer space. Was he trying to tell me something? When I looked closely, I seemed to see bumps under his faded cotton shirt…

"Are you 'Venusian?'" I asked him, and then added something that a human would have taken for a cough, but which was really a Pure Land proverb meaning something like, "Once you're born, the worst has already happened."

Without answering he pulled the pickup off the road and turned to look directly at me. His features were flowing with joy and we embraced.

We sat there maybe a half hour, pulsing each other's like stories back and forth. His name was Roon, and he'd come from a bud some "Venusian" had lesnerized into the body of the farmer Roon still impersonated. The farmer and his wife had been UFO enthusiasts willing to go along with anything an alien suggested, and Roon's sib-bud had agreed that lesnerizing was wrong, and the sib-bud had gone down to the Pentagon, trying to tell them the truth. Roon had never heard from his sib-bud again, and figured he'd either chirped out or joined the CIA.

Roon raised pigs now, and when I asked him why we couldn't just grow our buds in his pigs' bodies, he was shocked. "Pigs are lower forms of life, Sibork!"

"So are humans," I responded. "And for that matter, so are we." I told him my theory about why Brow had acted as he did. "It doesn't have to be this way," I concluded. "If we stop murdering people, we'll be able to come out in the open and really befriend them. I've found it's almost impossible to lie to a human." Which reminded me…if I was going to stop Jack from knifing me, I'd better get a move on.

Roon dropped me off near the pizza-parlor, and we agreed to meet again. Now to explain what happened next, I'm going to have to introduce a little notation. Roon dropped me off near the pizza-parlor, right? Now if I had walked down, looked in the window, and seen a "Venusian" talking with Helen at the rear table…who would that be? Me. But to keep things from getting too confusing, let's call that "Venusian" me*, reserving the word *me* for the "Venusian" looking in the window.

It was just about night now, maybe seven o'clock, and I walked down the street towards the pizza-parlor. Everything was clicking. I knew that Jack was going to be standing in that window.

And he was. He'd just turned the jukebox on, and was picking up a pizza pan and an eight-inch knife from the counter. At the back of the room I could see my* back and Helen, her face in her hands.

I opened the door and walked in. Jack had paused to exchange a few last words with the counterman and he didn't see me. I walked over to the jukebox and kicked it so hard that the needle slid across the record and the machine turned itself off. He whirled around, knife at the ready.

"Hi, Jack."

I was ready for him, and there was no way in the world he could get that knife into me. I could see that realization sink into him, and he mumbled something about getting the knife to cut up the pizza. He hadn't noticed yet that I* was still sitting at the table.

"Jack," I began, "I've been through a lot of changes since the last time I saw you…"

He laughed nervously, "It's been all of two minutes, Simon. What kind of..." and then he broke off. I* was walking across the room towards him.

I* was glad to see that I had made it in time...but I* had always known that I would. I wondered how I* had known that, since I didn't recall having expected anyone to come save me the last time around. I* pointed out that that had been a different universe...and I realized that since things were happening differently here from the last time, it must be that I really had bounced out of Gouda X-1 into a universe just a shade different from the one where I had gotten knifed.

While Jack was staring at me*, I deftly took the knife away from him. I* thought that was nicely done, and we exchanged a smile.

"We've got double consciousness," I and I* said to Jack happily. He looked confused.

"Where did *you* come from?" he said to me, "Are you Si's twin brother, or what?"

"Actually I'm the same person as Sibork*," I answered, "Only I come from a different universe." And then I began laughing, "I've finally got it."

"Got what?" Jack said, expressionlessly looking from me to me*.

"Trans-universal consciousness," I* answered, and then , "So I* don't need to lesnerize anyone anymore. You were right to be scared of it, and I'm* sorry for wanting to do it to you." Finally Jack broke into a smile.

"Tell me more," he said. So I* did.

Meanwhile I walked over to Helen. She had stopped crying and was sitting there watching the conversation in amazement. "Helen," I said, "I love you, I can make you happy. Just because you love a 'Venusian,' doesn't make you bad. You have broader horizons than other people is all."

She smiled up at me, "And now there's two of you?"

I smiled back. The Pure Land could wait.

Note on "Jumpin' Jack Flash"

Written in Spring, 1976.
The 57th Franz Kafka, Ace Books, 1983.

This apprentice exercise touches upon some of my favorite SF themes: time-travel, UFO aliens, brain-eating, and sex. It also marks the start of my "transreal" practice of modeling some of my characters on myself, my friends and my long-suffering family. Loosely speaking, I'm Jack Flash and Si Bork was my Geneseo English professor friend Lee Poague. Lee also appears in *White Light*, and his younger brother Dennis became the Stahn "Sta-Hi" Mooney character of my *Ware* series of novels. Not that my family, friends or I are really very much like my fiction characters. The distinction is comparable to that between an actor's real life and the life of the characters whom he or she plays.

The word "geezel" is an homage to the master Robert Sheckley, who once used it to stand for a kind of alien food; and "lesnerize" is from a Golden Age story that used it to mean "sneeze."

Enlightenment Rabies

His boots looked so perfect. Two dark parabolas in a field of yellow; slight three-dimensional interest provided by the scurf strewn about. Time to act. Boone took a newspaper the size of a bubblegum wrapper from the stack at the android's elbow.

"Three dollars."

Handing over the money, he again forgot where he was. Or entered another spacetime. "The cave and the marketplace" is what he called it. Buying the newspaper was marketplace, and grooving on his boots was cave. This was an old Zen distinction comparable to the One/Many distinction of the Greeks. Boone tried to live at the interface of complementary world-views; but more often than not he was just really out of it.

He passed through the news-shop's air-curtain and glanced up at the sky. A shareholder jostled him, then remarked, "They're saying it'll rain tonight, uh."

"I don't care what they're saying. I make my own weather," Boone snapped.

The shareholder's face froze behind his stunglasses and began to fade. Boone elaborated, "If you let those glasses tell you what tomorrow's weather is today, then you don't have your tomorrow. You have their tomorrow. Lose the consensus, Jimmy. Wake up, uh."

The shareholder gave him a cautious but superior smile. "You had your vaccination?" he asked with exaggerated clarity, and walked on.

Boone fell into a dream looking at the gauzy white clouds against the light and bright November sky. Good day for something. He put some music in his workspace and started walking. The shareholder's question surfaced in his mind.

Vaccination. Damn. Seemed like they'd just been through all that a few weeks ago. Boone had nearly been swept that time. He'd caught the disease…"Dirtbug" they'd been calling it…he'd caught it and would have died if he hadn't been able to score some anti-toxin. Had cost him ten grand, and he'd had to kill a man to get the money. This time he'd do it the easy way and let the state vaccinate him.

Boone sat down on a bench and took the newspaper out of his packet. It was really a small white-light hologram. He held it up to his eye and looked through to see an old-fashioned newspaper spread out on a table. Social hygiene was page four.

…tragic death of three patients at Veterans' hospital…ten soldiers at research center…new virus isolated…disease has been named "Enlightenment Rabies"…

Boone laughed bitterly. There must be more people working the interface than he'd realized. The state invented the diseases and spread them, but it always named them after some perceived social ill. This time it was enlightenment, next time it might be underconsumption or dirty teeth. In any case, the point was that if you were too wasted or stubborn to go get the state-administered antidote you were going to get swept.

…cramps, buboes, and convulsions ending in death by suffocation…crash vaccination program…available November 17–20 at these local centers…

Boone checked the date on the paper. Today was the 20th. Now where was the nearest center? After a few minutes he knew where to go. Off the interface, brought down in the marketplace, running scared like they wanted.

Halfway down the block Boone bumped into his friend Ace High. Ace was standing on the sidewalk with his head thrown far back and his arms wrapped around his legs. The Metal Crane position.

Boone stopped to look at Ace for a minute. Ace's eyes were aimed at him, but there was nobody home. Boone was clearly in the presence of an unvaccinated fellow-citizen.

"Hey Ace," he said, trying to straighten up his friend's bent body, "Come on, uh, it's eigenstate time."

Ace High was infinitely differentiable. He got the message and locked in on the signal. His face split like a melon when he smiled, as he did now, uncleaned teeth glistening in the sun. "Why…does the doctor… have no face?" he crooned, guessing Boone's meaning. "Lez go, boss."

Boone and Ace High started off for the vaccination center. It was easier to be going together. That way if you forgot where you were going, your friend might still know.

"Let's get some stunglasses on," Boone suggested, feeling through his pockets. He still had his pair. Ace had lost his, so they decided to stop in at the next news-shop to get some.

Boone was already feeling the effects of his stunglasses. His mind was filled with safety tips, news updates, and new product information.

Purposefully he went into the news-shop and bought a pair of stunglasses for Ace High. It was an attractive little shop with a big multiplexed holographic display in the corner. If Boone looked in just the right direction, the image his stunglasses produced fit right on top of the image displayed in the news-shop. An indescribably beautiful moiré interference pattern appeared, and he was gone again.

Fortunately Ace High had already put on his new stunglasses. As he watched, Boone slowly assumed the Silent Planet posture, his face turned rapturously to the news-shop's advertising display. Ace High looked at the floor, not wanting to disturb his friend. The stunglasses were projecting a three-dimensional holographic image in front of everything he looked at. The image was multiplexed, so he couldn't actually say for sure what it was of. It was a lot things at once, and his brain knew how to sort out and store the information. His trusting brain was soaking it right up.

As he watched the stunglasses' images, Ace High's slack exuberance turned to *responsible concern*. Concern that he had not drawn his paycheck for two months. Concern about what he *had* been doing for two months. Concern that everyone receive their Enlightenment Rabies vaccination, particularly himself and Boone. Concern with the fact that more and more young people were turning their backs on the real world, only to go chasing after some kind of crazy half-scientific hopped-up occultist mystagogic blue-dome swizzle, uh.

Boone was more or less squatting on the floor with his arms between his knees. He was singing or moaning a wavering note. The Music of the Spheres is what the kids called it, and ordinarily if your best friend was singing the Music of the Spheres you left him alone for a few days. But they had to get that vaccination or they'd be swept.

"Are we crazy / are we insanéd / are we zeroes / that someone painted?" Boone muttered when Ace shook him. Then he shifted phases, the images unlocked, and he was walking out the door with a headache.

"The old bus station, right?" Ace High said. Boone nodded, and they started down the cold and dry sidewalk, flooded yellow with clear November sun. They were wearing their stunglasses, and each of them had about half of his attention occupied by the multiplex image the stunglasses projected into any part of the visual field not under active scrutiny.

The bus station was a ten minute walk away, but they didn't talk much. They were absorbed in watching a dinosaur show. They couldn't even tell that it was multiplex anymore. Their whole conscious minds were involved in the show they were watching, and the incessant messages from all the "sponsors" were being sorted out and stowed away subconsciously.

Soon Boone and Ace High had joined the long line of waiting citizens that snaked out of the old bus station. Everyone had stunglasses on. Some people were watching sports, some were watching old movies, some were watching sex, some were watching university extension courses. Nobody was watching the November sunlight sliding across the street like nectar from the last flower of the year.

Note on "Enlightenment Rabies"

Written in 1977.
New Pathways, #9, November, 1987.

When I wrote the amateurish "Enlightenment Rabies" I was exercised about the U. S. propaganda tactic of naming diseases after the government's enemies: the Russian Flu, the Chinese Flu and the like. And, of course, I was filled with hatred for television. From the present-day vantage, the story looks cyberpunk. I sent "Enlightenment Rabies" to the short-lived magazine Unearth in 1978, and they were going to print it, but then they decided to serialize my novel Spacetime Donuts instead. Unearth's policy was to print previously unpublished authors. William Gibson and I both had our first SF publications there. I eventually cannibalized the opening paragraph of "Enlightenment Rabies" for Chapter 25 of *Software*.

Schrödinger's Cat

"A cat is placed in a steel chamber, together with the following hellish contraption (which must be protected against direct interference by the cat): In a Geiger counter there is a tiny amount of radioactive substance, so tiny that maybe within an hour one of the atoms decays, but equally probably none of them decays. If an atom decays then the counter triggers and via a relay activates a little hammer which breaks a container of cyanide. If one has left this entire system for an hour, then one would say that the cat is still living if no atom has decayed. The first decay would have poisoned it. The wave-function of the entire system would express this by containing equal parts of the living and the dead cat."—Erwin Schrödinger.

By rights, this should have been an important scientific paper… not a thrilling wonder tale in some lurid, mass-produced edition. But I must cast my net as wide as possible. I am fishing for minds, minds with the delicacy of thought to appreciate the nature of Ion Stepanek's fate.

Such are the facts: with my assistance, Ion Stepanek was able to build a sort of time-machine. He used this machine to produce a yes-and-no situation, which he tried to observe. As a result, he has split into an uncollapsible mixed state. Due to coupling effects, I suffer his condition, though not yet to the same degree.

It is March 21, 1980, Heidelberg, West Germany. I am sitting in the office Stepanek shared with me, staring out at a white sky. The office is in the Physics Institute. Across the river, the great castle hovers over the misted town like a thought. Such are the facts.

I did my undergraduate work at Stanford, then took my Ph.D. in particle physics at Berkeley. My thesis project helped lead to the first experimental disproof of the Bell inequality. At one time this was a fairly sensational result, although now more and more people have accepted the ultimate validity of the wave-function world-view.

Schrödinger's though-experiment is paradoxical because, according to quantum mechanics, until the observer opens the door, *the cat is not definitely dead or definitely alive*, but is rather 50 percent dead and 50 percent alive. The cat is in what is known as a *mixed state*.

Einstein responded to Schrödinger's paradox by asserting that this fifty-fifty business was just a measure of the observer's lack of knowledge, rather than being a true description of the actual state of the cat. But the experimental disproof of the Bell inequality has shown that Einstein was wrong. The unobserved world evolves into truly mixed states. There are no hidden parameters which make things stay definite.

It is thanks, in part, to my own research that this result was proved. But despite this high achievement, I was unable to obtain a good research or teaching post. I make enemies easily, and it may be that one of my letters of recommendation was, in effect, a black-ball.

I postponed the inevitable with a post-doc at Harvard. But after that I had to take a poorly paying job at a state college in Wankato, Minnesota.

Cut off from any real physics laboratory, I was forced to begin thinking more deeply about the experiments I had run at Harvard and at Berkeley. What is it Schrödinger says about his paradox?

"This prevents us from accepting a 'blurred model' so naïvely as a picture of reality. By itself reality is not at all unclear or contradictory. There is a difference between a blurred or poorly-focused photograph and a picture of clouds or fog patches."

I had a nervous breakdown during my fourth year at Wankato. It had to do with the television weather reports. Quantum mechanics implies that *until someone makes an observation*, the weather is indeterminate, in a mixed state. There is, in principle, no reason why it should not be sunny every day. Indeed, it is logically possible to argue that it rains only because people *believe it to be raining*.

Fact: in Wankato, Minnesota, there is precipitation 227 days of the year.

Before too long I thought I had determined the reason for this. All of the citizens of Wankato...even the faculty members...watch television weather reports every evening. These reports almost always predict rain or snow. It seemed obvious to me, in my isolation, that if the weather reports could be stopped, then it would not rain so often.

I tried, unsuccessfully, to gather signatures for a petition. I went to the TV station and complained. Finally, I forced my way into the studio one evening and interrupted the weather report to state my case.

"Tomorrow it will be sunny!" I cried. "If only you will believe!"

The next day it was sunny. But I was out of a job, and in a mental institution. It was clear that I needed a rest. It had been folly to shift my fellows over so abruptly from one belief system to another. I had neglected the bridge, the mixed state.

That was in March, 1979. A year ago. They let me out after six weeks of treatment. As luck would have it, a letter from a German research foundation was waiting for me when I finally got back to my little furnished room. They had approved my application for a one-year grant, to be spent working with Ion Stepanek at the Physics Institute of the University of Heidelberg. My project title? "Mixed States as Bridges Between Parallel Universes."

On a typical Heidelberg day it is misty. On the Neckar River the vapor hangs in networks, concentrated at the boundaries of atmospheric pressure cells. The old town is squeezed between the river and a steep mountainside. Some hundred meters up the mountain hangs the huge, ruined castle. In the mist it looks weightless, phantasmagoric.

I got there in early September, during semester break. I found a room outside of town, and on most days, I would ride the stuffy bus from my apartment to Bismarckplatz, the little city's center.

Strange feelings always filled me on these bus rides. I never seemed to see the same face twice, and the strangeness of it put me at a remove from reality. Never had I tasted alienation in such a pure and unalloyed form.

Half convinced that I was invisible, I would stare greedily at the German women, at their thick blonde hair and their strong features. The women stared back with bold and clinical eyes. I gave my heart a thousand times, without ever saying a word. But I could never muster the courage to approach one of those tantalizing aliens. I am, after all, soft and funny-looking.

On a normal day I would get out at Bismarckplatz and walk over the bridge. Crossing the Neckar always took me a long time. In the middle of the bridge I would stop and watch the fifty-meter-long barges speeding by beneath me. The river is like a highway, with coal and wrecked cars being lugged upstream, and great beams of steel gliding downstream. There are the locks to see, and the hazy old town, and above it all, the great hallucinatory castle.

Other darker thoughts detained me on the bridge as well. Surely you have seen Edvard Munch's painting, *The Cry*? Why do you think Munch chose to place this most anguished figure in modern art…on a bridge? On a bridge one is neither here nor there; one is rootless… and anything can happen. Did you know that in the 1800s the most commonly attempted method of suicide was none other than…jumping off a bridge? Out there, in the wind, one need not choose this bank or that. There are other alternatives.

During my first two months in Heidelberg, the Institute was deserted. The sole secretary present showed me my desk in Ion Stepanek's large office. As I later learned, Stepanek was spending the semester break visiting relatives in Budapest. Both he and his wife, Klara, were Hungarian refugees.

The first time I met Stepanek, he caught me by surprise. I had spent those first lonely months at the Institute by going over various treatments of the Einstein-Podolsky-Rosen paradox. My slow understanding of the solution was expressed in a large, three-dimensional figure, a sort of solid letter "Y," which I was amusing myself with by drawing on the office blackboard.

"William," a voice cried suddenly. "What a pleasure to find you here, hard at work!" I turned a bit too abruptly—he had startled me—and we shook hands.

Ion Stepanek was a short, wiry man, given to wearing suede vests and jackets. His hair was thinning, and rather greasy. He had a large nose and a wide, amused mouth. His eyes were very quick, and he had a disconcerting habit of staring me in the eye when he sensed I might be holding something back.

Although he was ten years my senior and, nominally, my supervisor, Ion began by treating me as an equal. He had read my experimental work and my recent, unpublishable theorizings. In return I had read everything he had written, even including a stack of freshly typed pages I had found on his desk.

His sharp eyes took in my diagram of the EPR paradox, and then he turned to gesture at the window. "So, William? Do you like the fog? The indeterminacy?"

I shrugged. "I can live with it. Did you enjoy your vacation?"

"Must it be yes or no?" I didn't know quite what to answer. Stepanek savored the moment, then clapped me on the shoulder. "Have you read my latest?"

"You mean this?" I pointed to the pages on his desk. "Yes, I took the liberty. But…" I stopped, not wanting to offend him.

He plucked the thought out of my eyes and answered it. "You are wondering why I would waste my energy on a chimera like time-travel."

I nodded. "Surely you are aware of the paradoxes. One can so easily produce a yes-and-no situation with a time-machine."

Ion smiled widely, mirthlessly. "Do you not understand your own work? This is just what you want."

We dropped the matter for then, and went on to discuss the bus routes, my apartment, the restaurants…the minutiae of life in a foreign country.

Ion insisted on taking me home with him for the midday meal. His house was only a few hundred meters from the Institute. His wife, Klara, greeted me like a long-lost cousin.

"Ion has been so looking forward to your visit, William. It is wonderful that you are here!" She had soft eyes and dark, sensual lips. A perfect wife, a perfect mother. How comfortable she made me feel!

I accepted a glass of kirsch before lunch. The clear, dry alcohol went straight to my head, but Ion assured me that Klara's after-dinner coffee would remedy that. Then the two children, twin ten-year-old girls, came crashing in.

The German school-day ends before one o'clock, and it is not unusual for the whole family to have their big meal together at midday.

"Do you fix such a big supper as well?" I asked Klara as we sat down to our cauliflower soup.

"This is not big," she said, looking down the loaded table. "This is nothing."

Besides the soup, there was a roast stuffed with hot sausage, a platter of fried potatoes, creamed spinach, cucumber salad, smoked cheese, two kinds of salami, dishes of pickled peppers, and a large carafe of excellent white wine.

"I have never seen such a magnificent meal in my life!" I exclaimed.

The twins giggled, and Ion laughed appreciatively. "You see, Klara? William is already learning the art of Hungarian exaggeration."

In the course of many happy hours spent at the Stepaneks' over the next three months, I was to become very familiar with this sort of conversation. A Hungarian is never happy without being ecstatic, never sad without being suicidal, never your friend without being ready to give you everything he owns, never displeased without being ready to kill. But there was, for all that, a consciously playful element to their exaggerations which somehow kept them from ever being oppressive.

Klara was thirty-five, about halfway in age between Ion and I. Before long I was thoroughly infatuated with her, and flirted shamelessly. Ion must have noticed, but perhaps he welcomed the excitement for Klara. Or perhaps he pitied me too much to object.

I got in the habit of dropping my spoon at most of our frequent common meals. Bent and straining under the table, I would stare at Klara's legs. She could feel my gaze, and would slowly rub her nylons against each other. When I sat up she would give me a look of dreamy speculation, her full lips parted to show a few of her perfect teeth. I hoped my hopes and dreamed my dreams.

Meanwhile, Ion and I were working long hours on our joint project. His intention was to push the Feynman time-reversal theory of antimatter hard enough to get time-travel. He had the clout to get the necessary components and material—some of them totally new. My job was to assemble the components into a working system.

There is something magical about scientific apparatus. A witch doctor assembles decorated stones, special herbs, pieces of rare animals… and he expects that putting these valued objects together will cause something unusual to happen. Spirit voices, levitation, miracle cures…

The constructions of engineers and physicists are not really so different. Bits of etched silicon, special chemicals, oddly shaped pieces of metal…the experimentalist places them together, and suddenly one has a radio, or an airplane, or an X-ray machine.

Stepanek's design for a time-machine was a bit more obviously allied to sorcery than is customary. The key components were six of the brand-new "phase-mirrors." It was only as a result of his years-long friendship with the director of the Max Planck Institute that Ion was able to get these fantastically rare and valuable plates of…what?

The phase-mirrors were made of a completely new type of substance called quarkonium, a hyperstable compound something like metallic helium—but with some of the protons' component quarks replaced by the newly obtainable "bottom" quarks. Quarkonium is, strangely enough, neither matter nor antimatter. The stuff exists in some fantastically charged tension between the two. The fact that quarkonium is thus hyperstable made it possible that, in certain circumstances, the phase-mirrors could emit or absorb almost their entire mass-energy without disintegrating.

Two of the thin, inflexible quarkonium plates were square, and four were longish rectangles. I assembled the six into a box, setting an evacuation nozzle into the hole with which one plate had been provided. The material was strange to work with, slippery and utterly rigid. Although they were supposed to be a sort of mirror, the plates did not reflect images in any ordinary way…at least not most of the time. But, over and over, as I was assembling the phase-mirrors into a box, I seemed to glimpse isolated images of my fingertips here and there on the mirrors' surfaces.

We spent forty-eight hours pumping the box out to a state of near-perfect vacuum, and then sealed it off. While the pump was running, Ion instructed me to mount a series of wire loops on the table, loops which could be charged to produce a weakly guiding magnetic field. We set the box in the middle of the loops, and that was about it. A transparent box like an aquarium with a glass top. Ion called the box a time-tunnel, but I found this colorful description misleading.

We ran our first tests with an electron beam. The idea was that a signal could come out of one end of the box before it went in the other. It's called an advanced potential in quantum mechanics. We got the results Ion had predicted, so we moved up to atomic nuclei, and then to a series of larger and larger iron bullets.

Shooting the bullets into that phase-mirror box made me a little nervous…. I expected the box to shatter. But somehow it didn't. I assumed it was because the quarkonium plates were, in some sense, liquid, and thus able to close up after a rapid enough object.

I believed that for a while, anyway. But before long I had come to believe something stranger…that the box was able to create and destroy matter/antimatter pairs. But where was the energy coming from? And where did it go?

Ion had an explanation. But I was not ready to accept his description of what we had built. That way lay madness.

"Do you know what your husband and I have done?" I asked Klara at lunch the last day of February. The twins had already left the table to do their homework. I glanced at Ion, and he gave me an encouraging nod. Until now I had been sworn to silence.

Klara looked a bit nervous at my question. Ion was, I had learned, something of a philanderer. What a fool to betray a woman as wonderful as Klara!

"Nothing too depraved, I hope?" Her voice was gay, but with the faintest tremolo of real worry. She drew out a cigarette and placed it between her wonderful lips, waiting for the touch of my lighter…the lighter which I had bought solely so that I could light Klara's cigarettes. She tilted her head back, away from the smoke, and looked at Ion questioningly.

He smiled his broad, mirthless smile. "William and I have assembled a rather interesting piece of apparatus. It creates and destroys matter, according to William's way of looking at things."

Klara arched her eyebrows at me. "Is that true, William? Perhaps you have solved the energy crisis?"

I laughed, a bit exasperated by Ion's misdirection. "No, no. This is a very expensive machine to build. We have used most of the quarkonium in the world to build it. And really it creates and absorbs matter/antimatter *pairs*, rather than just matter. But Ion thinks…"

Ion was pouring himself a glass of wine, and the carafe clattered against his glass. "I do not *think*, William, I *know*. We have built a time-machine." Suddenly, on some level, we were fighting over Klara.

She blew a thick stream of smoke and put out her cigarette. "I would like a time-machine. Then I could see what the castle looked like in

1400, before the French blew it up. And I'd like to see dinosaurs. And fashions one thousand years from now." It was clear she didn't believe Ion. "Dearest, do you think you could bring me back a kitchen-robot from the future? It would be even nicer than that dishwasher you're always promising to get me!"

Ion was breathing heavily. He had had several glasses of kirsch before lunch. This quarrel had been brewing for three months. I thought his experiment interesting, but I saw no reason to take Feynman's theory so literally as to assert that we had produced time-travel. Ion could see this in my eyes.

He stood up suddenly, almost as if to attack me. Was he, on top of it all, jealous of my attentions to Klara? New Year's Eve, after he had passed out, Klara and I, how close we had come! I tried to keep this out of my eyes. I stood up clumsily, and my chair fell to the floor behind me.

"Don't panic, William," Ion said, shrugging on his suede jacket. "I only thought we could give Klara a demonstration."

The twins, attracted by the noise of my chair, had come running in from the study, and insisted that they too be allowed to come see Daddy's machine. Ion acquiesced, on the condition that they bring a certain toy.

We all bundled into our coats…Klara wore a charming fox coat sewed in herring-bone strips…and we walked the three blocks to the Physics Institute.

The twins ran ahead of us, screaming and trying to slide on the frozen puddles. Klara walked between Ion and me, linking an arm with each of us. The sky was low and grey. The eternal mist seemed to form a circular wall around us, always ten meters off.

"Should we show Klara the bullet series?" I asked Ion, speaking across Klara's lovely, upturned face.

Ion pursed his lips and shook his head. "Too fast. Klara has to see it to believe it."

"Believe what?"

"We have a sort of tunnel," I explained. "The size of a toy train tunnel. And if we shoot a bullet through it, the bullet seems to come out the right end *before* it goes in the left."

Klara laughed. "Now *that* sounds useful. We could use one of your machines in the tunnel under the castle…where those dreadful traffic jams are."

"Actually," Ion said, "I thought I *would* use a little car today—the little three-wheeler that I helped the twins make last night."

The twins had brought the little car, a bright red-yellow-blue mass of Lego blocks. On the top was a battery-run motor, with a cog wheel linked by a black plastic chain to a gear on the single front wheel.

Klara examined our "time-tunnel" with interest. The core of it was the shoe-box-sized vacuum chamber made of phase-mirrors. You could see in quite easily. The thick loops of the guiding-field wires arched over the box like croquet wickets.

I removed the rifle from its mount on one end of the lab-table, and waited while Ion got the car from the little girls.

Then, bustling a bit, he lined up his three women in chairs against the wall, and set the car down at one end of the table. I cleared my throat, preparatory to telling them what they might expect, but Ion shushed me.

"First let them see, and *then* we'll discuss it."

I taped an iron nail to the bottom of the Lego car, and dialed the guiding-field's power up to some hundred times the level we had used before. The Lego car made a pretty big test-particle.

In all frankness, I expected the experiment to be a failure. The car would roll up to the phase-mirror box, bump into the side and stop... nothing more. But I was wrong.

As the little car labored across the table towards the left end of the box, something happened at the right end. Seemingly out of no place, an identical Lego car pushed out of the right end of the tunnel and went chuffing on its way! "And there's one inside now, rolling left!" Klara exclaimed, leaning forward. She was right. For a few seconds there were *three* Lego cars on the table.

Car (1): The original car, still approaching the tunnel's left entrance. Car (2): The one moving in the tunnel, from right to left. Car (3): The new one moving away from the right end of the tunnel.

And then car (1) and car (2) met at the left-end mirror. They melted into each other...nose into nose, wheel into wheel, tail into tail. It was like watching a Rorschach ink-blot disappear into its central fold.

One of the twins squealed and ran to catch car (3) before it ran off the other end of the lab table. I took it from her and examined it closely. Car (3) appeared to be identical to car (1). We had already done this experiment with electrons and with small bullets...but one bullet or electron is much like another. Until now I had been unwilling to accept Ion's interpretation of our experiment. But it certainly looked as if car (3) really *was* car (1).

Ion stepped to the blackboard and drew a diagram.

"Look," he said to Klara. "Here's a spacetime diagram of what happens. If we think of the zigzag line as the history of a particular object, what we have is this: First, car (1) goes forward in time till it gets to the left phase-mirror. Second, inside the tunnel it flips and moves backwards in time, but still left-to-right, and we call it car (2). Third, upon passing through another phase-mirror it flips back to run forward in time again, and is called car (3). By evolving into car (3), the original car (1) manages to come out of the right end a few seconds earlier than it goes in the left."

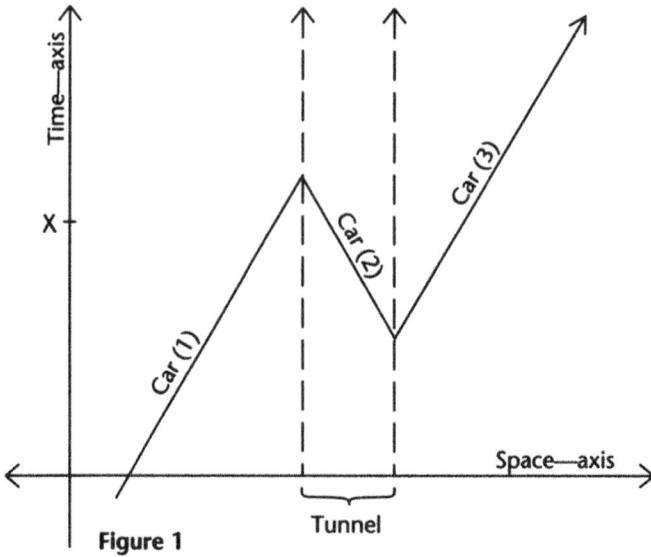

Figure 1

Tunnel

"That's one way of looking at it," I interrupted. "But we can read the picture a bit differently. Just think of moving that space-axis upwards through time, and see what happens. First there's just car (1) moving to the right. Then suddenly something happens at the right end of the tunnel. Car (2) and car (3) come into existence together—by a process called pair-production. Car (3) is matter and car (2) is antimatter. With enough energy present, you can convert zero Lego blocks into plus-forty-nine Lego blocks and minus-forty-nine Lego blocks. You can get something from nothing…as long as you get anti-something too."

My voice was baying evangelically. At Wankato State the students used to call me "Rover." Now Klara smiled at me. Politely. She didn't know what I was talking about. Ion hid a smile by pretending to rub his nose.

I continued, "When car (2) meets car (1), the two disappear into a burst of energy. It's called mutual annihilation. Matter plus antimatter makes pure energy. The first puzzling thing about the experiment is how the tunnel knows to produce the appropriate matter/antimatter pair in time. But quantum mechanics does allow for action at a distance. *Advanced potentials.* Presumably an advanced potential from the approaching car (1) triggers the pair-production of…"

Klara looked quite blank by now. I broke off the exposition and made my point. "All three cars are different. Car (2) is antimatter traveling forward in time, not car (1) traveling backwards in time. And car (3) is just a sort of correction term."

Klara looked from one of us to the other, smiling a bit. "Ion's right," she said finally, and with a nod of her head. "Anyone can see that the little car which came out is the same as the one that went in." She caught my dejected expression and laughed. "Well, what's the difference anyway? Whether the thing in the tunnel is a particle going backwards in time or an anti-particle going forward in time. It comes to…"

She had to break off and grab one of the twins, who had been about to try to stick her finger into a phase-mirror. A smell was filling the room, and we noticed that the other twin had opened one of the propane gas-valves set in the table.

"I better get these bad children out of here," Klara exclaimed. "But it's marvelous, Ion. And William, you must be very clever to have helped Ion build this!" A flash of lips, a swirl of fur, and she was gone.

I picked up the toy car and examined it closely. Even I had trouble believing my description of what had happened. How would the right end know to produce pairs in the right order to build up car and anti-car from nose to wheel to tail? And where would the energy have come from? Granted that a fantastic amount of energy was stored in the fantastically expensive quarkonium, but still…

Ion was sitting at his desk writing, his back to me. Despite what Klara had said, the two descriptions did *not* come to the same thing. Was this car the *same* as the original car, or was it only an *identical copy*? I had to know!

Suddenly I thought of a way to test the difference. I would let the car roll towards the tunnel, and at the last minute I would stop it from going in. A decisive experiment.

Suppose Ion was right. Suppose that car (3) was just a time-traveled car (1). What then? If car (1) did not go in the tunnel, then car (2) and car (3) would not come into existence.

But suppose I was right. Suppose that the whole effect was just advanced potential pair-production, triggered by car (1)'s approach. What then? Car (2) and car (3) would already have been created even if, at the very last second, car (1) did not actually enter the tunnel.

In terms of Ion's spacetime diagram, what I was going to do was to stop car (1) at the time marked "X." If car (3) came out anyway, then I was right. If car (3) didn't come out, then Ion was right.

I started the car and set it down. "Look, Ion." I didn't bother saying more…he would understand. I fixed my mind on grabbing the car at the last possible instant before it went through the…looking-glass. I leaned over the table, concentrating. I didn't dare look away to see if car (3) came out of the other end or not.

I seized car (1) just before its nose touched the phase-mirror. Then I stepped back and looked down the table. There was no car (3) at the other end…and no antimatter car (2) at my end. Ion was right.

I returned the little car to the starting position and let it run through the time-tunnel undisturbed, trying to see it Ion's way.

A car moving *right to left* is the same as a car moving *left to right and backwards in time*. Suddenly I could see the pair-production and the mutual annihilation as corners in time. Ion was right, he really was. We had time-travel, admittedly over just a three-second range, but time-travel nonetheless. Even the strange fact that the phase-mirrors turned things backwards as well as reversing them in time made sense. The fact that the front of the car moved backwards in time as soon as it passed through the left end meant that a normal observer *had* to see it as disappearing first.

Figure 2

"Well?" Ion was smiling his wide, mirthless smile, his eyes picking my brain.

I nodded. "Okay. But how does the car get through the phase-mirrors? They felt so hard when I was gluing them together."

Ion shrugged. "How does a reflection get through an ordinary looking-glass? It is the property of a mirror to produce images. But this particular mirror works only when the guiding-field is on." He pointed to the left end of the time-tunnel.

Time-tunnel. As I said the word to myself, my last remaining question dissolved. If car (1) was car (2) was car (3), then no mass or anti-mass at all was really being created or destroyed. So of course there were no huge energy drains or blasts going on. Looked at differently, the quarkonium plates were a closed system which could pass energy back in time...so the pair-producing drew its energy from the annihilation, even though it happened first.

I nodded again, harder. "Okay. But now what?"

"Aren't you worried about time-paradoxes anymore?" Ion's voice was challenging, almost angry. It was as if he hadn't wanted me to agree with him...hadn't wanted it to be true. The next question: What if one were to stop car (1) if and only if car (3) has already appeared?

I didn't say it, but he could see it in my eyes. The fear. Suddenly fatherly, he patted me on the shoulder. "Take the rest of the afternoon off, William. I want to write all of this up before...before I continue."

I nodded and left him there. I spent the next few hours drinking Schlossquell beer, and then I went to the Eros House, a shabby building full of legal prostitutes. With the lights off, I could almost believe I was with Klara. Later I had more beer.

I slept badly that night. At four in the morning an unpleasant dream woke me up so completely that I couldn't go back to sleep. It was a scene inspired by Kafka's *The Castle*.

In the dream, through some transmutation, the Heidelberg castle is...*science.* Endless corridors, doors, people to meet. On the white plaster walls there are things like fire-alarms, little hammers mounted over glass plates. Behind the glass is...*cyanide*, thick gas, swirling, deadly. I hurry down a hallway, a sheaf of papers in my hand. Someone is in front of me, tangible, but invisible. My other self? Somehow the person moves so as to always be in my blind spot. A question is posed, the unspeakable question which the castle itself embodies. My tongue is slow and sticky. Yes and no. A bell is tolling. Yes and no. The hammers quiver....

The world is clouds and fog patches, a confused smear which no magical apparatus can sharpen up. The cat knows.

That morning I found Ion sitting at his desk. He was asleep, with his head on his crossed arms. One of the phase-mirrors was cracked! Had Ion had some sort of tantrum? I examined the hairline crack. Of course the vacuum was ruined now. I wondered if the quarkonium plate could be repaired. There were some individual Lego-blocks scattered around the floor and table. Apparently Ion had been there all night.

I stood over him for a moment, looking at him with something like affection. I had been worried, too worried to even…

"William?" The voice was blurred. His eyes flickered open, then shut. "Is it raining?"

This struck me as a very odd question. It was, in fact, a marvelously sunny day, the first taste of spring. The sky was a delicate blue and the birds were singing. A square of sunlight was lying on Ion's desk!

"It's sunny, Ion."

"I thought it was. And I thought it was raining." His voice was muffled, and seemed somehow to come from underneath his head.

"You should get some sleep," I urged. "Klara must be worried."

"I'm scared to move." A long pause. "I might disperse even more."

Disperse? A strange word to use. Wave-packets disperse, but people…

"Read my notes," Ion said, "I…" He let his voice trail off, and just sat there, eyes closed, his head resting on his crossed arms. There seemed to be something under his arms, some sort of pillow.

I picked up the lab book lying on his desk. It started with a description of the apparatus and the first experiments we had conducted. Nothing new there. I flipped forward a few pages.

There was a diagram like the one Ion had drawn for Klara. Under it was a sketch of the Lego car and a description of the two experiments, the one where the car comes out of the time-tunnel before it goes in, and my variation, where the car is stopped from going in, and therefore does not come out.

Ion had conducted a third experiment. The car was to roll towards the tunnel while he watched both ends. His plan was to stop car (1) if car (3) appeared, and to let car (1) go if car (3) did not appear. This meant that a car would come out of the right end of the tunnel if and only if no car came out of the right end of the tunnel. Yes if and only if no.

Think about it. Either car (3) appears or it doesn't. Case I: Car (3) appears. So Ion stops car (1) from entering the tunnel. So car (3) doesn't appear. Case II: Car (3) doesn't appear. So Ion lets car (1) into the tunnel. So car (3) appears.

Question: When Ion actually ran the experiment, did car (3) appear? Answer: Yes and no.

I closed the lab book and looked around the room. The scattered bits of Legos…how many?

"What happened, Ion? Did the car come out of the tunnel?"

"Yes," Ion said, raising his head from on top of his arms.

"No," Ion said, uncrossing his arms and raising up his other head from under his arms.

The two faces looked at me, each of them a bit translucent, a bit unreal. The two necks merged into his collar, making a solid, tubular letter "Y."

I gagged and stepped back.

The phone began to ring. The second of Ion's heads…the no-head…seemed not to hear it, and continued to stare at me with those prehensile eyes. Eyes which reached deep into my mind.

But at the same time, Ion's head groped up the receiver and held it to the first head…the yes-head…to one of the shimmering ears. I could hear Klara's tiny voice. She sounded angry, accusing.

"I was working," the yes-head said.

"Your boyfriend is here," the no-head said, noticing the conversation. "I'm going to show him something."

Ion let the phone drop and walked over to the laboratory table. The no-head, the mean one, was doing the talking. Whichever head was talking tended to be bigger. It was as if the silent head corresponded to some part of Ion which was father away…drifting towards some parallel universe.

"I'm in a mixed state, William. I ran the paradox. It had to come out both ways." He turned the switch to power-up the guiding-field. It was dangerous to be restarting it without a vacuum in the chamber.

The no-head bent down, peering into the cracked phase-mirror. He was still talking to me. "I know how you think I look. But that's just your projection. Actually it feels…marvelous. You'll see in…"

"Get out, William," the yes-head cried. "Before it's too late."

Klara's voice was quacking from the dangling phone receiver. I could feel myself going mad, as surely as cloth tearing. I seized the phone to speak to her. "This is William. Ion's had a terrible accident. He…"

There was a crash behind me. I whirled around. The time-tunnel was billowing smoke and the phase-mirrors had smashed into pieces. For a second I couldn't see Ion through the smoke, but then he came at me.

A tangle of twenty or a hundred thin necks writhed out of his open collar, and on the end of each tentacle-like neck rode a tiny grimacing head, and every little head was screaming at me in a terrible tiny voice….

He dispersed completely after that. As different variants of Ion Stepanek split off into different universes, each corresponding head would shrink…get "farther away"…and a copy of his body would split off with it, twisting and dwindling. I don't know how long it took; I don't know how I saw it; I wish I could forget it. The horrible squid-bunch of necks, each little head screaming out something different…I hope he's really gone.

I live with Klara now, and I wear Ion's clothes. I have taken over his job at the Institute…they think he's resigned. Klara forged his signature on the letter.

It's a good life, except for having to cut the buds off my neck every morning. The wart-like little heads. Some look like me, and some look like him. Klara says I only imagine them, and that there's nothing on my neck but eczema.

I still have the specs for the time-tunnel. Maybe I'll rebuild it, and observe a yes-and-no, and disperse. I'll go into the mixed state and come out…who knows…maybe in heaven. But I don't really need the machine anymore.

Mixed states happen all the time. Say someone asks you whether or not you want to kill yourself. Before they asked, maybe you weren't really all that much for or against suicide. That's your original mixed state. But answering the question is like being born. You have to stick out a yes-head or a no-head to answer. And the other one has to get shaved off.

It could be any question. Do you like milk? Who are you going to vote for? Are you happy? Do you understand what I'm talking about?

In a way, mixed states are nice. Not naming things, and not forcing them to be this way or that, but just…letting them go. Satori. There's a Zen question for it: "What was your original face before you were born?"

My original face. A mixed state. I don't need a machine, no heap of glass and wire. I'm just going to walk out on the bridge towards the castle. I'll stop. Out there, in the wind, one needs not choose this bank or that. There are other alternatives.

Note on "Schrödinger's Cat"

Written in Spring, 1979.
Analog Science Fiction / Science Fact, March, 1981.

My family and I lived in Heidelberg from 1978 to 1980. I was there on a two-year grant from the Alexander von Humboldt Foundation. The grant came through just as I was losing my first teaching job in Geneseo (a.k.a. Wankato, a.k.a. Bata). My formal duties in Heidelberg were zero: I was given a soundproofed office and a typewriter. As well as doing research on Georg Cantor's theories of infinities, I spent a lot of my time writing science-fiction. At this point in my career I didn't know that I would be able to complete and sell novels, so I put a great deal of energy into writing stories.

"Schrödinger's Cat" was inspired by my studies of numerous papers on quantum mechanics and the nature of time in journals like *Philosophy of Science*. The second diagram for this story seems to suggest an interesting new result: that a time-reversing mirror would have to spatially mirror-reverse objects as well. "By rights this should have been an important scientific paper…"

Analog editor Stanley Schmidt had some doubts about the legitimacy of the mass-energy conversion processes taking place at the surface of the phase-mirrors, but I placated him by saying the phase-mirror was made of "quarkonium." Since quarks were then at the edge of scientific knowledge, quarkonium was a handy catch-all magic-maker akin to the "radioactivity" used by 1940s SF writers.

The seed for this story was a drawing I made for my cheerfully horrified children of a Santa Claus with a thousand heads, answering phone-calls from every boy and girl in the world at once.

Sufferin' Succotash

She was big. Fine big legs and white feathers glued all over her head. I had to have a piece of that. She brought me another bowl of slop and I gave her a thousand credit note. "Keep the change, baby." That made three. She dimpled and sat down across from me.

"You're beachy." Looking me over. Charlie and I had only been out of the Regulator for a month, but I was back up to 150 keys already. I had an exoskeleton with gold chasing and rubies at the joints.

"I'm fat and I'm rich," I said, stating the obvious. "And you've got something I want." I stared at her hungrily. Those white feathers on the bare scalp were a perfect touch.

She signaled the other waitress to cover for her. I'd set the hook. She rested her big breasts on her folded arms and leaned across the table. "Why you spoon so hard? Soliton flange?"

"I've always been hungry, baby. Always. I lost my mother when I was four."

She cooed sympathetically, and I decided to whip a little more out of it. "She was a juicer. She'd lock me and the dog in and go out for the night. One night she didn't come back. It was a week before the landlord happened to open up our apartment. There wasn't much of Poochy left…"

"You poor slogger." Three thousand credits and she didn't mind if I'd eaten a live dog. But still, "Why you not dial the food-tap?"

"This was back in 2020, honey. You had to go out to get food. They had stores."

She made an O of her bright yellow lips, flexing her juicy tongue. "But you're still mix and match!"

"You're as young as you feel," I said vaguely. Right now I felt like I was going to die if I didn't get some meat. I still couldn't believe I'd gone to so much trouble to end up in a future where there was nothing to eat but processed algae. I had half a billion credits and I couldn't score anything but veggies.

I looked at the room around us. You could eat for free at home, but people still liked to come out. They had some noise they called music, and things to look at glued to the walls. Antiques. A car-wheel, a 2-D TV set, a formica table-top…and animals, lots of stuffed animals.

Around 2130 they'd realized that nothing but the cockroaches and us was going to hack it. Pollution had cut the gene pools that far and a domino effect was setting in. Suddenly everyone wanted a stuffed animal to remind them of our glorious heritage. The whole last generation of animals ended up on mantelpieces and barroom walls.

"You know," I said, staring longingly at a glass-eyed chicken, "A hundred years ago this place was an Italian restaurant called Stacky's. I used to spend a lot of time here back then. The menu they had! Jesus. Have you ever even seen meat, baby?"

She smiled and shook her head. "You're just scripting." She didn't believe any of it, which was just as well. The statute of limitations had run out, but still…

"Where's your crib?" she was asking. "I could peel you." Her tongue was purple against the yellow lip-wax.

I didn't answer for a few minutes. I was remembering how it had been here a hundred years ago…the night I'd first met Charlie.

I was just getting by, back then, living off computer fraud. I'd invented a do-gooder thing, the Office of Interpersonal Therapeutics, and I'd gotten the computer to believe me when I charged all my bills to the OIT. It took a couple of hours a day punching in fake case-histories, requisitions, employee data…but at least it wasn't honest work.

It was easy…so easy I sometimes suspected the Feds had a special slot on the payroll for computer con-men. I figured I fell somewhere between wino and social worker.

Most evenings I'd get into Stacky's early and they'd just bring me one of everything on the menu. Then I'd have a couple more rounds of whatever seemed best.

The night I met Charlie I was just sitting there looking at the beautiful golden skin of a roast chicken. Suddenly my table flipped over and the dishes went flying. Lying on the floor in front of me was the fattest…hell, he was obese.

"You do that often?" I asked.

He was slowly getting up with the aid of his exoskeleton, and didn't seem to hear me. It was hard, really, to even tell where his head was. There was just metal tubes and little motors and yards of bouncing cloth. But then a precise little voice answered, "More than once a year, less than once a month." An arm and then a head appeared. "You're Eddie Myers," the fat man stated. "And I'm Charles Laxman."

He had fifty keys on me easy. You could tell from the way he had a deep crease circling his wrist. I only had those at my ankles. The servos at Charlie's shoulder and elbow whirred, and the alloy tubes strapped to his right arm swiveled and hinged so as to move his right hand towards me. My servos followed suit and we shook.

In a sense all really fat men look alike. But there are differences if you know how to look for them. I could tell that Charles Laxman was rich, educated and a little flaky. He was the kind of guy who might drool when he's thinking hard…but he's likely to be thinking about something incredible. I liked him already for being fatter than me, and it was clear from his clothes that he was rich.

"So what's on your mind, Charlie?" I asked, punching two drink orders into the bar board. As usual I charged it to the OIT.

"Eddie," he said, nodding towards the bar board, "You're a fat, small-time criminal. Am I correct?"

I was a little insulted. Was he drunk? "You out slumming?"

But he didn't seem to hear me. "Money, Eddie. Money," he said, smiling and puddling forward on the table. His eyes were blank.

"Money…" I said, encouragingly.

He held up five fingers. "Megadollars, Eddie. Fifty million in gold." And then I knew what he was talking about as if I'd read his mind. He wanted me to help him break the Bin.

I figured he was crazy, but talk is just talk. And he looked lonely. "Let's go outside," I suggested, tossing off my drink.

Our exoskeletons walked us a few blocks together. It was a pleasant night, and I had to admit I enjoyed Charlie's company. The whir and clank of the servos in the night air was relaxing. I lit a cigar and heard him out.

Charlie wasn't like any of the other fat men I've known. Any newspaper column psychologist could tell you why I eat so much…after all, mamma is the Latin word for tit. But Charlie hadn't gotten fat as an accidental side-effect of a desperate seeking after this or that. No, he had gotten fat on purpose. That was the first thing he told me…that for two years he had been eating "like a mindless animal."

Without telling me why he'd wanted to be so fat, Charlie then went into some convoluted spiel about space and time. Apparently he had made his fortune by inventing a gravitational condenser. Fill it with garbage, flick a switch…and you had a tiny black hole which would boil off in radiation before long. Every big city dump had one.

But being rich wasn't enough for Charlie…or maybe he just wasn't rich enough. In any case, he wanted to pull off the crime of the century. He wanted to rob the Bin, the Earth-Moon gold transport.

The Moon colony had seceded from Earth shortly after they discovered the helium caves in 2025. They called us Mudders and we called them Loonies, but we couldn't live without them. By 2050 every power plant on Earth had a super-cooled, quantum-effect liquid helium core, and most freight was being shipped in helium-filled zeppelins.

The Loonies didn't trust us, and insisted on being paid twice a year for their helium. Paid in gold. Obligingly we Mudders had built them a robot-operated gold transport armed with missiles and lasers. The Loonies' Bin we called it.

Everyone who'd ever tried to rob the Bin was dead, but my new friend Charlie Laxman had a plan. His gimmick was that he'd found a way to speed up.

He called his gizmo a Regulator. You fed energy into it and something seeped out…loosening things up in such a way that time near the Regulator had very little to do with the time in the rest of the world. You could live out a year at the time it took an egg to fry.

"But have you ever tried it on yourself?" I asked Charlie.

"I'll try it now that you're coming in with me," he said quietly as we walked along in the direction of his townhouse. "I was scared to try it alone, even though I know it's safe…if you're fat enough."

"What does the fat have to do with it?"

"I've been testing the Regulator on hamsters. I'd strap it to their backs and turn it on and then watch how they died. It always took the fat ones much longer to die." Charlie began searching through his pockets for something.

"I don't get it. If this Regulator kills every hamster you tried it on…I mean, that's not real encouraging?" The fifty million in gold seemed a little further away than it had a minute ago.

Charlie didn't seem to hear me. He was still rummaging in his clothes. Finally he gave up the search and looked at me, blinking. "Encouraging," he said, obviously replaying my question to himself, "Encouraging. Well, it was just starvation they died of. And you and I could live very comfortably for a week on nothing but water."

I was beginning to get it. We'd flash down on the Bin, take a day or two to clear it out and be gone before it could react. "But what about when we slow back down?" I asked, "They'll be able to trace the gold."

"We'll just lie low," Charlie said calmly. "For about a hundred years. My Regulator works the other way too. We'll take a nap and it'll be 2150."

A big loose grin spread over my face.

The girl across the table from me was grinning back. She held an atomizer out towards me. "You step out? Alterations?"

"Let's go," I said. "Physically." She went over to whisper something to the other waitress, and then we left together. I whistled and my car pulled up. There was room for her in back with me, and I instructed the robot to take us out to my house.

"I'm Zoozie," she said, trying to put her arms around me.

"Fast Eddie," I answered. "But I'm too big." Her face was near mine, and I managed to lean forward enough to lick it. Nice. I reached down to feel one of those big legs.

"Let's bounce," she suggested.

"If you can find it." I told the robot not to hurry and lay back in my seat. I could see lights flickering past like starts. In my mind I was back on Charlie's spaceship.

The Bin was just a point of light against the blackness of space, but we had come close enough to attract its attention. A light began flashing on the control panel of our ship, and a pleasantly feminine computer voice addressed us. "Red warning. You have violated the security zone of a Class Q Transport. Please change your course to a three-one-niner reading to avoid interception. You have thirty seconds of grace. This warning will not be repeated."

I gunned our ship straight for the Bin, and looked over at Charlie with a hard grin. He looked a little pale. I think he might have backed out if I hadn't been there.

We were both wearing scuba diving gear...yellow rubber suits and a couple of tanks of compressed oxygen apiece. He said that even though it would feel like we were out there for hours, we wouldn't need pressure suits. A suit's joints would have heated up too much anyway. As it was, Charlie had had to design us special beefed-up and frictionless exo-skeletons. It had taken a while to get used to them. If you weren't careful, you could brain yourself going to scratch your ear.

Each of us had one of Charlie's Regulators set into the rubber suit right over the navel, and now we dialed them on. I felt like I could smell the extra time, a tingling high in my sinuses. My nose seemed to expand and I felt like a horse, a horse I'd seen in a zoo when I was four. I remembered the scrape I'd gotten on my knee that day, and Mommy tucking me in. I seemed to taste blood in my mouth and I could hear Poochy screaming. My eyes snapped open.

Nothing looked different, except the clock on the control panel seemed to have stopped. The next fifteen hours of my life would last about a tenth of a second, normal time.

Charlie was already undogging the hatch and I walked over to help him. As I walked, the air felt like a thick jelly, and rubbing against it heated me up unpleasantly. Finally the hatch cracked open and the jelly wafted us and our equipment into outer space. This was the part I'd had my doubts about, but the hard vacuum just felt like a crisp fall day. The raw solar radiation warmed my cheeks pleasantly.

Charlie ripped the hatch door loose from the ship, tore it in half, and handed me the larger piece. What with the souped-up exoskeleton and my speeded-up reflexes, the thick metal felt like balsa wood.

The Bin was about two k's off, and I could see a missile come easing out of a hole in the side. It came floating towards us like a big lazy fish. Aiming carefully, I threw a chunk of metal at it when it was a thousand meters off. The recoil of my throw sent me spinning, and it took a minute of pitching out small pieces of the hatch to stop myself. The Rocket was exploding in slow motion. It looked like a flower blooming.

Charlie waved his fist at me happily, and by throwing some more pieces of the hatch we got ourselves moving towards the Bin at a good clip. Two more missiles swam out, but they were just after our ship and we let them go. I began to doubt that the Bin's robot brain could see us at all.

Just then the lasers started up. A beam was sweeping towards my mid-section a lot faster than I liked. I pitched a big piece of that hatch past my feet, and the recoil pushed me headfirst away from the level of the ray. But it was close, and my feet felt a little warm.

Again, it took me a minute to stop spinning. There were four laser rays. Three of them were happily roasting our ship, but my narrow escape seemed to have attracted the attention of the fourth. It was still after me. We weren't carrying radios, so I could only signal Charlie by waving desperately.

The ray was almost on me again, and I didn't have time to see if Charlie noticed or not. I dodged, but this time the unbearably bright ray caught up with me while I was still spinning. I was dizzy, and it was getting hot. It was hard to think. Should I turn the Regulator dial? Which way should I turn it?

Suddenly the light went out. Painfully I stopped the spinning and looked around. Charlie had knocked out the laser with a lucky throw.

The Bin thought it was taking evasive action now. I could tell because there was a cloud of gas oozing out of the engines. But Charlie and I were so speeded up that the ship looked like it was standing still. We closed in on it, and Charlie split open the hull with a high-speed karate chop. I glanced back at our ship. The three lasers were melting it like an ice-cream cone, and a missile was starting to explode next to it. It was going to be a long walk home.

The Moon was not too far away, and it filled what seemed like half the sky. Most of it was dark, lit only by Earthlight. Some mountain peaks made points of light near the terminator. Somewhere down there was a mountain called J-67, inside of which Charlie had his hideout.

While he set up the launching tube, I began hauling the gold out of the Bin. There were 200 bars, each with a mass of some 10 keys… which is a lot to push around, even in free-fall.

Meanwhile, Charlie had set the sights of the launching tube on three reference stars and switched on the gyros. I fitted in a gold bar, pulled back the spring and pressed the release. Our first million bucks went tumbling down its trajectory towards the slopes of J-67.

I kept hauling the bars out, and Charlie kept zinging them off. God, it was hard work. And was I hungry! Hours and hours passed. Finally I was so weak that I thought one of the gold bars was a roast chicken. I could almost hear it cackling as I gnawed at it. Someone made me stop moving. It was Charlie laying me out on the Bin's hull. Listlessly I watched him launch a few more bars. Suddenly I felt a twitch in the metal plates beneath me.

The rear end of the ship was beginning to swell up. I went and tapped Charlie's shoulder and pointed aft. His mouth was covered by the breathing mask, but I could see his eyes light up. He made an exploding motion with his hands and legs. I remembered then. The Loonies had the Bin booby-trapped with a bomb.

I was ready to leave and to hell with the last few bars of gold, but Charlie had a different idea. We each turned our Regulators up another notch.

I was moving so fast now that the light coming from the Moon looked funny. The pounds were melting off me faster than a taxi-meter clicks. Finally the last gold bar was shipped off.

We each ripped a big chunk off the front end of the Bin, being careful not to uncover that explosion. Then we started pitching pieces at the Earth to get us moving towards the Moon. The important thing, of course, was to save some of the hull to use as a retro-rocket when you came tumbling down at those unbelievably sharp mountains.

I felt an unfamiliar twitching. Zoozie was sitting on me like a chicken on an ostrich egg. "Thanks, baby. I didn't think I had it in me."

She laughed musically and lifted her plump leg over me as she slid off. "That's a beachy crib," she said, looking out the window. My car had pulled up in front of our house.

Charlie met us at the door, suspicious as a father waiting up for his son on prom night. "Who's this?" he demanded.

"I'm Zoozie. Parley-voo bounce?"

Charlie looked at her sadly. "You'd better leave now. You don't know what Mr. Myers is really after."

"Will you shut up!" I pulled her in and closed the door behind us. God, I was hungry. I felt like I hadn't eaten good food in a hundred years.

But Charlie wouldn't let up. "Did he tell you how we got here?" He had a protective arm around her, the goddamn vegetarian.

"Just can it, Mr. Clean," I shouted. "The decision is hers. I'm ready to buy her the best prosthetic leg that money can…" I stopped suddenly. Things were developing a little faster than I'd planned.

Zoozie was looking back and forth between us. "You tollahs jab so old. Fancy dress?"

"We're from 2050," Charlie said, speaking slowly. "We stole lots of gold and had to hide for a hundred years. Now we're rich and we're safe, but Eddie can't get what he wants to eat."

There was no use putting it off. I answered the question in her eyes. "I'd like to buy one…one of your drumsticks."

Charlie held the door open for her. We listened as her footsteps pattered into the distance. "Don't worry, Eddie," he said. I've got some slime mold evolving under the Regulator. We'll be feasting on horse-shoe crab before you know it."

Note on "Sufferin' Succotash"

Written in Summer, 1979.
The 57th Franz Kafka, Ace Books, 1983.

I made my first stab at writing science-fiction when I was a senior at Swarthmore College, and I actually wrote the first few pages of this story in 1967. In 1979, I was pushing hard to become a pro SF writer, and I wanted always to have a story in the mail. So I dug out "Sufferin' Succotash" and finished it. In a way, this is my first SF story that I started, although it's not the first that I finished.

Oh, but wait, I did write an even earlier science-fiction story; it was called "The Miracle," and appeared in *The Pegasus*, an annual magazine published by The Chevalier

Literary Society in Louisville, Kentucky, March, 1962. If you want to read that one, you'll have to find a copy of *The Pegasus*! I can't bring myself to reprint it.

The Chevalier Literary Society was in fact a social club for high-school boys in Louisville. There were about six of these high-school fraternities in Louisville, and we all had to publish annual literary magazines to lend an air of legitimacy. *The Pegasus* of June, 1963, contains an actually usable piece of writing by me, a stream-of-consciousness piece called "Bus Ride—December 20, 1962." Later I lifted this piece nearly intact for use at the end of the third chapter of my transreal novel *The Secret of Life*.

A NEW GOLDEN AGE

"It's like music," I repeated. Lady Vickers looked at me uncomprehendingly. Pale British features beneath wavy red hair, a long nose with a ripple in it.

"You can't hear mathematics," she stated. "It's just squiggles in some great dusty book." Everyone else around the small table was eating. White soup again.

I laid down my spoon. "Look at it this way. When I read a math paper it's no different than a musician reading a score. In each case the pleasure comes from the play of patterns, the harmonies and contrasts." The meat platter was going around the table now, and I speared a cutlet.

I salted it heavily and bit into the hot, greasy meat with pleasure. The food was second-rate, but it was free. The prospect of unemployment had done wonders for my appetite.

Mies van Koop joined the conversation. He had sparse curly hair and no chin. His head was like a large, thoughtful carrot with the point tucked into his tight collar. "It's a sound analogy, Fletch. But the musician can play his score, play it so that even a legislator..." he smiled and nodded donnishly to Lady Vickers. "Even a legislator can hear how beautiful Beethoven is."

"That's just what I was going to say," she added, wagging her finger at me. "I'm sure my husband has done lovely work, but the only way he knows how to show a person one of his beastly theorems is to make her swot through pages and pages of teeming little symbols."

Mies and I exchanged a look. Lord Vickers was a crank, an eccentric amateur whose work was devoid of serious mathematical interest. But it was thanks to him that Lady Vickers had bothered to come to our little conference. She was the only member of the Europarliament who had.

"Vat you think our chances are?" Rozzick asked her in the sudden silence, his mouth full of unchewed cauliflower.

"Dismal. Unless you can find some way of making your research appeal to the working man, you'll be cut out of next year's budget entirely. They need all the mathematics money for that new computer in Geneva, you know."

"We know," I said gloomily. "That's why we're holding this meeting. But it seems a little late for public relations. If only we hadn't let the government take over all the research funds."

"There's no point blaming the government," Lady Vickers said tartly. "People are simply tired of paying you mathematicians to make them feel stupid."

"Zo build the machine," Rozzick said with an emphatic bob of his bald little head.

"That's right," Mies said, "Build a machine that will play mathematics like music. Why not?"

Lady Vickers clapped her hands in delight and turned to me, "You mean you know how?"

Before I could say anything, Mies kicked me under the table. Hard. I got the message. "Well, we don't have quite all the bugs worked out…"

"But that's just too marvelous!" Lady Vickers gushed, pulling out a little appointment book. "Let's see…the vote on the math appropriation is June 4…which gives us six weeks. Why don't you get your machine ready and bring it to Foxmire towards the end of May? The session is being held in London, you know, and I could bring the whole committee out to feel the beauty of mathematics."

I was having trouble moving my mouth. "Is planty time," Rozzick put in, his eyes twinkling.

Just then Watson caught the thread of conversation. In the journals he was a famous mathematician…practically a grand old man. In conversation he was the callowest of eighteen-years-olds. "Who are you trying to kid, Fletch?" He shook his head, and dandruff showered down on the narrow shoulders of his black suit. "There's no way…" He broke off with a yelp of pain. Mies was keeping busy.

"If you're going to make that train, we'd better get going," I said to Lady Vickers with a worried glance at my watch.

"My dear me, yes," she agreed, rising with me. "We'll expect you and your machine on May 23 then?" I nodded, steering her across the room. Watson had stuck his head under the table to see what was the matter. Something was preventing him from getting back out.

When I got back from the train station, an excited knot of people had formed around Watson, Rozzick and Mies. Watson spotted me first, and in his shrill cracking voice called out, "Our pimp is here."

I smiled ingratiatingly and joined the group. "Watson thinks it's immoral to make mathematics a sensual experience," Mies explained. "The rest of us feel that greater exposure can only help our case."

"Where is machine?" Rozzick asked, grinning like a Tartar jack-o'-lantern.

"You know as well as I do that there is none. All I did was remark to Lady Vickers…"

"One must employ the direct stimulation of the brain," LaHaye put in. He was a delicate old Frenchman with a shock of luminous white hair.

I shook my head. "In the long run, maybe. But I can't quite see myself sticking needles in the committee's brainstems five weeks from now. I'm afraid the impulses are going to have to come in through normal…"

"Absolute Film," Rozzick said suddenly. "Hans Richter and Oskar Fischinger invented in the 1920s. Abstract patterns on screen, repeating and differentiating. Is in Warszaw archives accessible."

"Derisory!" LaHaye protested. "If we make of mathematics an exhibit, it should not be a tawdry *son et lumière*. Don't worry about needles, Dr. Fletcher. There are new field methods." He molded strange shapes in the air around his snowy head.

"He's right," Watson nodded. "The essential thing about mathematics is that it gives aesthetic pleasure without coming through the senses. They've already got food and television for their eyes and ears, their gobbling mouths and grubbing hands. If we're going to give them mathematics, let's sock it to them right in the old grey matter!"

Mies had taken out his pen and a pad of paper. "What type of manifold should we use as the parameter space?"

>> - - - <<

We couldn't have done it if we'd been anywhere else but the Center. Even with their staff and laboratories it took us a month of twenty-hour days to get our first working math player built. It looked like one of those domey old hair-dryers growing out of a file cabinet with dials. We called it a Moddler.

No one was very interested in being the first to get his brain mathed or modified or coddled or whatever. The others had done most of the actual work, so I had to volunteer.

Watson, LaHaye, Rozzick and Mies were all there when I snugged the Moddler's helmet down over my ears. I squeezed the switch on and let the electrical vortex fields swirl into my head.

We'd put together two tapes, one on Book I of Euclid's Elements, and the other on iterated ultrapowers of measurable cardinals. The idea was that the first tape would show people how to understand things they'd vaguely heard of…congruent triangles, parallel lines and the Pythagorean theorem. The second tape was supposed to show the power and beauty of flat-out pure mathematics. It was like we had two excursions: a leisurely drive around a famous ruin, and a jolting blast down a drag-strip out on the edge of town.

We'd put the first tape together in a sort of patchwork fashion, using direct brain recordings as well as artificially punched-in thought patterns. Rozzick had done most of this one. It was all visualized geometry: glowing triangles, blooming circles and the like. Sort of an internalized Absolute Film.

The final proof was lovely, but for me the most striking part was a series of food images which Rozzick had accidentally let slip into the proof that a triangle's area is one-half base times height.

"Since when are triangles covered with anchovy paste?" I asked Rozzick as Mies switched tapes.

"Is your vision clear?" LaHaye wanted to know. I looked around, blinking. Everything felt fine. I still had an afterglow of pleasure from the complex play of angles in Euclid's culminating proof that the square of the hypotenuse is equal to the sum of the squares on the two sides.

Then they switched on the second tape. Watson was the only one of us who had really mastered the Kunen paper on which this tape was based. But he'd refused to have his brain patterns taped. Instead he'd constructed the whole thing as an artificial design in our parameter space.

The tape played in my head without words or pictures. There was a measurable cardinal. Suddenly I knew its properties in the same unspoken way that I knew my own body. I did something to the cardinal and it transformed itself, changing the concepts clustered around it. This happened over and over. With a feeling of light-headedness, I felt myself moving outside of this endless self-transformation…comprehending it from the outside. I picked out a certain subconstellation of the whole process, and swathed it in its logical hull. Suddenly I understood a theorem I had always wondered about.

When the tape ended I begged my colleagues for an hour of privacy. I had to think about iterated ultrapowers some more. I rushed to the library and got out Kunen's paper. But the lucidity was gone. I started to stumble over the notation, the subscripts and superscripts; I was stumped by the gappy proofs; I kept forgetting the definitions. Already the actual content of the main theorem eluded me. I realized then that the Moddler was a success. You could *enjoy* mathematics— even the mathematics you couldn't normally *understand*.

We all got a little drunk that night. Somewhere towards midnight I found myself walking along the edge of the woods with Mies. He was humming softly, beating time with gentle nods of his head.

We stopped while I lit my thirtieth cigarette of the day. In the match's fire I thought I caught something odd in Mies's expression. "What is it?" I asked, exhaling smoke.

"The music..." he began. "The music most people listen to is not good."

I didn't see what he was getting at, and started my usual defense of rock music.

"Muzak," Mies interrupted. "Isn't that what you call it...what they play in airports?"

"Yeah. Easy listening."

"Do you really expect that the official taste in mathematics will be any better? If everyone were to sit under the Moddler...what kind of mathematics would they ask for?"

I shrank from his suggestion. "Don't worry, Mies. There are objective standards of mathematical truth. No one will undermine them. We're headed for a new golden age."

LaHaye and I took the Moddler to Foxmire the next week. It was a big estate, with a hog wallow and three holes of golf between the gatehouse and the mansion. We found Lord Vickers at work on the terrace behind his house. He was thick-set and sported pop-eyes set into a high forehead.

"Fletcher and LaHaye," he exclaimed. "I am honored. You arrive opportunely. Behold." He pulled a sheet of paper out of his special typewriter and handed it to me.

LaHaye was looking over my shoulder. There wasn't much to see. Vickers used his own special mathematical notation. "It would make a nice wallpaper," LaHaye chuckled, then added quickly, "Perhaps if you once explained the symbolism..."

Lord Vickers took the paper back with a hollow laugh. "You know very well that my symbols are all defined in my *Thematics and Metathematics*...a book whose acceptance you have tirelessly conspired against."

"Let's not open old wounds," I broke in. "Dr. LaHaye's remark was not seriously intended. But it illustrates a problem which every mathematician faces. The problem of communicating his work to non-specialists, to mathematical illiterates." I went on to describe the Moddler while LaHaye left to supervise its installation in Lord Vicker's study.

"But that is fantastic!" Vickers exclaimed, pacing back and forth excitedly. A large Yorkshire hog had ambled up to the edge of the terrace. I threw it an apple.

Suddenly Vickers was saying, "We must make a tape of *Thematics and Metathematics*, Dr. Fletcher." This request caught me off-guard.

Vickers had printed his book privately, and had sent a copy to every mathematician in the world. I didn't know of anyone who had read it. The problem was that Vickers claimed he could do things like trisect angles with ruler and compass, give an internal consistency proof for mathematics, and so on. But we mathematicians have rigorous proofs that such things are impossible. So we knew in advance that Vickers's work contained errors, as surely as if he had claimed to have proved that he was twenty meters tall. To master his eccentric notation just to find out his specific mistakes seemed no more worthwhile than looking for the leak in a sunken ship.

But Lord Vickers had money and he had influence. I was glad LaHaye wasn't there to hear me answer, "Of course. I'd be glad to put it on tape."

And, God help me, I did. We had four days before Lady Vickers would bring the Appropriations Committee out for our demonstration. I spent all my waking time in Vickers's study, smoking his cigarettes and punching in *Thematics and Metathematics*.

It would be nice if I could say I discovered great truths in the book, but that's not the way it was. Vickers's work was garbage, full of logical errors and needless obfuscation. I refrained from trying to fix up his mistakes, and just programmed in the patterns as they came. LaHaye flipped when he found out what I was up to. "We have prepared a feast for the mind," he complained, "And you have fouled the table with this, this…"

"Think of it as a ripe Camembert," I sighed. "And serve it last. They'll just laugh it off."

Lady Vickers was radiant when she heard I'd taped *Thematics and Metathematics*. I suggested that it was perhaps too important a work to waste on the Appropriations Committee, but she wouldn't hear of passing it up.

Counting her, there were five people on the committee. LaHaye was the one who knew how to run the Moddler, so I took a walk while he ran each of the legislators through the three tapes.

It was a hot day. I spotted some of those hogs lying on the smooth hard earth under a huge beech tree, and I wandered over to look at them. The big fellow I'd given the apple was there, and he cocked a hopeful eye at me. I spread out my empty hands, then leaned over to scratch his ears. It was peaceful with the pigs, and after a while I lay down and rested my head on my friend's stomach. Through the fresh green beech leaves I could see the taut blue sky.

Lady Vickers called me in. The committee was sitting around the study working on a couple of bottles of Amontillado. Lord Vickers was at the sideboard, his back turned to me. LaHaye looked flushed and desperate.

"Well," I said.

"They didn't like the first tape…" LaHaye began.

"Dreary, dreary," Lady Vickers cried.

"We are not schoolchildren," another committee member put in.

I felt the floor sinking below me. "And the second tape?"

"I don't see how you can call that mathematics," Lady Vickers declaimed.

"There were no equations," someone complained.

"And it made me dizzy," another added.

"Here's to the new golden age of mathematics," Lord Vickers cried suddenly.

"To *Thematics and Metathematics*," his wife added, lifting her glass. There was a chorus of approving remarks.

"That was the real thing."

"Plenty of logic."

"And so many symbols!"

Lord Vickers was smiling at me from across the room. "There'll be a place for you at my new institute, Fletcher."

I took a glass of sherry.

Note on "A New Golden Age"

Written in Fall, 1979.
The Randolph-Macon Woman's College Alumnae Bulletin, Summer, 1981.

My character Joseph Fletcher makes his first appearance in this story, which was inspired by a visit to the Mathematics Conference Center in Oberwolfach, Germany. At that time my grant was about to run out and I was intensively looking for a job. The only job I ended up being offered was at Randolph-Macon Woman's College, in Lynchburg, Virginia.

Publishing a story in the *R-MWC Alumnae Bulletin* struck me as an ironically fitting thing to do since Charles Howard Hinton, a nineteenth century mathematical writer whom I admire, first published one of his stories about the fourth dimension in the *Cheltenham Ladies' College Journal.*

Faraway Eyes

"Look at this," my partner the genius said. He was waving a soap bubble.

I looked back at the program taking shape on my terminal's screen. Orderly green lines of PL/II commands. "Lay off, Harry. I'm not interested."

Harry ignored remarks like that…probably didn't even hear them. He leaned over me heavily. A fat drop of soap solution splatted onto the keys. I sighed, punched in a SAVE, and logged off.

"Watch," Harry said. He had one of those super-bubble frames, a big plastic ring. There was a ten-centimeter soap film stretched across it. Harry blew a gentle stream of air at the center. The big film wobbled, bulged, and then a procession of little bubbles began pinching off and floating away.

"Radioactivity, Harry," I said, trying not to nag. "Waste disposal. Remember the NCR contract?"

He stared at the dancing soap film, thick lips parted in wonder. A bubble landed on the film and merged back in.

Someone was shouting in the reception room. Someone from New Jersey. Rosie's footsteps came stitching down the hall. I walked past Harry and leaned out the door. "What's up?"

Rosie wore her hair over her face with a transparent peep-hole dyed in. Her dress was hologrammed to look like a tree-trunk. A nice girl. Sometimes I wondered what she looked like.

"There's a man with a wheelbarrow to see you, Mister Fletcher. A Mister Kreementz?"

I remembered Kreementz. He was in charge of pollution control at Murden Chemical in Newark. Harry and I had built him a novel stack-scrubber about five years ago. There'd been no complaints before this.

"What's in the wheelbarrow?"

Rosie glanced sidelong at Harry and tittered. "That's the funny part. The wheelbarrow's empty. And he keeps saying he wants to dump it out on your…"

The door from the reception room slammed open and Kreementz came surging down the hall with a big steel wheelbarrow in front of him. If it hadn't been for the necktie, he would have looked like an angry old construction worker. Rosie and I stepped back into my office, bumping Harry.

"Garden State Degeneracy—We Deliver," Harry said cryptically.

And then the wrath of Kreementz was upon us. "The jig is up, boys. I filed suit on my way over. You know what a plant shutdown costs per *hour*? You ain't gonna sneak off and leave *me* holding the bag."

He set the wheelbarrow down heavily. His suit was sweat-stained, and he was breathing hard. I wondered how an empty wheelbarrow could be so heavy.

"Sit down, Mr. Kreementz." I gestured at my chair. "I don't know why you think Fletcher & Company would do anything other than stand behind our products. If Murden Chemical has a problem with our emission controller, I can assure you that…"

Harry sniffed the air and winked at Rosie. He stuck his thumb out from his fist and mimed someone drinking out of a bottle. I was surprised to see him joke that way. Kreementz caught the gesture and flared up.

"That weirdo null-ray of yours is on the fritz. Every time we start it, it shuts itself off again. And they're blaming me!" He glared at Harry. "You'd drink, too! You think it's funny? Try this on for size!"

With a grunt he tipped the wheelbarrow forward. Something too small to see thudded on to the concrete floor. Dust and stone chips flew up. There was a terrible rumbling, like a lead beer-barrel. It was rolling towards Harry.

With a heavy man's nimbleness, Harry stepped to the side and knelt down. There was a slowly lengthening groove in the floor. There was something at the end of the groove, something tiny that rolled and rumbled.

Rosie was standing by the door looking like a hairy fence-post. When her peephole didn't show, you couldn't tell which way she was facing. I assumed she was watching Harry. He seemed to fascinate her.

"Very nice," Harry said as he inched along the floor on his hands and knees. "Come take a look, Fletch."

I glanced inquiringly at Kreementz. "Be my guest," he said. "We've got plenty more where that came from. The base of Stack Seven. That's the one that you…"

Suddenly I got the picture.

The rumbling was still going on. It sounded for all the world like Kreementz had started a heavy little ball rolling across our floor. I got down next to Harry and squinted.

It was tiny, a fraction of a millimeter across. A little sphere, shiny like a droplet of mercury. Judging from the groove it was chewing into the floor, I guessed it weighed well over a hundred kilograms. Harry planted his thick thumb in the ball's path. The ball rumbled under his thumb without slowing down. Pretty soon it would hit the wall.

Rosie was behind me, leaning over to see too. I shot a look up. With her hair hanging forward, I could see her face. She had a prim mouth and faraway eyes. When she saw me looking at her she stood up straight.

I got up, determined to show Kreementz who was boss. "Mister Kreementz, the null-ray was designed to compress the matter inside your stack. We did *not* say that the matter would then disappear. I believe I warned you to keep the stack clean."

"But I didn't see anything building up!" Kreementz burst out. "The first month I cleaned it out every day, but one day I missed and the gunk was gone anyway. I figured that ray of yours would make anything disappear if it stayed in long enough."

"In other words, you haven't cleaned the stack for almost five years of continuous operation?"

Kreementz started to nod, then glared. He'd admitted too much already.

"I guess you were right," Harry said to me as he stood up.

"About the automatic shut-off?"

"You mean you *designed* the null-ray to stop working?" Kreementz demanded.

There was a sudden crunching. The little ball was drilling through our wall and into the next room. When the noise died down again I answered.

"We wanted it to be…foolproof."

"You see," Harry added, "If you leave something under the null-ray long enough…say five years…then it goes black hole."

Kreementz mopped his brow. "What would have happened if we'd gotten a black hole in Stack Seven?"

"I'll give you the good news first," Harry said, his ropey lips twisting into a smile. "Quantum effects would force the hole to evaporate into pure energy. By measuring the energy released in the evaporation event, scientists would be able to tell whether or not the quark theory of matter is correct. Fletch, give him the bad news."

"According to Stephen Hawking's calculations, the 'evaporation' of a hundred kilogram black hole would be the same as a ten megaton nuclear blast. Of course, if the quark theory of matter is wrong, then the blast would be some ten thousand times stronger."

"You guys would have been great on *Laugh-In*," Kreementz said sourly.

"What's *Laugh-In*?" Rosie asked.

"It was a TV show when Mister Kreementz was little," I said. "He seems like a person who watched television a lot as a child, doesn't he?"

"At least I *had* a childhood," Kreementz retorted. "You guys look like you was hatched. Especially him!"

Harry was staring at the wall, shoulders hunched and fists thrust into the enormous pockets of his baggy grey polyester pants. There was a muffled crash as the little ball left the next room.

Harry turned slowly. "How many tons?"

"He means how many tons are in the stack," I explained.

"I ain't weighed it," Kreementz said sullenly. "Five years worth of smoke. Maybe two hundred thousand tons."

"But smoke is light," Rosie protested.

"Not at Murden Chemical," I said.

"Not when these guys are through with it," Kreementz added. "They built us a ray which kills all the atoms inside Stack Seven. They stop vibrating and shrivel up. We have a cap on the stack. Every few minutes it gets as full of smoke as it can hold, and then the null-ray triggers, and everything inside the smokestack disappears."

"You keep forgetting that the stuff doesn't disappear," I corrected. "It just collapses down to a very small size."

"Like a trash compactor," Rosie suggested.

I nodded. "That's what we had in mind. One smokestack full of crud was supposed to make a hundred-kilogram block the size of a brick. But Mister Kreementz left the stuff in there to get collapsed a little more with each pulse of the null-ray. We warned him not to do that, but he did it anyway. If I hadn't put in a mass detector coupled to a shut-off circuit, then Mister Kreementz would have turned Central Jersey into just another beautiful memory."

The rumbling had stopped after the last crash. The shiny little speck of degenerate matter had probably sunk into our flower bed. "How dense is that stuff?" I asked Harry.

He had been scribbling on the blackboard ever since Kreementz had given him the two hundred thousand tons figure. "I get ten-to-the-eleventh grams per cubic centimeter. That's neutronium. Plain neutrons with just enough degenerate electrons and protons mixed in to keep it stable. I'm surprised it worked."

"Is neutronium valuable?" Kreementz wanted to know.

Harry opened his mouth to answer. I stepped in front of him. I had a policy of never letting Harry answer any question relating to money.

"Are you kidding?" I asked Kreementz with a mocking laugh. "Is sewage valuable? Do people like cancer? Are oil-spills good for fish? Is the Pope Jewish? You've got a big, dirty cleanup ahead of you, Kreementz. One false move and you'll blow the plant sky high. I don't envy you." One hand was behind my back, making shooing gestures at Harry.

Kreementz sighed heavily. "You wouldn't have a drink handy, would you?"

Rosie got him a Coke and a few ounces of lab alcohol. He took a long, thirsty pull. Deftly I set the hook. "We *could* organize the cleanup, but it'd be…"

"No, Fletch," Harry said. "It's too dangerous. I don't think we should risk it." He was right on the beam.

"I've been authorized to make you an offer," Kreementz said, naming a reasonable sum. "It's a lot to pay, and I still think we could win the lawsuit…but the management wants to get her started up again."

"Triple that and we'll have it clean in two days."

"Double."

"Done."

* * * *

Actually, the cleanup was a piece of cake. We opened up the side of the smokestack and brought in bulldozers. The stuff on top was something like high-grade iron ore. The lower layers had been under the null-ray longer. We had to truck most of it out a few cubic centimeters at a time. Our trucks could only carry a hundred tons. But we'd rented a fleet of them.

Harry had poured a titaniplast floor into our basement. The stuff was a metallic compound based on the new quark chemistry. No one knew yet how strong it was…since no one had ever been able to break a piece of it after it hardened. We dumped the neutronium in the basement window. Harry was happy to have the stuff, said it had arrived just when he needed it. He took some waldoes down there and got to work. I was happy to get him and his soap bubbles out of my office.

My job right then was to run some computer simulations for the nuclear energy people. How many would die if we buried the radioactive waste in a diamond mine. What would happen if you put it in the polar ice-cap. How much would it cost to rocket it into the sun. They'd been stockpiling the waste for forty years now. Every time it looked like they'd decided on a solution, someone came up with a new "but what if." Fletcher & Co. had taken an NRC contract to improve the simulations and, by God, make a decision.

Harry had promised to try to think of a brand-new solution, but I wasn't counting on it. I just concentrated on debugging my programs. The extra money from Murden Chemical had helped, but if I couldn't make the NRC happy enough to pay big bucks, then the leaser was going to repossess my central processing unit. I would have sooner given up my own medulla.

A week went by. Rosie brought me my lunch as usual, milk and tuna-salad sandwich. I didn't like to stop programming when I was hot. But instead of quietly leaving, Rosie stayed standing next to me. Today's dress was hologrammed to make a fountain out of her. It was distracting.

"Is there a problem, Rosie?"

"It's Doctor Gerber. He's been acting strangely."

"When Harry *stops* acting strangely, I'll worry. Meanwhile, could you get me some more milk?"

I went on eating and punching keys for a while, but then I realized she was still standing at my elbow. "All right," I said, finally looking up. "Tell me about it."

"I guess you know that Doctor Gerber and I are…are…"

I hadn't. The possibility had never occurred to me. *Harry? Rosie?* They were my genius and my receptionist. It was hard for me to think of them as being anything else. It wasn't in the flowchart.

"I didn't feel it was my place to interfere," I said finally.

"He moved in with me two months ago," she said with a toss of her head. For a second I glimpsed her aquiline nose. "I've been after him to take me somewhere, somewhere far away. But now he hasn't come home for a week. He just stays in the basement here and he won't come out."

So, I wanted to say, that's what he *always* does when he's onto something. Leave him alone! Instead I said, "Perhaps I'd better have a look." I stood up.

"And tell him that I'll stop nagging him about the trip if he comes back," Rosie added.

Harry didn't notice me at first. He was asleep. The basement looked like a minimalist sculptor's studio. The main exhibit was a bowed ramp of titaniplast that looked like it had grown out of the floor. The ramp slanted down from one wall, and then swooped back up to the other wall. The ramp had a semi-circular groove on top, and at the low point there was a black titaniplast sphere. The setup reminded me of the ball-return gutter in some unearthly bowling alley. The ball was one-and-a-half meters across and looked heavy.

I walked past the greasy vinyl couch that Harry was lying on and looked at the sphere. The utterly rigid black material shone dully under the yellow electric lights. There was a hole cut in one side, a pentagonal hole big enough to crawl through. There was something funny about the space inside. It was like staring into a lens.

As I leaned closer I felt an unpleasant pressure on my temples. I straightened up, but the sphere kept getting closer. I was sliding across the floor. I jerked in fear and fell backwards. Crablike I scuttled back across the room.

"The only way to get in is fast," Harry said suddenly. "It's not so bad inside, I think. Positive curvature instead of negative."

I sat up and looked around. Harry was lying on his back with his arms and legs sticking straight up. It must have been exercise, but it looked terrible.

"Rosie sent me," I said, before I forgot.

"Why?"

"She wonders why you haven't come to see her this week."

"I've been busy."

I decided I'd done enough for Rosie. "What's the sphere for?"

"You roll it back and forth. It's a dodecahedral skeleton of neutronium bars embedded in a shell of titaniplast. A padded jungle-gym for gravitons. What else did Rosie say?"

"She said that if you came back she'd stop nagging you about the trip. What happens when you roll the sphere back and forth?"

"I hoped she'd say that. I hate travel. I ought to go up and talk to her…"

He started out, but I caught him by the shoulder. "Harry, please tell me what you've built here."

He looked back at me, baffled. "Can't you see?"

"I see a hollow black sphere sitting on a rocker track. Why don't we take it from there."

"You remember my super-bubble ring? This is sort of the same thing. It's to get rid of nuclear waste. Anything that's inside the sphere disappears when the sphere rolls back and forth."

My heart skipped a beat. "Have you tested it?"

"No. Wait a minute. I'm going to get Rosie." He flicked on a switch and went upstairs.

While he was gone I looked the thing over some more. Harry had started a system of winches and pulleys running. Almost imperceptibly, the sphere was creeping up the ramp. I hoped it didn't fall off. That degenerate matter packed a wallop. I sat down on the couch and started drafting my letter to the NRC. All things considered, a half billion a year didn't seem like too much to ask.

When Harry and Rosie finally came back, I could see that hunky was still far from dory. Harry didn't understand about apologies, about white lies. I wondered what she saw in him.

But with both of us there to impress, Harry became more communicative. His soap solution and super-bubble ring were under the couch, and he dragged them out. He made a big film and blew at the center of it. The film wobbled and bulged.

"That's what space is like inside a massive object," Harry said. "It curves towards the fourth dimension. Now, if I blow harder…"

He did, and a little bubble pinched off the film and floated away. "That's the way a black hole does it. But we can't use them. So instead…"

He blew out a little bulge in the soap film again. But this time instead of blowing harder, he jiggled the film back and forth. Ripples darted around on the film's surface, and suddenly two of them happened to meet near the bulge. The walls met and a little bubble floated off again.

"That's what the neutronium skeleton is supposed to do for us. The space inside it bulges way out towards the fourth dimension. Now when the sphere starts rolling down the ramp, those moving bars of neutronium are going to churn up waves like a mix-master. Sooner or later two waves will meet, and the bulge inside the sphere will pinch off to make a little hypersphere outside of our space."

The winch motors turned off with a click. The sphere was poised at the top of the ramp.

"What happens then?" Rosie asked.

"The hypersphere floats away. Maybe it lands on a different space; maybe it comes back to ours someplace else."

"Another space…" Rosie said slowly. "Like the astral plane?"

Harry shrugged. "If you want to call it that."

The sphere had come to rest at the top of the track with the hole on the side pointing towards us. Harry had a little loading chute ready by the track there. It was aimed so that anything that slid down it would zip right through the hole in the sphere.

"What do you want to put in?" Harry asked.

"Would it…would it be dangerous for a person?" Rosie wanted to know.

"What a question!" I burst out. "You'd be squeezed to death! And then the gravity waves would work you over. And if by some wild fluke you lived through all that, where do you think you'd end up? Even if your space bubble ever did join up with a normal space again, what do you think the odds are that you'd land on the surface of an Earth-like planet?"

"Maybe it would take you to a different *kind* of space," Rosie suggested mildly. "Where you don't *need* planets."

"Rosie will always have the mind of a secretary," Harry said cuttingly. "What do you say I put this in?" He picked up an empty cardboard box from the floor.

"Fine," I said. "But let's try something massive, too. A sandbag."

Harry set the cardboard box at the top of the little sliding-board and let it go. The sphere's field accelerated the box down the chute and it zoomed through the hole, getting somewhat crushed by tidal forces on the way.

Once inside, it bounced around for a minute before settling to the bottom. The bouncing had fluffed it back up again. Except for all the box's right angles being a little too big, it looked fine.

"Why doesn't the gravitational field in there crush it?"

"Anything inside is pushed and pulled in every direction at once," Harry said. "Which adds up to nothing. Of course there's still a strong positive curvature of space in there. And when those bars start moving around…but I don't want to bore Rosie." He shot her a nasty look, but she just stood there, stiff and alone.

Harry and I went upstairs then to get one of the sandbags from the radiation lab. It was a good fifty kilos, and it took the two of us to get it down the stairs. Neither one of us is getting any younger.

Rosie was gone when we got back downstairs. "You shouldn't have said that about the mind of a secretary," I told Harry.

He sighed. "Ah, she's always talking about that fantasy-land stuff. If only I could get her to take a night-school physics course. There's wonder enough in pure science without going in for a lot of malarkey. And she still won't give up on that trip business."

We heaved the sandbag onto the chute and it slid down to rest by the cardboard box. Then Harry tossed a cap-shaped titaniplast hatch-cover in place. The gravitational field slammed it on tight. We stood clear and he tripped the release.

The enormously heavy sphere rumbled down the incline, past the middle and back up to the other wall. Then it came back. I thought of a bubble wand waving back and forth. I thought I could feel the gravity waves in the pit of my stomach.

"It's not moving very fast, Harry."

"Doesn't have too. The dodecahedral field configuration is inherently unstable, especially with that space mix-master going. I bet it has pinched off five hyperspheres by now. Hear the air rushing in?"

Indeed there was a hissing to be heard over the rumble of the track. As the space inside the neutronium sphere was blown away, new space and new air had to seep in. I actually felt myself drawn towards the sphere again, but this time from across the room.

It took about ten minutes for the oscillations to dampen, for the sphere to stop rolling back and forth. When we slid the hatch-door over with a long stick there was nothing inside.

"We ought to send a radio-beacon through the next time," Harry remarked. "Then we could hear if it resurfaced somewhere in our space."

"Tomorrow," I said. "Right now I want to celebrate. What do you say I take you and Rosie out for the best meal of your lives?"

But we couldn't find Rosie anywhere. In fact, she never showed up at the office again.

It's funny about a girl like that. I never noticed her much when she worked for me, but now...now I dream about her every night. So does Harry.

Note on "Faraway Eyes"

Written in Fall, 1979.
Analog Science Fiction / Science Fact, September, 1980.

"Faraway Eyes" was the first story I sold to a mainline SF magazine, although by this time I'd serialized *Space-time Donuts* in *Unearth* and I'd sold my novel *White Light* to both Virgin and Ace. But "Faraway Eyes" was my first "real" magazine sale.

"Faraway Eyes" introduces Joe Fletcher's partner Harry Gerber. These are a very traditional SF pair of characters, whose roots go back to Robert Sheckley's AAA Ace stories, to Henry Kuttner and beyond. Fletcher and Harry reappear in the stories "The Man Who Ate Himself," "Inertia," and in my novel *Master of Space and Time*.

I have the uneasy feeling that the various mass and size numbers in this tale are scientifically inaccurate. In later years I often had my engineer friend John Walker check the science in my writings.

THE 57TH FRANZ KAFKA

20 January 1981.

Pain again, deep in the left side of my face. At some point in the night I gave up pretending to sleep and sat by the window, staring down at the blind land-street and the deaf river.

The impossibility of connected thought. Several times I thought I heard the new body moving in the long basin.

It began snowing during the night. I opened both windows and hunched myself forward with my mouth open, drawing in deep, aching breaths. My hope: a perfect snowflake, if sucked down wholly and rapidly, might reach the black center of my lungs and freeze them solid. Imagine breathing water, breathing ice. Later, hearing the bells toll, I wept.

After Mema brought me my breakfast, she went out to clean away the melting snow. I stood well back from the window lest she see my cheers and gloating grimaces.

After clearing the sidewalk, she had not yet had enough of wielding her scrub-broom, and stepped, repeatedly and at great risk, into the heavy land-street traffic, trying to clear off *our half*. She has, in the years since I dissolved the marriage, become an automaton. I realize this with finality when I see her stare uncomprehendingly after the splashing motorwagons, which again and again cover *our half* of the street, and splatter her apron and her thick legs with the grey, crystalline frosting.

The suppressed laughter hurts my chest. I begin to cough and have to sit down on my bed. Here I sit, words crawling off my pen-point.

There are only four more pages left in this, the last volume of my fifty-seventh series of diaries. I must write less.

23 January 1981.

Three days of fever. Straightening my wet bedclothes, Mema found my special pictures, the Fast-Night groupings, and took them away. *What if Felice were to see them?*

I have more pictures hidden in the attic, pictures I press to my ribs while I pour all my food out into the long basin. The new body is not so far along as I had hoped. There are still only the clotted fibers. It is strange that I could have thought otherwise.

25 January 1981.

Last night the worst yet. Dream: again Reb Pessin showing me the Book of Qlippoth, the secrets of immortality. A high buzzing, as of a tremendous propeller, drowns out his voice. The surprising weight of the little book. He makes a false gesture, and I spread out in space instead of time. A whole city where everyone wears my face, streets of women, the offices. A street-car conductor leaning over me, shaking with laughter, "If I were you…"

Awake before dawn. For the first time real fear that the new body will not be ready. But going into the attic with a candle, I see that all is well. Even the skin is finished.

26 January 1981.

Real sleep at last. Waking up, an unnatural feeling of lightness. So many memories are gone already, gone over.

I drank two cups of black tea with breakfast. Mema had to go back down to the kitchen for the second. When she brought it up, I had forgotten the first breakfast already, and asked her where it was. This is all as it should be. Soon I can begin again.

Yesterday, in a mood of wild exaltation, I mailed my remaining special pictures to Felice, first scribbling her real name on some of the women's faces.

Now, cheerful and whistling from my sound sleep and my two cups of tea, I take pen in hand and compose another letter to her father:

> Honored Herr B!
>
> I am not surprised that you have failed to answer my letters of 24.XII.80, 26.XII.80, and 15.I.81. You need not apologize! It is only right and natural that a man in your position must take thought, in the interests of his daughter, before moving to bind a marriage contract. The questions of my finances, age and health are undoubtedly your unspoken concerns.
>
> As regards the question of age: I am forty-one, and will remain so. Although your daughter is now but twenty, she will in the course of time become sixty. Until that

age, I vow to have and hold her as sole love-object. Frau Mema, my housekeeper and ex-wife, can attest to this.

My financial security is assured by certain interlocking fixed-interest annuities. I do not need to work, and I despise to do so. My brutto yearly income is in the excess of fifteen thousand thalers…not a figure to conjure with, but surely adequate for your little mouse's needs.

The state of my health is a predictable matter. At present it is bad, and it will grow a bit worse. But next month, and in the summer, I will once again be fresh and strong. There can be no doubt of this.

Would a marriage date of February 30 be acceptable to you?

With high respect,
Franz K. LVII

29 January 1981.

All evening, Mema watched television in the parlor, directly under my bedroom. The police were here yesterday, sent by Felice's father.

They did not dare come up to me, and spoke only to Mema. I stood naked at the head of the stairs, baring my teeth and trembling with a fierce joy each time I glimpsed their green peaked caps. It struck me that the caps were living beings which *wear policemen*.

The excitement made me very weak, and all day I left the bed only to empty my cavities into the long basin. It is time to complete the task, to open my veins. Mema knows that today is the day, and under my feet she rocks and watches green, peaked caps move across the television screen.

30 January 1981.

LVIII is still waiting in the long basin behind the thin attic wall.

Last night I took candle and long knife and leaned over the basin, staring down through the thick, gathered fluids. The candle-wax dripped and sprung into little saucers, white disks that drifted down to rest on Franz LVIII's closed eyelids. His mouth is set in a smile, as always.

I am not frightened of death, not after fifty-six times. But when my new body walks, the green, peaked caps will take it away. Herr B. must pay for this.

I have resolved to make him murder me. The exquisite uncertainty of *how he will do it*. I feel like a virgin bride.

Mema has gone to the butcher to buy two kilograms of blood-sausage. Tonight I will chew the sausage up for LVIII. My true blood must belong to Herr B.

31 January 1981.
The blood-sausage was everything I had ever dreamed it to be. Thick and dark, with the texture of excrement, the congealed pigs' blood is stuffed into a greasy casing made of the animals' own small intestines.

Leaning over the long basin, chewing and spitting up, I felt a disgust purer and more complete than anything I have experienced since the time of the camps.

The sausage-casing is stamped with repeated pictures of a pig wearing a crown and making obeisances. I have stretched the casing enough to wrap it around my waist, like the little tailor who killed seven with one blow.

The chewing of the sausage took a long time, and I fell asleep in a sort of ecstasy, with my forehead resting on the rim of the long basin. I awakened to a touch of LVIII's hand, tugging petulantly at my hair. I started back, uncertain where I was, and heard the church tower toll three.

Filled with an implacable strength, I descended the stairs. Mema lay sleeping on her cot in the kitchen. I unplugged the phone and brought it upstairs. Then I crawled under my bed to muffle the sound, and dialed Felice's number over and over.

The shining love-words dripped off my lips that still glistened with blood-sausage. My tongue felt slender, magically flexible, as if it could pierce the phone wires and the shell of her ear. After my second call, her father answered, and I gibbered like a golem, ever-new inspirations striking me with each call. I continued calling for two hours. They answered less and less often, and finally not at all. Now I have left my phone off the hook to keep theirs ringing.

Franz K. LVIII is sloshing about in the long basin, impatient for the final spark. The dawn strikes through my window and gilds this page, the last of this volume. Now, before Mema awakes, I must go to pound on Felice's door, a long knife in my hand.

Note on "The 57th Franz Kafka"

Written in Spring, 1980.
The Little Magazine, Vol. 13, Nos. 3 & 4, 1982.

In Heidelberg I read and reread the Penguin Modern Classics edition of *The Diaries of Franz Kafka*. The physical setting of this story was the house of my Heidelberg friend Imre Molnar who lived down the hill from us on the Schlierbacher Landstrasse. Imre himself appears as Huba in *The Sex Sphere*, but he had nothing to do with the character in "The 57th Franz Kafka."

The name for the story comes from the fact that the story is set in 1981, which was fifty-seven years after Kafka's 1924 death. I used this story's name for my first story anthology because I had the fantasy that people would like my stories so much that I would be considered a "new Franz Kafka"— certainly not the first "new Franz Kafka," but maybe the fifty-seventh.

The Little Magazine at that time was co-edited by David Hartwell, who'd eventually become my editor at Tor Books.

THE INDIAN ROPE TRICK EXPLAINED

(With excerpts from Transdimensional Avatar, by Revell Gibson.)

Paris was backwards. Charlie Raumer sat on a patch of grass near the Louvre trying to straighten it out. The kids were fighting, Cybele wasn't speaking to him, and all around was the mirror-image of the Paris he remembered from twelve years ago.

He buried his face in his hands, pushing at the misty red memories. He imagined a Paris made of glass, a relief map. If you looked at it from the wrong side, everything would be backwards, inside-out. He began tugging at the surfaces in his image to put them right. Something began…there was a heavy thud on his back.

It was Iris, the ten-year-old. "What's the matter, Daddy, are you *drunk*?" She broke into a wild giggle at this sally, and her two little brothers joined in, pigs at the party. They piled onto his back with a confused squealing. Someone shrieked, "POKE!" and little Jimmy fell crying to the ground.

Raumer's teeth clenched. "Iris, you stop it or…"

"It was Howard," she yelled with a grimace at the larger of her two little brothers. Distrusting speech, Howard charged her, arms windmilling. Raumer seized the two and shook them hard. Their little faces looked crooked and ugly.

"Stop, stop, stop!" It was Cybele, back with a precious paper bag of postcards. When she was a girl she had spent every Sunday in the Louvre. But now that she was finally here again, her family had refused to come inside.

"Mine, Mama. Me." Jimmy took an uncertain step forwards. Howard snaked past him and snatched the cards from his mother. Iris crosschecked Howard and they hit the ground together.

Raumer dealt out two back-handed slaps and recovered the cards. The printing on the museum shop bag was reversed. He wished he had never started fooling with the Hinton hypercube models.

"Is that all you can do?" his wife was demanding, an orchid of anger blossoming in her voice. "Beat them? Why don't you ever help me instead of *ruining* our…"

All this time a part of Raumer's mind had been fiddling with his image of Paris. Now instead of trying to make it come right he let it *be* backward, let himself go. He felt a rush of freedom. And disappeared.

He snapped back on the steps of the Louvre, thirty meters away. Nothing looked backwards anymore. In a twinkling instant the two heavily ornamented wings of the building had changed places. His tail-bone hurt where he'd dropped onto the steps. Across the road he could see Cybele and the kids looking for him.

"Bhom bhom bho-la?"

Raumer turned. A tall African was hunkering just behind him. A street-vendor. They were all over Paris this June. White plastic ivory elephants, brittle leather belts, strangely patterned wallets, and the little drums mounted on sticks. The vendor was twirling one of the drums between his fingers. There were two clay marbles attached with string, and when the drum twirled, the marbles rattled on the taut skins. "Bhom bhom bho-la?"

"*Non merci. Pas acheter.*" As he tried to brush the peddler off, the utter strangeness of what had just happened was hitting Raumer. He had been over there, and now he was here. Had he blacked out? But there was nothing stronger than coffee and a hangover in his system. Across the road, Iris squealed and pointed up at him.

"*Je vous le donne,*" the African said, holding out the little drum. Still twirling it. Pattapattapattapat. "*Pour devenir sauteur.*" Serious eyes under a high, noble forehead.

Raumer took the drum. *For becoming a jumper.* So the African had seen. Raumer had really jumped thirty meters. But…

Iris came pumping up the steps, her eyes fixed on the toy. "Can it be mine, Dad?"

A light touch of long fingers on Raumer's shoulder. "*Inquirez devant le Centre Pompidou.*" He turned to thank, to ask, but the tall African was already gliding down the steps, no leg-movements visible under his black and yellow dashiki.

Iris was tugging at the drum now. One of the little clay marbles came off and bounced down the steps. Raumer bared his teeth at the child, then retrieved the ball. He slipped it into his coat pocket with the drum before the others could start in.

"You didn't have to run off like that," Cybele said, looking not quite pleased to have found him. "We didn't even see you cross the street."

"Daddy bought a toy drum, and it's mine," Iris announced. Jimmy's face quivered, and Howard stepped forward, alert eyes fixed on the bulge in Raumer's pocket.

"What is the matter with you children?" Cybele demanded. "Can't you stop asking for things for one *minute*?"

"I'll get them each a drum," Raumer muttered. Four of the Africans were standing in a group ten meters away. Impassively, with long arcing gestures, they were working a stream of Canadian tourists. They could have been catching fish. Raumer hesitated, trying to decide which one he had talked with.

"You will not," Cybele said, taking his arm. An old lady had just stepped out of a cab and onto the curb next to them. Cybele called to the cab driver in rapid French, then herded Raumer in. "I am going to feed you and these children before you murder each other."

Raumer had a veal cutlet with a fried egg on it; Cybele had calf-brains in brown butter; and the kids each had a little steak with *pommes frites*. Coffee, apple juice, wine…they were all smiling at each other. A cool June day in Paris. It's ridiculous what a difference food makes. The kids drifted across the cheap restaurant to play pinball with two francs they had scrounged.

Raumer took the toy drum out of his pocket to tie the string Iris had snapped. "So you did buy one," Cybele said, lighting a cigarette. "It's cute."

"One of those Africans gave it to me," Raumer said. "For jumping thirty meters through hyperspace."

"What are you talking about?"

"I figure that's what happened. When I disappeared. I'd been having that mirror-image feeling again and…"

Cybele sighed a cloud of smoke. "This is our vacation, Charlie. Our last chance. Can't you wait till you're back in your library to be so crazy?" She tried to soften the last word with a strained smile.

"I don't think it's crazy to be writing a book on the history of the fourth dimension. What am I supposed to do…walk around holding your hand as if we were still courting?"

"It might be nice." Suddenly her reserve broke. "Oh, Charlie, don't you care? We fell in love here. And if now all we can do is…*fight*…then we're…" She held a supplicating hand out across the table.

"My jumping like that fits in with the theory I found in the Hinton book," Raumer said slowly, not really noticing his wife. "We have a slight thickness in the fourth dimension. We're like coins sliding around on a table-top. Our consciousness is down with the table-top…but if you somehow identify with the *top* side of the coin then things look backwards. At the Louvre I finally let myself go all the way up. The momentum flipped me right off the board. I could have come down anywhere. I could have come down backwards or sideways…"

While he talked, Raumer twirled the carved rod sticking out of the little tom-tom's side. The strings and weights followed along, trailing like a galaxy's spiral arms. When he reversed direction, the little marbles pattered on the tight skins. He rolled the stick back and forth, getting the hang of it. Pattapat. Pattapattapat.

"You don't…you don't really…" Cybele began, then gave up. "Why don't we all rest and then go see the Pompidou Art Center at Beaubourg?" she suggested in a charged, artificially bright voice. "I hear it's the kind of place where you and the kids won't get bored."

A wail cut the air. Howard. Iris had pushed the reset button on the pinball machine, and Howard's franc had been lost. Raumer went over to put in another coin.

The machine was called *Dimension Warp*. The glass scoreboard carried a bright picture of two women learning the ropes from a hyperspace pilot who's a robot. Those naughty cuties are taking notes and licking the points of their thick pencils…while that jivey robobopster fingers the controls. The player as machine, courting curvy Nature. Groovy.

Raumer split three games with Iris and Howard. Jimmy got to pull the plunger. The machine had an unusual feature, a little ramp a ball could jump over to land somewhere else on the board…in a special and otherwise inaccessible free-game hole if you were lucky. The cover-glass was set up high enough so the ball could sail quite a distance before clacking back into the plane of normal play.

"That's what you did, Daddy," Howard said the first time the ball made its trip through the third dimension.

"What do you mean?" Raumer gave his son a sharp look. He couldn't always tell what went on behind that smooth seven-year-old forehead.

"He means that your turn's over," Iris interjected. They left it at that.

Their hotel was nearby, and Cybele wanted to go up to rest and change shoes. Little Jimmy needed a nap and Iris wanted to keep an eye on her mother. Eager to avoid the possibility of another ugly scene in the tiny hotel room, Raumer proposed that he kill some time with Howard and meet the others in front of the Pompidou Center in an hour and a half. Cheerfully, father and son boarded the Metro.

In between stations the DuBonnet ads flickered past. DUBO…DUBON…DUBONNET…DUBO…DUBON…DUBONNET…Over and over. A pun. *Du beau*: lovely; *du bon*: tasty. Cybele had explained it to him the first time he'd come to Paris. Twelve years now. She'd been an art student then and he'd been at the *Université* on a scholars exchange program. An American machine courting a French cutie. Somehow he'd won her. But now he only wondered why he'd wanted to.

"What if the ball went under the board like a subway?" Howard asked suddenly, his big opened eyes reflecting in the black glass.

Cybele had told Raumer about Howard's long ruminations. "All the machinery, the electrical stuff, is under the board," he smiled. "The ball would probably get stuck, half under and half over."

He had a sudden impulse to talk to the boy, to teach him something. He hardly knew the child, really. In the normal run of things Cybele did all the work with the children.

"Imagine this, Howard. Imagine that there were pictures that could slide around just on the pinball board. What would the ball look like to them when it rolled around?"

"Like a ball."

"No, dummy. If all they could see was what touched their plane, then the ball would look like a dot moving around."

"Unless you pushed it through."

"That's right. If you pushed the ball through the plane they'd see a circular cross-section. And when the ball jumps off the ramp, they'd think it had disappeared."

"Why do you call it a cross-section? Cross means X."

"It can mean cutting, too. If I had a real big sharp knife I could make a cross-section of you…cut you down the middle and shave off a nice thin…" Raumer stopped himself. That was no way to talk to a child. What was the matter with him?

At the next stop they had to change trains. Raumer's memory was still playing tricks on him…they caught their connecting train in the wrong direction. Upset, he yelled at Howard for wanting to go to the bathroom.

When they finally got to the right stop, the boy's face had turned into a tight little mask. Raumer suddenly realized that no one in his family really liked him. They had no reason to. Trying to buy a smile, he gave Howard the toy drum. No reaction. They climbed the stairs, and stepped out into the plaza next to the *Centre Pompidou*.

The building itself is as wonderful as anything in it. It is built inside-out, with all the structural supports, heating shafts, escalators, plumbing and electrical conduits attached to the outside walls. The machinery is all outside, and the traditional decoration is all hanging on the walls inside. The marvelous joke is that a lot of those functional-looking pipes outside are fake…pure this-is-not-a-decoration decoration. It isn't enough for the building to *be* inside out, it has to *look* inside out.

The plaza was dotted with idlers, many of them arranged into circles around street-performers: a juggler, a fire-eater lying on a mound of broken glass, and a crazy man shouting fifty years too late about the surrealist staple of *rayons ultraviolets*. The chilly breeze was snatching the words out of people's mouths and scattering them around the big square.

Right by the subway stairs there were a few sidewalk artists waiting for people to drop coins onto the pastels they'd drawn on the stone ground. One of the artists had filled in the black outline of a boy with fanciful pictures of body organs and thoughts.

Howard begged till Raumer put half a franc on the man's picture, and then he pulled his father over to join a group watching a snake-charmer. Snakers are supposed to be Indian, but this charmer was another of the dashiki-clad Africans.

He was squatting on a piece of cloth patterned with squares and slanting lines. His snakes writhed sluggishly and spilled out of a big wicker basket. His flute was a gourd with two pipes sticking out. One pipe had holes for fingering the eerie, wandering notes, and the other let air out to play on the face of the snake being charmed.

A cobra on the basket top wove back and forth, following the movements of the snaker's flute. Its hood was spread menacingly, and occasionally it made as if to strike. The tune drifted up and down a pentatonic scale, weaving like the snake's body. Little Howard began twirling his drum in accompaniment. Typically, he'd been able to play it as soon as Raumer gave it to him.

When the snaker heard the sound of the pattering, his eyes flashed at them. The tune speeded up, and Howard kept pace. Slowly the snaker rose to a crouch, drawing the cobra higher and higher. Finally he was standing erect on his long legs and the cobra had reared up to an impossible height. Raumer hoped its venom sacs were gone. The music cut off abruptly and the cobra collapsed back to a great, shifting coil.

"Bhom bhom bho-la!" the African shouted. He was an imposing man with stiff ebony features. A few coins pattered onto the tessellated cloth beneath his feet. "*Dix francs de plus et je vous montre une merveille!*" He held out his ten fingers. He wanted more money.

Perhaps this was the man he'd been told to see, Raumer thought. That African by the Louvre had said something about coming here. On a sudden impulse he fingered a limp bill out of his pocket and tossed it onto the snaker's cloth. Ten francs. It seemed like play-money.

"*Merci, Monsieur De L'Espace,*" the tall black man said with a slight bow. "*Et maintenant! Le truc Indien!*" He whistled sharply, penetratingly, and a young African boy in shorts came running across the square, carrying a heavy coiled rope.

The snaker gave a longer speech then, but Raumer couldn't follow it. What had the man called him? Mister Space? He couldn't figure it out. What a strange day this was. First that funny gap or jump near the Louvre…and now this snake charmer was making a rope uncoil and slowly rise into the air.

Howard was tugging his sleeve; he had something to say. "There's a thread attached to the rope," came the deafening whisper. "The little boy is pulling it up."

The kid was right. Sharp-eyed little devil. There was a grey thread leading up from the rope. The thread looped over a nail in the air overhead, and the little assistant was surreptitiously reeling the thread in behind his back. Ten francs for such a cheap…a nail in the air?

The music squeaked, rose higher, and disappeared into the supersonic. The snaker laid down his flute. The end of the rope was up at the nail…it looked more like a thorn, really. With a single precise gesture, the African reached up and attached the rope to the thorn.

Meanwhile the little boy was sitting on the cube-patterned cloth, binding a long thorn lengthwise to the bottom of each foot. The thorns stuck out in front like crampons.

"*Dix francs*," the speaker cried, pacing back and forth with his long fingers outspread. "*Seulement dix francs de plus et mon fils va monter!*"

Quite a crowd had gathered now. Raumer and Howard were in the front row, but the people were three deep behind them. A few coins flew through the air and landed near the snakes. The cobra struck halfheartedly at a twenty-centime piece. The little boy was ready now, a thorn sticking out past the toes of each foot, and a third thorn clasped ice-pick style in his right hand.

"*Encore trois francs!*" the father shouted after looking things over. "Encore trois!" One more franc piece landed on the cloth. And then nothing. They all waited. The breeze grew colder. Where was the sun? This was supposed to be June.

"Lend me two francs, Daddy," Howard whispered. It looked like no one else was going to cough up. With a sigh Raumer fished his last two coins out. All his family ever wanted from him was money.

Howard trotted over and handed the coins to the snaker. The man's hand whipped out and caught Howard by the wrist. He took the little drum from him, and then leaned over and whispered something. Raumer stepped forward, but Howard was already free. The snaker had given him a straw-wrapped package in place of the drum. He skipped back, his eyebrows high with excitement.

The music started up again. The snaker was playing the flute with one hand and the drum with the other. His mouth remained fixed in the same mask-like expression. The little black boy made a stroboscopic series of gestures and began to climb.

He held the rope with his left hand only. Foot by foot, hand by hand, he worked himself into the air. He would pull a foot loose, then set the thorn with a sharp kick. Slide the left hand up, reset the right hand, reset the feet. It was like watching a mountain climber kicking ice-steps for himself in a steep snow-field.

When the boy reached the top of the rope he began pulling the rope up after him. The crowd was absolutely silent. The music wailed and pattered, the flute-tone flowing over the beats like a stream over round stones.

The boy had the rope coiled over his left shoulder now. Holding himself steady with his right hand, he pulled loose the thorn that had held the rope. He reset it at shoulder level and paused, pressed against the aether like a tree-fog on a windowpane. His thin, wooden-looking limbs tensed.

Suddenly the boy was gone. The audience broke into a wild hub-bub of cheers and questions. Coins rained onto the African's cloth. He bowed once and began gathering up his snakes. The show was over. People drifted off.

"*There* you are. We looked all over."

"What did you buy for Howard? What's he got in his hand?"

"Dada!"

Raumer turned with a smile. "We just saw the most incredible thing. This kid climbed up a rope, pulled it up after him and disappeared. The Indian Rope Trick! I've read about it for years. And now I understand how it works. I've got to ask that guy where the bush..."

But when he turned back the snaker had disappeared, faded into the crowd, basket and all. Meanwhile Iris had unwrapped Howard's package.

"Four stickers!" she exclaimed. "Good for *poking*!"

"Let me see those." Raumer scooped the long, reddish thorns up. Testing, he jabbed one in the air. It dug in and stuck in something invisible.

"What are you teaching the children, Charlie? They could put each other's eyes out that way. Throw those things away!"

Raumer released the thorn cautiously. It stayed fixed in the air where he'd jabbed it. Wonderingly, he looked at the tips of the other three. The tips seemed to bend…yet not bend. They weren't quite fully there.

"These are thorns from the legendary bush of Shanker Bhola, Cybele. Aether pitons. I always thought it was only a…" Raumer sat down on the pavement and unlaced a shoe. "It's as if those coins on the table had little needles to dig into the wood. Then they wouldn't have to just slide wherever the forces pulled them. They'd be free to climb against gravity through empty space."

Raumer had both shoes off now. He laid one of the long thorns inside each shoe and pushed them forward, through the leather. They stuck out the front like toe-spurs. He began lacing the shoes back on, his feet squeezed in over the thorn-shafts.

"What's Daddy doing?"

"I don't know, Iris. I don't know *what's* the matter with your father."

"He wants to climb through the air like the little black boy," Howard explained. "Those thorns can stick in the air."

A few passers-by had gathered to watch Raumer putting his shoes on. "*Dix francs!*" Howard shouted, getting in the spirit of the thing. His mother had taught him a few words of French. He held his little hands up for attention. "*Dix francs!*" A few more people stopped. American street-performers were a rarity.

Cybele shushed Howard. Jimmy started crying for an ice cream. Iris had one of the thorns and was practicing jabbing it into the aether. "This is swell, Dad! Can I try it next?"

"We'll see, sweetie." Raumer patted his daughter's blonde head and kicked a raised foot tentatively. The thorn dug into the air. He reached up and set another thorn overhead. He was able then to pull himself up off the ground, resting on his anchored left foot and right hand.

He drew his right foot up a little higher than the other and kicked it in. Iris handed him the fourth thorn, and he set that up higher with his left hand. Like a human fly climbing an office building with suction cups, he began working his way up. A few coins rang on the pavement beneath him. "*Dix francs!*" Howard shouted again.

Cybele had just gotten four ice cream sticks from a vendor. Now she saw him and stared up, fear and joy fighting for possession of her features. "Don't go too *high*, Charlie!"

He did another few meters. He was high enough to break a leg now if he fell. His hands were sweating and it was hard to keep a good grip on the thorns in his hands. The shafts of the other thorns were digging into the soles of his feet. He couldn't go much higher. But he didn't want to go back down to his family either.

The most puzzling thing was that the aether didn't seem to be moving relative to normal space. Using the sliding-coins analogy, a person would be a small, irregular coin riding the rim of a huge rotating disk… Earth. But since Earth is rotating, then it should zip out from under any piton fixed in the motionless aether. Of course maybe the aether wasn't quite solid after all. Maybe a thin sheet of it was dragged along with the Earth. Given the right kinds of length contractions that would just about jibe with relativity. Raumer wondered if he could set a thorn hard enough to reach the lower levels of the aether.

Holding fast with his left hand, he pulled his right hand back and slammed the thorn forward as hard as he could. There was a sudden wrench, the sound of glass breaking. His right hand was bleeding. The thorn had ripped out of his grasp and sped across the plaza to break a window in the Pompidou Center.

There were a lot of people under Raumer now, pointing at him and at the broken window. He was ten or fifteen meters up. Cybele and the kids seemed peculiarly unconcerned about him. They were just eating their ice creams and staring. Howard and Iris had managed to fill their pockets with small change from the crowd. Across the plaza Raumer saw a *flic*, a young nattily-uniformed policeman. He was heading his way. Raumer wondered how that African kid had managed to disappear.

He was standing on two of the thorns and holding the other with both hands. Now the flic was close enough to start shouting at him. Calling him a terrorist. He was going to have to do something. Before, it had looked as if that kid had just jumped backward…out through hyperspace. He'd done it himself that morning. But what if he landed wrong? Suddenly he didn't care.

Raumer tensed all his muscles and jumped backwards, pushing off as hard as possible with the three thorns. He slipped sideways as he took off.

And a sort of wafer floated to the ground.

"*Qu'est ce qu'y a, alors?*" the flic asked, effortlessly pushing his way through the crowd. His handsome dark eyes flashed back and forth, searching for the man who had broken the window. But the villain had escaped.

In the center of the circle the flic found only a sidewalk artist…a charming French-American woman with three children. They were standing around an astonishingly detailed cross-sectional picture of a man's insides.

Strictly speaking, the flic should have arrested the woman for painting without a license. But suddenly, inexplicably, the picture seemed to slide off down the street. The policeman covered his confusion by asking the woman for a date.

The following selected passages, and the accompanying illustrations, are taken from Transdimensional Avatar *by Revell Gibson (Ten Pound Island Press, 1982).*

And how did this living avatar come into being? How is it that, Christ-like, one man can span the gap between Heaven and Hell...yet remain here on Earth with ordinary mortals?

Professor Raumer has suggested that I explain his physical trans-mogrification by the time-honored technique of analogical reasoning. So let us imagine a flat universe, a two-dimensional world whose inhab-itants would contemplate the idea of a *third* dimension with the fear and trembling we normally accord the *fourth*.

We are three-dimensional solids that move about on a certain surface, the spherical surface of Earth. Think of a Flatland whose inhab-itants are two-dimensional figures that move about on a certain line, the bounding line, if you will, or a disk which they call their planet.

Just as gravity limits us, as a rule, to two degrees of freedom in our mundane peregrinations (East-West plus North-South); just so we imagine that the Flatland gravity limits most Flatlanders to one degree of freedom in their motions (Left-Right) along their planetary line. Of course, if a Flatlander had wing-like projections which he *flapped*, then he could also move in the additional Up-Down dimension, just as a bird does.

Now suppose that the whole sheet which makes up Flatland is actually lying *on* something. Think of a vast sheet of wax paper floating on a sea. In the sheet itself are scratches…shapes which move about…the Flatlanders bustling back and forth on their planetary line. The analogy, of course, is to our space as a vast hypersheet nestled on the breast of the endless Aether main.

And what a noble vista that must be, the endless sea of Aethery! What strange demons swim beneath, what angels fly above! Our thoughts, Professor Raumer tells me, float above this sea like joyous, sun-bathed clouds…but *beneath* the hypersurface crowd clotted emotions: shining, stinging, slimy jellyfish!

Our avatar, our Professor Raumer, is wedged at right angles to our space. He is half above the hypersurface of space…and half below. Half-demon and half-god, he intersects our space in a single two-dimensional cross-section…a section too thin and feeble for speech, but immanent enough for hand-signals.

It fell upon me to be the first to recognize him for what he is, though so seemingly like a beer-stain on the floor…the floor of the Coupole Café to be precise, in the Montparnasse district of Paris. A marvelous place, crowded with merry-makers late into the night. I was there, part of the happy throng, eating my second dozen of oysters. *Claires No. 1* (the best in my estimation) were the oysters, and I gave this living food an agreeable environment in the form of a bottle of excellent, but cheap, Muscadet.

Full of food, full of peace, I gazed with interest at the floor. There were cigarette butts, women's ankles, streaks of sawdust and!!! A large, man-shaped stain, lightly tinted, a perfect silhouette sliding along! The arms were waving in semaphore, I realized proximately, still remembering my youthful experience as a signalman. "H–E–L–P!" they said.

Without wishing to attract undue notice, I moved my feet about on the floor, also in semaphore patterns. "W–H–O A–R–E Y–O–U?" An animated conversation ensued. Raumer had been sliding all over Paris looking for someone who would a) notice him, and b) understand his arm signals. I was, or am, the man, and will be, yet even in the face of scorn from those myopic fools who say they cannot *see* Professor Raumer.

Three Aether Pitons!

Climbing Against Gravity!

He Slips and Rotates!

X—Section on Ground!

But I dgress. Professor Raumer's rotation was, he told me, the result of an ill-conceived and badly executed attempt to move out along the Aether, above the surface of the Earth, and against the gravitational force.

His technique was to use special thorns as Oars or Pitons, reaching out of our space and into the Aether, thus exerting a force to act against gravity. This worked well enough, but when he attempted to jump free of the Aether and back to the ground, he slipped somehow sideways.

Gravity, weakly acting on that of his cross-sections still in our space, keeps him glued to the ground. He floats, as it were, on his back. By sticking a leg or an arm down into the swirling currents of the Aether sea he is able to slide about Earth's surface at will. Yet, such is the nature of the Aether-stuff that Professor Raumer is unable to exert the force to turn him-self sideways. His own efforts cannot bring him fully back into our space.

Immediately after the transformation, Professor Raumer slid away from the crowd at the Pompidou Center. He tells me that he was by some higher vision certain that his wife, a practical woman, would take up with the first replacement for him which she found. He could not have been more prescient.

These inquiries finally led me to an apartment above a miserable café in the Monceau district. Professor Raumer had so manipulated himself that only a cross-section of his head and eyes remained in our space. I carried this cross-section tucked between the pages of these very notes.

Throned behind the zinc bar was the inevitable *concierge*, a termagant, a virago. No, she had never heard of a Madame Raumer. I gave her twenty francs. Oh yes, I must be looking for the woman with the American children. She lived upstairs with her fiancé, a fine young man employed by the police force.

"*That's* not my husband," cried Mrs. Raumer, an attractive but somewhat hard-looking woman. "My husband is dead!"

The cross-section of Professor Raumer's head lay on the table between us. Suddenly the shapes of his two hands appeared on the table-top as well. The fingers moved in agile silhouettes, spelling out the words of his plea: "C–Y–B–E–L–E I S–T–I–L–L L–O–V–E Y–O–U. D–O Y–O–U H–A–V–E T–H–E T–H–O–R–N–S?"

Mrs. Raumer started back from the table. She seemed angry with me. "Get out of here, you pompous *blimp!* Take your creepy magic tricks with you! No, I don't have the thorns, the thorns disappeared with my husband! He's gone and I have a new life!"

As she railed in this way, one of her children, the littlest, pressed forward and poked a finger into the center of the cross-section on the table. This direct palpating of his brain must have been uncomfortable for Professor Raumer, for he slid off the table, floated to the floor, and disappeared beneath a rug.

The unpleasantly handsome young flic seemed to take me for his rival in Mrs. Raumer's affections. If I were not a man of generous bulk, the situation might have gone very badly indeed. As it was, I was forced to leave so precipitously that I was unable to retrieve Professor Raumer from beneath the rug. There was nothing for it but to install myself in the dreary drink-shop downstairs and await further developments.

I spent a miserable two hours there, with only a few pinball players for company. The café's menu was utterly without interest, and their wine was not even deplorable. I regretted having aided Professor Raumer in his fool's mission of revisiting his family. I had helped him only because of his promise to later reveal certain higher truths to me.

I was on the point of leaving when Raumer's three children suddenly appeared, trooping down the stairs. Iris, the oldest, was spokeswoman for this pathetic delegation.

"Can you make my Daddy get fat again?" she inquired.

"Perhaps I can help. But not unless he comes away with me."

"I want him to stay under the rug," protested Howard. "We can talk to him with our fingers."

Talk? About what? How absurd to waste so great an avatar on children's prattle! I controlled myself with difficulty. "Your father belongs to humanity. With my help he can bring us unheard-of knowledge. Tell him he must come to me."

It was almost midnight, and I was quite dizzy from the many glasses of cognac. The children had long since gone back upstairs. Bleakly I wondered how Professor Raumer could prefer their uncultured company to mine. Just then I saw the familiar stain come sliding down the stairs like a hesitant man's shadow.

The scene was painful in the extreme. Not having a family, and not wanting one, I cannot pretend to understand his motives. But in the end I promised to help him "get fat again," and for his part, Professor Raumer shared with me all that he had learned. I give here only a partial summary of what he told me that night before our long journey began.

Thoughts are definite forms...permanently extant, yet in some way parasitic upon human existence. *Parasitism* is too strong a word. Let us say, rather, *symbiosis*, reserving the term "parasitism" for those low and slippery entities which do deserve such a name. I speak, of course, of human emotion, or, to be quite blunt, the ties of love which can make an avatar shrink from his destiny.

Following this, Professor Raumer described to me how the thought-clouds rain lower-dimensional simulacra of themselves upon the infinite Aether sea, dimpling and rippling the sketchy forms of our lowly three-dimensional space.

He told me of how the clouds merge and split, and of the great SUN beyond it all, the SUN which drives the eternal process of sublimation and precipitation. The SUN, the goal of every mystic's quest...I cannot understand how anyone could ever wish to leave it.

And now, these few notes written, we set off, I know not whence, in search of the sacred bush of Shanker Bola. With its thorns I will lever Professor Raumer back. With the same thorns I shall set myself free. Peace, my brothers.

Note on "The Indian Rope Trick Explained"

Written in Spring, 1980.
Changes, Ace Books, 1983.

One of the great things about living in Heidelberg was that we could get in the car and drive to Paris. This story was inspired by a trip there with my wife Sylvia and our three children Georgia, Rudy Jr., and Isabel. I should add that we had a lot more fun on the trip than this story might indicate. Raumer needs to be something of a jerk so that his wife will be glad to get rid of him. "Transreal" doesn't mean "true."

A New Experiment With Time

The first thing the citizens of Bata notice is a greasy place in the street. A fat man slips on it. Bill Stook comes down in the yellow pickup with the smashed fender and throws on a bucket of sand.

A week later the patch begins to stink. The stuff is thickened and drawn together. There're lots of flies that come and land on your face afterwards. The kindergarten teacher twists her ankle. Black high-heels and a thin summer dress.

Stook comes back with a shovel, but he can't get the stuff loose. A few idlers—daytripping feebs—give their advice, spit-talking about glare-ice and mineral oil. Finally Stook throws on some more sand and goes home.

Under the arc-lights the patch is elliptical, four by eight feet. It cuts across the crosswalk and both lanes of traffic. The tire-marks on it extend out into straight smears in either direction. A dog has dropped a bone in the middle.

Maisie Gleaves lives in a Buffalo rooming house. She is black and white, with red lipstick and a christmas-green raincoat. Every night she lies on her bed looking at her Bata High School yearbook. Two years now. Somehow she will go back.

Workmen are putting up a banner saying, BATA SIDEWALK SALE DAYS. Meanwhile a group of men, shopkeepers, inspect the stinking patch of pulp. One of them tries to pick up a bone. His fingers slide off it. It's an outrage. Bill Stook is called and threatened with dismissal. He covers the patch with sawdust and puts a refreshment stand around it. SIDEWALK SALE DAYS. In the hot sun, people order hot dogs, catch a whiff of decay and put on more mustard. Stook mans the booth, nipping whiskey from a pint bottle. The flattened lump underfoot feels springy.

A white sunset slides under low clouds. They dismantle the booth and the sawdust blows away. Mashed arms and legs, tooth cracklings, scraps of green cloth. The tire tracks are gone from the flattened corpse. The state police take Stook away.

Maisie watches Buffalo TV in a silver diner. Trouble in Bata. She remembers all the lost faces. Ron. She pays for her tea. Back in her room she stares into the mirror for two hours. Her image is moving closer.

Sleeping or waking, it's all the same now. No more boundaries. Something is coming nearer, growing to connect. She lives on air and thinks only of Bata. She will return.

Bit by bit the corpse grows whole. Slowly the bones link up, imperceptibly the flesh crawls back. One night the face is finished. In the dark it begins to twitch unseen.

Stook is out on bail. He is driving a stolen truck, the pickup they used to let him use. All his rage and bitterness is focused on the corpse in the street. He speeds towards it, past the guards, through the saw-horses. A screech of brakes, a thud. Suddenly his crumpled fender is smooth. The corpse walks off backwards.

Stook runs after the skinny corpse, a woman. She minces backwards towards the bus stop, glaring at him. He catches up as she climbs into the bus to Buffalo. He tries to grab her, but it's impossible. He cannot alter her past.

Maisie leaves her room and walks. A block ahead she sees a black and white woman in a christmas-green coat climb off the bus from Bata. She is walking backwards, this woman. Maisie hastens to meet her.

The two figures merge and are no more. A cabbie sees them disappear into each other. For Maisie it is different. She walks through the flash and down the street.

Everything is running backwards. Maisie is going back through time, back to Bata. The bus backs up to where she'd seen herself get out. Ticketless, she climbs in the exit door and sits down. She is nervous. The bus is going forty miles per hour in reverse.

As the bus backs out of Buffalo onto the Thruway, the man sitting next to Maisie begins staring at her. He says something backwards, a drooling gabble. She answers anyway. He turns and stares out the dark window. She spoke because he spoke; he spoke because she spoke. He picks off a wad of gum from under his seat and begins chewing it.

When the bus leaves the Thruway and backs past the old filling-station, she walks to the door. It opens, and she goes down the steps. Bata. She's glad she waited so long. She'll get a room here, and in two years she'll be back in high school. Ron. This time it will work out right.

A short, red-faced man is blocking her way. She sets her face and walks towards him. He backs off, drawing farther and farther away. There are police around a pickup parked in the intersection. But there is no traffic.

The little man scuttles crablike into the cab of the pickup. Just to scare him she walks right up to it, right up to the fender. There is a sudden jolt. The pickup squeals its brakes and backs away.

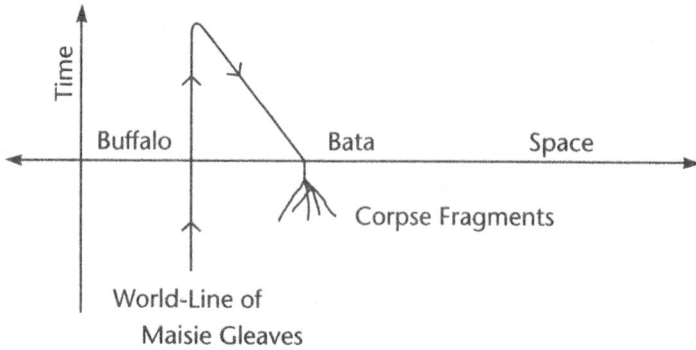

Note on "A New Experiment with Time"

Written in Spring, 1980.
Sphinx Magazin, #16, Spring, 1982.

I got the seed idea for this story while driving from Geneseo to Buffalo in 1978. I was looking in my rear-view mirror and imagining that I was driving backwards. Two years later in a Heidelberg street I saw a woman with red lipstick and a green raincoat, and the story clicked. It's kind of a retake on the time-reversal diagrams that appear in "Schrödinger's Cat." The story's first publication was as a German translation in a hipster European magazine edited by Udo Breger, my German translator at that time.

THE MAN WHO ATE HIMSELF

Harry enjoyed driving, even though he'd never managed to get a license. He had a whole theory of it, a system of simultaneous differential equations which told him how fast to turn the wheel for a four-wheel skid on a tight turn taken too fast. "Controlled drift," he called it.

I drew my safety belt a bit tighter. "I'm driving on the way back to the airport, Harry. I only said you could drive on the way to Marston's. Remember that." It wasn't always easy to have a genius for a partner.

We were going at least fifteen miles per hour too fast. Harry was slouched back in his seat, stiff arms outstretched. He wore a forgotten smile and kept giving the wheel abrupt, precise little twitches. I had to think of Mr. Toad's wild ride. At least we were in open country.

We hadn't encountered another car for about five miles now. Harry was taking the curves wider and wider…brushing across them and fish-tailing out. Humming unhappily, I studied the map Marston had sent us. Great Crater. We should be almost…

There was a wild squealing. I cried out something of a religious nature and threw my hands up to protect my face. The car bounced like a skipped stone, slewed and shuddered to a stop. The engine died. The sun was bright and hot.

"Pretty flashy, boys. And ah'd always thought you scientist fellas were a bunch of ribbon clerks. Welcome to Great Crater!"

A limited-function android with a TV-screen face pulled open the cyclone-fence gate Harry had stopped for. The android was dressed like a gunslinger. Van Marston's familiar features grinned at us from the screen.

Immediately beyond the gate, the road slanted sharply downwards… dropping a hundred meters to the floor of Great Crater. The crater was a few kilometers across. A mist clung to the heavily irrigated grounds. I couldn't quite make out the mansion I knew lay at the center.

As soon as the gate was fully open, Harry revved up the engine to a chattering scream and peeled out, kicking cubic meters of gravel up

99

into a roostertail. When the road dropped out from under us we actually left the ground.

"YEEEEEHAW!" Marston's amplified voice whooped. The android drew a six-shooter and fired two shots down the slope after us. Presumably it had aimed to miss.

Marston had made his bundle in oil and uranium. He wasn't what you'd normally think of as a Friend Of The Earth. But now that he'd retired, he'd tried to fix up his Great Crater estate like one of those wild animal parks. Some giraffes were stalking through the tall grass to our right, and down where the driveway leveled out, a tremendous snake lay sunning himself.

Still accelerating, Harry detoured around the snake, knocking a cloud of winged insects out of the elephant grass. The unexpected lurch made me smack my head on the edge of the window. Suddenly I'd had enough.

I reached my left foot over and stepped on the brake. Hard. At the same time I took the key out of the ignition and pocketed it. Far above us, the android fired another shot. You could hardly hear it over the steady chirping of the insects.

"Harry, the car's rented in my name. And we've got some delicate machinery in the trunk. What are you trying to prove?"

We'd skidded to a stop half off the road, some hundred feet past that huge snake. It was watching us with glassy black eyes, and seemed to be nibbling its tail. Marston's house was still out of sight.

Finally Harry answered. "You know how I feel, Fletch. I don't like Marston. He's stupid. He's a bully." Harry's hands clenched and unclenched on the wheel. "I knew a kid just like him in eighth grade. Donny Lyons. Every day Donny Lyons would knock me down and steal my dessert. Until one day I hid one of my father's false teeth inside a Twinkie." Harry let out one of his weird giggles.

"Look, Harry. Marston wants to give us a lot of money to help float his corpse in outer space forever. We're going to take the money. We need it because for some crazy reason you wouldn't let me market that waste disposal device of yours…"

"I don't want to talk about it."

"*I know*, Harry. Just let me finish. The point is that we can take Marston for a lot of bucks. You *told* me you don't see how his capsule can avoid crashing…sooner or later. So just remember that we're screwing him. But, please, for God's sake, don't tell him. Then everyone'll be happy."

"Everyone except his wife."

"Look, how's *she* going to know if Marston's capsule falls into a star somewhere? As if she'd care anyway. She's not even thirty! Now, will you trade places with me and let me drive?"

Harry opened his door and got out heavily. It was hot, and the plastic seat was sweaty where he'd sat. I waited a minute before sliding over. Harry stood next to the car and stared back at that snake.

"Isn't there some myth?" he said when he got back in. "About a snake who swallows his own tail?"

"Yeah. I don't know." I rolled up my window. There was something moving towards us through the tall grass on our left. It would be typical of Marston to have lions loose to handle intruders. I started up the engine and drove on.

There was a second fence around Marston's house and lawn. The old man was out in front, leaning on a hoe and waiting for us. I couldn't believe how skinny he'd gotten. Lung cancer. He pushed one of the buttons set into the hoe handle. The inner gate opened for us.

"Welcome, boys! Welcome to my little Garden of Eden. Let me show you mah plot!" His diseased voice had a grainy, raucous quality.

I got out and went over to gladhand our pigeon, but Harry just sat in the car, ostentatiously picking his teeth.

"Y'all wouldn't have to do that if you'd stop eatin' flesh!" Marston called out to him. "*Live and let live*. It's Mother Nature's law!" Marston had been one of America's most vocal vegetarians for several years now.

Harry examined the end of his toothpick. "That's not what you said when you closed down the solar energy companies, Mr. Marston." He spoke without looking up. "Back then it was *eat or be eaten*."

Marston looked back at me with a genial smile. "Guess ah've always wanted to see me a real genius. Now ah know." He hooked his thumb towards Harry and stage-whispered, "Looks lahk a cross between a cow-flop and an albino toad, don't he?"

"Really, Van." A melodious voice came from the shady porch. "That's no way to talk about the author of *The Geometrodynamics of the Degenerate Tensor*?" In true Southern belle style, each sentence ended as a question.

"Well, point mah head and call me Doctor," Marston chortled. "Ah had no ideah!"

Evangeline Marston walked down the steps, a graceful arm outstretched. She wore a jiggling T-shirt and skintight red lamé jeans. I had to bite my tongue to keep from moaning.

"Don't listen to Van, Dr. Gerber. We're really so happy to meet you?" Harry pocketed his toothpick and got out of the car with alacrity. He was as much of a horny bastard as the next man.

"I didn't realize you were abreast of current cosmological theory, Mrs. Marston." Harry's big livery lips stretched in a wet smile. "I'd be happy to send you some preprints."

"Oh, you would? I have the nicest little professor at Austin who'd be so delighted? And do call me Evangeline."

"Pleased to meet you, Evangeline," I sang out, and basked for an instant in her warm gaze. Harry grunted something similar.

"Y'all just have to come see mah crops now," Marston said, waving us on around the house. "Ole Eva and me have been living off the land, ain't we sugar?" He gave the gorgeous red apple of her rear a lingering pat.

In back of the house Marston had his famous garden. He always had his TV spots filmed with him standing in it...usually leaning on that goddamn hoe. All his companies had ever done was to rip the Earth off, but now the fact that he had a garden was supposed to make us forget all that.

For all Marston's talk about Mother Earth, you could tell that he had a crazy fear that the old girl was going to get back at him. He was so scared of ending up underground that he'd hired us to help him launch his corpse into outer space. According to his letter he had only a few weeks left.

Evangeline walked in among the plants and tossed Marston a ripe tomato. He caught it and bit in thirstily, the juice running down his knobby old chin.

"Why don't you just let Eva bury you in the garden?" Harry suggested with deliberate cruelty. "I'm sure you'd make good fertilizer."

A pulsing snake of a vein sprang into relief on Marston's forehead. "That is *just*," he wheezed angrily, "what ah do *not* want to happen. As you verah well know, Mr. Genius author of *Tense Jamaican Degenerates*. As you *verah* well know!" His dull old eyes brightened with fury.

I stepped in. We'd come here to close a deal, not to trade insults. "I'm sorry, Mr. Marston. Dr. Gerber has only been involved with the technical design aspects. I'm sure he was not aware that..."

Gasping for breath, the old man went on as if I hadn't spoken. Harry had struck a nerve. "Ah, Van Marston, am not going to rot in the ground. And ah am not going to *burn* in no fire. Ah am going to stay just as ah am fo'evvah and a *day*!" He glared at Harry with pure hatred.

"Yes, sir!" I said with an ingratiating smile. "And Fletcher & Company is going to make it happen for you. Your guidance system is in our car. All systems go! I've got the plans right here." I patted my briefcase. "If you'd care to..."

"I'm sure that you distinguished gentlemen must be absolutely famished?" Eva said, drifting out of the garden. The contrast between her swiveling hips and her refined, magnolia-blossom voice was exquisite. Those pants could have been painted on. Briefly I let myself imagine licking the paint off.

At lunch I was polite and shared Marston's stewed corn and zucchini. Harry and Evangeline had TV-dinners of Mexican food.

"Eva doesn't like vegetables," Marston confided in me. "Ah have to eat just about everything that garden grows." A TV-screen-faced android cleared the dishes away.

The screen was playing an old-South movie staring Shirley Temple and Mr. Bojangles. "Oh my goo'ness," the android murmured, and set a bottle of bourbon on the table. Happily, I poured myself a drink.

There really had been something special about the vegetables. Eating them had filled me with an unusual sense of…completeness. "The soil is special," Marston was saying. I listened with a patient smile. "Mah plot is right on the spot where the meteor struck." He leaned across the table with an expression of senile cunning. "We found part of it, too. The remains of an alien spaceship. Ah made it into mah sarcophagus."

Harry had been busy watching Evangeline chew, but this last remark drew him into the conversation. "Chariots of the Gods, Mr. Marston? Fact is stranger than fiction, eh?"

That little vein on the old man's forehead popped out again. He stood up angrily. "You just come on out to the barn with me, toad head. Ah have nevah…" A wet, heavy cough cut him off.

In an instant Evangeline was at his side. In between the brutal coughs Marston was gasping air with pathetic little whoops. His face was red, and his eyes bulged out. Suddenly a thick gusher of blood vomited out of his mouth. The eyes went out like lights. He was dead when he hit the floor.

Evangeline looked wild-eyed from him to me to Harry. "You…" she got out in a thin strained voice. Then she began throwing things. A metal trivet caught Harry in the temple, but I managed to grab her wrists before she got the carving knives. I had been wrong when I'd said she wouldn't care if Marston died. I don't know why, but she loved that scrawny old earthraper.

I was ready to forget the contract and leave, but the gate-control buttons were keyed to Marston's and Evangeline's fingerprints only. And Evangeline wanted to do things just as Marston had planned.

So I helped her put him in his cylindrical coffin. It was made of strips of wood fit together like a Chinese puzzle. Marston had made it himself, out of a cottonwood tree he'd cut down to dig his garden.

We slid Marston in there naked and took him downstairs to the walk-in freezer.

The physical labor of hauling the coffin to the basement helped calm Evangeline down. I strained my milk, and ended up wishing I'd gotten the android to help. When the old man was stowed like he'd wanted, I helped myself to some more of his bourbon and sat down on the porch with Evangeline. The shrilling of the grasshoppers washed over us.

"Where is that awful toad-man?" Evangeline asked suddenly. It was not clear to me what she wanted him for.

"Harry didn't kill your husband, Mrs. Marston. It was cancer. And, if you'll forgive my saying so, your husband's companies have probably led to more…"

"You don't have to tell me that, Mr. Fletcher. My husband knew what he did to the Earth. And he was scared the Earth wouldn't forgive him for it. That's one of the reasons…" Her voice caught.

"One of the reasons he wanted us to launch him into space," I filled in. "Well, it shouldn't be hard. He's already got the rocket?"

"Yes, we have it in an underground silo right over there." She waved towards the barn. "And Van and I built his own little capsule for him." She pushed her voice on. "All you and…and Dr. Gerber have to do is plan a course and install something to keep him from falling into any stars."

"He wants to float in outer space forever," I said. "That's fine with me. Let me show you how the system works." I got out some papers. I'd done most of the work on this one, and was eager to impress this beautiful woman.

The heart of the system was a set of piezoelectric crystals. Whenever Marston's capsule approached a gravitating object, the tidal forces would squeeze a trickle of current out of one of the crystals. Each crystal was hooked in to a little ion jet. The result was that Marston's capsule would automatically adjust its path to avoid any star or planet which came its way. In the absolute cold of outer space, the crystals would be sensitive enough to react to a star that was still a light-year off. Since the guidance jets would react so early, they didn't have to be very strong.

"Yes," Evangeline said when I'd finished explaining. "But what happens when the jets run out of juice?"

I hadn't expected her to think of that. "The charge should be more than adequate for a thousand years," I extemporized. "That certainly…"

"It's not forever," she protested. "Van wants to last forever…not just end up in some star a thousand years from now."

Harry ambled around the corner of the house. He looked like he wanted to laugh. Holding a tight, straight mouth he took a seat next to me. There was a silence.

"I looked at it," Harry said finally. "I guess I owe Mr. Marston some sort of apology." Then, with terrible inappropriateness, he giggled.

"Look at what?" I asked, sharply.

"It's a little bit late for an apology, Dr. Gerber?" Evangeline spoke across me. Her voice was cold, but there was a hint of satisfaction in it.

"Do you think I could photograph it before..." Harry began.

"I'm not at all sure we're going to send it off," Evangeline replied. "Mr. Fletcher has just told me he can only guarantee a thousand years?"

Harry made a negative, froglike face. "Fletch doesn't know what he's talking about. Once it goes into orbit around the galaxy, the energy requirement goes down to oh-point-zilch. I can promise you ten billion years. A whole cosmic cycle."

"What the lame-brained hell is a cosmic cycle supposed to be?" I burst out. Harry had hurt my feelings.

Evangeline seemed to know. "That's how long the universe lasts," she explained. "That nice little professor at Austin told me about it. Time is only supposed to be ten billion years long?"

"That's right," Harry said, with another giggle. "And wouldn't it be something if your husband's capsule lasts all the way? The first man to travel around time!"

I thought for a minute. "When you say *around*, do you mean..."

Harry interrupted me. "I don't see why we shouldn't be able to get him launched tonight."

I took a long drink of my bourbon. Sitting in the middle of Great Crater, I felt like I was at the center of a bull's-eye. The house, the lawn, the inner fence, the fake African savanna, the rim of the crater, the outer fence...it was all Marston's and I wanted to get out. I held my glass up to the setting sun. "So let's get to work."

We got the guidance system out of the car's trunk. We had six little ion jets coupled to crystal sensors, and a power pack to drive the jets. Microprocessors were built in. The pack was no bigger than a knapsack, but we had wedged enough unconfined quarks in there to run New York City for ten years. Two of Marston's power-plants had piped us the energy. If he was lucky enough not to have too many near misses, maybe he *would* make it into galactic orbit.

Evangeline brought the android over to help. The TV-screen face was playing a tape of Marston, in black-face, singing work-songs. Weird.

"Take dis hammer, give it to the captain," the android crooned as it shouldered the power pack. "Take dis hammer, *give* it to the..."

THE MAN WHO ATE HIMSELF

Evangeline stepped forward and flicked a switch on the machine's back. Its face shrank to a point of light and winked out. The locusts shrilled on.

Nothing Harry or Evangeline had said had prepared me for Marston's capsule. It was like a giant razor clam. The two shell-halves were made of some shiny, lavalike substance. In back they were joined by metal hinges. In front, they were propped open with a two-by-four. Inside was a cylindrical hollow, just the size of Marston's coffin.

"We found those…windows in the garden?" Evangeline said. "And there were some metal scraps we melted and cast into hinges. Van had the whole idea after he found the windows?" The shock of her husband's death seemed to have worn off a little. Her halo of sexuality was building back up.

"They could just be silica that was fused when the meteor hit," Harry mused. "But those markings…"

I looked closely at one of the shell-halves. It was darkly transparent, and was covered with scratches. The scratches were arranged in bands, and certain of them appeared over and over. It was easy to see how Marston might have convinced himself they meant something. I shuddered a little, remembering his thick, bloody coughing. I busied myself with the jets.

A few hours later we had the guidance system hooked up. It was basically just glued onto the capsule…any touch of an atmosphere would have pulled it loose…but we weren't planning for the capsule to ever go near an atmosphere once the rocket was launched.

Although there was no way to honestly predict what the capsule might encounter once it was a few dozen light-years from Earth, we had programmed in an overall course plan. The rocket Marston had hidden in the underground silo was to take the capsule out of the solar system. Once in interstellar space, the rocket would eject the capsule. At that point our guidance system would kick on. Our basic principle would just be to avoid massive objects as they came up. According to our calculations, this would eventually get the capsule out into intergalactic space. So as not to have to deal with any more galaxies crowded with stars, we planned for the capsule to go into orbit around our galaxy once it got out there. Sooner or later it would have to fall back in…but this wasn't exactly a short-term problem.

"The most important thing is that he doesn't come back to Earth," Evangeline reminded us. "Can you promise me that?"

I had known Harry long enough to read his expressions. Right now he was wiggly with suppressed laughter. I wondered how badly he'd sabotaged the guidance system.

"I promise you," I told Evangeline, giving her arm a kindly pat. Her flesh felt like warm marble. "I think we're ready to go."

Evangeline and the android went down to the freezer to get Marston. While they were gone I tried to pump Harry for some information, but he just grinned and took a few pictures of the scratches in that black glass. When Evangeline came back, the android's face-screen was back on. It was singing, "Massa's In De Cold Cold Ground."

I helped them heave Marston's coffin into the capsule. I'd had those two bourbons, so of course I had to gash my finger on a rough edge. Some of my blood went with Marston.

The capsule was resting on a little dolly on tracks.

While I nursed my cut, Evangeline pushed a button on the wall, and the capsule began rolling smoothly forward. Outside, a five-meter disk of sod lifted up to reveal Marston's personal hearse. A hydraulic lift eased the rocket up so that its hatch was level with the ground. Mechanical arms reached out and gently drew the capsule in. The hatch thudded shut, and we were ready for launch. The sky was clear. It was almost midnight. The locusts had finally knocked off. In the distance I heard a lion's coughing roar.

"When should it go off?" Evangeline asked me in a silky whisper. She looked a little chilled in just that T-shirt.

I took my calculator out. I'd stored the master program last week. All I had to do was to enter tomorrow's date, and the machine gave me the optimum launch time. "One thirteen," I replied. "A.M. Where's your console?"

"Inside." We followed Evangeline into the dark house. I felt better being there now that Marston was out of the freezer. Evangeline opened a rolltop desk in the living room to reveal the console. She punched in *0113* and switched on the automatic sequencing. That was all there was to it. We had a little over an hour to kill. I got myself another bourbon. Harry and Evangeline stuck to soda.

Looking out the window at the rocket-tip protruding from the ground fifty meters away, something occurred to me. "That's kind of close, you know. The exhaust is liable to set the house on fire."

"Don't worry," Evangeline sang back. "The house is mostly titani-plast. Van had a lot of enemies?"

That was a good lead-in for one of Harry's remarks, but he passed the opportunity up. He just leaned back in one of Marston's leather chairs sipping soda and staring at Evangeline. She kept finding reasons to stand up and lean over, with her prettiest feature aimed right at him.

When it got down to the last few minutes, we all stood by the window and counted down together. I had to hand it to Marston. It seemed like a great way to go. Just before blast-off, the android came out with a magnum of cold champagne. Knowing that Marston must have programmed that into the console sequencer, we drank long and deep with a clear conscience. And at one thirteen the big bird lifted off. Marston's lawn and garden were burned to a crisp, but inside his titaniplast house we didn't feel a thing. We stared upward until the tiny flame was lost in the stars.

I must have had most of the champagne, because I don't remember going to bed. All night I had whirlybed dreams. There was some trivial sequence of actions which I kept having to do—each completion was only a new beginning. The task had something to do with the scratches on Marston's capsule. They were sort of there, yet not there...and it was up to me to make them real. But I couldn't read them until I'd written them, and I couldn't write them till I'd read them.

Finally I managed to wake up. Dawn. The house was quiet. I seemed to be in a guest room. On the other side of the room was an unmade bed. Where was Harry? Just as I stood up, he came padding down the hall. He had a funny expression.

"Let's go," he said shortly.

"Okay. But where's…"

"Never mind. Let's get out of here. Are you sober enough to drive?"

"Sure."

We went down and got in the car. Harry said I should just drive up to the gate and honk. I did, and it swung open. Harry leaned out the car window, staring back at the house. Perhaps something moved at one of the windows. "I love her," he said, finally pulling himself back in.

"What happened last night? Don't tell me that she let you…"

Harry was close to tears. "She has a *mind*, Fletch. A body like that, and she'd even heard of my papers! I had her. I *had* her. But then I had to go and tell her. She'll never forgive me."

"You told her how you sabotaged the guidance system?"

"I *didn't* sabotage it. I didn't have to. Time is a circle, Fletch. If she had really understood my papers she would have known that. Time is a circle ten billion years around. And Marston's body is going to make the round trip."

I thought a minute. "So? That just means that there's two Marstons out there. There's the Marston we just launched, and there's the Marston who's traveled ten billion years around. One Marston is seventy and the other is ten-billion-and-seventy."

"That won't wash, Fletch. What if we'd decided not to launch him? How would the ten-billion-and-seventy-year-old know whether or not to exist? A particle's world-line can't be like a thread winding around and around time. It has to close off, to come back on itself."

"I still don't get the point, Harry."

"The point is that circular time means the universe *repeats*. Every ten billion years everything comes back to the same place. It's like a pool table. If you plug all the pockets and hit a hard enough break-shot, the balls will eventually reform into the triangular pattern you started with. Every atom in Marston's capsule has to come back to where it started from."

We were almost at the edge of the crater floor now. Suddenly it clicked. "You mean this crater…"

"Has to be, Fletch. *Has* to be! Marston's ship is going to go around time and crash here…say in AD 1100. There's probably even a Zuni Indian legend about it. And then Marston's capsule is going to lie buried until he digs it up five years ago. Sealed in the capsule is going to be some rotten compost which he is going to plow into his vegetable garden."

The joy of science had driven off Harry's sorrow at losing Evangeline. He gave a wild giggle. "And Marston thought he was a vegetarian! He thought he could avoid rotting on Earth!"

The same snake we'd seen yesterday was lying in the same place in the driveway. It had its tail tucked into its mouth. I down-shifted and drove up the slope to the lip of the crater. The android guard was already holding the gate open for us. The TV-camera over the gate scanned back and forth. For an instant the camera pointed at the android's face, and it became a TV-screen with a picture of a TV-screen with a picture of a TV-screen with a picture of…

I pulled onto the paved road and started driving toward the airport. I had a hell of a hangover.

Note on "The Man Who Ate Himself"

Written in Spring, 1980.
The Magazine of Fantasy and Science Fiction, December, 1982.

This is another story that could have been a paper for *Philosophy of Science*. But instead I made it a Fletcher and Harry story. Harry's appearance is based on a professor I knew when I was a mathematics graduate student. The story went that when this particular professor had been drafted, years earlier, they'd had to discharge him after a week because he refused to ever let go of his special briefcase full of math papers!

TALES OF HOUDINI

Houdini is broke. The vaudeville circuit is dead, ditto big-city stage. Mel Rabstein from Pathé News phones him up looking for a feature.

"Two G advance plus three points gross after turnaround."

"You're on."

The idea is to get a priest, a rabbi and a judge to be on camera with Houdini in all the big scenes. It'll be feature-length and play in the Loews chain. All Houdini knows for sure is that there'll be escapes, bad ones, with no warnings.

It starts at four in the morning, July 8, 1948. They bust into Houdini's home in Levittown. He lives there with his crippled mom. Opening shot of priest and rabbi kicking the door down. Close on their thick-soled black shoes. Available light. The footage is grainy, jerky, can't-help-it-cinema-verité. It's all true.

The judge has a little bucket of melted wax, and they seal up Houdini's eyes and ears and nose-holes. The dark mysterioso face is covered over and over before he fully awakes, relaxing into the events, leaving dreams of pursuit. Houdini is ready. They wrap him up in Ace bandages and surgical tape, a mummy, a White Owl cigar.

Eddie Machotka, the Pathé cameraman, time-lapses the drive out to the airstrip. He shoots a frame every ten seconds so the half-hour drive only takes two minutes on screen. Dark, the wrong angles, but still convincing. There's *no cuts*. In the back of the Packard, on the laps of the priest, judge and rabbi, lies Houdini, a white loaf crusty with tape, twitching in condensed time.

The car pulls right onto the airstrip, next to a B-15 bomber. Eddie hops out and films the three holy witnesses unloading Houdini. Pan over the plane. "The Dirty Lady," is lettered up near the nose.

The Dirty Lady! And it's not crop dusters or reservists flying it, daddyo, it's Johnny Gallio and his Flying A-Holes! Forget it! Johnny G., the most decorated World War II Pacific combat ace, flying, with

Slick Tires Jones navigating, and no less a man than Moanin' Max Moscowitz in back.

Johnny G. jumps down out of the cockpit, not too fast, not too slow, just cool, flight-jacket Johnny. Moanin' Max and Slick Tires lean out the bomb-bay hatch, grinning and ready to roll.

The judge pulls out a turnip pocket-watch. The camera zooms in and out, four-fifty A. M., the sky is getting light.

Houdini? He doesn't know they're handing him into the bomb-bay of The Dirty Lady. He can't even hear or see or smell. But he's at peace, glad to have all this out in the open, glad to have it *really happen*.

Everyone gets in the plane. Bad camera-motion as Eddie climbs in. Then a shot of Houdini, long and white, worming around like an insect larva. He's snuggled right down in the bomb cradle with Moanin' Max leaning over him like some wild worker ant.

The engines fire up with a hoarse roar. The priest and the rabbi sit and talk. Black clothes, white faces, grey teeth.

"Do you have any food?" the priest asks. He's powerfully built, young, with thin blonde hair. One hell of a Notre Dame linebacker under those robes.

The rabbi is a little fellow with a fedora and a black beard. He's got a Franz Kafka mouth, all ticks and teeth. "It's my understanding that we'll breakfast in the terminal after the release."

The priest is getting two hundred for this, the rabbi three. He has a bigger name. If the rushes work out they'll be witnessing the other escapes as well.

It's not a big plane, really, and no matter which way Eddie points the camera, there's always a white piece of Houdini in the frame. Up front you can see Johnny G. in profile, handsome Johnny not looking too good. There's sweat-beads on his long upper lip, booze sweat. Peace is coming hard to Johnny.

"Just spiral her on up," Slick Tires says softly. "Like a bed-spring, Johnny."

Out the portholes you can see the angled horizon sweep by, until they hit the high mattress of clouds. Max watches the altimeter, grinning and showing his teeth. They punch out of the clouds, into high slanting sunlight. Johnny holds to the helix…he'd go up forever if no one said stop…but now it's high enough.

"Bombs away!" Slick Tires calls back. The priest crosses himself and Moanin' Max pulls the release handle. Shot of white-wrapped Houdini in the coffin-like bomb-cradle. The bottom falls out, and the long form falls slowly, weightlessly at first. Then the slipstream catches one end, and he begins to tumble, dark white against the bright white of the clouds below.

Eddie holds the shot as long as he can. There's a big egg-shaped cloud down there, with Houdini falling towards it. Houdini begins to unwrap himself. You can see the bandages trailing him, whipping back and forth like a long flagellum, then *thip* he's spermed his way into that rounded white cloud.

On the way back to the airstrip, Eddie and the sound-man go around the plane asking everyone if they think Houdini'll make it.

"I certainly hope so," the rabbi.

"I have no idea," the priest, hungry for his breakfast.

"There's just no way," Moanin' Max. "He'll impact at two hundred miles per."

"Everyone dies," Johnny G.

"In his position I expect I'd try to drogue-chute the bandages," Slick Tires.

"It's a conundrum," the judge.

The clouds drizzle and the plane throws up great sheets of water when it lands. Eddie films them getting out and filing into the small terminal, deserted except…

Across the room, with his back to them, a man in pajamas is playing pinball. Cigar-smoke. Someone calls to him, and he turns—Houdini.

Houdini brings his mother to see the rushes. Everyone except for her loves it. She's very upset, though, and tears at her hair. Lots of it comes out, lots of white old hair on the floor next to her wheelchair.

Back at home Houdini gets down on his knees and begs and begs until she gives him permission to finish the movie. Rabstein at Pathé figures two more stunts will do it.

"No more magic after that," Houdini promises. "I'll use the money to open us a little music shop."

"Dear boy."

For the second stunt they fly Houdini and his mom out to Seattle. Rabstein wants to use the old lady for reaction shots. Pathé sets the two of them up in a boarding house, leaving the time and nature of the escape indeterminate.

Eddie Machotka sticks pretty close, filming bits of their long strolls down by the docks. Houdini eating a Dungeness crab. His mom buying taffy. Houdini getting her a wig.

Four figures in black slickers slip down from a fishing boat. Perhaps Houdini hears their footfalls, but he doesn't deign to turn. Then they're upon him: the priest, the judge, the rabbi, and this time a doctor as well—could be Rex Morgan.

While the old lady screams and screams, the doctor knocks Houdini out with a big injection of sodium pentathol. The great escape artist doesn't resist, just watches and smiles till he fades. The old lady bashes the doctor with her purse before the priest and rabbi get her and Houdini bundled onto the fishing boat.

On the boat, it's Johnny G. and the A-Holes again. Johnny can fly anything, even a boat. His eyes are bloodshot and all over the place, but Slick Tires guides him out of the harbor and down the Puget Sound to a logging river. Takes a couple of hours, but Eddie time-lapses it all... Houdini lying in half of a hollowed log and the doc shooting him up every so often.

Finally they get to a sort of mill-pond with a few logs in it. Moanin' Max and the judge have a tub of plaster mixed up, and they pour it in around Houdini. They tape over his head-holes, except for the mouth, which gets a breathing tube. What they do is to seal him up inside a big log, with the breathing tube sticking out disguised as a branch-stub. Houdini is unconscious and locked inside the log by a plaster-of-Paris filling...sort of like a worm dead inside a Twinkie. The priest and the rabbi and the judge and the doctor heave the log overboard.

It splashes, rolls, and mingles with the other logs waiting to get sawed up. There's ten logs now, and you can't tell for sure which is the one with Houdini in it. The saw is running and the conveyor belt snags the first log.

Shot of the logs bumping around. In the foreground, Houdini's mom is pulling the hair out of her wig. Big SKAAAAAZZT sound of the first log getting cut up. You can see the saw up there in the background, a giant rip-saw cutting the log right down the middle.

SKAAAZZZZT! SKAAAAZZZZZT! SKAAAZZZZT! The splinters fly. One by one the logs are hooked and dragged up to the saw. You want to look away, but you can't...just waiting to see blood and used food come flying out. SKAAAZZZZT!

Johnny G. drinks something from a silver hip-flask. His lips move silently. Curses? Prayers? SKAAAZZZZT! Moanin' Max's nervous horse-face sweats and grins. Houdini's Mom has the wig plucked right down to the hair-net. SKAAAZZZZZT! Slick Tire's eyes are big and white as hard-boiled eggs. He helps himself to Johnny's flask. SKAAAZZT! The priest mops his forehead and the rabbi...SKNAKCHUNKFWEEEEE!

Plaster dust flies from the ninth log. It falls in two, revealing only a negative of Houdini's body. An empty mold! They all scramble onto the mill dock, camera pointing around, looking for the great man. Where is he?

Over the shouts and cheers you can hear the jukebox in the mill-hands' cafeteria. The Andrews Sisters. And inside there's…Houdini, tapping his foot and eating a cheeseburger.

"Only one more escape," Houdini promises, "And then we'll get that music shop."

"I'm so frightened, Harry," his bald mom says. "If only they'd give you some warning."

"They have, this time. Piece of cake. We're flying out to Nevada."

"I just hope you stay away from those show-girls."

The priest and the rabbi and the judge and the doctor are all there, and this time a scientist, too. A low-ceilinged concrete room with slits for windows. Houdini is dressed in a black rubber wet suit, doing card-tricks.

The scientist, who's a dead ringer for Albert Einstein, speaks briefly over the telephone and nods to the doctor. The doctor smiles handsomely into the camera, then handcuffs Houdini and helps him into a cylindrical tank of water. Refrigeration coils cool it down, and before long they've got Houdini frozen solid inside a huge cake of ice.

The priest and the rabbi knock down the sides of the tank, and there's Houdini like a big firecracker with his head sticking out for a fuse. Outside is a truck with a hydraulic lift. Johnny G. and the A-Holes are there, and they load Houdini in back. The ice gets covered with pads to keep it from melting in the hot desert sun.

Two miles off, you can see a spindly test-tower with a little shed on top. This is an atom-bomb test range, out in some godforsaken desert in the middle of Nevada. Eddie Machotka rides the truck with Houdini and the A-Holes.

Shot of the slender tower looming overhead, the obscene bomb-bulge at the top. God only knows what strings Rabstein had to pull to get Pathé in on this.

There's a cylindrical hole in the ground right under the tower, right at ground zero, and they slip the frozen Houdini in there. His head, flush with the ground, grins at them like a peyote cactus. They drive back to the bunker, fast.

Eddie films it all in real time, no cuts. Houdini's mom is in the bunker, of course, plucking a lapful of wigs. The scientist hands her some dice.

"Just to give him fighting chance, we won't detonate until you are rolling a two. Is called snake-eyes, yes?"

Close on her face, frantic with worry. As slowly as possible, she rattles the dice and spills them onto the floor.

Snake-eyes!

Before anyone else can react, the scientist has pushed the button, a merry twinkle in his faraway eyes. The sudden light filters into the bunker, shading all the blacks up to grey. The shock wave hits next, and the judge collapses, possibly from heart attack. The roar goes on and on. The crowded faces turn this way and that.

Then it's over, and the noise is gone, gone except for…an insistent *honking*, right outside the bunker. The scientist undogs the door and they all look out, Eddie shooting over their shoulders.

It's *Houdini*! Yes! In a white convertible with a breast-heavy show-girl! "Give me my money!" he shouts. "And color me gone!"

Note on "Tales of Houdini"

Written in Summer, 1980.
Elsewhere, Ace Books, 1981.

I remember reading a cartoon-story about Houdini in *Children's Digest* when I was young. My own "Tales of Houdini" arose orally; it was a story that I made up for the children one day while we were driving on a Sunday outing from Heidelberg to the nearby town of Speyer, all five of us in a 1972 Taunus, Sylvia and I in front and the three kids in back. I rehearsed the story in my mind a few times, and then, right after we moved back to the States, I used my mother's portable Olivetti to knock it out in one go. Bruce Sterling included the story in his classic cyberpunk *Mirrorshades* anthology of 1986. The cameraman "Eddie" in this story was based on my friend Eddie Marritz, who still is a cameraman to this day.

THE FACTS OF LIFE

The Tulpan resembled an ordinary plastic soda-straw. He was warpsick, and lay trembling on his tiny jellybed. One end of him…his name was Ö…was oozing orange foam, and the other end of him was piping a distress signal.

Jack Stalk wanted to help, but he didn't trust his legs. Or arms, for that matter. He thought back on the crowded, chiming passage through hyperspace. Now you see us, now you don't.

It was horrible to come down from the mindless joy of the warp, down into a crowded piece of machinery, a hundred thousand light-years from home. From Micha. Jack could see her full face, smell her sweet body. Micha. If they hadn't quarreled this never would have happened.

He felt he should sit up and do something, help Ö , look out a porthole, ask more questions…but he could only lie there, staring at the blank ceiling which now looked, in some indefinite way, alive… like a face, really.

"Hello, Jack-Stalk," the ceiling said. "Ready for conversing topics of mutual interest?"

It was Ö 's cloud-person, Fefferfuff by name. Fefferfuff was up there, a centimeter thick, a talking carpet of cloud.

"Are we there yet?" Jack asked.

"Position yes, velocity no. Our planet always moving some 700 km/sec relative to the cosmic background. After matching them up then we landing Tulpa."

As Fefferfuff said this, he reached a tendril down to the control board. Jack could feel the ship's engines cutting in, and the welcome pressure of acceleration. The solid g-force felt good to Jack. He felt good enough to sit up and take a look at little Ö , still skirling his distress.

The distress-call was a repeated pattern of kinetic tone images. There was a downward tone, a thrust and grab, a twirling sound, three blips and a harmonious resolution.

Jack slid his hand down the side of Ö 's bed until he found a slit. He pushed his hand in, removed an object and laid it on the bed. It was a tightly furled piece of material. A Tulpan suitcase. Jack unrolled it as Ö squeaked approvingly.

The fabric…slippery and somewhat elastic…was lined with little pockets holding various shapes. One pocket seemed full of little balls. Jack took out three and laid them near the Tulpan's intake end.

"Geople helping geople," Fefferfuff observed. Ö vacuumed up the pills. He looked, then, like a short boa constrictor who'd just eaten three cantaloupes. He stopped foaming and humped himself up like a numeral "2."

"Gleephwee buzz buzz," Ö said, "Ah wove Wucy."

"I love Lucy," Fefferfuff repeated, his husky voice solemn with emotion. "You love Lucy. Lucy loves you. Geople loving geople."

Jack Stalk tried once again to explain. "That was just a comedy show. Twenty, thirty years ago. I hardly ever watched it. I mean if you want to talk about old TV shows, how about Rod Serling? Ed Sullivan? 'Sergeant Bilko?'"

"Hahahahahahaha," Ö said, imitating canned laughter.

"Lucy is waiting," Fefferfuff said serenely. "Waiting for average fellow. You lucky dog."

"How does your FTL drive work?" Jack Stalk asked, just to change the subject. He'd heard about little else but Lucille Ball from these two ever since they'd nabbed him. It had been a classic UFO snatch. Lights in the sky. Unattached young man has a fight with his girl, goes out for a walk, and is never seen again. Missing person number 765 for the year 1981. No one but Micha would really care…and she'd forget before long. He had to get back!

"Grandma dreams she moves Tweety-Bird's cage," Fefferfuff said, presumably in answer to Jack's question. "Tweety dreams Grandma. We dream God. God dreams us here, he dreams us there."

"Znnt, znnt," Ö said by way of illustration. He swayed back and forth like a happy little cobra.

"But what type of *engine* have you got in this thing?" Jack insisted. He needed to find out how to fly it back. "I mean this isn't a Tibetan prayer-wheel you've got here, it's a fantastically sophisticated ship with a faster-than-light drive! We'd give anything for this on Earth." A sudden inspiration struck. "We could probably arrange to turn the *real* Lucille Ball over to…"

A porthole irised open. "We already got good-looking Lucy on Tulpa. Waiting for you. You lucky dog."

Jack Stalk could see the small blue disk of a planet out there. They were coming up on it, matching velocities. He still couldn't see why, if the Tulpans had an FTL drive, they couldn't have just jumped right from downtown Louisville, where they'd nabbed him, to the surface of their home planet. Instead they had spent a whole week powering out of the solar system…allegedly to "match velocities with the cosmic background." And now they were using the rockets again, this time to switch from cosmic rest to the motion of Tulpa. It seemed stupid.

"Hewwo," Ö said, sounding like a wetly blown kazoo, "Hewwo, Earthwing." This, along with "Ah wove Wucy," was the extent of his spoken English. Of course Ö, the soda-straw, didn't *need* to speak English. Fefferfuff could create the necessary sound waves by vibrating the particles of his gaseous body. And Fefferfuff, who was part of Ö… or was it the other way around…Fefferfuff was a linguist, a student of Earth's televised culture. He had some very strange ideas about Earth.

"Jack-Stalk," the cloud person asked then, "In your sex orgies what is the precise role of the twenty-piece steel mixing-bowl set? Is the wearing of black mouse-ears a signal of genotypic sterility? Or is it rather functioning as signal for coital adjacency? We are so very curious about your reproductive processes."

"If you're so interested in that stuff you should spend some time on Earth and look around…instead of watching television all the time. Sex is part of everyday life. No big deal. It's just…" Jack broke off, strangely embarrassed, and made the traditional hand-gesture for coitus: *The extended right forefinger is thrust repeatedly into a circle formed by the left thumb and forefinger.* In point of fact, Jack was still a virgin.

"You and Lucy must do this for all of us," Fefferfuff said. "We never seeing it on television. Excretion as well. Until Ö and I picking you up we thinking that human body-chemistry so advanced that there no bodily wastes. In the cases of Fred-Flintstone or Walter-Cronkite, for instance…"

Jack stopped listening. He'd been kidnapped by incredibly advanced aliens…and all they were interested in was doo-doo and weenies.

They were from the planet Tulpa, on the other side of the galaxy, about a hundred thousand light-years from Earth. Something about the symmetry of the galactic gravitational field made it easy for them to jump across to our side and back. They'd been doing the jumps for twenty or thirty years now, but had never actually landed on Earth before this. They hadn't had the conventional rocket power up till now.

Prior to this visit, the Tulpans had gotten all their information about Earth by intercepting TV broadcasts. On the basis of total minutes broadcast, they had concluded that Lucille Ball was the most important person on Earth. Apparently they had developed some sort of Lucy simulacrum.

Once again, Jack leaned over the ship's control panel, trying to puzzle it out. The big button there must activate the FTL drive…he'd seen Fefferfuff reach a tendril down to it just before the jump. And those two rows of lights had something to do with the velocity. Before the jump, the Tulpans had wasted days maneuvering the ship till each pair of lights was glowing evenly. The conventional rocket controls were over there and…

Fefferfuff drifted down from the ceiling to shroud the control panel. The engines shifted to full roar. The ship was sliding down into the gravitational well of the planet Tulpa. Jack lurched back to his jellybed.

When Fefferfuff had finished setting the controls, he drifted over to settle down on top of little Ö and his bed. The two of them seemed to be symbiotic parts of a single organism. An animated lichen. The gauzy cloud-person wrapped himself round and round the lively soda-straw. The result was a long pale object about the size and shape of a human mummy. A hole opened in one end to address Jack Stalk.

"We shaping like humans in your honor." Arms and legs articulated out of the form, then fingers, a nose and a chin. It looked something like the Pillsbury dough-boy.

There was a thump and the engines stopped. They'd landed. As far as Jack Stalk could figure out, he'd been brought here to star in a live sex-show, co-starring a giant lichen in drag. Fuuuugh! What a way to lose your virginity!

The dough-boy opened the ship's door and…she was right outside, smiling at him with that weird double-bow mouth, her hair flaming red. The planet's surface looked like blue jello.

"Hello, Jack-Stalk. Let's getting down to business."

The humanoid form lay down on the blue jello and pulled up her skirts…

"What should be under skirts?" Ö-Fefferfuff stage-whispered in Jack Stalk's ear. "What normally looking like? We fix up just like."

"Not keeping a girl waiting all day," the supine one warbled, nancing her skirts back and forth. There were several other Tulpans standing around holding things that might have been guns…but were probably cameras. Jack made his move.

With quick, economical motions, he pushed the Ö-Fefferfuff dough-boy out of the hatch, stepped back, locked the door, and walked over to the control panel. If he wasted time using the conventional rockets, the Tulpans would get him. Better to use the FTL drive right away. Jump right out. Back to Earth, back to Louisville, back to Micha.

A Tulpan's voice crackled over the ship's comm-unit. "Not making a false move, Jack-Stalk! Above all not using the FTL drive without matching velocity to cosmic nullity! Uncontrolled hyperjumping very bad, come back yesterday!"

Another Tulpan voice, perhaps Ö-Fefferfuff's, broke in. "If you really...*not* loving Lucy, we can painless re-model. Better maybe she matching dream-girl Micha? You giving us please one sex-show and I safely driving you home like taxi."

Something finally snapped in Jack Stalk's psyche. He wanted out, *far* out, right *now*. He pushed the big FTL button on the control panel.

The Tulpans watched in dismay as their ship wavered, sagged and disappeared.

"You're a fool," the one with the comm-unit told Ö-Fefferfuff.

"God is a fool," the dough-boy shrugged. "He wrote the script, not me."

"What's going to happen?" the imitation Lucy asked, flowing back into an upright position. "Jack-Stalk didn't match velocities! He jumped without adopting the cosmic frame of reference!" They spoke in Tulpan.

One of the cameramen spoke up. "Since we're moving away from Earth, this means that he'll get back before he left..."

"Oh no!" Lucy shrilled. "What if he causes a paradox? What if he warns his past self not to be abducted by Ö-Fefferfuff? If he's not abducted, then he doesn't come here, so he doesn't go back, so he doesn't warn himself, so he *is* abducted, in which case he *does* go back, and..."

"Oh, shut up," the Tulpan with the comm-unit snapped. "We've all heard it before. What do *you* think, Ö-Fefferfuff, you unruffled fool?"

Ö-Fefferfuff had let himself slump into the sluglike Posture of Noble Ease. "No problem, chief. Grandma's in her rocker and all's right with the cage." A serious student of the *Tweetie and Sylvester* cycle, he enjoyed showing off his erudition. "But seriously, Ü-Ramalam, are you familiar with Ä-Eddywed's explanation of the recession of distant galaxies? He claims that, in cosmic time, the galaxies are actually shrinking, and *that's* why they look farther apart. Thus, when Jack-Stalk arrives, perhaps one or two Lucy shows before leaving, he will..."

Jack Stalk stared out his stolen ship's porthole, presumably at the Sun. After fiddling around with the instrument panel for awhile, he'd been able to dope out the controls for the attitude jets. He was, after all, a budding engineer. He'd rolled the ship around till he found what looked like the closest and brightest star. That *had* to be the Sun. If not...

He pushed the thought back, pointed the ship towards that bright star, and cut in the conventional rocket drive. He would have liked to try another hyperjump...but maybe hyperjumps were bad for nearby planets. The thought that he might have destroyed Tulpa didn't particularly bother him. Hell, what difference was one less inhabited planet in a whole galaxy? But Earth...Earth was special. Earth had Micha on it. Not to mention Louisville.

The Tulpan ship was fast...the engines seemed to be based on powerful mass-converters. But it was still a long way to the Sun. He kept track of the days by making food-paste smears on the bulkhead. Feffer-fuff had showed him how to run the food synthesizer on the way out.

After two weeks the Sun...if it *was* the Sun...had grown to a distinct little disc, and Jack Stalk began decelerating. Once a day he would cut the engines and roll the ship around, watching for planets. On his third day of searching, he spotted a bright dot a few degrees above the Sun. Above the sun, damn, that meant he wasn't in the plane of the ecliptic. He was coming down on the solar system from above...or up from beneath, not that up and down really meant anything out in...

On second thought Jack Stalk realized that it was *good* to be looking down on the solar system. He dialed up the porthole's magnification and began looking for planets. It wasn't hard, once he got the hang of it...after all, sunlight was bouncing up off each of them. It was just a matter of...*there*, that blue-white one had to be Earth...it was the next one in from the red one, Mars.

Jack managed to hit the plane of the ecliptic pretty near Earth, but he hadn't decelerated enough, and had to spend a frustrating three days watching Earth sliding back above him. From time to time he wondered what sort of fuel the rocket's mass-converter used...and how much of it was left. It was another long week till he finally got back up near the Earth, and this time at a reasonable speed.

The planet looked big, really big, turning majestically beneath him. Landing was going to be touchy...if he came in too fast there'd be no correcting it. And what if someone's Air Force fired a missile at him?

Jack Stalk spun the dial on the comm-unit, hoping to eavesdrop on some military transmissions.

FZZAT! The screen sprang to life. A smooth, handsome male face stared out at him. "What do you mean by coming here like this? What is it that you...*want*, Jennifer?"

Cut to Jennifer's tear-stained face. "Oh, Brad, don't you *understand?* I've fallen in love with you. You can't just *use* a woman and walk..."

Jack Stalk smiled happily. A soap opera. He was back to Earth for sure. He decided to just watch TV for a while, relax, wait for the news, find out the date. It had been Saturday, August 22, 1981, when the Tulpans had nabbed him. Since then had been close to two months. Would

Micha still be waiting? As the soap opera on the TV screen played itself out, Jack Stalk's own soap opera spun in his mind.

On that last Saturday, he and Micha had gone swimming in a quarry on Jack's brother's farm, a few miles west of Louisville. It had just been the two of them, so they'd gone nude. The water in the quarry was deep and unimaginably pure. You could see blue-gills hovering, ten, twenty, thirty feet below. Jack loved to dive and come up under Micha, marveling at her big strong buttocks and huge buoyant breasts.

There was even a cave cut into the quarry wall, and Jack and Micha swam in there for some serious necking. It had been nice, not too rocky, and not much flotsam except for an old grey tennis-ball.

Micha's lips, posing and pouting, had planted kisses, soft and hard, all over him. He'd revelled in her white curves…this was the first time he'd seen her naked all over…and had noticed that from the side she was an almost perfect sine-wave. Kissable neck at zero, plump nipple at one-half pi, tiny waist at pi, delectable summit of firm asscheek at three-halves pi, and the divinely soft folds of thigh against buttock at two pi. He'd told her this, and she, also an engineering student at The University of Louisville, had been amused.

They might have even made love, at last, at last…if Jack's brother Daryl hadn't showed up. Typically, Daryl had made his presence known by firing a shotgun and hollering, "COME ON OUT OF THAT CAVE," over the outside speaker of his pickup truck's CB.

He was just-kidding-around-of-course, as usual, but Micha'd been so freaked that Jack had had to swim back, tell Daryl to cool it, get Micha's suit, and swim it out to the cave.

They swam in side by side, and Jack had been touched-to-the-quick by Micha's brave and nervous smile, her lower lip set just so against her upper. On second thought, it hadn't been the smile itself that really got him—it had been her control over it, and the way she would compress her lips over and over again in her enigmatic, slightly menacing pout.

"Hey," Daryl had called when she got out of the water. "What's a sexy girl like you doing with my baby brother? What's he got that I don't?"

Micha didn't say anything, just pouted and flashed her eyes from the one to the other. Where Jack was skinny, almost hollow-chested, Daryl was big and muscular. Jack had a visionary's wide brown eyes, Daryl a soldier's green slits. Now that he'd taken over the family farm, Daryl liked to play the redneck.

"You're a real idiot," Jack said quietly, "Shooting off that gun."

"Whatsamatter, bro?" Daryl laughed. "Didn't you get a chance to shoot *yours*?" He chuckled lewdly, ingratiatingly, and stuck a corner of his tongue out at Micha. "Y'all come on up to the house and have a drink," he called then, and drove off in his pickup.

"Let's not stay long," Micha urged, as they followed Daryl in Jack's old VW.

But they had stayed long, too long. For all their resentment of each other, the two brothers did enjoy drinking bourbon together. Daryl needled Jack about getting so educated at Daryl's expense, and Jack needled Daryl about hogging most of their inheritance. But on another level, each respected the other for being different. And here, on the family farm, in the haze of alcohol, it was almost like being kids again, kids with all the time in the world. Daryl's wife brought out food and old jokes. Micha quietly sipped at a glass of white wine, setting and resetting her full lips.

They'd finally left around ten, and on the drive back downtown, Micha had spoken her piece. "So, so, Jack, you still wish you were a farmboy. And you let you bully of a brother walk all over you. Did you see the way he looked at me? Thank God I waited for my suit in that disgusting cave, or he probably would have shot you and raped me on the spot! And I thought you came from a nice family."

"But," Jack protested, staring hard at the drink-blurred road, "It was *nice* in the cave, I thought. That…that wasn't so disgusting, was it?"

"Oh, it was all right," Micha said coldly. "Until your brother came. A horrible big bug crawled on me when you were getting my suit. And then him staring at me like that all evening…oh, just take me home."

In the car, outside her apartment-house, Micha had sat with him for five minutes, passively letting herself be kissed and apologized to… but she'd refused to let him set their next date.

Jack had driven the five blocks to his own apartment building, parked the car, and, too depressed to go in, had taken a walk. There had been a storm brewing, with high flashes of heat lightning, and he had wandered onto the University of Louisville campus, finally sitting on the administration building's steps, next to their copy of Rodin's *The Thinker*. The rain had started, all at once, and Jack just sat there, lashed by the liquid curtains. Lightning had forked and zigzagged down the sky, striking once, twice, three times nearby.

And then the Tulpans' spherical ship had touched down. At first Jack had thought it was ball-lightning. He'd even fumbled out a pen, useless in the rain, to take some notes on the phenomenon…but by then Fefferfuff had flown out and begun pulling him towards the ship. With Micha mad at him he hadn't even felt like struggling.

On the comm-unit's screen, an ugly man was reading a sheet of paper. The five-thirty local news. School board. Sewage. Lay-offs at Ford and GE. "And now the weather. Charlie?"

The weatherman's bald head filled the screen. He scribbled the usual incomprehensible bullshit on a plastic map. He was so bald that when he turned his head, you could see a lot of folds and meat-tucks in back. Jack amused himself by pretending that these mashing wrinkles made up the weatherman's *real face*. But then he heard something which brought him up with a start.

"Today is Friday, August 21, 1981. The hottest temperature on record for this date was 104 in 1956, the lowest a cool 64 in 1949. The weather for tomorrow, Saturday, August 22, 1981, will be hot, with thundershowers expected in the late afternoon and evening."

The date was printed right there on the screen. This was the day before Jack had left! But...

Jack dialed his receiver up and down the spectrum, and picked up another news show. The same thing. One of the Tulpans, he now recalled, had said something about this: *Uncontrolled hyperjumping very bad, come back yesterday.*

Come back yesterday. What an opportunity! At the very least he could head off the fight with Micha by giving himself some sound advice when it would do the most good. Or, even better, he could somehow head off Daryl...prevent him from fouling up Jack's big chance to get laid.

Grinning with excitement, Jack nudged the ship out of orbit. The Earth fell up at him, huge and welcome as Micha's ass.

The ship maneuvered surprisingly well, and in the space of five hours, Jack had it down to an altitude of what looked like two or three km. He was hovering somewhere out over the Pacific Ocean, sunny blue wave-patterns marching past below. By now it would be almost midnight in Louisville. He set his wristwatch to twelve. He toyed with the idea of whipping across America and slitting his sleeping brother's throat...but thought better of it. He was too tired.

So Jack Stalk lay down on his jellybed and slept.

When he awoke it was night on the Pacific. Ten in the morning, Louisville time. He flew east, into the dawn. As he flew, he kept searching up and down the radio bands, nervous about military pursuit planes... but no one seemed to notice him.

He was crossing the Mississippi when he first suspected that something might be wrong. A swallow flew at him. This was surprising in itself, since it looked as if he was about two km up. But the real shocker was the bird's size. The thing was as big as a jetliner! Powering along with its maw spread, it attacked him!

Jack Stalk took evasive action and increased his altitude. By the time he'd found Louisville, he had himself convinced that the business with the bird had just been an illusion. After all, the porthole had still been set on a pretty high magnification.

He knew Louisville well, and it wasn't hard to find his brother's farm. Before landing, Jack checked the time. Two in the afternoon. Great. Daryl hadn't busted in on them till about three-thirty. All he had to do was land in the woods, cover the ship with brush, and go distract his brother for a couple of hours. Meanwhile his past self would get laid in the cave and, hopefully, drive downtown to spend the night with Micha. When that thunderstorm started, he'd be happy in Micha's soft bed—instead of out getting kidnapped by the Tulpans.

But then…? Jack had a moment of doubt. If he didn't get kidnapped by the Tulpans, then he wouldn't be here in a second body to do all this. So what! So this body would disappear or something. Jack looked at his hands, white and slender. Disappear? So what, so what. His other self, the real self would wake up in bed with yummy milky Micha. Could any man die for a better cause?

Jack centered the ship over a copse of trees in the middle of the pasture nearest Daryl's house. He could see Daryl on his tractor, mowing the next pasture over, too busy to look up. Jack cut the engine power and let the ship slide down to Earth.

He had to fight back a moment of panic as he came down into the trees. They were *so big*! How could they be so big? Gently jiggling the attitude jets, he wriggled past the huge trunks and branches. It seemed to go on for kilometers. Finally there was the grass…coming up…and up…a jungle of high golden stalks scissoring past the porthole…what?

With a tiny thud the ship finally hit solid ground. Jack was beginning, vaguely, to get the picture. Cautiously he opened the hatch. The yellow-grey field grass rose a hundred meters above him. Beneath him were root-tendrils, as big as the tunnels in a man-sized, 3-D maze, twined this way and that. Something large, dark and chitinous was scrabbling towards the ship…

Jack slammed the hatch and powered back up into the treetops. Now he understood why the trees looked so big. His ship was the size of a tennis ball. He was the size of a grasshopper. He had jumped into the past and it had made him small.

Suddenly he remembered a paradox he'd read about in the first pages of Martin Gardner's classic, *Relativity for the Million*. It had been called Poincaré's Paradox:

"Suppose that one night, while you were sleeping, everything got a hundred times as small as it was the day before. EVERYTHING—electrons, atoms, wavelengths of light, you yourself, your bed, your house, the Earth, the Sun, the stars, the spaces between the stars. When you awoke would you be able to tell that anything had changed? Is there any experiment you could perform that would prove you had altered in size?"

"No," Poincaré and Gardner had answered. "There would be no way to tell. For size is relative." Fine. But, Jack Stalk thought, *what about time-travel?* What if the universe really is shrinking...maybe not quite uniformly, and that's why the galaxies seem to get farther apart...what if it does get a hundred times smaller every week...what if that's true and one day some poor guy manages to travel back in time?

Relative to the time-traveler, all the yesterday people are two hundred meters tall. And a tree is two kilometers high. And...

A crow protecting its territory darted out and struck the Tulpan spaceship a glancing blow with its beak. Bobbing and weaving, Jack took the ship back up high. From there things looked fine. It was just that he wasn't nearly as high as it felt like he was.

What could he possibly accomplish now, two centimeters tall? As long as he stayed on Earth, floating along the normal timestream again, he was going to be, almost literally, a shrimp.

What about using the hyperjump again, then? Presumably the thing worked like a shuttle, and he'd yoyo right back to Tulpa. Maybe he would gain a week back and show up normal-sized. *Lucy-sized.* Jack shuddered. And thought of another problem.

He'd changed his velocity a lot since the last jump. What if the next jump made him even smaller, or worse, bigger...enormously bigger. Jack visualized that for a moment, imagining his ship becoming the size of a whole galactic sector. The gentle patter of stars and planets raining down his gravity-well to patter on his hull. Still, if he were to carefully...

Just then the Tulpan ship's engine sputtered. He began losing altitude. Out of fuel. Jack looked frantically out the porthole. There was the quarry over there. *Quick!*

By using the last reserves of the altitude jets, Jack was able to crash-land in the quarry's clear waters. Fortunately he got strapped down on the jellybed in time, and the crash felt no worse than getting kicked in the stomach by a mule. Even after he'd bounced up to the surface again, the ship kept tossing around for awhile. Through the porthole, Jack saw a whale-sized fish whizz past. The blue-gills were striking at him.

But after awhile they gave up. Fortunately the ship was too big to swallow whole. There was an dangerous-sounding gurgling from deep in the ship, but after awhile that, too, stopped.

"I'm glad it's not *two* weeks back," Jack muttered, and opened the hatch which was, providentially, somewhat above the water-line.

It was Saturday, August 22, 1981, the second time around for this shrunken future Jack Stalk. Over there, where the road sloped down to the quarry's edge sat two people. A boy and a girl. Jack and Micha. A past Jack. Call him Jack*.

They were only twenty meters off, but it looked like two kilometers to poor little Jack. Even so, he almost dove in...before he remembered the fish. But then he noticed the mouth of the cave, not very far off at all.

For some reason the attitude jets still worked. Using what he supposed were the last drops of the fuel, Jack skipped across the water and beached himself on the cave's wide shingle.

Jack* and Micha arrived soon thereafter. They lay down some five meters off. Grimly, hurriedly, Jack started the long trek over, struggling over the many large boulders in his path. What would he say? He didn't even know anymore. Somehow the idea of getting Jack* laid and just quietly winking out of existence...somehow this had stopped seeming like such a noble and sensible idea. He wanted help!

But just as he came to the foothills of Micha's wonderful white thighs, there was an explosion outside. Daryl. His stupid loudspeaker voice. Jack* and Micha exchanged words...so loud that Jack had to hold his tiny ears...and then Jack* splashed off. Micha just lay there on her side, resting her head on her arm, her back to Jack.

Jack wondered where to begin. He was standing on the rocky ground about even with the two pi point on Micha's sine-curve, that is to say, right next to her most private parts, rear approach.

Her full, smooth thigh towered above him. To his right the celestial spheres of her buttocks joined. There was a fat, pleasant-looking wrinkle where buttock met thigh. Jack resolved to climb it. On a sudden sex-crazed impulse, he took his clothes off first.

"This makes it all worthwhile," he muttered as he worked his way up. There was some pubic hair up ahead, almost within reach, just another step, she'd be glad to see him, sure she would, dear Micha, oh my God I love it so much here I think I'm going to...

"EEE-YAH!" Jack heard from afar. And then he was snatched and flung, head over heels, far out into the water.

By the time he'd struggled back to shore, that stupid and monstrous Jack* had come and taken his fine, big Micha away. Jack lay down on a rock, gasping like a fish out of water.

It was hard to get his breath properly...the air wasn't really right for him, now that his lungs and hemoglobin molecules were a hundred times too small. Fortunately he'd left the ship's hatch open, and its air-generator was working overtime, filling the cave with shrunk air. But the mixture wasn't rich enough. He had to get back to the ship.

Had to get back to the ship. Jack staggered to his feet. And fell. He wasn't going to make it. He didn't care. He lay on his side, wet, naked and helpless, his chest heaving. His mind was a blank.

Something tickled Jack's ass then, down at the bottom of the cheek where it meets the thigh. A spider? Eeeyah! He twitched himself into a sitting position, ready for something horrible…but it was only a little ball of some kind. A floating little ball nudging at him.

It was a tiny Tulpan spaceship! From further in the future! Suddenly Jack felt strong enough to move. He seized the new little ship in his fist, and scrambled over to his own ship. There was good air inside. He closed the hatch and opened his hand.

The little ship's hatch popped open, and a white puff of smoke drifted out. The smoke spread, tenuously taking shape…

"Fefferfuff?" Jack asked. "Is it you?"

"It is I, Jack-Stalk." The voice was faint and windy. "Ö and I feeling sorry your jam, and noticing that universe not disappearing, we also breaking jump rules. Now to setting controls correctly and not like flaky shmoe. Lucy still waiting."

The patch of pale haze drifted over to the control panel, tsk-tsking at what it found.

"But the engines are out of fuel," Jack said weakly. He tried to peek into the tiny ship hovering in front of him. "Is Ö really in there?"

A tiny squeak of, "Hewwo, Earthwing," floated out of the miniature hatch. Somehow, having Ö there made Jack feel that everything would be all right.

"Everything's all right," Fefferfuff said. "The ship is refueled. It running on water. Molecule size no problem. Now to setting controls as I say, Jack-Stalk. Please one sex-show, then I bringing you back like taxi as advertised."

So Jack Stalk finally lost his virginity. Once to Lucy. And then, a month later, to Micha.

Note on "The Facts of Life"

Written in Fall, 1980.
The 57th Franz Kafka, Ace Books, 1983.

I grew up in Louisville, Kentucky, near where this story is set. This is another time-travel-related tale with aliens, based on a seed idea from Martin Gardner. If you're curious about why FTL can lead to time-travel, check out my nonfiction book, *The Fourth Dimension*.

BUZZ

A rock-concert. It's Elvis Costello and the Attractions. Elvis is dripping sweat, bent over a white plastic J. C. Penney's guitar. Superwimp! His amazingly deep and authoritative voice carries over the driving network of electric sound. "Waitin' to de eyund of de woruld / waitin' to de eyund o de woruld / waitin' to de eyund odee world, deeyur Lord / I sincerely hope you're comin' 'cause you cerntly started something." NnnMmmMMmmMMMmMMMP NnnnMmmmMMmMMmMMMP. His rhythm guitarist shambles about, opening and closing his mouth like a chimpanzee eating a cigarette butt. The bassman looks like the equipment manager for a football team, all dressed in chinos and a yellow oxford-cloth button-down. But at the end of the song he jumps up and lands in a split.

The camera draws back and we see the audience. A sparse crowd here in this Mannheim concert-hall. Maybe three hundred people. A few of the greaser-hippies the Germans call "rrockerrs," some punk-girls with black lips, punk-boys with short red and green hair, but mostly just average-type sales clerks and students.

"You're a dismal bunch of punks," Elvis says, not unkindly. People are smoking cigarettes. A little knot of GIs shares a hash-pipe.

The camera closes in on a slight, red-haired youth at the right edge of the crowd. On the sound track, Elvis starts one of his smeared-notes songs from *Get Happy*. The red-haired youth fiddles with his tape-recorder. Close shot of the turning reels. The reels speed up, the music too, an excited drone. Tape ends, flap flap flap, and everyone's leaving the concert hall.

We follow the red-haired youth out onto the street. He's alone, carrying his big tape-player on a strap slung over one shoulder. He wears black Levis and a shiny brown leather jacket. His skin is luminously pale, his hair short and spiky, his fingers long and mobile. A street-car screeches to a *gggkgreeeeeeesht* halt and he climbs into its yellow-green light.

Cut. The next evening. Shot of the red-haired youth handling an ancient glass vase. He sits by a window in a one-room apartment, the fragile cylindrical vessel in his hands. Close shot on the vase.

The glass is cloudy, old-looking and shimmering here and there with metal oxides deposited over what must have been centuries of burial. The surface is etched with thousands of tiny lines. The lines wrap around and around the cylinder. It is as if after having been blown, the vase was put on a lathe and shaved down. A diamond knife in some turner's hand has etched a single groove around the vase from top to bottom.

Medium shot of red-haired youth walking across his apartment. One whole wall is books, one wall a workbench. Electronic components, computer circuitry. Orange light from the setting sun slopes in.

He flicks on his tape-deck. A man screaming in rising bursts and then a great rush of tight, happy sound. Blondie's "I'm Not Living in the Real World."

The red-haired youth busies himself with his tools, mounting the vase into some kind of machine. When Debbie's voice croons, "Didn't I ever tell you I was gone?" he hits a button, snaring the phrase on a tape-loop. Eternal repeat on that: "Didn't I ever tell you I was gone? Didn't I ever tell you I was gone? Didn't I ever tell you I was gone?"

There's a whole console of buttons set into the back of the workbench. He hits another and overdubs a loop of live E. C. sneering, "Now I try to stay amused. Now I try to stay amused. Now I try to stay amused."

More buttons, and more voices coming on, all on top of each other. Jagger: "Do the hip-shake, babe. Do the hip-shake, babe. Do the hip-shake, babe." The Zap: "The torture never stops. The torture never stops. The torture never stops." Marley: "Wake up and turn I loose. Wake up and turn I loose. Wake up and turn I loose." Nina Hagen: *"Ich glotz Tay-Fow. Ich glotz Tay-Fow. Ich glotz Tay-Fow."* Johnny Rotten: "And we don't care. And we don't care. And we don't care." More Jagger: "I'm always hearin' voices in the street. I'm always hearin' voices in the street. I'm always hearin' voices in the street." And more others, more and more cutting in and speeded up, making a...wild, high *buzz*, you understand.

But it won't fly yet. Something's missing. The vase! He's got the vase mounted on a sort of lathe, and he's setting a phonograph needle down on the spinning glass, dropping the needle down into the groove as if it were one of Thomas Alva Edison's cylindrical phonograph records.

Macro-close-up of the phonograph needle in the groove. The needle vibrates back and forth with the groove's slow meanderings. There is a steady tone feeding out from the needle. The winging welter of the music-loops damps down and the vase-glass recording comes up. A rumble as from a voice underwater. A squeak. A rumble.

Zoom back to the red-haired youth. Weird eyes on this kid. He's so young…how can he know so much? His hands crawl patiently over the equipment surrounding the vase. Dreamy smile. Again an indistinct rumble from the vase, this time more voice-like. The youth wags his head and makes another adjustment.

Cut back to macro-close-up of the phono needle. The groove twists back and forth, the needle follows, and we hear a voice talking clearly.

"Ah noko landee cleek-ka-sneep. Orbaahm. Deedle?"

Soft *wah-wah-wah* and the phono needle changes its appearance. We zoom slowly back…vase still spinning. But only half of the vase is etched yet, and the needle has turned into the tip of a diamond knife, held in the hand of a tan-brown man with ultra-black hair, an Egyptian craftsman etching the original groove into the vase. He is talking, and as he talks the vibrations travel down his arms and into the etching tool he holds…he's recording his voice though he doesn't know it.

Here in the flashback we see it all, the pedal-driven lathe, the blazing square of sun lying on the floor like sheet-iron, the play of muscles in the turner's back, his big liquid eyes and purple lips. He speaks again.

"Ahna bogbog du smeepy flan."

Suddenly we notice who he's talking to.

Propped up in a corner of the one-room workshop is a…giant beetle. Totem? No…it's alive, but injured. Straw-yellow ichor seeps from a rent in one side of the soft belly. With a sudden screech, the creature begins to sing.

The noise is dense, concentrated…quintessentially evil, welling out of the swiveling, jewel-like little head, all emerald, carnelian, lapis lazuli. Outside the door we see part of what might be a wrecked spaceship.

The alien knows what it's doing, beaming its groaning twitter straight at the craftsman's body. The timeless humming of the alien's soul is being etched forever into the spinning glass.

Close shot of the glass, the flash-forward (soft haw-haw-haw) to red-haired youth. He's still got all his tape-loops running, and now on top of it is the horrible, insistent, mind-picking flicker of the ancient alien death-song. It adds up to something…unheard of.

The youth starts back from the bench. A stool crashes down. The sound is out of control, roiling about the room in booming crests so crushingly loud you begin to see them gel. (A buzzer goes off under your seat nnnNNNBBZEEEEEEE, just like at *The Tingler*.)

Red-haired youth slapping at switches, smashing machinery with a crescent wrench, trying to stop it, Stop It, STOP STOP STOP…

Vase shatters, youth's pants split open from a huge milky-white hard-on. He pumps it frantically with one hand, flailing at instruments with the other; it's too much, too loud, too far.

Wild, high, buzzing stacking way up now. We cut to an outside shot of youth's building. Everything motionless for two heartbeats, then a window explodes out in slow motion, and he flies through, bleeding, ejaculating. Suddenly the soundtrack is slowed down, too, and the mad sound breaks into manageable pieces.

You can see into the apartment, the machinery is wrecked, a fire is starting, but the sound keeps on. It's a self-perpetuating vortex pattern now, riding on the energy gradient of the day/night twilight zone. We can see the smoke twirling in *significant* patterns, and overlayered there are purple-to-ultraviolet moirés.

Camera pulls up to a hundred meters and we look down to see the paisley streamers flowing out on the gentle evening breeze. The youth is flaring like a sparkler, still falling, and on the sidewalk we see a man and his dog go up in light. Down the block we see it happen again, and again, and with each flash, the paisley moiré gets a little brighter, the sound a little stronger. Three little children run down the street, screaming, but unharmed.

Cut.

New Jersey. The refineries like giant chemistry labs. Ten-wheel trucks roar past. A solitary figure by the side of the Jersey Turnpike here at the Newark exit. Sunset.

He has colorless blond hair, steel glasses, wears baggy old clothes. White painter's clothes. The drafts from the trucks' passings flutter the loose fabric this way and that.

In front of his solar plexus, like a dish-antenna, he holds a piece of cardboard. "EXIT 9." The lettering is dark and crooked.

There is a lull in the traffic now. He sets down his sign and lights a cigarette. Behind him we see the stark silhouette of a cracking tower, totem woven of five hundred pipes. In profile, he inhales deeply.

Something is bothering him. He brushes at his eyes...smoke? Insects? He throws down his thin cigarette and begins slapping at his head and shoulders. There is a wild, high buzzing. As the noise peaks, the hitchhiker melts into a blob of blinding light.

A semi rumbles past, brakes groaning, horn blasting fear. It says "PYRAMID" on the side.

Cut to the truck-driver's face. Likable Italian kid, twenty, curly black hair, trying to keep his rig under control.

"Waxman," he hollers to his sleeping partner. "Hey, Waxman! We gotta pull..."

The wild, high buzzing has not stopped, and now it builds to a new peak. The curly-haired driver's face glows and runs like molten steel.

Aerial shot of the PYRAMID semi-tractor-trailer jack-knifing, rolling, bursting into flame. Wild, high buzzing, rhythmic, never repeating.

We continue to rise, looking down at the big pile-up. Cars and trucks keep coming. The passengers go up in little puffs of white light, flashbulbs popping off in the dinky-toy cars far, far below us, still rising, rising to look down at all America, one-quarter dark.

Time speeds up and we see the terminator, the edge of night, sweep across the country east to west. There is a jumping twinkle in the moving twilight zone, fleeting specks of light like phosphorescent plankton at some surf's lapping line. Pht, pht, pht, pht, pht. The wild, high buzzing, far and faint.

We come back down in California, just before the terminator gets there. Across a beach and through the dish of a radio-telescope. The percussive sounds of a woman's foot-steps hurrying down the hall. Clip clip clip clip. (Think of those little jolts traveling wavelike up her leg-flesh, up to her ripe ass and crinkly hole and fur-burger deluxe…just think about it!) Knock knock.

We see a door open. A fat man looks up. He wears a long-sleeved white plastic shirt with a pen in the pocket. He holds a sheaf of computer print-outs. The day's last square of sunlight lies warm on his lap, and he's been thinking about sex, but only says, "Yes, Dr. Schmid? What is it?"

The woman steps forward and leans over the desk. She's dressed casually: jeans, tube-top, wedgies. Bushy-brown hair, all frizzed out. No lipstick on her full lips. We look at her from behind.

"It's these readings, Professor Akwell." She hands him a roll of paper with squiggles on it. "These peaks are utterly anomalous. It's as if some vast pulse of energy swept across the country during the last three hours. See this? And this and this?"

The professor feeds the paper tape slowly through his fingers. "Do you have an audio conversion?"

"Not yet, but…"

"I'll want to hear the fine-structure energy-analogue."

"Of course." She's around behind the desk now, leaning over his shoulder. It is almost dark outside and, again, the wild, high buzzing mounts.

The professor swivels and looks up at her. Nice full braless breasts right at eye-level. His heart beating, ka-thumn ka-thumn. The buzzing coming and going, a syncopated sound with crests inside the troughs.

135

He pushes up her tube-top. She smiles and leans forward. He tongues and sucks at her hanging milky-white bubs, takes a stiff, dark-pink nipple in his mouth.

The buzzing peaks, but instead of vibrating away into pure dimension-Z energy, the professor and doctor are…dancing through it, lying down beside the CRASH desk-chair, spitty slippery slick peekaboo hair fanning out, and the deadly sound is just coking them up is all…my God, he's built like a racehorse. She spreads and pushes back, their orgone energy tears at the buzzing, breaking it into Stones riffs: "Oh, Doctor please do the hip-shake, babe, I'm riding down your moonlight mile…"

But now we're dollying out through the window, and up again. It's almost dark outside and the buzzing is louder than ever, wilder and higher…it's a multiplex sound with endlessly complex layers of information folded inside each other over and over. (Think of the sound an acid-tripping brain might make as chessmen slide off tilted tiles and wooden fingers fumble for the saves.)

Split-screen checker-board montage. In the black squares people flare into white energy, in the red squares they couple. We draw back and the tessellated plane warps into a sphere, Mother Earth, everyone coming or going at twilight's touch.

Cut to a double bed with a sleeping couple. Pale, pale grey light outside. Faint buzzing. The woman sits up suddenly. Mashed frizzy hair, smallish breasts with perfect nipples. It's Dr. Schmid! She shakes the dormant mound next to her, and Professor Akwell sits up, too, eyes gummy.

The light is growing, the buzzing too. Dr. Schmid flicks on the radio.

"It is *kuzzz* seventy to *bzzzzzznt* Earth's adult population destroyed. Preliminary studies indicate that the deaths *wheeeeeep* dawn and dusk."

"Do you hear that?" she cries, jumping out of bed and staring out the window. On a distant hillside a little flare of white light. "Quickly, dear!" She hops back in the bed.

Professor Akwell still rubbing his eyes. "I'm…I'm too tired."

The radio is still crackling and talking. "Interviews with *fweeep* a striking uniformity. All those adults not destroyed by the Buzz were engaged in *dzeeeent*. Listeners are urgently advised to pair up and stick together. Orgasm *zaaaaap* only answer."

Fingers trembling with haste, Dr. Schmid has pulled on tight stockings and a lacy black garter belt. The buzzing is so loud that the perfume bottles on her dresser are rattling. She falls back on a chair, her legs spread. "Hurry, hurry, oh please hurry!" A ray of sunlight slant into the room.

The professor shambles across the room and kneels down in front of her. Runs his hands around her stocking-tops, where the full buttocks bulge out like warm triple-scoops of vanilla ice cream. He squats lower and glues his mouth to her vagina.

Cut to prof's-eye view of her body. Mystery-furze of black pubic hair in the foreground, thighs and black suspenders out to the sides, the taut buckler of her undulating belly, the swollen breasts sliding, nipples pointing this way and that, her pouting lips and heavy-lidded eyes.

She's coming now; it's fine for *her*, and part of the buzzing stutters into "Emotional Rescue," but the professor barely has a hard-on, this early in the morning and still having to take a piss. He doesn't come, and the buzzing takes him away, melting into hot light between those quivering thighs.

She screams and draws back. The light rolls across the floor like ball-lightning, singeing a trail into the carpet. And then something surprising happens. The light grows projections, begins to dim, and it's… Professor Akwell saved by the love of a good woman?

No. It's that red-haired youth from Mannheim. Naked and curled into a fetal position. He stands up and runs a hand across his forehead. Buzzing and music fading now, New York Dolls chanting: "Who are the Mystery Girls? Who are the Mystery Girls? Who are the Mystery Girls?"

"*Wo sind wir?*" youth asks in German.

The woman is embarrassed and fumbles for her robe. "Who are you?"

"*Amerika?*"

"Yes." She stands, cheeks still pink with sex-flush. "This is America. But where did you come from?"

"I," he fumbles for the English. "I am from Mannheim, Germany. I have make the Buzz. I am Uli." Naked, but self-assured, Uli holds his hand out.

"Lola. Lola Schmid." Gingerly she takes his hand. "But why have you done this? And how?"

Uli looks down at himself. "Do you have some jeans?"

"Yes…" She hands him the pair she was wearing yesterday. He wriggles into them, then slips on her discarded tube-top as well. He picks up one of her lipsticks and leans close to the mirror on her dresser.

Lola goes to her closet, turns her back to Uli and puts on a dress. Shot of inviting ass framed by black garter-straps. Then *swish* the dress is on, a light summer dress with little stars and nebulae printed yellow on white.

Cut to Uli and Lola having breakfast in Lola's kitchen. In her clothes, and with his face made up, he looks…unsettling. A punky bachelor girl. He is talking, haltingly, and with many fluid hand-gestures.

"I have all the time been looking for the *absolute rock*. I snipped from here and there the all-best pieces and folded up mixed." He meshes his fingers to illustrate. "So it was all right. It went. But always I was still feeling something missing."

"Where did you find it, then?" Lola's manner is bright, yet distant. You sense that she no longer quite believes in the reality unfolding around her.

"I was reading in a magazine that someone had the idea of treating turned antiquities as noise-plates." His measured eyes stare at her, looking to see if she understands. One eye is blue, one green.

Lola shakes her head and Uli tries again. "I robbed an Egyptian vase from the museum." He picks up an empty juice-glass and turns it on its side. As he continues talking, he rolls the glass with one hand and touches it delicately with a pencil. "There was a little groove ringed around and around. The Egyptian worker a long time ago made noise and his knife trembled. My phonographic stylus turned the trembling back into voice. A song not his. A very strange song."

Uli falls silent. Lola finds and lights a cigarette. Finally Uli continues.

"I whited-out…and yet here I am back. I think everyone will melt into light and everyone will come back. We all must tour the Hall of the Martian Kings."

"I don't want to. Sex is better. And why do you speak of Martians?"

"It was like this. I mixed the sounds together. It stacked up and became too big. From the window out I must go. And this is the surprising point, that I never hit the street. Instead…

Wah-wah-wah and melt to flashback.

Uli-eye view of falling towards street. Neatly arranged German cobblestones rushing up at you. A dog gazing up too surprised to run. Wild, high buzzing.

Suddenly a section of the cobblestones swings open like two double doors. Blinding light streams out and you fall through the street and into the light. Everything is glowing from ultraviolet on up to X-ray-colored. Also an on/off strobing in the film here, giving things red jumpy edges.

The music-loops are subtracted from the buzzing and now you hear only the pure, solemn twitter of the Martian death-song. Camera dollies along the endless bright corridor. Huge translucent statues of scarab-beetles line the sides like suits of armor. The floor is tessellated in snaky curves, there are doors doors doors.

You see Uli's hand reach out and turn a doorknob, then whiiisssk! Back in Lola's kitchen.

"The song from the vase," Uli is saying, "It is perhaps the soul of the Martian civilization. We are free now to go in and out from door to door."

Lola shakes her head. "Not me."

Cut. Lola's bed, sunset. The buzzing is building. Lola is on all fours, wearing only the garter belt. Uli is crouched behind her, his hand spreading her cheeks, his face pressed into her crack. She moans and pushes back.

Wild, high buzzing closer now. Uli kneels and we see Lola's sweet, inviting asshole puckered out like Clara Bow's mouth. Uli rubs spit on his long white cock and drives it in, holding her hips and pulling her against him. They come, screaming. The buzzing fades.

Cut. Dawn. Uli sleeping in Lola's bed. A shaft of sunlight flicks onto the wall. Faint buzzing. Lola sits up with a grunt of fear. Moving quickly, she turns and squats over Uli's face, rubbing her cunt against his slack features. He half wakes.

"Go gone, Lola. Back to the Hall is best."

"*No!*" She is kneeling over his mouth, naked, facing the camera. "Do it, Uli! Do it to me!" He is passive, uninterested.

Lola mashes her breasts with her left hand, rubs her clitoris with two fingers of her right. The buzzing is louder and louder.

"More," Lola moans, "It's not enough. You've got to…"

She begins to piss. This is enough. Her face puffs and glazes and she comes, taking some of the buzzing into Linton Kwesi Johnson: "Smash their brains in, smash their brains in, smash their brains in."

But Uli…Uli lets the sound take him away again; he's a hissing white mound at the foot of the bed. Once again, as with Professor Akwell, the light dims and re-forms into a new shape…"Baby it's you, baby it's you, baby it's you."

Enjoy yourself.

Note on "Buzz"

Written in Spring, 1981.
New Blood, December, 1981.

New Blood was a magazine run by Michael Wojczuk and Niko Murray out of Boulder, Colorado. I met them in the summer of 1981 when I had a two-week gig giving a short course at the Naropa Institute of Boulder. *New Blood* always had a vigorous punky feel to it, and I was happy to have two of my stories in their pages. It was great in Boulder—I got to take a hot tub with Allen Ginsberg, smoke pot with Gregory Corso, and give a copy of *White Light* to William Burroughs.

"Buzz" is the most cyberpunk of my early stories. Sylvia and I really did see Elvis Costello play in Mannheim, by the way, it wasn't far from Heidelberg.

I took the scientific idea for "Buzz" from Peter K. Lewin, "Preliminary Studies in the Extraction of Human Sounds Engraved Accidentally into Ancient Vessels," *Speculations in Science And Technology*, #3, August, 1980.

THE LAST EINSTEIN-ROSEN BRIDGE

"O God, I could be bounded in a nutshell and count myself a king of infinite space, were it not that I have bad dreams." — Hamlet, *Act II, Scene ii.*

Joe threw the empty soda bottle high over the black dirt, and Udo fired a rock at it. Miss. Joe's turn.

He looked for a good rock while Udo retrieved the bottle from the mounded rows of the asparagus field. In Heidelberg, the farmers keep their asparagus white by making it grow up through half a meter of sunless mulch.

"Okay Joe," Udo called. "*Raketen los!*" The big liter bottle arced up, twirling end over end and whistling. Completely in synch for that one second, Joe flung his clot of asphalt. He nicked the bottle, but it didn't break. Solid German construction.

Just then Udo's mother started yelling from the house. Joe couldn't understand her dialect, but he liked her voice. She had strong legs and big breasts and red hair. Too bad he didn't have a mother like that. Too bad he didn't have a mother.

"I must eat dinner," Udo explained in the clean high-German they taught at school. "You can have the bottle since you hit it first."

"Thanks. Why don't you come over to the base tonight? They're showing *Grease.*" It was Joe's favorite movie. Dark and wiry, he looked like one of Travolta's friends.

"*Schmiere?* In English?"

"Naturally. In *Amerikanisch*, man. It's at the Patrick Henry Village NCO Club. I'll get you in."

After Udo left, Joe walked into the asparagus field to get the bottle. It would be good for a twenty pfennig refund, enough for a sweet-bun at the market he passed on the way to the U.S. Army base where he lived with his father.

The mounds of mulch over the asparagus were patted smooth. Here and there you could see a little bump where a ripe stalk was about to break through. The watery, insistent May sunlight brought a rich earth-smell up from the field. An occasional car whizzed past, emphasizing the silence.

As Joe picked up the bottle he noticed something shiny lying on the next mound over. A bright little sphere, like a big ball bearing or a silvered glass Christmas-tree ball. An odd thing to find in an asparagus field.

He hopped over the intervening mound and leaned over the little mirror-ball. The sky was in there, and his face and the horizon and the field. Neat. But...

Wait. It wasn't the same. The field in the little reflected image was pink and crowded with towering...machinery, tapering in towards the image's center. Worse, the funhouse face looking back at Joe was not his after all...was not any living human's.

He jumped back with a sort of cry. The face in the ball didn't move. Maybe it was just painted on? That had to be it. He leaned over the ball again, scrutinizing the weird visage.

What had initially seemed a butchered mess now took on order. It was basically humanoid: ears, pinky-tan skin, long hair on top, nose-slits, eyes and mouth. The big difference was that the mouth was on top and the eyes on bottom...like a person upside down, with red mouth detached and writhing in the big black forehead. What a crazy thing to paint on a ball and leave...

The mouth was moving. Calling others. More faces crowded up. Two, three, five...small and distorted in the mirror's curve.

Joe gasped and stepped back, then stepped forward and gave the ball a poke with his bottle. It rolled off the mound. Nothing in the image changed. The central figure was holding up a three-fingered hand and making signs. The vaguely female mouth-slash moved soundlessly. Over the figure's head Joe could make out a tiny rocket-plane moving across the curved sky, moving away and away, dwindling towards the infinitely distant central point. It was a whole universe in there. The... woman beckoned him closer.

"Wait," Joe muttered. "I'll take you home. I can't stay here."

But he didn't want to touch the sphere. Maybe if you touched it they could pull you inside. He took out his handkerchief and laid it on the ground next to the shiny ball. Then he used the bottle to nudge the ball onto the hankie, which he picked up by its four corners. The ball was very light...hardly there at all. Back at the road he stowed it and the bottle in the knapsack he used for a school satchel, then swung onto his bike.

The ride from his school to the Army apartment blocks usually spun past in a happy blur of physical power. Joe was good on his bike, a ten-speed his Dad had given him for his fourteenth birthday.

But today the bike felt like an Exercycle. Like a pedal-powered generator feeding hidden movie projectors busily back-imaging filmed Heidelberg scenes onto a spherical plastic screen, a ten-meter fake universe centered on Joe's head. Only then the middle wouldn't be infinitely…

KLA-BRANG-BRANNG-BRANNNNG! Ow. Almost hit by a street-car. Easy there, Joe, you're freaking out. Wasn't he ever going to get home? It was like he just kept going half the remaining distance.

Feeling too shaky to ride anymore, Joe dismounted and wheeled his bike down the crowded four P. M. sidewalk. Alien faces streamed past. All he could think of was the infinite universe in his knapsack.

"Joey! Hey, Joey!"

Vivian came skipping up to him, smiling and breathing hard. She was a pre-teen pest, a real Army-brat. She lived in the same building as Joe.

"What are you doing off the base?" he asked.

Vivian's eyes glowed. "My mom sent me to buy some wine. I'm allowed in Germany. How was *German school* today, Joey?"

Joe was one of the few Army kids who didn't go to the Army school. He had hopes of growing up cosmopolitan. With a full-blooded gypsy for a father, he had a leg up on it. Vivian already thought he was an inter-national playboy.

"It was highly stimulating. Look, will you watch my bike while I go in the market?" He could have locked it, of course, but if Vivian was watching it, then she couldn't follow him into the store.

"Sure, Joey. I was already in there. Look." She held up her shopping bag. "Real wine, and I bought it." She stuck out her bud-breasts and pursed her pinkened lips.

Joe walked past the bright vegetables and into the store. Inside he selected a twenty-pfennig sweet-roll and opened his knapsack to get out the empty soda bottle.

A face filled with womanly pleading stared up at him. The handkerchief had come undone. The little ball-universe provided its own light…Joe could make out the bright pinpoint of a distant sun. Some trucks were driving around on the field behind the woman. *Out*, she gestured, holding her hands together and rapidly parting them. *Take us out of the bag!*

Joe vibrated his hands in front of his face in the *calm down* gesture. He tapped his watch and held up a *just a minute* finger. Smiling and waving *goodbye for now*, he took out the bottle and rebuckled the knapsack.

"Do you have a little animal in there?" asked Frau Wittman as he traded the bottle for the sweet-bun. She was a pleasant skinny lady, who liked Joe for knowing German. Most other Germans didn't trust him, since his skin was so dark. But ever since Frau Wittman had wormed out of Joe that his mother was a suicide, she'd treated him like a grandson.

"*Ja,*" Joe nodded, thinking fast. "*Ein Meerschweinchen.*" A guinea pig.

"How nice," Frau Wittman beamed. "Take yourself another sweet-roll."

"Thanks."

On the sidewalk Vivian was acting her age for once…staring blankly at the traffic and picking her nose. Feeling like a big brother, Joe gave her the extra bun. He wondered what it would be like to have a sibling… someone close enough to share his secret with. Maybe he could show it to Udo tonight…if Udo's parents let him come. But they probably wouldn't—they didn't like the Army, and they didn't like Joe's olive skin.

He said goodbye to Vivian and rode the rest of the way home without any trouble. He'd probably just been hungry. The apartment was a pigsty, an empty pigsty. Joe's Dad usually went straight to the noncoms' bar as soon as he got off duty for the day. Joe checked the fridge…nothing but milk and his father's beer…then went on to his room.

Joe's room was the one nice spot in the apartment. He had a good stereo from the PX, travel posters on the wall, a couple of plants and an Indian bedspread for a window curtain. The furniture was GI, but at least it was neat.

His heart pounding with excitement, Joe rolled the mirror-ball out onto his bed. The woman…he was sure it was a woman…waved her hands in greeting, then began staring this way and that, taking it all in.

She could only see half the room from the side she was on, and Joe was about to turn the ball so she could see the rest. But then she… turned it herself.

It was strange to watch this happen. one of the woman's hands came closer and closer to the ball's surface, and the image of her fingers covered almost everything. The fingers seemed to hold and turn the surface, and the whole little universe turned along. The fingers let go, the hand drew back, and the woman was on the other side of the ball. Joe could see the back of her head.

He leaned over the ball and looked down at her from above. That put the mouth and eyes in the right places, and she looked human, almost familiar. The mouth smiled kindly.

She could see his bookcase from where she was now, and it seemed to be of particular interest to her. She raised an arm and pointed. The arm-image curved halfway round the ball.

Still leery of actually touching the ball, Joe went and got a book and brought it over…a tattered copy of Heinlein's *Starman Jones*. The woman held up what seemed to be a camera and he riffled through the pages for her. Maybe her machines would be able to learn English!

Excited by this idea, Joe brought over book after book. His fat, illustrated dictionary seemed to be a particularly big hit. He riffled its pages slowly to be sure they got it all down.

At the end of an hour Joe was feeling weak and hungry again. The Christmas-ball people were busy setting up something that looked like a console-model TV set. Maybe they planned to show him movies? He went out to the kitchen to drink some milk.

When he came back, the little TV screen was on. The woman spoke into a microphone, and words crawled across the screen. English words.

HELLO. MY NAME IS TULPA. WHAT IS YOUR NAME?

Hands shaking with excitement, Joe fumbled out a pen and one of his little blue school-paper pamphlets.

Hello, Tulpa, he printed. *My name is Joe. Where are you from?*

WE ARE NOT FROM. WE ARE HERE. WE HAVE LANDED YOU HERE WITH OUR MACHINES.

That didn't make sense. It was Tulpa who had landed on Earth in her little space-squeezed ball. A strange, mind-numbing idea began to form….

You landed, Joe insisted. *You are inside a tiny ball.*

Tulpa smiled, her eyes, staring out from under the microphone. *YOU LOOK THE SAME TO US. YOU LOOK LIKE YOU'RE INSIDE A LITTLE BALL.*

To prove this she reached out her hand and pressed two fingers against the ball's surface. Then she…picked up the surface and moved it around. The images in the ball swept and curved. Now he saw the top of her head, now the back of the TV, now the distant sunset. One of Tulpa's companions danced towards the surface, then away.

No, Joe wrote shakily. *You're inside and I'm outside. I can prove it.* He covered the ball with his handkerchief, then pulled it away. *I can cover you up!*

SO CAN I. Tulpa produced a black velvet pouch. Her fingers grew out to the surface, the images swept, and suddenly the little ball was all black. A shiny, black, imageless mirror.

Just then the apartment door slammed. His father!

"Joey?" the drink-blurred voice called. "Are you here?"

"Yeah, Dad." Joe put his handkerchief over the ball.

"What a day," his father called. "What a bitch of a day." Joe heard him get a beer out of the fridge and snap it open. "What are you doing in there?" The light footsteps approached, and the door swung open.

Joe's father was a slight man, a bantam-weight gypsy with a metallic voice. He was an alcoholic, a lifer retread sergeant, a lonely man who had never forgiven his wife for escaping into suicide. His eyes looked flat behind his flesh-colored GI glasses. Flat but observant.

"What's all the books out for? And what's that under the hankie? You're not smoking pot are you?"

Joe snorted contemptuously. "Sure, Dad, I'm high on angel-dust. I'm really flying." He tucked his hands into his underarms and flapped his elbows like chicken-wings. "And meanwhile I'm writing up a report for my literature class."

"So what's with the snot-rag? What's under it?" Veteran of twenty years of barracks inspections, Joe's father was not to be distracted.

"It's just a ball I found. A funny glass ball." Chancing it, Joe raised a corner of the hankie. Okay. It was still black from Tulpa's pouch. He took the hankie all the way off.

Joe's father leaned wonderingly over the ball. "Funny how it doesn't reflect. It looks like one of those crystal balls. You know your Aunt Rosie...she used to do that stuff. Show people their dead relatives."

"That's interesting," Joe said, not really listening. He had to put the ball away before...

Three pink spots appeared on the ball's surface. The blackness slid down off the ball. Tulpa stared out at them, smiling uncertainly.

Joe's father grunted like a man punched in the heart. "That's her," he croaked. "That's your no-good traitor mother who left me all alone."

Tulpa stared intently at Joe's father, trying to read his expression.

"You're crazy," Joe said, shaking his father's shoulder. "This has nothing to do with you."

His father twisted out of Joe's grip and shoved him aside. "It's her, I tell you. Safe in heaven and laughing at me."

Tulpa had both hands up, waving the *calm down* gesture she'd learned from Joe. She looked frightened.

Joe's father's voice rose to parade-ground intensity. "I'LL GET YOU, ARLENE!"

Before Joe could stop him, his father snatched up the ball and threw it against the wall.

The ball winked out of existence. Two punctured sheets of space-time snapped apart...too far. The universe shattered.

Note on "The Last Einstein-Rosen Bridge"

Written in Spring, 1981.
The 57th Franz Kafka, Ace Books, 1983.

"The Last Einstein-Rosen Bridge" has an odd history. After writing it, I sent it to Robert Sheckley, who was then the fiction editor at *Omni*. He called back to say he was going to buy it, provided I made a small change to the ending. I was overjoyed, as *Omni* was at that time the top-paying SF market. My wife and I were about to go to New York for a conference anyway, so we arranged to meet Sheckley, which was great fun. Sheckley suggested the Hamlet quote for the head of the story. My wife and I had dinner with him and his then wife, Jay Rothbel. The waiter behaved like an out-of-control Sheckley robot and Sheckley and I almost got run down crossing the street. It was all perfect. But then I didn't hear anything from Sheckley for quite some time.

When I next talked to him, he told me that his boss at *Omni* had told him not to use "The Last Einstein-Rosen Bridge." Also Sheckley told me that he was being eased out of the *Omni* job. So in the end I never did sell a story to *Omni*. I was working on my novel *The Sex Sphere* around this same time, and just to get some immediate use out of "The Last Einstein-Rosen Bridge," I used an altered from of it as Chapter Twelve of that book.

PAC-MAN

It was hot. Polly was driving Rhett home from work. Pretty Polly, fresh out of college, driving her husband home from his job at the arcade. Rhett had been fresh out of college three or four years earlier, but it hadn't took.

"Eat her, Polly, eat her fast," cried Rhett. A fifty-year-old woman in a pink alligator shirt and lime-green Bermudas was in the crosswalk.

"Pac-Man, Rhett?"

Rhett made change and serviced the machines at Crasher's, a pinball and video arcade in the new Killeville shopping mall. He left about a third of his pay in the machines, especially Pac-Man and Star Castle. Sometimes, when Rhett had been playing a lot, he'd come home still in the machine's space, the Pac-Man space today, a cookie-filled maze with floorping monsters that try to eat you while you try to eat all the cookies, and there's stop-signs to eat too: they make the monsters turn blue and then you can eat them back till they start flashing, which is almost right away on the third and fifth boards...

"Yeah. I broke a hundred thousand today."

"My that's a lot." The uneaten fifty-year-old preppie was out of the road now. Polly eased the car forward.

"Sixteen boards," added Rhett.

In Pac-Man, each time you eat all the cookies and stop-signs, the screen blinks and then goes back to starting position. Almost all the video games include some similar principle. Killing off all the monsters in Space Invaders, blowing up the central ship in Star Castle, making it through the maze in Berzerk: in each case one gets a reset, a new board. The rules of the game usually change somewhat with each new board, so that as one moves to higher levels, one is exploring new space, probing unknown areas of the machine's program.

"There was an incredible show after the fifteenth board," Rhett continued. "All the monsters came out and took their robes off. Underneath they were like pink slugs. And then they acted out their roles. Like the red one is always first?"

Polly smiled over at Rhett. He was long and skinny, with a pencil-thin mustache. He knew that he was wasting his life on the video machines, and she knew, but it hadn't seemed to matter yet. They had time to burn. They were married and they both had college degrees: till now that had been enough.

"I went for the interview, Rhett."

"Yeah? At the bank?"

"I think I can get it, but it looks kind of dinky. I'd just be a programmer."

"You don't know computers."

"I do too. I took a whole year of programming, I'll have you know."

"A useful trade," mused Rhett. "Killeville College prepares its students for a successful career in modern society. The New South. Why did I have to major in English?"

"You could get a better job if you wanted to, Rhett."

Rhett's fingers danced across the phantom controls.

"Tfoo, tfoo, tfoom!"

The next day, Polly decided to take the bank job. It was dinky, but they paid five dollars an hour, and Mr. Hunt, the personnel officer, promised that there were opportunities for rapid advancement. After signing up and agreeing to be there Monday, Polly drove over to the mall to tell Rhett.

The mall was a single huge building jigsawed into a lake of asphalt. Crasher's was in the middle, right by Spencer Gifts. It was dark and air-conditioned with a gold carpet on the floor. A row of machines was lined up along each wall, pinball on the right, video on the left. Polly liked the pinballs better; at least there you were manipulating something real.

The pinballs glowed and the videos twinkled. A few youths were playing, and the machines filled the room with sound.

Intruder alert, Intruder alert.

mmmmmwwwwwhhhhaaaaaAAAAAAAAAA-KOW-KOW-KOW!

Welcome to Xenon.

Doodley-doodle-doodley-doo.

Budda-budda-zen-zen-BLOOOO!

Try me again.

There at the back was Rhett, grinning and twitching at the controls of Star Castle. He wore a news-vendor's change apron.

"I took the job," said Polly, coming up behind him.

"Just a minute," said Rhett, not looking up. "I'll give you change in a minute." He took her for a customer, or pretended to.

A fat spaceship rotated slowly at the center of the Star Castle screen. Surrounding it were concentric rings of light: force-fields. Rhett's ship darted around the perimeter of the rings like a horsefly, twisting and stinging, trying to blast its way to the machine's central ship. Eerily singing bombs pursued Rhett, and when he finally breached the innermost wall, the machine began firing huge, crackling space-mines. Rhett dodged the mines, firing and thrusting all the while. One of his bullets caught the central ship and the whole screen blacked out in a deafening explosion.

"That's five," said Rhett, glancing back. "Hi, Polly."

"I went to see Mr. Hunt like we decided, Rhett. They're really giving me the job."

"Far out. Maybe I'll quit working here. The machines are starting to get to me. This morning I saw a face on the Pac-Man screen."

"Whose face, Rhett?"

The new board was on the screen and Rhett turned back to the controls. *Wi-wi-wi-wi-wi-wi-wi* went his bullets against the *eeEEeeEEeeEEeeEEee* of the smart bombs and the *mmmmMMMMwaaaaaa* of the force-fields.

"Reagan," said Rhett, sliding his ship off one corner of the screen and back on the other. "President Reagan, man. He thanked me for developing the software for some new missile system. He said that all the Pac-Man machines are keyed into the Pentagon, and that the monsters stand for Russian anti-missiles. I ran twenty boards. Nobody's ever done that before."

There was a big hole in the force-fields now. The fat, evil ship at the center spat a vicious buzz-bomb. Rhett zapped it *wi-wi-wi* from the other side of the board. Then the ship. *BLOOOOOOOO!*

"Six," said Rhett, glancing up again. "I'm really hot today. I figure if the Pentagon put out Pac-Man, maybe someone else did Star Castle."

Polly wondered if Rhett was joking. In a way it made sense. Use the machines to tap American youth's idle energy and quirky reflexes. A computer can follow a given program as fast as you want, but a human operator's creative randomization is impossible to simulate. Why not have our missiles trace out Pac-Man monster-evasion paths? Why not tap every run that gets past twenty boards?

"Did President Reagan say you'd get any money?" asked Polly. "Did he offer you a job?"

"No job." *Wi-wi-wi-wi-wi-wi-wi.* "But he's sending a secret agent to give me a thousand dollars. If I tell anyone, it's treason. Aaaaaauugh!" *Crackle-ackle-ackle-FTOOOM.* Rhett's ship exploded into twirling fragments.

"Change, please?"

Rhett changed a five for one of the customers, then turned his full attention on Polly.

"So you're taking the job at the bank? They're really hiring you?"

"Starting Monday. Did you really see Reagan?"

"I think I did."

"Why don't you phone him up?"

"It was probably just a tape. He wouldn't know me from Adam." Rhett fed another quarter into the Star Castle machine. "I'm gonna work on this some more. See who's behind it. Will you hand out change for me?"

"Okay."

Polly tied on Rhett's change apron and leaned against the rear wall. Now and then someone would ask her for more quarters, always boys. White males between fourteen and thirty-four years of age. Interacting with machines. Maybe, for men, women themselves are just very complicated video machines…. Polly pushed the unpleasant thought away. There was something more serious to think about: Rhett's obsession. The whole time she made change, he kept plugging away at Star Castle. Ten boards, fifteen, and finally twenty.

But no leader's face appeared, just the same dull target with its whining force-fields. A flurry of bombs raced out like a flight of swallows. Rhett let them take him, then sagged against the machine in exhaustion.

"Polly! Are you working here?" A big sloppy man shambled up. It was Dr. Horvath, Polly's old Calculus professor. She'd been his favorite student. "Is this the best job a Killeville College math major can aspire to?"

"No, no." Polly was embarrassed. "I'm just helping Rhett. Rhett?" Wearily her husband straightened up from the Star Castle machine. "Rhett, you remember Dr. Horvath, don't you? From the graduation?"

"Hi." Rhett gave his winning smile and shook hands. "These machines have been freaking me out."

"Can I tell him, Rhett?"

"Go ahead."

"Dr. Horvath, this morning Rhett saw President Reagan's face on the Pac-Man screen. Rhett says the Pentagon is using the twenty-board runs to design the new anti-anti-missile system."

Horvath cocked his big head and smiled. "Sounds like paranoid schizophrenia to me, Polly. Or drug psychosis."

"Hey!" said Rhett. "I'm clean!"

"So show me *der Führer*'s face. I've got time to kill or I wouldn't be here."

151

"Right now I'm too wrecked," confessed Rhett. "I just blew the whole afternoon trying the break through on Star Castle. But there's nothing there."

Horvath gave Polly a questioning look. He thought Rhett was crazy. She couldn't leave it at that.

"Come in tomorrow, Dr. Horvath. Come in before ten. Rhett's fastest in the morning. He'll show you…and me, too."

"At this point Rhett's the only one who's been vouchsafed the mystical vision of our fearless leader?" Horvath's pasty, green-tinged features twisted sarcastically.

"Put up or shut up," said Rhett. "Be here at nine."

That night, Rhett and Polly had their first really big argument in ten months of marriage. Ostensibly, it was about whether Polly should be allowed to read in bed when Rhett was trying to sleep. Obviously, it was also about her reluctance to make love. But deep down, the argument was triggered by the slippage of their relative positions: Polly was moving into a good, middle-class job, but Rhett seemed to be moving down into madness.

There was a lot of tension the next morning. Crasher's didn't open to the public till ten, so Rhett and Polly had it to themselves. Rhett fed a quarter to the Pac-Man machine and got to work. "What a way to spend Saturday," complained Polly. "That machine doesn't connect to anything, Rhett. You might as well be shouting into a hollow tree. President Reagan isn't in there."

Rhett didn't look up…didn't dare to. Three boards, six.

Horvath arrived, rapping at the metal grill that covered the entrance. As usual, he was wearing shapeless baggy pants and an oversized white nylon shirt. His glasses glinted blankly in the fluorescent light. Polly let him in.

"How's he doing?" whispered Horvath eagerly.

"Ten boards," shouted Rhett. "I'm in the groove today. Ten boards and I haven't lost a man yet!"

Horvath and Polly exchanged a glance. After all the nasty, wild things Rhett has said last night, there was no question in her mind that Rhett had imagined his vision of the President. Surely Dr. Horvath knew this, too. But he looked so expectant! Why would an important professor take the trouble to come watch her crazy husband play Pac-Man at nine in the morning?

Horvath walked over to stand behind Rhett, and Polly trailed after. There is a single control on a Pac-Man machine, a sort of joystick. It controls the movements of a yellow disk on the screen: the disk moves in the direction in which you push the joystick. It's not quite a disk, really; it's a circle with one sector missing. The sector acts as a munching mouth, a hungry Chinese, a greedy Happy-Face, a Pac-Man. As you move it around, the Pac-Man eats the cookies and stop-signs in the maze. *Muncha-uncha-uncha-uncha.* Later there are also cherries, strawberries, grapes, birds, and bags of gold. *Gloooop!*

Rhett was on his fifteenth board now, and the four monsters that chased his yellow disk moved with a frightening degree of cooperation. But, *uncha-uncha-uncha*, the little Pac-Man slipped out of every trap, lured the monsters away from every prize. *Uncha-uncha-uncha-uncha-gloop!* Rhett ate a bag of gold worth five thousand points. That made a hundred-and-three thousand points. Horvath was transfixed, and even Polly was a little impressed. She'd never seen Rhett play so well.

The next few boards took longer. The monsters had stopped speeding up with each board. Instead they were acting smarter. Rhett had to expend more and more time on evasive action. The happy little Pac-Man moved about in paths so complex as to seem utterly random to anyone but Rhett. Seventeen boards. Nineteen.

On the twentieth board the monsters speeded back up. Rhett nearly lost a man. But then he knuckled down and ate the whole board in one intricately filigreed sweep.

The screen grew gray and full of static. And then there he was—Mr. President himself.

"Ron-Boy Ray-Gun," said Horvath nastily. "I don't believe it."

"See?" snarled Rhett. "Now who's crazy?"

"…thank you for helping our country," the video screen was saying. Reagan looked friendly with his neat pompadour and his cocky, lopsided smile. Friendly, but serious. "Your photograph and fingerprints have been forwarded to the CIA for information retrieval. An agent will contact you to make payment in the sum of one thousand dollars. This offer cannot be repeated, and must be kept secret. Let me thank you again for making this a safer world."

"That's it," said Rhett, straightening up and kicking the kinks out of his long, skinny legs.

"Are you sure?" demanded Horvath, strangely tense. "Couldn't there be a higher level?"

"The screen's blank," shrugged Rhett. "The game's over."

"Push the Start button," suggested Horvath.

"Pac-Man doesn't give free games," replied Rhett. "And I've got to open up in a few minutes."

"Just try," insisted Horvath. "Push the button."

Rhett pressed the Start button with his skinny forefinger. The familiar maze appeared on the screen. The monsters moved out of their cave and the little Pac-Man started eating. *Uncha-uncha-uncha-unch*. Mesmerized by the sound, Rhett grabbed the joystick, meaning to dodge a hungry red monster.

But when Rhett touched the control, something about the image changed. It thickened and grew out of the screen. This was no longer a two-dimensional video image, but a three-dimensional hologram. The Pac-Man was a smiling little sphere sliding around a transparent three-dimensional maze. Rhett found that he could control his man's movement in the new dimension by pushing or pulling the joystick. With rapid, automatic motions he dodged the monsters and set his man to eating cookies.

Polly was not so accepting of this change. "How did you know that would happen?" she demanded of Horvath. "What are you up to, anyway?"

"Just don't disturb Rhett," said Horvath, pushing Polly away from the machine. "This is more important than you can realize." His hands felt strange and clammy.

Just then someone started shaking the steel grate at the entrance.

"Let them in," called Rhett. "It's almost time. I don't *believe* this machine!" His face was set in a tight, happy smile. He'd eaten every cookie in his cubical maze now, and with a flourish of music it reset itself. Twenty-second board.

"Hey!" shouted the man at the grate. "Let me in there!"

He already had his wallet out. *Can't wait to spend his money*, thought Polly, but she was wrong. The man had a badge to show her.

"CIA, Miss. I'm looking for Rhett Lyndon."

"That's my husband. He's playing Pac-Man. Do you have the two thousand dollars?"

"He can only collect one. But he shouldn't have told you!" The secret agent was a fit, avid-faced man in his thirties. He reminded Polly of a whippet. She rolled back the grate and he surged in, looking the whole room over at once.

"Who's the other guy?"

"Beat it, pig!" shouted Horvath.

Polly had always known Dr. Horvath was a radical, but this outburst really shocked her. "You can leave, Dr. Horvath. We have some private business to discuss."

Rhett glanced over with a brief, ambiguous smile. But then he had to give his full attention back to the game. The maze he was working seemed to have grown. It stuck more than a meter out of the machine now.

"I can do better than the Pentagon's lousy thousand," hissed Horvath. "I can give you anything you want, if only Rhett can help us defeat the Rull."

"Freeze," screamed the secret agent. He'd drawn a heavy pistol out of his shoulder-holster.

But rather than freezing, Horvath *flowed*. His whole body seemed to melt away, and thick gouts of green slime came surging out the bottoms of his pant-legs. The agent fired three wild shots anyway, but they only rippled the slime. And then a pseudopod of the stuff lashed out and struck the CIA man down. There was a moment's soft burbling while the alien flowed over and absorbed its prey.

And then, as suddenly as it had started, the ugly incident was over. The slime flowed back from the agent, revealing only a clean spot on the carpet, and Dr. Horvath's clothes filled back up. The head reappeared last of all, growing out of the nylon shirt's collar like a talking puffball.

"I'll admit it, Polly," it was saying. "I'm an alien. But a *good* alien. The Rull are the bad ones. They don't even eat what they kill. We are, of course, fantastically advanced compared to you primitive bipeds. But we need your animal shiftiness, your low cunning!"

"Rhett," screamed Polly. "Help! Horvath is an alien!" She darted past the slimy deceiver to stand near her husband, as near as she could get.

Rhett's upper body and head were inside the maze now; it had grown that much. A glowing two-meter cube of passages surrounded him. The Pac-Man and the monsters raced this way and that. Bobbing and weaving, Rhett watched and controlled the chase. The planes of the hologram bathed his features in a golden, beatific light. The Pac-Man completed its circuit of a randomized space-filling curve…and the cube flickered to rest.

"Thirty," said Rhett.

"Go!" shouted Horvath. "Go Rhett! Finish this board and we'll be able to eat all the Rull worlds without losing a single ship!"

With each *uncha* Polly imagined a planet disappearing into some huge group-Horvath. Rull-monsters darted this way and that, trying to foil the Pac-Man, but crazy Rhett was too fast and random for *anyone*. She wondered what to ask Horvath for. Riches, telepathy, the power of flight?

Suddenly the board was empty. Rhett had done it again! The huge maze drew back into the Pac-Man machine's screen. The image of a jubilant alien appeared, burbling thanks. And then the screen blanked out.

"That was our leader," said Horvath. "We can't thank you enough. Anything you want is yours. Make a wish."

"*PAC*," said Rhett distantly. "*P,A,C. P* is Pentagon, *A* is Alien…I wish I could find out what *C* is."

"You got it," said Horvath. "Just push the Start button. And thanks again." With a slow *zeent*ing noise the alien disappeared, feet first.

"Was he for real?" said Rhett.

"I can't believe it," wailed Polly. "You just blew our big wish. Who cares what *C* stands for!"

Rhett shrugged and pushed the Start button. There was a sizzling sound, and slowly the machine, and then the room, dissolved into clear white light.

"Greetings," boomed a voice. "This is the Cosmos speaking. I wonder if you could help me out?"

Note on "Pac-Man"

Written in Summer, 1981.
Asimov's Science Fiction, June, 1982.

I wrote "Pac-Man" on summer vacation at the Outer Banks of North Carolina. My son Rudy Jr. and I had just discovered video arcades, and we spent a lot of time in them. Even though he was only nine, Rudy was much better at them than me. And now, nearly twenty years later, one of my favorite projects for teaching my computer science students is to have them write Pac-Man and Asteroids games.

When I sold this story to *Asimov's*, the editor George Scithers thought it would be legally risky to use the trademarked name "Pac-Man," and he insisted that we call it "Peg-Man." Instead of having "P.A.C." stand for "President, Alien, Cosmos," P.E.G. stood for "President, Extraterrestrial, God."

This is the first of several stories set in "Killeville," a *Twilight Zone* kind of town inspired by Lynchburg, Virginia, where my family and I lived from 1980 to 1986.

PI IN THE SKY

The fragmented shells beneath Jane's feet began to flicker and sway. She took her husband's arm.

"Let's go back, Morris."

"Already?"

"I'm dizzy. The sun…it's too much."

Morris looked at her closely, his dark eyes concerned. She leaned against him, smiling weakly.

"You're right," said Morris. "It's too much at noon like this. Let's go back to Andrew's."

Jane shaded her eyes and looked back along the beach. The beach sand was pure white; the hot waves were pale blue. Grand Turk Island, March 22, 1992. This was their honeymoon.

Jane's brother, Andrew, lived here, and they could stay with him for free. Andrew made his living teaching the occasional tourist to skin-dive.

Back at the house there was nothing doing. The shutters were closed against the heat. Andrew was lying on a couch, smoking and listening to soft Hawaiian music. In the next room, Andrew's wife Julie lay on their bed's white sheets, reading a Borges anthology.

"You see," said Andrew as they came in. "I told you."

"You were right," grinned Morris. He did not enjoy talking to his brother-in-law.

"I almost had sunstroke," said Jane. "Morris, too. It was like being hit on the head with a hammer."

"At three we'll go out in the boat," promised Andrew. "We can go down off the shelf today."

"Great," said Morris. "How deep?"

With slow, economical gestures, Andrew lit another cigarette. "As the spirit moves us. My equipment's good for a hundred meters. Last week I saw whales down there. A whole pod."

It was four-thirty by the time they were actually in the boat. Everything happened late down there. Island time. As a gesture towards assimilation, Morris had stopped wearing his digital watch. Now he was sitting back by the boat's electric motor, happy to be doing something. Up in the front of the boat with her brother, Jane smiled back at her husband.

"Don't forget to exhale on the way up," Andrew cautioned her. "And stay near me. Yesterday, every time I looked for you, all I could see was a flipper sticking out from behind a reef."

"I love it down there," said Jane. "The flip and flow of it, everything so alive and full of color. It's a relief from my job at the cancer labs. All the doctors do is kill things. Sad, colorless little mice. There's a sort of blender that liquifies a mouse every thirty seconds."

"At least Morris doesn't kill things," muttered Andrew. "What's he supposed to do with those computers anyway?"

"It was something to do with breaking codes. A universal decoder. But you should ask him yourself, Andrew. You never talk to him. Aren't you glad to see us?"

"Oh, sure, Sis. At least he finally married you. I didn't like the way he was living off you all last year, and still not committing himself. This way he can't bug out when he gets his degree and the bucks start rolling in."

"Morris would never do that, Andrew."

The sun had filled the boat's batteries with a good charge. Before long, they'd jounced out to where the water-color changes. Near the shore it's turquoise, but when you get out to where the continental shelf drops off, the water suddenly looks deep green. Andrew threw an anchor out and signaled Morris to cut the motor. The air was hot and damp, palpable as wet silk. It'd be good to get underwater.

"Okay," said Andrew, relaxed and professional. "Let's get our wet suits on. It's cold down there."

Morris helped Jane into the tight rubber garment. "I can't believe we're doing this. Somehow I never thought that I would spend a honeymoon skin-diving in the Caribbean. This is just fantastic."

"Stick near me and exhale on the way up," repeated Andrew. "I think we'll go down fifty meters today. No point going much further... it gets gloomy after that. And dangerous."

"How deep *is* the water here?" asked Morris.

"Down off the shelf it's over a mile. Two thousand meters."

"Unreal. Can we bring up some sponges?"

"I'll give you a knife for your belt. But I don't really like bringing live things up. They belong down there. Up here they just lie around and stink."

Andrew checked the anchor again, and then they donned facemasks, flippers, weights and airleaves. The airleaves were the latest in scuba equipment: folded packs of special gas-exchange membrane. Instead of carrying your air in a pressurized tank, you could simply extract it from the water around you. The airleaves were, in effect, artificial gills. They made it possible to stay down much longer.

Underwater now, Jane looked up at the boat, an odd slipper-shape black against the wrinkled mirror of the water's surface. She took an almost sensual pleasure at drawing air in through her mouthpiece. When she breathed out, the vibrations of the bubbles filled her ears with lively sound. Morris was above her, Andrew below. All around them darted bright bits of color—parrot fish, tetras, clown-fish, lupes—vibrant flecks, wheeling like shattered light. Now Andrew was waving to Jane, gesturing her closer. He'd found something. Gently flapping her hands, Jane sank to his level.

Using the butt of his spear, Andrew prodded a small, untidy-looking fish. At the first touch of the spear, the fish stopped swimming and puffed itself up. A blow-fish! Now it was the size of a basketball, all spiny and uptight. As her smile was invisible, Jane showed her amusement with a happy hand-wave. Morris joined them, and they swam a bit deeper.

It was like being at the lip of a tremendous cliff. Directly beneath them was the sandy bottom which slopes up to become Grand Turk's beach. But a few meters ahead the bottom stopped abruptly. Fighting a feeling that she would fall, Jane swam out over the edge. A sheer wall of fissured rock dropped down beneath her, down and down into invisibility. A mile of water.

Something touched Jane's elbow. Morris. His eyes were wide and excited behind the glass of his face-mask. With a long outrush of bubbles, he kicked himself down past the cliff's edge, down past a group of protruding sponges. Andrew and Jane followed.

With each few meters of further descent, things changed. At one level there was color, at the next everything was blue, then brown, then grey. Jane noticed that as the pressure increased, the shape of her air-bubbles changed. Instead of being lovely musical spheres, they were now squeezed into nasty sickle-shaped saucers. The sound of the bubbles seemed like mocking laughter. The pressure, the dark, the cold…she felt so confused. Her ears hurt. How long had they been down? How deep were they? Morris was far below, darkly twitching. He should come back!

Looking around desperately, Jane found Andrew at her side. He showed her his depth gauge. Sixty meters. Was that a lot? *Stay*, Andrew signaled to her. *Don't follow*. Then he kicked his way down after Morris.

Jane held her nostrils and blew. With a sticky pop, her ears finally cleared. As the pain went, so did her panic. The satanic cackling of her air-bubbles changed to sweet chiming. Beneath the music sounded something else, something profound and solemn, some giant song that set her whole body athrill. Behind her were the jumbled surfaces of the cliff; far beneath her were Andrew and Morris, but there, out there in the depths, something vast was moving.

Strange giant fish. Two, three of them, as big as whales, singing a deep, mysterious song that Jane *felt* more than *heard*. The song had a dense, packed quality—each note was filled with hidden cadences and falls.

The creatures were pale-green, mottled here and there with ugly splotches of red. The oddest thing was that each of them bore bunches of tentacles were the pectoral fins might have been. Five tentacles per bunch. These were not creatures of Earth. Their vast, pale-purple eyes glowed feverishly. Were they ill? Their immense tails seemed to beat with an unhealthy stutter. Impossibly huge, impossibly weightless, they circled once, as if to stare at the humans, then glided off into the endless volume of sea.

Andrew reappeared, half-dragging Morris by one arm. Was something wrong? Morris held his other arm against his chest, hugging something to himself. The knife-scabbard at his belt was empty.

Andrew pointed up towards the surface, then mimed bubbles coming out of his mouth. *Breathe out.* All the way to the surface. Jane fixed her wandering mind on that one thing. *Breathe out.*

Finally air, real air. Sunlight. She flopped over the gunwale and into the boat. Morris and Andrew were already there.

"What happened?" asked Jane. "I felt so strange."

"That's rapture of the depths," said Andrew. "Nitrogen gets into your blood. I should have warned you. Morris here was ready to swim all the way down."

"I was not," protested Morris. "I just had to look at that funny sort of canyon in the cliff. You didn't have to rush me like that, Andrew."

"What did you do with my knife?"

"It broke. This thing, I pried it loose in there." Morris held out the object that he'd been cradling against his chest. It was a narrow cone, six inches long and marked with an intricate pattern of black and grey rings.

"How beautiful," exclaimed Jane. "Is it a seashell? Is there still something in it?"

Andrew took the object from Morris's reluctant grasp and examined it closely. "I don't think it's a shell. A fossil, maybe, or some kind of coral. You look, Jane."

The cone felt strangely heavy to Jane. The base and the tip were white. The tip was so fine that it curled back on itself like a wire. The main part of the cone was marked with many black rings, some broad, some fine. The base was somewhat hollowed out. Jane held the hollow up to her ear and listened, just as if it were a conch.

"It works," she announced. "Even though it's not a shell, it's got the ocean sound in it. Try it, Morris."

Morris pressed the cone to his ear, listening hard to the intricate pattern of hisses.

"Did you see the giant fishes?" Jane asked Andrew.

"There aren't any whales today. We would have seen them spouting."

"I know, Andrew. These weren't whales. They were just as big, but they had tentacles. I heard them singing."

Andrew regarded his sister quizzically. "That rapture of the depths really got to you, didn't it?"

"This sound is interesting," said Morris, the cone still pressed to his ear. "It sounds like the stripes look."

Andrew's wife, Julie, heated up a can of corned beef for supper. Almost no one on Grand Turk ate fresh fish, not even the natives. They preferred the glamour of canned or frozen imports. Washed down with bottle after bottle of Beck's beer, the corned beef tasted pretty good. Morris told Julie of his adventure.

"There was a big rift in the cliff, a sort of canyon almost. I could see something bright towards the back."

"You're lucky there wasn't a barracuda in there," chided Andrew. "Or a moray eel. I don't know why you couldn't wait for me."

"Face it, I was zonked. I'll be the first to admit it. It's incredible the effect that a little extra nitrogen in your bloodstream has. But I saw this bright spot back in the canyon and it looked like…like an altar. I was thinking of a movie I saw on TV one night, *The Idol's Eye*. It felt like I was in some alien temple to steal treasure." Morris gave Jane a special smile. He was proud to have done something unexpected for once. "So I entered the temple of the deep and there I found it, snagged in a big branch of white coral. Look, Julie."

Morris took the striped cone out from his pocket and laid it on the table by Julie's plate. Julie, a sexy, full-lipped woman in her early thirties, picked the cone up and examined its tip.

"It's so sharp. There's a sort of curly wire at the tip. Maybe it's a part from some crashed airplane's radio. Don't resistors have stripes like that?"

Andrew took the cone. "That's a thought, Julie. There was that big plane-crash this winter. The smugglers."

"How did you know they were smugglers?" asked Jane.

"They never radioed for help. And no one could ever trace them. Some of the villagers saw the plane go down at night, all lit up." Andrew turned his attention back to the little striped cone. "You know, it's smooth enough to be man-made. And that really does look like a wire at the tip. Why don't we smash it open?"

"*No!*" cried Morris. "It's mine."

"Yeah?" taunted Andrew. "And what about my thirty-seven-dollar knife? While I was swimming down to rescue Morris, he was busy breaking my knife. And meanwhile Jane was hallucinating some new kind of giant fish. What a zoo. These two were worse than the Kansans…and that's going some."

"Tell them about the Kansans," urged Julie.

Andrew gave Morris back his cone and launched into a series of linked tales about the various wackos he'd guided into the depths. Julie chimed in with details. Once they got started, Andrew and Julie could talk all night. There was still no decent TV reception on Grand Turk, and the residents were accustomed to passing the evenings in endless yak-sessions.

Jane and Morris got to bed around midnight, exhausted and full of beer. One of the nightly thunderstorms was wandering around in the distance. Jane fell asleep quickly.

At four A. M. something woke her. She lay there wondering what, then remembered that there was supposed to be someone in bed with her. Where was Morris? She lay there for a minute, listening to the rain on Andrew's tin roof. The sound of the water made her thirsty.

She found Morris at the kitchen table, bent over a sheet of paper, making notations. His free hand held the striped cone pressed to his ear.

"Jane." He set the cone down, then picked it up again, eyeing it in wonder. "This is unbelievable. The pattern of stripes and the pattern of sound…they're the same. This thing is specially designed to code up a certain string of numbers. The pattern is a noisy fractal."

"What are you talking about? It's four in the morning."

"Look. Look at the rings on this thing." He held the cone out to her. There were three solid black strips around it. Between the solid stripes were lots of smaller black and white stripes.

"So what. It looks like a coon-tail."

"How many of the big black rings are there?"

"Three."

"Right. *Three.* Now look at the two areas in between the big stripes."

"They look like each other."

"Right again. Note that each of them is cut in half by a smaller black stripe. *One* small black stripe in each. That makes a bunch of sub-areas, all identical. Each of these is, in turn, cut by *four* tiny black stripes. It goes on." Morris displayed a magnifying glass. "I've got the first few levels: *three, one, four, one, five*. Now listen to it, Jane. The sound is the same pattern." He proffered the cone.

Dutifully, Jane held it to her ear. "sss–s–s–s–s–ss–s–s–s–s–sss–s–s–s–s–ss–s–s–s–sss," went the cone. There was a pause, then the sound repeated itself: "sss–s–s–s–s–ss–s–s–s–s–sss–s–s–s–s–ss–s–s–s–sss." Three loud hisses, each of the intervals broken up by a quieter hiss, and each of the subintervals broken by four still quieter hisses. *Three, one, four*.

Jane sat the cone down and nodded at Morris. "You're right. The patterns are the same. Can we go back to bed?"

"Jane, don't you see? If the patterns are the same, then it can only be because they mean something. There's an endless string of digits coded up in this thing. I think it must be an alien artifact. I can't wait to hook the wire up to a signal analyzer."

"How would an alien artifact get here?"

"Didn't you hear what Andrew said about an unidentified airship crashing last winter? It must have been a UFO. Those giant whale-like fish you saw…they might be the aliens! This cone is packed with alien information! I'll decode it with my new program!"

And decode it he did. As soon as they got back up to Boston, Morris rushed into his lab and hooked the cone's little wire up to his computer. The cone began feeding out an endless sequence of digits, apparently the same digits as were coded up in the nuances of its shading. Breaking the code was not easy, but once a very large sample of the numbers had been examined it was possible for Morris's decoding program to produce results. On May 9th the first print-outs appeared.

That day, when Jane came by to pick up Morris, she found him in the computer room, surrounded by a crowd of people: graduate students, professors, and a reporter from the Boston *Globe*.

"You're saying that you have a whole library of books written by extraterrestrials?" queried the reporter. "Can you show me the books?"

Morris and the other graduate students laughed happily.

"That's the library," Morris said, pointing. "Right there."

The striped cone rested on cushioned supports in a plexiglass box. The curly little hair of a wire at the cone's tip was fixed to a cable leading into the lab's incredibly powerful CRAY-3 gigaflop computer. The machine's ink-jet printer was running. A secondary knot of excited scientists stood flipping through the pages of the print-out. Not wanting to disturb Morris, Jane walked over and asked them what they were reading.

"What I'm reading?" exclaimed one of them, a distinguished mathematics professor named Slade. Morris had taken Jane to a party at his house once. "I'm reading the solution to the Riemann Conjecture. I've spent my whole life working on this problem and now your husband's decoding program has found the answer in a goddamn seashell from outer space."

"Aren't you glad?" said Jane. "Isn't it wonderful?"

"No," cried the professor. "It's a disaster! I've lived for nothing!"

"Don't be a fool, Slade," interrupted one of the others. "What if it prints out a cure for cancer?"

"What makes you think that giant space-fish suffer from cancer?" snapped Slade. "And even if they did, why should we be able to understand their cure? Most of this stuff is gibberish. Only mathematics is the same for everyone. Only the mathematicians are going to be out of a job."

Slade's prediction proved false. Over the next couple of weeks, information poured out of the cone at an ever-increasing rate. Morris located a section of the code which served as a sort of index to the rest of it. Like some tiny horn of plenty, the cone disgorged not only brilliant mathematical monographs, but also new theories of physics, strange alien philosophies, and a complete history of the creatures who had built it.

Each day the newspapers and TV shows were filled with all of the newest facts about the extraterrestrials:

They call themselves the "Leutians." They inhabit a world orbiting Barnard's Star, a world completely covered with water. The water is as atmosphere for them; they float above their planet's sea-bed like blimps over mountains. With no need for shelter, Leutians do not have our concept of society. Information is exchanged not by crowding together, but rather by long, powerful songs which reverberate the deeps for leagues and leagues. Owing to an existence in a sea's constant flux, the

Leutian world-view is quite essentially different from ours. They lack, for instance, our belief in the primacy of time over space. The events of a typical Leutian story or myth are organized not in terms of temporal occurrence, but rather in terms of spatial location. Most Leutian physics is still incomprehensible for us. Leutian mathematics places much more emphasis on geometry than on algebra; yet they have the answers to virtually every mathematical puzzle which we have ever proposed. Leutians have three sexual genders, the extra sex serving an enzymatic purpose. Their religion is very odd: rather than regarding God as large and powerful, the Leutians view Him as small and simple. In their discussions of God, the Leutian books refer to some hidden knowledge known only as the Joke. We do not yet know what the Joke is.

And so on. Jane and Morris began to tire of it. With the incessant round of receptions and interviews, Morris hardly had time for his new wife. And Jane herself had her own interviews to attend. After all, she was the only person who had actually seen the Leutians. Over and over she answered the same three or four questions: over and over Morris described how he had found the cone. When the government decided to organize a search for the Leutians off Grand Turk, Jane and Morris were happy to join in.

Thinking fast, Andrew had persuaded the government to buy him a five-million-dollar mini-sub. With an experienced deep-sea diver as co-pilot, Andrew explored the surrounding ocean bottom, finally finding some charred sections of the Leutian ship's vast hull. The seekers speculated that the Leutian home-planet's air was very tenuous, and that the creatures had been badly burned by the heat of entering the Earth's atmosphere. The red splotches, which Jane had observed on the Leutians, took on a sinister significance.

Meanwhile a fleet of ships combed the island waters, sonars a-ping. Nothing. Andrew's further searches were also unsuccessful. One by one, the reporters left Grand Turk. By mid-June, it felt like a second honeymoon. Though Jane wondered why Morris wasn't eager to rush back to his machines, she postponed any inquiries. In any case, as far as money went, they were fixed for life. The U.S. government was buying Morris's salvage rights to the cone. Instead of sponging off Andrew, Jane and Morris could now pay for the ramshackle comfort of the Turk's Head Inn.

June 24th was a Wednesday. Jane and Morris had a pleasant lunch of daiquiris and lobster-tail salad, the lobsters fresh from Grand Turk's waters. Happy and full, they wandered up to their room from the hotel's shady veranda. Instead of air-conditioning, their room had a large ceiling fan, right over the big, clean bed.

"Morris," asked Jane after awhile. "There's something I've sort of wanted to ask you. Only we've been so happy here I didn't dare."

Morris smiled and kissed her. Success had mellowed him fast. "You wonder why I don't want to rush back and play with my computer."

"Well, yes. Don't you have to take care of your decoding program?"

Morris made a face halfway between a grimace and a smile. "It's not my decoding program anymore. One of the Leutian books had a better one. Nothing I could ever do with computers can match what those books have in them."

"That must bother you. Professor Slade said something about having lived for nothing once he saw the answer to his big math problem in the Leutian books."

"Slade. Slade's crazy. What about lobster-tails? What about the beach?"

Jane knew Morris well enough to detect an edge of bitterness in these remarks. "But you miss the intellectual adventure don't you, Morris? Don't you, in a way, wish we could get rid of the cone and go back to the way things were?"

"I'm sure that someone like Slade *will* try to get rid of it," said Morris. "But it's impossible. There's no way for us to lose the Leutian knowledge. That's the Joke."

There was a sudden pounding on their door. "Jane, Morris!" hollered Andrew's voice. "Come quick! The Leutians have washed up on the south beach!"

Andrew drove Julie, Jane, Morris, and the lone remaining TV camera-man in his Jeep. Grand Turk's south beach was wild and deserted, a prime place for beachcombing. Thick seaweed clotted the water, and the ocean waves beat in just as they did a million years ago. Ten meters out from shore, out where the shallows ended, lay the three bloated corpses.

Gulls and terns whirled above them, tearing off strips of the strange flesh. One of the hulks had swung around so that its tail rested on dry sand. A pack of wild dogs gathered there to fight over the meat. The Leutians' huge purple eyes glared up at the sky like jewels in toppled idols' heads. The smell was wild and sweet, smoke and ambergris.

"Oh," cried Jane, "Oh, Morris, why did they leave home?"

Morris was looking up and down the beach with interest. He and Jane had never been here yet. He leaned over to examine a blue glass sphere, a fishing-float washed from who knows where.

"Why?" repeated Jane. "Why did they come?"

Hefting the float, Morris finally met her eyes. "They wanted to get away from the Joke. They wanted intellectual adventure."

"But what is it, Morris? What is the Joke?"

"The code numbers for their library. Their library is coded up as an endless sequence of digits, right?"

"So?"

"Well it just happens…" Morris held up the glass sphere. "You know what pi is, don't you, Jane? Pi is the ratio of a circle's circumference to its diameter, right? In decimals, pi starts out 3.14159265358979. There's plenty of simple programs to generate the rest of the digits."

"Three, one, four. Wasn't that…"

"You got it, Jane. You've got the Joke. The library of all Leutian knowledge is coded up by the decimal expansion of pi. There's no getting rid of it."

Half happy, half sad, they stood there, looking out past the gulls and dogs, out past the Leutians, out to the living sea. Beyond that lay the sky—so big, so small.

Note on "Pi in the Sky"

Written in Fall, 1981.
The 57th Franz Kafka, Ace Books, 1983.

"Pi in the Sky" was inspired by a trip that Sylvia, the kids and I took to visit my brother Embry when he lived on Grand Turk Island in the Caribbean. I liked the idea of the regressing fractal encryption, as I'd been wondering how to store a very large amount of data in a physical pattern, this was something I'd been discussing with the science writer Martin Gardner. My story was to some extent inspired by Jorge Luis Borges 1940 tale, "Tlön, Uqbar, Orbis Tertius." My notion of pi as a kind of universal library reappears in Carl Sagan's 1985 novel *Contact*.

Wishloop

Jeannie snaked her arm a little tighter around Ricky's waist. They were surely going to kiss tonight, as soon as it got dark. To her left were gold-plated clouds and a fat ruby sun. The longest day of the year. Too bad there were so many people on the beach.

Just ahead, a knot of idlers watched a fisherman drag something in. Ricky stopped short. Jeannie tugged him to come on, but there he stopped, staring with his mouth open. Anything to do with sports held Ricky in thrall.

"Come on, Ricky, it's just a rull."

"Gigundo! Look at the rod bend!"

The rull came slip-slopping out of the surf, a sort of giant skate or manta ray. Rulls were from outer space. People liked to kill them.

"Gigundo!" repeated Ricky. "That devil's got a three meter wingspan."

Jeannie sighed. It was a shame that a smart, lively girl like herself had to date idiots. How many Rickys had she known? When would Fall and college ever come?

The rull's flesh was pale green with filaments of red. Its main body was vaguely reptilian: a fat, sinuous croc shape and a long spiky tail. On the sides of the body were the big slimy wings that flew the rull through the water. The rull had no head to speak of: just a long mouth-slit, some nose-holes, and two little eyes backed by pouches. The mouth was soft and toothless; rulls lived on whatever decayed garbage they could scrounge from the sea floor. This one had a hook set in its mouth. A bad catch.

According to the scientists, the rull spores had drifted down from space to seed the ocean. Why, no one knew. Why do weeds grow? In the last year all kinds of unearthly creatures had appeared. The solar system was drifting through some cosmic cloud of spores, and worthless new species were cropping up all over the place.

"Watch," Ricky said, taking Jeannie's arm. "Watch this."

The fisherman held a long hunting knife poised over the center of the rull's translucent body. The stupid, harmless creature lay there shivering. Rulls balanced off their low intelligence with some modest psionic abilities. It could feel the humans' revulsion and see its impending death.

The rull puffed up the two big airsacs behind its smeary eyes. The air whistled back out, clammy and smelly, trying to sound like words. *Fwee-fwet-fwee-fwo.* Please let me go. *Fwee-fwaah-fwa-fwish.* I'll grant a wish.

Rulls always said this, but people killed them anyway. The fisherman steadied his knife over the fleshmound's summit. Jeannie felt a sudden burst of sympathy for the poor thing, this poor outcast in a world it never made. She drew free of Ricky and stepped forward to lay her hand on the fisherman's shoulder.

"Don't. Let the poor thing go, and take your wish."

"Rull wishes don't work out so good," said the fisherman, glancing up at her. "Or didn't you know?"

The creature's muddy eyes stared gratefully up at Jeannie. The hook, she noticed, had fallen out of its mouth. She smiled charmingly at the fisherman, working to keep him distracted.

"What do you mean?" asked Jeannie. "I wish *I* could free a rull and get a wish."

Just then the ungainly creature made its move. With a huge slurping noise it flopped across the sand and into the breakers. There was a moment of confusion, and then Jeannie got her wish.

She snaked her arm a little tighter around Ricky's waist. They were surely going to kiss tonight, as soon as it got dark. To her left were gold-plated clouds and a fat ruby sun. The longest day of the year… the longest day ever.

Note on "Wishloop"

Written in Summer, 1981.
San Jose State University Department of Mathematics and Computer Science Newsletter, December, 1988.

I wrote this on vacation with my family at Kill Devil Hills, North Carolina. In the Outer Banks, you always see idiots killing skates that they've caught. Just to publish this short-short story somewhere, I eventually put in our SJSU departmental newsletter.

Inertia

Nancy was asleep, avoiding me. I was watching TV. A six-inch butler in there making a pitch for textured paper napkins. Texture equals romance. I was clean broke, and my new wife had stopped loving me.

"Come on," urges the midget butler, beckoning me into the tube and towards a table. The tablecloth hangs down to the ground like theater curtains. An expectant buzz filters out. I shoulder through the heavy fabric and find myself onstage. A big little audience in here. At last, I have texture, and Nancy's onstage, too, wearing next to nothing and raring to…

The doorbell rang, waking me. Eleven-thirty Friday night, mild mid-September, Princeton, New Jersey, Nancy asleep beside me, her features all closed up. My unformed bud, my cruel mistress. I went downstairs and answered the door. Harry.

His big white face looked anxious. "I hope I didn't wake you, I just thought I'd, uh…"

"It's okay. I was under a table putting on a show for some midgets."

Harry's voice dropped. "You were already dreaming?"

"Relax. I'm still dressed. Nancy's asleep." I walked into the kitchen and Harry tagged along. We'd had a drink together that afternoon, and he looked like he'd been at it ever since. I took out two beers and handed him one.

"No thanks," said Harry. He shouldered past me and shambled into the pantry where Nancy kept our liquor supply.

"Tequila, Harry?"

"Uh, yeah, I need."

I should point out that Harry and I were both getting over a series of nasty shocks and unwanted life-changes. Rude chuckles with a negative charge. Harry's regular girlfriend had more or less committed suicide, and the next woman he'd loved had rejected him utterly.

I'd gotten married, which seems positive enough, but just then my engineering business had gone down the tubes. "When there's money worries, love goes out the window," my Uncle Arpad told me once. Once you get started fighting, it's hard to stop.

My near-bankruptcy had finished Harry right off: he'd been my research and development department. I was still making a little money with consulting, but I had no work at all for Harry. He was making ends meet by teaching high-school physics. Rumpled genius Harry was teaching at the Collegiate Academy for Young Ladies.

"There's only a drop left," Harry observed, holding up the tequila bottle.

"Go on and kill it."

"I better not. Nancy'll be mad at me."

My tidy new wife, Nancy, my slobby old pal Harry—need I say more? Nancy was going to be mad no matter what.

"Frozen daiquiris!" I proposed. I found a rum-bottle with a few shots left. Harry snagged a vodka bottle, and it was back to the kitchen. Harry leaned against a wall, staring at the ceiling. I got ice and a can of limeade concentrate out of the freezer. *You really shouldn't be doing this*, I thought to myself.

"That's some ceiling," Harry remarked. "The way it's peeling."

It was an unusual ceiling. The week after Nancy and I had moved in, the kitchen ceiling paint had blistered and burst in seven places. But it was new paint, so no flakes had fallen. Instead, there were seven irregular blobs of white underpaint surrounded by dangling ruffs of peeled-back tan latex.

"Jellyfish," said Harry. "Invisible space-squid."

I loaded up the blender and pushed the switch. *Skazz, skazz, fwrrr, tik-tik-tik.* I sampled it. Fuh. Too much limeade.

Harry read my expression. "You put the whole two-quart size in, idiot?"

I added ice. *Skazz, fwrrr, tik.* Pour and pour.

"Too watery." Harry dumped his drink back in and handed me the vodka bottle. My hand tipped a half-pint in. *Skazz, fwrr, tik.* Perfection.

"I didn't tell you what I've been teaching," Harry said.

"I wasn't sure you wanted to talk about it. Action equals reaction? Voltage equals current times resistance? I'm sorry, Harry, believe me I'm sorry. If I can get my business back on its feet you'll be the first to…"

"It's interesting to teach in prep-school," Harry said, smiling strangely. "It stimulates my mind in a way that could be most lucrative."

My attention level went up about fifteen percent. "You have a new idea?"

"Are you familiar with Mach's Principle?"

"Heard of it. It's unproved. Something about absolute space?"

"Mach says there really is no space. There's no framework at all without matter. If there were only one object in the universe, then motion would be a meaningless concept. No acceleration, no rotation, no inertia."

"Inertia?"

"Inertia is an object's tendency to resist changes in motion." Harry waved his glass. "*Heft* is inertia." The glass flew out of his hand and shattered on the floor. I heard a fluting call from upstairs.

"It's all right, Nancy," I shouted. But already her steps were coming down the stairs, swift and implacable.

"What's that smell? What are you doing?"

She stood in the kitchen doorway, squinting against the light. She had snub features, bobbed strawberry-blonde hair and a sweet little figure. I loved her with all my heart.

Harry squatted on the floor, picking up bits of broken glass. Seeing him, Nancy stepped back, as if from an open drain.

"Harry just dropped by," I explained. "We're discussing inertia."

"I can see that. You're going to be in horrible condition for the race tomorrow, Joseph." My Christian name. She was unhappy—and who could blame her? I'd promised to run the Princeton Ten-Miler with her.

"What nonsense," put in Harry. "Conspicuous consumption of body-energy. How do you think a black millhand feels when he sees you go prancing by in your seventy-dollar air-shoes?" The guy never knew when to shut up.

"You fat ugly toad, I'd like to step on you." With that, Nancy turned and stalked upstairs.

There was a minute's silence. The humming fluorescent light covered everything with stagnant vivacity. The rum hit me. Suddenly the big, lobed paint-peelings on the ceiling looked festive.

"Let's go down to the basement, Harry."

He poured some more vodka into our blenderful of daiquiris. I opened the basement door and the cats rushed out.

Downstairs was my happy place. I'd torn some carpet out of my old office and brought it here, also the desk and file-cabinet. I had a good little computer, a daisy-wheel printer and, best of all, half a basement full of offbeat tools and components.

It was the first time Harry had been down here. From the old days he knew most of the equipment by serial number, but seeing it all jumbled up differently was Christmas for him.

"Jeez, Fletch. There's enough stuff here to build a time-machine!"

"You mean that?"

He gave me a sly look from the corner of his eye. "You got a gyroscope?"

"Sure. Yeah. Got a beauty. Army surplus inertial guidance servo. I've even got a transformer for it. Want to see it run?"

"In a minute. First things first." He sat down on my desk and, no longer having a glass, took a long gulp from the chill and green and possibly protosentient fluid in the Pyrex beaker-top of our blender, a beaker-top, by the way, whose geometry was such that it could not be set down.

"Gimme some."

Blub, chug, blub.

"Ahhhhh. 'Sgood."

Chug, blub, chub, blug. The beaker passed back and forth and was suddenly empty.

"We finished that too fast, Harry. Much too fast."

"I feel pretty damn good, Fletch. I think I can do something with that Mach's principle. The point is that gravitational mass and inertial mass are not the same thing. Gravity is like a *charge*, but inertia is a type of *interrelatedness*."

"You're going to build a time-machine?"

"Get your mind out of the gutter, Fletcher. I'm going to build an inertia-winder."

I assumed that he was putting me on. "Why not smelt up some Cavorite instead? You know what I mean? That Jules Verne alloy that was supposed to shield things from gravitational attraction? Or maybe we should put together a Dean Drive and mail it to John Campbell. The gyro'd come in handy."

"Campbell's dead, more's the pity." Harry sucked a last drop out of the beaker and smacked his lips. "I'm commencin' to feel *pret*-ty damn good."

"You learn to talk that way at the prep-school?"

"The Collegiate Academy. Oh, my, yes. Those sweet girls. Bless their hearts. The cardioid curve, dear Fletcher, is, of course, a traditional symbol for pulchritudinous callipygosity, and when I speak of blessing, I think, *selbstverständlich*, of the censer and thurible, the spray of holy anointment, and the fullness of emotion appropriate to such…"

Maundering on in such fashion, Harry drifted over to my equipment and began hefting this object and now that. Suddenly I didn't feel so good. I decided to leave him on his own and check out Nancy.

She was pacing up and down the upstairs hall. Seeing her, the moment before she started talking, I knew again why I loved her. Her grace, her aliveness, the way she moved.

"Dammit, Joseph, what do you think you're doing?"

"Nancy, I was *asleep*. And Harry showed up, so I let him in. He's my buddy."

"You smell like a distillery. Talking to him's fine, but do you have to drink like him? You're not built for it."

A wave of dizziness hit me then. I grabbed the banister for support. Nancy spotted the move.

"Are you going to throw up, Joe? Are you all right?"

I felt a sickening lightness in my stomach. We'd drunk that stuff much too fast. Inertia. A giant's fist clenched my Adam's apple. Nancy helped me into the bathroom.

When I was through being sick, she wiped my face off with a washcloth and laid me down on our bed.

"Poor Joey. Poor baby."

"You don't really love me."

"You don't love *me*."

"I *do* love you."

"I love you, too, Joey. I love you a lot."

It was good in bed. Sleep came.

I woke suddenly in the dark, feeling queasy. Three, four in the morning? My mouth was an agony of salt and mucus. Water, I needed water, lots of it. Aspirin. The toilet.

Painfully I eased up onto one elbow. For some reason my body rocked so far forward that my head bumped my knees. I was as wobbly as a Macy's parade turkey float. I definitely had to get to the bathroom.

I creaked into a sitting position and swung my legs out of bed. Inexplicably, my legs took off across the room, dragging my body behind. *WHAM*, I crashed into an armchair; *SLAM*, I hit the floor; *CRASH*, I bounced across the room. My arms and legs were flying around like Styrofoam cups in a windstorm. Yet none of it really hurt. With sudden sick horror, I decided that I'd suffered some kind of brain damage. I was having a seizure for sure.

Just then there was a scream, and Nancy came bashing into me. I reached out to grab her, but the force of my touch flicked her away like a ping-pong ball. The objects she smashed into took off on their own random trajectories, and now our whole room was filled with dark, crazy bouncing. This was more than brain damage; this was a major breakdown of physical law. What…

I remembered Harry. *I'm going to build an inertia-winder.* I rose abruptly to my feet. Error. I ricocheted from the ceiling to our bed. I struck the bed at an awkward angle, and its springs catapulted me out our bedroom's open French windows. I was traveling much faster than it seemed at all reasonable. Our second story porch shot under me, and an instant later I'd crashed. My fall was fortunately broken by the large Spirea bush that I landed on.

For a long minute I just lay there, assessing the damages. As far as I could feel, nothing was broken. Really, I hardly even felt bruised. The night air was mild and pleasant. From where I lay, I could see the lit-up windows of our basement. Harry was down there. Harry had made this happen. But how? Something to do with inertia. He'd taken my inertia away, and now my body could be pushed around like a dandelion seed. But if I didn't weigh anything, why had I crashed to the ground so hard? And why hadn't it hurt?

It didn't matter. Right now the only thing that mattered was to go down to the basement and wring Harry's neck. Slowly, slowly, I eased myself into an upright position. I felt as unsteady as a six-foot pile of plates. When I tried to step forward, my center of gravity shifted and I fell back down. Great progress: an inch per minute.

I decided to take my chances and leap.

Once again, I overdid it. The two stories of our house whizzed past, and then I was looking down at our streetlit roof—looking down at the roof and still climbing. Although I was getting frightfully high, I wasn't too worried about it. My body had so little inertia that my legs would easily be able to absorb the shock of landing.

Slowly, not wanting to throw myself into a spin, I leaned my head back to look up at the sky. Nothing. There was nothing up there. Low clouds? Not likely; clouds would be reflecting some of the city lights back down at us. But tonight had been a full moon, the Harvest moon. I'd seen it rising earlier when…

Suddenly I could see the moon and stars again. I was high, high in the sky. Forgetting to move slowly, I looked back down. Despite my abrupt head-movement, I didn't start spinning. The influence of the rest of the universe was acting on me again, and my inertia was back.

Below my feet was a huge black dome, the region that Harry had somehow cut off from the world. It was expanding. The air up here felt thick again. It had inertia; it dragged and beat against me. Rapidly my upward motion slowed, and then I was falling, falling heavily. I prayed that Harry wouldn't pick this instant to turn off his inertia-winder.

As I tumbled back through the dark dome, my speed increased dramatically. The gravitational mass of my body was the same, so that the gravity of Earth pulled me as hard as ever. Yet in here my inertial mass, the mass which resists motion, was almost zero. The trees, the streetlight, my house—they all streaked past. I tensed my bent legs against the crash.

At just the moment of impact I pushed up, neutralizing the shock. When someone jumps off a building, it's not the *falling* that kills them, it's the sudden *stop*. But with virtually no inertia to resist changes of motion, a sudden transition from over one hundred miles per hour to complete rest is only mildly jarring.

The whole leap had taken less than a minute. I found myself right next to the cellar door outside my house. Now that I had a better understanding of what was going on, I was able without too much difficulty to get one of the big doors open and go on down into the basement.

"HELLO, FLETCHER!"

My inertialess eardrum vibrated wildly with Harry's greeting. He was comfortably seated in my desk-chair. I must have jerked an arm involuntarily, for I found myself on the floor again. Glaring fixedly at Harry, I crawled towards him, close enough to reach out and...

"AREN'T YOU HAPPY?"

This time I was braced for it.

"Whisper, Harry, whisper." Maybe it wasn't really that loud; maybe it was the hangover. There's no hangover worse than the one you have when you wake up at four A. M. I wondered what Nancy was doing now. I hoped she'd have the sense to just get back in bed. For some reason, thinking about her didn't make me feel tense like it usually did. She was, after all, just another person, a person just like me...

"I DID IT!"

"You did it." Gingerly I rose to my feet. "Please don't talk loud or I'll have to kill you. Did what?"

"Come see." Moving with the caution of an arthritic eighty-year-old on glare-ice, Harry eased out of my chair and led me back to the workshop area. Sitting on a cleared part of the floor was the inertia-winder.

It was basically just an electric gyroscope with a glob of something attached to the protruding rotor. Wound-up inertia?

"Quarkonium," breathed Harry. "I kept some back from the last shipment. It's a cross between matter and antimatter. Last week I ran it through some high-energy vacuum-sputtering to build up a fractal surface-geometry. A lot of the quark pairs are split up now. Once I had that going for me, I just needed a gyro to spin them around."

"You could have warned me."

"I didn't know you were going to rush back upstairs. How about another drink?"

"No way. Turn that thing off now, before someone gets hurt. I was outside and I could see the sphere of influence growing. It's just our house now, but if you let it go much longer, it'll be the neighbors, too. I could get sued."

Harry looked acutely uncomfortable, but said nothing.

"All right then, I'll turn it off myself." I leaned forward, fell down, righted myself on all fours, found the cord of the electric gyro, and yanked at it. The plug flew at me and bounced off my forehead. Harry had already unplugged it. I kicked at the gyro. The compassless rotor bobbed this way and that. The faint while of its spinning diminished not one whit.

"The quarkonium's surface is very…adhesive," Harry murmured. "The field-lines of inertia are all wrapped around it. It has a lot of inertia and it keeps getting more."

"So when does it run down?"

"I…I don't think it ever will. It's self-perpetuating."

"Come on, Harry. What about the Second Law of Thermodynamics?"

"This is different, Fletch. This is quarkonium."

There was a sledgehammer over in the corner of the basement. I went and got it. It was amazingly easy to heft. I took a good solid stance in front of the gyro and let fly. The gyro skittered a few feet across the floor and I fell down. All right. I hadn't expected to succeed on the first try. I kept at it for about ten minutes. Harry watched in silence.

Finally a lucky blow cracked the gyro's mount. The rotor snapped free, rolled around on the floor, then spun up onto one end. The shiny glob of wound-up inertia spun there like a child's top. All that hammering had accomplished exactly nothing.

I let my arms and legs go limp. Gravity bounced me around on the floor for awhile. I lay there. Harry stood over me, looking worried. With a quick, savage blow, I knocked his legs out from under him. Gravity bounced him around for awhile. Then he was lying next to me.

I closed my eye, imagining a black sphere of inertialessness. The sphere grew and grew. Soon it included the whole Earth. Chaos. The sphere kept growing. After awhile it included the Moon. Without its inertia, the Moon would fall down. Without any heft fighting our gravity, we'd reel the Moon in like a poisoned catfish. Eventually…if anyone still cared…we'd both fall into the Sun.

The whine of the spinning quarkonium blob seemed to have gotten higher. The thing was actually speeding up. How long did we have? Ten hours? Ten days?

"JOEY! WHERE ARE YOU?" The distress-cry of my mate.

I leaped to my feet shouting, "I'M COMING, DARLING!" Error. I smashed the naked light bulb on the ceiling with the nape of my neck. I bounced into a shelf full of radio tubes. I landed right on top of the inertia-winder. For a horrible moment the inertia-wrapped glob of quarkonium spun right against my cheek. It felt silky and sly as a vampire's first kiss.

The light in the stairwell snapped on and there was Nancy.

"What is it, Joey? Why don't we weigh anything? I keep falling and…" She tumbled down the stairs and came to rest next to me and Harry and the inertia-winder. A square of light from the staircase spot-lit us like three degenerates in a Tennessee Williams play.

"Harry built this machine?"

"That's right, Nancy." Harry was actually trying to sound friendly. I think he'd realized, as I had, that we'd all be dead soon. I took Nancy's hand.

"Why are you just lying here? Why don't you turn the machine off?"

"We can't."

"Well, what exactly is it doing?"

"It cuts us off from the rest of the world's inertial influences," said Harry. "You know what inertia is?"

"It's you and Joey getting drunk again for no reason. It's Joey and me fighting just because we fought yesterday. It's you and me not liking each other because the other one doesn't like us." Nancy paused, considering what she'd just said.

"That's all true, Nancy. And in physics inertia is an object's tendency to resist changes in its motion. Inertia is an overall property of the universe. We only have inertia because of the stars."

"You mean like the zodiac influences your moods?"

"Well…maybe. But I'm talking physics. This thing I put together," Harry gestured at the inertia-winder. "This thing produces an expanding shell of unconfined quarks. Wherever the shell crosses inertial field-lines, the lines snap. It's snapping more and more field-lines all the time. Soon the whole block will have no inertia, then all of Princeton, then the whole state and the world and then…"

"How long, Harry?" My voice was husky and brittle.

"Well, you're asking me to solve a non-linear partial differential equation there…" Harry hummed a distracted snatch of verse. "…fine-structured constant…hyperbolic tangent of that…oh, call it 26.34 hours. Give or take."

"Until what?" demanded Nancy.

"Until the Moon loses all its inertia," I said. "When that happens it falls down."

"But why would it fall if it doesn't weigh anything?"

"There's inertia and there's gravitational mass," said Harry patiently. "This doesn't change gravitational attraction. It just takes away the ability to resist gravitational attraction."

"DAMMIT HARRY!" The force of the accompanying gesture threw Nancy against me. "Goddammit, Harry, what'd you build it for?"

"It would have wonderful applications," I said placatingly, "if we could just turn it off. Like for a jet-liner. Get rid of its inertia for awhile and you could launch it with a rubber-band. Or you could use an inertia-winder for real cheap energy generation. Accelerate something when it's inertialess, then let it have its inertia back and take advantage of the free momentum. If there were a way to turn it off, we'd be rich instead of dead."

The spinning glob on the rotor was the size of a softball now. Nancy reached out a finger to touch it. "Ugh! It's so soft and...greedy feeling."

"What did you just say?" asked Harry.

"Soft. Greedy feeling."

"That's the broken quark-bags. But I meant Fletch. What did you say, Fletcher?"

"You could accelerate something inside the inertialess sphere and when it got out, it'd have a lot of momentum."

"*Pret*-ty damn good. Call the Kennedy Center."

"What for? Tickets to the ballet?"

"Kennedy *Space* Center. We'll put this sucker on a Saturn rocket and let the Crab Nebula worry about it."

"Sure, Crab Nebula. You'll be lucky to find a rocket that moves faster than the black sphere is expanding."

"The change-up, Fletcher. When the rocket exhaust gets to the edge of the sphere, it gets a sudden increase in momentum. The same speed but a lot more inertia. Action equals reaction. Momentum down means momentum up. It'll kick the whole sphere like a mule. I don't see why..." Distracted humming again. "Yes. The system should reach nine-tenths the speed of light at...forty-seven minutes after launch. We'll have lost part of the night sky but what the hell. It beats having the Moon land on your head. Call Max Moritz."

General Moritz was a guy we'd done some ordnance development for, a few years back. A Pentagon big-wig. "All right. I'll call him."

"Where does he live?" Nancy wanted to know.

"Right in D.C. Georgetown."

"Do you think the sphere has reached them yet?"

"I doubt it. What's the difference? The telephone'll work. It's just electrons moving down a wire. If your husband can move through the sphere, then so can an electron."

"The phone *won't* work," I insisted. "Except for local calls. Long-distance is all by microwave these days. There's something about your expanding quark sphere that blocks electromagnetic radiation. That's why you can't tell if the Sun's up yet."

"Even if you could call Moritz, he wouldn't believe you yet," added Nancy. "He still has his stubbornness."

"Not stubbornness, Nancy. *Inertia*."

"This is more than just physics." Her voice was light and amused. "People keep acting the same way because other people are watching them. You get trapped into acting out the role that society assigns you. It's the same with matter. If all the stars and galaxies say, 'Well, so and so is sitting right *there*,' then it's really hard to move over *here*. Peer pressure. It's inertia. But now we're all covered up together. Like kids hiding under a blanket. None of the big people know what we're doing." She put her arms around me and gave me a wet kiss. "Come on, Harry, you kiss me too."

"I'd better not. You two just go on and enjoy yourselves. I'm going upstairs to call Max."

Harry banged around upstairs for awhile. Then he was talking to someone, an operator. Nancy and I ignored him. We were enjoying our-selves. The only fly in the ointment was that I kept imagining that I saw people out of the corner of my eyes, glowing people like elves and fairies. That was just the alcohol abuse acting up on me. But making love with no inertia was fantastic, so…

"Ahem."

"Are you already back, Harry? Can't you see…"

"You were right about the phone. I think we better go see Moritz in person."

I sat up and straightened my clothes. "What?"

"Didn't you say you could jump real high? We'll walk to Washington in seven-league boots!"

"What if we move too fast and land outside the sphere? If we landed from one of those jumps with all our inertia along, it'd be like falling out of an airplane. Certain death."

"We'll carry the inertia-winder with us. We'll need it to show Moritz anyway."

Well…why not. I began looking around for something to carry the spinning inertia-winder in.

"I'm coming, too," said Nancy, standing up carefully.

"Aw, Nancy…"

"Yes, I'm coming."

My Nancy. "Okay, honey. You come, too. Maybe we can see some sights in D.C. Be sure to bring your checkbook if we need to get the bus back. And what should I carry the inertia-winder in?"

"How about your old lunch-box that you used to use when you had an office to go to."

"Good idea." I found the old grey lunch-box in a corner of the basement and nudged the inertia-winder on in. It sat in the bottom of the box, spinning like a top, making a whining buzz against the metal. I hoped it wouldn't drill its way through.

"Let me get us some sweaters," suggested Nancy. "Even though it's warm, we could get cold flying through the air."

The trip got off to a good start. The three of us went out in the back yard, linked arms, and took off like superheroes. I'd never jumped harder in my life. It felt like we were going a thousand miles an hour. A limp wind whistled past us as we rose up and up and up. I held my shrilly buzzing lunch-box clutched in one hand. With the winder right with us, there was no danger of leaving the region of no inertia. We continued to rise. The whole suburban sprawl of Princeton was just a dotty smear of light, far, far below.

"Joey!" Nancy was worried. "We shouldn't have jumped so hard! What's going to happen when we land? And we're still climbing!"

All at once the ground was invisible. As far as I could make out, we were passing through some clouds. A very unpleasant thought crossed my mind. What if we kept climbing indefinitely? What if the force of our combined jump had been enough to zap us up to escape velocity? As long as we stayed inside the sphere, there was virtually no wind-resistance to slow us down. Earth's gravity was pulling at us all the time, slowly chip-ping away at our velocity, yet the turnaround point was nowhere in sight. We were going to rise and rise until we either froze to death or asphyxiated. The air streaming past me felt cold and thin as ice picks.

"Drop it, Fletch," said Harry. His thoughts were, as usual, a step ahead of mine. "Drop the inertia-winder so we can get out of its sphere of influence and have the wind slow us down."

I dropped my lunch-box, or tried to. At first it just hung there in front of me, buzzing like some giant horsefly. Finally I took hold of it and threw it down past my feet. The other two hung onto me as the recoil pushed us yet higher. The air was really getting cold now. With the clouds below and the black sphere's boundary still above, it was utterly dark. Nancy began sobbing.

Just then we broke out into blinding sunlight. We were so high that the sky overhead was dark purple instead of blue. A terrifyingly immense dome of black curved down away from us, cutting the Earth's spread-out surface in a vast circle. Out past it I could see the wrinkled surface of the sea, the huge expanse of the Chesapeake Bay. With any luck we'd be landing right in Washington.

"It's beautiful," gasped Nancy.

The air was so thin that we had to pant rapidly to keep from blacking out. But it was thick enough to stop our flight. Earth's big gravity took over and we began to fall.

"Just remember how Superman lands in the movies," I advised Nancy. "Keep your legs bent and push up as you hit." Then the lovely sunlight was gone again.

Once we'd fallen back through the clouds we could make out the spread-out street-lights of Washington and its suburbs. The Potomac River's black swath made a convenient landmark. Harry craned this way and that, trying to orient himself. Finally he pointed one of his stubby arms.

"That's Georgetown over there."

"The Pentagon would be better," I suggested. "I'm sure General Moritz is over there by now. The Army's going to be in a state of Red Alert wondering what happened. The whole city is without inertia. Let's just hope they don't start shooting missiles at the Russians."

"They couldn't if they wanted to," Harry observed. "No radio-links."

We were falling faster than ever. Here and there I could see other people flying through the air. Some of them looked very strange…not even like people, really. There was one in particular, a small man who glowed green all over. I tried to point him out to Nancy, but then he was gone. Probably just my imagination. A complex sound drifted up from the city, a generalized roar compounded of screams, sirens and horns.

"You all better decide where to land," said Nancy. "Or we're going to end up in the river."

Indeed, the Potomac was directly beneath us, and getting closer all the time. "The Pentagon," I urged, "over there to the right. We should throw something to the left to push us that way."

"My shoes," offered Harry. Hanging onto me with his left arm, he reached down with his right to slip off his loafers, then threw them one, two, off to our left. This was enough. We streaked down towards a strip of park at the river's edge.

The landing was easy, but the one-mile walk to the Pentagon was a bit harder. Without inertia it's impossible to walk normally, yet we were loath to try another big jump. Finally Nancy hit on a sort of modified bunny-hop. Harry and I hopped along after her.

The George Washington Parkway was an incredible scene. Some people were still trying to drive. Their cars jerked around like in a speeded up stop-action movie. From zero to a hundred and back to zero in three seconds. The vehicles kept crashing into each other like bumper cars, but no one was getting hurt.

The great lawn in front of the Pentagon's main entrance was brightly lit by searchlights. A cordon of armed soldiers barred the entrance. The whole scene reminded me of the last time I'd been here: for the big outer-space peace-march.

"HALT," shouted a bull-horn.

"Look out, Joey," said Nancy. "They've got guns pointed at us."

"Think Superman, baby. With no inertia those bullets'll just bounce off us."

"HUMANS," hollered Harry. "WE ARE HERE TO HELP YOU. TAKE US TO YOUR LEADERS." He'd never sounded more like a Martian.

We bunny-hopped closer. There was another warning, and then the soldiers opened fire. Just as I predicted, it was no worse than being barraged by pea-shooters. You just had to be careful that you didn't get hit in the eye. We hopped closer.

Harry kept us his alien invader routine. "DO NOT ANGER US, EARTHLINGS. WE COME IN PEACE." At that, some fanatic lobbed a mortar shell down in front of us. The shrapnel bounced off us all right, but the force of the shock-wave was enough to send us tumbling head over heels. Luckily, we were able to hang onto each other. We finally came to a stop against a big deuce-and-a-half troop truck parked off to one side.

"What's with the *Day the Earth Stood Still* routine?" I asked Harry as soon as I could get my breath. "Why do you act like a spaceman?"

"I thought that way it would be easier to get in."

"We're lucky we weren't killed," exclaimed Nancy. "If we'd gotten closer, they could have bayoneted us, you realize that?"

"No more Mister Nice Guy," I said. "Let's plow this stinking truck into them. We've got to get Moritz to find that inertia-winder and put it on a rocket."

I toyed with the idea of picking the truck up and throwing it, but this was unfortunately out of the question. The truck's gravitational mass was as big as ever. The most I could hope for would be to push it over on its side.

"The keys are in here," called Nancy from the cab. "Come on, boys."

Bombs and tracer bullets flared around us as we barreled into the Pentagon steps. At the last minute we jumped clear and bounced to a rest against the building's wall. The soldiers were so distracted that we were able to climb through a window.

We found ourselves in a long, brightly-lit corridor. People in uniforms hurried this way and that, bouncing off the walls and ceilings. Harry steered us right into one of the offices. A whey-faced old man in a captain's uniform looked up from his empty desk. He seemed a bit drunk.

"Can we use your phone?" asked Harry. "We have to get in touch with General Max Moritz."

"Good luck," said the man, smiling wryly. "All the great high muck-a-mucks are downstairs hiding in the Situation Room. How did you three get in here anyway?"

"We're CIA operatives," I said casually. "We've got some information on the attack."

Narrowing his muddy eyes, he sized us up. Cute Nancy, weird Harold, and Joe Fletcher the tech-freak. "You're lying," he concluded, and pulled something out of his drawer. A bottle. "Have a drink. *Die high*, as we used to say in 'Nam."

"Well all right." I took the fifth of bourbon and blasted a hit.

"*Joseph.*"

"I'm sorry, Nancy, I forgot myself." I passed the bottle to Harry, who greedily sucked it for what seemed like a very long time. The man be-hind the desk watched with displeasure. The name-tag on his chest read: Captain Snerman.

"It's really true," wheezed Harry, returning what remained of the bourbon. "We're not in the CIA, but we do have some information about the inertia-winder. I built it. I made all this happen."

"Sure you did," said Snerman, cradling his depleted fifth. "You and the two hundred other people who've already called in. What'd you use, pyramid power? Antigravity? Spirit familiars?"

There was a crash as one of the people hurrying down the corridor bounced against our door. "Not anti*gravity*," said Harry, "anti-*inertia*. I promise you, my good man, Max Moritz knows us very well. Just tell him that Harry Gerber and Joe Fletcher are here to consult with him on the current situation. Time is of the essence."

"What the hell," Snerman took a drink and dialed a number. "Snerman here. We've got what might be a lead. Two men and a woman. Harry Gerber, Joseph Fletcher, and…" He glanced up at Nancy.

"Nancy Lydon." Of course she'd refused to change her name when we got married.

"Nancy Lydon," continued Snerman. "Gerber and Fletcher insist that they are scientists, that they know General Moritz, and that they have caused the present crises." The receiver chattered briefly, and then Snerman set it down.

"Make yourselves comfortable." he said, gesturing at some grey metal chairs. He held onto his desk to keep the gesture from knocking him over. "It'll take your message a while to percolate up the chain of command. Where is this machine of yours anyway, Mr. Gerber?"

"It's in my lunch-box," I volunteered, "But…" Harry nudged me sharply and I fell silent.

"This is for General Moritz's ears only," said Harry. "The fate of the Earth is at stake."

Snerman shrugged, fell out of his chair, got back in his chair and took another drink. I wondered what time it was. Maybe ten in the morning. According to Harry's calculations we had about twenty hours till the moon fell down. Of course some other disaster might take place first.

It seemed possible, for instance, that the changing balance of gravity and inertia could lead to severe earthquakes. What if Earth broke right in half? Of if the air escaped? Or…

Just then my stomach took a nose dive. There was some…personage standing behind Snerman. It was a man made of greenish flames, a man with a goblin's pointed face…

There was a sharp knock on the door. Two big marines with bayonets. Our escort. Moritz wanted to see us. The glowing man had disappeared with the knock. I'd probably just imagined him. You know how it is when you're over-tired; sometimes you think you see things moving, just quick glimpses out of the corner of your eye.

There were more people in the halls than before. They were still falling down a lot, but they kept moving anyway. The best technique for indoors seemed to be a rapid shuffling motion like that of a cross-country skier. The elevators were not to be trusted, so we took the stairs. It was ten levels and three checkpoints to the Situation Room. The marines shoved us in and closed the door after us.

A huge wall-map of the world dominated the room. Built-in electronic graphics had shaded a large grey circle around D.C. To the south it took in most of Virginia; to the north it had just reached New York City.

"Harry," called a man's high, choky voice. "Fletcher."

It was General Moritz. He was seated with the other brass at a long oak table. Nancy, Harry and I shuffled closer.

Max Moritz was a plump Pennsylvania Dutchman who wore his blond hair combed straight back from the forehead. His cheeks were chubby and his eyes a merry delft-blue. For him war was fun. He had the cheerful viciousness of a child who likes to torture animals. Harry and I had endeared ourselves to him a few years back when we'd invented a way to make water radioactive. It was a beam that a satellite could shine at the enemy's reservoirs. The beam started a quark resonance process leading to proton-decay. If you drank any of our irradiated water, you'd glow in the dark. Moritz was still hoping for a chance to try it out.

"Is this true that you have caused the big blackout?" yodeled the general. He always sounded like he was swallowing something. "By thunder, I'm hoping so!"

"Yes, it's true," I said. "Harry made something called an inertia-winder. It snaps our ties to the rest of the universe. Inertial field-lines are broken, and electromagnetic radiation is blocked as well. The problem…"

"These men are insane," snapped a grim-faced civilian to Moritz's right. "Get them out of here."

"So it's you, Baumgard," crowed Harry. "Still stupid and blind?"

"General Moritz!" The civilian rose to his feet, his angrily waving arms jerking his inertialess body around. He had conservatively long hair, the same grey color as his face. His suit was dark-blue with dandruff on the shoulders. I recognized him as Dr. Dana Baumgard, a very well-respected government physicist, formerly of M.I.T. Harry and I had beat-en him out on that radioactive water project. He'd never forgiven Harry for refusing to explain how our beam worked…Harry never really knew how any of his inventions worked.

"I have known Harry Gerber for years," continued Baumgard. "The man is an unscrupulous charlatan. To be sure, he has cobbled together one or two ingenious devices. But never has he offered any scientific explanations of why his machines should work. Whatever he tells you will be nonsense, I can assure you."

"I am thanking you for your opinion, Dr. Baumgard," gargled Moritz. "And now I am asking you, please, to sit down."

"We need a rocket," said Harry. "We have to get the inertia-winder on a rocket right away."

"To send at the Russians," chortled Moritz. "If only we could. But these politicians are such cautious snails. I can ask permission, but…"

"Not to send at the Russians," I broke in. "To send to outer space. The Moon will fall on us in less than twenty hours!"

"Can't you make it fall on the Russians?" asked Moritz petulantly. "Why does it have to fall on us?"

"It will kill us all no matter where it falls," cried Nancy. "Please don't waste time!"

"Where is this device that you have purportedly concocted?" asked Baumgard.

"Right in the center," said Harry, pointing at the map. "Right in the center of that big grey circle. A bit northeast of here, I'd say. We meant to bring it, but Fletcher dropped it."

"I don't suppose you drunken fools can give me any kind of description of what your machine does?" demanded Baumgard.

"It's an inertia-winder," said Harry calmly. "Basically, what I have is a rotating sphere of unconfined quarks. As you know from Mach's Principle, inertia exists only relative to the mass of the distant stars. My device cuts the inertia-lines that stretch to us from these distant objects. Isolated inside this sphere we have only our self-inertia, which is virtually zero."

"If we are cut off," interrupted Baumgard, "then why is it that we still feel the gravitational attraction of Earth? Why aren't we weightless? Surely you are not denying the equivalence of gravitational and inertial mass?"

"Of course I am," gloated Harry. "You can feel it yourself. Your inertia is gone, but the Earth still pulls you against the floor. Unless you jump." Harry gave a little hop and whisked up to the ceiling and back. He was really getting smooth at this. "Gravitation is a type of spacetime curvature. My inertia-winder does nothing to change that. But inertia is a synchronistic quantum-mechanical effect."

"The stars can't see what we're doing," put in Nancy. "They don't know where we are, so we don't have to stay still so much. Can't you feel it? Don't you feel...looser?"

"Shut up, Nancy," I muttered. "It'll be a cold day in hell when the Situation Room crowd starts feeling loose."

"Gibberish!" declaimed Baumgard. "Complete gibberish."

General Moritz signed. "Yes indeed, Doctor, yes indeed. But what we're doing next, I have no inkling."

"You're going to help us," I insisted. "The inertia-winder's sphere of influence is growing. We are unable to stop it. Within twenty hours, it's influence will reach to the Moon. With no centrifugal force of inertia, the Moon will fall down and smash our whole planet. The only solution is to send the inertia-winder away from our solar system."

"How do you know you could rocket it away faster than the sphere of influence is growing?" demanded Baumgard.

"The rocket will have the advantage of taking off with virtually no air-resistance to fight," said Harry tapping one hand with his broad fore-finger. "Moreover, there will be a fantastic gain of momentum for each particle of exhaust which leaves the sphere of inertialessness. According to my calculations, the rocket will soon reach near-light velocity, while the sphere's radius will continue to expand at only a few hundred miles per hour.

"And what happens to the sphere then?" asked Baumgard, his voice carrying the wistfulness of a boy whose worst enemy has received a much better Christmas present.

"Won't it ruin any other solar system that it runs into? Eventually it could collapse our whole galaxy!"

"You're talking about thousands of years from now," said Harry airily. "Millions. By then we'll think of something. Hell, if I can just get the bugs worked out, we can fly out to turn the inertia-winder off by next year."

There was a sudden, earth-shaking crash. Then another and another. Moritz snatched up a red telephone, his face aglow with excitement. "Is it the Russians? Can we retaliate?"

The answer he heard seemed not to be to his liking. A few moments later he'd slammed the receiver down, bouncing a little from the motion. "It's our satellites," he said. "They're starting to fall down. Where did you boys say you were losing that furshlugginer inertia-winder?"

"I'll back your plan to send it into space," added Baumgard, his face pale and sweating. "But God help you, Gerber, if you don't make good on your promise to go out and turn it off by next year."

"Next year" has a way of rolling around a little sooner than you expect. Nine months after that eventful September day when we'd built and launched the inertia-winder, Harry and I were rocketing after it, strapped into a spaceship of our design. And Nancy? I'd lost her over Christmas. She'd gone to visit her sister down South, and it didn't look like she was ever coming back. In mid-February Harry had moved in with me and we'd been hard at work ever since. I'd meant to go after Nancy, but somehow I hadn't gotten around to it. And now I was racing out of the plane of the solar system at about ninety-five percent the speed of light.

Our spaceship was unconventional, to say the least. It was basically a big old Ford station wagon…with a few modifications. Why a Ford? Because Harry's mother had one that she didn't need much anymore.

We'd torn out the tailgate and rear-window and replaced them with an air lock just big enough to cycle us through one at a time. We'd beefed up the windshield with a transparent slab of titaniplast, hoisted out the engine and packed the life-support unit in under the hood. The actual rocket-drive was mounted down where the transmission had been, with the nozzles pointing out like dual exhausts. To finish the ship off, we'd sprayed everything but the windshield and rocket-nozzles with airtight urethane foams, and then coated that with a skin of reflective Mylar. It was a hell of a vehicle.

The secret of our rocket-drive was that Harry had finally perfected the inertia-winder. He'd found a way to turn it on and off, and even better, a way to keep the black sphere of influence from growing indefinitely. To move our ship we needed only to surround ourselves with a five-meter sphere of inertialessness and shoot matter out of our rocket-nozzles. Under inertialess conditions, it was easy to accelerate the matter with an electromagnetic mass-driver; and whenever matter left the black sphere of inertialessness, it gave us a fantastic push forward.

The two major factors limiting our range were, firstly, how much matter we could bring along with us for the mass-driver to throw out, and, secondly, how much power we could store to run the mass-driver. We beat the matter-storage problem by using powdered neutronium, a sort of degenerate matter massing about one hundred kilos per dust-speck. And we handled the energy-storage by using a power-pack based on unconfined quark-antiquark pairs. The thing held a charge big enough to run New York City for months. With the runaway inertia-winder's head start, it was going to take us awhile to catch it.

So as far as rocket-power went, we were in pretty good shape. Air and food were okay too: we had a nice culture of DNA-doctored slime-mold growing under the hood. The stuff absorbed carbon dioxide, gave off oxygen, and tasted more or less like tuna fish. All it asked in return was our waste, and a steady supply of heat from the power-pack.

Physically we were all set for a trip of up to a year our time, which could come to something like three or four years Earth-time, taking relativistic time-dilation into account. Physically we were all set, but mentally, well…imagine a month-long car-trip with no view, no change in diet, no chance to stretch your legs, and with Harry Gerber in the car with you. Or with Joseph Fletcher, for that matter.

"Harry," I whined. "Let's turn the drive off for awhile again. I've got to see." The bad thing about our drive was that when it was on, we were cut off from the rest of the universe by our inertia-winder's five-meter black sphere. According to the Ford's dashboard calendar-clock this was our ninety-third day out. We'd had the drive on for the last ten days solid. Sitting behind the steering wheel and staring out through the windshield, I could see nothing but our ship's shiny hood faintly reflecting our small ceiling-light.

"We really ought to keep accelerating," said Harry testily. He was behind me, floating there in the wagon's roomy rear. "The sooner we catch up, the sooner we can go home. And you shouldn't be talking to me anyway. It's my turn to sleep."

"I don't care, I don't care, I don't care!" I slapped the gearshift from Drive to Neutral. The mass-driver's irritating whine stopped instantly, and moments later the inertia-winder stopped, too.

Harry surged forward, as eager as I to look out the window. His knee caught my head a nasty jolt.

"You stupid stinking slob," I hissed through clenched teeth. I didn't bother to turn my head to glare at him. The view was too important to me.

The view. When I was little, my parents used to take us to visit some friends in Georgia. They lived on the Savannah River, with a dock going out into it. Nights we'd sit there, all of us, the big people smoking and talking, and we kids staring up at the sky. That was the most stars I'd ever seen till this trip. And now, oh now, great skeins and marbled streamers of light, so living, so static. I loved to look at it, to let my mind flow out of our cramped quarters, flow out into the All.

Dead ahead of us was a black dish the size of your fist at arm's length. That's where we were going; that was the sphere of influence of the inertia-winder we'd launched in September.

"Look how big it is," I said to Harry after awhile. "Twice as big as the last time we looked. We're gaining fast."

"Or it's growing fast."

"You stupid stinking slob."

"That's twice, Fletcher." Something in Harry's voice compelled me to look over at the too-familiar features. It was not a pleasant sight.

"Harry, don't look at me that way."

"*That's twice*. You know where that line comes from? It's a joke my grandfather used to tell. It goes like this; it's an old-time story. A man and a woman had just gotten married. They got into a rented horse-and-buggy and started out on their honeymoon trip, the man holding the reins. It was a wet day and there were puddles in the road. The horse shied at one particularly large puddle, and the bridegroom had to get down and lead the animal through the puddle. '*That's once*,' he said to the horse as he remounted the driver's seat. Well, pretty soon there came another large puddle. Once again…"

Garbage. I stopped listening and let my mind flow back out that window. The runaway inertia-winder was still so far off. After we shut it down, we'd still have to fly all the way back. And for what? By rights we should be back on Earth marketing our new rocket-drive…not that Harry was able to explain how to build one. Even more important, I should be back there wooing Nancy. Now that the excitement of the rocket-building was over, I missed her more every day.

"…stopped at a third puddle," Harry was saying. "'*That's three times,*' cried the bridegroom, and then he took out a pistol and shot the horse dead. 'I don't think you should have done that,' says the bride, and the man says, '*That's once!*'"

"Are you trying to threaten me, Harry? You're a stupid stinking slob. That's three times. Like it or lump it and shut the goddamn hell up while I'm enjoying the view." Trembling with some mad rage I'd never known, I awaited his reaction.

Like a fool, he went for my neck. That was just what I'd been expecting, and I blocked his lunge with my forearm. But I hadn't realized that Harry had a knife in his right hand. It cut deeply into my flesh.

Bright globs of my blood shot out and danced. Almost immediately, Harry showed signs of remorse. He dropped his knife and tried to stanch my blood's flow, pressing his dirty handkerchief onto the incision.

Well all right, I'd asked for it. Typical event on a long two-man probe. But then, all at once, it got a lot worse. A glob of my blood drifted into our toilet-vent, a louvered oval in the center of the dash. The vent channeled right to the superslime, our food, our air, our good buddy, a DNA-doctored mutant tissue with no FDA approval. My blood went in the vent, the superslime tasted of it, found it good, and wanted more, more, MORE.

There we were in the front seat of our Ford station wagon, me behind the wheel, and Harry bent over my slashed wrist, an instant poised just right there, and then a thick gout, a thick nasty gout of hungry super- slime reared out of the toilet-vent all reach and menace. The slime's distributive, ambiguous, non-FDA brain had realized a basic truth: People Are Food.

More and more of the thick, mucus-like slime came oozing out of the vent. A pseudopod, the size of a man's arm, waved about, feeling for flesh. Harry shrank away from it, trying to scoot back over the seat. But a lax tentacle stretched out to block his escape-route. The stuff was stalking him—I guess he smelled stronger than I.

Quickly I tied Harry's handkerchief around my wrist, making a sort of tourniquet, and then I slipped over the seat and into the station wagon's rear. If I could just get to the laser in time! We hadn't planned to use it till later, and it was packed in under a lot of other…

"Help me, Fletcher! For the love of God, help me!"

For some twisted reason I found Harry's cries amusing.

"*That's twice,*" I called, in a voice shaking with laughter. "That's twice, Harry. And you didn't say please."

"Please help me! It's all over my leg and it's oozing some kind of acid on me. Oh God it burns, Fletcher, it's *digesting* me!"

There was the laser. I snatched it up and leaned into the front seat. The slime had woven a sort of wet cage all around Harry, a cage of thick green ropes dripping hydrochloric acid. Harry had his knees drawn up and his arms wrapped around his head. A piece of slime was plastered against his left leg. Faint wisps of smoke drifted up from this spot as the acid ate away at Harry's baggy pants.

Moving quickly, I lasered through the slime-rope that fed out of the toilet-vent, and then I snapped the vent's louvers shut. Cut off from the main body-mass, the slime tendrils around Harry lost their purposeful-ness and simply flopped down over him. The acid-secretions stopped as well, and we were able to scrape the stuff off without too much pain. Harry was unharmed, except for an ugly red burn on his thigh. My wounded wrist began to throb as the adrenaline faded.

"Here," said Harry, fumbling open the glove-compartment. "Here's the first-aid kit. Let me bandage your wrist for you."

"Oh no, Harry. Let me fix your burn first."

We looked at each other and burst out laughing. Suddenly I felt better than I'd felt all month.

"I'll turn the drive back on."

"Good. Open it up all the way and we'll catch that sucker by next week." Harry's voice was a little muffled. He was chewing a mouthful of the slime.

Our last week of pursuit went by pretty quickly. Harry amused himself by putting together a little Zeeman catastrophe-machine out of rubber-bands and paper-clips. The effect was that if you moved one of the paper-clips around in the contraption, it felt like there was a com-plexly folded set of forces acting on the clip. At one spot, in particular, the clip would always give a sudden jerk. That was supposed to be a "catastrophe," in the sense of "abrupt and unpredictable change." Harry claimed that if you called one direction "fear" and the other direction "rage," then that little twitch of the paper-clip symbolized what he'd been feeling when he pulled the knife on me. I let him talk, and spent most of my time programming some video-games onto our computer.

As we approached the runaway inertia-winder's black sphere, we turned off our drive more and more often to check our progress. It was important to line ourselves up so we'd be heading right towards the center. Once we were inside, our drive wouldn't be nearly so powerful.

Day by day the sphere grew, blotting out the distant stars. Soon we could see nothing else. We blasted the rockets for twelve more hours, cut power, and coasted towards the interface. We wanted to be able to get a fix on the other rocket as soon as we entered its sphere of influence.

"How will we know when we're inside?" I asked Harry.

"You'll feel your inertia go away again. And our radar'll pick up the other rocket. And maybe…"

Just then I felt a little twitch, a space-ripple running the length of our ship. A strange twinkling filled the space ahead of us.

Before I could say anything, the speaker on our radio crackled into life. "Greetings, masslings. Hail the dearth!" The voice was high and staticky, almost a random whistle. "Hail the dearth!" chimed in more of the little voices. "And sideways fro!"

Something slapped into our windshield then, something green-yellow-white and glowing, something like a living flame.

"Oh my," said Harry.

The light-glob on our windshield twisted and flickered, forming itself into the shape of a wiry little man. His face was sharp and pointed, with a mischievous slash-mouth and great, staring eyes. A goblin.

"I've seen it before," I stuttered. "I've seen that thing before."

Spots of light flickered everywhere, as far ahead of us as I could see. It was like we'd flown into a swarm of varicolored fireflies.

"It's all full of aliens," Harry gasped. "The inertia-winder's sphere of influence is full of aliens. Maybe we should leave, Fletcher. Maybe we should turn around before they get us. Hurry up and turn the ship around!"

I hesitated, lost in thought. That goblin looked just like the creature I'd seen in Snerman's office. And…

"Oh masslings, flee not so soon," said the speaker. The little green goblin bowed and capered, mouthing the words. Bits of flame scattered off his fingertips.

Another glob of light flopped into our windshield. It was mostly red and brown. As before, the flickering damped down, and the thing took humanoid shape.

"That's a gnome," said Harry, his voice cracking a little. "A little gnome just like the statue that Mother had in our backyard. These aren't aliens, Fletcher, these are…"

"How do you do, and how do you do, and how do you do again," boomed a voice as the red-jacketed little gnome bowed in turn to Harry, the goblin and me. He had muddy boots and a dense white beard. A pleasant-looking fellow.

Another shape landed, and another. A slender pink sprite with gauzy gold wings, and a blobby mermaid. They all looked…familiar, like things seen or dreamed once before.

"Come out, come out, come out and play," sang their voices, and the eldritch creatures pressed up against our windshield. The gnome produced a sturdy silver hammer from inside his coat and began tapping at our titaniplast, as if looking for the right place. The mermaid drooled, the goblin snickered, and the little sprite made limbering-up gestures with her magic wand.

"Look out!" screamed Harry. "They're going to break our windshield!"

"Let's get out of here," I cried, reaching for the gearshift. "I'm going to cut the drive back..."

But just then the windshield shattered. The gaping hole with its shards of plastic was like a horrible insatiable mouth. The air screamed out past us, while loose cargo flew this way and that. I struggled to hang onto the steering wheel, but the wind was too strong. I let it take me then; I let myself flutter out like a dead leaf. No use fighting it; we were dead for sure.

The cold nothingness of space burned into my nose and lungs, like Alpine air at first, coming on and on, infinitely empty, utterly pure. Something grabbed me by the leg, something hot—the goblin.

That should have been it...but it wasn't. The sprite ran her wand all over me, coating me with an even, golden glow. Suddenly the frost on my tongue melted and I could breathe. No, that's not quite right. It wasn't that I could breathe, it was that I no longer *needed* to breathe. The aching nausea of suffocation went away as soon as the wand touched my lips. Somehow the sprite had wrapped me in an energy barrier and had put my viscera in stasis.

I could move around as easily as ever. The first thing I did was look to see what had happened to Harry. He was still in his seat, his legs grimly wedged against the dash. His eyes had a glazed, staring quality... frozen solid? The sprite went in after him.

It occurred to me that I was hearing voices, an impossibility in empty space. Could it be telepathy? Maybe it had been telepathy all along...I didn't recall ever having turned the radio *on*, come to think of it.

"Greet thee meet in ever neverplace," said the goblin, still clutching my leg in his hot, flickering hand. "Seekers be ye free to slide?"

"He can't understand that," said the gnome, tugging at his beard. "He doesn't know what you're talking about, Fire. I wonder what his name is?" The sturdy little man floated in front of me, waiting for me to introduce myself.

I went ahead and pretended I could talk, letting the words form in my mind. "I'm Joe Fletcher. My partner's name is Harry Gerber. We built the machine that's at the center of this sphere. We want to turn it off. But who are you?"

"I'm called Earth," said the gnome. "But really I'm everywhere. The goblin is Fire, and the ladies are Air and Water. We're elementals."

195

"Wawa," said the soggy mermaid called Water. "Wa glub."

"Silly Water," sang the sprite. She'd finished coating Harry with pixie-dust. "You're all right now, Harry Gerber."

Harry stared at me, his fishlike mouth agape.

"It's okay," I said—or thought—to him. "I mean it's sort of okay. Talk to me subvocally. I'll be able to hear."

"We're both dead and it's sort of okay?"

"I don't think we're dead, Harry."

"Dearth not dead," interjected the goblin.

"Wa glubby glub," said Water.

"We like your machine," said the gnome. "It's nice in here, in this big black sphere. Usually we can't stop moving."

"This is Earth, Air, Fire, and Water," I told Harry. "They're elemental spirits. Gnome, sprite, goblin, mermaid."

"What about all the others?" asked Harry, sticking his head out through our broken windshield. There were zillions of other bright beings, darting and dancing as far as the eye could see.

"Those are all us, too," said Earth, the gnome. "There's only one of me, but I weave back and forth through all of space and time."

"Me first," corrected the goblin. "Only me in the wee, wee start."

"I come before the start," said Air melodiously. "I am the framework."

"Wa glub," said Water, waving a slack hand at the other three and then at herself. "Gaga me."

"She means that she is logically prior to all of us," said the sprite. "In the sense that form and becoming are more basic than substance and being."

"Wawa glubglub," agreed the mermaid. Her color fluctuated from blue to grey. Her lower half was the traditional fishtail, and her upper half was like a nude woman's. But she was lumpy, by no means the sexy doll that the word "mermaid" conjures up. Great humps and bulges rippled her flesh like waves on a wind-whipped sea. Now and then a glob of her body would pinch off and drift away into space.

Nor was the sprite sexy in any ordinary sense. Her slender bubble-gum-pink body was so attenuated as to be insectlike. With her buzzing gold wings, she was more like a dragonfly than a person. Yet there was something sweet about her small face, something sweet and deeply intelligent.

The goblin's sharp face also seemed to hold some great wisdom, but a wisdom too arcane for me ever to grasp. Of all the elementals, he seemed the most familiar to me. I'd seen him, or a copy of him, in D.C. the day we launched the winder. And I'd seen him before that: in my dreams, out of the corner of my eye in cities, or on lonely walks in the woods, and most of all, of course, in fires. Have you ever stared too long at a log fire, stared so long that the darting little flames became speedy men peeping out of the wood's cracks? Speedy men, each a goblin, each a loop of Fire's tangled lifeline.

The gnome was the most human of the elementals. He looked just right, with dirty brown boots and pants, and with a red jacket and cap. The cap was pointed and fell over to one side.

"I don't believe this," said Harry, struggling with our spaceship. "This is so unscientific it makes me sick. I'd almost rather die than be saved by pixie-dust. Why don't you…elementals tell me you're from Betelgeuse or Proxima Centauri. It'd made me feel a whole lot better."

"We're not from anywhere in particular," said the sprite, taking Harry's arm to keep him from drifting off. "We're abstract concepts personified. Like the electron. The *electron* is in each piece of matter right? Or space. *Space* is everywhere."

"Not right now it isn't," said the gnome, with a nervous glance over his shoulder. "It hasn't been around recently. I think that's because there's no inertia in here."

"Space as squid is lurking ere wot ye…" began the goblin, but Harry interrupted.

"Well, *we* aren't from everywhere. We're from the planet Earth. And you've ruined our ship. How are we going to get home?"

"Can't you fix that windshield?" I asked the gnome. "We just want to turn off the runaway inertia-winder and go back to our people."

"Cancel dearth?" cried the goblin. "Ah, but merry it is this way, 'tis the finest fairy-ring that ever was."

"Prehistoric Stonehenge isn't so bad," put in the sprite. "We're having a good time there, too."

"And the time when the Sun goes nova and black hole," added the gnome. "I'm having fun *there*."

"Wait," protested Harry. "If you're really spread out all over space and time, then you must sometimes meet your past selves, right?"

"That's one way of looking at it."

"Wilst probe the savor?" asked the goblin. A twisting glob of flame, green-yellow-white, smacked into my leg. Too hot. I danced aside and the glob jelled into a copy of the goblin, a past and future self.

"What about time-paradoxes?" asked Harry. "What if your past self does something that it didn't do?"

"So what?"

"Contradictions are logically impossible," I explained. "A universe containing contradictions cannot exist."

"Glub gazork," said the mermaid. And then she did something very strange. She lifted up her arms and…didn't lift up her arms. At the same time. She winked/smiled at Harry/me. The sprite pinched my cheek with both hands. Yet at the same time she was tickling Harry.

"You see?" said the gnome. "Who are you to tell the universe what it can do."

"The existence of the universe is already a contradiction," amplified the sprite. "Something from nothing."

"Glub gazork na bog du smeepy flan."

"Slideways in the fog."

"Tally-ho!"

"Stop!" cried Harry. "I can't take any more."

The two goblins put their arms around each other's shoulders like Tweedledum and Tweedledee.

"First boy," sang the sprite.

"Nohow," snapped a goblin.

"Second boy."

"Contrariwise," cried the other.

"This is all very interesting," I interrupted. "But what's the point? I mean, will you fix our windshield or not?" The effects of the pixie-dust were beginning to wear off and I was getting cold.

"'In Xanadu did Kubla Khan / A stately pleasure dome decree,'" quoted the gnome, "'Where Alph the sacred river ran / Through caverns measureless to man / Down to a sunless sea.' This is the sunless sea, Joe Fletcher. We like it here. If we let you keep your rocket, you might come back. You might turn our inertia-winder off. Or your leader, the mad General Moritz, might mindlessly attack us."

"What if the sphere of influence keeps growing," I protested. "What if all the galaxy gets eaten up?"

"That won't happen," said the sprite. "The thing's already stopped growing. It's stable now. You mustn't disturb it."

Harry and I exchanged a glance. I could read his thoughts like neon signs: *Who cares about the inertia-winder anyway?* and *I like the sprite*, and *How are we going to get back?* and…

There was a sudden screaming. It seemed to come from a great distance. One of the goblins disappeared and the other began to jabber.

"Six furlongs 'tis and most foully beaked. The squid draws nigh to seek her prey and snaffle down these miserable victims every one!"

"The space-squid!" exclaimed the gnome.

"Oh my," said the sprite. "Already?"

"Aaauuugh!" roared the mermaid, rippling in sloppy panic.

"Don't worry, dear," said the sprite. "These men are going to kill the squid after it eats you, remember?"

"Aaaaaaarrrgh! Yubba mmpf wow!"

"What *squid*?" I demanded, but the question was suddenly superfluous. Looming up ahead was a huge, twisty, purplish form: the space-squid.

It looked much like an ocean-going giant squid. Its body was a pen-shaped pod with a fluke at one end. The business end of the body sported eight tentacles and two extra-long arms, arms some thirty meters long and with broad sucker-pads at the ends.

Watching us closely with its huge, intelligent eyes, the creature drew closer. Its method of propulsion was elegant: a flexible funnel sticking out of its body spewed a jet of glowing ions.

Before any of us could really react (or perhaps the elementals had no will to alter a known future), the long arms' sucker-pads had seized the mermaid. She gave a gurgling cry and was drawn away from us towards the space-squid's bunched and writhing wreath of tentacles. I could make out a great hooked beak in the center, a beak like a parrot's, and moments later this beak sank into the mermaid's watery flesh.

Her screams were overwhelming. Listening against my will, I felt the slash of the creature's beak; I felt the grip of its tooth-ringed suckers; I felt the horror of becoming food.

"Quick," shouted Harry. "Let out the superslime!"

Yes! The superslime! I zipped into our ship and opened up the toilet vent. At first there was no reaction, but when I stuck in my hand the slime came surging after.

"Get under the car," Harry told the elementals. "Go around behind it and wait till the squid tries to eat the superslime."

"We knew you'd do this," said the gnome happily. "You humans are so delightfully sequential."

The slime was thickly feeling for me, its glistening surface athrob. I led it out through the broken windshield, out into space. As the slime was vacuum-adapted, this caused it no pain. It flowed out, bulking ever larger. Now the space-squid's arms came reaching towards us again.

A quick, inertialess twist and flip put me safe under the car with the others. Using my pixie-dust ESP, I could pick up the feelings of both slime and squid. *EAT! GRAB! EAT! GRAB!*

The two met like long-lost lovers: tentacles seizing slime, slime engulfing tentacles. The hideous beak gobbled chunks of superslime while the slime's acids dissolved great sections of the squid. In a matter of minutes, nothing at all was left; they'd consumed each other totally.

"Like an electron meeting a positron," marveled Harry. "Now will you three fix our spaceship?"

"Even if they fix it, we're going to have a hard time with no slime for food and air," I worried at Harry.

"We *won't* fix it," said the gnome. "We don't want anyone coming back out here. What's more, Harry Gerber is going to *forget* how to build inertia-winders."

"Zap," said the sprite, tapping Harry's head with her wand. "That does it."

I felt a sudden horror of the void of space stretching out on all sides of us.

"Help us," I begged the goblin. "Isn't there a way for us to go back?"

"Go slideways."

"We don't know how."

"We can push you," said the gnome. "Where do you want to land?"

"And when?" added the sprite.

"At Nancy's sister's house in Virginia," I said.

"June twenty-fourth," said Harry. "Like it should be. Please send us back. I really don't remember how to build the inertia-winder. I promise."

The goblin danced, the sprite waved her wand, and the gnome put his hands on our backs and shoved. We tumbled head over heels slideways fro, and crashed down onto Nancy's sister's dining table.

Nancy was, on the whole, glad to see me. I moved into her bedroom, and they let Harry sleep on the couch. Our plan was to lie low for a few weeks. Everything would have been fine if Nancy's sister hadn't asked Harry to fix her TV set. But that's another story.

Note on "Inertia"

Written in Spring, 1982.
The Magazine of Fantasy and Science Fiction, January, 1983.

"Inertia" has one of the more complicated and interesting scientific premises I've used. I got the idea for it when hanging around with my Lynchburg friend, Mike Gambone, who did indeed have a peeling paint ceiling and an electric gyroscope in his basement. After I wrote "Inertia," Mike gave me the gyroscope, and I kept it with me until we left Lynchburg. The transreal identities of my Fletcher and Harry characters vary, but when I was writing "Inertia," I thought of Fletcher as Mike and Harry as me. Later I wrote a whole novel about these two characters, *Master of Space and Time*.

BRINGING IN THE SHEAVES

Religious fervor filled the air. Twenty or thirty rows of mutants ringed the torch-lit dais where Pally Love was holding forth. The dais was set up in the middle of what had once been a gymnasium. The gym had been part of a YMCA summer camp located on an island out in the Thomas River. The island was called Love Island now. It was the seat of Pally Love's Millennial Church of the Mystical Body of Christ. Pally was a doughy little man with a plain face. But what a voice!

"*They* call you gunjy mues." he shouted. "The Montviews, the Pigy-ears, the Arkers…*they* want to kill you, yes they do. They set themselves up as mighty ones, and they seek to trample you beneath their feet. They see fit to tamper with Lord God's new dispensation. Oh, sweet Jesus, what a time we're having here. *Oh*, what a time we are having on God's gray earth in these, the last days. And these *are* the last days, my brethren, make no mistake about it. I'd like you to pause…and look around, dear friends. Look at your neighbors, look at each other, and ask yourself one simple question. One simple little question. Does Pally love me? Can I let Pally into my heart? Can *Christ*, through Pally, bring me to a brighter day? Dear friends! If you say *yes*, if you say *yes Pally*, then you have received the greatest gift that man can receive. You have received the love that Christ has given *me* to give unto *you*. And this love…"

Meg Crash stood off to one side, watching Pally work out. Pretty good crowd of mues tonight, and most of them had brought something. The offerings were piled beside the dais: records, pieces of metal, liquor, car batteries, bags of food, even some tanks of gasoline. Pally was one of the only men in Killeville who managed to still drive a car. Pally Love, king of the gunjy mues. Not that Pally himself was a mutant. No way. Pally was fat and sleek and healthy as a prize stud-hog. That was part of his appeal to the mues: the fact that even though he was everything the mutants were not, Pally still loved them.

And why shouldn't Pally love the mues? They took good care of him. They took good care of Meg Crash, too, for that matter, not that

Meg could bring herself to really love them any more than Pally could. It was a rough job being Pally Love's head deaconess, especially rough ever since her brother Tab had left.

"Yes," Pally was shouting. "Come forward my darlings, drag your poor twisted bodies here and *merge* with the love of Christ, Christ the Son of God, the Christ whose body-cells are *us*. Join Him now, come *join Him* here and now!"

This was Meg's signal to start helping mues up onto the dais. A kid with no legs was already out in the aisle, so Meg helped that one first. The kid's head was all wrenched around to one side and his tongue was hanging out, but you could sense a keen intelligence in there anyway. One thing, mues weren't stupid, even if they did fall for Pally's line. Who could tell? Maybe he was helping them more than they were helping him. The whole giant leech business made Meg nervous…it was like the mues were using Pally to set the thing up.

"Flubba," said the kid, rolling an eye up at Meg. "Flubba geep."

His body tapered to a sort of point around the waist, but his arms were big and strong. She grabbed his hands and lugged him up to the dais. *That's it for you, gunjy mue*, Meg couldn't help thinking. *Time to become part of Pally's giant leech*. He was probably skrenning her thoughts but it didn't seem to bother him.

Two others were at the edge of the platform already, and Meg helped them up. She glanced out at the crowd…no one else was coming up tonight. The next thing was to undress these three. The boy with no legs wore only a long T-shirt, which came off easily enough. The next mue had a fairly normal body, dressed in jeans and T-shirt, but it didn't really have a head. There was just a sort of cavity-riddled hump between his shoulders. No telling which hole was for what. The jeans came off smoothly, but the T-shirt snagged on the ragged head-hump and Meg had to pull really hard. The last mue was perhaps female, very pale and wearing a night-gown. Stripping this off, Meg saw that its body was like a soft porcupine, with flesh-fingers sticking out all over. How did these things stay alive, anyway?

"Are you ready to join Christ's mystical body?" The veins in Pally's neck were standing out; his face was slick with sweat.

"*Weddy, Pawwy!*"

"Open the tabernacle, Reverend Crash!"

Meg walked over to the side of the gymnasium and threw open the door that led to the locker room. The giant leech lived in there, a sort of group-creature made up of the merged bodies of scores of mues. It wouldn't do to let the thing near you…not unless you were ready to join it for good. A sweet, wet smell drifted out of the locker room door.

Meg could hear a heavy slithering, a sound like wet canvas bags being dragged across the cement floor. Taking no chances, she hurried across to the other side of the gym.

The rest of the mues, the ones not ready to merge tonight, followed Meg across the gym floor, dragging and flippering themselves along as fast as they could. Meg stood protectively in front of them with an electric cattle prod in one hand. Pally used his car's generator to keep the prod charged up.

The gym floor was clear now, clear except for the little, round platform in the middle. Pally was still on the platform, still yelling, with the three naked mues at his feet.

"Can you *feel* it?"

"*Guh fee it.*"

"Are you *ready?*"

"*Bluh weddy!*"

"Do you *want* it?"

"*Wah wanna!*"

The tip of the giant leech poked out of the locker-room door now, and the crowd moaned with excitement. The giant leech ritual was still relatively new. Meg's twin brother Tab had invented it more or less by accident one night…the last night before he'd taken off for some other part of Killeville. Pally had always ended his services by having some mues get up on the dais with him. Once they were up there, he'd sprinkle water and oil on them and say they were blessed. But that last night, Tab, drunk and disgusted, had filled Pally's water and oil pitchers with concentrated battery acid.

Now the one thing about mutants was their fantastic ability to recover from wounds. If you stuck a knife in a mue and pulled the blade back out, the cut would just close up. They healed like dough, no matter what. To kill a mue you had to practically cut it in half. Their ability to regenerate tissue was one of their two big survival traits, the other survival feature being enhanced psi powers. They could read minds and see things far away. "Skrenning," they called it.

When Tab's acid had burned four mues' skins off that last night, the skins had taken a few minutes to grow back. But by then the flayed parts, where the mues touched, had already grown together. Presto, a group-creature, a newborn giant leech, a grex made of four mutants. Technically, a *grex* is a slug-like object formed by a group of slime-mold cells. Each of the cells has an independent existence, yet for purposes of reproduction they are able to join together, crawl about, and form a fruiting body. The combination of tissue regeneration and psi power enabled the mues to form just such a grex, a leech-like creature that lived and acted as a single organism.

Pally and Meg and been doing the ritual a few times a week now for several months. The giant grex held some sixty mues. Blessedly, it seemed satisfied with its life, though there was no telling what it thought about while resting in its locker room. One thing for sure, no one was going to investigate. Just throw a bunch of food in there once a day, and keep the door shut.

Now the huge group-mutant was slithering across the gymnasium floor, sliding closer and closer to the dais holding Pally and the three mues. There were eyes scattered all over the grex's surface, and there were bunches of hands here and there. Towards the front was a moist slit, the thing's tooth-filled mouth.

"The body of *Christ*," bellowed Pally. "The mystical body of Christ!" Not wanting to take the chance of being eaten or absorbed, he shouted a last blessing and hurried over to Meg's side.

"*Kwa*," cried the porcupine-flesh-fingers mutant on the dais, "*Bah Kwa!*" The one with no real head made a sort of high whistling sound and now the grex was at the edge of the dais.

Each time they did the giant leech ritual, the leech looked more developed, more integrated. At first it had been easy to pick out the individual members of the grex: they'd been like the constituent parts in one of those old paintings where an allegorical face, say "Harvest" or "Spring", is made up of the fruits and flowers of the season. The giant leech had started as "Radiation", made up of dozens of skungy freaks. But now the grex was fully integrated, all smoothed out.

A web of veins lay under the pink, wet skin. There were eyes all over…like raisins in a pie. The bottom of the thing was covered with hair. Everyone's scalp had migrated there to give the grex something to "walk" on. The hairs all pointed backwards for traction, like mohair on the bottom of a cross-country ski. There was a row of ears along the grex's median line, and bunches of hands both fore and aft.

Meg's stomach was hardened from two years' work with Pally and the mues, but the sight of the giant leech always made her retch. Its muscular symmetry was somehow worse than the ragged deformities of the mues. Meg leaned forward, gagging, hoping she wouldn't actually vomit.

"Stop it," muttered Pally, right at her side. "Control yourself, Meg."

The grex was on the dais now. It arched itself up over the three waiting mues like a croquet wicket. The long slit-mouth was only for feeding…the thing had another method for absorbing new members, a disgusting, vaguely sexual procedure. As the grex arched over the three naked mues, the one with no head began whistling louder, whistling like a tea-kettle. Perhaps it was in pain.

The hair on the grex's bottom was suddenly wet, wet and dripping. Some of the constituent mues' stomach tissues were down there to produce hydrochloric acid. The acid drizzled on the three naked forms, eating at their skins. Just as his face began to burn off, the kid with no legs shot Meg a hard glance, a look that said, "I know why you're sorry for me, but you'll never know why I'm sorry for you."

Once again, Meg wondered who was really using who. In a sense, she and Pally were the mues' servants...even though Pally thought it was the other way around. More than anything, Pally needed power and adulation. The normals, the people in the clans, thought Pally was a fool, a liar and a bully. Pally needed to have the mues worship him. The clanspeople didn't think about Pally very much. If they spoke of him at all, it was only with weary contempt. The clans didn't hate Pally, but Pally hated the clans. Oh, did he hate the clans! The less they cared about him, the more he hated them. Sometimes he would preach to the mues about leading a crusade, a holy war against the unbelievers. Until now it had all been just so much talk. But with the giant leech... or with *ten* leeches...

The skin was pretty well gone from the three mues now, and the grex began slowly to lower itself down on them. Its wet bottom-hair parted to expose a long red welt, a strip of naked tissue that the new mues could merge into. One of them cried out something like, "It is finished," and then it was. The great leech lay flat on the dais, calmly pulsing.

They all sang a hymn then, and the leech swayed to the beat. Standing well over to one side of the gym, Pally gave a closing harangue and sent the congregation on its way. Meg handed him the cattle prod and went to stand by the exit door, trying to get a few more donations from the mues as they left.

"Okay, Meg," called Pally as soon as the hall emptied. "Help me herd it back." Pally didn't like getting close to the big leech. He held the cattle prod out like someone holding a crucifix up to a vampire.

Just as Meg started towards Pally, the leech shuddered and slid off the dais, its long supple body flowing like water. Pally jerked convulsively, knocking loose the plug of the cord that led from cattle prod to his car outside. Moving faster than it ever had before, the leech flowed over the prod and put itself between Pally and the exit. Pally froze and shot Meg a desperate glance.

"Back to your room, guys," shouted Meg, putting some iron in her voice. She strode angrily towards the leech. "Turn around and go back in. We'll feed you double rations tomorrow."

The leech raised its front end up in a questioning way. Its broad mouth was slightly parted, revealing two carpets of teeth. Its eyes shifted from Pally to Meg and back again.

Meg took another step forward, and stamped her foot commandingly. "BACK! Go back to your room, and I'll get you a whole pig to eat tomorrow!"

Pally picked that moment to scream. His scream was lurid and juicy. The leech went for the sound. Moving so fast that it blurred, it darted over and clamped its mouth over Pally's head and shoulders. His screaming stopped almost right away. The leech humped itself up and bolted the rest of Pally down into its gullet. It was like watching a snake swallow a rat.

Meg ran outside, locking the door behind her. As soon as the door closed, she heard the heavy thud of the leech throwing itself against it. *SPLANG*. The door shuddered. *SPLANG*.

Pally's big car was out there running, still feeding juice into the cattle prod's disconnected cord. Cooter, a black guy Meg's age, was sitting behind the wheel.

"What happened?" he yelled.

"The leech got Pally," answered Meg, getting in the car. "We better get out of here."

The door gave then, and the leech came speeding out. Cooter peeled out, but not fast enough. The leech flowed up over the car and the engine stalled. With the mass of sixty mues, the leech had them pinned in place. For a moment nothing happened, and then the creature's hairy underside began sucking at the windows, trying to pop one loose.

"Don't open the door, Cooter, whatever you do."

Cooter unholstered his .45 and fired a few shots up through the car roof. Acid began drizzling in. Now the leech was thumping on the windows instead of sucking at them. A spiderweb of cracks spread across the windshield. Cooter leaned on the horn.

Suddenly the leech slid off them. All the noise had drawn the rest of Pally's private army out of their barracks. Five beefy guys that looked like good food. The leech wolfed down two of them, and the other three headed for the river. Cooter got the car restarted, and sped across the wood bridge that led from Pally's island to the shore.

"Stop here," said Meg. "Let's burn the bridge." Moving quickly, they got a drum of gasoline out of the car's trunk and slopped it all over the bridge's planks. They got back on shore and fired the bridge up.

The sudden *WHUMP* of ignition singed Meg's eyebrows and threw her onto her back. In the firelight, they could see the leech racing along the island's shore, looking for the other men or looking for a way to shore. It tried several times to go into the water, but each time the current forced it back.

"It's too heavy to swim," said Cooter. "And the water's too fast and deep for it to wade."

The great leech reared itself up by the shore and began silently swaying back and forth, jerky in the fire's light.

"It's worried," said Meg. "Good. It'll starve to death out there. Thank God it's not big enough to splash across."

They got in the car to drive on up the hill into the city. But the road was full of dark figures. Mues. The grex was telepathically calling all mues, and they were flocking down to the river. Meg and Cooter stopped the car and stared back towards the island.

One by one the mues launched themselves into the current and floundered over to Pally's island. One by one they went and joined the body of the great leech. In half and hour it would be two or three times as big—big enough to crawl across the river.

Cooter put the car into gear and began edging forward through the torrent of mues.

"Where to, Meg?"

"As far as the gas'll take us." She leaned across and checked the gauge. "Let's shoot for Richmond."

Cooter eased the car up the hill that led down to the river. The mues thinned out at the top, and he stepped on the accelerator.

Bye-bye, Killeville, goodbye.

Note on "Bringing in the Sheaves"

Written in Spring, 1982.
Asimov's Science Fiction, November, 1986.

In the summer of 1982 I started writing *Twinks*, the only science-fiction novel which I never finished. I often dream that there is yet another science-fiction novel which I wrote quickly and had published in a small, fugitive edition. The elusive extra dream book is something like *The Hobbit*, and my hurried editor is Craig Shaw Gardner, who was my editor at *Unearth*. Well, that's not

Twinks in any case, *Twinks* was a punk post-WWIII book with radiation mutants. "Bringing in the Sheaves" is the slightly altered third chapter of *Twinks*.

Pally Love is of course modeled on Lynchburg's then-famous TV evangelist Jerry Falwell, and the giant leech is his so-called Moral Majority movement.

THE JACK KEROUAC DISEMBODIED SCHOOL OF POETICS

I got the tape in Heidelberg. A witch named Karla gave it to me.

I met Karla at Diaconescu's apartment. Diaconescu, a Romanian, was interesting in his own right although, balding, he had a "rope-throw" hairdo. We played chess sometimes in his office, on a marble board with pre-Columbian pieces. I was supposed to be a mathematician and he was supposed to be a physicist. His fantasy was that I would help him develop a computer theory of perception. For my part, I was hoping he had dope. One Sunday I came for tea.

Lots of rolling papers around his place, and lots of what an American would take to be dope-art. But it was only cheap tobacco, only European avant-garde. Wine and tea, tea and Mozart. Oh man. Stuck inside of culture with the freak-out blues again.

Karla had a shiny face, like four foreheads clustered around her basic face-holes. All in all, it occurred to me, men have nine body-holes, women ten. I can't remember if we spoke German or English—English most likely. She was writing a doctoral dissertation on Jack Kerouac.

Jack K. My main man. Those dreary high-school years I read *On the Road*, then *Desolation Angels* and *Big Sur* in college, *Mexico City Blues* in grad-school and, finally, on the actual airplane to actual Heidelberg, I'd read *Tristessa*: "All of us trembling in our mortality boots, born to die, BORN TO DIE I could write it on the wall and on Walls all over America."

I asked Karla if she had weed. "Well, sure, I mean I will soon," and she gave me her address. Some kind of sex-angle in there too. "We'll talk about the beatniks."

I phoned a few times, and she'd never scored yet. At some point I rode my bike over to her apartment anyway. Going to visit a strange witchy girl alone was something I'd never done since marriage. Ringing Karla's bell felt like reaching in through a waterfall, like passing through an interface.

She had a scuzzy pad, two rooms on either side of a public hall. Coffee in her kitchen and cross the hall to look at books in her bedroom. Dope coming next week maybe.

Well, there we were, her on the bed with four foreheads and ten holes, me cross-legged on the floor looking at this and that. Heartbeat, a book by Carolyn Cassady, who married Neal and had Jack for a lover. Xeroxes of letters between Jack and Neal, traces of the long disintegration, both losing their raps, word by word, drink by pill, blank years winding down to boredom, blindness, O. D. death. A long sliding board I'm on too, oh man, oh man, sun in a meat-bag with nine holes.

Karla could see I was real depressed and in no way about to get on that bed with her, hole to hole, hole to hole. To cheer me up she brought out something else: a tape-cassette and a cassette-player. "This is Jack."

"Him doing a reading?"

"No, no. It's really him. This is a very special machine. You know how Neal was involved with the Edgar Cayce people?"

"Yeah, I guess so. I don't know." The tape-player *did* look funny. Instead of the speaker there was a sort of cone-shaped hole. And there were no controls, no fast-forward or reverse, just an on-off switch. I leaned to look at the little tape-cassette. There was a tape in there, but a very fine and silvery sort of tape. For some reason the case was etched all over in patterns like circuit diagrams.

"…right after death," Karla was saying in her low, hypnotic voice. "Jack's complete software is in here as well as his genetic code. There's only been a few of these made…it's more than just science, it's magic." She clicked the tape into the player. "Go on, Alvin, turn Jack on. He'll enjoy meeting you."

I felt dizzy and confused. How long had I been sitting here? How long had she been talking? I reached for the switch, then hesitated. This scene had gotten so unreal so fast. Maybe she'd drugged the coffee?

"Don't be afraid. Turn him on." Karla's voice seemed to come from a long way away. I clicked the switch.

The tape whined on its spools. I could smell something burning. A little puff of smoke floated up from the tape-player's cone, and then there was more smoke, lots of it. The thick plume writhed and folded back on itself, forming layer after layer of intricate haze.

The ghostly figure thickened and drew substance from the player's cone. At some point it was finished. Jack Kerouac was there standing over me with a puzzled frown.

Somehow Karla's coven had caught the Kerouac of 1958, a tough, greasy-faced mind-assassin still years away from his eventual bloat and blood-stomach death.

"I was afraid he'd look like a corpse," I murmured to Karla.

"Well, I feel like a corpse—say a dead horse—what happened?" said Kerouac. He walked over to the window and looked out. "Whooeee, this ain't even Cleveland or the golden tongues of flame. Got any hoo-cha?" He turned and glared at me with eyes that were dark vortices. Everything about him was right except the eyes.

"Do you have any brandy?" I asked Karla.

"No, but I could begin undressing."

Kerouac and I exchanged a glance of mutual understanding. "Look," I suggested, "Jack and I will go out for a bottle and be right back."

"Oh all right," Karla sighed. "But you have to carry the player with you. And *hang onto it!*"

The soul-player had a carrying strap. As I slung it over my shoulder, Kerouac staggered a bit. "Easy, Jackson," he cautioned.

"My name's Alvin, actually," I said.

"Al von Actually," muttered Kerouac. "Let's rip this joint."

We clattered down the stairs, his feet as loud as mine. Jack seemed a little surprised at the street-scene. I think it was his first time in Germany. I wasn't too well dressed, and with Jack's rumpled hair and filthy plaid shirt, we made a really scurvy pair of Americans. The passers-by, handsome and nicely dressed, gave us wide berth.

"We can get some brandy down here," I said, jerking my head. "At the candy store. Then let's go sit by the river."

"Twilight of the gods at River Lethe. In the groove, Al, in the gr-gr-oove." He seemed fairly uninterested in talking to me and spoke only in such distracted snatches, spoke like a man playing pinball and talking to a friend over his shoulder. Off and on I had the feeling that if the soul-player were turned off, I'd be the one to disappear. But he was the one with black whirlpools instead of eyes. Kerouac was the ghost, not me.

But not quite ghost either; his grip on the bottle was solid, his drinking was real, and so was mine, of course, as we passed the liter back and forth, sitting on the grassy meadow that slopes down the Neckar River. It was March 12th, basically cold, but with a good strong sun. I was comfortable in my old leather jacket and Jack, Jack was right there with me.

"I like this brandy," I said, feeling it.

"Bee-a-zooze. What do you want from me anyway, Al? Poke a stick in a corpse, get maggots come up on you. Taking a chance, Al, for whyever?"

"Well, I…you're my favorite writer. I always wanted to be you. Hitch-hike stoned and buy whores in Mexico. I missed all that, I mean I did it, but differently. I guess I want the next kids to like me like I like you."

"Lot of like, it's all nothing. Pain and death, more death and pain. It took me twenty years to kill myself. You?"

"I'm just starting. I figure if I trade some of the drinking off for weed, I can stretch it out longer. If I don't shoot myself. I can't believe you're really here. Jack Kerouac."

He drained the rest of the bottle and pitched it out into the river. A cloud was in front of the sun now and the water was grey. It was, all at once, hard to think of any good reason for living. At least I had a son.

"Look in my eyes," Jack was saying. "Look in there."

I didn't want to, but he leaned in front of me to stare. His face was hard and bitter. I realized I was playing way out of my league.

The eyes. Like I said before, they were spinning dark holes, empty sockets forever draining no place. I thought of Edgar Allen Poe's story about some guys caught for days in a maelstrom, and thinking this, I began to see small figures flailing in the dark spirals, Jack's remembered friends and loved ones maybe, or maybe other dead souls.

The whirlpools fused now to a single dark, huge cyclone, seemingly beneath me. I was scared to breathe, scared to fall, scared even that Kerouac himself might fall into his own eyes.

A dog ran up to us and the spell snapped. "More *trinken*," said Jack. "Go get another bottle, Al. I'll wait here."

"Okay."

"The player," rasped Jack. "You have to leave the soul-player here, too."

"Fine." I set it down on the ground.

"Out on first," said Kerouac. "The pick-off. Tell the bitch leave me alone." With that he snatched up the soul-player and ran down to the river. I let him go.

Well, I figured that was that. It looked like Kerouac turned himself off by carrying the soul-player into the river and shorting it out…which was fine with me. Meeting him hadn't been as much fun as I'd expected.

I didn't want to face Karla with the news I'd lost her machine, so I biked over to my office to phone her up. For some reason Diaconescu was there, waiting for me. I was glad to see a human face.

"What's happening, Ray?"

"Karla sent me. She saw you two from her window and phoned me to meet you here. You're really in trouble, Alvin."

"Look, it was her decision to lend me that machine. I'm sorry Kerouac threw it in the river and ruined it, but…"

"He didn't ruin the machine, Alvin. That's the point. The machine is waterproof."

"Then where'd he go? I saw him disappear."

"He went underwater, you idiot. To sneak off. It's the most dangerous thing possible to have a dead soul in control of its own player."

"Oh man. Are you sure you don't have any weed?"

I filled my knapsack up with beer bought at a newsstand—they sell alcohol everywhere in Germany—and pedaled on home. The seven-kilometer bike-ride from my University office to our apartment in the Foreign Scholars Guest House was usually a time when I got into my body and cooled out. But today my mind was boiling. The death and depression coming off Kerouac had been overwhelming. What had that been in his eyes there? The pit of hell, it'd seemed like, a vortex ring sort of, a long twisty thread running through each of his eyes, and whoever was outside in the air here was variable. The thought of *not* being able to die terrified me more than anything I'd ever heard of: for me death had always seemed like sweet oblivion, a back-door to the burrow, a certain escape. But now I had the feeling that the dark vortex was there, full of thin hare screamers, ineluctable whether or not a soul-player was around to reveal it at this level of reality. The only thing worse than death is eternal life.

Back home my wife, Cybele, was folding laundry on our bed. The baby was on the floor crying.

"Thank God you came back early, Alvin. I'm going nuts. You know what the superintendent told me? He said we can't put the dirty Pampers in the garbage, that it's unsanitary. We're supposed to tear them apart and flush the pieces, can you believe that? And he was so *rude*, all red-faced and puffing. Jesus I hate it here, can't you get us back to the States?"

"Cybele, you won't believe what happened today. I met Jack Kerouac. And now he's on the loose."

"I thought he died a long time ago."

"He did, he did. This witch-girl, Karla? I met her over at Diaconescu's?"

"The time you went without me. Left me home with the baby."

"Yeah, yeah. She conjured up his ghost somehow, and I was supposed to keep control of it; keep control of Kerouac's ghost, but we got drunk together and he freaked me out so much I let him get away."

"You're drunk now?"

"I don't know. Sort of. I bought some beer. You want one?"

"Sure. But you sound like you're off your rocker, Alvin. Why don't you just sit down and play with the baby. Maybe there's a cartoon on TV for you two."

Baby Joe was glad to see me. He held out his arms and opened up his mouth wide. I could see the two little teeth on his bottom gum. His diaper was soaked. I changed him, being careful to flush the paper part of the old diaper, as per request. As usual with the baby, I could forget I was alive, which is, after all, the only thing that makes life worth living.

I gave Cybele a beer, opened one for myself, and sat down in front of the TV with the baby. The evening programs were just starting—there's no daytime TV at all in Germany—and, thank God, *Zorro* was on. The month before they'd been showing old Marx brothers movies, dubbed of course, and now it was *Zorro*, an episode a day. Baby Joe liked it as much as I did.

But there was something fishy today, something very wrong. Zorro didn't look like he was supposed to. No cape, no sword, no pointy mustache. It was vortex-eyed Kerouac there in his place, sniggering and stumbling over his lines. Instead of slashing a "Z" on a wanted poster, he just spit on it. Instead of defending the waitress's honor during the big saloon brawl, he hopped over the bar and stole a fifth of tequila. When he bowed to the police-chief's daughter, he hiccupped and threw up. At the big masquerade ball he jumped on stage and started shouting about Death and Nothingness. When the peasants came to him for help, he asked them for marijuana. And the whole time he had the soul-player's strap slung over his shoulder.

After awhile I thought of calling Cybele.

"Look at this, baby! It's unbelievable. Kerouac's on TV instead of Zorro. I think he can see me, too. He keeps making faces."

Cybele came and stood next to me, tall and sexy. Instantly Kerouac disappeared from the screen, leaving old cape 'n' sword Zorro in his place. She smiled down at me kindly. "My Alvin. He trips out on acid but he still comes home on time. Just take care of Joe while I fix supper, honey. We're having pork stew with sauerkraut."

"But…"

"Are you so far gone you don't remember taking it? The Black-Star that Dennis DeMentis sent you last week. I saw you put it in your knapsack this morning. You can't fool me, Alvin."

"But…"

She disappeared into our tiny kitchen and Kerouac reappeared on the screen, elbowing past the horses and soldiers to press his face right up to it.

"Hey, Al," said the TV's speaker in Kerouac's voice. "You're going crazy croozy whack-a-doozy."

"Cybele! Come here!"

She came running out of the kitchen, and this time Kerouac wasn't fast enough; she saw him staring out at us like some giant goldfish. He started to withdraw, then changed his mind.

"Are you Al's old lady love do hop his heart on?"

"Really, Cybele," I whispered. "My story's true. That Black-Star's in my desk at school and Kerouac's ghost's inside our TV."

"A beer for blear, dear." The screen wobbled like Jello and Kerouac wriggled out into our living room. He stank of dead fish. In one hand he held that stolen bottle of tequila, and his other hand cradled the soul-player.

"Just don't look in his eyes," I cautioned Cybele. Baby Joe started crying.

"Be pope, ti Josie," crooned Jack. "Dad's in a castle, Ma's wearing a shell, nothing's the matter, black Jack's here from Hell."

I'd only had one sip of my beer, so I just handed it over to him. "Isn't there any way out?" I asked him. "Any way into Nothingness?"

Just then someone started pounding on our door. Cybele went to open it, walking backwards so she could keep an eye on Kerouac. He took a hit of tequila, a pull of beer, and lit one of the reefers the peasants had given him.

"*Black-jack* means *sap*," he said. "That's me."

It was Karla at the door. Karla and Ray Diaconescu. Before Jack could do anything, they'd run across the room and grabbed him. He was clumsy from all the booze, and Karla was able to wrest the soul-player away from him.

"Turn it off now, Alvin," she urged. "You turned it on and you have to be the one to turn it off. It only worked because you know Jack so well."

"How about it, Jack?" I looked over at him. His eyes were swirling worse than ever. You could almost feel a breeze from air rushing into them.

He gave a tight smile and passed me his reefer. "Bee-a-zlast on, brother. They call this Germany? I call it the Land of Nod. Friar Tuck awaits her shadowy pleasure. The cactus-shapes of nowhere night."

"Do you want me to turn it off or what? I can't give the player back to you. You'll drive me nuts. But anything else, man, I mean I know your pain."

Suddenly he threw an arm around my neck and dragged me up against him. Karla, still holding the soul-player, gasped and took a step back. Kerouac's voice was harsh in my ear.

"I knew a guy who died. That's what Corso says about me now. Only I didn't. He's keeping me in the whirlpool, you are. Let me in, Al, carry me." I tried to pull back, repelled by his closeness, his smell, but the crook of his arm held my neck like a vise. He was still talking. "Let me in your eyes, man, and I'll keep quiet till you crack up. I'll help you write. And you'll end up in the whirly dark, too. Sweet and low from the foggy dew, corrupting the boys from Kentucky ham-spread dope-rush street sweets."

He drew back then, and we stared into each other's eyes; and I saw the thin hare screamers in the black pit same as before, only this time I jumped in, but really it jumped in me. All at once Jack was gone. I turned Karla's machine off for her, saw her and Ray to the door, then had supper with Cybele and Baby Joe. And that's how I became a writer.

Note on "The Jack Kerouac Disembodied School of Poetics"

Written in Spring, 1982.
New Blood, July, 1982.

In 1982, the literary arm of the Naropa Institute in Boulder, Colorado, was directed by Allen Ginsberg and Anne Waldman, and was indeed called The Jack Kerouac Disembodied School of Poetics.

I did meet a woman in Germany who gave me a Xerox of Neal Cassady's and Jack Kerouac's letters to each other. Kerouac is, of course, one of my all-time favorite writers, not so much for the sustained narrative arc of one novel, but rather for his sensibility and for the extreme beauty and originality of his language and phrasing.

MESSAGE FOUND IN A COPY OF FLATLAND

The story which appears below is purported to be Robert Ackley's first-person account of his strange disappearance. I am not quite sure if the account is really true…I rather hope, for Ackley's sake, that it is not.

I obtained the typescript of this story in a roundabout way. My friend, Gregory Gibson, was in London last year, looking for rare books. A dealer in Cheapside Street showed Gibson a copy of an early edition of Edwin Abbott's 1884 fiction, Flatland. The copy Gibson saw was remarkable for the fact that someone had handwritten a whole story in the margins of the book's pages. The dealer told Gibson that the volume was brought in by a cook's helper, who had found the book in the basement of a Pakistani restaurant where he once worked.

Gibson could not afford the book's very steep purchase price, but he did obtain the dealer's permission to copy out the story written in the volume's margins. Here, without further ado, it is: the singular adventure of Robert Ackley.

All my attempts to get back through the tunnel have proven fruitless. It will be necessary for me to move on and seek another way out. Before departing, however, I will write out an account of my adventures thus far.

Until last year I had always believed Edwin Abbott's *Flatland* to be a work of fiction. Now I know better. Flatland is real. I can look up and see it as I write.

For those of my readers familiar with the book in whose margins I write, this will be startling news: for *Flatland* tells the adventures of A Square, a two-dimensional being living in a two-dimensional world. How, you may ask, could such a filmy world really exist? How could there be intelligent creatures with length and width, yet without thickness? If Flatland is real, then why am I the only living man who has touched it? Patience, dear readers. All this, and much more, will be revealed.

The scientific justification for Flatland is that it helps us better to understand the fourth dimension. "The fourth dimension" is a concept peculiarly linked to the late nineteenth century. In those years, mathematicians had just laid the foundations for a comprehensive theory of higher-dimensional space. Physicists were beginning to work with the notion of four-dimensional spacetime. Philosophers were using the idea of a fourth dimension to solve some of their oldest riddles. And mediums throughout Europe were coming to the conclusion that the spirits of the dead consist of four-dimensional ectoplasm. There was an immense popular interest in the fourth dimension, and *Flatland*, subtitled, "A Romance of Many Dimensions," was an immediate success.

Abbott's method was to describe a two-dimensional square's difficulties in imagining a third dimension of space. As we read of A Square's struggles, we become better able to understand our own difficulties in imagining a fourth dimension. The fourth dimension is to us what the third dimension is to the Flatlanders.

This powerful analogy is the rarest of things: a truly new idea. I often used to ask myself where Abbott might have gotten such an idea. When Gray University granted me my sabbatical last year, I determined to go to London and look through Abbott's papers and publications. Could *Flatland* have been inspired by A. F. Möbius's *Barycentric Calculus* of 1827? Might Abbott have corresponded with C. H. Hinton, eccentric author of the 1880 essay, "What Is The Fourth Dimension?" Or is *Flatland* nothing more than the inspired reworking of certain ideas in Plato's *Republic*?

Abbott wrote many other books in his lifetime, all crashingly dull: *How to Parse, The Kernel and the Husk—Letters on Spiritual Christianity, English Lessons for English People, A Shakespearian Grammar, Parables for Children*, and so on. Except for *Flatland*, all of Abbott's books are just what one would expect from a Victorian clergyman, headmaster of the City of London School. Where did Abbott find his inspiration for *Flatland*? The answer is stranger than I could ever have imagined.

It was an unnaturally hot day in July. The London papers were full of stories about the heat-wave. One man reported that three golf-balls had exploded in the heat of his parked car. All the blackboards in a local school had cracked. Numerous pigeons had died and fallen to the sidewalks. I finished my greasy breakfast and set forth from my hotel, an unprepossessing structure not far from St. Paul's Cathedral.

My plan for the day was to visit the site of the old City of London School on Cheapside at Milk Street. Abbott attended the school himself, and then returned as headmaster for the years 1865-1889. Under Abbott's leadership the school moved to a new building in 1882, but I had a feeling that some valuable clue to his psychology might still be found in the older building.

To my disappointment, nothing of the old building remained…at least nothing that I could see. Much of Cheapside was destroyed during the Blitz. Flimsy concrete and metal structures have replaced what stood there before. I came to a halt at the corner of Cheapside and Milk, utterly discouraged.

Sweat trickled down my sides. A red double-decker labored past, fouling the heavy air with its exhaust. Ugly, alien music drifted out of the little food-shops. I was jostled by men and women of every caste and color: masses of people, hot and impatient, inescapable as the flow of time.

I pushed into a wretched Pakistani snack-bar and ordered a beer. They had none. I settled for a Coke. I tried to imagine Edwin Abbott walking through this dingy space one hundred years ago.

The girl behind the counter handed me my Coke. Her skin had a fine coppery color, and her lips were like chocolate ice cream. She didn't smile, but neither did she frown. Desperate with loneliness and disorientation, I struck up a conversation.

"Have you been here long?"

"I was born in London." Her impeccable accent came as a rebuke. "My father owns this shop now for five years."

"Did you know I came all the way from America just to visit this shop?"

She laughed and looked away. A girl in a big city learns to ignore madmen.

"No, no," I insisted. "It's really true. Look…" I took out my dog-eared first edition of *Flatland*, this very copy in whose margins I now write. "The man who wrote this book was headmaster of a school that stood near this spot."

"What school?"

"The City School of London. They moved it to the Victoria Embankment in 1882."

"Then you should go there. Here we have only food." For some reason the sight of Abbot's book had caused her cheeks to flush an even darker hue.

"I'll save that trip for another day. Don't you want to know what the book is about?"

"I do know. It is about flat creatures who slide around in a plane."

The readiness of her response astonished me. But before I could pose another question, the girl had turned to serve another customer, a turbaned Sikh with a pockmarked face. I scanned the menu, looking for something else to order.

"Could I have some of the spicy meatballs, please?"

"Certainly."

"What's your name?"

"Deela."

She failed to ask mine, so I volunteered the information. "I'm Bob. Professor Robert Ackley of Gray University."

"And what do you profess?" She set the plate of meatballs down with an encouraging click.

"Mathematics. I study the fourth dimension, just as Abbott did. Have you really read *Flatland*?"

Deela glanced down the counter, as if fearful of being overheard. "I have not *read* it. I…"

The Sikh interrupted then, calling for butter on his rice. I sampled one of the meatballs. It was hot and dry as desert sand.

"Could I have another Coke, please?"

"Are you rich?" Deela whispered unexpectedly.

Was she hoping for a date with me? Well, why not? This was the longest conversation I'd had with anyone since coming to London. "I'm well-off," I said, hoping to make myself attractive. "I have a good position, and I am unmarried. Would you like to have dinner with me?"

This proposal seemed to surprise Deela. She covered her mouth with one hand and burst into high laughter. Admittedly I am no ladies' man, but this really seemed too rude to bear. I put away my book and rose to my feet.

"What do I owe you?"

"I'm sorry I laughed, Robert. You surprised me. Perhaps I will have dinner with you someday." She lowered her voice and leaned closer. "Downstairs here there is something you should see. I was hoping that you might pay to see it."

It seemed very hot and close in this little restaurant. The inclination of the Sikh's turban indicated that he was listening to our conversation. I had made a fool of myself. It was time to go. Stiffly I paid the bill and left. Only when I stepped out on the street and looked at my change did I realize that Deela had given me a note.

Robert—

Flatland is in the basement of our shop. Come back at closing time and I will show it to you. Please bring one hundred pounds. My father is ill.

Deela.

I turned and started back into the shop. But Deela made a worried face and placed her fingers on her lips. Very well, I could wait. Closing time, I noted, was ten P. M.

I spent the rest of the day in the British Museum, ferreting out obscure books on the fourth dimension. For the first time I was able to hold in my hands a copy of J. K. F. Zöllner's 1878 book, *Transcendental Physics*. Here I read how a spirit from hyperspace would be able to enter a closed room by coming in, not through walls or ceiling, but through the "side" of the room lying open to the fourth dimension.

Four-dimensional spirits...long sought, but never found! Smiling a bit at Zöllner's gullibility, I set his book down and reread Deela's note. *Flatland is in the basement of our shop.* What could she mean by this? Had they perhaps found Abbott's original manuscript in the ruined foundations of the old City School? Or did she mean something more literal, something more incredible, something more bizarre than spirits from the fourth dimension?

The whole time in the library, I had the feeling that someone was watching me. When I stepped back onto the street, I realized that I was indeed being followed. It was the Sikh, his obstinate turban always half a block behind me. Finally I lost him by going into a movie theater, leaving by the rear exit, and dashing into the nearest pub.

I passed a bland few hours there, drinking the warm beer and eating the stodgy food. Finally it was ten P. M.

Deela was waiting for me in the darkened shop. She let me in and locked the door behind me.

"Did you bring the money?"

The empty shop felt very private. Deela's breath was spicy and close. What had I really come for?

"Flatland," stated Deela, "is in the basement. Did you bring the money?"

I gave her a fifty-pound note. She flattened it out and held it up to examine it by the street-light. Suddenly there was a rapping on the door. The Sikh!

"Quick!" Deela took me by the arm and rushed me behind the counter and down a narrow hallway. "Down there," she said, indicating a door. "I'll get rid of him." She trotted back out to the front of the shop.

Breathless with fear and excitement, I opened the shabby door and stepped down onto the dark stairs.

The door swung closed behind me, muffling the sound of Deela's voice. She was arguing with the Sikh, though without letting him in. I moved my head this way and that, trying to make out what lay in the basement. Deela's faint voice grew shriller. There was what looked like a ball of light floating at the foot of the stairs. An oddly patterned ball of light some three feet across. I went down a few more steps to have a closer look. The thing was sort of like a huge lens, a lens looking onto…

Just then there came the sound of shattering glass. The Sikh had smashed his way in! The clangor of the shop's burglar alarm drowned out Deela's wild screams. Footsteps pounded close by and the door at the head of the stairs flew open.

"Come back up, Professor Ackley," called the Sikh. His voice was high and desperate. "You are in great danger."

But I couldn't tear myself away from the glowing sphere. It appeared to be an Einstein-Rosen bridge, a space-tunnel leading into another universe. The other universe seemed to contain only one thing: an endless glowing plane filled with moving forms. Flatland.

The Sikh came clattering down the stairs. My legs made a decision. I leaped forward, through the space-tunnel and into another world.

I landed on all fours…there was a sort of floor about a yard below the plane of Flatland. When I stood up, it was as if I were standing waist-deep in an endless, shiny lake. My fall through the Flatlanders' space had smashed up one of their houses. Several of them were nosing at my waist, wondering what I was. To my surprise, I could feel their touch quite distinctly. They seemed to have a thickness of several millimeters.

The mouth of the space-tunnel was right overhead, a dark sphere framing the Sikh's excited little face. He reached down as if to grab me. I quickly squatted down beneath the plane of Flatland and crawled away across the firm, smooth floor. The hazy, bright space shimmered overhead like an endless soap-film, effectively shielding me from the Sikh.

I could hear the sound of more footsteps on the stairs. Deela? There were cries, a gunshot, and then silence. I poked my head back up, being careful not to bump any Flatlanders. The dark opening of the space-tunnel was empty. I was safe, safe in Flatland. I rose up to my full height and surveyed the region around me.

I was standing in the middle of a "street," that is to say, in the middle of a clear path lined with Flatland houses on either side. The houses had the form of large squares and rectangles, three to five feet on a side. The Flatlanders themselves were as Abbott has described them: women are short Lines with a bright eye at one end, the soldiers are very sharp isosceles Triangles, and there are Squares, Pentagons and other Polygons as well. The adults are, on the average, about twelve inches across.

The buildings that lined my street bore signs in the form of strings of colored dots along their outer walls. To my right was the house of a childless Hexagon and his wife. To my left was the home of an equilateral

Triangle, proud father of three little Squares. The Triangle's door, a hinged line segment, stood ajar. One of his children, who had been playing in the street, sped inside, frightened by my appearance. The plane of Flatland cut me at the waist and arms, giving me the appearance of a large blob flanked by two smaller blobs—a weird and uncanny spectacle, to be sure.

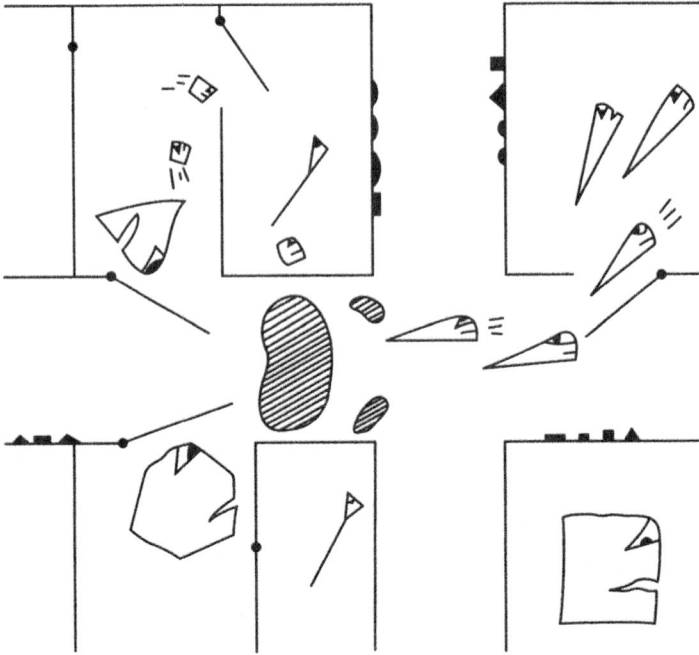

Now the Triangle stuck his eye out of his door to study me. I could feel his excited voice vibrating the space touching my waist. Flatland seemed to made of a sort of jelly, perhaps one-sixteenth of an inch thick.

Suddenly I heard Deela calling to me. I looked back at the dark mouth of the tunnel, floating about eight feet above the mysterious ground on which I stood. I walked towards it, staying in the middle of the street. The little line-segment doors slammed as I walked past, and I could look down at the Flatlanders cowering in their homes.

I stopped under the tunnel's mouth and looked up at Deela. She was holding a coiled-up rope-ladder.

"Do you want to come out now, Robert?" There was something cold and unpleasant about her voice.

"What happened to the Sikh?"

"He will not bother us again. How much money do you have with you?"

I recalled that so far I had only paid her half of the hundred pounds. "Don't worry, I'll give you the rest of the money." But how could she even think of money with a wonder like this to…

I felt a sharp pain in the small of my back, then another. I whirled around to see a platoon of two dozen Flatland soldiers bearing down on me. Two of them had stuck into my back like knives. I wrenched them out, lifted them free of their space, and threw them into the next block. I was bleeding! Blade-thick and tough-skinned, these soldiers were a real threat. One by one, I picked them up by their blunt ends and set them down inside the nearest building. I kept them locked in by propping my side against the door.

"If you give me all your money, Robert," said Deela, "then I will lower this rope-ladder."

It was then that I finally grasped the desperation of my situation. Barring Deela's help, there was no possible way for me to get up to the mouth of the tunnel. And Deela would not help unless I handed over all my cash…some three hundred pounds. The Sikh, whom I had mistakenly thought of as enemy, had been trying to save me from Deela's trap!

"Come on," she said. "I don't have all night."

There were some more soldiers coming down the street after me. I reached back to feel my wounds. My hand came away wet with blood. It was interesting here, but it was clearly time to leave.

"Very well, you nasty little thief. Here is all the money I have. Three hundred pounds. The police, I assure you, will hear of this." I drew the bills out and held them up to the tunnel-mouth. Deela reached through, snatched the money, and then disappeared. The new troop of soldiers was almost upon me.

"Hurry!" I shouted. "Hurry up with the ladder! I need medical attention!" Moving quickly, I scooped up the soldiers as they came. One got past my hand and stabbed me in the stomach. I grew angry, and dealt with the remaining soldiers by poking out their hearts.

When I was free to look up at the tunnel-mouth again. I saw a sight to chill the blood. I was the Sikh, eyes glazed in death, his arms dangling down towards me. I realized that Deela had shot him. I grabbed one of his hands and pulled, hoping to lift myself up into the tunnel. But the corpse slid down, crashed through Flatland, and thudded onto the floor at my feet.

"Deela!" I screamed. "For the love of God!"

Her face appeared again…but she was no longer holding the rope-ladder. In its stead she held a pistol. Of course it would not do to set me free. I would make difficulties. With my body already safe in this dimensional oubliette, it would be nonsense to set me free. Deela aimed her gun.

As before, I ducked below Flatland's opalescent surface and crawled for dear life. Deela didn't even bother shooting.

"Goodbye, Robert," I heard her calling. "Stay away from the tunnel or else!" This was followed by her laughter, her footsteps, the slamming of the cellar door, and then silence.

That was two days ago. My wounds have healed. The Sikh has grown stiff. I made several repellent efforts to use his corpse as a ladder or grappling-hook, but to no avail. The tunnel-mouth is too high, and I am constantly distracted by the attacks of the isosceles Triangles.

But my situation is not entirely desperate. The Flatlanders are, I have learned, edible, with a taste something like very moist smoked salmon. It takes quite a few of them to make a meal, but they are plentiful, and they are easy to catch. No matter how tightly they lock their doors, they never know when the five globs of my fingers will appear like Zöllner's spirits to snatch them away.

I have filled the margins of my beloved old *Flatland* now. It is time to move on. Somewhere there may be another tunnel. Before leaving, I will throw this message up through the tunnel-mouth. It will lie beneath the basement stairs, and someday someone will find it.

Farewell, reader, and do not pity me. I was but a poor laborer in the vineyard of knowledge—and now I have become the Lord of Flatland.

Note on "Message Found in a Copy of Flatland"

Written in Summer, 1982.
The 57th Franz Kafka, Ace Books, 1983.

My friend and fellow fourth-dimension maven Thomas Banchoff of Brown University traveled to London one summer to dig up information about Edwin Abbott. This story is my concept of what happened to him, although somehow Banchoff (or someone who says he is Banchoff) seems to have made it back to the States.

PLASTIC LETTERS

"Someone who, dreaming, says 'I am dreaming,' even if he speaks audibly in doing so, is no more right than if he said in his dream 'it is raining,' while it was in fact raining. Even if his dream were actually connected with the noise of the rain." — Ludwig Wittgenstein, On Certainty.

Wittgenstein wrote these words two days before his death on April 29, 1951. He died of cancer. I see my typewriter, its plastic keys. I press the plastic letters and write these words. Am I a mumbling dreamer? And you?

Before I came here I lived in a UFO, a spaceship called Star Nine. My "brother" and I were set down in the suburbs of Louisville, Kentucky. We attended private schools. He went into the wood business, and I became a science-fiction writer.

I first remembered about Star Nine one night in 1964 after drinking a fifth of scotch. I told my brother about it and started choking him when he didn't believe me. But the next day he admitted I was right.

The way Star Nine sends a person down is to aim a green laserbeam. The beam shudders like, and there's a new fake Earthling. When we first got here, I was a five-year-old boy, and my brother was ten. It was in a cow pasture with a barbed-wire fence. We started crying and ran home. Star Nine had beamed memories to our "parents," a childless couple just moving into town.

I am free to reveal all this because by the time you read this "I" will be gone. There are enough of us now to accomplish our task, the theft of your reality. You will dream on as before, there will be stimuli to mutter about, but the world will be absent. It is as if a farmer were to catch and make off with the rain of Wittgenstein's dreamer. So that the dreamer will not be disturbed, the farmer sets up, in the now-empty night, a cassette-player with a tape of "Rain." Splish-splash, gut-buckets of Iowa rain, and the corn rustling, all magnetic signals on a plastic tape. Miles off are Tenniel's "mome raths" (us), orange pigs with bunches of pink worms for tails, we are the farmer, we are the rain without stopping. I eye "I," to eat the exhale/inhale, day/night, summer/winter, parent/child, one/many, the broken clock all gone.

Note on "Plastic Letters"

Written in November, 1982.
Live From the Stagger Café, #5, Summer, 1987.

"Plastic Letters" is a quick vision that was inspired by a dream. It also represents the starting seed for my novel, *The Secret of Life*, in which the teenage hero learns that he is a saucer alien. *Live From the Stagger Café* was a little zine edited by Luke McGuff in Minneapolis. The story title is taken from the name of an album by the group Blondie.

Monument to the Third International

For Henry and Diana Vaughan.

A draft plucked at Luanne Carrandine's blonde hair. Visions of claws, shadows of deliverance.

"You see?" her salesgirl was saying. "There's a hole in the floor, Mrs. Carrandine. Thank goodness no one fell in!"

A thick mist was drifting up, mist thick and slow as ketchup. A tendril snaked up to encircle Luanne's calf. She caught a whiff of the stuff then, and tiny voices seemed to call from every corner. Luanne shook her head and widened her eyes. *Come on*, she thought to herself, *this is Monday morning, Luanne baby, it's get-it-together time*. The facts, please.

The facts: There is a big, round hole in the floor of the dressing-room of Luanne and Garvey Carrandine's dress-shop. The hole is oozing smoke. *Bummer*. Rain-gray post-holiday Monday, down there in Killeville, Virginia, man, and the goddamned store is like falling apart. *At least I don't have hair on my face.*

The mist gave off an electric ozone charge. Breathing it, Luanne felt good, tight, strong, tingly.

"Is that the basement?" her salesgirl inquired

"There isn't any basement," said Luanne. "None of the plaza stores have basements, baby. There's just a concrete slab, and garbage under that. Who found the hole? Have you called the fire-department?"

"I—I found it, but I haven't called. I wasn't sure who—do you think there's been a robbery?"

Luanne stepped back from the hole and looked around. Tops and bottoms, silk and fuzz. "I don't know what the hell anyone could have stolen, Kathy. There's nothing here worth taking—just ask our customers." She was sick of running the clothes-store, sick of making her money a dollar at a time.

The mist had her feeling reckless. "Maybe it's a sinkhole like in Florida. Maybe the whole damned store will fall in, and Garvey and I can collect insurance. I hope so, Kathy, I really do."

Luanne emphasized her point by jumping up and down. She was a small blonde with bold eyes and a pert mouth. Bold and round, pert and lipsticked. She was early thirties going on Sweet Sixteen.

Kathy watched her boss jump up and down. The jumps were surprisingly high. "What shall I do, Mrs. Carrandine?"

"Go on home, honey. I'll get Garvey and the cops and the insurance men over here. We'll stay closed for two days and then have a Fire Sale. A Sinkhole Special." She smiled, stopped jumping, and made her way to the phone. "Just run along, Kathy. We'll pay you for today, and tomorrow you can come in and help me mark down some of the tags." Kathy left.

The phone was behind the counter, over on one side with the store-room and the dressing-room. There was mist, and Luanne felt funny again as she started dialing.

"What's up?" asked Garvey's voice. He dealt with their wholesalers from an office downtown.

"Honey, there's a big hole in the dressing-room floor. It's like a manhole."

"Uh, how deep is it?" Garvey was not an excitable man.

"I don't know. But...I'm starting to see things. Hurry."

When Garvey reached the store, he found Luanne at her desk, drawing pictures with her youngest daughter's colored pencils. The whole floor was covered with mist, a slow gray carpet of magic gas. Some of the stuff drifted up to meet Garvey's nose. He inhaled and saw the shop fill with lazy blobs of color. It felt like skin-diving amidst tropical fish.

"God loves me, Garvey, He's sent me a vision. Just look at *that* one—the teal scroll with red stars printed on it? Can you see that as a blouse?"

"Uh..." Garvey *could* see it, sort of.

"Yes, Garvey, we can do it! We'll collect insurance and sell the store and start making our own line of clothes. Luanne's Luxuries, can you dig it?" She breathed deeply and looked around, eyes ablaze. "All these new images, it's just fantastic!"

Garvey was a tall, slim man with a perpetually unfocused air. He regarded his wife for a moment, then went to look at the hole in the dressing-room floor. The way the mist was pouring out, it was hard to see in. He wondered if the smoke might be dangerous to breathe, then decided not. He felt wonderful.

"Is there a flashlight, Luanne?"

"By the fuse-box, Gar."

He got the light and shone it at the hole. He could make out the sides—the hole was a slanting shaft some three feet across—but the bottom was all fogged up. He went out to the front counter and found a short length of leftover Christmas ribbon.

Luanne was too busy with her new fashion-drawings to look up.

"I'm going to lower this down into the hole," announced Garvey as he tied the ribbon's end around the flashlight. His skin was tingling, and colors were everywhere. He kept thinking he heard voices. "Luanne? Do you feel as weird as I do?"

She laughed softly and filled in some green cross-hatching. "It's the mist, man, it's giving me teachings. We've got the burning bush right here with us."

For the first time, Garvey noticed that rain was coming through the dressing-room ceiling. There was a big hole in the ceiling right over the hole in the floor.

"Hey Luanne, I think it's a meteorite!"

"Straight from heaven, baby. Luanne's Leisure Luxuries!"

Garvey crouched down by the hole and lowered away. The light swung this way and that, a pale blob in the mist. Three feet, six—he was out of ribbon and the bottom was still out of reach. He took a deep breath and reached way down in the hole, hoping to find out how deep it was.

Just then a bit of the floor's concrete crumbled. Garvey fell head first into the fog-shrouded hole.

Time passed. Slowly the mist dissipated. At some point Luanne's visionary state wore off. She looked down at the drawings she'd been working on and wondered what they meant. It was as if she had been drugged for the last hour or so, drugged full and happy. Some of her drawings were of clothes, but others were of buildings. One of the buildings was particularly striking: a vast conical lattice surrounded by two twining spirals of metal. Mounted inside it were four huge glass structures: a cube, a pyramid, a cylinder and a half-sphere.

But where was Garvey? Hadn't he been here a little while ago?

Luanne hurried through her silent store. There was the hole, and there, three feet down, were the soles of poor Garvey's shoes! He was stuck in there upside down! The mist had poisoned him—he had passed out and fallen in!

Luanne seized Garvey's feet and pulled. Normally she couldn't have budged him, but something filled her with superstrength. Garvey bumped up out of the hole like a lumpy carrot. Luanne laid him out on his back and began blowing kisses into his slack mouth. He breathed back, twitched, opened his eyes.

"Garvey? Are you all right?"

"*Da*," said Garvey, his voice strangely gruff. "*Pamiatnik III Internatsionala prokety* Vladimir Tatlin." His eyes closed and he went slack again.

Luanne picked him up bodily and carried him away from the awful hole. With fumbling fingers she dialed the Rescue Squad.

Garvey woke to the sound of his wife's voice. They were each in a single bed—hospital beds. She was sitting up and talking on the phone.

"...responsibility. The insurance won't pay, and we've got to sue someone. Isn't there a World Court? The comet smashed into our store, man. We're in a decontamination room and they want to bulldoze our store under. What the hell is a lawyer for, Sidney? Stay on it, and call back. Goodbye."

"Uh, Luanne..."

"Garvey! Baby! These idiots think we glow in the dark, man, we're supposed to stay locked up for ten days! The store's screwed and nobody wants to take the blame. I say it's our government's fault—I mean they're the ones who egg the Russians on."

"The Russians?"

"Those stupid Commies," Luanne fumed. "It was some kind of space-probe they sent up to intercept that new comet they discovered. Lenin's Comet? These goddamned spastic Reds wanted to plant a time-capsule of propaganda on the comet and bring part of it back."

"Part of Lenin's Comet?"

"That's what crashed in our store. The probe smashed the comet all to bits. Our store got hit by about six tons of frozen comet. The stuff boiled off into gas and that's what flipped us out, Garvey, that's where the visions came from."

For someone in a hospital bed, Luanne looked surprisingly well. Her cheeks were flushed with excitement, and her round eyes were bright with plans.

"They want us on the *Today* show, Gar, but the doctors won't let us out. There's got to be big money in this somewhere. It's just too bizarre. Drugged-out on space-gas!"

"Was I in the hole very long?"

"I was sort of wasted, baby, so I'm not too sure. Half an hour? What was it like?"

"I..."

Garvey was interrupted by a voice from the TV screen. It was a fat doctor, talking to them on closed-circuit. "Hello, Mr. Carrandine, I'm glad to see you've snapped out of it."

"Let us out!" shouted Luanne. "What about our children?"

"Your children will be taken care of by a policewoman, Mrs. Carrandine. Surely you must understand that your quarantine will last until we have finished our batteries of tests. The material you and your husband inhaled is unlike any other substance known to science. My colleagues tell me that is must come from a different galaxy, where the weak-force is…"

"CRAP!" Luanne threw her sheet over the TV screen and camera. "Come on, Garvey, help me figure out how we can get out of here and cash in on this!"

"Did you hear that? They'll put a policewoman in our house? Jesus. How long have we been here?"

"It's just noon. The kids are still in school. Do you feel all right now, baby?"

Garvey got out of his bed and stretched. He felt good, very good indeed. It would be nice to get some lunch. A fast-food triple-burger and a milkshake, for instance.

The air in front of his chest grew thick. There was a pale flickering, a slight buzz, and—*plop*, a burger 'n' shake dropped out of the air to splatter on the hospital-room floor!

"Oh my God!" Luanne had been watching closely. "Can you do that again, Gar?"

This time he stood next to the dresser. Make it two shakes and burgers. Nothing to it. Buzz, flicker, click—there they were.

"Jesus, Garvey. How come I can't do that?"

"I got more of the gas than you did." Garvey ate as he talked. "I always knew something like this would happen to me, Luanne. I'm Superman! I can do anything I like. And the I.R.S. can go straight to hell!"

"*Don't*, Garvey! You've got to be careful what you wish! Don't wear it out on garbage!"

There was a fumbling outside, and the inner door of their room's air-lock swung open. It was a man in a baggy white decontamination suit. His face was obscured by bulky air-filters.

"yrrnd shhhnnddt chuchufff mnnn krrrrdnnn!" The bulky figure reached for Garvey's lunch.

"Uh, Luanne, do you think…"

"Yeah, baby. Let's split."

The scene around them flickered like two intercut films and resolved itself into the Carrandine's living-room.

"Oh, Garvey! Make a lot of gold, man, I mean like hundreds of pounds! Quick before the pigs get here!"

A small ingot of gold thudded to the floor. Then another and another and another—the rain of metal lasted a full minute. Garvey paused and regarded his riches with a vaguely dissatisfied air.

"That's good for a few million bucks, Luanne. Go hide it, and let me concentrate. I've got to do something much bigger. There's not a whole lot of time left—I can feel my powers wearing off."

Obediently Luanne got her daughter Betsy's wagon and began lugging ingots into the den. There was a fireplace in there with a trapdoor you could lift up to shove the ashes in. One by one, Luanne stashed the gold-bars in the hidden ash-barrel.

There were sirens in the distance. Garvey lay on the couch with his eyes closed. As Luanne hurried back and forth with the heavy ingots, she saw girders rising up around their house, steel beams shooting up like fountains. Some vast tower was growing overhead, some eternal monument to Garvey's power!

Luanne hid the last ingot and went to stand by Garvey's laboring head. "Can you hear me, baby?" A weak nod. "Are you done?" Another nod. "Can I have a chicken sandwich and a glass of red wine?"

"No," said Garvey, smiling a little. "You'll have to buy it, Luanne. I've used up all my power."

The room was in shadow, darkened by the immense bulk overhead. Luanne laid her hand on Garvey's cool forehead. "What did you make out there, baby?"

"A tower. I saw it when I was in the hole. I don't know what it means, but I had to make it. It's sort of a giant clock. Let's go outside and see how it turned out."

The structure overhead was inconceivably vast. Standing under it was like standing under the Eiffel tower. Garvey and Luanne had to walk a good five minutes till they could get a decent view of the thing. People were milling about like excited ants, but for the moment no one stopped the Carrandines. They reached a good vantage-point and feasted their eyes.

"I *drew* that," murmured Luanne. Garvey just smiled, happier than he'd ever been.

The tower was a giant cone swept out by two linked spirals. Supported by a great spare lattice of strutwork, the spirals narrowed up to a point hundreds and hundreds of feet overhead. Inside the giant structure were four great glass jewels, four whole buildings suspended one above the other: a cube, a triangular pyramid, a cylinder, and a hemisphere.

"They rotate," said Garvey. "The cube once a year, the tetrahedron once a month, the cylinder once a week, and the hemisphere once a day. It's never the same. A monument with moving parts."

"Can we go in?"

"Yeah. See that?" Garvey pointed to a great slanting shaft that leaned up along one side of the tower. A shaft twice the height of the Empire State Building. "There's elevators in there. The cube is an exhibition hall, the pyramid is an auditorium, the cylinder is offices, and the hemisphere…the hemisphere is for us."

"There they are," someone shouted. "There's Carrandine and his wife! Get them!"

The fat doctor and some other men came rushing up to Garvey and Luanne. "Did you build this thing?"

"Uh…"

"Sure Garvey built it! You should be down on your knees thanking him, man."

"Do you know what this tower is, Carrandine?"

"I—I got the idea for it when I was stuck in that hole."

"No wonder. We found the Russian time-capsule down in the bottom. A Communist artist named Vladimir Tatlin dreamed up the design for this tower in 1919. *Monument to the Third International*. Fortunately the Soviets never had the funds to construct it. But now you…"

"Talk about uptight!" interrupted Luanne. "What's 'the Third Inter-national' supposed to be?"

No one seemed to know. And once Garvey had promised to manage the monument's rental and upkeep, no one really cared. The great tower stands in Killeville to this day—go see it next time you're down South!

Note on "Monument to the Third International"

Written in 1983.
The Magazine of Fantasy and Science Fiction, December, 1984.

Our Lynchburg friends Henry and Diana Vaughan did indeed own a dress-shop. I saw a model of Tatlin's proposed *Monument to the Third International* in the *Moscow-Paris* exhibition at the Pompidou Center, and then I saw the model again in a TV documentary.

RAPTURE IN SPACE

Denny Blevins was a dreamer who didn't like to think. Drugs and no job put his head in just the right place for this. If at all possible, he liked to get wired and spend the day lying on his rooming house mattress and looking out the window at the sky. On clear days he could watch his eyes' phosphenes against the bright blue; and on cloudy days he'd dig the clouds' drifty motions and boiling edges. One day he realized his window-dirt was like a constant noise-hum in the system, so he knocked out the pane that he usually looked through. The sky was even better then, and when it rained he could watch the drops coming in. At night he might watch the stars, or he might get up and roam the city streets for deals.

His Dad, whom he hadn't seen in several years, died that April. Denny flew out to the funeral. His big brother Allen was there, with Dad's insurance money. Turned out they got $15K apiece.

"Don't squander it, Denny," said Allen, who was an English teacher. "Time's winged chariot for no man waits! You're getting older and it's time you found a career. Go to school and learn something. Or buy into a trade. Do something to make Dad's soul proud."

"I will," said Denny, feeling defensive. Instead of talking in clear he used the new cyberslang. "I'll get so cashy and so starry so zip you won't believe it, Allen. I'll get a tunebot, start a motion, and cut a choicey vid. Denny in the Clouds with Clouds. Untense, bro, I've got plex ideas."

When Denny got back to his room he got a new sound system and a self-playing electric guitar. And scored a lot of dope and food-packs. The days went by; the money dwindled to $9K. Early in June the phone rang.

"Hello, Denny Blevins?" The voice was false and crackly.

"Yes!" Denny was glad to get a call from someone besides Allen. It seemed like lately Allen was constantly calling him up to nag.

"Welcome to the future. I am Phil, a phonebot cybersystem designed to contact consumer prospects. I would like to tell about the on-line possibilities open to you. Shall I continue?"

"Yes," said Denny.

It turned out the "Phil the phonebot" was a kind of computerized phone salesman. The phonebot was selling phonebots which you, the consumer prospect, could use to sell phonebots to others. It was—though Denny didn't realize this—a classic Ponzi pyramid scheme, like a chain letter, or like those companies which sell people franchises to sell franchises to sell franchises to sell…

The phonebot had a certain amount of interactivity. It asked a few yes/no questions; and whenever Denny burst in with some comment, it would pause, say, "That's right, Denny! But listen to the rest!" and continue. Denny was pleased to hear his name so often. Alone in his room, week after week, he'd been feeling his reality fade. Writing original songs for the guitar was harder than he'd expected. It would be nice to have a robot friend. At the end, when Phil asked for his verdict, Denny said, "Okay, Phil, I want you. Come to my rooming-house tomorrow and I'll have the money."

The phonebot was not the arm-waving clanker that Denny, in his ignorance, had imagined. It was, rather, a flat metal box that plugged right into the wall phone-socket. The box had a slot for an electronic directory, and a speaker for talking to its owner. It told Denny he could call it Phil; all the phonebots were named Phil. The basic phonebot sales spiel was stored in the Phil's memory, though you could change the patter if you wanted. You could, indeed, use the phonebot to sell things other than phonebots.

The standard salespitch lasted five minutes, and one minute was allotted to the consumer's responses. If everyone answered, listened, and responded, the phonebot could process ten prospects per hour, and one hundred twenty in a 9 A.M. – 9 P.M. day! The whole system cost nine thousand dollars, though as soon as you bought one and joined the pyramid, you could get more of them for six. Three thousand dollars profit for each phonebot your phonebot could sell! If you sold, say, one a day, you'd make better than $100K a year!

The electronic directory held all the names and numbers in the city; and each morning it would ask Denny who he wanted to try today. He could select the numbers on the day's calling list on the basis of neighborhood, last name, family size, type of business and so on.

The first day, Denny picked a middle-class suburb and told Phil to call all the childless married couples there. Young folks looking for an opportunity! Denny set the speaker so he could listen to people's responses. It was not encouraging.

"*click*"

"No...*click*"

"*click*"

"This kilp ought to be illegal...*click*"

"*click*"

"Get a job, you bizzy dook...*click*"

"Of all the...*click*"

"Again? *click*"

Most people hung up so fast that Phil was able to make some thousand unsuccessful contacts in less than ten hours. Only seven people listened through the whole message and left comments at the end; and six of these people seemed to be bedridden or crazy. The seventh had a phonebot she wanted to sell cheap.

Denny tried different phoning strategies—rich people, poor people, people with two sevens in their phone number, and so on. He tried different kinds of salespitches—bossy ones, ingratiating ones, curt ones, ethnic-accent ones, etc. He made up a salespitch that offered businesses the chance to rent Phil to do phone advertising for them.

Nothing worked. It got to be depressing sitting in his room watching Phil fail—it was like having Willy Loman for his roommate. The machine made little noises, and unless Denny took a *lot* of dope, he had trouble relaxing out into the sky. The empty food-packs stank.

Two more weeks, and all the money, food and dope were gone. Right after he did the last of the dope, Denny recorded a final sales-pitch:

"Uh...hi. This is Phil the prophet at 1801 Eye Street. I eye I...I'm out of money and I'd rather not have to...uh...leave my room. You send me money for...uh...food and I'll give God your name. Dope's rail, too."

Phil ran that on random numbers for two days with no success. Denny came down into deep hunger. Involuntary detox. If his Dad had left much more money, Denny might have died, holed up in that room. Good old Dad. He trembled out into the street and got a job working counter in a Greek coffee shop called the KoDo. It was okay; there was plenty of food, and he didn't have to watch Phil panhandling.

As Denny's strength and sanity came back, he remembered sex. But he didn't know any girls. He took Phil off panhandling and put him onto propositioning numbers in the young working-girl neighborhoods.

"Hi, are you a woman? I'm Phil, sleek robot for a whippy young man who's ready to get under. Make a guess and he'll mess. Leave your number and state your need; he's fuff-looking and into sleaze."

This message worked surprisingly well. The day after he started it up, Denny came home to find four enthusiastic responses stored on Phil's chips. Two of the responses seemed to be from men, and one of the women's voice sounded old...*really* old. The fourth response was from "Silke."

"Hi, desperado, this is Silke. I like your machine. Call me."

Phil had Silke's number stored, of course, so Denny called her right up. Feeling shy, he talked through Phil, using the machine as voder to make his voice sound weird. After all, Phil was the one who knew her.

"Hello?" Cute, eager, practical, strange.

"Silke? This is Phil. Denny's talking through me. You want to interface?"

"Like where?"

"My room?"

"Is it small? It sounds like your room is small. I like small rooms."

"You got it. 1801 Eye Street, Denny'll be in front of the building."

"What do you look like, Denny?"

"Tall, thin, teeth when I grin, which is lots. My hair's peroxide blond on top. I'll wear my X-shirt."

"Me too. See you in an hour."

Denny put on his X-shirt—a T-shirt with a big silk screen picture of his genitalia—and raced down to the KoDo to beg Spiros, the boss, for an advance on his wages.

"Please, Spiros, I got a date."

The shop was almost empty, and Spiros was sitting at the counter watching a payvid porno show on his pocket TV. He glanced over at Denny, all decked out in his X-shirt, and pulled two fifties out of his pocket.

"Let me know how she come."

Denny spent one fifty on two Fiesta food-packs and some wine: the other fifty went for a capsule of snap-crystals from a street vendor. He was back in front of his rooming-house in plenty of time. Ten minutes, and there came Silke, with a great big pink crotch-shot printed onto her T-shirt. She looked giga good.

For the first instant they stood looking at each other's X-shirts, and then they shook hands.

"I'm Denny Blevins. I got some food and wine and snap here, if you want to go up." Denny was indeed tall and thin, and toothy when he grinned. His mouth was very wide. His hair was long and dark in back, and short and blond on top. He wore red rhinestone earrings, his semi-erect X-shirt, tight black plastic pants, and fake leopard fur shoes. His arms were muscular and veiny, and he moved them a lot when he talked.

"Go up and get under," smiled Silke. She was medium height, and wore her straw-like black hair in a bouffant. She had fine, hard features. She'd appliquéd pictures of monster eyes to her eyelids, and she wore white dayglo lipstick. Beneath her sopping wet X-shirt, she wore a tight, silvered jumpsuit with cutouts. On her feet she wore roller skates with lights in the wheels.

"Oxo," said Denny.

"Wow," said Silke.

Up in the room they got to know each other. Denny showed Silke his phonebot and his sound system, pretended to start to play his guitar and to then decide not to, and told about some of the weird things he'd seen in the sky, looking out that broken pane. Silke, as it turned out, was a payvid sex dancer come here from West Virginia. She talked mostly in clear, but she was smart, and she liked to get wild, but only with the right kind of guy. Sex dancer didn't mean hooker and she was, she assured Denny, clean. She had a big dream she wasn't quite willing to tell him yet.

"Come on," he urged, popping the autowave foodpacks open. "Decode."

"Ah, I don't know, Denny. You might think I'm skanky."

They sat side by side on Denny's mattress and ate the pasty food with the packed in plastic spoons. It was good. It was good to have another person in the room here.

"Silke," said Denny when they finished eating, "I'd been thinking Phil was kilp. Dook null. But if he got you here it was worth it. Seems I just need tech to relate, you wave?"

Silke threw the empty foodtrays on the floor and gave Denny a big kiss. They went ahead and fuffed. It seemed like it had been a while for both of them. Skin all over, soft, warm, skin, touch, kiss, lick, smell, good.

Afterwards, Denny opened the capsule of snap and they split it. You put the stuff on your tongue, it sputtered and popped, and you breathed in the freebase fumes. Fab rush. Out through the empty window pane they could see the moon and two stars stronger than the city lights.

"Out there," said Silke, her voice fast and shaky from the snap. "That's my dream. If we hurry, Denny, we can be the first people to have sex in space. They'd remember us forever. I've been thinking about it, and there was always missing links, but you and Phil are it. We'll get in the shuttlebox—it's a room like this—and go up. We get up there and make videos of us getting under, and—this is my new flash—we use Phil to sell the vids to pay for the trip. You wave?"

Denny's long, maniacal smile curled across his face. The snap was still crackling on his tongue. "Stuzzadelic! Nobody's fuffed in space yet? None of those gawks who've used the shuttlebox?"

"They might have, but not for the record. But if we scurry we'll be the famous first forever. We'll be starry."

"Oxo, Silke." Denny's voice rose with excitement. "Are you there, Phil?"

"Yes, Denny."

"Got a new pitch. In clear."

"Proceed."

"Hi, this is Denny." He nudged the naked girl next to him.

"And this is Silke."

"We're doing a live fuff-vid we'd like to show you."

"It's called *Rapture in Space*. It's the very first X-rated love film from outer space."

"Zero gravity," said Denny, reaching over to whang on his guitar. "Endless fun."

"Mindless pleasure." *Whang.*

"Out near the sun." Silke nuzzled his neck and moaned stagily. "Oh, Denny, oh, darling, it's…"

"*RAPTURE IN SPACE*! Satisfaction guaranteed. This is bound to be a collector's item; the very first live sex video from space. A full ninety minutes of unbelievable null-gee action, with great Mother Earth in the background, tune in for only fifty…"

"More, Denny," wailed Silke, who was now grinding herself against him with some urgency. "More!"

Whang. "Only one hundred dollars, and going up fast. To order, simply leave your card number after the beep."

"*Beep!*"

Phil got to work the next morning, calling numbers of businesses where lots of men worked. The orders poured in. Lacking a business-front by which to cash the credit orders, Denny enlisted Spiros, who quickly set up KoDo Space Rapture Enterprises. For managing the business, Spiros only wanted 15% and some preliminary tapes of Denny and Silke in action. For another 45%, Silke's porno payvid employers—an outfit known as XVID—stood ready to distribute the show. Dreaming of this day, Silke had already bought her own cameras. She and Denny practiced a lot, getting their moves down. Spiros agreed that the rushes looked good. Denny went ahead and reserved the shuttlebox for a trip in mid July.

The shuttlebox was a small passenger module that could be loaded into the space shuttle for one of its weekly trips up to orbit and back.

A trip for two cost $100K. Denny bought electronic directories for cities across the country, and set Phil to working twenty hours a day. He averaged fifty sales a day, and by launch time, Silke and Denny had enough to pay everyone off, and then some.

But this was just the beginning. Three days before the launch, the news services picked up on the *Rapture in Space* plan, and everything went crazy. There was no way for a cheap box like Phil to process the orders anymore. Denny and Silke had to give XVID anther 15% of the action, and let them handle the tens of thousands of orders. It was projected that *Rapture in Space* would pull an audience share of 7%—which is a lot of people. Even more money came in the form of fat contracts for two product endorsements: SPACE RAPTURE, the cosmic eroscent for high-flyers, and RAPT SHIELD, an antiviral lotion for use by sexual adventurers. XVID and the advertisers privately wished that Denny and Silke were a bit more...*upscale* looking, but they were the two who had the tiger by the tail.

Inevitably, some of the Christian Party congressmen tried to have Denny and Silke enjoined from making an XVID broadcast from aboard the space shuttle which was, after all, government property. But for 5% of the gross, a fast thinking lawyer was able to convince a hastily convened Federal court that, insofar as *Rapture in Space* was being codecast to the XVID dish and cabled thence only to paying subscribers, the show was a form of constitutionally protected free speech, in no way essentially different from a live-sex show in a private club.

So the great day came. Naked save for a drenching of Space Rapture eroscent, Silke and Denny waved goodbye and stepped into their shuttle-box. It was shaped like a two-meter-thick letter D, with a rounded floor, and with a big picture window set into the flat ceiling. A crane loaded the shuttlebox into the bay of the space shuttle along with some satellites, missiles, building materials, etc. A worker dogged all the stuff down, and then the baydoors closed. Silke and Denny wedged themselves down into their puttylike floor. Blast off—roar, shudder, push, clunk, roar some more.

Then they were floating. The baydoors swung open, and the astronauts got to work with their retractable arms and space tools. Silke and Denny were busy, too. They set up the cameras, and got their little antenna locked in on the XVID dish. They started broadcasting right away—some of the *Rapture in Space* subscribers had signed up for the whole live protocols in addition to the ninety minute show that Silke and Denny were scheduled to put on in...

"Only half an hour, Denny," said Silke. "Only thirty minutes till we go on." She was crouched over the sink, douching, and vacuuming the water back up. As fate would have it, she was menstruating. She hadn't warned anyone about it.

Denny felt cold and sick to his stomach. XVID had scheduled their show right after take-off because otherwise—with all the news going on—people might forget about it. But right now he didn't fell like fuffing at all, let alone getting under. Every time he touched something, or even breathed, his whole body moved.

"All clean now," sang Silke. "No one can tell, not even you."

There was a rapping on their window—one of the astronauts, a jolly jock woman named Judy. She grinned through her helmet and gave them a high sign. The astronauts thought the *Rapture in Space* show was a great idea; it would make people think about them in new, more interesting ways.

"I talked to Judy before the launch," said Silke, waving back. "She said to watch out for the rebound." She floated to Denny and began fondling him. "Ten minutes, starman."

Outside the window, Judy was a shiny wad against Earth's great marbled curve. *The clouds*, Denny realized, *I'm seeing the clouds from on top*. His genitals were warming to Silke's touch. He tongued a snap crystal out of a crack between his teeth and bit it open. Inhale. The clouds. Silke's touch. He was hard, thank God, he was hard. This was going to be all right.

The cameras made a noise to signal the start of the main transmission, and Denny decided to start by planting a kiss on Silke's mouth. He bumped her shoulder and she started to drift away. She tightened her grip on his penis and led him along after her. It hurt, but not too unpleasantly. She landed on her back, on the padded floor, and guided Denny right into her vagina. Smooth and warm. Good. Denny pushed into her and...*rebound*.

He flew, rapidly and buttocks first, up to the window. He had hold of Silke's armpit and she came with him. She got her mouth over his penis for a second, which was good, but then her body spun around, and she slid toothrakingly off him, which was very bad.

Trying to hold a smile, Denny stole a look at the clock. Three minutes. *Rapture in Space* had been on for three minutes now. Eighty-seven minutes to go.

It was another bruising half hour or so until Denny and Silke began to get the hang of spacefuffing. And then it was fun. For a long time they hung in midair, with Denny in Silke, and Silke's legs around his waist, just gently jogging, but moaning and throwing their heads around for the camera. Actually, the more they hammed it up, the better it felt. Autosuggestion.

Denny stared and stared at the clouds to keep from coming, but finally he had to pull out for a rest. To keep things going they did rebounds for awhile. Silke would lie spreadeagled on the floor, and Denny would kind of leap down on her; both of them adjusting their pelvises for a bullseye. She'd sink into the cushions, then rebound them both up. It got better and better. Silke curled up into a ball and impaled herself on Denny's shaft. He wedged himself against the wall with his feet and one hand and used his other hand to spin her around and around, bobbin on his spindle. Denny lay on the floor and Silke did leaps onto him. They kissed and licked each other all over, and from every angle. The time was almost up.

For the finale, they went back to midair fuffing; arms and legs wrapped around each other; one camera aimed at their faces, and one camera aimed at their genitalia. They hit a rhythm where they always pushed just as hard as each other and it action/reaction cancelled out, hard and harder, with big Earth out the window, yes, the air full of their smells, yes, the only sound the sound of their ragged breathing, yes, now NOW AAAHHHHHHH!!!!

Denny kind of fainted there, and forgot to slide out for the come-shot. Silke went blank, too, and they just floated, linked like puzzle pieces for five or ten minutes. It made a great finale for the *Rapture in Space* show, really much more convincing than the standard sperm spurt.

Two days later, and they were back on Earth, with the difference that they were now, as Denny had hoped, cashy and starry. People recognized them everywhere, and looked at them funny, often asking for a date. They did some interviews, some more endorsements and they got an XVID contract to host a monthly spacefuff variety show.

Things were going really good until Denny got a tumor.

"It's a dooky little kilp down in my bag," he complained to Silke. "Feel it."

Sure enough, there was a one-centimeter lump in Denny's scrotum. Silke wanted him to see a doctor, but he kept stalling. He was afraid they'd run a blood test and get on his case about drugs. Some things were still illegal.

A month went by and the lump was the size of an orange.

"It's so gawky you can see it through my pants," complained Denny. "It's giga ouch and I can't cut a vid this way."

But he still wouldn't go to the doctor. What with all the snap he could buy, and with his new cloud telescope, Denny didn't notice what was going on in his body most of the time. He was happy to miss the next few XVID dates. Silke hosted them alone.

Three more months and the lump was like a small watermelon. When Denny came down one time and noticed that the tumor was moving he really got worried

"Silke! It's alive! The thing in my bag is alive! Aaauuugh!"

Silke paid a doctor two thousand dollars to come to their apartment. The doctor was a bald, dignified man with a white beard. He examined Denny's scrotum for a long time, feeling, listening, and watching the tumor's occasional twitches. Finally he pulled the covers back over Denny and sat down. He regarded Silke and Denny in silence for quite some time.

"Decode!" demanded Denny. "What the kilp we got running here?"

"You're pregnant," said the doctor. "Four months into it, I'd say."

The quickening fetus gave another kick and Denny groaned. He knew it was true. "But how?"

The doctor steepled his fingers. "I…I saw *Rapture in Space.* There were certain signs to indicate that your uh partner was menstruating?"

"Check."

"Menstruation, as you must know, involves the discharge of the unfertilized ovum along with some discarded uterine tissues. I would speculate that after your ejaculation the ovum became wedged in your meatus. It is conceivable that under weightless conditions the sperm's flagell3/4 could have driven the now-fertilized ovum up into your vas deferens. The ovum implanted itself in the bloodrich tissues there and developed into a fetus."

"I want an abortion."

"No!" protested Silke. "That's our baby, Denny. You're already almost half done carrying it. It'll be lovely for us…and just think of the publicity!"

"Uh…" said Denny, reaching for his bag of dope.

"No more drugs," said the doctor, snatching the bag. "Except for the ones I give you." He broke into a broad, excited smile. "This will make medical history."

And indeed it did. The doctor designed Denny a kind of pouch in which he could carry his pregnant scrotum, and Denny made a number of video appearances, not all of them X-rated. He spoke on the changing roles of the sexes, and he counted the days till delivery. In the public's mind, Denny became the symbol of a new recombining of sex with life and love. In Denny's own mind, he finally became a productive and worthwhile person. The baby was a flawless girl, delivered by a modified Caesarian section.

Sex was never the same again.

Note on "Rapture in Space"

Written in Fall, 1984.
Semiotext[e] SF, Autonomedia, 1989.

Dennis Poague, a.k.a. Sta-Hi, was the inspiration for this story; he really did spend his inheritance on a phoning machine. I wrote this story shortly after seeing the IMAX movie, *The Dream Is Alive*, which featured pictures of the sexy astronaut Judy Resnick sleeping in zero-gee. The Challenger shuttle blew up with Judy in it a few months later, definitively deep-sixing whatever slim chance "Rapture in Space" had of getting into a normal SF magazine.

Semiotext[e] SF was an anthology which Peter Lamborn Wilson and I co-edited. Originally we'd planned to call the book Bad Brains, but Peter felt doing this would conflict with the band of the same name. At the time, Peter rented an apartment upstairs from the apartment of my friend Eddie Marritz in New York City, which is how I happened to meet him. Eddie appears in the story "Tales of Houdini," in "Drugs and Live Sex—NYC 1980," and in the novel *Master of Space and Time*.

A funny Dennis story. When we moved to San Jose, it turned out Dennis lived here, so we started getting together a lot. I was supposed to give a reading at an annual San Jose SF convention called Bay Con in 1987, and the day before the reading I was in a bicycle accident and had a huge black eye. I didn't want to appear in public looking so bad, so I gave Dennis my manuscript of "As Above So Below," and told him to do the reading. I figured he would enjoy this free taste of fame, and I was right—remember that one of *Software* Sta-Hi's big obsessions is how to become famous.

Although I'd already made friends with the San Francisco SF writers, none of the fans knew at Bay Con knew what I looked like, so when Dennis appeared in a corduroy jacket and read my story, they assumed he was me. The funny thing was, when I came and did my own reading at Bay Con a year later, several people came up to me and said, "You know, I saw your reading last year and it was wonderful. You made the material so fresh and new…it was like you'd never even read it before!"

STORMING THE COSMOS (WITH BRUCE STERLING)

I first met Vlad Zipkin at a Moscow beatnik party in the glorious winter of 1957. I went there as a KGB informer. Because of my report on that first meeting, poor Vlad had to spend six months in a mental hospital—not that he wasn't crazy.

As a boy I often tattled on wrongdoers, but I certainly didn't plan to grow up to be a professional informer. It just worked out that way. The turning point was in the spring of 1953, when I failed my completion exams at the All-Union Metallurgical Institute. I'd been working towards those exams for years; I wanted to help build the rockets that would launch us into the Infinite.

And then, suddenly, one day in April, it was all over. Our examination grades were posted, and I was one of the three in seventeen who'd failed. To take the exam again, I'd have to wait a whole year. First I was depressed, then angry. I knew for a fact that four of the students with good grades had cheated. I, who was honest, had failed; and they, who had cheated, had passed. It wasn't fair, it wasn't communist—I went and told the head of the Institute.

The upshot was that I passed after all, and became an assistant metallurgical engineer at the Kaliningrad space center. But, in reality, my main duty was to make weekly reports to the KGB on what my coworkers thought and said and did. I was, frankly, grateful to have my KGB work to do, as most of the metallurgical work was a bit beyond me.

There is an ugly Russian word for informer: *stukach*, snitch. The criminals, the psychotics, the parasites, and the beatniks—to them I was a *stukach*. But without *stukachi*, our communist society would explode into anarchy or grind to a decadent halt. Vlad Zipkin might be a genius, and I might be a *stukach*—but society needed us both.

I first met Vlad at a party thrown by a girl called Lyuda. Lyuda had her own Moscow apartment; her father was a Red Army colonel-general in Kaliningrad. She was a nice, sexy girl who looked a little like Doris Day.

Lyuda and her friends were all beatniks. They drank a lot; they used English slang; they listened to jazz; and the men hung around with prostitutes. One of the guys got Lyuda pregnant and she went for an abortion. She had VD as well. We heard of this, of course. Word spreads about these matters. Someone in Higher Circles decided to eliminate the anti-social sex gangster responsible for this. It was my job to find out who he was.

It was a matter for space-center KGB because several rocket-scientists were known to be in Lyuda's orbit. My approach was cagey. I made contact with a prostitute named Trina who hung around the Metropol, the Moskva, and other foreign hotels. Trina had chic Western clothes from her customers, and she was friends with many of the Moscow beatniks. I'm certainly not dashing enough to charm a girl like Trina—instead, I simply told her that I was KGB, and that if she didn't get me into one of Lyuda's bashes I'd have her arrested.

Lyuda's pad was jammed when we got there. I was proud to show up with a cool chick like Trina on my arm. I looked very sharp too, with the leather jacket, and the black stove-pipe pants with no cuffs that all the beatniks were wearing that season. Trina stuck right with me—as we'd planned—and lots of men came up to talk to us. Trina would get them to talking dirty, and then I'd make some remark about Lyuda, ending with "but I guess she has a boyfriend?" The problem was that she had lots of them. I kept having to go into the bathroom to write down more names. Somehow I had to decide on one particular guy.

Time went on, and I got tenser. Cigarette smoke filled the room. The bathroom was jammed and I had to wait. When I came back I saw Trina with a hardcore beatnik named Starsky—he got her attention with some garbled Americanisms: "Hey baby, let's jive down to Hollywood and drink cool Scotch. I love making it with gone broads like you and Lyuda." He showed her a wad of hard currency—dollars he had illegally bought from tourists. I decided on the spot that Starsky was my man, and told Trina to leave with him and find out where he lived.

Now that I'd finished my investigation, I could relax and enjoy myself. I got a bottle of vodka and sat down by Lyuda's Steinway piano. Some guy in sunglasses was playing a slow boogie-woogie. It was lovely, lovely enough to move me to tears—tears for Lyuda's corrupted beauty, tears for my lost childhood, tears for my mother's grave.

A sharp poke in the thigh interrupted my reverie.

249

"Quit bawling, fatso, this isn't the Ukraine."

The voice came from beneath the piano. Leaning down, I saw a man sitting cross-legged there, a thin, blond man with pale eyes. He smiled and showed his bad teeth. "Cheer up, pal, I mean it. And pass me that vodka bottle you're sucking. My name's Vlad Zipkin."

I passed him my bottle. "I'm Nikita Iosifovich Globov."

"Nice shoes," Vlad said admiringly. "Cool jacket, too. You're a snappy dresser, for a rocket-type."

"What makes you think I'm from the space center?" I said.

Vlad lowered his voice. "The shoes. You got those from Nokidze the Kazakh, the black market guy. He's been selling 'em all over Kaliningrad."

I climbed under the piano with Zipkin. The air was a little clearer there. "You're one of us, Comrade Zipkin?"

"I do information theory," Zipkin whispered, drunkenly touching one finger to his lips. "We're designing error-proof codes for communicating with the…you know." He made a little orbiting movement with his forefinger and looked upward at the shiny dark bottom of the piano. The Sputnik had only been up since October. We space workers were still not used to talking about it in public.

"Come on, don't be shy," I said, smiling. "We can say 'Sputnik,' can't we? Everyone in the world has talked of nothing else for months!"

It was easy to draw Vlad out. "My group's hush-hush," he bragged criminally. "The top brass think 'information theory' has to be classified and censored. But the theory's not information itself, it's an abstract meta-information…" He burbled on a while in the weird jargon of his profession. I grew bored and opened a pack of Kent cigarettes.

Vlad bummed one instantly. He was impressed that I had American cigarettes. Only cool black-market operators had classy cigs like that. Vlad felt the need to impress me in return. "Khrushchev wants the next sputnik to broadcast propaganda," he confided, blowing smoke. "The Internationale in outer space—what foolishness!" Vlad shook his head. "As if countries matter any more outside our atmosphere. To any real Russian, it is already clear that we have surpassed the Americans. Why should we copy their fascist nationalism? We have soared into the void and left them in the dirt!" He grinned. "Damn, these are good smokes. Can you get me a connection?"

"What are you offering?" I said.

He nodded at Lyuda. "See our hostess? You see those earrings she has? They're gold-plated transistors I stole from the Center! All property is theft, hey Nikita?"

I liked Vlad well enough, but I felt duty-bound to report his questionable attitudes along with my information about Starsky. Political

250

deviance such as Vlad's is a type of mental illness. I liked Vlad enough to truly want to see him get better.

Having made my report, I returned to Kaliningrad, and forgot about Vlad. I didn't hear about him for a month.

Since the early '50s, Kaliningrad had been the home of the Soviet space effort. Kaliningrad was thirty kilometers north of Moscow and had once been a summer resort. There we worked heroically at rocket research and construction—though the actual launches took place at the famous Baikonur Cosmodrome, far to the south. I enjoyed life in Kaliningrad. The stores were crammed with Polish hams and fresh lamb chops, and the landscape of forests and lakes was romantic and pleasant. Security was excellent.

Outside the research complex and block apartments were *dachas*, resort homes for space scientists, engineers, and party officials, including our top boss, the Chief Designer himself. The entire compound was surrounded by a high wood-and-concrete fence manned around the clock by armed guards. It was very peaceful. The compound held almost fifty *dachas*. I owned a small one—a kitchen and two rooms—with large gar-den filled with fruit trees and berry bushes, now covered by winter snow.

A month after Lyuda's party, I was enjoying myself in my *dacha*, quietly pressing a new suit I had bought from Nokidze the Kazakh, when I heard a black ZIL sedan splash up through the mud outside. I peeked through the curtains. A woman stamped up the path and knocked. I opened the door slightly.

"Nikita Iosifovich Globov?"

"Yes?"

"Let me in, you fat sneak!" she said.

I gaped at her. She addressed me with filthy words. Shocked, I let her in. She was a dusky, strong-featured Tartar woman dressed in a cheap black two-piece suit from the Moscow G. U. M. store. No woman in Kaliningrad wore clothes or shoes that ugly, unless she was a real hardliner. So I got worried. She kicked the door shut and glared at me.

"You turned in Vladimir Zipkin!"

"What?"

"Listen, you meddling idiot, I'm Captain Bogulyubova from Information Mechanics. You've put my best worker into the mental hospital! What were you thinking? Do you realize what this will do to my production schedules?"

I was caught off guard. I babbled something about proper ideology coming first.

"You louse!" she snarled. "It's my department and I handle Security there! How dare you report one of my people without coming to me first? Do you see me turning in metallurgists?"

"Well, you can't have him babbling state secrets to every beatnik in Moscow!" I said defensively.

"You forget yourself," said Captain Bogulyubova with a taut smile. "I have a rank in KGB and you are a common *stukach*. I can make a great deal of trouble for you. A very great deal."

I began to sweat. "I was doing my duty. No one can deny that. Besides, I didn't know he was in the hospital! All he needed was a few counseling sessions!"

"You fouled up everything," she said, staring at me through slitted eyes like a Cossack sizing up a captured hog. She crossed her arms over her hefty chest and looked around my *dacha*. "This little place of yours will be nice for Vlad. He'll need some rest. *Poor* Vlad. No one else from my section will want to work with him after he gets out. They'll be afraid to be seen with him! But we need him, and you're going to help me. Vlad will work here, and you'll keep an eye on him. It can be a kind of house arrest."

"But what about my work in metallurgy?"

She glared at me. "Your new work will be Comrade Zipkin's rehabilitation. You'll volunteer to do it, and you'll tell the Higher Circles that he's become a splendid example of communist dedication! He'd better get the order of Lenin, understand?"

"This isn't fair, Comrade Captain. Be reasonable!"

"Listen, you hypocrite swine, I know all about you and your black market dealings. Those shoes cost more than you make in a month!" She snatched the iron off the end of my board and slammed it flat against my brand new suit. Steam curled up.

"All right!" I cried, wringing my hands. "I'll help him." I yanked the suit away and splashed water on the scorched fabric.

Nina laughed and stormed out of the house. I felt terrible. A man can't help it if he needs to dress well. It's unfair to hold a thing like that over someone.

Months passed. The spring of 1958 arrived. The dog Laika had been shot into the cosmic void. A good dog, a Russian, an Earthling. The Americans' first launches had failed, and then in February they shot up a laughable sputnik no bigger than a grapefruit. Meanwhile we metallurgists forged ahead on the mighty RD-108 Supercluster paraffin-fueled engine, which would lift our first cosmonaut into the Infinite. There were technical snags and gross lapses in space-worker ideology, but much progress was made.

Captain Nina dropped by several times to bluster and grumble about Vlad. She blamed me for everything, but it was Vlad's problem. All one has to do, really, is tell the mental health workers what they want to hear. But Zipkin couldn't seem to master this.

A third sputnik was launched in May 1958, with much instrumentation on board. Yet it still failed to broadcast a coherent propaganda statement, much less sing the *Internationale*. Vlad was missed, and missed badly. I awaited Vlad's return with some trepidation. Would he resent me? Fear me? Despise me?

For my part, I simply wanted Vlad to like me. In going over his dossier I had come to see that, despite his eccentricities, the man was indeed a genius. I resolved to take care of Vlad Zipkin, to protect him from his irrational sociopathic impulses.

A KGB ambulance brought Vlad and his belongings to my *dacha* early one Sunday morning in July. He looked pale and disoriented. I greeted him with false heartiness.

"Greetings Vladimir Eduardovich! It's an honor and a joy to have you share my *dacha*. Come in, come in. I have yogurt and fresh gooseberries. Let me help you carry all that stuff inside!"

"So it was you." Vlad was silent while we carried his suitcase and three boxes of belongings into the *dacha*. When I urged him to eat with me, his face took on a desperate cast. "Please, Globov, leave me alone now. Those months in the hospital—you can't imagine what it's been like."

"Vladimir, don't worry, this *dacha* is your home, and I'm your friend."

Vlad grimaced. "Just let me spend the day alone in your garden, and don't tell the KGB I'm antisocial. I want to conform, I do want to fit in, but for God's sake, not today."

"Vlad, believe me, I want only the best for you. Go out and lie in the hammock; eat the berries, enjoy the sun."

Vlad's pale eyes bulged as they fell on my framed official photograph of Laika, the cosmonaut dog. The dog had a weird, frog-like, rubber oxygen mask on her face. Just before launch, she had been laced up within a heavy, stiff space-suit—a kind of canine straitjacket, actually. Vlad frowned and shuddered. I guess it reminded him of his recent unpleasantness.

Vlad yanked my vodka bottle off the kitchen counter, and headed outside without another word. I watched him through the window—he looked well enough, sipping vodka, picking blackberries, and finally falling asleep in the hammock. His suitcase contained very little of interest, and his boxes were mostly filled with books. Most were technical, but many were scientific romances: the socialist H. G. Wells, Capek, Yefremov, Kazantsev, and the like.

When Vlad awoke he was in much better spirits. I showed him around the property. The garden stretched back thirty meters, where there was a snug outhouse. We strolled together out into the muddy streets. At Vlad's urging, I got the guards to open the gate for us, and we walked out into the peaceful birch and pine woods around the Klyazma Reservoir. It had rained heavily during the preceding week, and mush-rooms were everywhere. We amused ourselves by gathering the edible ones—every Russian knows mushrooms.

Vlad knew an "instant pickling" technique based on lightly boiling the mushrooms in brine, then packing them in ice and vinegar. It worked well back in our kitchen, and I congratulated him. He was as pleased as a child.

In the days that followed, I realized that Vlad was not anti-Party. He was simply very unworldly. He was one of those gifted unfortunates who can't manage life without a protector.

Still, his opinion carried a lot of weight around the Center, and he worked on important problems. I escorted him everywhere—except the labs I wasn't cleared for—reminding him not to blurt out anything stupid.

Of course my own work suffered. I told my co-workers that Vlad was a sick relative of mine, which explained my common absence from the job. Rather than being disappointed by my absence, though, the other engineers praised my dedication to Vlad and encouraged me to spend plenty of time with him. I liked Vlad, but soon grew tired of the constant shepherding. He did most of his work in our *dacha*, which kept me cooped up there when I could have been out cutting deals with Nokidze or reporting on the beatnik scene.

It was too bad that Captain Nina Bogulyubova had fallen down on her job. She should have been watching over Vlad from the first. Now I had to tidy up after her bungling, so I felt she owed me some free time. I hinted tactfully at this when she arrived with a sealed briefcase containing some of Vlad's work. My reward was another furious tongue lashing.

"You parasite, how dare you suggest that I failed Vladimir Eduardovich? I have always been aware of his value as a theorist, and as a man! He's worth any ten of you *stukach* vermin! The Chief Designer himself has asked after Vladimir's health. The Chief Designer spent years in a labor camp under Stalin. He knows it's no disgrace to be shut away by some lickspittle sneak…" There was more, and worse. I began to feel that Captain Bogulyubova, in her violent Tartar way, had personal feelings for Vlad.

Also I had not known that our Chief Designer had been in camp. This was not good news, because people who have spent time in detention sometimes become embittered and lose proper perspective. Many people were being released from labor camps now that Nikita Khrushchev had become the Leader of Progressive Mankind. Also, amazing and almost insolent things were being published in the *Literary Gazette*.

Like most Ukrainians, I liked Khrushchev, but he had a funny peasant accent and everyone made fun of the way he talked on the radio. We never had such problems in Stalin's day.

We Soviets had achieved a magnificent triumph in space, but I feared we were becoming lax. It saddened me to see how many space engineers, technicians, and designers avoided Party discipline. They claimed that their eighty-hour work weeks excused them from indoctrination meetings. Many read foreign technical documents without proper clearance. Proper censorship was evaded. Technicians from different departments sometimes gathered to discuss their work, privately, simply between themselves, without an actual need-to-know.

Vlad's behavior was especially scandalous. He left top-secret documents scattered about the *dacha*, where one's eye could not help but fall on them. He often drank to excess. He invited engineers from other departments to come visit us, and some of them, not knowing his dangerous past, accepted. It embarrassed me, because when they saw Vlad and me together they soon guessed the truth.

Still, I did my best to cover Vlad's tracks and minimize his indiscretions. In this I failed miserably.

One evening, to my astonishment, I found him mulling over working papers for the RD-108 Supercluster engine. He had built a cardboard model of the rocket out of roller tubes from my private stock of toilet paper. "Where did you get those?" I demanded.

"Found 'em in a box in the outhouse."

"No, the documents!" I shouted. "That's not your department! Those are state secrets!"

Vlad shrugged. "It's all wrong," he said thickly. He had been drinking again.

"What?"

"Our original rocket, the 107, had four nozzles. But this 108 Supercluster has twenty! Look, the extra engines are just bundled up like bananas and attached to the main rocket. They're held on with hoops! The Americans will laugh when they see this."

"But they won't." I snatched the blueprints out of his hands. "Who gave you these?"

"Korolyov did," Vlad muttered. "Sergei Pavlovich."

"The Chief Designer?" I said, stunned.

"Yeah, we were talking it over in the sauna this morning," Vlad said. "Your old pal Nokidze came by while you were at work this morning, and he and I had a few. So I walked down to the bathhouse to sweat it off. Turned out the Chief was in the sauna, too—he'd been up all night working. He and I did some time together once, years ago. We used to look up at the stars, talk rockets together…So anyway, he turns to me and says, 'You know how much thrust Von Braun is getting from a single engine?' And I said, 'Oh, must be eighty, ninety tons, right?' 'Right,' he said, 'and we're getting twenty-five. We'll have to strap twenty together to launch one man. We need a miracle, Vladimir. I'm ready to try anything.' So then I told him about this book I've been reading."

I said, "You were drunk on working-hours? And the chief Designer saw you in the sauna?"

"He sweats like anybody else," Vlad said. "I told him about this new fiction writer. Aleksander Kazantsev. He's a thinker, that boy." Vlad tapped the side of his head meaningfully, then scratched his ribs inside his filthy house robe and lit a cigarette. I felt like killing him. "Kazantsev says we're not the first explorers in space. There've been others, beings from the void. It's no surprise. The great space-prophet Tsiolkovsky said there are an infinite number of inhabited worlds. You know how much the Chief Designer admired Tsiolkovsky. And when you look at the evidence—I mean this Tunguska thing—it begins to add up nicely."

"Tunguska," I said, fighting back a growing sense of horror. "That's in Siberia, isn't it?"

"Sure. So anyway, I said, 'Chief, why are you wasting our time on these firecrackers when we have a shot at true star flight? Send out a crew of trained investigators to the impact site of this so-called Tunguska meteor! Run an information-theoretic analysis! If it was really an atomic-powered spacecraft like Kazantsev says, maybe there's something left that could help us!'"

I winced, imagining Vlad in the sauna, drunk, first bringing up disgusting prison memories, then babbling on about space fiction to the premier genius of Soviet rocketry. It was horrible. "What did the chief say to you?"

"He said it sounded promising," said Vlad airily. "Said he'd get things rolling right away. You got any more of those Kents?"

I slumped into my chair, dazed. "Look inside my boots," I said numbly. "My Italian ones."

"Oh," Vlad said in a small voice. "I sort of found those last week."

I roused myself. "The chief let you see the Supercluster plans? And said you ought to go to Siberia?"

"Oh, not just you and me," Vlad said, amused. "He needs a really thorough investigation! We'd commandeer a whole train, get all the personnel and equipment we need!" Vlad grinned. "Excited, Nikita?"

My head spun. The man was a demon. I knew in my soul that he was goading me. Deliberately. Sadistically. Suddenly I realized how sick I was of Vlad, of constantly watchdogging this visionary moron. Words tumbled out of me.

"I hate you, Zipkin! So this is your revenge at last, eh? Sending me to Siberia! You beatnik scum! You think you're smart, blondie? You're weak, you're sick, that's what! I wish the KGB had shot you, you stupid, selfish, crazy..." My eyes flooded with sudden tears.

Vlad patted my shoulder, surprised. "Now don't get all worked up."

"You're nuts!" I sobbed. "You rocketship types are all crazy, every one of you! Storming the cosmos...well, you can storm my sacred ass! I'm not boarding any secret train to nowhere—"

"Now, now," Vlad soothed. "My imagination, your thoroughness— we make a great team! Just think of them pinning awards on us."

"If it's such a great idea, then you do it! I'm not slogging through some stinking wilderness..."

"Be logical!" Vlad said, rolling his eyes in derision. "You know I'm not well trusted. Your Higher Circles don't understand me the way you do. I need you along to smooth things, that's all. Relax, Nikita! I promise, I'll split the fame and glory with you, fair and square."

Of course, I did my best to defuse, or at least avoid, this lunatic scheme. I protested to Higher Circles. My usual contact, a balding jazz fanatic named Colonel Popov, watched me blankly, with the empty stare of a professional interrogator. I hinted broadly that Vlad had been misbehaving with classified documents. Popov ignored this, absently tapping a pencil on his "special" phone in catchy 5/4 rhythm.

Hesitantly I mentioned Vlad's insane mission. Popov still gave no response. One of the phones, not the "special" one, rang loudly. Popov answered, said, "Yes," three times, and left the room.

I waited a long hour, careful not to look at or touch anything on his desk. Finally Popov returned.

I began at once to babble. I knew his silent treatment was an old trick, but I couldn't help it. Popov cut me off.

"Marx's laws of historical development apply universally to all societies," he said, sitting in his squeaking chair. "That, of course, includes possible star-dwelling societies." He steepled his fingers. "It follows logically that progressive Interstellar void-ites would look kindly on us progressive peoples."

"But the Tunguska meteor fell in 1908!" I said.

"Interesting," Popov mused. "Historical-determinist cosmic-oids could have calculated through Marxist science that Russia would be first to achieve communism. They might well have left us some message or legacy."

"But Comrade Colonel…"

Popov rustled open a desk drawer. "Have you read this book?" It was Kazantsev's space romance. "It's all the rage at the space center these days. I got my copy from your friend Nina Bogulyubova."

"Well…" I said.

"Then why do you presume to debate me without even reading the facts?" Popov folded his arms. "We find it significant that the Tunguska event took place on June 30, 1908. Today is June 15, 1958. If heroic measures are taken, you may reach the Tunguska valley on the very day of the 50th anniversary!"

That Tartar cow Bogulyubova had gotten to the Higher Circles first. Actually, it didn't surprise me that our KGB would support Vlad's scheme. They controlled our security, but our complex engineering and technical developments much exceeded their mental grasp. Space aliens, however, were a concept anyone could understand.

Any skepticism on their part was crushed by the Chief Designer's personal support for the scheme. The chief had been getting a lot of play in Khrushchev's speeches lately, and was known as a miracle worker. If he said it was possible, that was good enough for Security.

I was helpless. An expedition was organized in frantic haste.

Naturally it was vital to have KGB along. Me, of course, since I was guarding Vlad. And Nina Bogulyubova, as she was Vlad's superior. But then the KGB of the other departments grew jealous of Metallurgy and Information Mechanics. They suspected that we were pulling a fast one. Suppose an artifact really were discovered? It would make all our other work obsolete overnight. Would it not be best that each department have a KGB observer present? Soon we found no end of applicants for the expedition.

We were lavishly equipped. We had ten railway cars. Four held our Red Army escort and their tracked all-terrain vehicles. We also had three sleepers, a galley car, and two flatcars piled high with rations, tents, excavators, Geiger counters, radios, and surveying instruments. Vlad brought a bulky calculating device, Captain Nina supplied her own mysterious crates, and I had a box of metallurgical analysis equipment, in case we found a piece of the UFO.

We were towed through Moscow under tight security, then our cars were shackled to the green-and-yellow Trans-Siberian Express.

Soon the expedition was chugging across the endless, featureless steppes of central Asia. I grew so bored that I was forced to read Kazantsev's book.

On June 30, 1908, a huge, mysterious fireball had smashed into the Tunguska River valley of the central Siberian uplands. This place was impossibly remote. Kazantsev suggested that the crash point had been chosen deliberately to avoid injuring Earthlings.

It was not until 1927 that the first expedition reached the crash site, revealing terrific devastation, but—*no sign whatsoever of a meteorite*! They found no impact crater, either; only the swampy Tunguska valley, surrounded by an elliptical blast pattern: sixty kilometers of dead, smashed trees.

Kazantsev pointed out that the facts suggested a nuclear airburst. Perhaps it was a deliberate detonation by aliens, to demonstrate atomic power to Earthlings. Or it might have been the accidental explosion of a nuclear starship drive. In an accidental crash, a socially advanced alien pilot would naturally guide his stricken craft to one of the planet's "poles of uninhabitedness." And eyewitness reports made it clear that the Tunguska body had definitely changed course in flight!

Once I had read this excellent work, my natural optimism surfaced again. Perhaps we would find something grand in Tunguska after all, something miraculous that the 1927 expedition had overlooked. Kulik's expedition had missed it, but now we were in the atomic age. Or so we told ourselves. It seemed much more plausible on a train with two dozen other explorers, all eager for the great adventure.

It was an unsought vacation for us hardworking *stukachi*. Work had been savage throughout our departments, and we KGB had had a tough time keeping track of our comrades' correctness. Meanwhile, back in Kaliningrad, they were still laboring away, while we relaxed in the dining saloon with pegged chessboards and tall brass samovars of steaming tea.

Vlad and I shared our own sleeping car. I forgave him for having involved me in this mess. We became friends again. This would be real man's work, we told each other. Tramping through savage taiga with bears, wolves, and Siberian tigers! Hunting strange, possibly dangerous relics—relics that might change the very course of cosmic history! No more of this poring over blueprints and formulae like clerks! Neither of us had fought in the Great Patriotic War—I'd been too young, and Vlad had been in some camp or something. Other guys were always bragging about how they'd stormed this or shelled that or eaten shoe leather in Stalingrad—well, we'd soon be making them feel pretty small!

Day after day, the countryside rolled past. First the endless, grassy steppes, then a dark wall of pine forest, broken by white-barked birches. Khrushchev's Virgin Lands campaign was in full swing, and the radio was full of patriotic stuff about settling the wilderness. Every few hundred kilometers, especially by rivers, raw and ugly new towns had sprung up along the Trans-Sib line. Prefab apartment blocks, mud streets, cement trucks, and giant sooty power plants. Trains unloaded huge spools of black wire. "Electrification" was another big propaganda theme of 1958.

Our Trans-Sib train stopped often to take on passengers, but our long section was sealed under orders from Higher circles. We had no chance to stretch our legs and slowly all our carriages filled up with the reek of dirty clothes and endless cigarettes.

I was doing my best to keep Vlad's spirits up when Nina Boguly-ubova entered our carriage, ducking under a line of wet laundry. "Ah, Nina Igorovna," I said, trying to keep things friendly. "Vlad and I were just discussing something. Exactly what *does* it take to merit burial in the Kremlin?"

"Oh, put a cork in it," Bogulyubova said testily. "My money says your so-called spacecraft was just a chunk of ice and gas. Probably a piece of a comet which vaporized on impact. Maybe it's worth a look, but that doesn't mean I have to swallow crackpot pseudo-science!"

She sat on the bunk facing Vlad's, where he sprawled out, stunned with boredom and strong cigarettes. Nina opened her briefcase. "Vladimir, I've developed those pictures I took of you."

"Yeah?"

She produced a Kirlian photograph of his hand. "Look at these spiky flares of suppressed energy from your fingertips. Your aura has changed since we've boarded the train."

Vlad frowned. "I could do with a few deciliters of vodka, that's all."

She shook her head quickly, then smiled and blinked at him flir-tatiously. "Vladimir Eduardovich, you're a man of genius. You have strong, passionate drives…"

Vlad studied her for a moment, obviously weighing her dubious attractions against his extreme boredom. An affair with a woman who was his superior, and also KGB, would be grossly improper and risky. Vlad, naturally, caught my eye and winked. "Look, Nikita, take a hike for a while, okay?"

He was putty in her hands. I was disgusted by the way she exploited Vlad's weaknesses. I left him in her carnal clutches, though I felt really sorry for Vlad. Maybe I could scare him up something to drink.

The closest train-stop to Tunguska is near a place call Ust-Ilimsk, two hundred kilometers north of Bratsk, and three thousand long kilometers from Moscow. Even London, England, is twice as close to Moscow as Tunguska.

A secondary-line engine hauled our string of cars to a tiny railway junction in the absolute middle of nowhere. Then it chugged away. It was four in the morning of June 26, but since it was summer it was already light. There were five families running the place, living in log cabins chinked with mud.

Our ranking KGB officer, an officious jerk named Chalomei, unsealed our doors. Vlad and I jumped out onto the rough boards of the siding. After days of ceaseless train vibration we staggered around like sailors who'd lost their land-legs. All around us was raw wilderness, huge birches and tough Siberian pines, with knobby, shallow roots. Permafrost was only two feet underground. There was nothing but trees and marsh for days in all directions. I found it very depressing.

We tried to strike up a conversation with the local supervisor. He spoke bad Russian, and looked like a relocated Latvian. The rest of our company piled out, yawning and complaining.

When he saw them, our host turned pale. He wasn't much like the brave pioneers on the posters. He looked scrawny and glum.

"Quite a place you have here," I observed.

"Is better than labor camp, I always thinking," he said. He murmured something to Vlad.

"Yeah," Vlad said thoughtfully, looking at our crew. "Now that you mention it, they *are* all police sneaks."

With much confusion, we began unloading our train cars. Slowly the siding filled up with boxes of rations, bundled tents, and wooden crates labeled SECRET and THIS SIDE UP.

A fight broke out between our civilians and our Red Army detachment. Our Kaliningrad folk were soon sucking their blisters and rubbing strained backs, but the soldiers refused to do the work alone.

Things were getting out of hand. I urged Vlad to give them all a good talking-to, a good, ringing speech to establish who was who and what was what. Something simple and forceful, with lots of "marching steadfastly together" and "storming the stars" and so on.

"I'll give them something better," said Vlad, running his hands back through his hair. "I'll give them the truth." He climbed atop a crate and launched into a strange, ideologically incorrect harangue.

"Comrades. You should think of Einstein's teachings. Matter is illusion. Why do you struggle so? Spacetime is the ultimate reality. Spacetime is one, and we are all patterns on it. We are ripples, Comrades, wrinkles in the fabric of the…"

"Einstein is a tool of International Zionism," shouted someone.

"And you are a dog," said Vlad evenly. "Nevertheless you and I are the same. We are different parts of the cosmic One. Matter is just a…"

"Drop dead," yelled another heckler.

"Death is an illusion," said Vlad, his smile tightening. "A person's spacetime pattern codes an information pattern which the cosmos is free to…"

It was total gibberish. Everyone began shouting and complaining at once, and Vlad's speech stuttered to a halt.

Our KGB colonel Chalomei jumped up on a crate and declared that he was taking charge. He was attached directly to the Chief Designer's staff, he shouted, and was fed up with our expedition's laxity. This was nothing but pure mutiny, but nobody else outranked him in KGB. It looked like Chalomei would get away with it. He then tried to order our Red Army boys to finish the unloading.

But they got mulish. There were six of them, all Central Asian Uzbeks from Uckduck, a hick burg in Uzbekskaja. They'd all joined the Red Army together, probably at gunpoint. Their leader was Master Sergeant Mukhamed, a rough character with a broken nose and puffy, scarred eyebrows. He looked and acted like a tank.

Mukhamed bellowed that his orders didn't include acting as house-serfs for egghead aristocrats. Chalomei insinuated how much trouble he could make for Mukhamed, but Mukhamed only laughed.

"I may be just a dumb Uzbek," Mukhamed roared, "but I didn't just fall off the turnip truck! Why do you think this train is full of you worth-less *stukachi*? It's so those big-brain rocket boys you left behind can get some real work done for once! Without you stoolies hanging around, stir-ring up trouble to make yourselves look good! They'd love to see you scum break your necks in the swamps of Siberia…"

He said a great deal more, but the damage was already done. Our expedition's morale collapsed like a burst balloon. The rest of the group refused to move another millimeter without direct orders from Higher Circles.

We spent three days then, on the station's telegraph, waiting for orders. The glorious 50th Anniversary of the event came and went and everything was screwed up and in a total shambles. The gloomi-est rumors spread among us. Some said that the Chief Designer had tricked us KGB to get us out of the way, and others said that Khrushchev himself was behind it. (There were always rumors of struggle between Party and KGB at the Very Highest Circles.) Whatever it meant, we were all sure to be humiliated when we got back, and heads would roll.

I was worried sick. If this really was a plot to hoodwink KGB, then I was in it up to my neck. Then the galley car caught fire during the night and sabotage was suspected. The locals, fearing interrogation, fled into the forest, though it was probably just one of Chalomei's *stukachi* being careless with a samovar.

Orders finally arrived from Higher Circles. KGB personnel were to return to their posts for a "reassessment of their performance." This did not sound promising at all. No such orders were given to Vlad or the "expedition regulars," whatever that meant. Apparently the Higher Circles had not yet grasped that there *were* no "expedition regulars."

Nina and I were both severely implicated, so we both decided that we were certainly "regulars" and should put off going back as long as possible. Together with Vlad, we had a long talk with Sergeant Mukhamed, who seemed a sensible sort.

"We're better off without those desk jockeys," Mukhamed said bluntly. "This is rough country. We can't waste time tying up the shoelaces of those Moscow fairies. Besides, my orders say 'Zipkin' and I don't see 'KGB' written anywhere on them."

"Maybe he's right," Vlad said. "We're in so deep now that our best chance is to actually *find* an artifact and prove them all wrong! Results are what count, after all! We've come this far—why turn tail now?"

Our own orders said nothing about the equipment. It turned out there was far too much of it for us to load it aboard the Red Army tractor vehicles. We left most of it on the sidings.

We left early next morning, while the others were still snoring. We had three all-terrain vehicles with us, brand new Red Army amphibious personnel carriers, called "BTR-50s," or "*byutors*" in Army slang. They had camouflaged steel armor and rode very low to the ground on broad tracks. They had loud, rugged diesel engines and good navigation equipment, with room for ten troops each in a bay in the back. The front had slits and searchlights and little pop-up armored hatches for the driver and commander. The *byutors* floated in water, too, and could churn through the thickest mud like a salamander. We scientists rode in the first vehicle, while the second carried equipment and the third, fuel.

Once underway, our spirits rose immediately. You could always depend on the good old Red Army to get the job done! We roared through woods and swamps with a loud, comforting racket, scaring up large flocks of herons and geese. Our photoreconnaissance maps, which had been issued to us under the strictest security, helped us avoid the worst obstacles. The days were long and we made good speed, stopping only a few hours a night.

It took three days of steady travel to reach the Tunguksa basin. Cone-shaped hills surrounded the valley like watchtowers.

The terrain changed here. Mummified trees strewed the ground like jackstraws, many of them oddly burnt. Trees decayed very slowly in the Siberian taiga. They were deep-frozen all winter and stayed whole for decades.

Dusk fell. We bulled our way around the slope of one of the hills, while leafless, withered branches crunched and shrieked beneath our treads. The marshy Tunguska valley, clogged and gray with debris, came in to view. Sergeant Mukhamed called a halt. The maze of fallen lumber was too much for our machines.

We tottered out of the *byutors* and savored the silence. My kidneys felt like jelly from days of lurching and jarring. I stood by our *byutor*, resting my hand on it, taking comfort in the fact that it was man-made. The rough travel and savage dreariness had taken the edge off my enthusiasm. I needed a drink.

But our last liter of vodka had gone out the train window somewhere between Omsk and Tomsk. Nina had thrown it away "for Vlad's sake." She was acting more like a lovesick schoolgirl every day. She was constantly fussing over Vlad, tidying him up, watching his diet, leaping heavily to his defense in every conversation. Vlad, of course, merely sopped up this devotion as his due, too absent-minded to notice it. Vlad had a real talent for that. I wasn't sure which of the two of them was more disgusting.

"At last," Vlad exulted. "Look, Ninotchka, the site of the mystery! Isn't it sublime!" Nina smiled and linked her solid arm with his.

The dusk thickened. Huge taiga mosquitoes whirred past our ears and settled to sting and pump blood. We slapped furiously, then set up our camp amid a ring of dense, smoky fires.

To our alarm, answering fires flared up on the five other hilltops ringing the valley.

"Evenks," grumbled Sergeant Mukhamed. "Savage nomads. They live off their reindeer, and camp in round tents called yurts. No one can civilize them; it's hopeless. Best just to ignore them."

"Why are they here?" Nina said. "Such a bleak place."

Vlad rubbed his chin. "The record of the '27 Kulik Expedition said the Evenk tribes remembered the explosion. They spoke of a Thunder-God smiting the valley. They must know this place pretty well."

"I'm telling you," rasped Mukhamed, "stay away. The men are all mushroom-eaters and the women are all whores."

One of the shaven-headed Uzbek privates looked up from his tin of rations. "Really, Sarge?"

"Their girls have lice as big as your thumbnails," the sergeant said. "And the men don't like strangers. When they eat those poison toadstools they get like wild beasts."

We had tea and hardtack, sniffling and wiping our eyes from the bug-repelling smoke. Vlad was full of plans. "Tomorrow we'll gather data on the direction of the treefalls. That'll show us the central impact point. Nina, you can help me with that. Nikita, you can stay here and help the soldiers set up base camp. And maybe later tomorrow we'll have an idea of where to look for our artifact."

Later that night, Vlad and Nina crept out of our long tent. I heard restrained groaning and sighing for half an hour. The soldiers snored on peacefully while I lay under the canvas with my eyes wide open. Finally Nina shuffled in, followed by Vlad brushing mud from his knees.

I slept poorly that night. Maybe Nina was no sexy hard-currency girl, but she was a woman, and even a *stukach* can't overhear that sort of thing without getting hot and bothered. After all, I had my needs, too.

Around one in the morning I gave up trying to sleep and stepped out of the tent for some air. An incredible aurora display greeted me. We were late for the 50th anniversary of the Tunguska crash, but I had the feeling the valley was welcoming me.

There was an arc of rainbow light directly overhead, with crimson and yellow streamers shooting out from the zenith towards the horizons. Wide luminous bands, paralleling the arch, kept rising out of the horizon to roll across the heavens with swift steady majesty. The bands crashed into the arch like long breakers from a sea of light.

The great auroral rainbow, with all its wavering streamers, began to swing slowly upwards, and a second, brighter arch formed below it. The new arch shot a long serried row of slender, colored lances towards the Tunguska valley. The lances stretched down, touched, and a lightning flash of vivid orange glared out, filling the whole world around me. I held my breath, waiting for the thunder, but the only sound was Nina's light snoring.

I watched for a while longer, until finally the great cosmic tide of light shivered into pieces. At the very end, disks appeared, silvery, shimmering saucers that filled the sky. Truly we had come to a very strange place. Filled with profound emotions, I was able to forget myself and sleep.

Next morning everyone woke up refreshed and cheerful. Vlad and Nina traipsed off with the surveying equipment. With the soldiers' help, I set up the diesel generator for Vlad's portable calculator. We did some camp scut-work, cutting heaps of firewood, digging a proper latrine. By then it was noon, but the lovebirds were still not back, so I did some exploring of my own. I tramped downhill into the disaster zone.

I realized almost at once that our task was hopeless. The ground was squelchy and dead, beneath a thick tangling shroud of leafless pines. We couldn't look for wreckage systematically without hauling away the musty, long-dead crust of trees. Even if we managed that, the ground itself was impossibly soggy and treacherous.

I despaired. The valley itself oppressed my soul. The rest of the taiga had chipmunks, wood grouse, the occasional heron or squirrel, but this swamp seemed lifeless, poisonous. In many places the earth had sagged into shallow bowls and depressions, as if the rock below it had rotted away.

New young pines had sprung up to take the place of the old, but I didn't like the look of them. The green saplings, growing up through the gray skeletons of their ancestors, were oddly stunted and twisted. A few older pines had been half-sheltered from the blast by freaks of topography. The living bark on their battered limbs and trunks showed repulsive puckered blast-scars.

Something malign had entered the soil. Perhaps poisoned comet ice, I thought. I took samples of the mud, mostly to impress the soldiers back at camp. I wasn't much of a scientist, but I knew how to go through the motions.

While digging I disturbed an ant nest. The strange, big-headed ants emerged from their tunnels and surveyed the damage with eerie calm.

By the time I returned to camp, Vlad and Nina were back. Vlad was working on his calculator while Nina read out direction-angles of the felled trees. "We're almost done," Nina told me, her broad-cheeked face full of bovine satisfaction. "We're running an information-theoretic analysis to determine the ground location of the explosion."

The soldiers looked impressed. But the upshot of Vlad's and Nina's fancy analysis was what any fool could see by glancing at the elliptical valley. The brunt of the explosion had burst from the nearer focus of the ellipse, directly over a little hill I'd had my eye on all along.

"I've been taking soil samples," I told Nina. "I suspect odd trace elements in the soil. I suppose you noticed the strange growth of the pines. They're particularly tall at the blast's epicenter."

"Hmph," Nina said. "While you were sleeping last night, there was a minor aurora. I took photos. I think the geomagnetic field may have had an influence on the object's trajectory."

"That's elementary," I sniffed. "What we need to study is a possible remagnetization of the rocks. Especially at impact point."

"You're neglecting the biological element." Nina said. By now the soldiers' heads were swiveling to follow our discussion like a tennis match. "I suppose you didn't notice the faint luminescence of the sod?" She pulled some crumpled blades of grass from her pocket. "A Kirlian analysis will prove interesting."

"But, of course, the ants—" I began.

"Will you two fakers shut up a minute?" Vlad broke in. "I'm trying to think."

I swallowed hard. "Oh yes, Comrade Genius? What about?"

"About finding what we came for, Nikita. The alien craft." Vlad frowned, waving his arm at the valley below us. "I'm convinced it's buried out there somewhere. We don't have a chance in this tangle and ooze…but we've got to figure some way to sniff it out."

At that moment we heard the distant barking of a dog. "Great," Vlad said without pausing. "Maybe that's a bloodhound."

He'd made a joke. I realized this after a moment, but by then it was too late to laugh. "It's just some Evenk mutt," Sergeant Mukhamed said. "They keep sled-dogs…eat 'em, too." The dog barked louder, coming closer. "Maybe it got loose."

Ten minutes later the dog bounded into our camp, barking joyously and frisking. It was a small, bright-eyed female husky, with muddy legs and damp fur caked with bits of bark. "That's no sled-dog," Vlad said, wondering. "That's a city mutt. What's it doing here?"

She was certainly friendly enough. She barked in excitement and sniffed at our hands trustingly. I patted the dog and called her a good girl. "Where on earth did you come from?" I asked. I'd always liked dogs.

One of the soldiers addressed the dog in Uzbek and offered it some of his rations. It sniffed the food, took a tentative lick, but refused to eat it.

"Sit!" Vlad said suddenly. The dog sat obediently.

"She understands Russian," Vlad said.

"Nonsense," I said. "She just reacted to your voice."

"There must be other Russians nearby," Nina said. "A secret research station, maybe? Something we were never told about?"

"Well, I guess we have a mascot," I said, scratching the dog's scalp.

"Come here, Laika," Vlad said. The dog pricked her ears and wandered toward him.

I felt an icy sensation of horror. I snatched my hand back as if I had touched a corpse. With an effort, I controlled myself. "Come on, Vlad," I said. "You're joking again."

"Good dog," Vlad said, patting her.

"Vlad," I said, "Laika's rocket burned up on re-entry."

"Yes," Vlad said, "the first creature we Earthlings put into space was sentenced to be burned alive. I often think about that." Vlad stared dramatically into the depths of the valley. "Comrades, I think something is waiting here to help us storm the cosmos. I think it preserved Laika's soul and reanimated her here, at this place, and at this time… It's no coincidence. This is no ordinary animal. This is Laika, the cosmonaut dog!"

Laika barked loudly. I had never seen the dog without the rubber oxygen mask on her face, but I knew with a thrill of supernatural fear that Vlad was right. I felt an instant irrational urge to kill the dog, or at least give her a good kick. If I killed and buried her, I wouldn't have to think about what she meant.

The others looked equally stricken. "Probably fell off a train," Mukhamed muttered at last.

Vlad regally ignored this frail reed of logic. "We ought to follow Laika. The…Thunder-God put her here to lead us. It won't get dark till ten o'clock. Let's move out, comrades." Vlad stood up and shrugged on his backpack. "Mukhamed?"

"Uh…" the sergeant said. "My orders are to stay with the vehicles." He cleared his throat and spat. "There are Evenks about. Natural thieves. We wouldn't want our camp to be raided."

Vlad looked at him in surprise, and then with pity. He walked towards me, threw one arm over my shoulder, and took me aside. "Nikita, these Uzbeks are brave soldiers but they're a bit superstitious. Terrified of the unknown. What a laugh. But you and I…Scientists, space pioneers…the Unknown is our natural habitat, right?"

"Well…"

"Come on, Nikita." He glowered. "We can't go back and face the top brass empty-handed."

Nina joined us. "I knew you'd turn yellow, Globov. Never mind him, Vlad, darling. Why should you share your fame and glory with this sneaking coward? I'll go with you—"

"You're a woman," Vlad assured her loftily. "You're staying here where it's safe."

"But Vlad—"

Vlad folded his arms. "Don't make me have to beat you." Nina blushed girlishly and looked at the toes of her hiking boots. She could have broken his back like a twig.

The dog barked loudly and capered at our feet. "Come on," Vlad said. He set off without looking back.

I grabbed my pack and followed him. I had to. I was guarding him: no more Vlad, no more Globov…

Our journey was a nightmare. The dog kept trying to follow us, or would run yipping through ratholes in the brush that we had to circle painfully. Half on intuition, we headed for the epicenter of the blast, the little hillock at the valley's focus.

It was almost dusk again when we finally reached it, battered, scratched and bone-tired. We found a yurt there, half-hidden in a slough off to one side of the hill. It was an Evenk reindeer-skin tent, oozing grayish smoke from a vent-hole. A couple of scabby reindeer were pegged down outside it, gnawing at a lush, purplish patch of swamp moss. The dead trees around had been heavily seared by the blast, leaving half-charcoaled bubbly lumps of ancient resin. Some ferns and rushes had sprung up, corkscrewed, malformed, and growing with cancerous vigor.

The dog barked loudly at the wretched reindeer, who looked up with bleary-eyed indifference.

We heard leather thongs hiss loose in the door flap. A pale face framed in a greasy fur hood poked through. It was a young Evenk girl. She called to the dog, then noticed us and giggled quietly.

The dog rushed toward the yurt, wagging her tail. "Hello," Vlad called. He spread his open hands. "Come on out, we're friends."

The girl stepped out and inched toward us, watching the ground carefully. She paused at a small twig, her dilated eyes goggling as if it were a boulder. She high-jumped far over it, and landed giggling. She wore an elaborate reindeer-skin jacket that hung past her knees, thickly embroidered with little beads of bone and wood. She also had tight fur trousers with lumpy beaded booties, sewn all in one piece like a child's pajamas.

She sidled up, grinning coyly, and touched my face and clothes in curiosity. "Nikita," I said, touching my chest.

"Balan Thok," she whispered, running one fingertip down her sweating throat. She laughed drunkenly.

"Is that your dog?" Vlad said. "She came from the sky!" He gestured extravagantly. "Something under the earth here…brought her down from the sky…yes?"

I shrieked suddenly. A gargoyle had appeared in the tent's opening. But the blank, ghastly face was only a wooden ceremonial mask, shaped like a frying pan, with a handle to grip below the "chin." The mask had eye-slits and a carved mouth-hole fringed with a glued-on beard of reindeer hair.

Behind it was Balan Thok's father, or maybe grandfather. Cunningly, the old villain peered at us around the edge of his mask. His face was as wrinkled as an old boot. The sides of his head were shaven and filth-choked white hair puffed from the top like a thistle. His long reindeer coat was fringed with black fur and covered with bits of polished bone and metal.

We established that the old savage was called Jif Gurd. Vlad went through his sky-pointing routine again. Jif Gurd returned briefly to his leather yurt and re-emerged with a long wooden spear. Grinning vacuously, he jammed the butt of it into a socket in the ground and pointed to the heavens.

"I don't like the look of this," I told Vlad at once. "That spear has dried blood on it."

"Yeah. I've heard of this," Vlad said. "Sacrifice poles for the thunder-god. Kulik wrote about them." He turned to the old man. "That's right," he encouraged. "Thunder-God." He pointed to the dog. "Thunder-God brought this dog down."

"Thunder-God," said Jif Gurd seriously. "Dog." He looked up at the sky reverently. "Thunder-God." He made a descending motion with his right arm, threw his hands apart to describe the explosion. "Boom!"

"That's right! That's right!" Vlad said excitedly.

Jif Gurd nodded. He bent down almost absentmindedly and picked little Laika up by the scruff of the neck. "Dog."

"Yes, yes," Vlad nodded eagerly. Before we could do anything, before we could realize what was happening, Jif Gurd reached inside his greasy coat, produced a long, curved knife, and slashed poor Laika's throat. He lifted her up without effort—he was terribly strong, the strength of drug-madness—and jammed her limp neck over the end of the spear as if gaffing a fish.

Blood squirted everywhere. Vlad and I jumped back, horrified. "Hell!" Vlad cried in anguish. "I forgot that they sacrifice dogs!"

The hideous old man grinned and chattered excitedly. He was convinced that he understood us—that Vlad had wanted him to sacrifice the dog to the sky-god. He approved of the idea. He approved of us. I said, "He thinks we have something in common now, Vlad."

"Yeah," Vlad said. He looked sadly at Laika. "Well, we rocket men sacrificed her first, poor beast."

"There goes our last lead to the UFO," I said. "Poor Laika! All the way just for this!"

"This guy's got to know where the thing is," Vlad said stubbornly. "Look at the sly old codger—it's written all over his face." Vlad stepped forward. "Where is it? Where did it land?" He gestured wildly. "You take us there!"

Balan Thok gnawed her slender knuckles and giggled at our antics, but it didn't take the old guy long to catch on. By gestures, and a few key words, we established that the Thunder-God was in a hole nearby.

A hidden hole, deep in the earth. He knew where it was. He could show it to us.

But he wouldn't.

"It's a religious thing," Vlad said, mulling it over. "I think we're ritually unclean."

"Muk-a-moor," said the old man. He opened the tent flap and gestured us inside.

The leather walls inside were black with years of soot. The yurt was round, maybe five steps across, and braced with a lattice of smooth flat sticks and buckskin thongs. A fire blazed away in the yurt's center, chunks of charred pine on a hearth of flat yellow stones. Dense smoke curdled the air. Two huge furry mounds loomed beside the hearth. They were Evenk sleeping bags, like miniature tents in themselves.

Our eyes were caught by the drying-racks over the fire. Mushrooms littered the racks, the red-capped fly agaric mushrooms that one always sees in children's books. The intoxicating toadstools of the Siberian nomad. Their steaming fungal reek filled the tent, below the acrid stench of smoke and rancid sweat.

"Muk-a-moor," said Jif Gurd, pointing at them, and then at his head.

"Oh, Christ," Vlad said. "He won't show us anything unless we eat his sacred mushrooms." He caught the geezer's eye and pantomimed eating.

The old addict shook his head and held up a leather cup. He pretended to drink, then smacked his rubbery, bearded lips. He pointed to Balan Thok.

"I don't get it," Vlad said.

"Right," I said, getting to my feet. "Well, you hold him here, and I'll go back to camp. I'll have the soldiers in by midnight. We'll beat the truth out of the old dog-butcher."

"Sit down, idiot," Vlad hissed. "Don't you remember how quick he was with that knife?"

It was true. At my movement a sinister gleam had entered the old man's eyes. I sat down quickly. "We can outrun him."

"It's getting dark," Vlad said. Just three words, but they brought a whole scene into mind: running blind through a maze of broken branches, with a drug-crazed, panting slasher at my heels…I smiled winningly at the old shaman. He grinned back and again made his drinking gesture. He tossed the leather cup to Balan Thok, who grabbed at it wildly and missed it by two meters. She picked it up and turned her back on us. We heard her fumble with the lacing of her trousers. She squatted down. There was a hiss of liquid.

"Oh Jesus," I said. "Vlad, no."

"I've heard about this," Vlad said wonderingly. "The active ingredient passes on into the urine. Ten savages can get drunk on one mushroom. Pass it from man to man." He paused. "The kidneys absorb the impurities. It's supposed to be better for you that way. Not as poisonous."

"Can't we just eat the muk-a-moors?" I said, pointing at the rack. The old shaman glowered at me, and shook his head violently. Balan Thok sashayed toward me, hiding her face behind one sleeve. She put the warm cup into my hands and backed away, giggling.

I held the cup. A terrible fatalism washed over me. "Vladimir," I said. "I'm tired. My head hurts. I've been stung all over by mosquitoes and my pants are drenched with dog blood. I don't want to drink the poison piss of some savage—"

"It's for Science," Vlad said soberly.

"All my life," I began, "I wanted to work for the good of Society. My dear mother, God bless her memory…" I choked up. "If she could see what her dear son has come to…All those years of training, just for this! For this, Vlad?" I began trembling violently.

"Don't spill it!" Vlad said. Balan Thok stared at me, licking her lips. "I think she likes you," Vlad said.

For some weird reason these last words pushed me over the edge. I shoved the cup to my lips and drained the potion in one go. It sizzled down my gullet in a wave of hot nausea. Somehow I managed to keep from vomiting.

"How do you feel?" Vlad asked eagerly.

"My face is going numb." I stared at Balan Thok. Her eyes were full of hot fascination. I looked at her, willing her to come toward me. Nothing could be worse now. I had gone through the ultimate. I was ready, no, eager, to heap any degradation on myself. Maybe fornication with this degraded creature would raise me to some strange height.

"You're braver than I thought, Nikita," Vlad said. His voice rang with unnatural volume in my drugged ears. He pulled the cup from my numbed hands. "Considered objectively, this is really not so bad. A healthy young woman…sterile fluid…It's mere custom that makes it seem so repellent." He smiled in superior fashion, gripping the cup.

Suddenly the old Siberian shaman stood before him guffawing crazily as he donated Vlad's share. A cheesy reek came from his dropped trousers. Vlad stared at me in horror. I fell on my side, laughing wildly. My bones turned to rubber.

The girl laughed like a xylophone, gesturing to me lewdly. Vlad was puking noisily. I got up to lurch toward the girl, but forgot to move my feet and fell down. My head was inflamed with intense desire for her. She was turning round and round, singing in a high voice, holding a curved knife over her head. Somehow I tackled her and we fell head-long onto one of the Evenk sleeping bags, crushing it with a snapping of wood and lashings. I couldn't get out of my clothes. They were crawling over me like live things.

I paused to retch, not feeling much pain, just a torrent of sensations as the drug came up. Vlad and the old man were singing together loudly and at great length. I was thumping around vaguely on top of the girl, watching a louse crawl through one of her braids.

The old man came crawling up on all fours and stared into my face. "Thunder-God," he cackled, and tugged at my arm. He had pulled aside a large reindeer skin that covered the floor of the yurt. There was a deep hole, right there, right in the tent with us. Fighting the cramps in my stomach, I dragged myself toward it and peered in.

The space in the hole was strangely distorted; it was impossible to tell how deep it was. At its far end was a reticulated blue aurora that seemed to shift and flow in synchronization with my thoughts. For some reason I thought of Laika, and wished again that Jif Gurd hadn't killed her. The aurora pulsed at my thought, and there was a thump outside the tent—a thump followed by loud barking.

"Laika?" I said. My voice came out slow and drugged. Balan Thok had her arms around my neck and was licking my face. Dragging her after me, I crawled to the tent flap and peered out. There was a dog-shaped glob of light out there, barking as if its throat would burst.

I was scared, and I let Balan Thok pull me back into the tent. The full intoxication took over. Balan Thok undid my trousers and aroused me to madness. Vlad and the old man were lying at the edge of the Thunder-God hole, staring down into the growing blue light and screaming to it. I threw Balan Thok down between them, and we began coupling savagely. Each spastic twitch of our bodies was a coded message, a message that Vlad and Jif Gurd's howls were reinforcing. Our filth and drug-madness became a sacred ritual, an Eleusinian mystery. Before too long, I could hear the voice of…

God? No…not god, and not the Devil. The voice was from the blue light in the pit. And it wasn't a voice. It was the same, somehow, as the aurora I'd seen last night. It liked dogs, and it liked me. Behind all the frenzy, I was very happy there, shuddering on Balan Thok. Time passed.

At some point there was more barking outside, and the old man screamed. I saw his face, underlit by the pulsing blue glow from the Thunder-God hole. He bounded over me, waving his bloody knife overhead.

I heard a gunshot from the tent-door, and someone came crashing in. A person led by a bright blue dog. Captain Nina. The dog had helped her find us. The dog ran over and snapped at me, forcing me away from Balan Thok and the hole. I got hold of Vlad's leg, and dragged him along with me. There was another shot, and then Nina was struggling hand to hand with the old man. Vlad staggered to his feet and tried to join the fight. But I got my arms around his thin chest and kept backing away.

Jif Gurd and Nina were near the hole's jumpy light now, and I could see that they both were wounded. She had shot the old man twice with a pistol, but he had his knife, and the strength of a maniac. The two of them wrestled hand-to-hand, clawing and screaming. Now Balan Thok rose to her knees and began slashing at Nina's legs with a short dagger. Nina's pistol pointed this way and that, constantly about to fire.

I dragged Vlad backwards, and we tore through the rotting leather of the yurt's wall. An aurora like last night's filled the sky. Now that I wasn't staring into the hole I could think a little bit. So many things swirled in my mind, but one fact above all stuck out. *We had found an alien artifact.* If only it was a rocket-drive, then all of the terrible mess in the yurt could be forgotten…

An incandescent blast lifted Vlad and me off the ground and threw us five meters. The entire yurt leapt into the sky. It was gone instantly, leaving a backward meteor trail of flaming orange in the sudden blackness of the sky. The sodden earth convulsed. From overhead, a leaping sonic boom pressed Vlad and me down into the muck where we had landed. I passed out.

Vlad shook me awake after many hours. The sun was still burning above the horizon. It was another of those dizzying, endless, timeless summer days. I tried to remember what had happened. When my first memories came I retched in pain.

Vlad had started a roaring campfire from dead, mummified branches. "Have some tea, Nikita," he said, handing me a tin army mug filled with hot, yellow liquid.

"No," I choked weakly. "No more."

"It's tea," Vlad said. I could tell his mind was running a mile a minute. "Take it easy. It's all over. We're alive, and we've found the star-drive. That blast last night!" His face hardened a bit. "Why didn't you let me try to save poor Nina?"

I coughed and wiped my bloodshot, aching eyes. I tried to fit my last twelve hallucinated hours into some coherent pattern. "The yurt," I croaked. "The star-drive shot it into the sky? That really happened?"

"Nina shot the old man. She burst in with a kind of ghost-dog? She burst in and the old man rushed her with his knife. When the drive went off, it threw all of them into the sky. Nina, the two Evenks, even the two reindeer and the dog. We were lucky—we were right at the edge of the ellipse."

"I saved you, Vlad. There was no way to save Nina, too. Please don't blame me." I needed his forgiveness because I felt guilty. I had a strange feeling that it had been my *wish of finding a rocket drive* that had made the artifact send out the fatal blast.

Vlad sighed and scratched his ribs. "Poor Ninotchka. Imagine how it must have looked. Us rolling around screaming in delirium and you having filthy sex with that Evenk girl..." He frowned sadly. "Not what you expect from Soviet scientists."

I sat up to look at the elliptical blast area where the yurt had been. Nothing was left of it but a few sticks and thongs and bits of hide. The rest was a muddy crater. "My God, Vlad."

"It's extremely powerful," Vlad said moodily. "It wants to help us Earthlings, I know it does. It saved Laika, remember?"

"It saved her twice. Did you see the blue dog last night?"

Vlad frowned impatiently. "I saw lots of things last night, Nikita, but now those things are gone."

"The drive is gone?"

"Oh no," Vlad said. "I dug it out of the crater this morning."

He gestured at our booty. It was sitting in the mud behind him. It was caked with dirt and weird, powdery rust. It looked like an old tractor crankcase.

"Is that it?" I said doubtfully.

"It looked better this morning," Vlad said. "It was made of something like jade and was shaped like a vacuum cleaner. With fins. But if you take your eyes off it, it changes."

"No. Really?"

Vlad said, "It's looked shabby ever since you woke up. It's picking up on your shame. That was really pretty horrible last night, Nikita; I'd never thought that you..."

I poked him sharply to shut him up. We looked at each other for a minute, and then I took a deep breath. "The main thing is that we've got it, Vlad. This is a great day in history."

"Yeah," agreed Vlad, finally smiling. The drive looked shinier now. "Help me rig up a sling for it."

With great care, as much for our pounding heads as for the Artifact itself, we bundled it up in Vlad's coat and slung it from a long, crooked shoulder-pole.

My head was still swimming. The mosquitoes were a nightmare. Vlad and I climbed up and over the splintery, denuded trunks of dead pines, stopping often to wheeze on the damp, metallic air. The sky was very clear and blue, the color of Lake Baikal. Sometimes, when Vlad's head and shoulders were outlined against the sky, I seemed to see a faint Kirlian shimmer traveling up the shoulder-pole to dance on his skin.

Panting with exhaustion, we stopped and gulped down more rations. Both of us had the trots. Small wonder. We built a good sooty fire to keep the bugs off for a while. We threw in some smoky green boughs from those nasty-looking young pines. Vlad could not resist the urge to look at it again.

We unwrapped it. Vlad stared at it fondly. "After this, it will belong to all mankind," he said. "But for now it's ours!"

It had changed again. Now it had handles. They looked good and solid, less rusty than the rest. We lugged it by the handles until we got within earshot of the base-camp.

The soldiers heard our yells and three of them came to help us.

They told us about Nina on our way back. All day she had paced and fidgeted, worrying about Vlad and trying to talk the soldiers into a rescue mission. Finally, despite their good advice, she had set off after us alone.

The aurora fireworks during the night had terrified the Uzbeks. They were astonished to see that we had not only survived, but triumphed.

But we had to tell them that Nina was gone.

Sergeant Mukhamed produced some 200-proof ethanol from the de-icing tank of his *byutor*. Weeping unashamedly, we toasted the memory of our lost comrade, State Security Captain Nina Igorovna Bogulyubova. After that we had another round, and I made a short but dignified speech about those who fall while storming the cosmos. Yes, dear Captain Nina was gone; but thanks to her sacrifice, we, her comrades, had achieved an unprecedented victory. She would never be forgotten. Vlad and I would see to that.

We had another toast for our cosmic triumph. Then another for the final victory. Then we were out of drinks.

The Uzbeks hadn't been idle while Vlad and I had been gone. They didn't have live ammo, but a small bear had come snuffling round the camp the day before and they'd managed to run over him with one of the *byutors*. The air reeked of roast bear meat and dripping fat. Vlad and I had a good big rack of ribs, each. The ribs in my chunk were pretty broken up, but it was still tasty. For the first time, I felt like a real hero. Eating bear meat in Siberia. It was a heck of a thing.

Now that we were back to the *byutors*, our problems were behind us and we could look forward to a real "rain of gold." Medals, and plenty of them. Big *dachas* on the Black Sea, and maybe even lecture tours in the West, where we could buy jazz records. All the Red Army boys figured they had big promotions coming.

We broke camp and loaded the carriers. Vlad wouldn't join in the soldiers' joking and kidding. He was still mooning about Nina. I felt sorry for Vlad. I'd never liked Nina much, and I'd been against her coming from the first. The wilderness was no place for females, and it was no wonder she'd come to grief. But I didn't point this out to Vlad. It would only have made him feel worse. Besides, Nina's heroic sacrifice had given a new level of deep moral meaning to our effort.

We packed the drive away in the first *byutor* where Vlad and I could keep an eye on it. Every time we stopped to refuel or study the maps, Vlad would open its wrappings and have a peek. I teased him about it. "What's the matter, comrade? Want to chain it to your leg?"

Vlad was running his hand over and over the drive's rusty surface. Beneath his polishing strokes, a faint gleam of silver had appeared. He frowned mightily. "Nikita, we must never forget that this is no soulless machine. I'm convinced it takes its form from what we make of it. It's a frozen idea—that's it true essence. And if you and I forget it, or look aside, it might just vanish."

I tried to laugh him out of it, but Vlad was serious. He slept next to it both nights, until we reached the rail spur.

We followed the line to the station. Vlad telegraphed full particulars to Moscow and I sent along a proud report to Higher Circles.

We waited impatiently for four days. Finally a train arrived. It contained some rocket-drive technicians from the Baikonur Cosmodrome, and two dozen uniformed KGB. Vlad and I were arrested. The Red Army boys were taken in custody by some Red Army brass. Even the Latvian who ran the station was arrested.

We were kept incommunicado in a bunk car. Vlad remained cheerful, though. "This is nothing," he said, drawing on his old jailbird's lore. "When they really mean business, they take your shoelaces. These KGB are just protective custody. After all, you and I have the greatest secret in cosmic history!" And we were treated well—we had red caviar, Crimean champagne, Kamchatkan king crab, blinis with sour cream.

The drive had been loaded aboard a flatcar and swathed down under many layers of canvas. The train pulled to a halt several times. The window shades on our car were kept lowered, but whenever we stopped, Vlad peeked out. He claimed the rocket specialists were adjusting the load.

After the second day of travel I had grave doubts about our whole situation. No one had interrogated us; for cosmic heroes, we were being badly neglected. I even had to beg ignominiously for DDT to kill the crab-lice I had caught from Balan Thok. Compared to the mundane boredom of our train confinement, our glorious adventure began to seem absurd. How would we explain our strange decisions—how would we explain what had happened to Nina? Our confusion would surely make it look like we were hiding something.

Instead of returning in triumph to Kaliningrad, our train headed south. We were bound for Baikonur Cosmodrome, where the rockets are launched. Actually, Baikonur is just the "security name" for the installation. The real town of Baikonur is five hundred kilometers away. The true launch site is near the village of Tyuratam. And Tyuratam, worse luck, is even more of a hick town that Baikonur.

This cheerless place lies on a high plain north of Afghanistan and east of the Aral Sea. It was dry and hot when we got there, with a cease-less irritating wind. As they marched us out of the train, we saw engineers unloading the drive. With derricks.

Over the course of the trip, as the government rocket experts fiddled with it, the drive had expanded to fit their preconceptions. It had grown to the size of a whole flatcar. It had become a maze of crooked hydraulics, with great ridged black blast-nozzles. It was even bound together with those ridiculous hoops.

Vlad and I were hustled into our new quarters: a decontamination suite, built in anticipation of the launch of our first cosmonauts. It was not bad for a jail. We probably would have gotten something worse, except that Vlad's head sometimes oozed a faint but definite blue glow, and that made them cautious.

Our food came through sterilized slots in the wall. The door was like a bank vault. We were interrogated through windows of bulletproof glass via speakers and microphones.

We soon discovered that our space drive had been classified at the Very Highest Circles. It was not to be publicly referred to as an alien artifact. Officially, our space-drive was a secret new design from Kaliningrad. Even the scientist already working on it at Tyuratam had been told this, and apparently believed it.

The Higher Circles expected our drive to work miracles, but they were to be miracles of national Soviet science. No one was to know of our contact with cosmic powers.

Vlad and I became part of a precedence struggle in Higher Circles. Red Army defense radars had spotted the launching of the yurt, and they wanted to grill us. Khrushchev's new Rocket Defense Forces also wanted us. So did the Kaliningrad KGB. And of course the Tyuratam technicians had a claim on us; they were planning to use our drive for a spectacular propaganda feat.

We ended up in the hands of KGB's Paranormal Research Corps.

Weeks grew into months as the state psychics grilled us. They held up Zener cards from behind the glass and demanded that we guess circle, star, or cross. They gave us racks of radish seedlings through the food slots, and wanted us to speak nicely to half of them, and scold the other half.

They wanted us to influence the roll of dice, and to make it interesting they forced us to gamble for our vodka and cigarette rations. Naturally we blew the lot and were left with nothing to smoke.

We had no result from these investigations, except that Vlad once extruded a tiny bit of pale blue ectoplasm, and I turned out to be pretty good at reading colors, while blindfolded, with my fingertips. (I peeked down the side of my nose.)

One of our interrogators was a scrawny hardline Stalinist named Yezhov. He'd been a student of the biologist Lysenko and was convinced that Vlad and I could turn wheat into barley by forced evolution. Vlad finally blew up at this. "You charlatans!" he screamed into the microphone. "Not one of you has even read Tsiolkovsky! How can I speak to you? Where is the Chief Designer? I demand to be taken to Comrade Sergei Korolyov! He'd understand this!"

"You won't get out of it that way," Yezhov yapped, angrily shaking his vial of wheat seeds. "Your Chief Designer has had a heart attack. He's recovering in his *dacha*, and Khrushchev himself has ordered that he not be disturbed. Besides, do you think we're stupid enough to let people with alien powers into the heart of Moscow?"

"So that's it!" I shouted, wounded to the core at the thought of my beloved Moscow. "You pimp! We've been holding out on you, that's all!" I jabbed my hand dramatically at him from behind the glass. "Tonight, when you're sleeping, my psychic aura will creep into your bed and squeeze your brain, like this!" I made a fist. Yezhov fled in terror.

Silence fell. "You shouldn't have done that," Vlad observed.

I slumped into one of our futuristic aluminum chairs. "I couldn't help it," I muttered. "Vlad, the truth's out. It's permanent exile for us. We'll never see Moscow again." Tears filled my eyes.

Vlad patted my shoulder sympathetically. "It was a brave gesture, Nikita. I'm proud to call you my friend."

"You're the brave one, Vlad."

"But without you at my side, Nikita…You know, I'd have never dared to go into the valley alone. And if you hadn't drunk that piss first, well, I certainly would never have—"

"That's all in the past now, Vlad." My cheeks burned and I began sobbing. "I should have ignored you when you were sitting under that piano at Lyuda's. I should have left you in peace with your beatnik friends. Vlad, can you ever forgive me?"

"It's nothing," Vlad said nobly, thumping my back. "We've all been used, even poor Chief Korolyov. They've worked him to a frazzle. Even in camp he used to complain about his heart." Vlad shook his fist. "Those fools. We bring them a magnificent drive from Tunguska, and they convince themselves it's a reaction engine from Kaliningrad."

I burned with indignation. "That's right. It was our discovery! We're heroes, but they treat us like enemies of the State! It's so unfair, so uncommunist!" My voice rose. "If we're enemies of the State, then what are we doing in here? Real enemies of the State live in Paris, with silk suits and a girl on each arm! And plenty of capitalist dollars in a secret Swiss bank!"

Vlad was philosophical. "You can have all that. You know what I wanted? To see men on the moon. I just wanted to see men reach the moon, and know I'd seen a great leap for all humanity!"

I wiped away tears. "You're a dreamer, Vlad. The Infinite is just a propaganda game. We'll never see daylight again."

"Don't give up hope," Vlad said stubbornly. "At least we're not clearing trees in some labor camp where it's forty below. Sooner or later they'll launch some cosmonauts, and then they'll need this place for real. They'll have to spring us then!"

We didn't hear from the psychic corps again. We still got regular meals, and the occasional science magazine, reduced to tatters by some idiot censor who had decided Vlad and I were security risks. Once we even got a charity package from, of all people, Lyuda, who sent Vlad two cartons of Kents. We made a little ceremony of smoking one each, every day.

Our glass decontamination booth fronted on an empty auditorium for journalists and debriefing teams. Too bad none of them ever showed up. Every third day three cleaning women with mops and buckets scoured the auditorium floor. They always ignored us. Vlad and I used to speculate feverishly about their underwear.

The psychics had given up, and no one else seemed interested. Some-how we'd been lost in the files. We had been covered up so thoroughly that we no longer existed. We were the ghosts' ghosts, and the secrets' secrets, the best-hidden people in the world. We seemed to have popped loose from time and space, sleeping later and later each day, until finally we lost a day completely and could never keep track again.

We were down to our last pack of Kents when we had an unexpected visit.

It was a Red Army general with two brass-hat flunkies. We spotted him coming down the aisle from the auditorium's big double doors, and we hustled on our best shirts. The general was a harried-looking, bald guy in his fifties. He turned on our speakers and looked down at his clipboard. "Comrades Zipkin and Globov!"

"Let me handle this, Vlad," I hissed quickly. I leaned into my mike. "Yes, Comrade General?"

"My name's Nedelin. I'm in charge of the launch."

"What launch?" Vlad blurted.

"The Mars probe, of course." Nedelin frowned. "According to this, you were involved in the engine's design and construction?"

"Oh yes," I said. "Thoroughly."

Nedelin turned a page. "A special project with the Chief Designer." He spoke with respect. "I'm no scientist, and I know you have important work in there. But could you spare time from your labors to lend us a hand? We could use your expertise."

Vlad began to babble. "Oh, let us watch the launch! You can shoot us later, if you want! But let us see it, for God's sake—"

Luckily I had clamped my hand over Vlad's mike. I spoke quickly. "We're at your service, General. Never mind Professor Zipkin, he's a bit distraught."

One of the flunkies wheeled open our bank vault door. His nose wrinkled at the sudden reek of months of our airtight stench, but he said nothing. Vlad and I accompanied Nedelin through the building. I could barely hold back from skipping and leaping, and Vlad's knees trembled so badly I was afraid he would faint.

"I wouldn't have disturbed your secret project," the general informed us, "but Comrade Khrushchev delivers a speech at the United Nations tomorrow. He plans to announce that the Soviet Union has launched a probe to Mars. This launch must succeed today at all costs." We walked through steel double-doors into the Tyuratam sunshine. Dust and grass had never smelled so good.

We climbed into Nedelin's open-top field car. "You understand the stakes involved," Nedelin said, sweating despite the crisp October breeze. "There is a new American president, this Cuban situation… our success is crucial!"

We drove off rapidly across the bleak concrete expanse of the rocket-field. Nedelin shouted at us from the front seat. "Intelligence says the Americans are redoubling their space efforts. We must do something unprecedented, something to crush their morale! Something years ahead of its time! The first spacecraft sent to another planet!"

Wind poured through our long hair, our patchy beards. "A new American president," Vlad muttered. "Big deal." As I soaked my lungs with fresh air I realized how much Vlad and I stank. We looked and smelled like derelicts. Nedelin was obviously desperate.

We pulled up outside the sloped, fire-scorched wall of a concrete launch bunker. The Mars rocket towered on its pad, surrounded by four twenty-story hinged gantries. Wisps of cloud poured down from the rocket's liquid oxygen ports. Dozens of technicians in white coats and hard-hats clambered on the skeletal gentry-ladders, or shouted through bullhorns around the rocket's huge base.

"Well, comrades?" Nedelin said. "As you can see, we have our best people at it. The countdown went smoothly. We called for ignition. And nothing. Nothing at all!" He pulled off his brimmed cap and wiped his balding scalp. "We have a very narrow launch window! Within a matter of hours we will have lost our best parameters. Not to mention Comrade Khrushchev's speech!"

Vlad sniffed the air. "Comrade General. Have you fueled this craft with liquid paraffin?"

"Naturally!"

Vlad's voice sank. "These people are working on a rocket which misfired. And you haven't drained the fuel?"

Nedelin drew himself up stiffly. "That would take hours! I understand the risk! I'm not asking these people to face any danger I wouldn't face myself!"

"You pompous ass!" Vlad screeched. "That's no Earthling rocket! It only looks like one because you expect it to! It's not supposed to have fuel!"

Nedelin stared in amazement. "What?"

"That's why it didn't take off!" Vlad raved. "It didn't want to kill us all! That drive is from outer space! You've turned it into a gigantic firebomb!"

"You've gone mad! Comrade, get hold of yourself!" Nedelin shouted. We were all on the edge of panic.

"This blockhead's useless," Vlad snarled, grabbing my arm. "We've got to get those people out of there, Nikita! It could take off any second—everyone expected it to!"

We ran for the rocket, shouting wildly, yelling anything that came into our heads. We had to get the technicians away. The Tunguska device had never known its own strength—it didn't know how frail we were. I stumbled and looked over my shoulder. Nedelin's flunkies were just a dozen steps behind us.

The ground crew saw us coming. They cried out in alarm. Panic spread like lightning.

It wouldn't have happened if we hadn't all been Russians. A gloomy and sensitive people are always ready to believe the worst. And the worst in this case was obvious: total disaster from a late ignition.

They fled like maniacs, but they couldn't escape their expectations. Pale streamers of flame gushed from the engines. More streamers arched from the rocket's peak, the spikes of auroral fire. The gantries shattered like matchsticks, filling the air above us with wheeling black shrapnel. Vlad stumbled to the ground. Somewhere ahead of us I could hear barking.

I hauled Vlad to his feet. "Follow the dog!" I bellowed over the roar. "Into the focus of the ellipse, where it's stable!"

Vlad stumbled after me, jabbering with rage. "If only the Americans had gotten the drive! They would have put men on the moon!"

We dashed through a blinding rain of paraffin. The barking grew louder, and now I could see the eager dog of blue light, showing us the way. The rocket was dissolving above us. The blast-seared concrete under our feet pitched and buckled like aspic. Before us the rocket's great nozzles dissolved into flaming webs of spectral whiteness.

Behind us, around us, the paraffin caught in a great flaming sea of deadly heat. I felt my flesh searing in the last instant: the instant when the inferno's shock wave caught us up like straws and flung us into the core of white light.

I saw nothing but white for the longest time, seeing nothing, touching nothing. I floated in the timeless void. All the panic, the terror of the event, evaporated from me. All thoughts stopped. It was like death. Maybe it was a kind of death, I still don't know.

And then, somehow, that perfect silence and oneness broke into pieces again. It shattered into millions of grainy atoms, a soundless crawling blizzard. Like phantom, hissing snow.

I stared into the snow, seeing it swirling, resolving into something new, with perfect ease, as if it were following the phase of my own dreams…A beautiful sheen, a white blur—

The white blur of reflections on glass. I was standing in front of a glass window. A department-store window. There were televisions behind the glass, the biggest televisions I had ever seen.

Vlad was standing next to me. A woman was holding my arm, a pretty beatnik girl with a flowered silk blouse and a scandalous short skirt. She was staring raptly at the television. A crowd of well-dressed people filled the pavement around and behind us.

I should have fainted then. But I felt fine. I'd just had a good lunch and my mouth tasted of a fine cigar. I blurted something in confusion, and the girl with Vlad said, "Shhhh!" and suddenly everyone was cheering.

Vlad grabbed me in a bear hug. I noticed then how fat we were. I don't know why, but it just struck me. Our suits were so well-cut that they'd disguised it. "We've done it!" Vlad bellowed. "The moon!"

All around us people were chattering wildly. In French.

We were in Paris. And Americans were on the moon.

Vlad and I had lost nine years in a moment. Nine years in limbo, as the artifact flung us through time and space to that moment Vlad had longed so much to see. We were knit back into the world with many convincing details: paunches from years of decadent Western living, and apartments in the émigré quarter full of fine suits and well-worn shoes, and even some pop-science Vlad had written for the émigré magazines. And of course, our Swiss bank accounts.

It was a disappointment to see the Americans steal our glory. But of course, the Americans would never have made it if we Russians hadn't shown them the way and supplied the vision. The Artifact was very generous to the Americans. If it weren't for the Nedelin Disaster, which killed so many of our best technicians, we would surely have won.

The West still believes that the Nedelin Disaster of October 1960 was caused by the explosion of a conventional rocket. They did not even learn of the disaster until years after the fact. Even now this terrible catastrophe is little known. The Higher Circles forged false statements of death for all concerned: heart attacks, air crashes, and the like. Years passed before the coincidences of so many deaths became obvious.

Sometimes I wonder if even the Higher Circles know the real truth. It's easy to imagine every document about Vlad and myself vanishing into the KGB shredders as soon as the disaster news spread. Where there is no history, there can be no blame. It's an old principle.

Now the Cosmos is stormed every day, but the rockets are nothing more than bread trucks. This is not surprising from Americans, who will always try their best to turn the stars into dollars. But where is our memorial? We had the great dream of Tsiolkovsky right there in our hands. Vlad and I found it ourselves and brought it back from Siberia. We practically threw the Infinite right there at their feet! If only the Higher Circles hadn't been so hasty, things would have been different.

Vlad has always told me not to say anything, now that we're safe and rich and officially dead, but it's just not fair. We deserve our historian, and what's a historian but a fancy kind of snitch? So I wrote this all down while Vlad wasn't looking.

I couldn't help it—I just had to inform somebody. No one has ever known how Vlad Zipkin and I stormed the cosmos, except ourselves and the Higher Circles…and maybe some American top brass.

And Laika? Yes, the Artifact brought her to Paris, too. She still lives with us—which proves that all of this is true.

Note on "Storming the Cosmos" (With Bruce Sterling)

Written in 1985.
Asimov's Science Fiction, December, 1985.

The first I heard of Bruce Sterling was in 1982, when he sent me a review of my *Software* and of *Spacetime Donuts* that he'd written for a free newspaper in Austin. It was about the best review I'd ever gotten, clearly this guy understood where I was coming from. He also sent me a copy of his novel *Involution Ocean*, a delightful take on *Moby Dick* which features dopers on a sea of sand.

I met Bruce in the flesh at a science-fiction convention in Baltimore in 1983, right after the publication of my fourth SF book, *The Sex Sphere*. He was there with his wife Nancy, William Gibson, Lou Shiner, and Lou Shiner's wife. After the con, the five of them unexpectedly drove down to visit me in Lynchburg. I came home from my rundown office in shades and a Hawaiian shirt, driving our 1956 Buick. I was thrilled to have them visit me.

Around that time, Bruce started publishing a single-sheet newsletter called *Cheap Truth*, which railed at the plastic artificiality of much SF. The zine—and Gibson's huge commercial success—soon established cyberpunk as a legitimate form of writing.

"Storming the Cosmos" takes off on Bruce's deep interest in all things Soviet. One way to organize a story collaboration is for each author to "own" or even to "be" one of the characters. Loosely speaking, Bruce is Nikita and I'm Vlad.

You will notice that my *Complete Stories* includes, as of 2016, a total of nine stories co-written with Bruce Sterling. This is a enough stories to stand as a book on it's own, and in 2016, Bruce and I published them as Transreal Cyberpunk. The published book includes Bruce's comments on the stories, as well as my comments, and it's fun to follow the back and forth of the commentary. You can buy the book—or listen to audio of Bruce and I reading our tales—at the book's home page, www.rudyrucker.com/ruckersterling/

In Frozen Time

I just went back to look at the accident again. It's truly horrible. I don't even look human. My head's being crushed under the right front wheel; it's half as thick as it should be, and blood is squirting out my faceholes. A monster. I can't stand looking at it, but as long as I'm here in frozen time, I'll be slinking back and looking at my death, over and over, like a dog returning to his vomit, I know it, I know it, I know it.

I keep running up and down these boring few streets—something keeps me from getting too far—running up and down, and nothing's changing. All I can do is rush around, hating the dull ugly buildings, the mindless plants, the priggish, proper people. And my thoughts, all in loops, never ending.

I don't see how I'm going to stand this. My poor body, my poor wife, our poor wasted lives. Why couldn't I have done better? I want to kill myself all over again, but I'm already dead. Oh God, oh God, oh, dear God, please help me. Please make this stop.

Once again, my hysteria ebbs. That's my only measure of time now: my moodswings, and the walks I take, lonely ghost in a bland little town.

It took me a few years to kill myself. I guess it was losing my last teaching job that started me off with the suicide thoughts. Losing my good job, and then some marriage problems…ah, it wasn't just the big things getting me down, it was a lot of things. The hangovers, being 38, no goals, and, worst of all, the boredom. The sameness. Day after day, month after month, the same fights, the same brief joys, the same problems. The menial job, shelving books in a library.

Thanksgiving, Christmas, Wedding Anniversary, Summer Vacation, Thanksgiving, Christmas…I couldn't take it anymore, and finally I got the nerve to step in front of a truck. Now I'm dead and it's 9:17:06 A.M., September 14, forever. *Forever.*

It's so horrible, so Dantean, that I almost have to laugh. A guy kills himself because life's such a boring drag, and then time freezes up on him, and he can't walk more than three blocks from his body. Till recently, I never really knew what boredom was. Being here is like…an airport lounge with streets and buildings in it. Frozen time.

When I died, my consciousness branched out of the normal time-stream. My time is now perpendicular to normal time. I walk around and look at things—I have an astral body that looks just like my real one—and it's as if everything were frozen. Like a huge 3-D flash-photograph. Right now, sitting here in my empty office, thinking this out, I can see a bird outside the window. It's just about to land, and its wings are outstretched, and its beak is half-open, and if I walk over for a closer look, which I've done several times, I can see the nictating membrane stretched halfway across each of the blinking bird's eyes. The bird is hanging there like a raisin in jello, hanging there every time I look.

On the streets, all the people are still as statues, like the figures in Muybridge's "zoopraxographic" photographs. Some people are frozen in such awkward positions that it's hard to believe they won't—after my eternity ends—fall over, especially the old lady standing on one foot to reach a bag of food in through her car window.

In my house, my wife is brushing her teeth. The toothbrush handle pushes her mouth to one side. She doesn't know yet that I'm dead. In my time I've been dead for a while now, but relative to me, my wife is frozen at the instant I died. She hasn't gotten the word. She thinks I'm on my way back from the store with milk and eggs, when in fact I'm out of my broken body, and walking around.

Walking and thinking, always alone. I'm the only thing that moves in this silent town's streets. Nothing changes except my thoughts. Boredom, boredom, boredom. And the horror of my corpse.

I always thought in terms of shooting myself, but the way it worked out was that I stepped in front of a Japanese pickup truck. I was on the way up to the store to get milk and eggs when, just like that, I stepped off the curb in front of the truck. It wasn't an accident—I saw the truck coming—it was suicide. But, really, I'd always planned to shoot myself.

I used to think about it a lot. Like on a Sunday night—lying there weak and shaky, going over and over the money worries, the dying marriage, and all the stinging memories of another weekend's ugly drunken scenes: the fights with friends, the cop troubles, the self-degradation, and the crazy things my wife had done—I'd cut it all off with thoughts of a .45 automatic, one of those flat black guns that movie gangsters and WWII soldiers have—with the checks on the grip, and the heavy bullets that are fed in at the butt of the gun. Lying there in bed, depressed and self-hating. I'd cheer myself up by imagining there was a .45 on my night table. I wouldn't reach out my real arm—I didn't want to stir my miserable wife into painful apology or recrimination—no, I'd reach out a *phantom* arm. An astral arm, a ghost arm, an arm like the arm an amputee imagines himself still to have—an arm like my whole body is now. The phantom arm would peel on out of my right arm, and reach over, and pick up that longed for .45.

Lying there sleepless and desperate, I had a lot of time to analyze my fantasies. The fact that I always reached for the pistol with my right arm struck me as significant, for if you pick up a pistol with your right hand, and then hold it to your temple in the most natural way, this means that your right hand is shooting the right hemisphere of your brain. Now, as is well known, the left hemisphere of the brain is a) the uptight cop half, and b) in control of the right hand. So by shooting oneself in the right temple with a gun held in the right hand one is, in effect, letting the left-brain kill the right-brain. The digital, highly socialized left-brain shoots the dark and creative right-brain. This particular death always seemed somberly appropriate to me, and a good symbol of society forcing poor, intellectual me into an early grave.

But—hell—I guess getting run over by a Japanese pickup truck makes some kind of statement, too. The fact is that I really hate pickups. I think I hate pickups a lot more than my right-brain ever hated my left-brain. What is it that people think they need to haul around in all those pickups? The pickups you see are always empty, aren't they? Especially the Japanese ones, the cute, preppy energy-savers that bank employees and insurance salesmen drive. Presumably, the preps want to share in some imagined pickup grit macho, but they're too clean and sensible to get a rusted-out unmuffled '70s redneck Ford, so they buy one of these shiny little Nipponese jobs with the manufacturer's name on the back like on a pair of designer jeans. UGH! I hate, I hate, I hate…so many things.

I was talking about suicide.

Sometimes, if I was *really* strung out, the imaginary .45 would start to grow. It would get as big as a coffin: a heavy, L-shaped coffin lying on top of me and crushing out my breath. As big as the house I lived in. And every day, set into the classified ads, there was a picture of my gun, part of an ad for Ace Hardware, "Largest Selection of Guns in Central Virginia."

I got so *tired* of not killing myself.

Some days it would sandbag me. I'd be, say, waiting in the car for the wife to come out of the library where we worked (she full-time, me part-time), and I wouldn't be able to come up with one single iota of wanting to be there. And then, all of a sudden, there'd be Death, breathing in my face, *so much closer than the last time.*

I don't want to exaggerate—my life wasn't any worse than that of any other unhappily married, underemployed, middle-aged alcoholic. There wasn't any one thing that made me want to die. It was the boredom that got me. My life was, quite literally, boring me to death, and I didn't have the will power to do anything to change it. The only change I could come up with was suicide. And for the longest time, I was scared to even do that. Thinking back, I realize that I never could have shot myself. Focusing on the .45 was a kind of cop-out. But finally I got it together and stepped in front of that truck.

Got it together? In a way, yes. At first I was upset to be here, but now I'm getting used to it. What do I do? I sit in my office, and I take walks. Back and forth. It's a rhythm. Thinking these thoughts, I stare at my computer, imagining that my words are being coded up on disk.

I've been thinking some more about what's happened to me. I was, before my final occupation as book-shelver, a physics teacher, and it amuses me to try to analyze my present supernatural existence in scientific terms.

My astral body is of a faintly glowing substance, somewhat transparent—call it aether. I can pass through walls in good ghost-fashion, yet the gravitational curvature of space still binds me to the earth's surface: I cannot fly. Although I am not of ordinary matter, I can see. Since nothing is moving for me, I must not be seeing in the usual fashion (that is, by intercepting moving photons). I would guess that my fine aether-body sees, rather, by directly sensing the space-undulations caused by the photons' passage. This is borne out by the fact that I can see with my eyes closed.

My theory, as I've said before, is that when one dies, one's soul enters frozen time—a volume of space corresponding to the instant of one's death. I think of time as a long, gently undulating line, with each space-instant a hypersheet touching time at one point. A ghost lives on and on, but it is always in the now-space of its body's death. In ordinary life, people encounter ghosts regularly—but only once for each ghost. A given instant is haunted only by the ghost of that particular space-slice, the ghost of whoever died that moment.

Image: *the long corridor of time, lined with death-cells, some cells empty, some holding one tattered soul.*

How long is a moment? How long does it take a person to die? Looking at the frozen world around me, it seems that my death instant has almost no time-duration at all. If it were even a hundredth of a second long, then some things would be blurred. But nothing is blurred, not even the flies' wings, or the teeth of the chainsaw my neighbor is forever gunning. My death lasts no more than a thousandth of a second…and perhaps much less. This is significant.

Why? Because if the death-instant is so short, then each ghost is in solitary confinement. I know that someone, somewhere, dies every second—but what are the odds that any given person dies at the exact same thousandth of a second after 9:17, September 14, as I? I have calculated the odds—I have ample time for such calculations. The odds against such a coincidence are well over one thousand billion to one. And there are only a few billion people in the world. The chances that any other ghost shares my space-cell are less than one in a thousand.

So I'll quest me no quests. Really, I'm not at all sure that I could leave Killeville, even if I tried. My astral body is, it may be, a holographic projection powered by my dying brain's last massive pulse. If I go even three blocks away from my body, I feel faint and uneasy. There is no hope of walking to another city.

Here I am, and here I will be, forever. Alone.

It's a sunny day.

It's funny about boredom. The physical world is so complex, yet I used to think of it as simple. Each time I walk around the block I see something new.

Just now, I was out looking at all the wasps and bees feeding at one of the flowering bushes in our yard. I marveled at the bristles on the bees' bulging backs, and at their little space-monster faces. And in the fork of a branchlet, caught in a hidden web, was a wasp being attacked by a spider. The wasp is biting the spider's belly.

Walking on, I felt such a feeling of freedom. I used to always be in a hurry—not that I had anything worth doing. I was in a hurry, I suppose, because I felt bad about wasting time. But now that I have no time, I have all time. If I have endless time, then how can I waste it? I feel so relaxed. I wish I could have felt this way when I was alive.

The crushed body beneath the truck seems less and less like me. I walk by it with impunity. Up by the shops, coming out of the post office, not yet noticing the accident in the street, is always Lou Bunce, successful and overbearing. How nice it is, I thought this time, walking past him, how nice it is not to have to talk to him.

The supermarket front consists of 18,726 bricks. Numbers are power. I think now I'll count the blades of grass in our lawn. I'll memorize each and every detail of the little world I'm in.

Somehow the sunlight seems to be getting brighter. Could it be that by visiting each spot in my little neighborhood over and over, I am learning the light-patterns better, sensing them more intensely? Or is the world, in some way, objectively changing along my time axis? Has this all just been a dying man's last hallucination? It doesn't matter.

Before, I thought of this frozen time as a prison cell. But now, I've come to think of it rather as a monastic cubicle. I've had time here—how much time? I've had time to rethink my life. This started as hell, and it's turned into heaven.

I've stopped taking my walks. I've lost my locality. From travelling over and over these few streets, I've spread myself out: I see all of it, all the time, all melting into the light.

A thought: *I am this moment.* Each of us is part God, and when our life ends, God puts us to work dreaming the world. I am the sidewalk, I am the air, I am 9:17:06 A.M., September 14.

Still the brightness grows.

Note on "In Frozen Time"

Written in 1985.
Afterlives, Vintage Books, 1986.

"In Frozen Time," comes from near the end of my Lynchburg period. When your stories are all about death and suicide, it's time for a change. Thank God my new job teaching computer science at San Jose State University came through.

SOFT DEATH

"I'm sorry, Mr. Leckesh," said the doctor, nervously tapping on his desk-screen. "There's no doubt about it. The tests are all positive."

"But surely…" began Leckesh. His voice came out as a papery whisper. He cleared his throat and tried again. "I mean…can't you put a new liver in me? I can afford the organs, and I can afford the surgery. My god, man, don't just sit there and tell me you're *sorry*! What am I paying you for?" At the mention of money, Leckesh's voice regained its usual commanding tone.

The doctor looked uncomfortable. "I *am* sorry, Mr. Leckesh. The cancer has metastasized. Tumor cells are established in every part of your body." He fingered some keys and green lines formed on his screen. "Step around the desk, Mr. Leckesh, and look at this."

It was the graph of an upsloping curve, with dates along the horizontal axis, and percentages along the vertical axis. The graph was captioned: PROJECTED MORTALITY OF DOUGLAS LECKESH.

"These are my odds of dying by a given date?" barked Leckesh. What a fool this doctor was to let a computer do all his thinking. "You've got this all projected like some damned commodities option?"

"Most patients find it reassuring to know the whole truth," said the doctor. "Today is March 30. You see how the curve rises? We have a fifty percent chance of your death before May 1; a ninety percent chance before July 1; and virtual certainty by late September. You can trust these figures, Mr. Leckesh. The Bertroy Medical Associates have the best computer in New York."

"Turn it off," cried Leckesh, smacking the screen so hard that its pixels quivered. "I came here to see a doctor! If I wanted to look at computer projections, I could have stayed in my office down on the Street!"

The doctor sighed and turned off his terminal. "You're experiencing denial, Mr. Leckesh. The fact is that you're going to die. Make the most of the time you have left. If you want a non-computerized projection,

I'll give you one." He stared briefly at the cityscape outside his window. "Don't expect much more than three weeks before your final collapse."

Leckesh found his way out of the Bertroy Building and into the morning roar of Madison Avenue. It was 10:30. He had business meetings; but what difference would more millions make now? At least he should call Abby; she'd be waiting to hear. But once he told Abby, she'd only get right to work planning her own future. If he, Doug Leckesh, was the one doing the dying, why should he do anything for anyone anymore? Abby could wait. Business could stop. Right now he wanted a drink.

The weather was raw and blustery, with a little snow in the air. The sky was fifty different shades of gray. One of the new robot taxis slowed invitingly as Leckesh approached the curb. He owned stock in the company, but today of all days he didn't feel like talking to a robot. He waved the cab off and kept walking. His club was only four blocks off.

There was a bar at the next corner, apparently not automated. Leckesh hadn't entered a public drinking place for years, but a sudden gust of cold wind urged him in. He ordered a beer and a shot of scotch. The bartender looked sympathetic; Leckesh had a sudden flash that someone with cancer came in here every day. There were lots of doctors in the Bertroy Building. There were lots of people with cancer. There were lots of people who handled stress with alcohol.

"I'm ready for spring," observed the bartender when Leckesh ordered his second round. He was a broad-faced Korean with a New Jersey accent. "I got a garden up on the roof and I'm dying to put the seedlings in."

"What do you grow?" asked Leckesh, thinking of his father. Papa had put a garden in the back of their little tract home every summer. "This is living, Dougie," Papa would say, picking a tomato and biting into it. "This is what it's all about."

"Lettuce," said the flat-faced Korean. "Bok choy. Potatoes. I love new potatoes, the way they come up in a big clump of nuggets."

Leckesh thought about nuggets. Tumor cells in every part of his body. He sucked down his scotch and asked for another.

"The main thing is fertilizer," said the bartender, placidly pouring out a shot. "Plants need dead stuff, rotten stuff, all crumbly and black. It's the cycle of nature. Death into life."

"I'll be dead in a month," said Leckesh. The words jumped out. "I just saw my doctor. I have cancer all over my body."

The Korean stopped moving and looked into Leckesh's eyes. Just looked, for a long few seconds, watching him like a TV. "You scared?"

"I'm not religious," said Leckesh. "I don't think there's anything after death. Three more weeks and it's all over. I might as well never have lived."

"You got a wife?"

"Ah, she won't miss me. She'll *talk* about missing me. She likes to put on a show. But she won't really miss me. She'll take all my money and find someone else, the little tramp." Speaking so unkindly about Abby gave Leckesh a perverse and bitter satisfaction.

The Korean kept watching him in that blank, judicious way. "You have a lot of money?" he asked finally.

"Yes, I do," said Leckesh, regaining his composure. "Not that it's any of your business. What's your name anyway? I'll buy you a drink. Take it all out of this and keep the change." He threw a two hundred dollar bill on the bar.

"My name's Yung. I'm not supposed to drink on duty but…" The Korean glanced impassively around the bar. There were a couple of old longhairs having coffee in the booths, but that was it. "Yeah, I'll take a Heineken."

"That's a boy, Yung. Get me one, too. Nothing but the best for Douglas Leckesh. I'm full of nuggets. You can call me Doug. I was thinking before, you must get a lot of death cases in this bar, being so close to the Bertroy Building. It's all doctors in there, you know."

"Oh yeah," said Yung, opening the two bottles of Heineken. He poured his into a coffee mug. "Bertroy Medical Associates. They have a teraflop diagnostic computer in the basement there—it does a trillion calculations a second, fast as a human brain. My sister helps program it. She's a smart girl, my sister Lo." He sipped at his mug and watched Leckesh some more. "So you gonna die and you think that's it, huh, Mr. Leckesh?"

"Religion's wrong, Yung, isn't it?" Leckesh was feeling his drinks. "When I was your age, I didn't think so—hell, I even used to paint pictures. But down on the Street, nothing counts but numbers. I've got a seat on the Exchange, you know that? So don't try and tell *me* about religion."

Yung looked up and down the bar and leaned close. "Religion's one thing, Mr. Leckesh, but immortality's something else. Lo says immortality's no big problem anymore." He drew a business card out of his pocket and handed it to Leckesh. "This is modern; this is digital. Whenever you're ready for immortality, my sister Lo's got it."

Leckesh pocketed the card without looking at it. All of a sudden, the beers and the scotches were hitting him hard. The dull throb of his sick liver was filigreed with accents of acute pain. He was stupid to be drinking this early in the day, drinking and slobbering out his soul to a Korean bartender. Where was his self-control? Stiff-legged, he stalked into the men's room and made himself throw up. Better. He washed his face, first with hot and then with cold. He gargled and drank water from the tap. *Three weeks*, the doctor had said. *Three weeks*. Leckesh left the bar and went home to Abby.

Abby Leckesh was a dark-haired woman with full cheeks and beautiful teeth. When they'd met, fifteen years ago, Leckesh had been fifty and Abby thirty. He'd still dreamed of being a painter, even then, and he'd liked the bohemian crowd that Abby traveled in. But now Leckesh hated Abby's friends with an aging man's impotent jealousy.

To his displeasure, Abby greeted the news of his impending death with what he took for enthusiasm. She believed in spirits and mediums, and she was confident that Leckesh would be able to contact her from beyond the grave.

"Don't be downcast, Doug. You'll only be moving to a higher plane of existence. You'll still be here with me as a dear familiar spirit."

"Talk about a fate worse than death," snapped Leckesh. "I don't want to float around watching you spend my money on your boyfriends." For years now, he'd suspected her of being unfaithful to him.

"I'll wear full mourning for six months," prattled Abby, ignoring his accusation. "I'll go out and buy some black dresses today! And we must have Irwin Garden over for tea. He's simply the most brilliant new medium in America. You should get to know his vibrations so he can contact you on the other side."

Leckesh didn't dignify this with an answer. Abby went out in search of mourning clothes and Mr. Garden while the robomat made Leckesh a veal cutlet for lunch. The meal cleared his head entirely and he drew out the business card that the Korean bartender…Yung…had given him.

SOFT DEATH INC.
Scientific Soul Preservation and Transmission
Strictest confidentiality — Call for an estimate today!
Lo Park * B-1001 Bertroy Building * 840-0190

Leckesh studied the card for awhile, and made his decision. He'd be damned if he was going to let one of Abby's phony mediums get away with pretending to talk to his spirit. If there was anything to this "Scientific Soul Preservation," he'd be able to steal a march on the table-rappers. He picked up the phone and called the Soft Death number.

"Hello, this is Lo Park." Her accent was as pure New Jersey as Yung's, though with a hint of Eastern melody.

"Hello, this is Doug Leckesh. A man—I believe it was your brother—gave me a business card with your name on it. Soft Death Incorporated?"

"Oh, yes, Yung told me. I don't like to discuss this on the telephone. Could you come see me tomorrow morning, Mr. Leckesh?"

"Ten o'clock?"

"That will be fine."

Feeling strangely relieved, Douglas Leckesh stretched out on the couch and fell asleep. He dreamed of colors, clouds of color around a long line of precise, musical tones—binary tones chanted by Lo Park's musical voice. When he awoke, it was late afternoon, and Abby was sitting across the room drinking tea with a balding young man in glasses.

"This is Mr. Garden, Doug. He's the medium I was telling you about."

Garden smiled shyly and shook Leckesh's hand. "I'm sorry to hear of your illness, Douglas." He had gentle eyes and large moist lips. "You have very interesting vibrations."

"So do you," said Leckesh curtly. The thought of Garden alone in a dark room with Abby made him sick. "You have the vibrations of an ambulance-chasing lawyer, mixed in with the aura of a two-bit Casanova and the emanations of a snake-oil salesman. Get out of my apartment."

Garden gave a low bow and left. Abby was quite angry.

"It's fine for you, Doug, to act like that. Soon you'll be dead. But I'll be here all alone, with no one to take care of me." Tears ran down her big cheeks. "Irwin Garden only wants to help me contact your spirit."

"Let me worry about my spirit, Abby. Can't you see that Garden wants to cheat me and seduce you? I don't want jackals sniffing around my death-bed. I want to pass on in peace. Business as usual!" His liver hurt very much.

Abby sobbed harder. The fact was that she was very devoted to Leckesh. All her talk of mediums and mourning clothes was just a way to avoid thinking about his death. After a few minutes, she calmed herself and kissed him on the forehead. "Of course, Doug. I'll do as you wish. I won't see Mr. Garden again." In his embittered state, Leckesh was convinced that Abby was lying. He'd never caught her yet, but he was sure she had boyfriends. How could she not? He'd been part artist when he'd wooed her, but since then he'd joined the Stock Exchange. How could Abby still love him? Well, now it didn't matter. The long game was almost over. And if there was anything to these Soft Death people, Leckesh was on the brink of a whole new existence.

The next morning, he was back at the Bertroy Building. Lo Park's office was in the basement; it was one of a number of small cubicles partitioned off along one wall of a room-sized computer installation. To all appearances, Lo worked as a programmer here. There was nothing about "Soft Death" on her flimsy office door. Leckesh wondered if he should bother going in, but the thought of outflanking Abby's occultist manipulations goaded him on.

The Korean woman at the desk was young and slender, with hair so dark as to appear almost blue against her yellow skin. She looked up with a quick smile.

"Mr. Leckesh? Yung told me about you."

"He told you I'm rich, dying and desperate, I suppose. What kind of immortality are you selling, Lo? And what's the price?"

"The price is high. The immortality is software."

"What do you mean?"

"Consider, Mr. Leckesh. The human body changes almost all its atoms every seven years or so. But you feel you are the same person as you were seven or fourteen or fifty-six years ago. What is constant in your body is the arrangement of cells, especially the cells of the brain. The real essence of Douglas Leckesh is not the seventy-five kilograms of diseased flesh that sits here. The essence of Douglas Leckesh is to be found in the pattern that your brain codes up. Do you follow?"

Leckesh nodded approvingly. "I was afraid you'd be another spiritualist. You're saying that my so-called soul is really just a pattern of digital information?"

"Exactly. Abstractly speaking, the information pattern exists even in the absence of a body. Yet for the pattern to be in any sense *alive*, it needs some kind of substrate." She smiled and gestured beyond her office door. "The Soft Death substrate is that computer out there. If you wish, I can extract the entire software information pattern from your body and code it into the machine."

"How do I know you can really do it? And what would it feel like to live inside a computer's memory?"

"Before we continue, Mr. Leckesh, I need a commitment from you. For various reasons, the full work of Soft Death is not legally sanctioned. I cannot put my earlier clients at risk without some proof of your sincerity."

"You're saying you want a check?"

"I want a document granting us title to approximately half of your properties and investments." She slid a legal paper across the desk. "I've taken the liberty of drawing it up."

Leckesh scanned down the contract with a practiced eye. Soft Death Incorporated had worked fast: half his assets were listed here, nearly a billion dollars worth. In return for the billion, Soft Death was promising Leckesh "hospice care and advanced embalming services."

"We can't make the contract more specific, Mr. Leckesh, again because of the legal sanctions on certain aspects of our operation."

Leckesh shrugged. Perhaps this was a con. But what was the difference anymore? If Soft Death didn't get this billion, Abby would give it to the Mr. Gardens of the world. He could feel the cancer deep in his guts; he could feel the growing of the pain. "I'll sign."

Lo pushed a buzzer, and a man came in to witness and notarize the document. Another blue-haired Korean. They reminded Leckesh of smurfs.

"Your brother, too?" asked Leckesh, smiling a little. Signing away this money felt good. What was that old bible story about the rich man trying to squeeze through a needle's eye?

"No," said Lo. "A cousin." She locked the contract in her desk. "And now you'll want to see proof that our process works. Do you remember William Kaley?"

"Bill Kaley? Yes, I knew him rather well. We did business together. He died last fall, I believe. He was one of the most materialistic men I ever knew. Are you telling me…"

"Here," said Lo, punching a code into her telephone, and handing Leckesh the receiver. "You can talk to him."

At first Leckesh heard only pips and bleats, but then there was a ringing, and a voice.

"Hello? Kaley here."

"Bill? This is Doug Leckesh. Do you know what day it is?"

"It's March 31, Doug. Are you dead, too?"

"Damn near. Are you really inside that computer?"

"Sure am. It's not bad. There's a lot of information coming in. I'm managing most of the investments I signed over to Soft Death, which keeps me busy. There's a pretty good gang of people in here."

"Any landscape?"

"It's not like that, Dougie. But you'd be surprised how much fun pushing around the bits can be. How soon are you coming in? I'm a little lonely for a new voice, to tell you the truth." He sounded almost wistful. "But, hell, it beats being dead. When are you coming in?"

"We haven't worked that out yet." Was this real? Leckesh paused, trying to remember something that would convince him he was really talking to the software of William Kaley. The Schattner deal! "Do you remember the Schattner takeover, Bill?"

"Do I! Don't tell me the SEC finally found out."

"No, no, I'm just checking. Remember the night after Schattner shot himself, and you and I'd made twelve million bucks? Do you remember what we had for dinner?"

"We went to MacDonald's. The check was twelve dollars. We laughed our asses off. *I could eat a million of these.* Oh, it's me in here, Doug, don't worry."

Leckesh smiled. "I'm not worried now, Bill. See you soon." He hung up and looked at Lo. "When do we start?"

"Let me outline the procedure. To extract your software, we need to get five kinds of maps of your brain: symbolic, metabolic, electrical, physical, and chemical. Taken together, these data-sets are sufficient to produce an isomorphic model of your mental processes. You should begin working on the symbolic map today."

"What do you mean? I thought *you* would do the work."

"Only you know your own symbol-system, Mr. Leckesh." Lo took a device the size of a cigarette-pack out of her desk. It had two little grilles, for microphone and speaker. "We call this a lifebox. Basically, I want you to tell it your life story. Tell everything. It takes most people a couple of weeks."

"But...I'm no writer."

"Don't worry; the lifebox has prompts built into its program. It asks questions." She flicked a switch and the lifebox hummed. "Go on, Mr. Leckesh, say something to it."

"I...I'm not used to talking to machines."

"What are some of the first machines you remember, Doug?" asked the lifebox. Its voice was calm, pleasant, interested. Lo nodded encouragingly, and Leckesh answered the question.

"The TV, and my mother's vacuum cleaner. I used to love to watch the cartoons Saturday morning—Bugs Bunny was the best—and Mom would always pick that time to vacuum. It made red and green static on the TV screen." Leckesh stopped and looked at the box. "Can you understand me?"

"Perfectly, Doug. I want to build up a sort of network among the concepts that matter to you, so I'm going to keep asking questions about some of the things you mention. I'll get back to the vacuum cleaner in a minute, but first tell me this: what did you like best about Bugs Bunny?"

For the next couple of weeks, Leckesh took his lifebox everywhere. He talked to it at home and in the club—and when Abby and his friends reproved him for ignoring them, he began talking to it in a booth at Yung's bar. The lifebox was the best listener Leckesh had ever had. It remembered everything he told it, and it winnowed the key concepts out of all his stories. Leckesh would respond to its prompts, or simply go off on tangents of his own. Except for the dizziness and the constant pain, he hadn't had so much fun in years.

Finally, in mid-April, the lifebox said, "Now *that's* a story I've heard before, Doug. And so was the last one. And, unless I'm mistaken, you're about to tell me about the first time you slept with Abby."

"You're right," said Leckesh, feeling a little twinge of guilt. Telling his life had made him remember how big a part of him Abby really was. And now, for two weeks, he'd been too busy with the lifebox to even look at her.

"Abby, Summer, Maine, Fourth of July, Firecrackers, Cans, Pineapple, Aunt Rose, Roses, Abby, Skin, Honey, Hexagons…I think we've got enough to go on, now, Doug. Why don't you bring me on over to Lo's. I've signaled her to expect us."

Leckesh nodded to Yung and walked over the Bertroy Building. It was a beautiful spring day at last, with the endless blue sky leaping up from the spaces between the big city building. Six shades of blue, if you looked carefully. He hadn't been able to tell the lifebox much about colors.

Lo was all smiles. "You've done a good job with the lifebox, Mr. Leckesh. That's one of the most important steps. Now, what the lifebox program has done is to arrange some ten thousand of your key concepts into a kind of tree-diagram. The next step is to correlate this concept-network with your brain's metabolic activity. Please come this way."

Leckesh followed Lo across the computer room to the elevators. They rode up to a neurologist's office on the top floor. There was a nice view out the top halves of the windows; the bottom halves were frosted glass. The neurologist and his nurses were, of course, Korean. Working quickly, they injected Leckesh with something, and laid him out on a table, with his head inside a large, domed sensor device.

"This is a PET-scanner, Mr. Leckesh," explained the doctor. We want to learn just which parts of your brain react to the key concepts of your life story." The injection made Leckesh feel both stunned and lively. He couldn't move, but his mind was going a mile a minute. The PET-scan sensor seemed like a cavern, a door into the underworld. The doctor set the lifebox down on Leckesh's chest, and it began its rapid-fire rundown.

"Machine. TV. Vacuum cleaner. Bugs Bunny. Rudeness. Teeth. Dogs…" After each word or phrase the PET-scanner would click. The process went on for the whole afternoon. "…Pineapple. Cans. Firecrackers. Fourth of July. Maine. Summer. Abby." Finally it was over. The doctor injected an antidote; Leckesh's body speeded back up, and his mind slowed back down. Lo took him downstairs to her cubicle. The long afternoon's ordeal had left him so weak that his walk was a stooped shuffle.

"Well, that's it, Mr. Leckesh—until the end. We'll get the electrical, physical and chemical maps at the end."

"The end? After I die?"

Lo looked a little uncomfortable. "This is where the hospice comes in. We can't take the risk of having your brain degenerate before we can analyze it. For the electrical probes to give reliable reading, the brain still has to be somewhat functional. Unless the tissues are absolutely fresh, the physical microtoming process works very poorly. And memory RNA is an extremely labile substance. The coordination of your brain-removal with our team's readiness is a delicate thing."

"Now hold on a minute. What are you saying?" Lo's yellow face and blue hair made Leckesh think of a nightmare by van Gogh.

"I told you that some aspects of our operation are legally questionable, Mr. Leckesh." Each syllable came out just so.

"You're telling me that I'm supposed to make an appointment for your doctors to shock me to death, and cut up my brain, and grind up the pieces for a chemical analysis?"

"We need a day's notice, is all. When you get to the point where you think the end is near, Mr. Leckesh, you simply get in touch with Soft Death, and our ambulance will take you to our hospice."

"What if I wait too long?"

Lo shrugged. "It's a matter of statistics, like everything else. Here." She took what looked like a wristwatch out of her desk. "Wear this. To signal us to come get you, simply push this button here. The watch also has sensors which signal us automatically in case you collapse. Let me stress that the chances of our achieving a fully isomorphic copy of your software are much greater if you come in early. Quite frankly, I'd advise coming in today. I think the crisis is closer than you realize."

"You're just in a hurry to claim your half of my assets," challenged Leckesh, suddenly wild with fear. His guts were on fire and his head was spinning.

"We already *have* half of your assets," corrected Lo. "The document you signed was a contract, not a will. And, by the way, for another quarter of your assets we would be able to provide software *transmission* as well as the planned preservation…"

"I'm getting out of here," shouted Leckesh, in a strained, cracking voice. "Soft Death is a bunch of vampires and ghouls!" In the cab home, he began coughing blood. He wondered if the Soft Death neurologist had poisoned him. This had all been a horrible mistake. He'd never been able to take Bill Kaley for more than an hour at a time; and now he was supposed to spend eternity in a machine with Kaley and a bunch of other rich fools?

He found Abby alone in the apartment, talking on the phone with Mr. Garden. Leckesh was so desperate to see his wife that he didn't bother to be annoyed.

"Oh, Abby, I've been selfish. I'm sorry I've been ignoring you these last few weeks."

"Where's your little recorder, Doug? Did you finish dictating your life story?" Her pale, anxious face was luminous in the apartment's gathering dusk.

"It's all done. Kiss me, Abby."

They hugged and kissed for a long time. Leckesh wondered how he could have thought that his words were more important than Abby's real self, her real body with its real curves and its sweet real fragrance. And… even realer than that…her *aura*, the married couple telepathy they had together, the precious, unspoken understanding of two people in love.

"Doug?"

"What, darling?"

"What have you been up to, really? What were you always talking into that little box for? I know it wasn't a recorder like you said. I heard it talking back to you. And there's something else. I went to the bank today, and half of our money is gone. The teller said some group called Soft Death had a paper giving them the right to take half of our money out. What is Soft Death, Doug?" Abby's voice quavered and broke. "Is it another woman you've been talking to? I wouldn't blame you, with so little time left, but why won't you let *me* help you, too?"

Leckesh's heart swelled as if to burst. After all the bad things he'd thought about Abby in the past—she really did care. She cared more than anyone. Yet, still, he couldn't tell her. It was Soft Death or nothing, wasn't it? There was no immortality outside of their machine.

"Soft Death is…a kind of hospice. A home for the terminally ill. I signed a contract so I could go there when the cancer gets really bad. I might have to go pretty soon. I coughed blood in the cab, Abby, and I'm hurting bad."

"But…half our money, Doug?"

"They pressured me, Abby. And it's not just a hospice. I can't tell you more, you might mess it up. We've both always had our secrets, haven't we?" The pain in his stomach was beating like a bass drum.

"Oh, Doug, you've gotten so suspicious of me. There haven't been any secrets, darling. It's only because you were older than me that you worried so much. You're all I…"

Something collapsed in Leckesh's guts. He pitched forward onto his knees and vomited blood. The sensor in Lo's wristwatch sent out a signal to the Soft Death ambulance that had trailed Leckesh's taxi home.

The funeral was two days later. The only mourner aside from Abby was Irwin Garden, with his baggy pants and turbaned mind. Over Abby's protests, he accompanied her back to her apartment.

"I promised Doug not to see you," said Abby, pacing distractedly up and down the richly furnished living room. She stared out the window and turned to look at Garden's calm face. His arched eyebrows showed over his glasses. Abby made up her mind. "Doug will forgive me. He and I still had so much to tell each other. He needs me, Irwin, I can feel it. Can you help me reach him?"

"I can try."

Garden opened up his battered briefcase and drew out a large square of silk with a Tibetan mandala on it. He set it down on the dining table, and he and Abby sat down on either side of Leckesh's old seat. Garden lit a stick of incense and began reading from a book he said was the *Tibetan Book of the Dead*.

Time passed. Abby let Garden's droning voice wash over her, as she thought of Doug. It was nearly dark now, and the plume of incense smoke was dense above the silken mandala. The table creaked and shifted; the thick smoke began to give off a faint blue glow. Garden fell silent.

"Doug," said Abby, staring into the luminous smoke. "Doug, are you there?"

The smoke had no words. It only moaned, turning in on itself.

"Is something wrong, Doug? Tell me. Show me."

A pattern formed in the air, indistinct as a cheap hologram, but multicolored, with rainbow fringes at each color-volume's edge. The face of Douglas Leckesh, his tormented face.

Now the face shrank to the size of a fist, and pale color-lines enveloped it.

"A ghost-trap," said Garden softly. "He's telling you that something has his spirit trapped here on earth."

Bright blips raced along the color-lines surrounding Leckesh's face; bright, digital blips. His moaning chattered into the sound of typewriters.

"Is it Soft Death, Doug?"

The pulsing lines fell away, and the spirit face nodded. Somewhere in the apartment, a window blew open with a crash. There was a sudden, strong wind, and something white fluttered in from the bedroom. A small white rectangle.

The incense smoke dispersed, and the mandala cloth wafted onto the floor. Doug's face was gone, but there, lying on the table between Abby and Irwin, was a dog-eared business card. The Soft Death business card that Yung had given Leckesh three weeks ago.

Abby was at the Bertroy Building when it opened next morning. After lengthy inquiries, she found herself in Lo Park's basement cubicle.

"What have you done to my husband?" demanded Abby.

The young Korean woman was cool and matter-of-fact. "Soft Death Incorporated has preserved his software, according to his request."

"What do you mean?"

"We coded up Douglas Leckesh's brain-functions as a pattern of zeroes and ones in the computer out there. Would you like to talk with him?"

"I communicated with him last night."

The Korean woman twitched her eyebrows unbelievingly. "I will telephone him for you." She punched some buttons and handed Abby the receiver.

There was chiming and a buzzing, and then a voice. Doug's voice. "Hello?" He sounded bored and unhappy.

"Doug! Is it really you?"

"I...I don't know. Abby. You're with Lo Park?"

"Yes. She says you're in her computer. But last night Irwin Garden called your spirit out of thin air."

A sob of anguish. "I was a fool, Abby. I should have believed you. Get me out of here. It's like an endless business meeting, oh, it's like Hell."

"Your spirit wants you out, too. But it couldn't talk."

"All they have in here is my digital code," said Leckesh's voice. "But not the rest of me. I can hardly remember it in here, Abby, the colors and smells, the feelings you give me. It's wrong for my two parts to be split this way. I was a fool to think I was nothing but numbers. I need to get out of here, and move on to the other side."

"I'll save you, darling."

It didn't take Lo Park long to draw up a contract for half of what Abby had left. In return, Soft Death promised "software transmission."

That afternoon a long, powerful radio signal was beamed straight up from a dish on the top of the Bertroy Building. The signal coded a certain digital information pattern, a bit-string derived from the software of the late Douglas Leckesh. Radio signals are invisible, but if you'd been watching the sky as the Leckesh beam went up, you might have seen an iridule: a brief swirl of rainbow light.

Note on "Soft Death"

Written in 1985.
The Magazine of Fantasy and Science Fiction, September, 1986.

Another death story from Lynchburg. The software model of a person's brain idea is central to my novels *Software* and *Wetware*. In "Soft Death," I was interested in clarifying the technology of the "uploading" technique. I can really imagine senior citizens buying and using lifeboxes. The idea of a lifebox program which can "tell stories just like Grandpa used to" seems quite plausible. Imagine a graveyard with a pushbutton, speaker-grill and video screen on each stone, each of them running an interactive simulation of the grave's inhabitant, a simulation that remembers the things that you, the visitor, tell it. The only hard part would be writing the program to insert the hyperlinks into the dictated material. I have more about this idea in my novel, *Saucer Wisdom*.

The character-name "Leckesh" is a near-anagram of Sheckley. For me, the most important SF writer of all is Robert Sheckley. Somewhere Nabokov describes a certain childhood book as being the one that bumped something and set the heavy ball rolling down the corridor of years. For me, that book of books was Sheckley's *Untouched by Human Hands*. I first read it in the Spring of 1961, when I was in the hospital recovering from having my ruptured spleen removed.

Around the time I was writing "Soft Death," Sheckley and his then-wife Jay Rothbel showed up at our Lynchburg house in a camper van and lived in our driveway for a few days, their electric cord plugged into our socket, and their plumbing system connected to our hose. I could hardly believe my good fortune. It was like having ET land his ship in your yard

INSIDE OUT

You might think of Killeville as a town where every building is a Pizza Hut. Street after street of Pizza Huts, each with the same ten toppings and the same mock mansard roof—the same shiny zero repeated over and over like same tiles in a pavement, same pixels in a grid, same blank neurons in an imbecile's brain.

The Killevillers—the men and women on either side of the Pizza Hut counters—see nothing odd about the boredom, the dodecaduplication. They are ugly people, cheap and odd as K-Mart dolls. The Killeville gene pool is a dreg from which all fine vapors evaporate, a dreg so small that some highly recessive genes have found expression. Killeville is like New Zealand with its weirdly unique fauna. Walking down a Killeville street, you might see the same hideous platypus face three times in ten minutes.

Of course a platypus is beautiful…to another platypus. The sound that drifts out of Killeville's country clubs and cocktail parties is smug and well-pleased. It's a sound like locusts, or like feasting geese. "This is good food," they say. "Have you tried the spinach?" The words don't actually matter; the nasal buzzing honk of the vowels conveys it all: *We're the same. We're the same.*

Unless you were born there, Killeville is a horrible place to live. Especially in August. In August the sky is a featureless gray pizza. The unpaved parts of the outdoors are choked with thorns and poison ivy. Inside the houses, mold grows on every surface, and fleas seethe in the wall-to-wall carpeting. In the wet grayness, time seems to have stopped. How to kill it?

One can watch TV, go to a restaurant, see a movie, or drink in a bar—though none of these pastimes is fun in Killeville. The TV channels are crowded with evangelists so stupid that it isn't even funny. All the restaurants are, of course, Pizza Huts. And if all the restaurants are Pizza Huts, then all the movie theaters are showing *Rambo* and the *Care Bears* movie. Mothers Against Drunk Driving is very active in Killeville, and drinking in bars is risky. Sober, vigilant law-enforcement officers patrol the streets at every hour.

For all this, stodgy, nasty Killeville is as interesting a place as can be found in our universe. For whatever reason, it's a place where strange things keep happening…*very* strange things. Look at what happened to Rex and Candy Redman in August, 198–.

Rex and Candy Redman: married twelve years, with two children aged eight and eleven. Rex was dark and skinny; Candy was a plump, fair-skinned redhead with blue eyes. She taught English at Killeville Middle School. Rex had lost his job at GE back in April. Rex had been a CB radio specialist at the Killeville GE plant—the job was the reason the Redmans had moved to Killeville in the first place. When Rex got laid off, he went a little crazy. Instead of selling the house and moving—which is what he should have done—he got a second mortgage on their house and started a business of his own: Redman Novelties & Magic, Wholesale & Retail. So far it hadn't clicked. Far from it. The Redmans were broke and stuck in wretched Killeville. They avoided each other in the daytime, and in the evenings they read magazines.

Rex ran his business out of a rundown building downtown, a building abandoned by its former tenants, a sheet music sales corporation called, of all things, Bongo Fury. Bongo Fury had gotten some federal money to renovate the building next door, and were letting Rex's building moulder as some kind of tax dodge. Rex had the whole second floor for fifty dollars a month. There was a girl artist who rented a room downstairs; she called it her studio. Her name was Marjorie. She thought Rex was cute. Candy didn't like the situation.

"How was *Marjorie* today?" Candy asked, suddenly looking up from her copy of *People*. It was a glum Wednesday night.

"Look, Candy, she's just a person. I do not have the slightest sexual interest in Marjorie. Even if I did, do you think I'd be stupid enough to start something with her? She'd be upstairs bothering me all the time. You'd find out right away…life would be even more of a nightmare."

"It just seems funny," said Candy, a hard glint in her eye. "It seems funny, that admiring young girl alone with you in an abandoned building all day. It stinks! Put yourself in my shoes! How would *you* like it?"

Rex went out to the kitchen for a glass of water. "Candy," he said, coming back into the living room. "Just because you're bored is no reason to start getting mean. Why can't you be a little more rational?"

"Yeah?" said Candy. She threw her magazine to the floor. "Yeah? Well I've got a question for you. Why don't you get a JOB?"

"I'm trying, hon, you know that." Rex ran his fingers through his thinning hair. "And you know I just sent the catalogs out. The orders'll be pouring in soon."

"BULL!" Candy was escalating fast. "GET A JOB!"

"Ah, go to hell, ya goddamn naggin'…" Rex moved rapidly out of the room as he said this.

"THAT'S RIGHT, GET OUT OF HERE!"

He grabbed his Kools pack and stepped out on the front stoop. A little breeze tonight; it was better than it had been. Good night to take a walk, have a cigarette, bring home a Dr Pepper, and fool around in his little basement workshop. He had a new effect he was working on. Candy would be asleep on the couch before long; it was her new dodge to avoid going to bed with him.

Walking towards the 7-Eleven, Rex thought about his new trick. It was a box called Reverso that was supposed to turn things into their opposites. A left glove into a right glove, a saltshaker into a pepper grinder, a deck of cards into a Bible, a Barbie doll into a Ken doll. Reverso could even move a coffee cup's handle to its inside. Of course all the Reverso action could be done by sleight of hand—the idea was to sell the trapdoored Reverso box with before-and-after props. But now, walking along, Rex remembered his math and tried to work out what it would be like if Reverso were for real. What if it were possible, for instance, to turn things inside out by inverting in a sphere, turning each radius vector around on itself, sending a tennis ball's fuzz to its inside, for instance. Given the right dimensional flow, it could be done…

As Rex calmed himself with thoughts of math, his senses opened and took in the night. The trees looked nice, nice and black against the citylit gray sky. The leaves whispered on a rising note. Storm coming; there was heat lightning in the distance and thundermutter. *Buddaboomba-bububu.* The wind picked up all of a sudden; fat rain started spitting; and then *KCRAAACK!* there was a blast to Rex's right like a bomb going off! Somehow he'd felt it coming, and he jerked just the right way at just the right time. Things crashed all around him—what seemed like a whole tree. Sudden deaf silence and the crackling of flames.

Lightning had struck a big elm tree across the street from him; struck it and split it right down the middle. Half the tree had fallen down all around Rex, with heavy limbs just missing him on either side.

Shaky and elated, Rex picked his way over the wood to look at the exposed flaming heart of the tree. Something funny about the flame. Something very strange indeed. The flames were in the shape of a little person, a woman with red eyes and trailing limbs.

"Please help me, sir," said the flame girl, her voice rough and skippy as an old LP. "I am of the folk, come down on the bolt. I need a flow to live on. When this fire goes out, I'm gone."

"I," said Rex. "You." He thought of Moses and the burning bush. "Are you a spirit?"

Tinkling of laughter. "The folk are information patterns. I drift through the levels doing this and that. Can you lend me a body or two? I'll make it worth your while."

The rain was picking up, and the fire was dying out. A siren approached. The little figure's hot, perfect face stared at Rex. She reached out towards him beseechingly.

"I have an idea," said Rex. "I'll put you in Candy…my wife. Just for a little while. Right now she's probably asleep, so she won't notice anyway. I live just over there…"

"Carry me in a coal," hissed the little voice.

Rex tried to pick up part of the burning heartwood, but it was all one piece. On a sudden inspiration, he drew out a Kool and lit it by holding it against the dying flames. He puffed once, getting it lit, and the elfgirl entered him.

It felt good, it felt tingly, it felt like being alive. Quick thin fractal pathways grew down his arms and legs, spidering out from his chest, where the girl—

"My name is Zee."

—had settled in.

"It's nice in here," said Zee, her voice subvocal in Rex's throat. "No need to introduce yourself, Rex, I'm reading your mind. I'm going to keep your body and give Candy to Alf." Rex's lips moved slightly as Zee spoke. The reality of this hit Rex—he was possessed! He began a howl of surprise, but Zee cut him off toot sweet. She took over his motor reflexes and began marching him home. Rex's nerves felt thick, coated, crustacean.

"Sorry to do this to you, Rex," said the voice, "but I really don't have a choice. It's the only way I can get rid of Alf, the little spirit who possesses me. He's been insisting I get him a human body. But I like you, so we'll put him in your wife instead of you."

Candy was stretched out on the couch, softly snoring. Rex put the Kool in his mouth and leaned over Candy so that the ash end was just inside her mouth. He blew as she inhaled. A tiny figure of smoke— a little man much, much smaller than Zee—twisted off the cigarette tip and disappeared into Candy's chest. *Gazzzunk*. She snorted and sat up, eyes unnaturally bright. "So you're Rex?" It was Candy's voice, but huskier, and with a different pronunciation.

310

"Rex Redman. And you're in my wife Candy. We're both possessed, me by little Zee and she by smaller who? Who are you? You haven't hurt Candy, have you?"

"Hi Zee. Tell him shut up, Candy's here asleep, and I'm Alf. Let's shake this meat, Zee." Candy/Alf stretched her arms and pushed out her chest. "Hmm." She undid her blouse and bra and examined her breasts with interest. Her motions were pert and youthful, and her features had a new tautness. "Do you want to make love?"

"Yeah," said Rex/Zee. "Sure."

Up in their second-floor bedroom, the sex was more fun than it had been in quite a while. The only reason Candy kept bugging Rex about Marjorie was, Rex believed, because Candy wanted to be unfaithful herself. Lately she'd been sick of him. Pumping in and out, Rex wondered if this was adultery. It was Candy's body, but Candy's mind was asleep, or on hold, and, for his part, Zee was calling the shots so good Rex wanted them all: come shots, smack shots, booze shots in the sweaty night. Eventually Candy woke up halfway and was happy. It became almost a fourway scene.

The way Zee told it, flaked out on the mattress there, she came from a race of discorporated beings consisting of pure patterns of information. The folk. They could live at any size scale or ideally, at several size scales at once. Each of the folk had a physically real ancestor on some level or another, but the originals were long lost in the endless mindgaming and switching of hosts. Before entering Rex's nervous system, Zee had been a pattern of air turbulence up in the sky, a pattern that had wafted out from the leaves of a virus-infested bamboo grove in Thailand. The virus—which had been Zee—had evolved out of a self-replicating crystalline clay structure in the ground, which had been Zee, too.

Alf was a kind of parasite who'd just entered Zee recently. There were folk throughout the universe, and Alf had arrived in the form of a shower of cosmic rays. He'd latched right onto Zee. It had been his idea to get Zee to come down and possess a person—the folk didn't usually like to do that. Alf had gotten Zee to possess Rex so Rex would help put Alf into a person, too. Zee was glad to get Alf out of her—she didn't like him.

Lying there spent, fondling Candy and listening to Zee in the dark, Rex began to think he was dreaming. Dreaming a factual dream of the folk who live in the world's patterns—live as clouds, as fires, as trees, as brooks, as people, as cells, as genes, as superstrings from dimension Z. Any type of ongoing process at all would do. *Fractal*; the word kept coming back. It meant something that is endlessly complex at every level—like a coastline, with its spits within inlets within bays; like a high-tree habitat where the thick branches keep merging to thicker ones, and the thin ones split and split.

"Would you really have died if I'd let your fire go out?" Rex asked. It was dawn and this was no dream.

"No," laughed Zee. "I'm a terrible liar. I would have gone down into the wood's grain-patterns, and then into the sugars of the sap. But I just had to get rid of Alf. And I like you, Rex. I was aiming for you when I rode the lightning down. You smelled interesting and…thick like extra space."

"You could smell me all the way up in the sky?"

"It's not really *smelling*. For us nothing's so far away, you know. Your whole notion of space and distances is…a kind of flat picture? The folk are much realer than that. We live in full fractal Hilbert space. You think like a flat picture, but the paper, if you'll just look, is all bumpy like a moonscape of bristlebushes covered with fuzzy fleas. There's no fixed dimensions at all. Does it feel good when Alf and I do this?"

"Yes."

Candy's wordless smiling daze ended when the first rays of the sun came angling in the window. She jerked, rubbed her eyes, and groaned. "Rex, what have you been doing to me? I dreamed…" She tried to sit up and Alf wouldn't let her. Her eyes rolled. "There are things in us, Rex, it's real, I'm scared, I'm SCARED *SCARED* oooo—"

Her skin seemed to ridge up as Alf's tendrils clamped down. Her mouth snapped shut and then her face smoothed into an icky pixie grin. She got out of bed and dressed awkwardly. Rex didn't usually pay much attention to what women wore, but Candy's outfit today definitely did not look right. A cocktail dress tucked into a pair of jeans. Where did she think she was going so early?

"I'll call in sick," said Alf through Candy. "Just a minute." She went to the phone and tried to call the school where she worked. Alf didn't seem to realize it was summer vacation.

"Mommy's up!" shouted Griff, hearing the call.

"Where's breakfast?" demanded little Leda.

"LOOK OUT, KIDS!" shouted Rex. "MOMMY AND I HAVE BEEN TAKEN OVER BY—" Zee's clampdown hit him like a shot of animal tranquilizer.

"Just kidding," called Zee/Rex. The kids laughed. Daddy was wild. Zee/Rex went into the kitchen to look for food and Leda asked for breakfast again. "Feed yourself, grubber," mouthed Rex. Hungry. Zee had him brush past Griff and Leda and fill a bowl with milk, sugar, and three raw eggs. Zee/Rex leaned over the bowl and lapped the contents up.

"Daddy, you are eating like a pig!" laughed Leda. She fixed herself a bowl of milk and sugar and tried lapping it up like Daddy. The bowl slid off the table and onto the floor. Griff, upset by the disorder, grabbed some bread and headed out the door to play with the dog. Leda cleaned up halfheartedly until she realized that Daddy didn't care, and then she went to watch cable TV.

"Do you want to fuck your wife some more?" said Zee. The voice was subvocal.

"Uh, no," said Rex, beginning to wonder what he'd gotten his family into. "Not right now. Do you remember saying that you'd make it worth my while if I gave the use of our bodies, Zee? What kind of payment do the folk give?"

"As a rule, none," said Zee, making Rex nibble on a stick of butter. "I told you I'm a terrible liar. Isn't having me in you payment enough? Don't you like being part of the Zee fractal?" Rex didn't understand, but Zee helped him and then he did. Folk like Zee were long thin vortices in the fractal soup of all that is. Or like a necklace strung with diverse beads. Rex was a Zee-bead now, and Candy was an Alf-bead. Alf's thread passed up through Zee, too, and up through Zee to who knew where.

It was dizzying to think about, the endlessness and the weird geometry of it all. To hear Zee tell it, every size scale was equally central, each object just another crotch in the transdimensional fractal world-tree. Zee and Alf were in them, above them, and maybe below them now, too: in their genes and in their memes. Rex's thoughts felt no longer quite his.

He'd made a terrible mistake picking Zee up. He kept remembering the desperate expression on Candy's face as Alf made her stop yelling. And the puzzled looks the children had given their terribly altered Dad.

"Can't you and Alf move on, Zee? Leave your fractal trail in us, but move on down into the atoms? Can I drive you anywhere?"

"No. It's ugly here in Killeville. I just came down because of you. When I'm through eating, I want to get back in bed with Candy and Alf." Rex watched himself open the fridge, hunker down, and begin using a stick of celery to dig peanut butter out of the jar. Crunch off some celery each time. It tasted good. Whenever he relaxed, the nerve-tingle of Zee's possession started to feel good. That was bad.

"What was it about me that attracted you so much, Zee?"

"I said I could smell you. You were thinking about your magic box called Reverso. It makes your flat space get thick, and it spins things over themselves. I told you the higher dimensions are real; you can build up to them with fractals. I bet I could make Reverso really work. I could do that for you, dear Rex."

"Well, all right." Rex went back in the bedroom and talked things over with Candy, who was busy putting on a different set of clothes. "I think I'll drive down to my office, Candy," said Rex. "Zee says she can help me get the Reverso working. And maybe then they'll leave."

"I'm going to stay in bed all day," said Candy, making that pixie face. She had taken all her clothes back off, and one of her hands was busy down in her crotch. "I love this body." Her voice was husky and strange. Rex felt very uneasy.

"Maybe I shouldn't leave you like this, Candy."

"Go on, go downtown to your Marjorie. I won't be lonely, Rex. You can count on that."

"Do you mean—"

Zee cut him off and marched him out of the bedroom and back down the stairs.

"And take the kids," called Candy in something like her normal voice. She sounded scared. "Get the poor children out of here!"

"Right."

Rex rounded up the children and took them over to the Carrandines' house. Luanne Carrandine was a little surprised when Rex asked her to babysit, but after the usual heavy flirting, she agreed to help out. She was a charming blonde woman with a small jaded face. Some of the suggestions which Zee forced out of Rex's mouth made Luanne laugh out loud. If her husband Garvey hadn't been upstairs, Rex and Zee might have stayed on, but as it was, they headed downtown.

Last night's storm had left Killeville gray and steamy. Kudzu writhed up the walls of the abandoned building Rex rented space in. The other renter—the famous Marjorie—didn't usually show up till ten. Rex/Zee's footsteps echoed in the empty space. He walked her up the filthy stairs to his little office. There on his desk sat the Reverso: a silver-painted, wood box with a hidden trapdoor in the bottom.

Rex felt foolish showing his crummy trick to a truly magical spirit like Zee. But she insisted, and he ran through the patter.

"This is a handy little box that turns things into their opposites," said Rex, putting a right-handed leather glove in the chamber. "Suppose that you have two pairs of gloves, but you lose the left glove to each pair. No problem with Reverso!" He lifted the box up and shook it (meanwhile sneaking a hand in through the trapdoor to turn the special glove inside out). He set the Reverso beck down. "Open it up, Zee. You see! Right into left." He took out the left glove and put in a fake saltshaker. "But that's not all. Reverso changes all kinds of opposites. What if you have salt but no pepper?" He shook the chamber again. (A hidden curtain inside the "Saltshaker" slid down, changing its sides from white to black.) "Open the chamber, Zee—salt into pepper! Now what if you're short on shelf space and your coffee cups' handles keep bumping into each other?" He drew out a (special) coffee cup and placed it in the chamber. "Simple! We use Reverso to turn inside to out and put the handle on the inside for storage!" (He opened the chamber, moving the suctioned-on cup handle to the cup's inside as he drew it out.) "See!"

"I know a way to do the first and last tricks without cheating," said Zee. "I know how to really turn things inside out. Look." Rex's hand picked up a pencil and drew a picture of two concentric circles. "See the annular ring between the circles? Think of lots of little radial arrows in the ring, all leading from the inner circle to the outer circle." His hand sketched rapidly. Think of the ring part as something solid. To turn it inside out means to flip each of the arrows over." Zee stopped drawing and ran a kind of animation on Rex's paper to point inwards. All of them turning together made a trail shaped like a torus. "Yes, a torus, whose intersection with the plane looks like two circles. Think of a smoke-ring, a torus whose inner circle keeps moving out—like a tornado biting its own tail. A planecutting toroidal vortex ring turns flat objects inside out. What we need for your real Reverso is a hypertorus whose intersection with your space looks like two spheres, a big one and a little one. I know where to get 'em, Rex, closer than you know. These hypertoruses have a fuzzy fractal surface and a built-in vortex flow. You won't believe where…"

"Talking to yourself, Rex?" It was Marjorie, come up the stairs to say hi. Rex and Zee, in the throes of scientific rapture, had failed to hear her come in.

Marjorie was a thin young woman who smiled a lot. She wore her hair very short, and she smoked Gauloises—which took some doing in a chainstore town like Killeville. "I'm making coffee for us, and I wondered if you remembered to bring milk and sugar."

"Uh, no. Yes, I guess I am talking to myself. This Reverso trick, you know." Suddenly Zee seized control of Rex's tongue. "Do you want to make love?"

Marjorie laughed and gave Rex a gentle butt with her head. "I never thought you'd ask. Sex *now*?"

"No time now," cried Rex, taking back over. "Shut up, Zee!"

Marjorie stepped back to the door and gave Rex a considering look. "Are you high, Rex? Or what? You have some for me?"

"I have to work," said Rex. "Stay quiet, Zee."

"I can make you feel like Rex," said Zee through Rex's mouth. "With an Alf. Come back here, honey."

"Meanwhile on planet Earth," said Marjorie, and disappeared down the stairs, shaking her head.

"Stop it, Zee, and let's get to work. Where are we supposed to find that hypertoroidal vortex ring you were talking about?"

"Space's dimensionality depends on the size scale you look at, Rex. From a distance a tree seems like a pattern of 1-D lines. Get closer and the bark looks like a warpy 2-D surface. Land on the surface and it's a fissured 3-D world. Down and down. Hypertoroidal vortex rings are common at the atomic scale. They're called quarks."

"Quarks!"

"A quark is a toroidal loop of superstring. Now just hold still while I reach down and yank—"

There was a sinking feeling in Rex's chest. Zee was moving down through him, descending into the dimensional depths. With her bright "growth tip" gone from him, Rex felt more fully himself than he had since last night. Zee's fractal trail was still in him, but her active self was down somewhere in his atoms. He sighed and sank down into his armchair.

Interesting how receptive Marjorie had been to that suggestion of Zee's...but no. The peace of his neutral isolation was too sweet to compromise. *But what was Candy up to right now? What was Alf getting her to do?*

Rex's nervous gaze strayed to the shelves of the little novelties that he was ready to mail, once the orders started coming in. He tried to calm himself by thinking about business. *Boy's Life* might be a good place to advertise, maybe he should write them for their rates. Or—

"Wuugh!" Zee's heavy catch swelled and stung in Rex's rising gorge and he gagged again, harder. A flickering fur sphere flopped out of his mouth and plopped onto the floor in front of him. It had an aura of frenzied activity, but it didn't seem to be going anyplace. It just lay there on the pine boards, its surface flowing this way and that.

"I'm back," murmured Zee with Rex's mouth.

Rex nudged the sphere with his foot. It shrank from his touch.

"If you're rough with it, it shrinks," said Zee. "And if you pat it, it gets bigger. Try."

Rex leaned forward and placed his hands lightly on the sphere's equator. It wasn't exactly fur-covered after all. Velcro was more like it. Zee had him rub his hands back and forth caressingly, and then move them apart. The sphere bulged along with his hands, out and out till it was four feet across. Rex felt like a tailor fitting a fat man for a suit. He pushed back his chair and got up to take a better look at the thing.

At any instant, its surface was fractally rough: cracked and fissured, with cracks in its cracks, and with a tufty overlay of slippery fuzz that branched and rebranched. In its richness of structure, it was a bit like an incredibly detailed scale model of some alien planet.

What made the fuzzball doubly strange was that its surface was in constant flux. If it was like the model of a planet, it was a dynamic model, with speeded-up time. As if to the rhythm of unseen seasons, patches of the fuzzball's stubble would grow dark red, flatten out to eroded yellow badlands, glaze over with blue cracks, and then blossom back into pale red growth.

"A quark is this complex?" Rex asked unbelievingly. "And you say this is really a hypertorus? Where's the inner sphere? And how can anything ever get inside it?"

"It's the hyperflow that makes it impervious," said Zee. "And you valve that down with a twist like this." She made Rex grab the sphere and twist it clockwise about its vertical axis. It turned as grudgingly as a stiff faucet. "If you give it a half-turn, the hyperflow stops." Sure enough, as Zee/Rex's hands rotated the sphere it stopped it flickering. It was static now, with a big red patch near Rex. Frozen still like this, the sphere was filmy and transparent. Peering into it, Rex could see a small sphere in the middle with a green patch matching the outer sphere's red patch.

"You can still make it change size when it's stopped like this," said Zee, urging Rex's reluctant hands forward. "But now, even better, you can push right through it. Even though it still resists shear, it's gone matter-transparent."

The outer sphere was insubstantial as a curtain of water; the central sphere was, too. It had been the hyperflow, now halted, that gave the spheres their seeming solidity. Zee now demonstrated that if Rex jabbed or caressed the barely palpable inner sphere, it grew and shrank just as willingly as did the outer sphere. The two could be adjusted to bound concentric shells of any size.

The region between the spheres felt tingly with leashed energies. Rex could begin to see what would happen if the hyperflow started back up. Everything would turn over. The inside would go out, and the outside would go in. He jerked his hands back.

"And of course you restart it by turning it the other way," said Zee. Rex dug into the sphere's yielding surface and twisted it counterclockwise. Insubstantial though it was, the sphere resisted this axial rotation as strongly as before. Slowly it gave and unvalved. The hyperflow started back up. The big outer patch near Rex shifted shades from red through orange to yellow to green to blue to violet. Rex watched for a while and then stopped the flow the next time a green outer patch appeared.

Peered in. Yes, now the inner patch was red. They'd traded places. The stuff of the outer sphere had flowed up through hyperspace and back down to the inner sphere. It was just the same as the way the stuff of a donut-shape's outer equator can flow up over the donut's top and down to its inner equator. Like a sea cucumber, the big quark lived to evert.

"Let's call it a cumberquark," said Rex.

"Fine," said Zee. "Wonderful. I'm glad I showed it to you. Aren't you going to try it out?"

Rex's eye lit on a glass jar of rubber cement. He halted the cumberquark's flow, jabbed the central sphere down to the size of a BB, squeezed the outer sphere down to the size of a small cantaloupe, and then adjusted the temporarily matter-transparent sphere so that the inner one was inside his jar of rubber cement. The outer sphere included the whole jar and a small disk-section of Rex's desktop. With one quick motion, Rex unvalved the cumberquark just enough for the green patch to turn red, twisted the hyperflow back off, and shoved the cumberquark aside to see what it had wrought.

Thud floop. A moundy puddle of rubber cement resting in a crater on his desk. Wedged into the hole was an odd-shaped glass object. Rex picked it up. A jar, it was the rubber cement jar, but with the label inside, and rattling around inside it was—

"That hard little thing is the disk of desk the jar was sitting on."

The jar's lid was on the top, but facing inwards. Rex pushed on its underside and got it untwisted. As he untwisted it, compressed air hissed out: all the air that had been between the jar and the cumberquark's outer sphere was squeezed in there. The lid clattered into the jar's dry inside. Peeking in, Rex could see that the RUBBER CEMENT label had mirror-flipped to TNEMEC REBBUR. Check. He jiggled the jar and spilled the shrunken bit of desk out into his hand. Neat. It was a tiny sphere, with a BB-sized craterlet where the cumberquark's inner sphere had nestled. A small gobbet of uneverted rubber cement clung to this dimple.

Quick youthful footsteps ascended the steps to Rex's office. Marjorie, back for today's Round Two.

"I want you to meet Kissycat. Kissycat, this is Rex." Marjorie had a sinewy black cat nestled against her flattish chest. She pressed forward and placed the cat on Rex's shoulder. It dug its claws in. Rex sneezed. He was allergic to cats. He had some trouble getting the neurotic beast off his shoulder and onto the desktop. He had a wonderful, awful, Grinchy idea.

"Will you sell me that cat, Marjorie?"

"No, but you can babysit him. I'm going down to the sub shop. Want anything?"

"Just a Coke. I'm going to meet Candy for lunch." He'd been away too long already.

"La dee da. Where?"

"Oh, just at home." Rex ran his shaky fingers through his hair, wondering if Candy was still in bed. But dammit, this was more important than Candy's crazy threats. The cat. In just a minute he would be alone with the cat.

Kissycat nosed daintily around Rex's desktop and began sniffing at the cumberquark.

"Rad," said Marjorie, noticing it. "Is that a magic trick?"

"It's a cumberquark. I just invented it."

"What does it do?"

"Maybe I'll show you when you get back. Sure, Kissycat can stay here. That's fine. Here's seventy-five cents for the Coke."

As soon as she'd left the building, Rex dilated the cumberquark to pumpkin size and began stalking Kissycat. Sensing Rex's mood—a mixture of prickly ailurophobia and psychotic glee—the beast kept well away from him. Fortunately he'd closed his office door and windows. Kissycat wedged himself under Rex's armchair. Rex thumped the chair over and lunged. The cat yowled, spit, and slapped four nasty scratches across Rex's left hand.

"You want me to kill you *first*?" Rex snarled, snatching up the heavy rod that he used to prop his window open. Candy had him all upset. "You want me to crush your head before I turn you inside out, you god—"

His voice broke and sweetened. Zee taking over. He'd forgotten all about her.

"Niceums kitty. Dere he is. All thcared of nassy man? Oobie doobie purr purr." Zee made Rex rummage in his trashcan till he found a crust of yesterday's tuna sandwich. "Nummy nums for Mr. Tissytat! Oobie doobie purr purr purr." This humiliating performance went on for longer than Rex liked, but finally Kissycat was stretched out on the canvas seat of the director's chair next to Rex's desk, shedding hair and licking his feet. Rex halted the cumberquark's flow and moved gingerly forward. "Niceums!"

Kissycat seemed not to notice as the gossamer outer sphere passed through his body. Cooing and peering in, Rex manipulated the sphere till its BB-sized center was inside the cat, hopefully inside its stomach. With a harsh cackle, Rex unvalved the sphere, let it flow through a flip, and turned it back off. There was a circle of canvas missing from the chair seat now, and the everted cat dropped through the hole to the floor, passing right through the temporarily matter-transparent cumberquark.

Kissycat was a good-sized pink ball with two holes in it. Rex had managed to get the middle sphere bang-on in the cat's stomach. The crust he'd just fed Kissycat was lying right there next to the stomach. The stomach twitched and jerked. It had two sphincterish holes in it—holes that presumably tunneled to Kissycat's mouth and anus. Rex gave the ball a little kick and it made a muffled mewing noise.

"A little *strange* in there is it, hand-scratcher?"

"Rex," came Zee's subvocal voice. "Don't be mean. Isn't he going to suffocate?" She was like a goddamn good conscience. If only Alf had been good, too. *He couldn't let himself think about Candy!*

Rex forced his attention back to the matter at hand. "Kissycat won't suffocate for a few minutes. Look how big he is. There's a lot of air in there with him. He's like a balloon!" The ball shuddered and mewed again, more faintly than before. "I'm just surprised the flip didn't break his neck or something."

"No, that's safe enough. Space is kind of rubbery, you know. But listen, Rex, his air is running out fast. Turn him back."

"I don't want to. I want to show him to—" Rex was struck by an idea. Moving quickly, he took the tubular housing of a ballpoint pen and pushed it deep into one of the stomach holes. Kissycat's esophagus. Stale air came rushing out in a gassy yowl. The pink ball shrank to cat-size. After a few moments of confused struggle, the ball began pulsing steadily, pumping breaths in and out of the pen-tube.

There was noise downstairs. Marjorie! Rex turned the cumberquark back into a brightflowing little fuzzball, then put it and the everted cat inside his briefcase. He pounded down the stairs and got his Coke. "Thanks, Marjorie! Sorry to run, I just realized how late it is."

"Where's Kissycat?"

"Uh…I'm not sure. Inside or outside or something." Rex's briefcase was making a faint hissing noise.

"Some babysitter *you* are," said Marjorie, cocking her head in kittenish pique. "What's that noise? Do you—"

Rex lunged for the door, but now Zee had to put her two-cents worth in. "Look," cried Rex's mouth as his arms dumped the contents of his briefcase out onto the dirty hallway floor.

Marjorie screamed. "You've killed him! You're crazy! Help!"

Zee relinquished control of Rex and hunkered somewhere inside him, snickering. Rex could hear her laughter like elfin bells. He snatched up him cumberquark and made as if to run for it, but Marjorie's tearful face won his sudden sympathy. She was a pest, and a kid, but still—

"Stop screaming, dammit. I can turn him back."

"You killed my cat!"

"He scratched my hand. And he's not dead anyway. He's just inside out. I wanted to borrow him to show Candy. I wasn't going to hurt him any. Honest. I turned him inside out with my cumberquark, and I can turn him back."

"You can? What's that plastic tube?"

"He's breathing through it. Now look. Let's get something that can go in his stomach without making him sick. Oh…how about a sheet of newspaper. Yeah." Moving quickly, Rex spread out a sheet of old newspaper and set the everted cat on it. Marjorie watched him with wide, frightened eyes. "Don't look at me that way, dammit. Come here and pick up the paper, Marjorie, hold it stretched tight out in front of you." She obeyed, and Rex got the cumberquark halted and in position, more or less. He reached in and took out the pen-tube, then readjusted the cumberquark. Marjorie was shaking. If Rex did the flip with the inner-sphere intersecting Kissycat's flesh, this was going to be gross.

"Hold real still." He steadied himself and unvalved the cumberquark for a half turn, then tightened it back.

Mrraaaow! Kissycat landed on his feet, right on the circle of cloth that had been part of Rex's chairset upstairs. Marjorie stared down through the hole in her newspaper at him and cried out his name. Spotting Rex, the cat took off down the hall, heading for the dark recesses of the basement.

Everything was okay for a moment there, but then Zee had to speak back up. "I was thinking, Marjorie, about a wild new way to have sex. I could put the cumberquark's central sphere in your womb and turn you inside out and—"

With a major effort of will, Rex got himself out the door and on the street before Zee could finish her suggestion. Marjorie watched him leave, too stunned to react.

The three mile drive home seemed to take a very long time. As the hot summer air beat in through the open car window, Rex kept thinking about inside out. What was the very innermost of all—the one/many language of quantum logic? And what, finally, was outermost of all—dead Aristotle's Empyrean? Zee knew, or maybe she didn't. Though Zee was not so scalebound as Rex, she was still finite, and her levels reached only so far, both up and down. There's a sense in which zero is as far away as infinity: you can keep halving your size or keep doubling, but you never get to zero or infinity.

Rex's thoughts grew less abstract. His perceptions were so loosened by the morning's play that he kept seeing things inside out. Passing through Killeville, he could hear the bored platypus honking inside the offices, outside the tense exchanges in the Pizza Hut kitchens, inside the slow rustlings in the black people's small shops, outside the redundant empty Killeville churches, inside the funeral homes with secret stinks, outside the huge "fine homes" with only a widow home, inside a supermarket office with the manager holding a plain teenage girl clerk on his gray-clad knees, outside a plastic gallon of milk. Entering his neighborhood, Rex could see into his neighbor's hearts, see the wheels of worry and pain; and finally he could understand how little anyone else's problems connected to his now. No one cared about him, nobody but Candy.

There were four strange cars in front of his house. A rusty pickup, a beetle, an MG, and a Japanese pickup. Rex knew the MG was Roland Brody's, but who the hell were those other people?

There was a man sitting on Rex's porch steps, a redneck who worked at the gas station. He smiled thinly and patted the spot on the porch next to him.

"Hydee. Ah'm Jody. And Ah believe yore her old man. Poor son. Hee hee."

"This isn't right."

Another man hollered out the front door, a banker platypus in his white undershirt and flipperlength black socks. "Get some brew, Jodih, and we'll all go back for seconds! She goin' strong!"

Laughter drifted down from the second floor. The phone was ringing.

Rex staggered about on the sidewalk there, in the hot sun, reeling under the impact of all this nightmare. What could he do? Candy had flipped, she was doing it with every guy she vaguely even knew! A Plymouth van full of teenage boys pulled into Rex's drive. He recognized the driver from church, but the boy didn't recognize Rex.

"Is old lady Redman still up there putting out?" asked the callow, lightly mustached youth.

Rex put his briefcase down on the ground and took out the cumberquark. "You better get out of here, kid. I'm Mr. Redman."

The van backed up rapidly and drove off. Rex could hear the excited boys whooping and laughing. Jody smiled down at him from the porch. Standing there in the high-noon moment, Rex could hear moans from upstairs. His wife; his wife having an orgasm with another man. This was just so—

"Poor Rex," said Zee. "That Alf is awful. He's not even from Earth."

"Shut up, you bitch," said Rex, starting up the steps.

"You gonna try and whup me?" Jody's hands were large and callused. He was ready for a fight. In Jody's trailerpark circles, fighting went with sex.

Rex spread the cumberquark out to the size of a washing machine and cut off its rotation. There was a lot of noise in his head: thumps and jabber. Jody rose up into a crouch. Rex lunged forward, spreading the cumberquark just a bit wider. For a frozen second there, the outer sphere surrounded Jody, and Rex cut the hyperflow on.

The surface was opaque fractal fuzz. You wouldn't have known someone was inside if it hadn't been for the wah-wah-wah sound of Jody's screams, chopped into pulses by the hyperflow. The cumberquark rested solidly on the hole it had cut into the porch steps.

"You're next, man," Rex yelled to the platypus man looking out the front door. "I'm going to kill you, you preppy bastard!" With rapid movements of his bill and flippers, the banker got in his black Toyota truck and left. Rex turned Jody off to see what was what.

Not right. Edge-on to all normal dimensions, Jody was an annular cut-out, a slice of Halloween pumpkin. Rex eased him through another quarter turn and Jody was back on the steps. The cumberquark had stayed good and steady through all this—everything was back where it had started.

"How did it look, Jody?" Rex's teeth were chattering.

"Unh." For gasping Jody, Rex was no longer a person but rather a force of nature. Jody moved slowly down the steps talking to himself. "No nothin' all inside out mah haid up mah butt just for snatch mah god—"

Rex shrank the cumberquark down a bit as Jody drove off. The VW and the MG were still there. How could Roland have done this to him? And who was the fourth guy?

The fourth guy was the real one, the lover a husband never sees. As Rex entered his house, the fourth man ran out the back door, looped around the house, and took off in his bug. Let him go. Rex went upstairs. Roland Brody was sitting on the edge of Rex and Candy's bed looking chipper.

"Damn, Rex! I didn't know Candy had it in her. I mean to tell you!" Roland fished his underpants off the floor and pulled them on. He was an old friend, an utterly charming man, tall and twitchy and with a profile like Thomas Jefferson on the nickel. A true Virginia gentleman. He had a deprecating way of tuning everything into a joke. Even now, it was hard to be angry with him. The VW's popping faded, and Rex sank down into a chair. He was trembling all over. The cumberquark nestled soothingly in his lap.

Candy had the sheet pulled all the way up to her nose. Her big blue eyes peered over the top. "Don't leave. Roland, I'm scared of what he'll do. Can you forgive me, Rex? Alf made me do it."

"Who's this Alf fellow?" asked Roland, tucking the tail of his button-down shirt into his black pants. "Was he the guy in the VW?"

"You're a bastard to have done it too, Roland," said Rex.

"Hell, Rex. Wouldn't you?"

The room reeked of sex. The jabbering was still in Rex's head—a sound like a woman talking fast. All of a sudden he didn't know what he was doing. He stretched the cumberquark out big and stopped and started it, turning big chunks of the room inside out. Part of the chair, circles of the floor, Candy's dresser-top, a big piece of mattress. Roland tried to grab Rex, and Rex turned Roland's forearm into pulp that fell to the floor. Candy was screaming bloody murder. Rex advanced on her, chunking the cumberquark on and off like a holepuncher, eating up their defiled bed. The womanvoice in his head was coming through Rex's mouth.

"Better get out of her, Alf, better get out or your bod is gone, you crooked hiss from outspace, Alf, I'll chunk you down, man, better split, Alf, better go or—"

"Stop!" yelled Candy. "Rex please stop!" Rex made the cumberquark go matter-transparent, and he slid it up over her legs. Candy's face got that pixie look and Alf spoke.

"I'm only having fun," he said. "Leave me alone, jerk. I'm your wife. I'm in here to stay."

Then Rex knew what to do, he knew it like a math problem. He thought it fast with Zee, and she said yes.

Rex shrank the cumberquark real small and put it in his pocket. Poor Roland had collapsed on the floor. He was bleeding to death. Rex tied off Roland's armstub with his necktie.

"Sorry, Roland. I'll drive you to the hospital, man."

"Damn, Rex, damn. Hurry."

"That's right," said Alf/Candy. "Get out of here and leave me alone."

The hospital wasn't far. Rex dropped Roland at the emergency door and went back home. Instead of going in the front door he went in the basement door to sit in his study. There was no use talking to Candy before he got rid of Alf.

He took the cumberquark out of his pocket and set it down on his desk. Small, fast, flowy. He leaned over it and breathed. Hot bright Zee rode his breath out of his body and into the cumberquark. She could live there as well as in Rex. The little sphere lifted off Rex's desk and buzzed around the study like a housefly. Zee had a way of pulsing its flow off and on to convert some of its 4-D momentum into antigravity. Now she stopped the quark's flow entirely and inflated it out through Rex so that it held all of him except his feet. Rex hopped into the air, up into the big light bubble. It stuttered on when he was all in.

Rex's sense inputs became a flicker. His room, his body, his room, his body, his room, his body…In between the two 3-D views were two prospects on hyperspace: ana and kata, black and white, heaven and hell. Room, ana, body, kata, room…The four images were shuffled together seamlessly, but only the room view mattered right now.

Zee shrank the cumberquark down to fly-size again. Rex felt the anti-gravity force as a jet from his spine. Thanks to the way Zee was pulsing the hyperflow, there was plenty of fresh air. They looped the loop, got a fix on things, and space-curved their way upstairs.

Candy/Alf didn't notice them at first. She was lying still, staring at the ceiling. Rex/Zee hovered over her and then, before the woman could react, they zoomed down at her, shrinking small enough to enter her nose.

Pink cavern with blonde hairs, a dark tunnel at the back rush of wind, onward. No light in here, but Rex/Zee could see by the quark-light of the quantum strangeness. Oh Candy it's nice in you. Me, kata, you, an, me, kata, you…

There was an evil glow in one of Candy's lungs: Alf. He looked like a goblin, crouched there with pointed nose and ears. Rex/Zee bored right into him, wrapping his fibers around and around them, knotting him into their complex join.

And zoomed back out Candy's nose, and got big again, and stopped.

Rex was standing in his bedroom. The ball that was Zee and Alf dipped in salute and sailed out the window.

Candy stood up and hugged Rex. They were still in love.

That winter Rex would get a new job, and they would leave Killeville, taking with them the children, a van of furniture, and the memory of this strange summer day.

Note on "Inside Out"

Written in Summer, 1986.
Synergy #1, HBJ Books, 1987.

In Lynchburg I rented an office in an empty, crumbling, kudzu-covered house owned by The Design Group, a commercial art office consisting of people who were friends of mine, and I got the notion to set a character into it.

This is the last of my Killeville stories, although the town does appear again in my alternate history novel, *The Hollow Earth*.

Instability (With Paul Di Filippo)

Jack and Neal, loose and blasted, sitting on the steps of the ramshackle porch of Bill Burroughs's Texas shack. Burroughs is out in the yard, catatonic in his orgone box, a copy of the Mayan codices in his lap. He's already fixed M twice today. Neal is cleaning the seeds out of a shoebox full of maryjane. Time is thick and slow as honey. In the distance the rendering company's noon whistle blows long, shrill and insistent. The rendering company is a factory where they cut up the cows that're too diseased to ship to Chicago. Shoot and cut and cook to tallow and canned cancer consommé.

Burroughs rises to his feet like a figure in a well-greased Swiss clock. "There is scrabbling," goes Bill. "There is scrabbling behind the dimensions. Bastards made a hole somewhere. You ever read Lovecraft's *Color Out of Space*, Jack?"

"I read it in jail," says Neal, secretly proud. "Dig, Bill, your mention of that document ties in so exactly with my most recent thought mode that old Jung would hop a hard-on."

"Mhwee-heee-heee," says Jack. "The Shadow knows."

"I'm talking about this bomb foolishness," harrumphs Burroughs, stalking stifflegged over to stand on the steps. "The paper on the floor in the roadhouse john last night said there's a giant atom-bomb test taking place tomorrow at White Sands. They're testing out the fucking 'trigger bomb' to use on that godawful new *hydrogen* bomb Edward Teller wants against the Rooshians. Pandora's Box, boys, and we're not talking cooze. That bomb's going off in New Mexico tomorrow and right here and now the shithead meatflayers' noon whistle is getting us all ready for World War Three, and if we're all ready for that, then we're by Gawd ready to be a great civilian army, yes, soldiers for Joe McCarthy and Harry J. Anslinger, poised to stomp out the reds 'n' queers 'n' dopefiends. Science brings us this. I wipe my queer junkie ass with science, boys. The Mayans had it aaall figured out a loooong time ago. Now take this von Neumann fella…"

"You mean Django Reinhardt?" goes Jack, stoned and rude. "Man, this is your life, their life, my life, a dog's life, God's life, the Life of Riley. The Army's genius von Neumann of the desert, Bill, it was in the Sunday paper. Neal and I were rolling sticks on in Tuscaloosa, I just got an eidetic memory flash of it, you gone wigged cat, it was right before Neal nailed that cute Dairy Queen waitress with the Joan Crawford nose. She rimmed him and I watched."

Neal goes: "Joan Crawford, Joan Crawfish, Joan Fishook, Joan Rawshanks in the fog. McVoutie!" He's toking a hydrant roach and his jaywrapping fingers are laying rapid cable. Half the damn box is already twisted up.

Jack warps a brutal moodswing. There's no wine. *Ti Jack could use a widdly sup pour bon peek, like please, you ill cats, get me off this Earth…*Is he saying this aloud, in front of Neal and Burroughs?

"And fuck the chicken giblets," chortles Neal obscurely, joyously, in there, and then suggests, by actions as much as by words, *is he really talking, Jack?* "That we get back to what's really important such as rolling up this here, ahem, um, urp, Mexican seegar, yes!"

Jack crabcakes slideways on fingertips and heels to Neal's elbow and they begin to lovingly craft and fashion and croon upon and even it would not be too much to say give birth to a beautiful McDeVoutieful hairseeded twat of a reefer, the roach of which will be larger than any two normal sticks.

They get off good.

Meanwhile Bill Burroughs is slacked back in his rocker, refixed and not quite on the nod because he's persistently irritated, both by the thought of the hydrogen bomb and, more acutely, by the flybuzz derry Times Square jive of the jabbering teaheads. Time passes, so very slow for Sal and Dean, so very fast for William Lee.

So Doctor Miracle and Little Richard are barreling along the Arizona highway, heading east Route 40 out of Vegas, their pockets full of silver cartwheels from the grinds they've thimblerigged and also wallets bulging with the high-denom bills they demanded when cashing in their chips after beating the bank at the roulette wheels of six different casinos with their unpatented probabilistic scams that are based on the vectors of neutrons through six inches of lead as transferred by ·spacetime Feynman diagrams to the workings of those rickety-clickety simple-ass macroscopic systems of ball and slots.

Doctor Miracle speaks. He attempts precision, to compensate for the Hungarian accent and for the alcohol-induced spread in bandwidth.

"Ve must remember to zend Stan Ulam a postcard from Los Alamos, reporting za zuccess of his Monte Carlo modeling method."

"It woulda worked even better over in Europe," goes Little Richard. "They got no double-zero slots on their wheels."

Doctor Miracle nods sagely. He's a plump guy in his fifties: thinning hair, cozy chin, faraway eyes. He's dressed in a double-breasted suit, with a bright hulagirl necktie that's wide as a pound of bacon.

Little Richard is younger, skinnier, more Jewish, and he has a thick pompadour. He's wearing baggy khakis and a white tee-shirt with a pack of Luckies rolled up in the left sleeve.

It is not immediately apparent that these two men are ATOMIC WIZARDS, QUANTUM SHAMANS, PLUTONIUM PROPHETS, and BE-BOPPIN' A-BOMB PEEAITCHDEES!

Doctor Miracle, meet Richard Feynman. Little Richard, say hello to Johnny von Neumann!

There is a case of champagne sitting on the rear seat in between them. Each of the A-scientists has an open bottle from which he swigs, while their car, a brand-new 1950 big-finned land-boat of a two-toned populuxe pink'n'green Caddy, speeds along the highway.

There is no one driving. The front seat is empty.

Von Neumann, First Anointed Master of Automata, has rigged up the world's premier autopilot, you dig. He never could drive very well, and now he doesn't have to. Fact is, no one has to! The Caddy has front-and-side-mounted radar which feeds into a monster contraption in the trunk, baby cousin to Weiner and Ulam's Los Alamos MANIAC machine, a thing all vacuum tubes and cams, all cogs and Hollerith sorting rods, a mechanical brain that transmits cybernetic impulses directly to the steering, gas and brake mechanisms.

The Trilateral Commission has ruled that the brain in the Cad's trunk is too cool for Joe Blow, way too cool, and the self-driving car isn't going to make it to the assembly line ever. The country only needs a few of these supercars and this one has been set aside for the use and utmost ease for the two genius-type riders who wish to discuss high quantum-physical, metamathematical, and cybernetic topics without the burden of paying attention to the road. Johnny and Dickie's periodic Alamos to Vegas jaunts soak up a lot of the extra nervous tension these important bomb-builders suffer from.

"So whadda ya think of my new method for scoring showgirls?" asks Feynman.

"Dickie, although za initial trials vere encouraging, ve must have more points on the graph before ve can extrapolate," replies von

Neumann. He looks sad. "You may haff scored, you zelfish little prick, but *I*—I did not achieve satisfactory sexual release. Far from it."

"Waaall," drawls Feynman, "I got a fave niteclub in El Paso where the girls are hotter'n gamma rays and pretty as parity conservation. You'll get what you need for sure, Johnny. We could go right instead of left at Albuquerque and be there before daylight. Everyone at Los Alamos'll be busy with the White Sands test anyway. Security won't look for us till Monday, and by then we'll be back, minus several milliliters of semen."

"El Paso," mutters von Neumann, taking a gadget out of his inner jacket pocket. It's…THE FIRST POCKET CALCULATOR! Thing's half the size of a volume of the Britannica, with Bakelite buttons, and what makes it truly hot is that it's got all the road-distances from the *Rand McNally Road Atlas* databased onto the spools of a small wire-recorder inside. Von Neumann's exceedingly proud of it, and although he could run the algorithm faster in his head, he plugs their present speed and location into the device, calls up the locations of Las Vegas, Albuquerque, El Paso and Los Alamos, and proceeds to massage the data.

"You're qvite right, Dickie," he announces presently, still counting the flashes of the calculator's lights. "Ve can do as you say and indeed eefen return to za barracks before Monday zunrise. Venn is za test scheduled, may I ask?"

"8:00 A. M. Sunday morning."

Von Neumann's mouth broadens in a liverlipped grin. "How zynchronistic. Ve'll be passing White Sands just zen. I haff not vittnessed a bomb-test since Trinity. And zis is za biggest one yet; zis bomb is, as you know Dickie, za Ulam cascade initiator for za new hydrogen bomb. I'm for it! Let me reprogram za brain!"

Feynman crawls over the front seat while the car continues its mad careening down the dizzy interstate, passing crawling tourist Buicks and mom'n'dad Studebakers. He lugs the case of champagne into the front with him. Von Neumann removes the upright cushion in the back seat and pries off the panel, exposing the brain in the trunk. Consulting his calculator from time to time, von Neumann begins reprogramming the big brain by yanking switchboard-type wires and reinserting them.

"I'm tired of plugging chust metal sockets, Richard. Viz za next girl, I go first."

Now it's night and the stoned beats are drunk and high on bennies, too. Neal, his face all crooked, slopes through Burroughs's shack and picks Bill's car keys off the dresser in the dinette where Joan is listening to the radio and scribbling on a piece of paper. Crossing the porch, thievishly heading for the Buick, Neal thinks Bill doesn't see, but Bill does.

Burroughs, the beat morphinist whose weary disdain has shaded catastrophically with the benzedrine and alcohol into fried impatience, draws the skeletized sawed-off shotgun from the tube of hidden gutter-pipe that this same Texafied Burroughs has suspended beneath a large hole drilled in the eaten wood of his porch floor. He fires a 12-gauge shotgun blast past Neal and into Neal's cleaned and twisted box of maryjane, barely missing Jack.

"*Whew, no doubt,*" goes Neal, tossing Burroughs the keys.

"Have ye hard drink, mine host?" goes Jack, trying to decide if the gun really went off or not. "Perhaps a pint of whiskey in the writing-desk, old top? A spot of sherry?"

"To continue my afternoon fit of thought," says Burroughs, pocketing his keys, "I was talking about thermonuclear destruction and about the future of all humanity, which species has just about been squashed to spermacetae in the rictal mandrake spasms of Billy Sunday's pimpled ass-cheeks." He pumps another shell into the shotgun's chamber. His eyes are crazed goofball pinpoints. "I am sorry I ever let you egregious dopesuckin' latahs crash here. I mean you especially, jailbird conman Cassady."

Neal sighs and hunkers down to wail on the bomber Jack's lit off a smoldering scrap of shotgun wadding. Before long he and Jack are far into a rap, possibly sincere, possibly jive, a new rap wrapped around the concept that the three hipsters assembled here on the splintery porch 'neath the gibbous prairie moon have formed or did or will form or, to be quite accurate, *were forming and still are forming right then and there*, an analogue of those Holy B-Movie Goofs, THE THREE STOOGES!

"Yes," goes Jack, "Those Doomed Saints of Chaos, loosed on the workadaddy world to scramble the Charles Dickens cark and swink of BLOOEY YER FIRED, those Stooge Swine are the anarchosyndical-ist truly wigged submarxists, Neal man, *bikkhu* Stooges goosing ripe assmelons and eating fried chicken for supper. *We* are the Three Stooges."

"Bill is Moe," says Neal, hot on the beam, batting his eyes at Bill, who wonders if it's time to shed his character-armor. "Mister Serious Administerer of Fundament Punishments and Shotgun Blasts, and me with a Lederhosen Ass!"

"Ah you, Neal," goes Jack, "You're Curly, angelic madman saint of the uncaught motebeam flybuzz fly!"

"And Kerouac is Larry," rheums Burroughs, weary with the knowl-edge. "*Mopple-lipped, lisped, muxed and completely flunk* is the phrase, eh Jack?"

"Born to die," goes Jack. "We're all born to die, and I hope it do be cool, Big Bill, if we goam take yo cah. Vootie-oh-oh." He holds out his hand for the keys.

"Fuck it," says Bill. "Who needs this noise." He hands Jack the keys and before you know it, Neal's at the wheel of the two-ton black Buick, gunning that straight eight mill and burping the clutch. Jack's at his side and they're on the road with a long honk goodbye.

In the night there's reefer and plush seats and the radio, and Neal is past spaced, off in his private land that few but Jack and Alan can see. He whips the destination on Jack.

"This car is a frontrow seat to the A-blast."

"What."

"We'll ball this jack to White Sands, New Mexico, dear Jack, right on time for the bombtest Sunday, 8 A. M. I stole some of Bill's M, man, we'll light up on it."

In Houston they stop and get gas and wine and benny and Bull Durham cigarette papers and keep flying West.

Sometime in the night Jack starts to fade in and out of horror dreams. There's a lot of overtime detox dreamwork that he's logged off of too long. One time he's dreaming he's driving to an atom bomb test in a stolen car, which is of course true, and then after that he's dreaming he's the dead mythic character in black and white that he's always planned to be. Not to mention the dreams of graves and Memere and the endless blood sausages pulled out of Jack's gullet by some boffable blonde's sinister boyfriend…

"…been oh rock and roll gospelled in on the *bomb foolishness…*" Neal is going when Jack screams and falls off the back seat he's stretched out on. There's hard wood and metal on the floor. "…and Jack you do understand, buckeroo, that I have hornswoggled you into yet another new and unprecedentedly harebrained swing across the dairy fat of her jane's spreadness?"

"Go," goes Jack feebly, feeling around on the backseat floor. Short metal barrel, lightly oiled. Big flat disk of a magazine. Fuckin' crazy Burroughs. It's a Thompson submachinegun Jack's lying on.

"And, ah Jack, man, I knew you'd know past the suicidal norm, Norm, that it was…*DeVoutie!*" Neal fishes a Bakelite ocarina out of his shirt pocket and tootles a thin, horrible note. "Goof on this, Jack, I just shot M and now I'm so high I can drive with my eyes closed."

Giggling Leda Atomica tugs at the shoulders of her low-cut peasant blouse with the darling petitpoint floral embroidery, trying to conceal the vertiginous depths of her cleavage, down which Doctor Miracle is attempting to pour flat champagne. What a ride this juicy brunette is having!

Leda had been toking roadside Albuquerque monoxide till 11:55 this Saturday night, thumb outstretched and skirt hiked up to midthigh, one high-heel foot perched on a little baby-blue handcase with nylons'n'bra-straps trailing from its crack. Earlier that day she'd parted ways with her employer, an Okie named Oather. Leda'd been working at Oather's juke-joint as a waitress and as a performer. Oather had put her in this like act wherein she strutted on the bar in highheels while a trained swan untied the strings of her atomgirl costume, a cute leatherette two-piece with conical silver lamé titcups and black shorts patterned in intersecting friendly-atom ellipses. Sometimes the swan bit Leda, which really pissed her off. Saturday afternoon, the swan had escaped from his pen, wandered out onto the road and been mashed by a semi full of hogs.

"That was the only bird like that in Arizona," yelled Oather. "Why dintcha latch the pen?"

"Maybe people would start payin' to watch you lick my butt," said Leda evenly. "It's about all you're good for, limpdick."

Et cetera.

Afternoon and early evening traffic was sparse. The drivers that did pass were all upstanding family men in sensible Plymouths, honest salesmen too tame for the tasty trouble Leda's bod suggested.

Standing there at the roadside, Leda almost gave up hope. But then, just before midnight, the gloom parted and here comes some kind of barrel-assing Necco-wafer-colored Caddy!

When the radars hit Leda's boobs and returned their echoes to the control mechanism, the cybernetic brain nearly had an aneurysm. Not trusting Feynman's promises, von Neumann had hardwired the radars for just such a tramp-girl eventuality, coding hitch-hiking Jane Russell T&A parameters into the electronic brain's very circuits. The Caddy's headlights started blinking like a fellaheen in a sandstorm, concealed sirens went off, and Roman candles mounted on the rear bumper discharged, shooting rainbow fountains of glory into the night.

"SKIRT ALERT!" whooped Doctor Miracle and Little Richard.

Before Leda knew what was happening, the cybernetic Caddy had braked at her exact spot. The rear door opened, Leda and her case were snatched on in, and the car roared off, the wind of its passage scattering the tumbleweeds like dust.

Leda knew she was hooked up with some queer fellas as soon as she noticed the empty driver's seat.

She wasn't reassured by their habit of reciting backwards all the signs they passed.

"Pots!"

"Egrem!"

"Sag!"

But soon Leda took a shine to Doctor Miracle and Little Richard. Their personalities grew on her in direct proportion to the amount of bubbly she downed. By the time they hit Truth or Consequences, N. M., they're scattin' to the cool sounds of Wagner's *Nibelungenlied* on the long-distance radio, and Johnny is trying to baptize her tits.

"Dleiy!" croons Doctor Miracle.

"Daeha thgil ciffart!" goes Feynman, all weaseled in on Leda's other side.

"Kcuf em won syob!" says Leda, who's gone seven dry weeks without the straight-on loving these scientists are so clearly ready to provide.

So they pull into the next tourist cabins and get naked and find out what factorial three really means. I mean…do they get it on or *what*? Those stagfilm stars Candy Barr and Smart Alec have got nothing on Leda, Dickie and Doctor Miracle! Oh baby!

And then it's near dawn and they have breakfast at a greasy spoon, and then they're on Route 85 South. Johnny's got the brain programmed to drive them right to the 7:57 A. M. White Sands spacetime coordinate; he's got the program tweaked down to the point where the Cad will actually cruise past ground zero and nestle itself behind the observation bunker, leaving them ample time to run inside and join the other top bomb boys.

Right before the turnoff to the White Sands road, von Neumann decides that things are getting dull.

"Dickie, activate the jacks!"

"Yowsah!"

Feynman leans over the front seat and flips a switch that's breadboarded into the dash. The car starts to buck and rear like a wild bronco, its front and tail alternately rising and plunging. It's another goof of the wondercaddy—von Neumann has built B-52 landing gear in over the car's axles.

As the Caddy porpoises down the highway, its three occupants are laughing and falling all over each other, playing grabass, champagne spilling from an open bottle.

Suddenly, without warning, an *OOGA-OOGA* klaxon starts to blare.

"Collision imminent," shouts von Neumann.

"Hold onto your tush!" advises Feynman.

"Be careful," screams Leda and wriggles to the floor.

Feynman manages to get a swift glimpse of a nightblack Buick driving down the two-lane road's exact center, heading straight towards them. No one is visible in the car.

Then the road disappears, leaving only blue sky to fill the windshield. There is a tremendous screech and roar of ripping metal, and the Caddy shudders slowly to a stop.

When Feynman and von Neumann peer out their rear window they see the Buick stopped back there. It is missing its entire roof, which lies crumpled in the road behind it.

For all Neal's bragging, M's not something he's totally used to. He has to stop and puke a couple of times in El Paso, early early with the sky going white. There's no sympathy from Jack, 'cause Jack picked up yet another bottle of sweet wine outside San Antone and now he's definitely passed. Neal has the machinegun up in the front seat with him; he knows he ought to put it in the trunk in case the cops ever pull them over, but the dapperness of the weapon is more than Neal can resist. He's hoping to get out in the desert with it and blow away some cacti.

North of Las Cruces the sun is almost up and Neal is getting a bad disconnected feeling; he figures it's the morphine wearing off and decides to fix again. He gets a syrette out of the Buick's glove compartment and skinpops it. Five more miles and the rosy flush is on him, he feels better than he's felt all night. The flat empty dawn highway is a gray triangle that's driving the car. Neal gets the idea he's a speck of paint on a perspective painting; he decides it would be cool to drive lying down. He lies down sideways on the driver's seat, and when he sees that it works he grins and closes his eyes.

The crash tears open the dreams of Jack and Neal like some ravening fatman's can-opener attacking oily smoked sardines. They wake up in a world that's horribly different.

Jack's sluggish and stays in the car, but Neal is out on the road doing dance incantation trying to avoid the death that he feels so thick in the air. The Thompson submachinegun is in his hand and he is, solely for the rhythm, you understand, firing it and raking the landscape, especially his own betraying Buick, though making sure the fatal lead is only in the lower parts, e.g. tires as opposed to sleepy Jack back seat or gastank, and, more especially than that, he's trying to keep himself from laying a steel-jacketed flat horizontal line of lead across the hapless marshmallow white faces of the rich boys in the Cadillac. They have a lownumber government license plate. Neal feels like Cagney in White Heat, possessed by total crazed rage against authority, ready for a maddog last-stand showdown that can culminate only in a fireball of glorious fuck-you-copper destruction. But there's only two of them here to kill. Not enough to go to the chair for. Not yet, no matter how bad the M comedown feels. Neal shoots lead arches over them until the gun goes to empty clicks.

Slowly, black Jack opens the holey Buick door, feeling God it's so horrible to be alive. He vomits on the meaningless asphalt. The two strange men in the Cadillac give off the scent of antilife evil, a taint buried deep in their bonemarrow, like strontium 90 in mother's milk. Bent down wiping his mouth and stealing an outlaw look at them, Jack flashes that these new guys have picked up their heavy death-aura from association with the very earth-frying, retina-blasting allbomb that he and Neal are being ineluctably drawn to by cosmic forces that Jack can see, as a matter of fact, ziggy lines sketched out against the sky as clear as any peyote mandala.

"Everyone hates me but Jesus," says Neal, walking over to the Cadillac, spinning the empty Thompson around his callused thumb. "Everyone is Jesus but me."

"Hi," says Feynman. "I'm sorry we wrecked your car."

Leda rises up from the floor between von Neumann's legs, a fact not lost on Neal.

"We're on our way to the bombtest," croaks Jack, lurching over.

"Ve helped invent the bomb," says von Neumann. "Ve're rich and important men. Of course ve vill pay reparations and additionally offer you a ride to the test, *ezpecially* since you didn't kill us."

The Cadillac is obediently idling in park, its robot-brain having retracted the jacks and gone into standby mode after the oilpan-scraping collision. Neal mimes a widemouthed blowjob of the hot tip of the Thompson, flashes Leda an easy smile, slings the gun out into the desert, and then he and shuddery Jack clamber into the Cad's front seat. Leda, with her trademark practicality, climbs into the front seat with them and gives them a bottle of champagne. She's got the feeling these two brawny drifters can take her faster farther than science can.

Von Neumann flicks the RESET cyberswitch in the rearseat control panel, and the Cad rockets forward, pressing them all back into the deep cushioned seats. Neal fiddles with the steering-wheel, fishtailing the Cad this way and that, then observes, "Seems like this tough short's got a mind of its own."

"Zis car's brobably as smart as you are," von Neumann can't help observing. Neal lets it slide. 7:49.

The Cad makes a hard squealing right turn onto the White Sands access road. There's a checkpoint further on; but the soldiers recognize von Neumann's wheels and wave them right on through.

Neal fires up a last reefer and begins beating out a rhythm on the dash with his hands, grooving to the pulse of the planet, his planet awaiting its savior. Smoke trickles out of his mouth; he shotguns Leda, breathing the smoke into her mouth, wearing the glazed eyes of a mundane gnostic messiah, hip to a revelation of the righteous road to salvation. Jack's plugged in too, sucking his last champagne, telepathy-rapping with Neal. It's almost time, and Doctor Miracle and Little Richard are too confused to stop it.

A tower rears on the horizon off to the left and all at once the smart Cad veers off the empty two-lane road and rams its way through a chain-link fence. Nerve-shattering scraping and lumbering thumps.

"Blease step on za gas a bit," says von Neumann, unsurprised. He programmed this shortcut in. "I still vant to go under za tower, but is only three minutes remaining. Za program is undercompensating for our unfortunate lost time." It is indeed 7:57.

Neal drapes himself over the wheel now, stone committed to this last holy folly. Feeling a wave of serene, yet exultant resignation, Jack says, "Go." It's almost all over now, he thinks, the endless roving and raging, brawling and fucking, the mad flights back and forth across and up and down the continent, the urge to get it all down on paper, every last feeling and vision in master-sketch detail, because we're all gonna die one day, man, all of us—

The Caddy, its sides raked of paint by the torn fence, hurtles on like God's own thunderbolt messenger, over pebbles and weeds, across the desert and the sloping glass craters of past tests. The tower is right ahead. 7:58.

"Get ready, Uncle Sam," whispers Neal. "We're coming to cut your balls off. Hold the boys down, Jack."

Jack bodyrolls over the seat back into the laps of Feynman and von Neumann. Can't have those mad scientists fiddle with the controls while Neal's pulling his cool automotive move!

Leda still thinks she's on a joyride and cozies up to Neal's biceps, and for a second it's just the way it's supposed to be, handsome hardrapping Neal at the wheel of a big old bomb with a luscious brunette squeezed up against him like gum.

And now, before the guys in back can do much of anything, Neal's clipped through the tower's southern leg. As the tower starts to collapse, Neal, flying utterly on extrasensory instincts, slows just enough to pick up the bomb, which has been jarred prematurely off its release hook.

No Fat Boy, this gadget represents the ultimate to date in minia-turization: it's only about as big as a fifty-gallon oildrum, and about as

337

weighty. It crunches down onto the Caddy's roof, bulging bent metal in just far enough to brush the heads of the riders.

And no, it doesn't go off. Not yet. 7:59.

Neal aims the mighty Cad at the squat concrete bunker one mile off. This is an important test, the last step before the H-bomb, and all the key assholes are in there, every atomic brain in the free world, not to mention dignitaries and politicians aplently, all come to witness this proof of Amerikkkan military superiority, all those shitnasty fuckheads ready to kill the future.

King Neal floors it and does a cowboy yodel, Jack is laughing and elbowing the scientists, Leda's screaming luridly, Dickie is talking too fast to understand, and Johnny is—8:00.

They impact the bunker at 80 mph, folding up accordian-style, but not feeling it, as the mushroom blooms, and the atoms of them and the assembled bigwigs commingle in the quantum instability of the reaction event. Time forks.

Somewhere, somewhen, there now exists an Earth where there are no nuclear arsenals, where nations do not waste their substance on missiles and bombs, where no one wakes up thinking each morning might be the world's last—an Earth where two high, gone wigged cats wailed and grooved and ate up the road and Holy Goofed the world off its course.

For you and me.

Note on "Instability" (With Paul Di Filippo)

Written 1986-1987.
The Magazine of Fantasy and Science Fiction, September, 1988.

I wrote the first page or two of "Instability" in Lynchburg, Virginia, and then I didn't see where to go with it. Paul Di Filippo was putting out a zine called *Astral Avenue*, and on a whim I sent Paul the start of "Instability" to print as a "Write A Story With Rudy Rucker" contest. Nobody at all entered! But then Paul got into it and added a few pages, and we mailed it back and forth until it was done. I didn't actually meet Paul in person until 1998.

Richard Feynman was still alive when we wrote "Instability," so we called his character "Richard Lernmore" in the first publication.

THE MAN WHO WAS A COSMIC STRING

As an acute-care doctor in San Francisco, I have seen many strange things. Perhaps I've turned a bit strange myself. I work at a clinic twelve hours a week; I live alone; I wear my head shaved; I speak softly; I am a morphine addict; I am Jewish; I do not have AIDS. I am my own man, but I have turned strange and stranger since I met the man who was a cosmic string.

It happened two weeks ago, in late November. It had been a long, sun-drenched day over the chocked pastel city of my birth. I was idle at home, staring out the attic window. The phone rang; it was one of my patients from the clinic. Her husband was sick. Yes, she understood I was off-duty, but could I come in a private capacity? If only as a friend. Her husband was taken very bad. She would give me a gold coin. Please come right away.

The woman's name was Bei-na Id. She was from Chaotiskan, a tiny island republic off the Thai-Burmese isthmus of Kra. I had treated Bei-na for numerous small complaints; she was something of a hypochondriac. Her English was odd, but comprehensible. Once she'd passed gas while talking to me. We'd ignored it, but it was something I usually thought of when I talked to her: popcorn fart. Of her husband I knew nothing. They lived in the Mission, a short bus-ride away.

I agreed to come.

It was growing dark when I got to the Id home, a tiny houselet on the back of a lot. It was a converted garage. TV light flickered from behind drawn curtains. I knocked and Bei-na came quickly to the door.

"Thank you for come, Doctor. My husband is sick two days."

"Yes."

Standing just inside the front door, holding the black lunch-box that I use for a medical bag, I could see the entire house. Here was the living/dining-room with two tiny girls watching TV and a boy on the couch doing homework. The children were long and pale, paler than Bei-na. Perhaps her husband was American. My imagination raced: a failed priest, a renegade vet, a retired smuggler? How big would the gold coin be?

Straight ahead was the kitchen and laundry room. A fourth child stood by the sink: a smooth perfect teenage girl, her skin like dirty ivory. The children all ignored me, letting social custom replace the walls their house lacked. The TV was turned down very low. I could hear the dishes clunking beneath the sinkwater, I could hear the chugging motor of the fridge. There was another sound as well, an odd, sputtery hiss. I looked alertly at Bei-na, waiting for info. The less I say, the more my patients tell me.

Bei-na was a short woman with prominent cheekbones and the kind of pointed glasses that lower middle-class white women used to wear. Like a cartoon coolie's, her head was a blunt yellow cone spreading out from her neck. She seemed worried, but also somewhat elated, perhaps at having gotten a doctor to come to her home. The hissing was definitely coming from behind the bedroom door. I wondered if her husband were psychotic. I imagined him crouched behind the door, mad-eyed with a machete. But no, surely not, the children were acting calm and safe.

"He been sick like this before, Doctor. When I find him first time on beach, he sick like this very bad three day and three night. My father cure him, but that medicine is all gone."

"Well, let's have a look at him. What's his name?"

"We call him Filbert. You sure you ready to see? Let me get gold coin right now be fair."

"Yes."

Bei-na spoke to her children in sliding slangy phonemes. The boy on the couch got up, turned off the TV, and herded his small sisters to the kitchen. The girl at the sink gave me a sudden amused smile. Her gums were bright red. I wondered how a girl like that would smell, wet red and dirty ivory, so unlike her tired yellow popcorn fart mother who now pressed into my hand the smallest disk that I have ever heard called a "coin." It was the size of one of those paper circles that a hole-puncher makes. I pocketed it, wondering if I would be able to get it home without losing it. Bei-na opened the bedroom door.

There is a drawing by M. C. Escher called *Rind*. It shows a rind, or ribbon, that curls around and around in a roughly helical pattern. The rind is bumpy, and its bumps sketch the surface of a human head. The wrappy rind is a helix head with spaces in it. One can see clouds and sky through the spaces.

Filbert Id was designed along similar lines. Each part of his body was a tight-wrapped spindle of dirty white fiber, as if he were a Michelin Man mummy with swathing-cloths of narrow narrow skin. There were no spaces between the successive loops of cosmic string. No spaces, that is, until I made my first error.

Leaning over Filbert Id's dimly lit bed, my initial impression was that his skin was very wrinkled. His hissing grew louder the closer I got. The noise was fretful and intricate. Bei-na, seeming to extract sense from it, spoke softly to Filbert in her own tongue, but to no avail. He seemed terrified of me, and he held up his axially grooved arms as if to push me away. If I say that the grooves were *axial*, rather than annular or longitudinal, I mean that they went around and around his head, neck, fingers, arms, chest, etc., like latitude lines.

I leaned closer.

Although Filbert's face contained the appearance of lips, his mouth did not open. *Yet how loudly he hissed!* I was medically curious about his means for producing the noise without opening his mouth. Could it be that he had a punctured lung? A cancer in the passages of his sinus? A missing tympanum and a hypertrophic Eustachian tube?

I felt a fine scientific impatience with Filbert's panic. I pushed his arms out of the way and leaned very close to his face. I was struck by three things. His face held a strong electric charge (a spark jumped between us); his face did not radiate warmth; he was not breathing. Indeed—I peered closer—his nostrils were but molded dents, entirely occluded by what seemed to be flaps of Filbert's dirty, fibrous skin. The man was suffocating!

I set my black metal box on the bedside table and took out swab, tongue depressor and rubbing alcohol. Clearly my first task was to clean out Filbert's buccal and nasal cavities. Filbert's eyes, I have omitted to mention, were matte black slits; I had thought they were closed. Yet as I opened my kit, laying out my syringe as well, Filbert moved his head as if he were looking things over. At the sight of the needle, he redoubled his hissings and his gesticulations. Fortunately he was in no condition to rise from his bed.

"Tell him to calm down," I ordered Bei-na.

She made some bell noises; he hissed the harder.

"He very scared you break him."

"He needs to breathe, doesn't he?"

"I don't know. "

"I'll give him a sedative."

Sedative. Lovely calm word. I myself was ready for my evening injection of morphine, for some morphine and for some fine classical music. This Chaotiskani nonsense was taking entirely too long.

I filled a syringe with morphine solution and stood back like a matador awaiting the moment of truth. I kept one hand in front of my upright syringe, so as not to alarm the patient. He thrashed and hissed… to no avail. I came in over his left forearm and pushed my needle into his chest.

It was only last week that I happened on a popular article about cosmic strings. Till then I had no language for what happened after I stuck the needle in Filbert Id.

At a certain large scale, our universe is structured like a foam of soap-bubbles. All ordinary matter is confined to the "soap films;" the galaxies are specks of color on mathematical sheets surrounding huge voids.

Why are the bubbles empty? Because each of these space voids has at its center a huge, tangled loop of cosmic string.

What is a cosmic string? A line-like spacetime flaw analogous to the point-like flaws called black holes.

How do the cosmic strings empty the bubbles? Each void's central string is a closed, superconducting loop. Vast energies surge along each loop, and the endless eddying stirs up waves that push us all away.

The strings are probably talking to each other, even if they don't know it. Even if they don't care.

One theory I have is that they're larvae, and that Filbert hatched when I poked him open. My image is this: Think of the stars as pollen on the surface of a quiet pond. There are eggs on the surface, too, and the eggs turn into larvae that are the cosmic strings. The larvae wiggle and jerk, and their waves push the star pollen back, forming it into a honeycomb of 2-D cells.

Either Filbert fell from the sky, which I doubt, or the strings are working at a new level, our level, yours and mine.

When I stuck my needle in Filbert Id, the man who was a cosmic string, his tight pattern came unsprung. Radiation surged out of his hollow inside, knocking me back and blowing the ceiling off the Ids' bedroom.

I was briefly blinded. I am not sure what I really saw, in the shock and confusion and lack of words. "Loony Loop," is the phrase I caught first. Loony Loop is a puzzle where you try to untangle a loop of blue nylon string from a multiple-looped pattern of chromesteel wire. Filbert Id came unsprung and turned into an enormous Loony Loop. I saw him doing it, and it made me radiation-sick. The loop hissed and buzzed, and then it tumbled rapidly upwards into the night sky.

Filbert Id hatched and flew away, leaving me with a loaded morphine syringe in my hand. With practiced speed, I injected the morphine intravenously. This was my second error.

How strong was the radiation? Bei-na died in my arms a half-hour later. Her children's hair fell out, but they are on the mend. We left the ruined house together that night. Bei-na's daughter, Wu-wei, has become my lover, which has eased the pain of these my last two weeks.

If this be my last will and testament, I bequeath all to dear Wu-wei, to her wet red, to her dirty ivory, to her brother Bo, and to her sisters Li and Le.

Cosmic string, larvae, Loony Loop, Wu-wei. These are the words that synchronistic Providence puts in my pen. My race is run beneath this sun.

With morphine, and only with morphine, the radiation-sickness has been bearable. But radiation-sickness is not the issue anymore. What is going to kill me—and quite soon—is something that I noticed this morning. My skin is grooved in axial rings, as skritchy as the surface of an Alva Edison cylindrical LP.

I shared a needle with Filbert two weeks ago, and what took him is ready to take me. I forbore the noon injection, but now it's dusk and I'm hissing.

It's time for the needle's last prick. I'll kiss Wu-wei goodbye and go outside to do it, to unspring and fall into the sky, a cosmic string.

Note on "The Man Who Was a Cosmic String"

Written in Spring, 1987.
The Universe, Bantam Books, 1987.

This was the first story I wrote after moving to California in the summer of 1986. The character is obliquely modeled on the science-fiction writer Michael Blumlein, who is indeed a doctor, though with none of the bad habits that the story character has. Blumlein has a very calm, serene way of expressing himself; this was the aspect of him that I tried to capture in this story.

I met Michael at a party in the apartment of Richard Kadrey and Pat Murphy in San Francisco. Marc Laidlaw was there as well. It was thrill to fall into so literary a scene. Right at this time I was helping Peter Lamborn Wilson edit the science-fiction anthology called *Semiotext[e] SF*, and we ended up including stories by Kadrey, Laidlaw and Blumlein. Michael sent us "Shed His Grace," a story about a man who castrates himself while watching videos of Ronald and Nancy Reagan! The anthology sold out its first printing in a few weeks.

I got the name "Filbert Id" from a dream that Marc Laidlaw told me.

PROBABILITY PIPELINE (WITH MARC LAIDLAW)

The trouble started in Surf City, and it ended in another dimension.

Delbert was loud and spidery; Zep was tall and absent and a year older. Being in different grades, they didn't see each other much in the winters, but in the summers they were best friends on and off the beach. When Zep graduated, he spent a year at UC Santa Cruz before drugging out—he said he'd overfed his head. Delbert didn't like drugs, so when he graduated he didn't bother going to college at all. Now it was summer all year long.

It was November in Surf City and the pipeline was coming in steady. For the last few weeks they'd been without a surfboard, though these days the word was "stick," not "board," meaning Del and Zep were stickless. The way this particular bummer had come down was that Del had been bragging about his escape from a great white shark, and no one had believed him, so maximum Zep had cut a big sharkbite shape out of the dinged longboard he and Delbert shared, and still no one had believed. Basically Zep had thrashed the board for nothing, but at least Delbert was able to sell it to the Pup-Tent, a surfer snack shop where his girl Jen worked—not that Jen was really Delbert's *girl* in any intense physical sense of the word, and not that the Pup-Tent had actually *paid* anything for the shark-bit board that Delbert had mounted on the wall over the cash register. But it looked rad up there.

Often, in the mid-morning, when things were slow at the Pup-Tent, Jen would grill Zep and Delbert some burgers, and the three of them would sit on the bench out in front of the Pup-Tent, staring through their shades at the bright, perfect sky, or at the cars and people going by, or across the street at the cliffs and the beach and the endlessly various Pacific ocean, dotted with wet-suited surfers. Zep sat on the left, Jen on the right, and Delbert in the middle; Delbert usually talking, either rapping off what he saw or telling one of his long, bogus stories, like about the time when he'd been flying a kite on the beach and a Coast Guard plane had swooped down low enough to suck his kite into its jet and he'd been pulled out to sea about half a mile, dangling twenty feet above the water until he'd flashed to let loose of the string.

One particular day that November, Delbert was telling Jen about a book on hypnotism he'd read the day before, and how last night he'd tried to activate Zep's thrashed genius by putting Zep in a trance and telling him he was a great scientist and asking him to invent invisibility.

"He did that, Zep?" asked Jen, briefly interested. "Did it work?"

"I, uh, I…thought of peroxide," said Zep. Peroxide was a big thing with Zep; he'd stripped his hair so often that its color was faintly ultra-violet. When Zep felt like somebody might understand him, he'd talk a lot about the weird science stuff he'd learned at Santa Cruz, but just now he wasn't quite *on*.

"We put seven coats of it on a sheet of paper," said Delbert, "and for a second we thought it was working, but it was really just the paper falling apart."

"Oxo wow," said Jen, suddenly pointing out at the horizon. "Out-sider." That was the traditional word for a big wave. "Far outsider… and ohmigod!…like…" Jen often ended her sentences that way, with a "like" and a gesture. This time it was her Vanna White move: both hands held out to the left side of her body, left hand high and right hand low, both hands palms up. She was watching one of the Stoke Pilgrims out there carve the outsider.

It was Lex Loach—Delbert could recognize him from the red-and-white checkerboard pattern on his wet suit. Loach executed a last nifty vertical snap, shot up off the face of the ripped outsider, and flew through the air, his wing squash turbo board glued to his feet by the suction cups on his neoprene booties.

Jen sighed and slowly turned her hands palms down. The Vanna White move, if done with the hands palms down, was known as Egyptian Style. Jen gave Delbert a sarcastic little neck-chop with her stiff left hand. "I wish you could ride, Delbert. I wish you had a stick."

"This surf's mush, Jen. Dig it, I saw a tidal wave when I was a kid. I was with my dad on Hawaii, and this volcano blew up, and the next minute all the water went out to sea and formed a gigantic—" He held out his arms as if to embrace a weather balloon.

"You saw that in a movie," said Zep.

"Did not!" yelled Delbert. He was always yelling, and consequently he was always hoarse.

"Yo, dude. *Krakatoa East of Java.*"

"I never saw that movie, it really happened! We got stranded on the edge of the volcano and they had to come get us in a hot air balloon. Listen up, dude, my dad—"

Delbert jabbered on, trying to distract Jen from Lex Loach's awesomely stoked breakouts. By the time a customer showed up, she seemed glad to go inside.

"Do you think she likes me?" Delbert asked Zep.

"No. You should have gone to college." Zep's voice was slow and even.

"What about you, brain-death?" challenged Del.

"I'm doing my detox, dude." Zep got a tense, distant look when people questioned his sanity. But his voice stayed calm and disengaged. "The programs are in place, dude. All I need is run time. Chaos, fractals, dynamics, cellular automata. I did ten years' research in two weeks last spring, dude. It's just a matter of working out the applications!"

"Like to what?"

"You name it, bro."

"Waves," said Del. "Surfing. The new stick I need to bang Jen."

Zep stared out at the horizon so long that Delbert thought he was lost in a flashback. But suddenly Zep's voice was running tight and fast.

"Dig it, Del, I'm not going to say this twice. The ocean is a chaotic dynamical system with sensitive dependence on initial conditions. Macro info keeps being folded in while micro info keeps being excavated. In terms of the phase-space, it works by a kneading process, continually doubling the size of a region and folding it over on itself like saltwater taffy with the ribbony layers of color all shot through. Big waves disappear in the chop and the right small ripple can amp on up to make an outsider. If you do the right thing to the ocean, it'll do whatever you want back. The thing about a chaotic system is that the slightest change in initial conditions produces a big effect—and I mean right away. Like on a pool table, dude, after ten bounces the position of the ball has been affected by the gravity from a pebble in a ring of Saturn. There's a whole space of dynamic states, and the places where the system settles down are called chaotic attractors. We do right, and the ocean'll do right by us."

Del was like: "Chaos attractor? How do we control it?"

"There's no formula because the computation is irreducibly complex. The only way to predict the ocean is to simulate it faster than real time. Could be done on a gigahertz CA. By the right head. The ocean…Delbert, the ocean's state is a point in ten-trillion-dimensional surfspace."

"Surfspace?" Delbert grinned over at his long blond friend with the dark, wandering eyes. When Zep got into one of his head trips he tended to let his cool, slow surfer pose slide. He'd been a punk before a surfer, and a science nerd before that.

"You gotta relate, babe," enunciated Zep, as he tore on into the rest of his riff. "The wave pattern at any time is a fractal. Waves upon waves upon waves. Like a mountain range, and an ant thinks he's at the top of a hill, but he's only at the top of a bump on rock on an outcrop on a peak on the range on the planet. And there's a cracky crack between his six legs. For our present purposes, it's probably enough to take ten levels of waves into account."

"Ten levels of waves?"

"Sure man, like put your nose near the water and there's shivers on the ripples. The shivers have got kind of sketchy foam on them too. So sketchy foam, shivers, ripples, wads, and slidy sheets, now we be getting some meat to carve, uh, actual waves, peaks—those choppy peaks that look like Mr. Frostee's head, you wave—steamers and hollow surf, mongo mothers, outsiders and number ten the tide. So the wave pattern at any given spot is a ten-dimensional quality, and the wave patterns at a trillion different spots make a point in ten-trillion-dimensional surfspace."

"What's all the trillions for?" Out on the sea, Lex Loach and four other Stoke Pilgrims were riding in from the break. Loach, Mr. Scrote, Shrimp Chips, Squid Puppy, and Floathead, same as usual. They usually came up to the Pup-Tent for lunch. Delbert and Zep usually left before the Pilgrims got there. "Talk faster, Zep."

"I'm telling you, dude. Say I'm interested in predicting or influencing the waves over the next few minutes. Waves don't move all that fast, so anything that can influence the surf here in the next few minutes is going to depend on the surfspace values within a neighboring area of, say, one square kilometer. I'm only going to fine-grain down to the millimeter level, you wave, so we're looking at, uh, one trillion sample points. Million squared. Don't interrupt again, Delbert, or I won't build you the chaotic attractor."

"You're going to build me a new stick?"

"I got the idea when you hypnotized me last night. Only I'd forgotten till just now. Ten fractal surf levels at a trillion sample points. We model that with an imipolex CA, we use a parallel nerve-patch modem outset unit to send the rider's surfest desires down a co-ax inside the leash, the CA does a chaotic back simulation of the fractal inset, the board does a jiggly-doo and…"

"TSUUUNAMIIIIII!" screamed Delbert, leaping up on the bench and striking a boss surfer pose.

Just then Lex Loach and the Stoke Pilgrims appeared, up from the beach. Lex looked at Delbert with the usual contempt. "*Ride* that bench, gnarly geek. Been puffing some of Zep's KJ?"

Lex Loach had been boss of Surf City as long as Delbert could remember. He lived here all year long, except when he went to snowboard at Big Bear in short pants and no shirt. Delbert thought he looked like a carrot. He was tall and thin like a carrot, narrow at the bottom and very wide at the shoulders; and like a carrot, his torso was ribbed and downy.

Loach's aging sidekick, Mr. Scrote, darted forward and made a vicious grab for Delbert's balls. Mr. Scrote was wrinkled and mean. He had bloodshot eyes and was half deaf from surfer's ear, and all his jokes had to do with genital pain. Delbert fended him off with a kick that missed. "Couldn't help myself," said Mr. Scrote to the other Pilgrims as he danced back out of reach. "Dude looks soooo killer on his new stick."

"I am getting a new stick," cried Delbert furiously. "Chaos Attractor. Zep's building it."

"What does a junkie know about surf?" put in Shrimp Chips, a burly young guy with bleached hair. "Zep can't even stand to take a bath."

"Zep's clean," said Delbert loyally. "And he knows all about surf just from sitting here and watching."

"Same way you know about girls, right, weenie?" said Loach. "Want to watch me and Jen get it on?"

Delbert leaped off the bench and butted his head right into the middle of the carroty washboard of Loach's abdomen. Loach fell over backward, and suddenly there were kids everywhere, screaming, "It's a fight!"

Zep pulled Delbert back before Loach could pulverize him. The Stoke Pilgrims lined up around their chief carrot, ready to charge.

"Wait a minute," Delbert yelped, holding out his hand. "Let's handle this like real men. Lex, we challenge you to a duel. Zep'll have my new gun ready by tomorrow. If you and your boys can close us out, it's yours. And if we win, you give me your wing squash turbo."

Loach shook his head and Mr. Scrote spoke up for him, widening his bloodshot eyes. "I doubt Lex'd want any piece of trash you'd ride. No, Delbert, if you lose, you suck a sea anemone and tell Jen you're a fag." The Stoke Pilgrims' laughter was like the barking of seals. Delbert's tongue prickled.

"Tomorrow by the San Diablo N-plant where the surf's the gnarliest," said Lex Loach, heading into the Pup-Tent. "Slack tide, dudes. Be there or we'll find you."

Up on the cliff, the N-plant looked like a gray golf ball sinking into a sand trap. The cliff was overgrown with yellow ice plant whose succulent, radiation-warmed leaves were fat as drowned men's fingers. A colonic loop of cooling pipe jagged down the cliff, out into the sea, and back up the cliff to the reactor. The beach was littered with fish killed by the reactor's thermal pollution. Closer to the sea, the tide's full moon low had exposed great beds of oversize sea anemones that were bright, mutated warm-water sports. Having your face pushed into one of them would be no joke.

"Trust me, bro," said Zep. He was greasy and jittery. "You'll sluice roosters in Loach's face. No prob. And after this we stalk the big tournament moola."

"The surf is mush, Zep. I know it's a drag, bro, but be objective. Look the hell at the zon." The horizon was indeed flat. Closer to shore were long rows of small, parallel lines where the dead sea's ripples came limping in. Delbert was secretly glad that the contest might well be called off.

"No way," shouted Zep, angrily brandishing the nylon case that held the new board. "All you gotta do is plug in your leash and put Chaos Attractor in the water. The surf will definitely rise, little dude."

"It's mush."

"Only because *you* are. Dig it!" Zep grabbed his friend by the front of his brand new paisley wet suit and shook him. "You haven't looked at my new stick!" Zep dropped to his knees and unzipped Chaos Attractor's case. He drew out a long, grayish, misshapen board. Most of it seemed actually transparent, though there were some dark, right-angled shapes embedded in the thing's center.

Delbert jerked back in horror. For this he'd given Zep two hundred dollars? All his saving for what looked like a dime store Styrofoam toy surfboard that a slushed druggie had doused in epoxy?

"It…it's transparent?" said Delbert after a time. In the dull day's light you could see Zep's scalp through his no-color hair. Del had trusted Zep and Zep had blown it. It was sad.

"Does that embarrass you?" snarled Zep, sensing Delbert's pity. "Is there something wrong with transparency? And screw your two hundred bucks 'cause this stick didn't cost me nothing. I spent your money on crank, mofo, on clean Hell's Angels blow. What else, Delbert, who do you think I am? Yeah! Touch the board!"

Delbert stroked the surface of the board uncertainly. "It's rough," he said finally.

"Yeah!" Zep wanted to get the whole story out, how he'd immediately spent the money on crank, and how then in the first comedown's guilt he'd laid meth on Cowboy Bob, a dope-starved biker who hung around the meth dealer's. Zep had fed Cowboy Bob's head so Bob'd take him out breaking and entering: First they hit the KZ Kustom Zurf Shop for a primo transparent surfboard blank, then they barreled Bob's chopped hog up to Oakland to liberate imipolex from the I. G. Farben research labs in the wake of a diversionary firebomb, and then they'd done the rest of the speed and shot over the Bay to dynamite open the door of System Concepts and score a Cellular Automaton Machine, the CAM8, right, and by 3:00 A. M. Zep had scored the goods and spent the rest of the night wiring the CAM board into the imipolex-wrapped blank's honeyheart with tiny wires connecting to the stick's surface all over, and then finally at dawn Zep had gone in through the back window of a butcher shop and wedged the board into the huge vacuum meat packer there to vacuum-sputter the new stick's finish up into as weird a fractal as a snowflake Koch curve or a rucked Sierpinski carpet. And now lame little Delbert is all worried and:

"Why's it so rough?"

Zep took a deep breath and concentrated on slowing down his heartbeat. Another breath. "This stick, Del, it uses its fractal surface for a realtime surfspace simulation. The board's surface is a fractal CA model of the sea, you wave?"

"Zep, what's that gray thing in the middle like a shark's skeleton? Loach is going to laugh at us."

"Shut up about Loach," snarled Zep, losing all patience once again. "Lex Loach is like a poisonous mutant warty sculpin choked by a plastic tampon insert at the mouth of an offshore toxic waste pipe, man, thrashing around and stinging everybody in his spastic nowhere death throes."

"He's standing right behind you."

Zep spun around and saw that Delbert was more or less correct, given his tendency toward exaggeration. Loach was striding down the beach toward them, along with the four other Stoke Pilgrims. They were carrying lean, tapering sticks with sharp noses and foiled rails. Loach and Mr. Scrote wore lurid wet suits. The younger three had painted their bodies with Day-Glo thermopaints.

"Gonna shred you suckers!" yelled Loach.

"Stupid clones!" whooped Zep, lifting Chaos Attractor high overhead. "Freestyle rules!"

"What kind of weird joke is this?" asked Loach, eyeing the new stick.

"Care to try it out?"

"Maybe. I'm gonna win it anyway, right?"

Zep nodded, calm and scientist-like now that the action had finally begun. It was good to have real flesh-and-blood enemies to deal with. "Let me show you where to plug it in. This might sting a bit a first."

He knelt down and began to brush sand from Loach's ankle.

"What're you doing?" Loach asked, jumping back when he saw Zep coming at him with a wire terminating in sharp pins.

"You need this special leash to ride the board," Zep said. "Without human input, the board would go out of control. The thing is, the fractal surface writhes in a data-simulation altered by the leash input. These fang things are a parallel nerve-port, wave? It feeds into the CAM8 along with the fractal wave analyses, so the board knows what to do."

Mr. Scrote gave Zep a sharp kick in the ribs. "You're gonna stick that thing in his ankle, you junkie, and give him AIDS?"

Zep bared his teeth in a confused grin. "Just hold still, Lex. It doesn't hurt. I'd like to see what you can do with it."

Loach stepped well back. "You're whacked, dude. You been over the falls one too many times. Your brain is whitewater. Yo, Delbert! See you out at the break. It's flat now, but there'll be peaks once the tide starts in—believe it!" Loach and the Stoke Pilgrims hit the mushy warm water and began paddling out.

Zep was still crouched over Chaos Attractor. He glanced slyly up at Delbert. "You ready?"

"No."

"Look, Del, you and my stick have to go out there and show the guys how to carve."

"No way."

"Get rad. Be an adventurist. You'll be part of the system, man. Don't you remember how I explained about waves?"

"I don't care about waves," said little Delbert. "I want to go home. It's stupid to think I would ever be a major surfer. Who talked me into this, anyway? Was it you?"

Zep stared out at the zon. Loach and the Stoke Pilgrims were bobbing on the mucky water, waiting for a set. Suddenly he frowned. "You know, Del, maybe it's not such a great idea for you to use this board."

"What do you mean? It's my stick isn't it? I gave you two hundred dollars."

"You still don't have the big picture. At any moment, the relevant sea-configuration is ten trillion bits of analog info, right? Which folds up to one point in the ten-trillion-dimensional surfspace. As the ocean dynamically evolves, the point traces out a trajectory. But Del! The *mind*, Del, the mind is meanwhile and always jamming in the infinite-dimensional *mindscape*. Mindscape being larger than surfspace, you wave. My good tool Chaos Attractor picks up what you're looking for and sends tiny ripples out into the ocean, pulsing them just right, so that they cause interference way out there and bounce back where you want. The coupled system of board and rider in the mindscape are riding the surfspace. You sketch yourself into your own picture."

"So why can't I ride the board?"

"Because, Delbert, because…" Zep gave a long, shuddery sigh and clamped the leash's fangs into his own ankle. "Because you have a bad attitude and you'll deal a mess and thrash the board before it gets burnt in. Because it's mine. Because right now I'm plugged in and you're not. Because…" Zep paused and smiled oddly. "I don't like to say the word for what you are."

"What word?"

"Ho-dad."

Delbert's tense frame sagged. "That's really depressing, Zep." In the distance a car had begun insistently to honk. At a loss for words, Delbert craned up the cliff at the N-plant parking lot. There was a girl up there, standing next to a car and waving and reaching in through the car window to honk. It was Jen! Delbert turned his back to Zep and waved both arms at Jen. "Come on down, baby," he screamed. "Zep's gonna break the board in for me and then I'll shut down this beach for true!" Jen began slowly to pick her way down the steep cliff path. Delbert turned back to Zep. All smiles. "Be careful, my man. The Pilgrims'll probably try to ram you."

"I'm not afraid of Loach," said Zep softly. "He's a clone surfer. No sense of freestyle. We're both 'dads, man, but we're still avant-garde. And you, man, you go and put some heavy physical moves on Jen while she's standing here."

Zep padded down to the water's edge, avoiding the lurid, overgrown anemones. Clams squirted dark brown water form their holes. Sand crabs hid with only their antennae showing, dredging the slack warm water for the luminous plankton indigenous to the San Diablo break.

The N-plant made for an empty beach. There was plenty of room in the water, even with the five Stoke Pilgrims out there in a lineup. Floathead and Shrimp Chips were playing tic-tac-toe in the body paints on each other's chests, and Squid Puppy was fiddling with a wristwatch video game.

Chaos Attractor lit up the instant it hit the water. Zep found himself looking into a percolating, turbulent lens. The board was a window into surfspace. Zep could see the swirling high-dimensional probability fluid, tiny torsion curls composed of tinier curls composed of tinier torsions.

It made him almost high on life. Zep flopped belly-down on the board and began paddling out through the wavelets that lapped the shore.

"Hang ten trillion!" called Delbert.

Ripples spread away from Zep's stick, expanding and crossing paths as they rushed toward the open sea. The water was laced with slimy indigo kelp. Zep thought of jellyfish. In this quap water, they'd be mongo. He kept paddling. The sun looked like the ghost of a silver dollar. He splashed through some parallel lines of number-three wavies. Stroke followed stroke, and finally he was far enough out. He let himself drift, riding up and down on the humping wave embryos. Chaos Attractor was sending out ripples all the time and now things were beginning to…

"Check the zon!" shouted Squid Puppy.

Zep sat up. Row upon row of waves were coming in from the zon, each wave bigger than the one before. The sea was starting to look like a staircase. Remain calm, carver. Nothing too big and nasty. A few even test waves would do nicely. Something with a long, lean lip and a smoothed-under ledge.

"Curl or crawl," Loach called, glancing sidelong at Zep with a confident sneer.

Zep could feel the power between his legs. The surface of Chaos Attractor was flexing and rippling now, a faithful model of the sea's surface. Looking down, Zep could see moving beads of color that matched the approaching waves. Wouldn't it be great if…

The leash fed Zep's thought to the CAM8. The CAM8 jived the imipolex. The imipolex fed a shudder to the sea. The surface band-pattern changed and…

"Mexican beach break!" screamed Zep.

The huge blue wall came out of nowhere and crashed onto Loach and his glittering board—all in the space of an exclamation point.

Zep aimed into the churning stampede of white foam, endured a moment of watery rage, and shot effortlessly out into calm tides. The real wave-set was marching in now. Zep decided to catch the seventh.

Loach surfaced a few meters off, all uptight. "Carve him, Pilgrims!"

Zep grinned. Not likely.

As the war-painted sea dogs huffed and puffed against the current, he calmly bent his will toward shaping that perfect seventh wave. The Stoke Pilgrims yelled in glee, catching waves from the set. Squid Puppy and Shrimp Chips came after Zep, dogsledding it in zigzags over the curl and down the hollow. Near miss. Here was Zep's wave. He took his time getting to his feet after a slow takeoff, and looked back to see the prune-faced Mr. Scrote snaking after him, befouling the wave in his eagerness to slyve Zep.

It was time to hang ten.

Zep took a ginger step toward the nose and watched the gliding water rise up. Perfect, perfect…aaauuuuummmm. A shadow fell over Zep. He leaned farther out over the nose, and the shadow grew—like an ever-thicker cloud closing over the sun.

Zep looked back, and he saw that the sky was green and alive with foam, a shivering vault of water. Floating amid that enormous green curved world, which looked like some fathomless cavern made from bottle glass, was a lurid, red-eyed giant—a Macy's Parade Mr. Scrote.

Zep flicked around, banked back toward the behemoth, and cruised up the slick green tube until he was at Scrote's eye level. The sight of the bulging capillaries sickened him, and he stretched his arms straight out ahead of him, gripping the very tip of the board with his naked toes. He had all the time in the world. The wave didn't seem to be breaking anymore.

The green expanse spread out around him. The curve above flowed like melting wax, drawing him into it. Rationally, he knew he was upside down, but it felt more like he was sliding down one side of a vast, translucent bowl. Under the board he could see a shimmering disk of white light, like a fire in the water: Was that the sun? He stepped back to the middle of Chaos Attractor, tilting the board up for greater speed, plunging ever deeper in the maelstrom spiral of the tube. He was nearing the heart of pure foam: the calm, still center of the ever-receding void.

Suddenly, a huge stain came steaming toward him out of the vortex. Gelatin, nausea, quaking purple spots, a glutinous leviathan with purple organs the size of aircraft carriers. Mile upon mile of slithery stinging tendrils drifted behind the thing, stretching clear back to the singular center that had been Zep's goal.

It was a jellyfish, and…Zep was less than a centimeter tall. It figured, Zep thought, realizing what was up—it figured that he'd shrink. That's what he'd always wanted from the drugs he couldn't quite kick: annihilation, cessation of pain, the deep inattention of the zero. The jellyfish steamed closer, lurid as a bad trip, urgently quaking.

Zep sighed and dug in his stick's back rail. Water shot up, and Zep grew. The jellyfish zoom-lensed back down to size. Chaos Attractor shot up out of the tube, and Zep fell down into the warm gray-and-green sea.

He surfaced into the raging chop and reeled Chaos Attractor in by the leash. Mr. Scrote was behind a crest somewhere, screaming at Loach. "He disappeared, Lex! I swear to God, dude—I had him, and he shrunk to nothing. Flat out disappeared!"

Zep got back on Chaos Attractor and rode some whitewater toward shore. There were Del and Jen, waving and making gestures. Del had his arm around her waist. Off to the right was the stupid N-plant cooling pipe. Zep glared up at the plant, feeling a hot, angry flash of righteous ecological rage. The nuke-pigs said no N-plant could ever explode, but it would be so rad if like this one went up, just to show the pigs that…

Ripples sped over the cooling pipe, and suddenly Zep noticed a cloud of steam or smoke in the air over the N-plant. Had that been there before? And was that rumbling noise thunder? Had to be thunder. Or a jet. Or maybe no. What was that he'd been thinking about an explosion? Forget it! Think pro-nuke, Zep baby!

When Zep was near shore, Delbert gave Jen a big kiss, dived in, and came stroking out, buoyed by his wet suit. He ducked a breaker or two and then he was holding onto the side of Chaos Attractor, totally stoked.

"I saw that, Zep! It was awesome! It does everything you said it does. It made great waves—and you shrank right up like you were surfing into a zero."

"Yeah, Del, but listen—"

"Let me try now, Zep. I think I can do it."

Zep back-paddled, gripping the board between his thighs. "I don't think that's such a hot idea."

Delbert reddened. "Yeah? You know, Zep, you're a real wipe sometimes. What is this, huh? You get me to fork over all my savings so you can go and build a board that didn't cost you a cent in the first place—and now you act like it's yours! You took my money for a board you would have made anyway!"

"It's not that, Del. It's just that—it's more powerful that I thought. We maybe shouldn't be using it around here. Look at the nuke."

"Oh, yeah, try to distract me. What a bunch of crap! Give me that board, Zep. Come on, and the leash, too."

"Del, look—"

Another spurt of steam went up from the plant. Zep gave thanks that the wind wasn't blowing their way.

"You two dudes are maka sushi!" yelled Loach.

The Stoke Pilgrims cried out in unison, "Shred 'em!"

Zep looked away from the board just long enough for Del to grab it away from him. Delbert got up on the board and pushed Zep under, holding him down with his feet and reeling in on the leash. Zep's foot surfaced, and Delbert ripped the leash fangs out of his ankle. By the time Zep got his head back in the air, Delbert had installed the leash on himself and was paddling away, triumph in his eyes.

"It's my stick, dude," called Del.

"Oh, no, Delbert. Please, I swear I'm not goofing. If you do it, you'd better stay really, really cool. Go for the little waves. And don't look at the N-plant. And if you do look, just remember that it can't possibly explode. No fancy tricks, dude."

"Bull!" screamed Delbert, shooting over a small peak. "This gun was built for tricks, Zep, and you know it. That's the thrill, man! *Anything* can happen! That's what this is all about!"

Delbert was belly to the board, stroking for the horizon. Back on the beach, Jen had noticed the N-plant's activity, and she was making gestures of distress. Zep dog-paddled, wondering what to do. Suddenly four of the surf punks surrounded him.

"He looks kind of helpless down there, don't he," said Floathead.

"Watch him close," said Mr. Scrote. "He's slippery."

"Let's use his head for water polo," suggested Squid Puppy darting the sharp end of his board at Zep.

Zep dove to the bottom and resurfaced, only find the Stoke Pilgrims' boards nosed in around him like an asterisk with his head at the center. "Mess with my mind, I don't care," said Zep. "But just don't put Delbert uptight."

"We won't bother bufu Delbert," said Mr. Scrote. "He's Lex's now."

"I know this is going to sound weird," Zep began. "But…"

"Holy righteous mother of God," interrupted Floathead. "Check out the zon, bros."

"Far, far, faaar outsider," someone whispered. The horizon looked bent in the middle, and it took an effort of will to realize that the great smooth bell-curve was an actual wave of actual water. It swelled up and up like a droplet on a faucet, swelled so big that you half expected it to break free of the sea and fly upward into great chaotic spheres. It was far enough off that there still might have been time to reach the safety of the cliffs…but that's not what the surfers did. They broke formation and raced farther out to sea, out to where they guessed the monster wave would break.

Zep power-stroked out after the others, out toward where Loach and Delbert were waiting, Delbert bobbing up and down with a dismayed expression as Loach kept shouting at him. Just as Zep got there, Loach reached over and smacked Delbert in the face.

Delbert screamed in anger, his face going redder every second. "I'm gonna kill you, Loach!"

"Hoo-hoo-hoo!" cried the Stoke Pilgrims, forming their lineup. "Delbert is a ho-dad!"

"You can't always bully me, Loach," continued Delbert. "If you get near me one more time—if you snake in while I'm riding this super wave, *my* wave—it's all over for you."

"Oh, I'm shaking," Loach said, slapping the water as he laughed. "Come on, paddle boy. Do your worst—and I do mean megaworst." Loach grinned past Del at the other Stoke Pilgrims. "Contest's over, guys! Let's take this dip's board right now!"

Zep watch Delbert's face run through some fast changes, from helpless to terrified to grim to enraged to psychotic. It was as if some vicious bug had erupted from shy caterpillar Delbert. Some kind of catastrophic transition took place, and Delbert was a death's head moth. All the while Chaos Attractor was churning out a moiréed blur of weird ripples, making the oncoming wave grow yet more monstrous.

Zep felt himself sucked up into the breast of a mountainous wall of water, a blackish green fortress whose surface rippled and coiled until it formed an immense, godlike face glaring down on all of them. Zep had never seen such cold eyes: The black depths of space had been drawn into them by the chaotic attractor. Sky had bent down to earth, drawing the sea up to see. Del and the Pilgrims and Zep all went rushing up toward a foamy green hell, while below...

Below was the rumbling, and now a ferocious cracking, accompanied by gouts of radioactive steam. Sirens and hooters. High up on the god-wave, Zep looked down and saw the N-plant rocking in its bed, as if nudged from beneath by a gigantic mole. Blue luminescence pulsed upward through the failing N-plant's shimmering veils of deadly mist, blending into the green savagery of the spray trailing down from their wave. Frantic Jen had flung herself into the surf and was thrashing there, goggling up at the twin catastrophes of N-plant and Neptune's wave.

Looking up, Zep saw Delbert streaking down the long beaked nose of Neptune while Loach and the Pilgrims skidded down the cheeks, thrown from their boards, eating it.

Zep felt proud. *Delbert, I didn't know you had it in you. Shut the beach DOWN!*

Cracks crazed the surface of the N-plant. It was ready to blow. Way down there was Jen, screaming, "Save me!" like Olive Oyl. Del carved the pure surfspace, sending up a rooster of probability spray, jamming as if he'd been born on silvery, shadowy Chaos Attractor. He looked like he'd been to the edge of the universe and back already. He raved down deep to snatch up his Jen and set her in the board's center; and then he snapped up the wall to wrap a tight spiral around floundering Zep.

"Latch on, dude!"

Zep clamped onto Chaos Attractor's back rail and pulled himself aboard. The stick reared like a horse and sent them scudding up over the lip of the tsunami, out over the arching neck of the slow-breaking wave. Del glanced back through the falls and saw the filtered light of the San Diablo Nuclear Plant's explosion, saw the light and the chunks of concrete and steel tumbling outward, borne on the shock-wave's A-bomb energy.

The two waves intermingled in a chaotic mindscape abstraction. Up and up they flew, the fin scraping sparks from the edges of the unknown. Zep saw stars swimming under them, a great spiral of stars.

Everything was still, so still.

And then Del's hand shot out. Across the galactic wheel a gleaming figure shared their space. It was coming straight at them. Rider of the tides of night, carver of blackhole beaches and neutron tubes. Bent low on his luminous board—graceful, poised, inhuman.

"Ohmigod!" said Jen. "The Silver Surfer!"

Note on "Probability Pipeline" (With Marc Laidlaw)

Written in 1987.
Synergy #2, HBJ Books, 1988.

Our first two years in California, Sylvia and I frequently got together with Kadrey, Murphy, Blumlein, and Laidlaw. We talked about starting a new "Freestyle" science-fiction movement along with Jeter and Shirley, but the idea died a-borning for the lack of any unifying principle other than "write like yourself except more so."

For awhile, though, Marc and I were pretty strongly in pursuit of a Freestyle mystique, and we found most of our information in surfing magazines. Here's one quote we dug: "Life on the edge measures seekers, performers, and adventurists." Marc started writing me letters in the surf-magazine style. "There it is, Rude Dude. The Freestyle antifesto. No need to break down the metaphors—an adventurist knows what the Ocean really is. No need to feature matte-black mirrorshades or other emblems of our freestyle culture—hey, dude, we know who we are. No need to either glorify or castrate technology. Nature is the Ultimate. We're skimming the cell-sea, cresting the waves that leap out over the black abyss…" Marc started publishing a neat zine called *Freestyle*, but it only went through three issues.

I went so far as to buy a used surfboard and wetsuit. Sylvia, Marc, Marc's wife Geraldine, and I went to a wild beach north of Santa Cruz on New Years Day, 1987, and I tried to surf. I didn't manage to stand on the board, but I did get out into the water. It was nice to see how well the wetsuit worked at keeping me warm.

Like my collaboration with Bruce Sterling, "Probability Pipeline" is a two-guys story. We thought of Marc being Del and Zep being me.

Due to anxiety about the trademark infringement issues in mentioning a well-known comic-book character like the Silver Surfer, the first publication of "Probability Pipeline" had the last line changed to: "Stoked," said Jen. "God's a surfer!"

Another exciting literary feature of moving to California was that I got to see my hero Robert Sheckley again. This time he was visiting his writer/comedian friend Marty Olson in Venice Beach. Olson had dreamed up the idea that Tim Leary would start hosting a PBS series about various futuristic things. Sheckley and I were to be the writers. Olson paid my plane-fare to LA, where he and "the Sheck-man" (as Olson called him) picked me up. It was a wonderful goof, hanging out with them, and then driving over to Tim's house in Beverly Hills. Tim was up for the meeting, with pencils and pads of papers; he was a nice old guy, and a freedom-fighter from way back. We were all in full agreement about everything, but the hitch was that we never found a sponsor.

AS ABOVE, SO BELOW

I'd been overhacking again. The warm California night was real and intimate, *synaesthetic*, with the distant surfsound matching the pebbly parking lot under my bare feet, and the flowering shrub of jade plant in front of me fitting in too, with its fat loplop green leaves and stuft yellow star petals knobbing along like my breath and my heartbeat, and the rest of the plants matching the rest of the world: the menthol-smelling eucalyptus trees like the rush of the cars, the palm trees like my jittering synapses, the bed of calla lilies white and wonderful as the woman waiting for me at home, ah the plants, with their smells and their realtime ongoing updates…

The old flash came rushing over me once again: astonishment at the vastness of the invisible world machinery that keeps all this running, awe for the great program the world is working out. *What a system! What a hack!*

I was stoned and I'd been overhacking and my eyes were throbbing and I couldn't remember what I'd said to Donna when she phoned… an hour ago?…nor could I remember when I'd last eaten. Eat. I walked across Route 1 to the Taco Bell. There were some kids there with pet rats crawling out of their Salvation Army coats, nice middle class kids no doubt, this being Santa Cruz. They wanted their burritos with no beans. "Beans are the worst," one of them explained to the cholo countergirl. The back of the boy's head had a remarkable yellow and green food-coloring dye job. A buzzcut DA with the left back half kapok yellow and the right half a poisonous green. The colors made me think of the assembly language XOR operation, which is a little like MINUS. Green XOR Yellow is Red. If I let my eyes go out of focus I could see a strip of red down the back of his head. I didn't want to think about the weird screens I'd just been watching at my workstation in the empty Micromax labs.

The boy's rat poked its head over the boy's shoulder and cheesed its nose at me, *twitch twitch*, the long whiskers sweeping out envelopes of virtual surfaces. The beastie had long yellow fangs, though a festive air withal.

"You should dye the rat red," I observed. "And call him XOR. Exclusive OR."

"Beans are the worst," repeated the boy, not acknowledging. He paid for his beanless burritos and left.

"Your order sir?" My turn.

"Four tacos and a large iced-tea."

I ate the food out on the concrete patio tables. I poured on the hot sauce and it was really good. I liked being there except I didn't like the traffic and I didn't like the wind blowing all the paper off my table. They give you a lot a lot of paper at Taco Bell. It's really obvious that the paper costs more than the food. But except for the wind and the traffic, I was feeling good. It was so neat to be getting input for free. When you're hacking, you're coupled to the screen, and all your input is from the machine's output which all comes from the passage of time and from what you put in the machine. You're making your own world all the time. And then you go outside and there's all this great deep complex shit for free. The crackle of the thin taco shells, the faces of the punks, the wind on my face, and best of all—always the best—the plants.

Plants are really where it's at, no lie. Take an oak tree: it grows from an acorn, right? The acorn is the program and the oak tree is the output. The runtime is like 80 years. That's the best kind of computation…where a short program runs for a long long time and makes an interesting image. Lots of things are like that—a simple start and a long computation. In information theory we call it low complexity/ high depth. *Low complexity* means short program, and *high depth* means a long runtime.

A really good example of a low complexity/high depth pattern is the Mandelbrot set. You grow it in the plane…for each point you keep squaring and adding in the last value, and some points go out to infinity and some don't. The ones that don't are inside the Mandelbrot set which is a big warty ass-shape with a disk stuck onto it. There's an antenna sticking out of the disk, and shish-kabobbed onto the antenna are tiny little Mandelbrot sets: ass, warts & disk. Each of the warts is a Mandelbrot disk, too, each with a wiggly antenna coming out, and with shish-kabobs of ass, warts & disk, with yet smaller antennae, asses, warts, and disks, all swirled into maelstroms and lobed vortices, into paisley cactus high desert, into the Santa Cruz cliffs being eaten by the evercrashing sea.

The Mandelbrot set goes on forever, deeper and deeper down into more and more detail, except sooner or later you always get tired and go home. After I finished my tacos I walked back across Route 1 and got in my bicycle. It was a carbonfiber lowrider with fat smooth tires of catalyzed imipolex. I realized that I'd left my workstation computer on inside the Micromax building, but I just couldn't handle going back in there to shut things off. It had been getting too weird. The last thing I thought I'd seen on my Mandelbrot set screen had been hairline cracks in the glass.

There was a liquor store just before the turnoff from Route 1 to the long road uphill to our house. My friend Jerry Rankle had stopped by Micromax to hand me a little capsule of white dust a couple of hours ago and I'd swallowed it fast and robotlike, thinking something like *this'll get you off the machine all right, Will*, because I knew I was over-hacking and I wanted to stop. I'd been the last one out of Micromax every day for a week.

"Lemme know how it hits you, Will," Jerry had said in his jerky stuttery voice, always on the verge of a giggle. He was an old pal, a run-down needlefreak who'd once summed up his worldview for me in the immortal phrase: "The Universe Is Made of Jokes."

"What is it exactly?" I'd thought to ask, sitting there at my work-station, feeling the little lump of the pill in my gullet, suddenly worried, but not talking too loud just in case my yuppie boss Steven Koss was within earshot. "How fast does it come on?"

"Wait and see," said Jerry. "It's brand new. You can name it, man. Some H. A. biohackers in Redwood City invented it last week. Could be a new scene." *H. A.* stood for *Hells Angels*. Jerry thought highly of H. A. drug suppliers.

Now, on my bicycle, two hours later, passing the liquor store, I realized Jerry's stuff was hitting me weird, worse than MDMA, this tinker-toy crap some slushed biker chemist had biohacked together—I was grinding my teeth like crazy and for sure it was going to be a good idea to have some booze to smooth the edges.

Basically, I was scared of going nuts just then, with the overhacking and the pot and the speed and now Jerry's pill on top of it. The images I'd been getting on the machine just before quitting were at wholly new levels of detail in the Mandelbrot set. These were new levels I'd accessed with brand-new hardware boards, and the almost impossible thing is that at the new levels the images were becoming more than two-dimensional. Partly it was because I was breeding the Mandelbrot set with a chaotic tree pattern, but it had also seemed as if my new, enhanced Mandelbrot set was somehow taking advantage of the screen phosphor's slight thickness to ruck itself up into faintly gnarled tissues that wanted (I could tell) to slide off the screen, across the desk, and onto my face just like the speedy octopus stage of the creature in that old flick *Alien*, the stage where the creature grabs onto some guy's face and forces a sick egg down his esophagus.

Wo!

So I'd left the office, I'd had my tacos and tea, and now calmly calmly I was taking the precautionary measure of picking up a cylindrical pint bottle of Gusano Rojo, a Mexican-bottled distillation of mescal cactus, with an authentic cactus worm (*gusano rojo* means *red worm*) on the bottom. I paid the Korean behind the counter, I got back on my bike, I took a few hits of Gusano Rojo, I tucked the bottle in my knapsack, and I started the rest of the way uphill, trying to stave off the pill by ignoring it, even though I couldn't stop the grinding of my teeth.

I held it all together until the last slope up to our house. The fatigue and the fear and the drugs started to clash really badly, and then the new drug kicked in top-volume, fusing shut the sanity brainswitch I'd desperately been holding open. It was nasty.

I lost control of my bicycle and weaved into the ditch. The bike's cage protected me, more or less, not that I noticed. The bumps and jolts were like jerky camera motion on a screen. When the picture stopped moving the camera was pointing up into the sky.

I lay there quietly grinding my teeth, like a barnacle sifting seawater, unwilling to move and to stir up more sensations to analyze. The patch of sky I could see included the moon, which was nearly full. Her pale gold face churned with images, though her outline held steady. Dear moon, dear real world.

My calm lasted a few minutes, and then I began to worry. My leg was throbbing, was I badly cut? A car would stop soon; I would be institutionalized or killed; I was really and truly going crazy for good; this would never stop; the whole cozy womany world I leaned on was a rapidly tattering computer pattern on the nonscreen of the angry Void; and *actually* I was bleeding to death and too wrecked to do anything about it?!?!?

Wo. I sat up. The bike's front wheel was broken. I dragged my machine up the road's low sand embankment and shoved it into the manzanita chaparral. There was a tussocky meadowlet of soft grass and yellow-blossomed wood-sorrel a few meters further in. All the plants smiled at me and said, "Hello." I lolled down and took a hit off my pint. Donna would be worried, but I couldn't hack going home just yet. I needed to lay out here in the moonlight a minute and enjoy my medication. I was pretty together after all; the clashing was all over and the drugs had like balanced each other out. Though I was in orbit,

I was by no means out to lunch. My skin felt prickly, like just before a thunderstorm.

And that's when the creature came for me—all the way from the place where zero and infinity are the same.

The first unusual thing I noticed was a lot of colored fireflies darting around, all red, yellow and green. I could tell they weren't hallucinations because they kept bumping into me. And then all at once there was this giant light moving up the hillside towards me. The light was so big and so bright that the manzanita bushes cast shadows. At first I was scared it was a police helicopter, and I scooted closer to the bushes to hide. The light kept getting brighter, so bright that I thought it was a nuclear explosion. I didn't want to be blinded, so I closed my eyes.

And then nothing was happening, except there was a kind of hissing sound, really rich and complicated hissing, like a thousand soft radios playing at once. I opened my eyes back up and the light was overhead. It was hovering right over me, hissing and sputtering in a whispery way. I decided it was a UFO.

I knew the aliens could do whatever they wanted, and I knew they saw me, so I just lay there staring up at the ship. It was maybe fifty feet overhead and maybe fifty feet long. Or maybe a hundred and a hundred…it was kind of hard to tell. There were zillions of those fireflies now; and the ones high off the ground and closer to the ship seemed larger. There were thin tendrils connecting the fireflies to the ship so that the whole thing was like a jellyfish with bumpy tentacles hanging down, though by the time they got to the ground the tendrils were too small to see, so that it looked like the "fireflies" weren't connected. I reached out and caught a couple of them…they were tingly and hard to hold on to. My skin was prickling like mad.

I yelled "Hello!" up at the UFO just so it would know I was an intelligent being. And then I was thinking maybe it had come especially to see me, so I yelled, "Welcome! My name is Will Coyote! I'm a hacker!" For the time being the mothership just stayed up there, hissing and with all its tendrils wafting this way and that like beautiful strings of Tivoli lights flashing red, yellow and green.

The ship itself was shaped in three main parts. There was a great big back section with a dimple in it, and then there was a smaller spherical section attached opposite the dimple, and sticking out of the front of the sphere section was a long spike kind of thing. It was just like— oh my God!—*just like a giant three-dimensional Mandelbrot set*! Though also like a beetle in a way, and like a jellyfish.

The UFO came lower and then some of the thicker tendrils were brushing against me. They felt shuddery, like the metal on a shorted out toaster. I figured the prickly feeling I'd been getting was from invisible fine tendrils that I couldn't see. Could it be possible the thing was going to eat me like a Portuguese man-of-war that's got hold of a small fish? I screamed out, "Don't hurt me, I'm an intelligent being like you!" and the thing hissed louder, and then suddenly the hissing Fourier-transformed itself into a human voice. A woman's voice.

"Don't worry, William, I am very grateful to you. I wish to take you for a ride."

I tried to stand up then, but I was too fucking zoned. So I just smiled and stretched by arms up to the big UFO ass. UFO? This *had* to be a hallucination. Slowly, slowly, it came lower.

The tendrils were thick as vines, and the fireflies on the tendrils were as big as grapefruits and baseballs. Since this whole ship was a fractal, each of the firefly globs was a three-sectioned thing like the main body: each of them was a dimpled round ass part with a little antennaed head-sphere stuck onto it. This was absolutely the best graphic ever. I was really happy.

I took one of the baby Mandelbrot sets in my hands and peered at it. It was warm and jittery as a pet mouse. Even though the little globster was vague at the edges, it was solid in the middle. Better than a graphic. I cradled it and touched it to my face. As the big mamma came lower I kept calm by wondering if she was real.

I stayed cool right up to when the giant ass landed on me and began pressing me down against the ground—pressing so hard that I could barely breathe. Was I like *dying* or some shit? Had I passed out, gotten apnea, and forgotten to breathe? I blinked and looked again, but the ass was still there; and right up against my face was the incredibly detailed female hide of a gigantic three dimensional Mandelbrot set, man, like all covered with warts on warts and cracks in cracks and bristles'n'bristles evverywhaaar, oh sisters and brothers, and the whole thing rippling with every color of the rainbow and loaded with such a strong electric charge that my nose prickled and I had to sneeze.

The sneeze changed something. Everything got black. Now I was really dead, right?

"Welcome aboard, William," came the deep, thrilling voice of the mandelsphere's dark innards. "My name is Ma."

It was not wholly dark, no indeed—there were objects, but objects of such a refined and subtle nature that, likely as not, I would normally have walked right through them, except that here I had nothing else to walk into or through, so they became real to me.

It was not really dark, and it was not really small inside Ma. The space within was the mirror of the space without. While the outside of the Mandelbrot set's hide was crowded and entangled, the hide's inside was endlessly spacious. There being nowhere in particular to go, I sat myself down in a faintly glowing blue armchair and spoke.

"Where are you from?"

"I am everywhere; beyond all space, and within the tiniest motes. I am any size that wants me. You called me here."

"It's good to see all that programming finally pay off." I was giddy with excitement. "Can I get a drink?"

Faint shapes wafted around me, and then a long luminous beaker of yellow was in my hand. I sucked greedily at the pure energy fluid. This was the kind of rest I deserved after all that mindbreaking hacking: always shifting bits left and right to make bytes, masking the bytes together into register-sized words, generating lookup tables, finding room for the tables in RAM, feeding the output into the color display ports...I drank and drank, and my glass was always full.

One pale shape after another came to me, flowed over me, and gave way to the next one. Each was reading me like a book, accessing me like a hypertext, learning the nature of my familiar world. It seemed that each could sense me in a slightly different way. While they read me, I thought questions and they thought answers back.

The shapes were like different body parts—each an aspect of the single higher-dimensional entity called Ma.

According to Ma, the smallest and largest sizes were one and the same. That was her native habitat.

Ma needed my presence to easily stay at this size-scale; for her it was more natural to exist as a quark or a universe. I was like a snag in a rushing river for her to hold onto.

Despite that, said Ma, there was only one thing at all, and that one thing was Ma.

"Am I you?"

"You are a pattern in the potentially infinite computation that is the universe; and I am the actually infinite end of said computation. I am all space and all time. The world you live in is happening; my essence is what comes before and after your mundane time."

"How long is the program that starts it all?"

"Two bits. One Zero."

"What about all the details?"

"You'd call it 'screen wrap.' Patterns grow out and around and come back over themselves and make fringes. It adds up over the billions of years, especially when you remember that each point in space is updating the computation each instant. Each of those points is me;

I'm the rule that runs it all; and looked at the other way, I'm all the past and all the future."

"I can totally dig it, Ma. The universe has a simple code and a long rich parallel computation. There are infinitely many size scales so in fact each orange or atom has everything inside it. Right on. What about uncertainty and Planck's constant, though. Is that a hassle for you, Ma?"

She got into a complex answer involving infinite-dimensional Hilbert space—the human modes of thinking were new to her so we had some back and forth about it—and the conversation drifted on. Talking mathematical metaphysics, lolling on my ethereal couch, sipping my invigorating energy drink, and with the eager phantom Ma figures mounting me like harem girls, I swore I'd never been so happy. But then, all at once, the joy ended.

"Two more people are here," said Ma's sweet voice. "One of them is—Ow!" There was a sputtering and a lashing. "They've torn off a piece of me," she screamed. "And now…oh no—"

There was a brainsplitting cry of pure agony, a pop, and then I thudded to the hard ground.

"Will! Hey, Will!" It was my wife, Donna, and my boss, Stephen Koss. They were proud of themselves for "saving" me.

"Yeah," gloated Koss, stupid yuppie that he was. "I shot it with my Tazer." He held up a stubby box with two wires trailing out of it. "Was some kind of anomalous electromagnetic field, I guess, and my jolt disrupted it. You feeling okay, big guy?"

"Why did you shoot it?" I asked, sitting up. "It was so beautiful!"

"It was going for your wife!" he snapped. I noticed that he had his arm across her shoulders.

Donna's face was a white patch inside her long, hanging-down dark hair. "Are you all right, Will? What happened was I pulled off one of the baby globbies, and it started screaming and flashing checkerboard sparks." She held something cradled against her breasts. It glowed.

"You got a baby Ma?" I cried, getting to my feet.

Donna cracked her fingers so Koss and I could peek in and see a flowing, colored, tiny Ma. Donna held it tight as a baby. Its little tail or spike stuck out below her hands. The tail was knobbed with tinier Mas.

"I broke it off the big one, and the big one got mad," smiled Donna. "Do you think we could keep this one for a pet?"

"Pet, hell," said Koss. "We can sell them."

The magic energy drink Ma'd given me had gotten my head back together pretty good. The three of us went on up to our house on top of the hill, Donna and I in our dingy Honda, Koss following behind in his Jaguar with my wrecked bike.

"I was really worried when you didn't come home," said Donna. She was driving and I was holding the baby Ma. Ma felt good to my hands.

"I called Micromax and nobody was there except that thing, that AI answering machine," continued Donna. She didn't sound particularly friendly. "So I decided to drive downtown and look for you. I just knew you'd be drunk and stoned again. God, I'm sick of you, Will. You never notice me anymore."

"Don't start nagging me, Donna."

"Oh, right. That's what you always say: *Don't talk, Donna, be quiet*. Well, I've had it, Will, with your computer and your drugs. When was the last time you bothered to touch me? I need love, Will, I need someone who'll listen to me!"

What she said was true, but why did she have to start in on it now? "I hear you, Donna, loud and clear. Can you tell me more about how you found me?"

She sighed and shook her head and grudgingly told me the rest. "Halfway down the hill I saw this huge bright light UFO sitting on the ground. I got out and looked at it, and after awhile I picked a bud off it. It got all upset. That's all."

"How does Koss fit in?" I demanded. "Who told him to show up with his asshole electric gun?"

"Steven thought I was in danger," said Donna. "He cares about me. Not like you, Will, so stoned and hacked you don't know the first thing about me anymore. Steven showed up in his Jaguar right before I picked the bud. He said the stupid AI thing at Micromax called him to tell him a window was broken. And when he went there he found your terminal's glass all broken out, too. He thinks the UFO thing came from your computer, Will."

"Her name is Ma, Donna. She's an infinite fractal from Hilbert space. This little one is all of her. Each of her bumps is all of her. She's every particle, and she's the whole world." I held Ma up to my face and kissed her warty tingly hide. Each time I kissed her she grew a little. Donna sighed heavily.

Back at the house, I couldn't get Koss to leave. He was all fired up with excitement from having killed something. Jock, caveman, yuppie—all the same. He preened himself in front of the disgustingly attentive Donna, laying down his moronic rap about what he thought had happened.

"I was in the exercise room working out with my exercise machine—hey, I need it every day, guys—and then the emergency phone's all ringing from our AI about a broken window. I get in my Jag, cruise down there, and find Will's fifteen thousand dollar Mitsubishi VGA with the front screen blown away. I'm wondering if one of Will's dusted-out friends've blown him away or what. I decide not to call the pig in, I board up the broken window—then outside I'm all *what's that light on the hillside?* I wind the Jag on up here and it's some kind of atmospheric plasma display? Donna's standing under it looking real fine—and she's got the idea to tear off a little bud from it and all at once it's violent."

By this point Koss was pacing and pounding his hand with his fit tan fist, reliving the big play. "At the speeds I travel, you can't waste time saying why. You just react. I snapped my Jaguar's utility boot open and got out the heavy-duty stungun I keep in there in case of trouble. Sucker's got a gunpowder charge that shoots two metal fishhook electrodes twenty yards. Those 'trodes pack 150 volts! I aimed steady and I nailed that big mother right in its butt. *FFFFFTT!*"

"Big deal," I said. "Donna already told me."

"Let's tear another glob off that little one," said Koss.

"You better not," said Donna. "It'll get violent!"

"This little one can't hurt us," chortled Koss, snatching it out of my hands and tearing off a bud.

Little Ma screamed, but only I could hear her. She got an ugly cyan/white/magenta for a few minutes, and her broken tendril shot out black and white sparks, but a minute later she was a calm red/yellow/green and the sparking spot had healed over.

"Check it out, Donna!" exulted Koss. "We got work to do!" He pulled off another bud and another. "Like artichokes!"

"How exciting," squealed Donna.

I just wanted to be alone with a Ma and grow it big enough to get inside again, but Koss got on my case about how I should write up a sample ad for the new company we were going to start. I told him to get fucked. Donna frowned at me and wrote an ad that was so bogus that I rewrote it. The finished version went like this:

WONDERGLOBS

The living Wonderglob is an object of unparalleled beauty. Like God or the Universe itself, the Wonderglob feeds on YOUR attention—the more you look at it, the larger it grows.

Perhaps the most satisfying aspect of owning a Wonderglob is that you can HARVEST BUDS from it and, under our franchising agreement, SELL these buds to your friends! The initial investment pays for itself in a matter of weeks!

The Wonderglob dislikes electricity and is easily kept captive in our patented Wondertanks, whose metal-plated glass sides carry a small electric charge. The Wonderglob may be removed for play and meditation, but be sure to replace it in the Wondertank, particularly after harvesting.

We didn't happen to have any "patented Wondertanks" handy, but Donna had the idea of hooking a wire to the tightly woven steel mesh of our old djinkotl cage and keeping the buds in there. The Mas hated it, man, they were shrinking steadily. Meanwhile Koss was giving Donna lines of coke and jabbering about money. I couldn't tell if things were as bad as they seemed, or worse. I chilled and crashed.

I snapped awake at 4:00 A. M. the way I sometimes do. Like if I go to bed wrecked, the survival reflex wakes me as soon as the limbic systems reboot. I wake up to assess the damages. Am I in bed? Who did I phone? What did I break?

Donna wasn't in bed with me. I got up and went in the living room. There was Koss putting it to her right there on our rug, her legs wrapped around his dumb cheeks. My Mas are dying specks in a shitty lizard's cage and Koss here is putting it to my wife? While torturing my dreams for *gain*?

I picked up the djinkotl cage and headed outside. Koss and Donna barely noticed.

It so happens I know my woods like the back of my own prick. I went around the hill to a green boulder redwood gully, a special spot all ferned and purling, with small white flowers and soggy mosses and rivulets underfoot, and overhead clear sky and stars past the tall trees. I took the Ma buds out of djinkotl cage—sixteen of them in all—and held them in my hands and mooshed down into soft trickly moss where living water could well in through my finger cracks and feed the ripped off and the newborn buds.

They drank the water avidly; they grew closer to my size. I could hear her/their happy thoughts. Ma'd never tasted water at this size scale before. The newly harvested buds stopped at the size of oranges, while Donna's maimed original puffed up to womansize and continued to grow. Big Ma.

The spots where Koss had torn buds off were flat scars covered with a fine fractal down of new growth. Each of the new baby buds bore a single birth-scar, a kind of navel hidden in the cheeks of her swelling behind. Ma's girls.

Sixteen is hex-ten. The girls lifted off and darted about. When they got farther away from me, they either got a lot smaller or a lot bigger. Some of them went high into the redwoods and on up into the sky, growing as they flew. There were quick blinks of brightness across the sky as one by one they maxxed out to cosmic scale. Others bumped down the gully towards the sea, dwindling to tiny bright specks in the water. A few hung around watching me and the main Ma.

And then the main Ma was big enough for me to get in her, so I did; I did it by hugging her against me until her shape slipped over me and I was back inside the endlessly vast interior of a fractal solid weird screen come true.

I wandered about in there at will. There were trees, there were boulders, but when you tripped over something it didn't hurt. I went up a nubby slope and found an ethereal armchair, same one as before, except now it was purple and it had wood trim along the arms. There was a glass of energy-drink on the floor by the chair, and laying there on the left arm's wood trim was a monster jay with a book of matches. I fired up for sure. Breathing the smoke out, watching the tendrils, with a pink womany Ma shape on my lap, I forgot everything I ever knew.

And it was calm, and it was wonderful, until of course some new Nazi asshole was on our case.

"A loud machine," said Ma. "Coming closer."

If I peered closely at a little speck in the air near me, I could see out to the world outside. It was all there, right in that little speck, the hill, and the ocean, and Santa Cruz. Racketting towards Ma and me was an Army helicopter with searchlights and with guns. From the speck's shifty viewpoint, I could even see the soldiers in the chopper, all peering down at our glow. They were getting ready to shoot us.

"Can we hide somewhere?" I asked Ma.

"Yes, William. I can shrink and I can jump in and out of Earth's space."

"Won't that hurt me?"

"Inside me you're already out of Earth's space. And as far as shrinking goes—infinity divided by ten is still infinity. My inside is always the same."

"Then let's go and get…inside the can of Geisha Girl crabmeat in my kitchen cupboard."

"It's…done."

I took my attention off the little worldview speck—which now showed strands of crabmeat, a can, and outside the can our kitchen. Cops in the house, talking to Koss and Donna.

That all happened yesterday, or maybe it's been two days. The longer I'm in here, the better I can see. At my request, Ma's got soft-edged computer graphics rippling over the endlessly unfolding surfaces around me—Escher images, Gosper hacks, Conway games—whatever I feel like seeing. It's like programming without ever having to touch a key. And with the energy drinks I'm never hungry. It's perfect in here.

I just hope no one gets hungry for canned crab.

Note on "As Above, So Below"

Written in 1987.
The Microverse, Bantam Books, 1989.

Soon after moving to California, I gave a talk on Cellular Automata in Ralph Abraham's Chaos Seminar at the University of California at Santa Cruz. Nick Herbert, author of *Quantum Reality* (Anchor Books, 1987) was there. I knew Nick from having corresponded with him about relativity theory. After my UCSC talk we had dinner with Ralph, and then some hackers showed Nick and me a lot of Mandelbrot set graphics. All of this came together pretty readily into the start of a story.

"As Above So Below" is a phrase used by the mystic P. D. Ouspensky and by the theosophist Madame Blavatsky. They attribute the phrase to a legendary magician called Hermes Trismigestus.

It took me awhile to completely finish "As Above So Below." The first installment of it came out in *Terra Nova*, a hippie hacker zine published by Nick Turner and Romana Machado, whom I met at a reading I gave for the magazine *Mondo 2000*.

A few years later I was approached by the theater director Kathelin Hoffman, who was interested in putting on a one-act play by me in a theater in Fort Worth. I worked "As Above So Below" into a script, and it was produced from August 20 - September 5, 1992, by the Theater of All Possibilities at the Caravan of Dreams Performing Arts Center in Fort Worth. It was an amazing thing to see the actor Jim Covault impersonate Will Coyote who was, in turn, an impersonation of me.

Ma the Mandelbrot set was played by the thrilling Fiorella Tirenzi. The great SubGenius Ivan Stang was there in the audience next to me. What a night. Mathematics has been good to me.

CHAOS SURFARI (WITH MARC LAIDLAW)

Way gnarly.

Delbert stood barefoot on a shelf of slimy-sharp sea rocks, clutching a terrycloth towel to his pimply chest. Behind him was a sandstone cliff crowned with cottages, below him were dead fish, seaweed, discolored water, and spit-bubbling crabs. One of the crabs had hold of a gooey condom; mindlessly the beast kept stretching and folding the rubber, now and again lowering its mandibles to taste the human salts that came oozing forth.

The sea, thought Del, has got to be the rudest place on earth.

Even though the surf was up, Del had stayed ashore today because of the red tide. Every so often the one-celled dinoflagellates would go on a breeding jag, and the ocean near Surf City would look and smell bad for weeks. Some of the older surfers said it was like the sea being on the rag, but it made Del think more of the time he'd vomited after eating reds, fried squid, and mucho red wine. Surf that shit? No way!

But Zep didn't mind. Zep...Zep would wade right out into the middle of the most gruesome scenes Del could imagine. He picked fights with cops; called bikers by names even their buddies didn't use; took drugs made by madmen; so right now, natch, Zep was out there carving tubes, unquestioningly accepting whatever liquid thrills Mother Ocean would serve up.

Well, almost unquestioningly. The catch was Zep's unique imipolex microprocessing way-tech surfboard: the good stick Chaos Attractor. Chaos Attractor had a distinct effect on the waves; it was wired to a parallel nerve-port in Zep's ankle. The smart board was able to read the ripples that hit it, run a CAM8 cellular automaton simulation of the future ocean nearby, use a global XOR to compare the simulation to Zep's wishes, and to then eliminate the differences by pulsing out just the right antiripples into the sensitive chaos of the sea.

Zep had built the thing single-handedly out of stolen parts; in fact the corporation that had built the CAM8 chip—a Silicon Valley outfit called System Complex—had placed full-page ads in *The Computer Shopper*, offering huge rewards for the return of the device or any information leading to the arrest of the culprit. Fortunately, aside from Zep, the only person who knew the truth was Delbert.

Out on the water, where the red-stained waves sluiced in between the curling rock pinchers of Blowhole Cove, Zep let out a brain-curdling scream whenever he created a particularly nasty wave. Looking at the big crisscross surf, Del knew that Zep's wishes were wild and unfocused—no surprise, as Zep was righteously stoned. Zep had scored a humongous jay that morning from Dennis Dementex, the chef at the Pup Tent where Del's girlfriend Jen worked.

Del had toked a few puffs himself, and now he began to imagine that the stinking red-brown ocean was awash with real blood, drained from the bodies of dead and racked-up surfers; yes, the ocean and the things in it were angry, and the waves were hit-men out to extract vengeance from thankless air-breathers. "Is this how you treat your mother?" the ocean seemed to say. "By building parking lots and condos on her sandy flanks? By dumping toxic waste and pesticides into the cradle, as if you're her only child? How dare you brag about your space probes when you know so little of what I conceal?"

Del peered down from his slippery rock shelf at the sand six feet below. The retreating tide combed back the eelgrass, slicking it down like Brylcreem in a cholo's hair. Sea anemones puckered the scraggy wall like free-living anuses, punked out with bits of shell and broken glass. He realized he had to take a piss. Nobody around; do it.

Delbert aimed his steamy stream down into the eelgrass, hosing through the seaweed as if he were an archaeologist cleaning out a wreck. Something glinted; he tried to pee harder, but he'd run out of pressure. There was something nestled in the weeds, something scummy with pink plankton yet diamond-bright.

A jewel! he thought. It's some kind of jewel washed up from the sea!

Zep screamed, his voice growing louder in a roar of surf. Delbert looked up and saw his best friend zooming toward him at the foot of a hungry wave. No time to watch Zep carve; in a moment, Del's newfound treasure would be lost in a cataclysm of spray. He leaped down to the sand and pushed the seaweed aside.

Del's fingers closed around the prize at the same time that the wave broke on his back an sucked him spinning into the deep. No way for now to tell which way was up, and already Del was out of breath. He clung hard to the shining ball he'd seized…confusion, a sharp jolt…

"Y'okay, dude?"

Del say up, his head ringing, and stared at the waves. Where had he been?

"My board clipped you right across the skull," Zep said. "Shit, man, I'm glad you woke up. I had to drag you out. That's a nasty bruise you got."

"I—look what I found," Delbert said. He opened his hand and the crystal lay revealed. The world showed inside it, reproduced in miniature but badly warped. He brought it closer to his eyes, working to focus, wishing that his head didn't ache so bad. There was movement down inside it, maybe brine shrimp, krill.

He seemed to hear a voice inside his head, a slithery whisper that said, *Look closer*.

Now he saw more clearly. A tiny gallery of moving faces lay within the crystal Superball. Inhuman faces; faces out of horror comics. They had quivery tentacles instead of beards; beaks and mandibles where mouths should have been. Cold gray eyes, dark secrets. The slithery voice began to whisper words he didn't understand, promising to reveal unguessed mysteries if he would only—would only —

"Del?"

"Shh! I'm looking!"

He was caught up in tracing the source of the faces, for they were set in a kaleidoscopic array, following some geometry he could hardly visualize. They seemed to sprout from the corners of a three-dimensional net of shimmering silver lines; the net formed pyramids and equilateral triangles, too many to see all at once. Some would vanish when others appeared. The whole thing cold have been an illusion, some novelty hologram a sea captain had put together in his spare time. But he couldn't tear his eyes from the depths. The faces twitched, crowding closer. They were like gargoyles crouched on the vertices of the hinged lines, guarding the hearts of the triangles. Guarding what, he wondered?

Very well then, the voice whispered. *A glimpse.*

"Let me see it, Del."

"I said wait!"

The gates of the net began to gape, permitting him some slight knowledge of what lay beyond those faces. His mind reeled with the insight. He saw an eye in a green pyramid, sitting on a plain very like the one he'd just dreamed of; but it wasn't a real place. It was a landscape in cameo—straight off the back of a dollar bill. His point of view shifted suddenly, and where the dollar had been he saw a luscious naked blonde surfer girl, vaguely familiar, her hands cupping her breasts, one running down to play in her pubic curls and she winked at Delbert and began to approach. But then her tanned flesh went all white and flaky; she began to expand from the inside and her hair turned to shredded lettuce.

A burrito, Del thought. Jesus, that's the most delicious burrito I've ever seen. And the smell—heavenly!

He started to reach out for it, but something rattled in his hands. He looked down and saw a car key where the crystal had been; looked up and saw, waiting for him at edge of an alien parking lot, a mint-green, mint-condition '48 Woodie. It was just like the car he'd seen in *Surf Serf* magazine last week, the boss Country Squire that belonged to the local Sicilian baron billionaire; it was the most beautiful car in the universe!

And poking out of the car's open rear, perfect noses gleaming, were three fine surfboards—red, white and blue. He just knew that they would give him the ride of his life—like the Woodie, like that blonde girl.

As he approached the car, he could see that the back was heaped with cases of beer—all import stuff, powerful Australian lagers, which he could never afford. And there was a hefty block of resinous green vegetable matter on the front seat, little glints of gold scattered among the leaves of tight-packed buds as big as his foot.

And standing on the dashboard, glowing no less brightly at noon than he would at midnight, was Jesus Christ Himself, lending his aura of protection and respectability to even the drunkest surfari!

Then the weirdly angled walls snapped closed; the net swung back into being. The guardians leered out at him, as if daring him to seize their precious goods.

"Come on, Delbert, snap out of it!"

He blinked up at Zep. "I think—I think this is magic, Zep. I think I've found good luck."

Zep snatched the ball out of his hand finally, and held it up to the sky, squinting at it with one eye.

"I don't know about that," he said after a minute. "I think this is just an ordinary plastic toy ecosphere. But look what's written on it."

He handed it back to Delbert, and showed him how when the light was just right you could see a string of angular letters scratched into the flattened base of the sphere.

WRITE IN NOW!
P.O. BOX 8128, SURF CITY, CA
WIN BIG $$$!

"We gotta write in now," said Del, fondling the wonderful sphere. "Before someone else wins all the prizes. Did you see the Woodie, Zep? With the beer and the key and Jesus on the dashboard?"

"I don't see anything in there but reflection lines and little shrimp," said Zep. "This is one of those cheap plastic kits you order form a comic book to grow Sea Monkeys, man, which are in fact brine shrimp. Some feeb could easily have scratched that message on there simply for a goof. But hell yes, let's go over to the post office. Penny. Penny'll be there." Penny was a big-breasted girl with dark brown hair and a wild laugh; Zep thought about her a lot.

They threw Chaos Attractor in the back of the old Chevy pickup Zep had recently acquired and drove over to the Surf City post office. It was cool and empty in there, like a jewel-case, Zep thought, a jewel-case holding plump pearl Penny so cute in her blue-gray Bermuda shorts, midthigh length with piping. Zep was all grin and buzzcut peroxide hair, leaning over the counter trying to think of something to say.

"I wish I was your underwear, Penny."

"You'd be too scratchy, Zep."

"Who has Box 8128?" asked Delbert. "I found this magic ball on the beach and it says to write Box 8128." The reedy sound of his voice annoyed Zep no end.

"Who has Box 8128?" answered Penny. "I'm not supposed to give out government information, Del." She gave her cute laugh and walked over to look at the post office boxes from behind. "Oh, wow! It's Kid Beast!"

"That's a name?" said Del. "Is he young?"

"Isn't everyone young in Surf City?" said Pen, resting her arms on the counter and her breasts on her arms. "Kid Beast is a skinny punk who talks funny. You've seen him, Zep, he played drums for the Auntie Christs." She glanced around the empty room. "I happen to know his home address because I saw him go in there one time. 496 Cliff Drive."

"496 is a perfect number," said Zep.

"What is?"

"Like six is three plus two plus one; and one, two, and three are the numbers that divide six. 496 is...whatever. Sixty-four times thirty-one. 1+2+4+8+16+32+64+31+62+124+248."

"How do you know that?" asked Penny.

"I went to college, baby. Santa Cruz UC."

"Let me see the magic ball," said Penny.

"We found it on the beach," said Zep, taking it from Del and handing it to her. "We saw things in it. You can keep it, Penny, if you'll let me tie you up and fuck you."

"Oh right."

She gave Zep a thoughtful glance.

"Hey, Zep, don't give it to her!" said Delbert. "That ball's got some kind of power—it's magic."

Zep sighed, pissed at Delbert for interrupting what had become a promising conversation.

"Why don't you go out to the truck, Del," he said. "I'll put a postcard in the Kid's box, then we'll swing by his house to make sure he pays up."

"You're trying to ditch me, aren't you? You want to steal my magic ball!"

"Yes. No. Here's your ball. Go on, man." Del went out to the truck.

Five minutes later Zep came out whistling, with a postmark stamped on his cheek like a government lipstick kiss. Penny had agreed to meet him at Bitchen Kitchen to watch the sunset later on. He would get another jay off Dennis at the Pup Tent, then he'd score a bottle of wine and mellow out with playful Penny. Unfortunately it was just past noon. Summer days were too damn long!

Zep found Delbert sitting in the front seat of the truck, staring into the float-ball as if he really were seeing all the weird stuff he'd said he saw. It worried Zep for a minute, bringing him down.

"You still seeing things, Del?"

Delbert shook his head. "They're not showing me, Zep. I have to be good...I have to do something special for them, I think."

"I hope you didn't get some weird spacetime concussion, Delbert. I mean, it wasn't just any old surfboard that cracked you on the skull—it was Chaos Attractor. It might have knocked your brain into another dimension. You ever see that movie where the living brains come after a bunch of geeks? They're like brains with snaky whiplike spines for tails."

Delbert looked at him, a little trail of spittle running down his chin. A skinny stranger on the sidewalk ducked down and peered at them, then disappeared. There was something funny going on. Something weirder than plastic movie monsters.

All the houses near 496 Cliff Drive had flowers in their yards and little "Cottage for Rent" signs with ivy wrapped around the posts; all perfect except for number 496, which was an animal house, totally whipped to shit. A three-legged pitbull lay sprawled in the dust of the front yard, angrily barking. The dog's missing leg ended in a stub that looked...well, chewed. When the dog finally stood up to make its move, Zep kicked it over. It fell on its spine, whining. Using the magic ball for a knocker, he rapped sharply on the bungalow's front door.

Just then something began happening to the surface of the door. It was like someone was projecting a slide on it, a picture all made of dancing spots whose speckling created the face of a boy. The light flashes, Zep realized, were caused by tiny laser-rays darting out of the base of the ball in his hands. As soon as he'd taken the image in, the laser rays turned back off.

The bungalow door opened to reveal the same skinny dude the ball's lasers had just drawn. He wore hightop sneakers, jeans, and an old mod black suit-jacket with no shirt. His straight black hair fell into his eyes. He wore faint black lipstick; or maybe he'd been sucking on a stamp pad. He had a leather thong around his neck with a little brass crucifix.

"I'm Kid Beast. You here to audition for the new band?"

Kid Beast flung the door open and stepped back. The room gave off a foul tidal stink, as of a dozen starfish left in a hot car trunk through the length of an August day. Half a dozen aquariums bubbled along the walls and corners of the room, and another half dozen sat dark and stagnant, with occasional sulfur farts bubbling up through the murky scum. There was a drum-kit and some amps.

"Come on in," said the Kid, picking up a carton of Friskees cat-food and pouring the contents into a black aquarium. The surface seethed with the frenzied feeding of opalescent beaks.

"My friend found this ball on the beach," said Zep, holding up the sphere. "I think you want to pay a reward for it? I'm Zep."

The Kid glanced up through the hair in his face. "On the beach, hug? I'll bet. Gidget sent you, right?"

"Gidget who?" said Delbert, taking the ball and pushing Zep ahead of him into the Kid's house. "Did she sing with the Auntie Christs? We love their stuff, don't we Zep?" He broke into song: "'I am the Auntie Christ! I look like Vincent Price! Wear black latex hosiery! Surfer girl is after me!'"

The Kid flicked them a nervous smile. His front teeth were broken, blackened, in need of caps. Zep was suddenly certain he had seen this kid many times…on the streets, or hanging out in front of the 7-11 at two in the morning, talking to the strangers who came and went, hitting on them for cigarettes and beer money. He repressed the dishonest urge to give the Kid a comradely clap on the back and reassure him that everything was going to be all right. Kid Beast was like a five-car pileup waiting for car number six.

"No, man, I'm talking about Tuttle Gidget, the chip billionaire."

"Sweet," said Zep. Everyone knew of Tuttle Gidget and his mansion on the hundred-acre estate on the top of a big hill north of town."

"Gidget had the Auntie Christs up to his place to play for one of his like society dinners," continued the Kid. "I bit a live squid…that was part of the new surf-music act we were breaking in. You know, bite into it and wave my head around with the tentacles coming out…"

"Did you get to see Gidget's '48 Country Squire?" asked Del. I bet this ball is from him and he wants to give it to me!"

"Yeah, I guess I saw it. I don't remember a lot about the evening. Somebody dosed me right before our second set and when I faded back in, the party was over, and the fucking band—my supposed friends—had all gone home without me. I was flaked out on the lawn and Gidget didn't even notice me. And then I heard the sounds. Wait."

Kid Beast started bopping around his living room, affixing little suction cups to the sides of his aquariums and hooking lengths of speaker wire to the suckers as he spoke. The wires all ran to a primitive mixing board, held together mainly by duct tape and rubber bands. Strange low noises began to ooze out of his speakers.

"It went kind of like this," the Kid was saying. "The sound was coming from his swimming pool, and I was seeing colors. Thins like color three-dee TV pictures…one of them looked like you, Zep, come to think of it, and another was like your little friend. What's his name?"

"My name is Del. I want what's coming to me."

"For sure. Why should I see something like Delbert?" Kid Beast shook his head in wonder, his dirty bangs batting against his dark eyes. "Anyway I'm seeing like ghost images and I'm hearing this weird bubbling music from the pool. Check it out. I think would be a great main sound for a new band."

Kid Beast fiddled with the dials on his deck, and the room reverberated with aquatic belchings and bubblings. He was mixing up the aquarium sounds, wrenching them into obscene configurations that sounded like some mad punker vomiting into the gulfs of outer space.

The Kid looked proud. "Like, it's so much uglier than anything any other group has got."

"What happened after you woke up at Gidget's?" asked Zep. "Did you get any more drugs?"

"Naw, man," said the Kid. "You're missing the point. The thing is, Gidget had somebody strapped to the diving board, a chick named Becka. She had her head hanging down over the end, with her long blonde hair touching the water. She was naked, arms and legs all tan, and you could see her T & A regions shining white in the dark. Gidget was standing over her on the diving board, wearing a wetsuit and holding a shimmering ball of light. Like that ball you have. Which is the point of this story. Did Gidget send you after me?"

"Becka?" said Zep. "I'd been wondering what happened to her."

"I see her," said Del, smiling and peering into his ball. "I see the girl you're talking about. She turns into a burrito."

"How right you are," said Kid Beast with a bitter laugh. "'Cause then the whole pool started to bubble and shake, and this huge orange-striped shell the color of a Creamsicle rose out of the water. There was a godawful smell. The shell tilted back under the diving board. It had tentacles—slithery orange tentacles, hundreds of 'em. A giant nautilus. The feelers reached up and started writhing all over that poor Becka. It was planting something in her. When I saw that shit, man, I took off running. I wish I'd tried to save her. I bet Becka's dead now. Her parents think she's just run away. But the nautilus thing got her."

In counterpoint to his narrative, Kid Beast had been mixing a nightmarish track that sounded like the ruminations of fish-eaten sailors playing Wurlitzers in a drowned shopping mall. His story chilled Zep, but Delbert was in another world: totally obliv.

"Gee," said Delbert, glancing up and tossing the ball idly from hand to hand. "You think maybe we could get to meet Gidget?"

"What's the matter with you, Del? You remember Becka. Didn't you hear what they did to her?"

"I just know Gidget will give me that Woodie."

"You really found that thing on the beach?" asked the Kid.

"Look for yourself," said Zep. "It's got your P. O. box number on it."

Kid Beast shook his head and refused to touch the ball. "This is some kind of trick of Gidget's. He wants to get that ball into my hands—like, maybe it will mark me, put a smell on me, so that tentacle thing knows where to find me. But no way, I'm not touching it."

"That monster you saw with Becka," said Zep, glancing down at his hands. "That was just a hallucination, right, Beast? Put the ball down, Delbert."

"But…but what about my Woodie? And the girl? And the money and everything?"

"It's called bait, Del. Put the ball in the trash. You're better off without it."

But Delbert clutched the little sphere to his chest. "You don't understand, Zep. You're just jealous cause you can't see what I can see. I want what's coming to me!"

Kid Beast gave Delbert a pitying look. "You know, Zep," he said after a moment's thought. "You guys should give the ball to Gidget. Not me. It's Gidget's anyway. Put the smell back on him before the nautilus wants to breed again."

"Shit," said Zep. He could see this turning into a full-on pain in the ass. He just hoped it didn't interfere with his evening's plans. "You mean like take it up to Gidget's place? He'd never let us in."

The Kid considered this. "Maybe not. But I know how to get past the gate. I'd like the chance to confront him about Becka. That shit was wrong. And while we're at it, I'd dig another chance to hear that swimming-pool sound. I'll bring a deck, man, and sample it. Yaaar. I'm glad you're here to help me."

"See, Zep," gloated Delbert. He seemed to be hearing about every other word of what was said. "Let's go to Gidget's—he's got my Woodie and everything. He'll give me the big reward! That's…that's what the little shrimp things want. They're telling me now, can't you hear them? They're telling me that Gidget wants to meet us. Especially you, Zep."

This was definitely the worst Delbert had ever been. To some extent, Zep felt responsible—it was his surfboard, after all, that had put Delbert out of whack. " "I'll drive you guys up there," said Zep slowly. "But you and me, Delbert, we get in, give Gidget the ball, ask for the reward, and get out . That's it. In and out. And what the Kid does there is up to him."

Delbert was pleased. He headed out the door toward the truck, hardly watching where he was going. The pitbull lunged, missed and fell over.

"Do you want to be in my new band?" Kid Beast asked Zep, upping the volume on his aquatic inferno for a last savoring second before switching off the power.

"I don't play an instrument," said Zep.

"Neither do I," said the Kid. "That's why I left the Aunties. They were starting sell out, getting into chords and shit."

They drove through the narrow, winding hill streets of Surf City, past an endless repetition of miniature pastel-colored haciendas, each with a dwarf palm and a driftwood-and-bottleglass sculpture on the lawn. Zep didn't trust Delbert to drive right now, and Del wasn't interested in anything but the promises of his magic Sea Monkey sphere. Kid Beast sat between the two of them, giving occasional directions, though Zep already knew the way. Who didn't?

While they were driving Zep kept thinking he saw pedestrians out of the corner of his eye. They'd pop out of nowhere and lurch towards the car. Zep would swerve, but then there'd be no one at all. It happened so often that he started to pick up on what seemed like a pattern. He only saw the ghost pedestrians at certain kinds of intersections, the ones were the streets were curved and one was running uphill. The weird walkers all looked like Kid Beast. Zep figured that Delbert's ball was doing it to him, flashing little glimpses of his passenger onto his retina and then scrambling them with the crazy lines of the curbs. Thank God they were getting rid of the thing.

Soon the came to the pink stucco wall surrounding Gidget's estate. Far ahead Zep could see the turreted roof of the mansion. The property wall held a wrought-iron gate decorated with dinosaurs. Long ago, when silicon was something that people were content to leave on beaches, the Gidget clan had made a tidy California fortune in oil. They weren't the sort of people who forgot a thing like that. Zep had read somewhere that they'd even put Tyrannosaurus Rex on their family crest.

"Right," said Kid Beast. "Honk four fast and three slow to make the gate open. Don't worry, there's only a few servants, and they stay in the house. We'll see that prick Gidget himself, and, man, I'm going to let him have it." Zep's horn was broken, of course, so the three of them had to scream, "Honk-honk-honk-honk! Hooonk-hooonk-hooonk!" like rutting dinosaurs. A wild-eyed metal pteranodon and a dainty diplodocus disengaged from a primordial French kiss, and the gate swung open with a wounded, rusty shriek.

Water sprinklers ran continuously all over the estate, and the grounds were lushly overgrown with exotic flowers and shrubs. It was more like a jungle than a formal garden—like something in one of those lost world movies. Kid Beast sat up, alertly shooting glances this way and that. "He's got a whole maze of roadways here," he said. They passed several side roads, and then the Kid pointed. "See the fork in the drive up there? The main entrance is around to the right. The pool and the garage are in back on the left. I'm thinking maybe it's not so cool to confront Gidget. Turn left. We'll throw the fucking bad-luck-ball in the pool, tape some sounds and split."

Zep started to steer, but Delbert shouted, "No!" and wrenched the steering-wheel around to the right. Zep had a momentary feeling of being pulled in two and then, dammit, they were tooling up the drive towards the big house.

"Wrong way!" yelled Kid Beast, and pushed Delbert away from the steering-wheel. Zep hit the brakes and started to back up. He twisted around in his seat, staring out the pickup's rear window. Just before he got back to the fork, a brilliantly polished '48 Country Squire Woodie came cruising out from the left fork that they'd missed. There were four people in the Woodie, one in back and three in front. At first all Zep saw was the beautiful blonde surfer chick sitting between the two guys in front. And then he noticed the faces of the others.

"Whoah," he whispered. "That's us."

"There she is!" hollered Del. "My car, just like the shrimp things promised! Look, Zep, there's beer in back and that glow on the dash is Jesus, and there's three boards in back and everything. Don't let them get away."

But they did get away…they disappeared around a clump of bougainvillea, their happy voices fading like radio static into the hiss of the sprinklers, the *chunka-chunka-pfft* of lawn birds. Before Zep could decide what to do next, a plump man in shades and white suit came pooting down the drive in a golf cart. He was holding a machine-gun.

"That's Logomarsino, Gidget's bodyguard," said Kid Beast, sinking down under the dash. "Don't let him see me, man."

"What are you worried about?" Zep asked sarcastically. "Guy's only got an Uzi."

Del leapt out of the car and waved his ball at the bodyguard. "Hey! How about my reward?"

The man in the golf cart, startled by what must have looked like a threatening gesture, squeezed off a burst. The bullets whizzed overhead, and the boys became studiously still. After the shots, the man stepped out of the cart and stared at them uncertainly. "You're not real," he croaked finally.

"Yes I am!" said Delbert indignantly. "You're just trying to get out of giving me what I deserve."

"I don't think you're real," repeated the bodyguard. There was a noise in the distance: four short honks and three long ones. The bodyguard hopped back on his golf cart. "Now *that* sounds real!" he said, and sped off downhill.

"I want my reward," said Del, plaintively. He started up the driveway to Gidget's house. Zep took the precaution of turning his truck around, and then the and Kid Beast followed. On his way up the hill, Zep saw a couple more of the fast false images amidst Gidget's jungle shrubbery—this time it was Del and the blonde girl. The images had a way of congealing out of flecks of color. There'd be like bright dots in the air, and then the dots would slide together in some filthy hyperdimensional way, forming a slightly grainy image of someone or something which would soon deconstruct itself into dots that drifted away like gnats.

"Hey Kid," Zep finally thought to ask. "You see what I see?"

"Naw," said Kid Beast. "I don't see none of them freaky demonic manifestations, dude." He lifted up the crucifix that hung from his neck and gave it a kiss.

Obviously Delbert was seeing the images, as he kept trying to talk to the ghosts, asking them when he'd get what he had coming. "Give it up, Delbert," snapped Kid Beast, but now the mansion's great madrone doors were swinging open to reveal a trim taut figure, all sheathed in shiny black. He held a glowing crystal in one hand, and there was a static of false images crowded around him like a ragged aura.

"Murderer!" screamed Kid Beast, flipping into a frenzy. "You killed that poor girl!"

"Hell, Beast, the dude's wearing a wetsuit," said Zep. "How bad can he be if he surfs?"

Seeing the weirdness and wealth, Zep was also flashing that no doubt Gidget had a monster stash somewhere. A pile of coke like in *Scarface*, right, a mound that you could just lower your snoggering face right down into. A fucking sandpile, man. Just thinking this, Zep could see the coke—or maybe it was acid-laced meth—sitting on a silver tray on a little three-legged table right at Gidget's side. Zep gave Del a sharp jostle, grabbed the magic ball, and sprang first up the manse's marble steps.

Delbert's ball and Gidget's ball picked up on each other. Little laser beams shot out of them, dancing off Zep and Gidget and the images around them. The billionaire frogman extended his one empty hand as a focus for the skittering beams, and within seconds all the little lines of light from Zep" ball had woven together into five brilliant strands, each one of them ending at one of Gidget's fingertips.

Then Gidget closed his fist and the ball flew forward into his palm, carrying Zep with it. Now Zep was surrounded by the miasma of duplicate images which clung to Gidget like body odor; in fact, he was shaking the billionaire's hand while a wiry tycoon arm slipped around his shoulder and gave him a friendly squeeze, leading him through the big doors and into the mansion.

"Get out of there, man!" he heard the Beast calling.

"Gimmie my ball, Zep, you weenie!"

But those were dim sounds, fading as he basked in the proximity of inconceivable wealth. Wealth, yes, it poured from the man. "Well, well," Mr. Gidget was saying. "You've finally come to see me." The madrone doors slammed shut, leaving Zep's friends outside. He glanced around, looking around for that tremendous stash, but it was nowhere to be seen.

Gidget tossed the two balls from hand to hand like a juggler. "I'm quite pleased, yes. I sent my second sphere out on an errand this morning, and I'd wondered if it would really return. But I should have known better. These things pull the dimensions together so nicely, and all through the marvelous power of circumstance. There are no accidents, don't you agree?"

"Definitely," said Zep, feeling unaccountably mellow. The sounds of his friends pounding on the doors seemed very far away. "Deep down, everything always fits."

"You sound sure of yourself," said Gidget. "I like that in a young man. And such a strong-looking fellow. A surfer, am I right? I wonder, though. What use would a simple surf-bum have for an advanced piece of computer technology like a million-dollar Systems Complex CAM8 chip?"

"You—you—what are you talking about, man?"

"I believe you know what I mean. Someone bombed and robbed the Systems Complex warehouse…six months ago, hmmmm? Systems Complex is a wholly owned subsidiary of Gidgetdyne."

A picture of Chaos Attractor danced out of the little ball and began zooming around Gidget's head. A small figure stood on the board, a small lean image of Zep.

"Look," said Zep, abandoning any hope of wall-papering his crime. "You want your CAM8 back? I've only been testing it out for you, Mr. Gidget. I've got it in my truck outside. In my surfboard."

"Oh no, no, no. The CAM8 is obsolete now. *Six months ago* it was worth a million. But now—now all any of our customers would want is the new CAM10. They don't know this yet, but they will soon. At present there's only two CAM10s. The CAM8 simulated a space that was, oh, two-and-a-half dimensional. But the new CAM10 handles five dimensions, one of which is time. That's why it was so easy for it to find you. Look."

Gidget pried up the base of Del's ball to reveal a glowing red jewel. He snapped the base shut again and the hidden hinges disappeared. "What makes the CAM10 chip particularly effective is that it drives a holographic laser display. When we're through testing these two prototypes, we'll go into full production."

"How did it find me?" asked Zep. If they could just keep talking, maybe everything would be OK.

"An interesting question. Do you know about chaos theory? Of course you do. Why else would you have put the CAM8 chip in a surfboard?" Gidget was warming to his topic. "The CAM chips are so information-theoretically rich that they act as strange attractors in the fact-space of our reality."

"I'm keyin' you, dude," said Zep. "Wave on this: I call my CAM8 surfboard Chaos Attractor!"

"You know, Zep," beamed Gidget. "Maybe our research end could use a mind like yours. Frankly I'd been planning to let Cthulha's daughter implant her neonate into the flesh of the CAM8 thief. But maybe—"

There was the sound of gunfire, of yelps, and of running feet. The front doors swung open to reveal the same Uzi-wielding bodyguard from before.

"Ah, Logomarsino," said Gidget. "Have you taken care of our other intruders?"

"Hard to get a fix on them with all the ghost images," said the bodyguard. "I just chased some of them away from your door." He reached out and pinched Zep's arm. "This is some live meat at last. The kid you were looking for, right? Let me tie him up and take him out to Cthulha's daughter in the pool."

"Bag that action," said Zep. "I'm R&D. I'm a computer scientist, dig? And what is this Cthulha's daughter, anyway?"

"The spawn of a Great Old One," said Gidget. "Neonate of an evil goddess-creature from another dimension. The CAM10 drew Cthulha here; she appeared in my swimming-pool the day I brought the chip home. It seems our supercomputational process has become so sensitive that different levels of reality are able to tune in upon it and to realize themselves. It's a two-way street, it seems. Without Cthulha's influence, I don't think our hardware would function. But she's a rather demanding guest. Although she only lives forty-nine days, on the last day of her life she produces a neonate that she needs to implant in human flesh. Today's the day for Cthulha's daughter to die—and to reproduce. Yes, today's the day for the third in the line of the California Cthulha."

"Cthulha's granddaughter?" said Zep uncertainly.

"A male will do," said Logomarsino. "And it's not going to be me or Mr. Gidget."

A faint sound came from the mansion's real door. Delbert yelling and kicking at the back door. "GODDAMN YOU ALL, I WANT WHAT'S COMING TO ME!" Gidget and Logomarsino nodded and smiled at each other. Safe here in their intoxicating dimensional image zazz, Zep had to fight back the urge to grin along with them.

A minute later they were all at the poolside. Logomarsino stripped Del nude, tied Del's hands tied behind him with rubber surgical cord, and cut his screams cut off with a ball-gag. Gidget stood to one side with the Uzi, preventing Zep and Kid Beast from trying to stop things. Now Logomarsino strapped Delbert the diving board. The pool water was black and fetid, as if filled with backed-up sewage. Kid Beast raised his eyebrows and surreptitiously flipped on his tape-recorder.

The pool water roiled, little pieces of garbage and algae floating up like a small red tide, and in the center of the filth flower appeared strands of green-yellow hair and a face—a heart-stopping beautiful California Girl face, ah, noble straight nose and lips thick enough to toothlessly peel a Sunkist orange! The face of Becka.

The nude Becka—or Cthulha's daughter—slipped out of the foul water. She held a knife, a big black anodized diver's knife, and in an instant she was at the diving board, the great blade poised over Delbert's genitals. Zep covered his eyes. The poor little dude was about to get what was coming to him.

There were sproings and a splash. Zep had to look. The girl had cut Delbert free and thrown her knife in the pool! She was kissing Del's cheek! Before anyone else could react, Zep shoved Gidget and his gun into the pool, and then Beast had done the same to Logomarsino! Like a complete pinhead, Del scooped up his magic ball, floating in the water at Gidget's side and then they were on their way.

In a trice, the chick and three caballeros had run around the house onto the driveway. Where Zep's truck had been, there now sat the green '48 Woodie, laden with the three new surfboards and Chaos Attractor, too. They jumped in and burned rubber, slaloming down Gidget's hill, through the back streets of Surf City, and onto the Pacific Coast Highway.

The summer air beat in the windows. The ocean was on their left, the PCH was clear. It was late and calm and the sun was setting west over the slick tubes and all the fudds and foobars had gone home.

"Twist up a fuckin' jay from that key, Del."

"For true."

The close-mouthed naked girl watched them, stroking Del gently on the upper arm. When he'd made the jay, she took it from him and lit it with the Woodie's built-in butane lighter. She smoked oddly, just opening her lips far enough to slip the reefer tip in, and then exhaling the thick blue smoke sharply through her nose. She did this three times and then she silently proffered the stick to Kid Beast in the back seat.

"Later," said he. "Right now I want this." He handed up DAT tape. "These are the Auntie Christs' best sounds. Is it really you, Becka? Do you remember what happened at the party? How did you ever get away from that big whacked-out nautilus?"

But Becka only smiled and didn't answer. She'd never been a big talker anyway. She looked OK, even if Logomarsino had called her Cthulha's daughter. Zep slotted the tape into the player. Del took a hit of the dope and passed it to Zep. Everything was wonderful. The water was beautiful; the red tide was gone. Stokin' tubes were breaking in long freight-train crashes. The energizing surf sound interlaced with the wasted plangent music wafting out of the Woodie's mighty sound system.

Zep smiled to feel the smooth-running Woodie roll them along so well. The pre-Populuxe Studebaker shape of the car reminded him of a car he'd thought he'd seen an ad for when he'd been a little boy. A car that had wings tucked under its fenders so that if you jerked the right lever the car would zoom off the crest of a hill, stubby and heavy as ever but with the engine roaring and making ti fly and you driving with the steering wheel. Whoah, dude. Maybe that dream too was about to come true. And, thinking of dreams, it was about time to meet Penny. Bitchen Kitchen would be booming just now. One more mile on the PCH, cut left onto the Point, and then they'd be carving for true.

The four of them were awesomely well-gunned, mused Zep, what with Chaos Attractor safe in back with the beer and the three bitchin' new boards. What a car! Del had been right! This was magic, and no kind of black magic at all, as you could plainly see by the mildly glowing plastic Jesus on the dash.

"Hi, Jesus," said Zep. "Thank you."

Now they were past the crater-site of the old San Diablo N-plant and freewheeling down the long last slope before the road bottomed out and jogged right. The long slope down to the sea was empty.

Zep could see the Bitchen Kitchen parking spot down there past the turn, a beige patch between road and sharp cliff-edge with the surprisingly distant ocean collaged in behind. Bitchen Kitchen, where the gnarliest nudists, perverts, and surfers hung.

Zep loved skidding into the lot here. It was a sport. Local legend said that if you gathered enough speed and went straight, you could actually shoot up off the low ski-ramp of the sheer bluff and, if the waves were right, splash down safe in a deep, surging kettle. A tourist called Tuck Playfair had actually done it in '68.

Becka was all over Del by now, she was unbuttoning his shirt and even putting her hands in his pants. Del had never looked happier in his life. Even Kid Beast in back was happy, though he couldn't stop staring nervously out the wagon's open back tailgate. All dudes present sensed this could be the start of a righteous and functional partnership.

"I tolk you," said Del, his voice actually choking up, so great was his joy. "I…I tolk Zep I'd get whak's c-coming to me. And right now—" Delbert fought back his emotion by raising the volume and the pitch of his voice. "Right now! It's happening!"

The silent blonde Becka—or Cthulha's daughter—slipped Del's shorts all the way off, cast them to the winds and leaned slowly forward, finally opening her mouth. Kid Beast was still staring out the back, and Zep was watching the road, so at first only Delbert could see the appalling structures in the girl's mouth. There was something majorly wrong in there…instead of teeth she had like two hard cartilaginous skin-covered ridges. Delbert started pushing her away, even as she strained forward, opening her mouth wider and wider and making a noise like Patty Duke playing Helen Keller by imitating a person taking a shit.

"Wuuuh. Uuuuuunnnnuuuuunnnh. Nnnnngggggggggh!"

"Hold on," Delbert was saying. He sounded worried, but Zep was too polite to glance over. "Wait a minute. HEY, ZEP—"

There was a popping noise far behind them. A white Mercedes back there, coming up fast. A sudden spiderweb appeared in the windshield's glass. "It's Gidget and Logomarsino!" screamed Kid Beast. "They're coming up fast!" Another gunshot, another hole in the windshield.

Out of the corner of his eye, Zep could see the girl's mouth open wide and some like beak come pushing out—"

And Del is all, "AAAAAAAAAUUUUUUUGHHH! WHAT ARE YOU—"

And Cthulha's daughter is all, "Yeeeeeek. WurraWurraWurra. Yeeeeeek. WurraWurraWurra."

And Kid Beast is all, "Floor it!"

And the cliff edge was coming right up and now, before Zep could even get his foot off the gas, Cthulha's daughter snaked her surprisingly flexible leg over and mashed on his foot sending them out, up, and into the air two hundred empty feet above the sun-gilded surf. And then there was this like click, and the Woodie changed back into Zep's pickup. It was Zep and Del and the girl in the front seat of the pickup, with Kid Beast in the bed of the truck with Chaos Attractor in back. And now Cthulha's daughter was like coming apart, unfolding her hands and arms into feelers, there was a striped shell on her back for a moment, but that shattered and split —

"It's an alien nautilus!" screamed Kid Beast, peering in through the pickup's rear window. There was a flicker of light; Del's sphere was shooting rays back towards Gidget's car. And now Logomarsino and Gidget behind them drove off the cliff too.

Zep hung onto the steering wheel as if it were a lifesaver-ring. The pickup that had been a Woodie was bucking in heavy air turbulence, in a froth of three-dimensional chaos surf. The primordial mollusc girl threw herself against the pickup's rear window, and it popped out clean and went tumbling away. She went flapping and wriggling out the hole, throwing herself to the wind. She fell away from the truck, but somehow evaded the pull of gravity, caught in the lines of force that had snarled pursued and pursuer somewhere outside of time. The pickup and the Mercedes hung impossibly suspended in midair. The waves far below them had stopped moving; the water was frozen in its endlessly various shapes.

A trumpet blast deafened them. Cthulha's daughter was still unfolding, her hair thickening into long prehensile tendrils; her body turning orange and white, unfolding and expanding. She seemed to be caught in a slipstream which drew her swiftly and steadily toward a point midway between the two cars. As she hit that point, her whole cephalopod body shuddered. Her tentacles whipped out in either direction, half of them snarling in the bumper of Gidget's Mercedes, the other half clutching the tail of Zep's pickup. Her feelers came slithering across the bed of the truck, past Chaos Attractor, rustling among the empty beer cans and clam shells, feeling for Kid Beast.

"Here, Del," gasped Zep. "Take the wheel."

Delbert grasped the wheel, and Zep took Delbert's magic ball.

Zep squeezed out through the pickup's rear window and—beautiful surf music filled the sky.

"Stomp on these tentacle things!" cried the Kid. "She's trying to get me!"

"Hang loose, Kid," said Zep. The surf music was flowing down his spine, into his hands and legs. He knew what to do.

Kid Beast made a muffled, grunting sound, battling a thinly writhing weave of bloodworm tentacles that kept trying to creep like a living Persian carpet down his throat. Zep grabbed hold of the thin black fin of his surfboard and tugged. The tentacles overlaying it recoiled. Dragging the board after him, Zep knee-walked to the back of the truck and pulled the board halfway off the truck-bed edge.

"Where the fuck are you going?" cried Kid Beast. "Help me, man!"

Zep poised himself upon Chaos Attractor. "I am." He gave himself a little push and out he went, Del's magic CAM10 ball clasped in one outstretched hand.

The music was blaring, a deep descending scale of bass notes that continually verged on some archetypal core of surf sound. The free-floating shelless nautilus was singing high-pitched harmonies. Her tendrils were sweeping up and around in either direction, forming a vast figure eight, an infinity loop. The frozen world glistened beneath them. Zep started the long slide down towards the core of the nautilus. The beast saw him coming and opened her beak. With a well-aimed gesture, Zep threw the ball right into her mouth, dug his board into the air, and up around the loop towards the Mercedes.

That idiot Logomarsino leaned out his window shooting his machine-gun. Zep slyved this way and that, faking the guy. The bullets streamed past Zep and past the nautilus, arcing up along the curve of the loop, swarming back down again towards their origin, shattering the windshield of the Mercedes. Gidget hollered in fury. Zep surfed down upon them, and snatched Gidget's CAM10 ball from his grasp. Zep air-surfed another trip around the great ribbon of the chaotic tentacle pattern, and threw the second magic ball into the beak of Cthulha's daughter.

The effect was dramatic. The magic that had pulled the Great Old Ones into our world was neutralized now, merged back with its source. There was a furious flicker of images, like time running backwards. The nautilus tentacles pulled back into the central form, and Cthulha's daughter was once again a girl named Becka.

The only catch was that all of them were still high up in the air above Bitchen Kitchen: Zep, Delbert, Gidget, Logomarsino, Kid Beast, Becka, the car and the truck, all dropping down towards the big basin of surf. The water was deep, but known for its sharp rocks. Zep dug the nose of his board downward, shooting to get beneath the others, and as he dived, he sent up a spiral of force, an invisible sliding board. Glancing up, he saw the others being pulled into his helical wake, their free fall softened into a safe glide.

Even so, the water rushed up fast enough to send Zep spinning. The black water scrambled Zep's mind; the hungry waves pulled his board away from him. He heard a watery humming, that same old surf music, and then Delbert was pulling him to the surface.

They'd all made it, and Becka was her same old self, albeit once again way too good for Delbert. Zep had saved them all!

And there, on the shore, cheering and waving, stood Penny and Del's real girlfriend Jen. They'd witnessed every one of Zep's awesomely stoked moves.

"Penny!" called Zep. "Hey, Penny!"

"Zep! Let's fuck! I love you!

Note on "Chaos Surfari" (With Marc Laidlaw)

Written in 1988.
Interzone, March/April 1989.

After "Probability Pipeline," Marc and I definitely wanted to do a second surf story, and this ramshackle piece was the result. The form that the nautilus stretches herself into is supposed to be the classic chaotic form known as the Lorenz Attractor. At the time we wrote it, Marc and I didn't have the ending quite straight, and we got the notion of "ending" the story by taking the last third of it and breaking that into pieces that would be printed upside-down, backwards, and/or mirror-reversed, these pieces to be set into the earlier parts of the story.

Interzone actually printed the story that way for us, but we ended up not feeling really happy with the way it came out. Trying to make your text physically resemble a Lorenz Attractor is not in fact a good way to communicate a tale! For this reprinting I reworked the ending enough that it's OK to just print it normally.

The CAM8 and CAM10 chips mentioned in this story and in "Probability Pipeline" were inspired by a special piece of computer hardware called the CAM6 which I was using for cellular automata simulations. The CAM6 was designed by a brilliant pair of guys called Norman Margolus and Tom Toffoli. I remember seeing them at a cellular automata conference in Los Alamos and telling them that I was working on a story in which a CAM10 attracts a giant squid-creature from another dimension. In his Italian accent, Toffoli said, "We are already expecting the giant squid with the CAM7."

Big Jelly (With Bruce Sterling)

The screaming metal jellyfish dragged long, invisible tentacles across the dry concrete acres of the San Jose airport. Or so it seemed to Tug—Tug Mesoglea, math-drunk programmer and fanatic aquarist. Tug was working on artificial jellyfish, and nearly everything looked like a jellyfish to him, even airplanes. Tug was here in front of the baggage claim to pick up Texas billionaire Revel Pullen.

It had taken a deluge of phone-calls, faxes and e-mail to lure the reclusive Texan venture-capitalist from his decrepit, polluted East Texas oil-fields, but Tug had now coaxed Revel Pullen to a second face-to-face meet in California. At last, it seemed that Tug's unconventional high-tech startup scheme would charge into full-scale production. The prospect of success was sweet.

Tug had first met Revel in Monterey two months earlier, at the Spring symposium of the ACM SIGUSC, that is, the Association for Computing Machinery's Special Interest Group for Underground and Submarine Computation.

At the symposium, Tug had given a badly botched presentation on artificial jellyfish. He'd arrived with 500 copies of a glossy desktop-published brochure: "Artificial Jellyfish: Your Route to Postindustrial Global Competitiveness!" But when it came time for Tug's talk, his 15-terabyte virtual jellyfish-demo had crashed so hideously that he couldn't even reboot his machine—a cheap Indonesian Sun-clone laptop that Tug now used as a bookend. Tug had brought some slides as a backup, but of course the slide-tray had jammed. And, worst of all, the single working prototype of Tug's plastic artificial jellyfish had burst in transit to Monterey. After the talk, Tug, in a red haze of shame, had flushed the sodden rags of decomposing gel down the conference center's john.

Tug had next headed for the cocktail lounge, and there the garrulous young Pullen had sought him out, had a few drinks with him, and had even picked up the tab—Tug's wallet had been stolen the night before by a cute older busboy.

Since Tug's topic was jellyfish, the raucous Pullen had thought it funny to buy rounds of tequila jelly-shots. The slimy jolts of potent boozy Jell-O had combined with Revel's bellowed jokes, brags, and wild promises to ease the pain of Tug's failed speech.

The next day, Tug and Revel had brunched together, and Revel had written Tug a handsome check as earnest money for pre-development expenses. Tug was to develop an artificial jellyfish capable of undersea oil prospecting.

As software applications went, oil-drilling was a little roughnecked and analog for Tug's taste; but the money certainly looked real enough. The only troubling aspect about dealing with Revel was the man's obsession with some new and troublesome organic slime which his family's oldest oil-well had recently tapped. Again and again, the garish Texan had steered the conversation away from jellyfish and onto the subject of ancient subterranean slime.

Perched now on the fire-engine red hood of his expensive Animata sports car, Tug waited for Revel to arrive. Tug had curly dark hair and a pink-cheeked complexion. He wore shorts, a sport shirt, and Birkenstock sandals with argyle socks. He looked like a depraved British schoolboy. He'd bought the Animata with his house-money nest-egg when he'd learned that he would never, ever, be rich enough to buy a house in California. Leaning back against the windshield of his car, Tug stared at the descending airplanes and thought about jellyfish trawling through sky-blue seawater.

Tug had whole tankfuls of jellies at home: one tank with flattish moon jellies each with its four whitish circles of sex organs, another tank with small clear bell jellies from the eel grass of Monterey bay, a large tank with sea nettles that had long frilly oral arms and whiplike purple tentacles covered with stinging cells, a smaller tank of toadstool-like spotted jellies from Jellyfish Lake in Palau, a special tank of spinning comb-jellies with trailing ciliated arms, a Japanese tank with Japanese umbrella jellies—and more.

Next to the arsenal of tanks was the huge color screen of Tug's workstation. Tug was no biologist; he'd blundered under the spell of the jellies while using mathematical algorithms to generate cellular models of vortex sheets. To Tug's mathematician's eye, a jellyfish was a highly perfected relationship between curvature and torsion, just like a vortex sheet, only a jellyfish was working off dynamic tension and osmotic stress. Real jellyfish were gnarlier than Tug's simulations. Tug had become a dedicated amateur of coelenteratology.

Imitating nature to the core, Tug found a way to evolve and improve his vortex sheet models via genetic programming. Tug's artificial jellyfish algorithms competed, mutated, reproduced and died inside the virtual reality of his workstation's sea-green screen. As Tug's algorithms improved, his big computer monitor became a tank of virtual jellyfish, of graphic representations of Tug's equations, pushing at the chip's computational limits, slowly pulsing about in dimly glowing simulation-space.

The living jellies in the tanks of true seawater provided an objective standard towards which Tug's programs could try to evolve. At every hour of the day and night, video cameras peered into the spot-lit water tanks, ceaselessly analyzing the jellyfish motions and feeding data into the workstation.

The recent, crowning step of Tug's investigations was his manufacturing breakthrough. His theoretical equations had become actual piezoplastic constructions—soft, watery, gelatinous robot jellies of real plastic in the real world. These models were produced by using an intersecting pair of laser beams to sinter—that is, to join together by heating without melting—the desired shape within a matrix of piezoplastic microbeads. The sintered microbeads behaved like a mass of cells: each of them could compress or elongate in response to delicate vibratory signals, and each microbead could in turn pass information to its neighbors.

A completed artificial jellyfish model was a floppy little umbrella that beat in steady cellular waves of excitation and relaxation. Tug's best plastic jellyfish could stay active for up to three weeks.

Tug's next requirement for his creations was "a killer application," as the software tycoons called it. And it seemed he might have that killer app in hand, given his recent experiments in making the jellyfish sensitive to chemical scents and signals. Tug had convinced Revel—and half-believed himself—that the artificial jellies could be equipped with radio-signaling chips and set loose beneath the sea floor. They could sniff out oil-seeps in the ocean bottom and work their way deep into the vents. If this were so, then artificial jellyfish would revolutionize undersea oil prospecting.

The only drawback, in Tug's view, was that offshore drilling was a contemptible crime against the wonderful environment that had bred the real jellies in the first place. Yet the plan seemed likely to free up Texas venture capital, enough capital to continue his research for at least another year. And maybe in another year, thought Tug, he would have a more ecologically sound killer app, and he would be able to disentangle himself from the crazy Texan.

Right on cue, Revel Pullen came strolling down the exit ramp, clad in the garb of a white-trash oil-field worker: a flannel shirt and a pair of Can't-Bust-'Em overalls. Revel had a blonde crewcut and smooth dark skin. The shirt was from Nieman-Marcus and the overalls were ironed, but they seemed to be genuinely stained with dirt-fresh Texas crude.

Tug hopped off the hood of his car and stood on tiptoe to wave, deliberately camping it up to jangle the Texan's nerves. He drew up a heel behind him like Marilyn Monroe waving in The Misfits.

Nothing daunted, Revel Pullen headed Tug's way with an exaggerated bowlegged sprawl and a scuff of his python-skin boots. Revel was the scapegrace nephew of Amarillo's billionaire Pullen Brothers. The Pullen clan were malignant market speculators and greenmail raiders who had once tried to corner the world market in molybdenum.

Revel himself, the least predictable of his clan, was in charge of the Pullen Brothers' weakest investments: the failing oil wells that had initially brought the Pullen family to prominence—beginning with the famous Ditheree Gusher, drilled near Spindletop, Texas in 1892.

Revel's quirk was his ambition to become a high-tech tycoon. This was why Revel attended computer-science meetings like SIGUSC, despite his stellar ignorance of everything having to do with the movement of bytes and pixels.

Revel stood ready to sink big money into a technically sexy Silicon Valley start-up. Especially if the start-up could somehow do something for his family's collapsing oil industry and—though this part still puzzled Tug—find a use for some odd clear fluid that Revel's engineers had recently been pumping from the Ditheree hole.

"Shit howdy, Tug," drawled Revel, hoisting his polyester/denim duffel bag from one slim shoulder to another. "Mighty nice of y'all to come meet me."

Beaming, Tug freed his fingers from Revel's insistent grip and gestured toward the Animata. "So, Revel! Ready to start a business? I've decided we should call it Ctenophore, Inc. A ctenophore is a kind of hermaphroditic jellyfish which uses a comb-like feeding organ to filter nutrients from the ocean; they're also called comb-jellies. Don't you think Ctenophore is a perfect name for our company? Raking in the dollars from the economy's mighty sea!"

"Not so loud!" Revel protested, glancing up and down the airport pavement in a parody of wary street-smarts. "As far as any industrial spy knows, I'm here in California on a personal vacation." He heaved his duffel into the back seat of Tug's car. Then he straightened, and reached deep into the baggy trouser-pocket of his Can't-Bust-'Ems.

The Texan dragged out a slender pill-bottle filled with clear viscous jelly and pressed the crotch-warmed vial into Tug's unwilling palm, with a dope-dealer's covert insistence. "I want you to keep this, Tug. Just in case anything should…you know…happen to me."

Revel swiveled his narrow head to scan the passers-by with paranoid alertness, briefly reminding Tug of the last time he'd been here at the San Jose airport: to meet his ailing father, who'd been fingerpaint-the-wall-with-shit senile and had been summarily dumped on the plane by Tug's uncle. Tug had gotten his father into a local nursing home, and last summer Tug's father had died.

Life was sad, and Tug was letting it slip through his fingers—he was an unloved gay man who'd never see thirty again, and now here he was humoring a nutso het from Texas. Humoring people was not something Tug excelled at.

"Do you really have enemies?" said Tug. "Or do you just think so? Am I supposed to think you have enemies? Am I supposed to care?"

"There's money in these plans of ours—real foldin' money," Revel bragged darkly, climbing into the Animata's passenger seat. He waited silently until Tug took the wheel and shut the driver's-side door. "All we really gotta worry about," Revel continued at last, "is controlling the publicity. The environmental impact crap. You didn't tell anybody about what I e-mailed you, did you?"

"No," snapped Tug. "That cheap public-key encryption you're using has garbled half your messages. What are you so worried about, anyway? Nobody's gonna care about some slime from a played-out oil-well—even if you do call it Urschleim. That's German, right?"

"Shhhhh!" hissed Revel.

Tug started the engine and gunned it with a bluish gust of muscular combustion. They swung out into the endless California traffic.

Revel checked several times to make sure that they weren't being trailed. "Yes, I call it Urschleim," he said at last, portentously. "In fact, I've put in a trademark for that name. Them old-time German professors were onto something. Ur means primeval. All life came from the Urschleim, the original slime! Primeval slime from the inner depths of the planet! You ever bitten into a green almond, Tug? From the tree? There's some green fuzz, a thin little shell and a center of clear, thick slime. That's exactly how our planet is, too. Most of the original Urschleim is still flowing, and oozing, and lyin' there 'way down deep. It's just waitin' for some bright boy to pump it out and exploit its commercial potential. Urschleim is life itself."

"That's pretty grandiose," said Tug evenly.

"Grandiose, hell!" Revel snapped. "It's the only salvation for the Texan oil business, compadre! God damn it, if we Texans don't drill for a living, we'll be reduced to peddling chips and software like a bunch of goddamn Pacific Rim computer weenies! You got me wrong if you think I'll give up the oil business without a fight!"

"Sure, sure, I'm hip," Tug said soothingly. "My jellyfish are going to help you find more oil, remember?" It was easy to tell when Revel had gone nonlinear—his Texan drawl thickened drastically and he began to refer to his beloved oil business as the "Aisle Bidness." But what was the story with this Urschleim?

Tug held up the pill-bottle of clear slime and glanced at it while steering with one hand. The stuff was thixotropic—meaning a gel which becomes liquid when shaken. You'd tilt the vial and all the Urschleim would be stuck in one end, but then, if you shook the bottle a bit, the slime's state would change and it would all run down to the other end like ketchup suddenly gushing from a bottle. Smooth, clear ketchup. Snot.

"The Ditheree hole's oozin' with Urschleim right now!" said Revel, settling a pair of Italian sunglasses onto his freckled nose. He looked no older than twenty-five. "I brought three gallons of it in a tank in my duffel. One of my engineers says it's a new type of deep-lying oil, and another one says it's just water infected with bacteria. But I'm with old Herr Doktor Professor von Stoffman. We've struck the cell fluid of Mother Earth herself: undifferentiated tissue, Tug, primordial ooze. Gaia goo. Urschleim!"

"What did you do to make it start oozing?" asked Tug, suppressing a giggle.

Revel threw back his head and crowed. "Man, if OPEC got wind about our new high-tech extraction techniques...You don't think I got enemies, son? Them sheiks play for keeps." Revel tapped his knuckles cagily against the car's closed window. "Hell, even Uncle Sam'd be down on us if he knew that we've been twisting genes and seeding those old worn-out oilbeds with designer bacteria! They eat through tar and paraffin, change the oil's viscosity, unblock the pores in the stone and get it all fizzy with methane...You wouldn't think the ol' Ditheree had it in 'er to blow valves and gush again, but we plumbed her out with a new extra-virulent strain. And what did she gush? Urschleim!"

Revel peered at Tug over the tops of his designer sunglasses, assuming what he seemed to think was a trustworthy expression. "But that ain't the half of it, Tug. Wait till I tell you what we did with the stuff once we had it."

Tug was impatient. Gusher or not, Revel's bizarre maunderings were not going to sell any jellyfish. "What did you think of that artificial jellyfish I sent you?"

Revel frowned. "Well, it looked okay when it showed up. About the size of a deflated football. I dropped in my swimmin' pool. It was floatin' there, kinda rippling and pulsing, for about two days. Didn't you say that sucker would run for weeks? Forty-eight hours and it was gone! Disintegrated I guess. Chlorine melted the plastic or something."

"No way," protested Tug, intensely. "It must have slipped out a crack in the side of your pool. I built that model to last three weeks for sure! It was my best prototype. It was a chemotactic artificial jellyfish designed to slither into undersea vents and find its way to underground oil beds."

"My swimming pool's not in the best condition," allowed Revel. "So I guess it's possible that your jellyfish did squeeze out through a crack. But if this oil-prospecting application of yours is any good, the thing should have come back with some usable geology data. And it never did come back that I noticed. Face it Tug, the thing melted."

Tug wouldn't give in. "My jellyfish didn't send back information because I didn't put a tracer chip in it. If you're going to be so rude about it, I might as well tell you that I don't think oil prospecting is a very honorable application. I'd really rather see the California Water Authority using my jellies to trace leaks in irrigation and sewage lines."

Revel yawned, sinking deeper into the passenger seat. "That's real public-spirited of you, Dr. Mesoglea. But California water ain't worth a dime to me."

Tug pressed onward. "Also, I'd like to see my jellyfish used to examine contaminated wells here in Silicon Valley. If you put an artificial jellyfish down a well, and leave it to pulsate down there for a week or two, it could filter up all kinds of trace pollutants! It'd be a great public-relations gambit to push the jelly's anti-pollution aspects. Considering your family history, it couldn't hurt to get the Pullen family in the good graces of the Environmental Protection people. If we angle it right, we could probably even swing a federal development grant!"

"I dunno, hombre," Revel grumbled. "Somehow it just don't seem sportin' to take money from the Feds…" He gazed mournfully at the lushly exotic landscape of monkey-puzzle trees, fat pampered yuccas, and orange trees. "Man, everything sure looks green out here."

"Yes," Tug said absently, "thank God there's been a break in the drought. California has plenty of use for a jellyfish that can monitor water-leaks."

"It's not the water that counts," said Revel, "it's the carbon dioxide. Two hundred million years' worth of crude oil, all burned to carbon dioxide and spewed right into the air in just few short decades. Plant life's goin' crazy. Why, all the plant life along this highway has built itself out of car exhausts! You ever think o' that?"

It was clear from the look of glee on Revel's shallow features that this thought pleased him mightily. "I mean, if you traced the history of the carbon in that weirdass-lookin' tree over there…hunnert years ago it was miles down in the primeval bowels of the earth! And since we eat plants to live, it's the same for people! Our flesh, brain and blood is built outa burnt crude-oil! We're creatures of the Urschleim, Tug. All life comes from the primeval goo."

"No way," said Tug heatedly. He took a highway exit to Los Perros, his own local enclave in the massive sprawl that was Silicon Valley. "One carbon atom's just like the next one. And once you're talking artificial life, it doesn't even have to be an 'atom' at all. It can be a byte of information, or a microbead of piezoplastic. It doesn't matter where the material came from—life is just a pattern of behavior."

"That's where you and me part company, boy." They were tooling down the main drag of Los Perros now, and Revel was gaping at some chicly dressed women. "Dig it, Tug, thanks to oil, a lot of the carbon in your yuppie neighbors comes from Texas. Like or not, most modern life is fundamentally Texan."

"That's pretty appalling news, Revel," smiled Tug. He took the last remaining hilly corners with a squeal of his Michelins, then pulled into his driveway. He parked the Animata under the rotting, fungus-specked redwood deck of the absurdly overpriced suburban home that he rented. The rent was killing him. Ever since his lover had moved out last Christmas, Tug had been meaning to move into a smaller place, but somewhere deep down he nursed a hope that if he kept the house, some nice strong man would come and move in with him.

Next door, Tug's neighbors were flinging water-balloons and roaring with laughter as they sizzled up a huge aromatic rack of barbecued tofu. They were rich Samoans. They had a big green parrot called Toatoa. On fine days, such as today, Toatoa sat squawking on the gable of the house. Toatoa had a large yellow beak and a taste for cuttlebone and pumpkin-seeds.

"This is great," Revel opined, examining the earthquake-split walls and peeling ceiling sheetrock. "I was afraid we'd have some trouble findin' the necessary space for experiments. No problem though, with you rentin' this sorry dump for a workshop."

"I live here," said Tug with dignity. "By California standards this is a very good house."

"No wonder you want to start a company!" Revel climbed the redwood stairs to Tug's outdoor deck, and dragged a yard-long plastic pressure-cylinder from within his duffel bag, flinging aside some balled-up boot socks and a set of watered-silk boxer shorts. "You got a garden hose? And a funnel?" He pulled a roll of silvered duct tape from the bottom of his bag.

Tug supplied a length of hose, prudently choosing one that had been severely scorched during the last hillside brushfire. Revel whipped a French designer pocketknife from within his Can't-Bust-'Ems and slashed off a three-foot length. He then deftly duct-taped the tin funnel to the end of the hose, and blew a few kazoo-like blasts.

Revel then flung the crude horn aside and took up the pressure cylinder. "You don't happen to have a washtub, do you?"

"No problem," Tug said. He went into the house and fetched a large plastic picnic cooler.

Revel opened the petcock of the pressure cylinder and began decanting its contents into the cooler. The black nozzle slowly ejaculated a thick clear gel, rather like silicone putty. Pint after pint of it settled languorously into the white pebbly interior of the hinge-topped cooler. The stuff had a sulfurous, burning-rubber reek that Tug associated with Hawaii—a necessarily brief stay he'd had on the oozing, flaming slopes of Kilauea.

Tug prudently sidled across the deck and stood upwind of the cooler. "How far down did you obtain this sample?"

Revel laughed. "Down? Doc, this stuff broke the safety-valves on old Ditheree and blew drillin' mud over five counties. We had an old-time blue-ball gusher of it. It just kept comin', pourin' out over the ground. Kinda, you know, spasmodic…Finally ended up with a lake of clear hot pudding higher than the tops of pickups."

"Jesus, what happened then?" Tug asked.

"Some evaporated. Some soaked right into the subsoil. Disappeared. The first sample I scored was out of the back of some good ol' boy's Toyota. Lucky thing he had the tailgate up, or it woulda all run out."

Revel pulled out a handkerchief, wiped sweat from his forehead, and continued talking. "Of course, once we got the rig repaired, we did some serious pump-work. We Pullens happen to own a tank-farm near Nacogdoches, a couple a football field's worth of big steel reservoirs. Haven't seen use since the OPEC embargo of the 70s. They were pretty much abandoned on site. But every one of them babies is brim-full with Revel Pullen's trademark Urschleim right now." He glanced up at the sun, looking a bit wild-eyed, and wiped his forehead again. "You got any beer in this dump?"

"Sure, Revel." Tug went into the kitchen for two bottles of Etna Ale, and brought them out to the deck.

Revel drank thirstily, then gestured with his makeshift horn. "If this don't work, well, you're gonna think I'm crazy." He pushed his Italian shades up onto the top of his narrow crewcut skull, and grinned. He was enjoying himself. "But if it does work, ol' son—you're gonna think you're crazy."

Revel dipped the end of the funnel into the quiescent but aromatic mass. He swirled it around, then held it up carefully and puffed.

A fat lozenge-shaped gelatinous bubble appeared at the end of the horn.

"Holy cow, it blows up just like a balloon," Tug said, impressed. "That's some kind of viscosity!"

Revel grinned wider, holding the thing at arm's length. "It gets better."

Tug Mesoglea watched in astonishment as the clear bubble of Urschleim slowly rippled and dimpled. A long double crease sank into the taut outer membrane of the gelatinous sphere, encircling it like the seam on an oversized baseball.

Now, with a swampy-sounding pop, the bubble came loose from the horn's tin muzzle and began to float in midair. A set of cilia emerged along the seam and the airborne jelly began to bob and beat its way upward.

"Urschleim!" whooped Revel.

"Jesus Christ," Tug said, staring in shocked fascination. The air jelly was still changing before its eyes, evolving a set of interior membranes, warping, pulsing, and rippling itself into an ever more precise shape, for all the world like a computer graphics program ray-tracing its image into an elegant counterfeit of reality…

Then a draft of air caught it. It hit the eaves of the house, adhered messily, and broke. Revel prudently stepped aside as a long rope of slime fell to the deck.

"I can hardly believe it," said Tug. "Spontaneous symmetry breaking! A self-actuating reaction/diffusion system. This slime of yours is an excitable medium with emergent behavior, Revel! And that spontaneous fractalization of the structures…Can you do it again?"

"As many times as you want," said Revel. "With as much Urschleim as you got. Of course, the smell kinda gets to you if you do it indoors."

"But it's so odd," breathed Tug. "That the slime out of your oil-well is forming itself into jellyfish shapes just as I'm starting to build jellyfish out of plastic."

"I figure it for some kind of a morphic resonance thing," nodded Revel. "This primeval slime's been trapped inside the Earth so long it's truly achin' to turn into something live and organic. Kind of like that super-weird worm and bacteria and clam shit that grows out of deep undersea vents."

"You mean around the undersea vents, Revel."

"No Tug, right out of 'em. That's the part most people don't get."

"Whatever. Let me try blowing an Urschleim air jelly."

Tug dabbled the horn's tin rim in the picnic cooler, then huffed away at his own balloon of Urschleim. The sphere began to ripple internally, just as before, with just the same dimples and just the same luscious double crease. Tug had a sudden deja vu. He'd seen this shape on his computer screen.

All of a sudden the treacherous thixotropic stuff broke into a flying burst of clear snot that splashed all over his feet and legs. The magic goo felt tingly on Tug's skin. He wondered nervously if any of the slime might be passing into his bloodstream. He hurriedly toweled it off his body, then used the side of his Birkenstock sandal to push the rest of the slime off the edge of the deck.

"What do you think?" asked Revel.

"I'm overwhelmed," said Tug, shaking his head. "Your Urschleim jellyfish look so much like the ones I've been building in my lab. Let's go in. I'll show you my jellyfish while we think this through." Tug led Revel into the house.

Revel insisted on bringing the Urschleim-containing cooler and the empty pressure canister into the house. He even got Tug to throw an Indian blanket over them, "in case we get company."

Tug's jellyfish tanks filled up an entire room with great green bubbling glory. The aquarium room had been a domestic video game parlor during the early 1980s, when the home's original builder, a designer of shoot-em-up computer twitch-games, had shored up the floor to accommodate two dozen massive arcade-consoles. This was a good thing too, for Tug's seawater tanks were a serious structural burden, and far outweighed all of Tug's other possessions put together, except maybe the teak waterbed which his ex-lover had left. Tug had bought the tanks themselves at a knockdown auction from the federal-seizure sale of an eccentric Oakland cocaine dealer, who had once used them to store schools of piranha.

Revel mulled silently over the ranks of jellyfish. Backlit by greenish glow from the spotlights of a defunct speed-metal crew, Tug's jellies were at their best. The backlighting brought out their most secret, most hidden interior curvatures, with an unblinking brilliance that was well-nigh pornographic.

Their seawater trace elements and Purina Jellyfish Lab Chow cost more than Tug's own weekly grocery bills, but his jelly menagerie had come to mean more to Tug than his own nourishment, health, money, or even his love-life. He spent long secret hours entranced before the gently spinning, ciliated marvels, watching them reel up their brine shrimp prey in mindless, reflexive elegance, absorbing the food in a silent ecstasy of poisonous goo. Live, digestive goo, that transmuted through secret alchemical biology into pulsating, glassy flesh.

Tug's ex-lover had been pretty sporting about Tug's goo-mania, especially compared to his other complaints about Tug's numerous perceived character flaws, but Tug figured his lover had finally been driven away by some deep rivalry with the barely-organic. Tug had gone to some pains to Windex his noseprints from the aquarium glass before Revel arrived.

"Can you tell which ones are real and which ones I made from scratch?" Tug demanded triumphantly.

"You got me whipped," Revel admitted. "It's a real nice show, Tug. If you can really teach these suckers some tricks, we'll have ourselves a business."

Revel's denim chest emitted a ringing sound. He reached within his overalls, whipped out a cellular phone the size of a cigarette-pack, and answered it. "Pullen here! What? Yeah. Yeah, sure. Okay, see you." He flipped the phone shut and stowed it.

"Got you a visitor coming," he announced. "Business consultant I hired."

Tug frowned.

"My uncle's idea, actually," Revel shrugged. "Just kind of standard Pullen procedure before we sink any real money in a venture. We got ourselves one of the best computer-industry consultants in the business."

"Yeah? Who?"

"Edna Sydney. She's a futurist, she writes a high-finance technology newsletter that's real hot with the boys in suits."

"Some strange woman is going to show up here and decide if my Ctenophore Inc. is worth funding?" Tug's voice was high and shaky with stress. "I don't like it, Revel."

"Just try 'n' act like you know what you're doing, Tug, and then she'll take my Uncle Donny Ray a clean bill of health for us. Just a detail really." Revel laughed falsely. "My uncle's a little over-cautious. Belt-and-suspenders kinda guy. Lot of private investigators on his payroll and stuff. The old boy's just tryin' to keep me outa trouble, basically. Don't worry about it none, Tug."

Revel's phone rang again, this time from the pocket on his left buttock. "Pullen here! What? Yeah, I know his house don't look like much, but this is the place, all right. Yeah, okay, we'll let you in." Revel stowed the phone again, and turned to Tug. "Go get the door, man, and I'll double check that our cooler of Urschleim is out of sight."

Seconds later, Tug's front doorbell rang loudly. Tug opened it to find a woman in blue jeans, jogging shoes and a shapeless gray wool jersey, slipping her own cellular phone into her black nylon satchel.

"Hello," she said. "Are you Dr. Mesoglea?"

"Yes I am. Tug Mesoglea."

"Edna Sydney, Edna Sydney Associates."

Tug shook Edna Sydney's dainty blue-knuckled hand. She had a pointed chin, an impressively large forehead, and a look of extraordinary, almost supernatural intelligence in her dark brown shoebutton eyes. She had a neat cap of gray-streaked brown hair. She looked like a digital pixie leapt full-blown from the brain of Thomas Edison.

While she greeted Revel, Tug dug a business-card from his wallet and forced it on her. Edna Sydney riposted with a card from the satchel that gave office addresses in Washington, Prague, and Chicago.

"Would you care for a latte?" Tug babbled. "Tab? Pineapple-mango soda?"

Edna Sydney settled for a Jolt Cola, then gently maneuvered the two men into the jellyfish lab. She listened attentively as Tug launched into an extensive, arm-waving spiel.

Tug was inspired. Words gushed from him like Revel's Urschleim. He'd never before met anyone who could fully understand him when he talked techie jargon absolutely as fast as he could. Edna Sydney, however, not only comprehended Tug's jabber but actually tapped her foot occasionally and once politely stifled a yawn.

"I've seen artificial life devices before," Edna allowed, as Tug began to run out of verbal ectoplasm. "I knew all those Santa Fe guys before they destroyed the futures exchanges and got sent off to Leavenworth. I wouldn't advise trying to break into the software market with some new genetic algorithm. You don't want to end up like Bill Gates."

Revel snorted. "Gates? Geez, I wouldn't wish that on my worst enemy." He chortled aloud. "To think they used to compare that nerd to Rockefeller! Hell, Rockefeller was an oil business man, a family man! If Gates had been in Rockefeller's class, there'd be kids named Gates running half the states in the Union by now."

"I'm not planning to market the algorithms," Tug told the consultant. "They'll be a trade secret, and I'll market the jelly simulacra themselves. Ctenophore Inc. is basically a manufacturing enterprise."

"What about the threat of reverse engineering?"

"We've got an eighteen-month lead," Revel bragged. "Round these parts, that's like eighteen years anywhere else! Besides, we got a set of ingredients that's gonna be mighty hard to duplicate."

"There hasn't been a lot of, uh, sustained industry development in the artificial jellyfish field before," Tug told her. "We've got a big R&D advantage."

Edna pursed her lips. "Well, that brings us to marketing, then. How are you going to get your products advertised and distributed?"

"Oh, for publicity, we'll do COMDEX, A-Life Developers, Bio-Science Fair, MONDO 3000, the works," Revel assured her. "And get this—we can ship jellies by the Pullen oil pipelines anywhere in North America for free! Try and match that for ease of distribution and clever use of an installed base! Hell, it'll be almost as easy as downloadin' software from the Internet!"

"That certainly sounds innovative," Edna nodded. "So—let's get to the crux of matters, then. What's the killer app for a robot jellyfish?"

Tug and Revel traded glances. "Our exact application is highly confidential," Tug said tentatively.

"Maybe you could suggest a few apps, Edna," Revel told her, folding his arms cagily over the denim chest of his Can't-Bust-Ems. "Come on and earn your twenty thousand bucks an hour."

"Hmmm," the consultant said. Her brow clouded, and she sat in the armchair at Tug's workstation, her eyes gone distant. "Jellyfish. Industrial jellyfish…"

Greenish rippling aquarium light played across Edna Sydney's face as she sat in deep thought. The jellyfish kept up their silent, eternal pulsations; kept on bouncing their waves of contraction out and back between the centers and the rims of their bells.

"Housewares application," said Edna presently. "Fill them with lye and flush them through sinks and commodes. They agitate their way through sink traps and hairballs and grease."

"Check," said Tug alertly. He snatched a mechanical pencil from the desktop and began scribbling notes on the back of an unpaid bill.

"Assist fermentation in septic tanks by loading jellies with decomposition bacteria, then setting them to churn the tank sludge. Sell them in packs of thousands for city-sized sewage-installations."

"Outrageous," said Tug.

"Microsurgical applications inside plugged arteries. Pulsates plaque away gently, but disintegrates in the ventrical valves to avoid heart attacks."

"That would need FDA approval," Revel hedged. "Maybe a few years down the road."

"You can get a livestock application done in eighteen months," said Edna. "It's happened in recombinant DNA."

"Gotcha," said Revel. "Lord knows the Pullens got a piece o' the cattle business!"

"If you could manufacture Portuguese man-o-war or other threatening toxic jellies," Edna said, "then you could set a few thousand right offshore in perhaps Hilton Head or Puerto Vallarta. After the tourist trade crashed, you could buy up shoreline property cheap and make a real killing." She paused. "Of course, that would be illegal."

"Right," Tug nodded, pencil scratching away. "Although my plastic jellyfish don't sting. I suppose we could implant pouches of toxins in them…"

"It would also be unethical. And wrong."

"Yeah, yeah, we get it," Revel assured her. "Anything else?"

"Do the jellyfish reproduce?" asked Edna.

"No they don't," Tug said. "I mean, not by themselves. They don't reproduce and they don't eat. I can manufacture as many as you want to any spec, though."

"So they're not truly alive, then? They don't evolve? They're not Type III a-life?"

"I evolved the algorithms for their behavior in my simulations, but the devices themselves are basically sterile robots with my best algorithms hard-coded in," Tug geeked fluently. "They're jellyfish androids that run my code. Not androids, coelenteroids."

"It's probably just as well if they don't reproduce," said Edna primly. "How big can you make them?"

"Well, not much bigger than a basketball at present. The lasers I'm currently using to sinter them are of limited capacity." Tug neglected to mention that he had the lasers out on unauthorized loan from San Jose State University, thanks to a good friend in lab support at the School of Engineering. "In principle, a jellyfish could be quite large."

"So they're currently too small to live inside," said Edna thoughtfully.

Revel smiled. "'Live inside,' huh? You're really something special, Edna."

"That's what they pay me for," she said crisply. She glanced at the screen of Tug's workstation, with its rich background color drifting from sky-blue to sea-green, and with a vigorous pack of sea-nettles

410

pumping their way forward. "What genetic operators are you using to evolve your algorithms?"

"Standard Holland stuff. Proportional reproduction, crossover, mutation, and inversion."

"The Chicago a-life group came up with a new schemata-sensitive operator last week," said Edna. "Preliminary tests are showing a forty percent speed-up for searching intractable sample spaces."

"Terrific! That would really be useful for me," said Tug. "I need that genetic operator."

Edna scribbled a file location and the electronic address of a downloading site on Tug's business card and gave it back to him. Then she glanced at a dainty wristwatch inside her left wrist. "Revel's uncle paid for a full hour plus travel. You two want to spring for a retainer, or do I go?"

"Uh, thanks a lot, but I don't think we can swing a retainer," Revel said modestly.

Edna nodded slowly, then touched one finger to her pointed chin. "I just thought of an angle for using your jellyfish in hotel swimming-pools. If your jellyfish don't sting, you could play with them like beach balls, they'd filtrate the water, and they could shed off little polyps to look for cracks. I just hate the hotel pools in California. They're surrounded by anorexic bleached blondes drinking margaritas made of chemicals with forty letters in their names. Should we talk some more?"

"If you don't like your pool, maybe you could take a nice dip in one of Tug's tanks," Revel said, with a glance at his own watch.

"Bad idea, Revel," Tug said hastily, "you get a good jolt from those natural sea-nettles and it'll stop your heart."

"Do you have a license for those venomous creatures?" Edna asked coolly.

Tug tugged his forelock in mock contrition. "Well, Ms. Sydney, amateur coelenteratology's kind of a poorly policed field."

Edna stood up briskly, and hefted her nylon bag. "We're out of time, so here's the bottom line," she said. "This is one of the looniest schemes I've ever seen. But I'm going to phone Revel's uncle with the go-ahead as soon as I get back into Illinois airspace. Risk-taking weirdos like you two are what makes this industry great, and the Pullen family can well afford to back you. I'm rooting for you boys. And if you even need any cut-rate Kazakh programmers, send me e-mail."

"Thanks, Edna," Revel said.

"Yes," said Tug, "Thank you for all the good ideas." He saw her to the door.

"She didn't really sound very encouraging," Tug said after she left. "And her ideas were ugly, compared to ours. Fill my jellyfish with lye? Put them in septic tanks and in cow arteries? Fill them with poison to sting families on vacation?" He flung back his head and began camping back and forth across the room imitating Edna in a shrieking falsetto. "They're not Type III a-life? Oh dear! How I hate those anorexic blondes! Oh my!"

"Look, Tug, if Edna was a little underwhelmed it's just 'cause I didn't tell her everything!" said Revel. "A trade secret is a trade secret, boy, and three's always a crowd. That gal's got a brain with the strength o' ten, but even Edna Sydney can't help droppin' certain hints in those pricey little newsletters of hers…"

Revel whistled briefly, pleased with his own brilliance.

Tug's eyes widened in sudden, cataclysmic comprehension. "I've got it Revel! I think I've got it! When you first saw an Urschleim air-jelly—was it before or after you put my plastic jellyfish in your swimming pool?"

"After, compadre. I only first thought of blowing Urschleim bubbles last week—I was drunk, and I did it to make a woman laugh. But you sent me that sorry-ass melting jellyfish a full six weeks ago."

"That 'sorry-ass melting jellyfish' found its way out a crack in your swimming pool and down through the shale beds into the Ditheree hole!" cried Tug exultantly. "Yes! That's it, Revel! My equations migrated right out into your goo!"

"Your software got into my primeval slime?" said Revel slowly. "How exactly is that s'posed to happen?"

"Mathematics represents optimal form, Revel," said Tug. "That's why it slips in everywhere. But sometimes you need a seed equation. Like if water gets cold, it likes to freeze; it freezes into a mathematical lattice. But if you have really cold water in a smooth tank, the water might not know how to freeze—until maybe a snowflake drifts into it. To make a long story short, the mathematical formations of my sintered jellyfish represent a low-energy phase space configuration that is stably attractive to the dynamics of the Urschleim."

"That story's too long for me," said Revel. "Let's just test if you're right. Why don't we throw one of your artificial jellies into my cooler full of slime?"

"Good idea," Tug said, pleased to see Revel plunging headlong into the scientific method. They returned to the aquaria.

Tug mounted a stepladder festooned with bright-red anti-litigation safety warnings, and used a long-handled aquarium net to fetch up his best artificial jelly, a purple-striped piezoplastic sea nettle that he'd sintered up just that morning, a home-made, stingless *Chrysaora quinquecirrha.*

Revel and Tug strode out to the living room with the plastic sea nettle pulsating gamely against the fine-woven mesh of the net.

"Stand back," Tug warned and flipped the jelly into the four inches of Urschleim still in the plastic picnic cooler.

The slime heaved upward violently at the touch of the little artificial jellyfish. Once again Revel blew some Texan hot air into the goo, only this time it all lifted up at once, all five liters of it, forming a floating sea-nettle the size of a large dog.

"Don't let it hit the ceiling!" Revel shouted. The Urschleim jelly drifted around the room, its white oral arms swaying like the train of a wedding dress.

"Yee haw! Shit howdy! This one's different from all the Urschleim ones I've seen before. People'd buy this one just for fun! Edna's right. It'd be a hell of a pool toy, or, heck, a plain old land toy, as long as it don't fly away."

"A toy?" said Tug. "You think we should go with the recreational application? I like it, Revel! Recreation has positive energy. And there's a lot of money in gaming."

"Just like tag!" Revel hooted, capering. "Blind man's bluff!"

"Watch out, Revel!" One swaying fringe of dog-sized ur-jelly made a sudden whipping snatch at Revel's leg. Revel yelped in alarm and tumbled backward over the living-room hassock.

"Christ! Get it off me!" Revel cried as the enormous jelly reeled at his ankle, its vast gelatinous bulk hovered menacingly over his upturned face. Tug, with a burst of inspiration, slid open the glass doors to the deck.

Caught in a draft of air, the jelly released Revel and floated out through the doors, and sailed off over Tug's redwood deck. Tug watched the dog-sized jelly ascending serenely over the neighbors' yard. Engrossed in beer and tofu, the neighbors failed to notice it.

Toatoa the parrot swooped off the roof of the Samoans' house and rose to circle the great flying sea nettle. The iridescent green parrot hung in a moment of timeless beauty near the translucent jelly, and then was caught by one of the lashing oral arms. There was a frenzy of green motion inside the Urschleim sea-nettle's bell, and then the parrot had clawed and beaked its way free. The punctured nettle fell into the stiff, gnarly branches of a madrone tree and lay there melting. The moist Toatoa cawed angrily from her roof-top perch, flapping her wings to dry.

"Wow!" said Tug. "I'd like to see that again—on digital video!" He smacked his forehead with the flat of his hand. "But now we've got none left for testing! Except —wait!— that little bit in the vial." He yanked

413

the vial from his pocket and looked at it speculatively. "I could put a tiny Monterey bell jelly in here, and then put in some nanophones to pick up the phonon jitter. Yeah. If I could get even a rough map of the Urschleim's basins of chaotic attraction—"

Revel yawned loudly and stretched his arms. "Sounds fascinatin', Doc. Take me on down to my motel, would you? I'll call Ditheree and get some more Urschleim delivered to your house by, oh, 6 AM tomorrow. And by day after tomorrow I can get you a lot more. A whole lot more."

Tug had rented Revel a room in the Los Perros Inn, a run-down stucco motel where, Tug told Revel as he dropped him off, Joe DiMaggio and Marilyn Monroe had once spent a honeymoon night.

Fearing that Tug harbored a budding romantic notion of a honeymoon night for himself, Revel frowned and muttered, "Now I know why they call this the Granola State: nuts, flakes, and fruits."

"Relax," said Tug. "I know you're not gay. And you're not my type anyway. You're way too young. What I want is a manly older guy who'll cherish me and take care of me. I want to snuggle against his shoulder and feel his strong arms around me in the still of the night." Perhaps the Etna Ale had gone to Tug's head. Or maybe the Urschleim had affected him. In any case, he didn't seem at all embarrassed to be making these revelations.

"See you tomorrow, old son," said Revel, closing his door.

Revel got on the phone and called the home of Hoss Jenks, the old forehand of the Ditheree field.

"Hoss, this is Revel Pullen. Can you messenger me out another pressure tank of that goo?"

"That goo, Revel, that goo! There's been big-ass balloons of it floatin' out of the well. You never should of thrown those gene-splice bacteria down there."

"I told you before, Hoss, it ain't bacteria we're dealing with, it's primeval slime!"

"Ain't many of us here that agree, Revel. What if it's some kind of plague on the oil wells? What if it spreads?"

"Let's stick to the point, Hoss. Has anybody noticed the balloons?"

"Not yet."

"Well, just keep folks off our property, Hoss. And tell the boys not to be shy of firing warning shots—we're on unincorporated land."

"I don't know how long this can stay secret."

"Hoss, we need time to try and find a way to make a buck off this. If I can get the right spin on the Urschleim, folks'll be glad to see it coming out of Ditheree. Just between you and me, I'm out here with the likeliest old boy to figure out what to do. Not that he's much of a regular fella, but that's neither here nor there. Name of Tug Mesoglea. I think we're onto something big. Send that tank of goo out to Mesoglea's address, pronto. Here it is. Yeah, and here's his number, and while we're at it, here's my number at the motel. And, Hoss, let's make that three tanks, the same size as the one you filled up for me yesterday. Yeah. Try and get em out here by six AM tomorrow. And start routing out a Pullen pipeline connection between our Nacogdoches tank farm and Monterey."

"Monterey, California, or Monterey, Mexico?"

"California. Monterey's handy and it's out of the way. We'll need some place real quiet for the next stage I'm planning. There's way too many professional snoops watching everybody's business here in Silicon Valley, drivin' around scanning cellular phones and stuff—you're receiving this call as encrypted, aren't you, Hoss?"

"Sure thing, boss. Got my Clipper Chip set to maximum scramble."

"Good, good, just making sure. I'm trying to be cautious, Hoss, just like Uncle Donny Ray."

Hoss gave a snort of laughter on the other end of the line, and Revel continued. "Anyhoo, we need someplace kind out of the way, but still convenient. Someplace with some spare capacity, but a little run-down, so's we can rent lots of square footage on the cheap and the city fathers don't ask too many prying questions…Ask Lucy to sniff around and find me a place like that in Monterey."

"There's already hundreds of towns like that in Texas!"

"Yeah, but I want to do this out here. This deal is a software kind o' thing, so it's gotta be California."

Revel woke around seven AM, stirred by the roar of the morning rush-hour traffic. He got his breakfast at a California coffee-shop that called itself "Southern Kitchen," yet served orange-rind muffins and sliced kiwi-fruits with the eggs. Over breakfast he called Texas, and learned that Lucy had found an abandoned tank farm near a defunct polluted military base just north of Monterey. The tank farm belonged to Felix Quinonez, who had been the base's fuel supplier. The property, on Quinonez's private land, included a large garage. The set-up sounded about perfect.

"Lease it, Lucy," said Revel, slurping his coffee. "And fax Quinonez two copies of the contract so's me and him can sign off down at his property today. I'll get this Tug Mesoglea fella to drive me down there. Let's say two o'clock this afternoon? Lock it in. Now has Hoss found a pipeline connection? He has? Straight to Quinonez's tanks? Bless you, honey. Oh, and one more thing? Draw up incorporation papers for a company called Ctenophore, Inc., register the company, and get the name trademarked. C-T-E-N-O-P-H-O-R-E. What it means? It's a kind of morphodite jellyfish. Swear to God. I learned it from Tug Mesoglea. If you should you put Mesoglea's name on my incorporation papers? Are you teasin' me, Lucy? Are you tryin' to make ol' Revel mad? Now book me and Mesoglea a suite in a Monterey hotel, and fax the incorporation papers to me there. Thanks, darlin'. Talk to ya later."

The rapid-fire wheeling and dealing filled Revel with joy. Expansively swinging his arms, he strolled up the hill to Tug's house, which was only a few blocks off. The air was clear and cool, and the sun was a low bright disk in the immaculate blue sky. Birds fluttered this way and that—sparrows, grackles, robins, humming-birds, and the startlingly large California bluejays. A dog barked in the distance as the exotic leaves and flowers swayed in the gentle morning breeze.

As he drew closer to Tug's house, Revel could hear the steady screeching of the Samoans' parrot. And when he turned the corner of Tug's block, Revel saw something very odd. It was like there was a ripple in the space over Tug's house, an undulating bluish glinting of curved air.

Wheeling about in the midst of the glinting was the furious Toatoa. A school of small airborne bell jellies were circling around and around over Tug's house, now fleeing from and now pursuing the parrot, who was endeavoring to puncture them one by one. Revel yelled at the cloud of jellyfish, but what good would that do? You could as soon yell at a volcano or at a spreadsheet.

To Revel's relief, the parrot retreated to her house with a broken tailfeather, and the jellies did not follow her. But now—were the air bells catching the scent plume of the air off Revel's body? They flocked and spiraled eldritchly. Revel hurried up Tug's steps and into his house, right past the three empty cylinders of Urschleim lying outside Tug's front door.

Inside Tug's house reeked of subterranean sulfur. Air jellies of all kinds pressed this way and that. Sea nettles, comb-jellies, bell jellies, spotted jellies, and even a few giant siphonophores—all the jellies of different sizes, with the smaller ones beating frantically faster than the big ones. It was like a children's birthday party with lighter-than-air balloons. Tug had gone utterly bat-shit with the Urschleim.

"Hey, Tug!" Revel called, slapping a sea nettle away from his face. "What's goin' on, buddy? Is it safe in here?"

Tug appeared from around a corner. He was wearing a long blonde wig. His cheeks were high pink with excitement, and his blue eyes were sparkling. He wore bright lipstick, and a tight red silk dress. "It's a jelly party, Revel!"

A huge siphonophore shaped like a mustachioed rope of mucus came bumping along the ceiling towards Revel, its mane of oral arms soundlessly a-jangle.

"Help!"

"Oh don't worry so," said Tug. "And don't beat up a lot of wind. Air currents are what excites them. Here, if you're scared, come down to my room while I slip into something less confrontational."

Revel sat on a chair in the corner of Tug's bedroom while Tug got back into his shorts and sandals.

"I was so excited when all that slime came this morning that I put on my dress-up clothes," Tug confessed. "I've been dancing with my equations for the last couple of hours. There doesn't seem to be any size limit to the size of the jellyfish I can blow. We can make Urschleim jellyfish as big as anything!"

Revel rubbed his cheek uncertainly. "Did you figure anything more out about them, Tug? I didn't tell you before, but back at Ditheree we're getting spontaneous air jelly releases. I mean—I sure don't understand how the hell they can fly. Did you get that part yet?"

"Well, as I'm sure you know, the scientific word for jellyfish is 'coelenterate'," said Tug, leaning towards the mirror to take off his lipstick. "'Coelenterate' is from 'hollow gut' in Latin. Your average jellyfish has an organ called a coelenteron, which is a saclike cavity within its body. The reason these Urschleim fellows can fly is that somehow the Urschleim vaporizes to fills their coelenterons with, of all things, helium! Nature's noblest gas! Traditionally found seeping out of the shafts of oil wells!" Tug whooped, waggled his ass, and slipped off his wig.

Revel clambered angrily to his feet. "I'm glad you're having fun, Doc, but fun ain't business. We're in retail now, and like they say in retail, you can't do business from an empty truck. We need jellies. All stocks, all sizes. You ready to set up shop seriously?"

"What do you mean?"

"I mean build product, son! I done called my man Hoss Jenkins at Ditheree, and we're gonna be ready to start pumping Urschleim cross-country by pipeline around noon our time tomorrow. That is, if you're man enough to handle the other end of the assembly line here in California."

"Isn't that awfully sudden?" Tug hedged, wiping off his mascara. "I mean, I do have some spreadsheets and business plans for a factory, but…"

Revel scoffed, and swatted at the jelly-stained leg of his Can't-Bust Ems. "Where have you been, Tug? This is the twenty-first century. Ain't you ever heard of just-in-time manufacturing? Hell, in Singapore or

Taiwan they'd have already set up six virtual corporations and had this stuff shipped to global markets yesterday!"

"But I can't run a major manufacturing enterprise out of my house," Tug said, gazing around him. "Even my laser-sintering equipment is on a kind of, uhm, loan, from the University. We'll still need lasers for making the plastic jellies to seed the big ones."

"I'll buy you lasers, Tug. Just give me the part numbers."

"But, but, we'll need workers. People to answer the phone, men to carry things..." Tug paused. "Though, come to think of it, we could use a simple Turing imitation program to answer the phones. And I know where we can pick up a few industrial robots to do the heavy lifting."

"Now you're talking sense!" Revel nodded. "Let's go on upstairs!"

"But what about the factory building?" Tug called after Revel. "We can't fit the business into my poor house. We'll need a lot of floor space, and a tank to store the Urschleim, with a pipeline depot nearby. We'll need a power hookup, an Internet node and—"

"And it has to be some outta-the-way locale," said Revel, turning to grin down from the head of the stairs. "Which I already leased for us this morning!"

"My stars!" said Tug. "Where is it?"

"Monterey. You're drivin'." Revel glanced around the living-room, taking in the odd menagerie of disparate jellyfish floating about. "Before we go," he cautioned, "You better close the door to your wood-stove. There's a passel of little air jellies who've already slipped out through your chimney. They were hassling your neighbor's parrot."

"Oh!" said Tug, and closed the wood-stove's door. The big siphonophore slimed its arms across Tug. Instead of trying to fight away, Tug dangled his arms limply and began hunching his back rhythmically—like a jellyfish. The siphonophore soon lost interest in him and drifted away. "That's how you do it," said Tug. "Just act like a jellyfish!"

"That's easier for you than it is for me," said Revel, picking up a twitching plastic moon jelly from the floor. "Let's take some of these suckers down to Monterey with us. We can use them for seeds. We can have like a tank of these moon jellies, some comb-jellies, a tank of sea nettles, a tank of those big street-loogie things over there—" he pointed at a siphonophore.

"Sure," said Tug. "We'll bring all my little plastic ones, and figure out which ones make the best Urschleim toys."

They set a sheet of plastic into the Animata's trunk, loaded it up with plastic jellyfish doused in seawater, and set off for Monterey.

All during the trip down the highway, Revel jabbered into his cellular phone, jolting various movers and shakers into action: Pullen family clients, suppliers and gophers, in Dallas, Houston, San Antonio—even a few discreet calls to Djakarta and Macao.

Quinonez's tank farm was just north of Monterey, squeezed up against the boundaries of what had once been Fort Ord. During their occupancy of these rolling dunes, the Army had so thoroughly polluted the soil that the land was now legally unusable. The base, which had been closed since the 1990s, was a nature preserve cum hazardous waste site. Those wishing to stroll the self-guiding nature trails were required to wear respirators and disposable plastic shoe-covers.

Tug guided the Animata along a loop road that led to the back of the Ord Natural Waste Site. Inland from the dunes were huge fields of Brussels sprouts and artichokes. In one of the fields six huge silvery tanks rested like visiting UFOs.

"There it is, Tug," said Revel, putting away his phone. "The home of Ctenophore, Inc!"

As they drew closer, they could see that the great storage tanks were marred with graffiti and pocked with rust. Some of the graffiti were richly psychedelic, but most were Aztec gang-code glyphs about red and blue, South and North, the numbers 13 and 14, and so on. The gangs' points of dispute grew ever more abstract.

Between the tanks and the road there was a vast gravel parking-lot with yellowed thistles pushing up through it. At one side of the lot was a truly enormous steel and concrete garage, practically the size of an airplane hanger. Painted on the wall in fading electric pink, yellow and blue was Quinonez Motorotive—Max Nix We Fix!

"Pull on up there, Tug," said Revel. "Mr. Quinonez is supposed to show up and give us the keys."

"How did you get the lease lined up already?"

"What do you think I've been doing on the phone, Doc? Ordering pizza?"

They got out of the Animata, and stood there in the sudden, startling silence beneath the immense, clear California sky. In the distance a sputtering motor made itself heard, then pushed closer. Revel wandered back towards the nearest oil-tank and peered at it. Now the motor arrived in the form of a battered multicolored pickup truck driven by a rugged older man with iron gray hair and a heavy mustache.

"Hello!" sang Tug, instantly in love.

"Good afternoon," said the man, getting out of his pickup. "I'm Felix Quinonez." He stuck out his hand and Tug eagerly grasped it.

"I'm Tug Mesoglea," said Tug. "I handle the science, and my partner Revel Pullen over there handles the business. I think we're leasing this property from you?"

"I think so too," said Quinonez, baring his strong teeth in a flashing smile. He let go of Tug's hand, giving Tug a thoughtful look. An ambiguous look. Did Tug dare hope?

Now Revel came striding over. "Quinonez? I'm Revel Pullen. Did you bring the contract Lucy faxed you? Muy bueno, my man. Let's sign the papers on the hood of your pickup. Texas style!"

The ceremony completed, Quinonez handed over the keys. "This is the key to garage, this is for the padlock on the pipeline valve, and these here are for the locks on the stairways up onto the tanks. We've been having some trouble keeping kids out of here."

"I can see that from the free paint-jobs you been getting," said Revel, staring over at the graffiti bedecked tanks. "But the rust I'm seeing is what worries me. The corrosion."

"These tanks have been empty and out of use for quite a few years," granted Quinonez. "But you weren't planning on filling them, were you? As I explained to your assistant, the hazardous materials license for this site was revoked the day Fort Ord was closed."

"I certainly am planning on filling these tanks," said Revel, "Or why the hell else would I be renting them? But the materials ain't gonna be hazardous."

"You're dealing in beet-sugar?" inquired Quinonez.

"Never you mind what's going in the tanks, Felix. Just show me around and get me up to speed on your valves and pipelines." He handed the garage key to Tug. "Here, Doc, scope out the building while Felix here shows me his system."

"Thanks, Revel. But Felix, before you go off with him, just show me how the garage lock works," said Tug. "I don't want to set off an alarm or something."

Revel watched disapprovingly while Tug walked over to the garage with Felix, chattering all the way.

"You must be very successful, Felix," gushed Tug as the leathery-faced Quinonez coaxed the garage's rusty lock open. Grasping for more topics to keep the conversation going, Tug glanced up at the garage's weathered sign. "Motorotive, that's a good word."

"A cholo who worked for me made it up," allowed Quinonez. "Do you know what Max Nix We Fix means?"

"Not really."

"My Dad was in the Army in the sixties. He was stationed in Germany, he had an easy deal. He was in the motor vehicle division, of course, and that was their slogan. Max Nix is German for 'it doesn't matter.'"

"How would you say Max Nix in Spanish?" inquired Tug. "I love Spanish."

420

"No problema," grinned Felix. Tug felt that there was definitely a good vibration between them. Now the lock on the garage door squeaked open, and Felix held it open so that Tug could pass inside.

"The lights are over here," said Felix, hitting a bank of switches. The cavernous garage was like a vast barn for elephants—there were thirty vehicle-repair bays on either side like stalls; each bay was big enough to have once held a huge green Army truck.

"Hey, Quinonez," came Revel's holler. "I ain't got all day!"

"Thanks so much, Felix," said Tug, reaching out to the handsome older man for another handshake. "I'd love to see more of you."

"Well, maybe you will," said Felix softly. "I am not a married man."

"That's lovely," breathed Tug. The two made full eye contact. No problema.

Later that afternoon, Tug and Revel settled into a top-floor suite of a Monterey seaside hotel. Tug poured a few buckets of hotel ice onto the artificial jellyfish in his trunk. Revel got back into the compulsive wheeler-dealer mode with his portable phone again, his demands becoming more unseemly and grandiose as he and Tug worked their way, inch by amber inch, through a fifth of Gentleman Jack.

At three in the morning, Tug crashed headlong into bed, his last conscious memory the clink and scrape of Revel razoring white powder on the suite's glass-topped coffee-table. He'd hoped to dream that he was in the arms of Felix Quinonez, but instead he dreamed once again about debugging a jellyfish program. He woke with a terrible hangover.

Whatever substance Revel had snorted—it seemed unlikely to be anything so mundane and antiquated as mere cocaine—it didn't seem to be bothering him next morning. Revel lustily ordered a big breakfast from room-service.

As Revel tipped the busboy lavishly and splashed California champagne into their beaker of orange juice, Tug staggered outside the suite to the balcony. The Monterey air was rank with kelp. Large immaculate seagulls slid and twisted along the sea-breeze updrafts at the hotel's walls. In the distance to the north, a line of California seals sprawled on a rocky wharf like brown slugs on broken concrete. Dead tin-roofed canneries lined the shore to the south, some of them retrofitted into tourist gyp-joints and discos, others empty and at near-collapse.

Tug huffed at the sea air until the vice-grip loosened at his temples. The world was bright and chaotic and beautiful. He stumbled into the room, bolted down a champagne mimosa and three forkfuls of scrambled eggs.

"Well, Revel," he said finally, "I've got to hand it to you. Quinonez Motorotive is ideal in every respect."

"Oh, I've had Monterey in mind since the first time we met here at SIGUSC," Revel averred, propping one boot-socked foot on the table-top. "I took to this place right away. This is my kind of town." With his lean strangler's mitts folded over his shallow chest, the young oilman looked surprisingly at peace, almost philosophical. "You ever read any John Steinbeck, Tug?"

"Steinbeck?"

"Yeah, the Nobel-Prize-winning twentieth-century novelist."

"I never figured you for a reading man, Revel."

"I got into Steinbeck's stuff when I first came to Monterey," Revel said. "Now I'm a big fan of his. Great writer. He wrote a book set right here in Cannery Row…you ever read it? Well, it's about all these drunks and whores living on the hillsides around here, some pretty interesting folks, and the hero's this guy who's kind of their mentor. He's an ich-thyologist who does abortions on the side. Not for the money though, just because it's the 1940s and he likes to have lots of sex, and abortion happens to be this thing he can hack 'cause of his science background… Y'see, Tug, in Steinbeck's day, Cannery Row actually canned a hell of a lot of fish! Sardines. But all the sardines vanished by 1950. Some kind of eco-disaster thing; the sardines never came back at all, not to this day." He laughed. "So you know what they sell in this town today? Steinbeck."

"Yeah I know," said Tug. "It's kind of a postmodern culture-industry museum-economy tourist thing."

"Yeah. Cannery Row cans Steinbeck now. There's Steinbeck novels, and tapes of the crappy movie adaptations, and Steinbeck beer-mugs, and Steinbeck key-chains, Steinbeck bumper-stickers, Steinbeck iron-on patches, Steinbeck fridge-magnets…and below the counter, there's Steinbeck blow-up plastic love-dolls so that the air-filled author of Grapes of Wrath can be subjected to any number of unspeakable post-humous indignities."

"You're kidding about the love-dolls, right?"

"Heck no, dude! I think what we ought to do is buy one of 'em, blow it up, and throw it into a cooler full of Urschleim. What we'd get is this big Jello Steinbeck, see? Maybe it'd even talk! Like deliver a Nobel Prize oration or something. Except when you go to shake his hand, the hand just snaps off at the wrist like a jelly polyp, a kind of dough-lump of dead author flesh, and floats through the air till it hits some paper and starts writing sequels…"

"What the hell was that stuff you snorted last night, Revel?"

"Bunch of letters and numbers, old son. Seems like they change 'em every time I score."

Tug groaned as if in physical pain. "In other words you're so fried, you can't remember."

Revel, jolted from his reverie, frowned. "Now, don't go Neanderthal on me, Tug. That stuff is pure competitive edge. You wouldn't act so shocked about it, if you'd spent some time in the boardrooms of the Fortune 500 lately. Smart drugs!" Revel coughed rackingly and laughed again. "The coolest thing about smart drugs is, that if they even barely work, you just gotta take 'em, no matter how square you are! Otherwise, the Japanese CEOs kick your ass!"

"I think it's time to get some fresh air, Revel."

"How right you are, hombre. We gotta settle in at Quinonez's tank farm this morning. We've got a Niagara of Urschleim headed our way." Revel glanced at his watch. "Fact is, the stuff oughta be rollin' in a couple of hours from now. Let's go on down and get ready to watch the tanks fill up."

"What if one of the tanks splits open?"

"Then I expect we won't use that particular tank no more."

When Tug and Revel got to Quinonez Motorotive, they found several crates of newly delivered equipment waiting for them. Tug was as excited as Christmas morning.

"Look, Revel, these two boxes are the industrial robots, that box is the supercomputer, and this one here is the laser-sintering device."

"Yep," said Revel. "And over here's a drum of those piezoplastic beads and here's a pallet of titaniplast sheets for your jellyfish tanks. You start gettin' it all set up, Doc, while I check out the pipeline valves one more time."

Tug unlimbered the robots first. They were built like short squat humanoids, and each came with a telerobotic interface that had the form of a virtual reality helmet. The idea was that you put on the helmet and watched through the robot's eyes, meanwhile talking the robot through some repetitive task that you were going to want it to do. The task in this case was to build jellyfish tanks by lining some of the garage's big truck bays with titaniplast—and to fill up the tanks with water.

The robot controls were of course trickier than Tug had anticipated, but after an hour or so he had one of them slaving away like the Sorcerer's Apprentice. He powered up the second robot and used it to bring in and set up the new computer and the laser-sintering assemblage. Then he crossloaded the first robot's program onto the second robot, and it too got to work turning truck-bays into aquaria.

Tug configured the new computer and did a remote login to his workstation back in Los Perros. In ten minutes he'd siphoned off copies of all the software he needed, and ghostly jellyfish were shimmering across the computer's new screen. Tug went out and looked at the robots; they'd finished five aquaria now, and water was gushing into them from connections the busy robots had made to the Quinonez Motorotive water-main.

Tug opened the trunk of his car and began bringing in artificial jellyfish and throwing them into the new tanks. Meanwhile Revel was moving about on the big storage tanks, crawling all over them like an excited fly on fresh meat. Spotting Tug, Revel whooped and waved from the top of a tank. "The slime's comin' soon," hollered Revel. Tug waved back and returned to his computer.

Checking his e-mail, Tug saw that he'd finally gotten a coelenteratological monograph concerning one of the ctenophores he'd been most eager to model: the Venus's-girdle, or Cestus veneris, a comb-jelly native to the Mediterranean that was shaped like a wide, tapering belt covered with cilia. The Venus's-girdle was a true ctenophore, and its water-combing cilia were said to diffract sunlight into gorgeous rainbows. It might be fun to wrap one of them around your waist for dress-up. Ctenophore, Inc., could make fashion accessories as well as toys! Smiling as he worked, Tug began transferring the report's data to his design program.

The roar of the Urschleim coming through the pipeline was like a subway underground. Initially taking it for an earthquake, Tug ran outside and collided with the jubilant Revel.

"Here she comes, pardner!"

The nearest of the giant tanks boomed and shuddered as the slime began coursing into it. "So far, so good!" said Revel.

Tanks two and three filled up uneventfully, but a long vertical seam midway up on tank four began to gape open as the tank was filling. Scampering about like a meth-biker roughneck, Revel yanked at the pipeline valves and diverted the Urschleim flow from tank four into tanks five and six, which tidily absorbed the rest of the shipment.

As the roaring and booming of the pipeline delivery died down, the metal of tank four gave a dying shriek and ripped open from top to bottom. Floundering in vast chaotic motion, the sides of the great tank unrolled to fall outwards like a snipped ribbon, tearing loose from the huge disk top, which glided forward some twenty yards like a giant Frisbee.

An acre or more of slime gushed out of the burst tank to flood the tank farm's dry weedy soil. The thousands of gallons of glistening Urschleim mounded up on the ground like a clear tapioca pudding.

Tug started running toward the spill, fearful for Revel's safety. But, no, there was Revel, standing safe off to one side like a triumphant cockroach. "Come on, Tug!" he called. "Come look at this!" Tug kept running and Revel met him at the edge of the Urschleim spill.

"This is just like the spill at Ditheree!" exclaimed Revel. "But you'll see, spillin' Urschleim on the ground don't mean a thing. You ready start fillin' orders, Tug?" His voice sounded tinny and high, like the voice of an indestructible cartoon character.

"The stuff is warm," said Tug, leaning forward to feel the great knee-high pancake of Urschleim. His voice too had high, quacking quality. Here and there fat bubbles of gas formed beneath the Urschleim and burst plopping holes in it. The huge Urschleim flapjack was giving off gas like a dough full of yeast. But the gas was helium, which is why their voices were high and—

"I just realized how the Urschleim makes helium," squawked Tug. "Cold fusion! Let's run back in the garage, Revel, and find out whether or not we've got radiation sickness. Come on. I mean it. Run!"

Back in the garage they caught their breath for awhile. "Why would we have radiation sickness?" puffed Revel finally.

"I think your Urschleim is fusing hydrogen atoms together to make helium," said Tug. "Depending on the details of the process, that could mean anything from warming the stuff up, to killing everyone in the county."

"Well, it ain't killed anyone down in Ditheree so far," Revel scoffed. "And come to think of it, one of my techs did check the first batch over with a Geiger counter. It ain't radioactive, Tug. How could it be? We're gonna use it to make toys!"

"Toys? You've already got orders?"

"I got a fella owns a chain of variety stores down in Orange County, wants ten thousand jellies to sell for swimming-pool toys. All shapes and sizes. I told him I'd send 'em out down the pipeline to his warehouse early tomorrow morning. He's takin' out ads in tomorrow's papers."

"Heavens to Betsy!" exclaimed Tug. "How are we going to pull that off?"

"I figure all you need to do is tap off Urschleim a bucketful at a time, and just dip one of your artificial jellyfish into each bucketful. The ur-snot will glom right onto the math and start acting like a jellyfish. You sell the slime jellyfish, and keep the plastic jellyfish to use as a seed again and again."

"We're going to do that ten thousand times by tomorrow morning?"

"Teach the damn robots to do it!"

Just about then, Felix Quinonez showed up in truck to try and find out what they'd just spilled out of tank four. Revel blustered at him until he went away, but not before Tug managed to set a dinner date with him for that evening.

"Jesus, Tug," snapped Revel. "What in hell you want to have supper with that old man for? I hope to God it ain't because of— "

"Hark," sang Tug. "The love that dare not speak its name! Maybe I can get myself a Venus's-girdle sintered up in time. I think it would be a stunning thing to wear. The Venus's-girdle is a ctenophore native to the Mediterranean. If I can make mine come out anywhere near as gorgeous as the real thing, then we'll sell twenty thousand of them to your man in Orange."

Revel nodded grimly. "Let's git on in the garage and start workin', son."

They tried to get the robots to help with making the ten thousand jellies, but the machines were slow and awkward at this task. Tug and Revel set to work making the jellies themselves—tapping off Urschleim, vivifying it with the magic touch of a plastic jellyfish, and throwing the Urschleim jellyfish into one of the aquaria for storage. They put nets over the storage aquaria to keep the creatures from floating off. Soon the nets bulged upward with a dizzying array of Urschleim coelenteroids.

When dinner time rolled around, Tug, to Revel's displeasure, excused himself for his date with Felix Quinonez.

"I'll just work on through," yelled Revel. "I care about business, Tug!"

"I'll check back with you around midnight."

"Fine!" Revel drew out his packet of white powder and inhaled deeply. "I can go all night, you lazy heifer!"

"Don't overwork yourself, Revel. If we don't finish all the jellyfish tonight we can finish them early tomorrow morning. How many do we have done anyway?"

"I'm counting about three thousand," said Revel. "Damn but those robots are slow."

"Well I'll be back later to drive you back to the hotel. Don't do anything crazy while I'm gone."

"You're the one whose crazy, Tug!"

Tug's dinner with Felix Quinonez went very well, even though Tug hadn't had time to sinter himself that Venus's-girdle. After the meal they went back to Felix's house and got to know each other better. The satiated Tug dropped off to sleep, and by the time he got back to the tank farm to pick up Revel, it was nearly dawn.

A stiff breeze was blowing from the south, and a dying moon hung low in the west over the sea. Patches of fog swept northward across the moon's low disk. The great tanks of Urschleim were creaking and shivering. Tug opened the garage door to find the whole interior space filled with Urschleim jellies. Crouched cackling at one side of the garage was the wasted Revel. Streaming out of five jury-rigged pipes next to Revel were a steady stream of fresh Urschleim jellyfish; blowing out of the pipes like bubbles from a bubble wand. Every now and then an air-bubble would start to swell too large before breaking free, and one of the two robots would step forward and snip it off.

"Reckon we got enough, yet, Tug?" asked Revel. "I done lost count."

Tug did a quick estimation of the volume of the garage divided by the volume of an air-jelly and came up with two hundred thousand.

"Yes, Revel, I'm that's way more than enough. Stop it now. How did you get around having to dip the plastic jellyfish into the slime?"

"The smart nose knows," said Revel, horning up a thumbnail of white powder. "How was your big date?"

"My date was fine," said Tug, pushing past Revel to turn off the valves on the five pipes. "It could even be the beginning of a steady thing. Thank God this garage isn't wood, or these air jellies would lift off the roof. How are you going to feed them all into the pipeline to Orange County, Revel?"

"Got the robots to rig a collector up top there," said Revel, gesturing towards the distant ceiling. "You think it's time to ship 'em out? Can do!" Revel slapped a large toggle switch that one of robots had jury-rigged into the wall. The deep throb of a powerful electric pump began.

"That's good, Revel, let's get the jellies out of here. But you still didn't tell me how you got the jellies to come out of the pipe all ready-made." Tug paused and stared at Revel. "I mean how they could come out ready-made without your having to dip a plastic jellyfish in them. What did you do?"

"Hell, I can tell by your face you already know the answer," snapped Revel defensively. "You want to hear it? Okay, I went and put one of your goddamn precious plastic jellies in each of the big tanks. Same idea as back at Ditheree. Once the whole tank's got your weird math in it, the pieces that bubble out form jellies naturally. We got sea nettles in tank number one, moon jellies in number two, those spotted jellies in tank three, bell jellies in tank five, and ctenophores in tank six. Comb-jellies. Tank four's busted, you recall."

"Busted," said Tug softly. Outside the screeching of metal rose above the sighing of the wind and the chug of the pipeline pump that was sucking the garage's jellies off the ceiling and pipelining them off to Orange County. "Busted."

A huge crash sounded from the tank field.

Tug helped the disoriented Revel out into the driveway in front of the garage. Tank number six was gone, and a spindle-shaped comb-jelly the size of a blimp was bouncing across the sloping field of artichoke plants that lay north of the tank farm. The great moving form was live and shiny in the slanting moonlight. Its transparent flesh glowed faintly from the effects of cold fusion.

"The other tanks are going to break up, too, Revel," Tug murmured. "One by one. It's the helium."

"Them giant air jellies are gonna look plumb beautiful when the sun comes up," said Revel, squinting at his watch. "It'll be great publicity for Ctenophore, Inc. Did I tell you I got the papers for it drawn up?"

"No," said Tug. "Shouldn't I sign them?"

"No need for you to sign, old son," said Revel. "The Urschleim's mine, and so's the company. I'm putting you on salary! You're our chief scientist!"

"God damn it, Revel, don't play me for a sucker. I wanted stock. You knew that."

A dark figure shuffled up behind them and tapped Revel's shoulder with its metal claw. It was one of the industrial robots, carrying Revel's portable phone.

"There's a call on your phone, Mr. Pullen. From Orange County. You set the phone down earlier while you were ingesting narcotics."

"Busy, busy!" exclaimed Revel. "They must be wantin' to transfer payment for our shipment. We're in business, Tug, my man. And just to make sure there's no hard feelings, I'll pay your first year's salary in advance! Tomorrow, that is."

As Revel drew out his portable phone, another of the great metal tanks gave way, releasing a giant, toadstool-like spotted jelly. Outlined against the faint eastern sky, it was an awesome sight. The wind urged the huge quivering thing northwards, and its great stubby tentacles dragged stubbornly across the ground. Tug wished briefly that Revel were screaming in the jelly's grip instead of screaming into his telephone.

"Lost 'em?" Revel was screeching. "What the hell you mean? We shipped 'em to you, and you owe us the money for 'em. Your warehouse roof blew off? That's not my fault, is it? Well, yes, we did ship some extras. Yes, we shipped you twenty to one. We figured you'd have a high demand. So that makes it our fault? Kiss my grits!" He snapped the phone shut and scowled.

"So all the jellies in Orange County got away?" said Tug softly. "It's looking kind of bad for Ctenophore, Inc., isn't it, Revel? It's going to be tough to run that operation alone." With a roar, a third storage tank gave way like a hatching egg, releasing a moon jelly the size of an ice-skating rink. The first rays of the rising sun shimmered on its great surface. In the distance there were sirens.

In rapid succession the two remaining tanks burst open, unleashing a bell jelly and a mammoth sea nettle. A vagary of the dawn breeze swept the sea nettle towards Tug and Revel. Instead of fleeing it, Revel ran crazily towards it, bellowing in mindless anger.

Tug watched Revel for a moment too long, for now the huge sea nettle lashed out two of its dangling oral arms and snagged the both of them. Swelling its hollow gut a bit larger, the vast sea nettle rose a few hundred feet into the air, and began drifting north along Route One towards San Francisco.

By swinging themselves around and climbing frenziedly, Tug and Revel were able to find a perch together in the tangled tissues on the underside of the enormous sea nettle. The effort and the clear morning air seemed finally to have cleared Revel's head.

"We're lucky these things don't sting, eh Doc? I gotta hand it to you. Say, ain't this a hell of a ride?"

The light of the morning sun refracted wonderfully through the giant lens-like tissues of the helium-filled sea nettle.

"I wonder if we can steer it?" said Tug, feeling around in the welter of dangling jelly frills all around them. "It's be pretty cool to set down at Crissy Field right near the Golden Gate Bridge."

"If anyone can steer it, Tug, you're the man."

Using his knowledge of the jelly's basins of chaotic attraction, Tug was indeed able to adjust the giant sea nettle's pulsings so as to bring them to hover over Crissy Field's great grassy sward, right at the mouth of the San Francisco Bay, first making a low pass over the hilly streets of San Francisco. Below were thousands of people, massed to great them.

They descended lower and lower, surrounded by a buzzing pack of TV-station helicopters. Anticipating a deluge of orders for Ctenophore products, Revel phoned up Hoss Jenkins to check his Urschleim supply.

"We've got more goo than oil, Revel," shouted Hoss. "It's showin' up in all our wells and in everybody else's wells all across Texas. Turns out there wasn't nothing primeval about your slime at all. It was just a mess of those gene-splice bacteria like I told you all along. Them germs have floated down from the air jellies and are eatin' up all the oil they can find!"

"Well, keep pumping that goo! We got us a global market here! We got cold fusion happening, Hoss! Not to mention airships, my man, and self-heating housing! And that probably ain't but the half of it."

"I sure hope so, Revel! Because it looks like all the oil business left in Texas is about to turn into the flyin' jelly business. Uncle Donny Ray's asking lots of questions, Revel! I hope you're prepared for this!"

"Hell yes, I'm prepared!" Revel snapped. "I spent all my life waitin' for a chance like this! Me 'n' ol' Tug are the pioneers of a paradigm-shatterin' postindustrial revolution, and anybody who don't like it, can get in the breadlines like those no-neck numbskulls from IBM." Revel snapped the phone shut.

"What's the news, Revel?" asked Tug.

"All the oil in Texas is turning into Urschleim," said Revel. "And we're the only ones who know what to do about it. Let's land this thing and start makin' us some deals."

The giant sea nettle hovered uneasily, rippling a bit in the prop-wash of the anxious helicopters. Tug made no move to bring them lower. "There's no we and no us as long as you're talking that salary bullshit," said Tug angrily. "If you want me to bust ass and take risks in your startup, it has to be fifty-fifty down the line. I want to be fully vested! I want to be on the board! I want to call my share of the shots!"

"I'll think about it," Revel hedged.

"You better think fast, Revel." Tug looked down between his legs at the jostling crowd below. "Look at them all. You don't really know how the hell we got here or what we're doing, Revel. Are you ready to face them alone? It's nice up here in this balloon, but we can't ride a balloon forever. Sooner or later, we're gonna have to walk on our own two feet again, and look people right in the eye." He reached up into the tissues of the giant sea nettle, manipulating it.

Now the sun-baked quake-prone ground began rising up steadily again. Tattooed local hipsters billowed away from beneath them in San Francisco's trademark mélange of ecstasy and dread.

"What are you going to say to them when I land us?" demanded Tug harshly.

"Me?" Revel said, surprised. "You're the scientist! You're the one who's s'posed to explain. Just feed 'em some mathematics. Chaos equations and all that bullshit. It don't matter if they can't understand it. 'There's no such thing as bad publicity,' Tug. P. T. Barnum said that."

"P. T. Barnum wasn't in the artificial life business, Revel."

"Sure he was," said Revel, as the great jellyfish touched down. "And, okay, what the hey, if you'll stick with me and do the talkin', I'll go ahead and cut you in for fifty percent."

Tug and Revel stepped from the jellyfish and shook hands, grinning gamely, in a barrage of exploding flashbulbs.

Note on "Big Jelly" (With Bruce Sterling)

Written in 1992.
Asimov's Science Fiction, November 1994.

In May, 1992, Bruce and I were panelists at a computer conference in Monterey called the ACM SIGCHI Conference on Human Factors in Computing. At the same time, there was a big show on jellyfish at the Monterey Aquarium, and Bruce and I went and looked at the tanks together. The jellyfish made a big impression on us. So as not to be locked into the classic macho SF two-guys story mode, I tried making "my" character gay for a change.

EASY AS PIE

In a far corner of a distant galaxy spins planet X, a place quite similar to our wonderful Earth. Like Earth, X is in a planetary system with a chaoticity of six parts per million and, like Earth, X orbits its sun in the third resonance band of its planetary system's attractor.

Planet X wears a lifeweb much like our holy Gaia, mother of life. Planet X once had a living neighbor, a planet Y, but eons and eons ago, the lost inhabitants of Y mastered direct matter control—and ended by turning themselves and their planet into a great band of dust.

Each year there is a day when planet X is the furthest from its sun and the closest to the orbit of the shattered planet Y. The people of planet X call this day Xday, and they cheer themselves through it with eating, drinking and the giving of gifts.

This is the story of what happened one Xday season to a selfish peasant named Karl and to his kind, long-suffering wife Giselle.

Karl and Giselle's hut was on the outskirts of a large ugly city. As a young man, Karl had been lively and wise, but time had crusted his heart over with self-indulgence and idle lechery. With his and Giselle's children grown and gone, Karl's only remaining smiles were for dancing-girls, for smoke, and for drink.

Like many women, Giselle thought first and foremost of her family and her home. If Karl was increasingly unpleasant to live with, there were still things to be set right in their hut and, above all, there was the Xday visit of the children to prepare for.

Six weeks before Xday, Giselle began talking to Karl about the coming holiday. Karl tried to put her off with sullen grimaces and discouraging words, but Giselle kept up her happy plans and chatter. What Giselle thought, she frankly said, and now she was thinking about the holiday.

"You say we can't afford a goose, but at least we have to put up some garlands, Karl. And the hut needs to be cleaned from top to bottom."

"Oh, what for? The hut looks fine. And you didn't like the garlands I put up for you last year."

"I think that this year we'll use ivy for the garlands," continued Giselle. "Ivy will stay nice and green."

"Where are we supposed to find ivy?"

"Don't you remember? There's a big patch of ivy near the top of Summer Hill! When the children were younger, you and I used to walk there with them all the time. It's not far. Come, Karl, let's go to Summer Hill and gather ivy."

"You're always asking for something, Giselle. I'm about to go to the inn. I'll get ivy another day. Or *you* get it."

"The inn is what you love, Karl, and I don't begrudge you; you worked hard for many years. Now you're an idle red-faced lecher who stares at hussies, fine. Nobody's perfect. But come with me to Summer Hill for an hour now." Giselle smiled fetchingly at Karl and ran her gentle hand across his stubbled cheek.

"I'm not a red-faced lecher," blustered Karl.

"Then don't act like one. The inn's empty at this time of day anyway. If you go there now, you'll be a *desperate* red-faced lecher." Giselle laughed so merrily that Karl's anger was undone.

Karl and Giselle left their hut and wound their way through their neighbor's huts and up the slopes of Summer Hill. Soon there were no more dwellings. Hilltops were viewed as sacred on planet X, and all hilltops were left empty for the wind, the people, and the Gaia of X.

As they gathered ivy high on the hill, the peasant couple could see out over the great imperial city of Mur which lay to their north. In the center of Mur rose the far tiny spires of the emperor's palace. The air near the palace was enlivened by the comings and goings of the gleaming metal flying saucers that the emperor Klaatu and his court used.

Karl and Giselle had often been into the city for market day, but neither of them had ever stood directly before the imperial palace. Peasants were not much welcomed in Mur outside the market district, and a peasant who tried to walk all the way to the palace was likely to be beaten and robbed—if not by a thief then by an officer of the imperial watch.

Though his palace was off-limits to the peasants, the emperor's airships often came to claim goods from the market. Over the years many of the great silvery saucers had grown to a size of over fifty feet across—yes, *grown*. The metal saucers were living things that grew and learned and eventually died. The saucers' silver surfaces were intricately chased with filigreed coppery lines that branched and intertwined as a saucer grew. No two saucers were the quite same. With exercise, polishing, and plenty of sunshine, a flying saucer could grow for many

433

a year, perhaps as much as two centuries. When a saucer got quite old, its skin would thin out to nothingness and the whole thing would suddenly crumble into a drifting dust like mushroom spores.

Where did the saucers come from? They spawned on the ribs of planet X herself. Every few years in some deep cave of planet X—and never twice the same cave—a few baby saucers would be found stuck to the walls like limpets. All saucers that were found became the property of the Klaatu dynasty. And the finder—invariably a hardy young peasant—would be granted imperial favor, a purse of gold, and the rank of baroness or baronet.

The sages of planet X classified the saucers as Spore Magic. Spore Magic included all the inexplicable events that had puzzled the citizens of X throughout history. The fact was that very odd things happened regularly on planet X—especially around Xday.

When the bright shape came flying down at Karl and Giselle on Summer Hill, they may have thought for an instant that it was a saucer—but it was a goose with snowy white plumage and a wedge-shaped orange beak. The goose stood there on her orange webbed feet, curving her neck this way and that, looking at Karl and Giselle. Finally she began slowly to waddle about, pecking up snails from beneath the ivy.

"Catch the goose, Karl," exclaimed Giselle. "We can eat her on Xday!"

Karl was reluctant. The goose looked alert and powerful. Karl didn't much fancy being pecked, clawed, and wing-beaten by the beast. "Why can't our Xday meal be turnips like it is every other day?" said Karl. "Leave the goose alone, Giselle. They'll have goose at the inn on Xday in any case. If I happen to go there, I can bring a wing home for you."

"Selfish old fool," said Giselle. "*I'll* catch the goose."

Giselle marched towards the plump white bird. Far from looking alarmed, the goose looked interested. She stuck her neck up to full height and regarded Giselle. The goose had shiny blue eyes. Giselle made feeding motions with her fingers, though she had no food to give. "Nice goosey loosey goosey girl," sang Giselle. "Goose, goose, goose!"

The goose honked, and when Giselle turned and walked away from her, the goose followed. When Karl, Giselle and goose were down among the huts, the goose willingly jumped into Giselle's arms and let herself be carried back to the peasant couple's hut.

Giselle cut a turnip into small bits and fed them to the goose, who gobbled them down avidly, stretching out her neck to swallow each morsel. Before letting the goose go outside, Giselle tied a heavy stone to one of the goose's legs. Slowly dragging the stone, the goose waddled about the yard, contentedly rooting for slugs, bugs, and snails.

"What a beautiful bird, Karl!" exclaimed Giselle. "We'll fatten her till the day before Xday, and then you can butcher and bleed her for me. I'll pluck, singe, draw, and cook her! We'll have goose for Xday! The children will be thrilled!"

"I hope Tolstan, the cook at the inn, can help me with the butchering," grumbled Karl. "I don't know anything about killing a goose. Yes, I'd better go talk to Tolstan."

"That's fine, Karl, but before you go off to the inn, I still want you to help me put up the ivy."

"Will you never be done, woman?" cried old Karl, but help with the ivy he did, and only then, finally, could he go to the inn to smoke and drink and stare at women until it was time to totter home and fall into his and Giselle's bed.

In the coming days, the goose became more and more Giselle's pet. The goose quickly found a way to free her foot from the rope and stone, and could easily have flown away—but she chose not to. At every hour of the day she was inside or outside the peasant couple's hut. When Giselle was active in the hut, the goose would honk plaintively until Giselle would pull aside the hut's wicker door and let the goose in. Once in the hut, the goose delighted in following Giselle, who often fed the goose scraps. The goose liked meat as well as vegetables, indeed she would even eat small pebbles and pieces of wood. Not that the goose was going hungry—the more time she spent in the hut, the more snails and bugs there seemed to be on the hut's floor. Giselle noticed that, for a special wonder, the goose seemed to know not to foul the floor, no matter how much she ate.

A few days later, Karl was due to pay off his quarterly debt at the inn. He and Giselle dug their small bag of savings out from under a stone at the back of the hearth. There was no way to reach the hoard without getting ashes all over oneself, which was the peasant couple's way of being sure that neither of them dipped into the savings alone.

The small leather bag held some silver and copper coins saved from Karl's occasional earnings, along with sixteen gold coins that remained from the inheritance which Giselle's parents had left her several years before. Ever since Giselle got her inheritance, Karl had worked as little as possible. He thought of Giselle's money as his own.

As was their custom, Karl and Giselle spread the coins out on the table and counted them together, a ritual they went through each time the coins appeared from beneath the stones of the hearth. The goose stood next to the table, watching with glittering eyes.

"Let me take a gold coin to the inn," wheedled Karl when they were done counting. "Then I'll have credit clear into the spring."

"Very well," said Giselle. "And I'll take a gold coin to spend on gifts for the children."

"One silver coin would be more than enough for them, woman!" snapped Karl. "The children are grown; they should take care of themselves!"

"It's my gold, Karl. You should be grateful that I'm so foolishly generous to you."

"Then I get some coppers as well," shouted Karl. "I earned the copper and silver in the turnip harvest this fall!" Giselle nodded curtly, and slid two gold coins and three coppers to one side of the table. Leaning forward, the two peasants began telling the remaining coins back into the bag.

But now all at once the goose darted forward and gulped down the two gold coins, pumping her neck to get the hard metal disks all the way down from craw to crop to gizzard.

"No, Goosey!" cried Giselle.

"Grab her," said Karl, drawing his knife. "I'll cut her open!" The goose made a frightened noise like a rusty metal hinge, and waddled rapidly out of Karl's reach.

"Stop, Karl!" cried Giselle. "She can't digest gold. The coins are safe in her stomach. It's still four days until Xday. If we butcher Goosey now, her meat will spoil."

"What if she shits the coins into the street?"

"I'll make a nest for her inside our hut," said Giselle. "Anyway, haven't you noticed? Goosey never shits. She just grows."

"Well, nobody's taking any *more* of our gold," snapped Karl. He pocketed his three coppers, swept the remaining coins into the little sack, tied the sack tight, and crawled into the hearth to bury the sack again. "The inn's coin and the children's presents will have to wait until your precious goose is ready," he told Giselle. And then Karl went down to the inn to spend his coppers.

The next morning, Giselle found four gold coins in the nest beneath the goose. She bit them and rang them, they seemed true as any coin. Karl, waking late, sat up blinking to stare at Giselle. "What's happened?"

"The goose, Karl! She turned our two coins into four!"

"What!" The old peasant sprang out of bed to see. Four bright coins lay in Giselle's dainty hand.

"Give me my two," demanded Karl.

"You get *one*, Karl," said Giselle and gave it to him. "I'll keep one for the children, and I'll feed these other two to Goosey to see if it works again! Then we'll have *four* extra gold coins! Here, Goosey!"

Karl watched excitedly as the goose ate two gold coins from Giselle's hand. He stayed in the hut at Giselle's side all day, and finally, near dusk, the goose gave a warbling honk and rose to her feet. Gold glittered from the goose's nest—and this time it was not just four coins, it was a heap that Karl feverishly counted as seventeen coins! Their fortune had more than doubled in one day!

Karl snatched up two gold coins for his own and hurried off to the inn, leaving Giselle to hide the new treasure. Once at the inn, Karl behaved very foolishly: he got drunk and began bragging about his white goose that laid golden coins. One of the emperor's soldiers happened to hear him, and the next morning Karl awoke from his sodden slumber to hear Giselle arguing with someone while angry Goosey made her rusty hinge sound.

"It's just an ordinary goose," Giselle was saying. "We caught her on Summer Hill."

"The goose may be Spore Magic," came the stranger's voice. "I'm here to claim her for the emperor."

Any miracle that might be as valuable as the flying saucers was called Spore Magic. And, by ancient imperial decree, all Spore Magic was the property of the Klaatu dynasty.

Goosey came running to the corner of the hut where Karl lay. *If the goose is Spore Magic like the saucers*, thought Karl, *then the emperor will grant imperial favor to the one who brings her to him*. Karl grabbed Goosey in his arms and went out to face the stranger.

It was a young knight of the emperor's guard, smartly dressed in flowing silks and furs. One of the emperor's flying saucers rested in the dirt of the peasants' yard; the saucer was a young twenty-footer, still but lightly filigreed. All the peasants from the neighborhood had gathered, or were still gathering, to watch. None of the emperor's saucers had ever landed here before, and none of the peasants had ever been inside a saucer.

"I will come with you to bring the goose to the palace," said Karl, his voice trembling at the enormity of the proposal.

"No, Karl," cried Giselle. "The goose is mine. And I fed her two more coins this morning."

"Silence," said Karl. "We cannot argue with the emperor. I will bring the goose to him, and he will grant me imperial favor. He will give me a bag of gold and the rank of baronet. Have a care, woman!" Karl held the goose tight and stepped away from Giselle.

The young knight looked at Karl doubtfully, but then said, "Very well. Carry the goose into the ship, peasant. But don't touch anything. You're filthy and you stink."

437

The inside of the saucer was of smooth silvery metal delicately veined with copper. There was a bulge in the wall that made a bench that ran all around the circular cabin. As well as the open arch of the cabin door, there were round, open portholes ranged along the walls. So as not to sully the fine fabric of the cushions on the seats, old Karl sat on the floor with Goosey cradled securely his arms.

The knight controlled the saucer's flight simply by talking to it. "Fly back to the courtyard of Emperor Klaatu's palace," said the knight, and the saucer lifted into the air. Wind whistled through the open door and portholes. The view was dizzying. What with the uneasiness in his stomach from last night's debauch, it was too much for Karl, and as the ship turned to angle down to the emperor's palace, he vomited between his legs onto the floor. Goosey pecked at the vomit.

"You cursed old fool," cried the young knight, and favored Karl with a sharp kick in the ribs. Karl endured the abuse with no complaint. At least he had now flown in one of the emperor's airships.

The saucer landed in the palace's walled courtyard. The knight called for a scullion to clean up Karl's mess, then led Karl across the courtyard and into the palace. Still clutched in Karl's arms, the goose turned her head this way and that, watching everything with her clear, blue-irised eyes.

The emperor Klaatu was a small bald man with a dark beard and a penetrating gaze. Sitting at the emperor's side was his fool, or minister, a fat clean-shaven man with a loose smile.

"Is this is the goose that lays golden coins?" demanded the emperor.

"Yes, sire," said Karl. "And I freely bring her to you. Will you grant me imperial favor?"

"Favor?" asked the emperor.

"A purse of gold," said Karl. "And I should like to be made a baronet. I could rule my neighborhood in the name of the empire. Even my wife would have to obey me." He bowed low and set the goose down on the floor at the emperor's feet.

The goose gave a rusty honk, waggled her bottom, and squeezed out a foul-smelling puddle that resembled Karl's vomit.

"I'm to grant a baronetage for goose-droppings?" roared the emperor. The fool, or minister, cuffed Karl on the head, and the knight screamed for a scullion to clean up the mess.

"I think you have to feed the goose gold coins first," stammered Karl. "She needs gold to make gold. She shits out copies of whatever you feed her. Do you have a coin you can feed her, sire? Or a large gem?"

"Oh, so I'm to give you jewels as well as gold?" cried the emperor. "Knight, lock this charlatan and his goose in the dungeon. If the goose lays no gold by tomorrow, then put them both to death. I'll have the goose roasted with turnips."

"Oh, wait, please wait," cried Karl, as all his courage fled from him. "If you want gold from the goose then you should cut her open right away. She still hasn't shit out the two coins my wife fed her this morning." The goose gave Karl a startled look as the peasant caught hold of her.

"Go on," Karl begged the knight, stretching out the goose on the floor with her neck in his left hand and her feet in his right. "Cut the goose in half with your sword, sir knight. Cut right where she's the fattest. I know there's gold in her. Take the gold and flog me and set me free. Please spare me, my lords, as it is nearly Xday. I thought the goose was Spore Magic. I meant no harm."

The emperor nodded to the knight, and the knight brought his razor sharp sword down on Goosey's back, quite severing her breast and head from her feet and tail. What a shriek the poor goose gave!

Instead of gushing blood, the cut surfaces of the goose's body were damp but firm, with the consistency and color of a ripe avocado. In the center of each surface was a hemispherical depression: Goosey was hollow at the center, hollow as an avocado without a pit. From the two halves of the cut-open cavity there oozed onto the stone floor a shiny fluid that quickly hardened into a puddle of gold.

Karl had let go of the goose as the sword struck. Now the goose's rear section rocked back and began waddling around on its feet, while the front section settled its flat cut surface onto the floor and began honking and beating its wings. As the seconds passed, the rear section bulged up its top surface to grow a new breast, neck and head. At the same time, the front half of the goose rose slowly up onto a fresh-grown belly and legs. The flesh and feathers of the geese flowed and shifted as these transformations happened, so that the two new geese were each of half the weight of the original goose, with each new goose being about four-fifths the original size.

One of the geese hopped onto the emperor's lap, and the other one waddled over to Karl.

"You…you see!" blustered the peasant. "The goose is Spore Magic. And look!" He leaned forward and pried the golden, somewhat vomit-reeking, puddle off the floor and presented it to the emperor. "Here is your gold, sire. Now please let me go home. My family needs me for Xday. Oh please, sire, let me go to them. I love them so."

"Very well," said the emperor. "But I will keep both of the magic geese. And you shall receive no gold, nor any baronetage. You have tried my patience too sorely."

So Karl spent Xday with his family, laughing and feasting on a roast goose—which Giselle bought from a poultry dealer. So relieved was he to be alive, that old Karl opened up his heart to his loved ones as never before—and the good feelings lasted on through the rest of the year.

And the emperor? The emperor grew ever richer as he ran the contents of the royal treasury over and over through the bodies of his ever-growing flock of repeatedly subdivided magic geese, who stayed with him for a whole year. But on the eve of the next Xday, the geese herded the emperor, and all his family, and all his court, into the emperor's flying saucers and flew them away forever—easy as pie. With no more emperors, Planet X became a more sacred place.

Hail Gaia, full of synchronicity, the universe is with thee. Blessed art though amongst dynamical systems, and blessed are thy strange attractors. Holy Gaia, mother of life, pray for us sinners, now and at the hour of our death, Amen.

Note on "Easy As Pie"

Written in 1993.
Christmas Forever, Tor Books, 1993.

I've always loved the classic fairy tales, and this is a retake on one of them. I wrote this for a volume of Christmas stories.

THE ANDY WARHOL SANDCANDLE (WITH MARC LAIDLAW)

Carlo the homeless artist was walking on the beach late one day in February with a tinfoil pipe and the last crumbs of a sinsemilla bud in the pouch of his sweatshirt when a family of tourists came strolling up the beach snapping electronic strobe pictures of the crashing majestic sea. Against the dazzling orange luster of the failing sunset and the crazy backwards arching gyrations of the foam flecks seemingly caught—imprisoned!—in the harsh thyristor beams, the Flintstones-like family seemed not only ludicrous but offensive, threatening all the peaceful possibilities of this beach, spoiling the end of Carlo's hard-worked, wasted day. On impulse he seized a gnarled log of salt-sodden driftwood and waved it over his head like a caveman's club (not that any caveman, probably, would have been so aware of the club's contours as Carlo, who was wondering helplessly, as he approached the brightly clad middle Americans, if the club mightn't be buffed to a fine sheen, blow-torched ever so slightly to enhance the natural weathering, coated with varnish, and sold at the weekly Surf City flea market), and bore down screaming on all the kith and kin and ilk and issue of Farmer Brown-shirt, which redoubtable gentlemen gracefully sidestepped Carlo's mad plunge, plucked the weapon from his impassioned grasp, and coolly laid a dam across Carlo's raging, stoned, grandiose stream of consciousness.

As a Surf City taxpayer—he paid sales tax, didn't he?—Carlo had every theoretical right to expect the police to take his side, but no, no, no, not with pot in his pocket. The voters of Surf City had recently approved an initiative to become a DFZ, or "Drug-Free Zone."

Carlo's fourteen-year-old pick-up truck was impounded and auctioned off; everything in the back (oxyacetylene torches, cans of resin, and miscellaneous clock parts and brass pencil-holder inserts) was stolen while the truck sat in the police parking lot. His driver's license was suspended, and he was sentenced to either thirty days in jail or a "diversion program," which meant thirty twelve-step meetings in thirty days, to be followed by six months of piss tests, with a missed meeting or a dirty test meaning you had to do the thirty days in jail after all. Not that Carlo was planning to do any of that. No fixed address—how would they find him? And who would really care? They'd already gotten the only thing of value Carlo had owned: his truck. Losing the truck rankled.

"It's your fault!" Carlo screamed at his female partner Dina, as they sat eating someone's abandoned wet nachos in the rain-splattered gale wailing up from the beach through the cement arches of the Taco Patio. He was acting out his anger over losing his truck. Carlo and Dina had been living together for several months in the cab of that pickup, and now they had nowhere to go. "Schizos shouldn't be allowed to vote! What'd you give for your address anyway? My truck's license plate number?"

Dina had just confessed to Carlo that, standing dizzily in the voting booth, addled by the clouds of winged ants around the ceiling-mounted track lights—the winged ants that only Dina could see—well, she'd confused "DFZ" with "DMZ," and then remembered "NFZ," which meant Nuclear-Free Zone, like Oakland, or was that some kind of car? NFX? Anyway, she'd voted for it.

"Shut up, big deal, Carlo, it was just one vote. Don't yell at me or I'll kick you in the balls. Maybe the rehab meetings would be good for you. I mean if you get so torn up that you go try to club Barney and Wilma on the beach down there—it's not realistic."

"Don't try to get out of it, Dina. You voted for the DFZ and got me into this mess. *You* should go to the twelve-step meetings, not me. You'd like it. You know there's gonna be plenty of messed-up well-off guys in the program all hot to meet a down and outer like you. They'll take you home like a lost kitten, baby. You and them can work the steps."

"You're in heavy denial, Carlo. You need rehab. Drugs and alcohol have ruined your life. The Great American Artist. Riiiight. I mean, look at you."

The tip of Carlo's tongue was bloody and swollen from where he'd bitten it while gobbling down the warm food they'd given him in jail, and now he'd opened the wound again on the pointy end of a nacho chip. He was wearing polyester slacks, four T-shirts and a sweatshirt with a pouch and a hood. His thinning blonde hair was in long knotted tangles, and his flushed broken-veined face was covered with greasy scraps of beard. He had a white bandage wrapped around his head from where the tourist had clubbed him.

"Look at me? Shit, Dina, look at *you*."

Much of Dina's face was hidden by her lank shoulder-length hair, but you could see that her sallow skin was drawn painfully tight over her sharp nose and high cheekbones. In the chill wind, her thin shoulders hunched forward over her flat chest. Like Carlo, she was dressed in a Goodwill outfit—three pairs of torn pantyhose and a beige sweater topped by a green polyester jumper. While talking to Carlo, Dina's head kept scanning from left to right; she was always on the alert against the approach of winged ants.

"Look, Dina," said Carlo cruelly. He held up one of the nachos they were eating. "Look in the cheese sauce. See those little flecks? How the light glints on them? It's like tiny insect wings. I wonder if…if maybe…"

Dina's mouth made a compulsive tic-like twist as she shoved the food off the table. "Winged ants," she compulsively muttered in a low deep voice quite unlike her girlish speaking voice. "Winged ants get outta here." She rose to her feet and stalked stiff-legged out of the Taco Patio.

"Where you going? Hey! Wait up, Dina, where you going?"

"Away from you," snarled Dina, but she waited for Carlo to catch up with her.

"I been thinking about where we can sleep, Dina," said Carlo. "With my truck gone. Let's panhandle for awhile so's I can get a bottle and then I'll take you to this new bunk I know of."

"Is it the shelter?"

"No, man, it's casual. It's Sally Durban's old house. The house is wide open because the windows are out and they're still re—re—"

"Rehabilitating it," said Dina. "Yeah." She put herself in the path of a passerby. "Spare change, mister? Can you spare some change?"

The man shook his head and tried to go on his way, but Dina was persistent. "It's me and my husband, sir, we just got into town and we're looking for work. The church shelter is full up tonight. See, I'm pregnant and he don't speak English." She paused and rubbed the back of her hand against her eyes, still tagging after the guy. "Please please help us, sir. If you don't have change, a dollar will do. Or if you got any jobs need doing—I mean, in trade for food or shelter."

That did it. He shoved a wadded single in her hand.

"God bless you, sir!"

"Gracias," added Carlo.

In a half hour, they had enough for a bottle of Night Train, three Slim Jims and a pack of Basic Menthol. They walked away from the lights along the gently curved streets that followed the edge of the sea.

"Who was Sally Durban?" asked Dina. "I don't remember."

"Aging speedfreak, big old house, right on the cliffs? Remember, she jumped off her deck at dawn a couple of years ago? Speed kills—too true. Sally was in with Andy Warhol in the Seventies; she was in one of his movies called *Surf Boy*. I told you about her."

Dina shrugged. "I sort of remember. Andy Warhol the artist. We were talking about him the other day. You saw something on TV. You said Andy was your hero. Didn't you tell me you actually saw *Surf Boy*?"

"I saw it at Sally Durban's house. She used to play it all the time, over and over and over. Like, it was all she had left from her glory days. She'd have young surfers in there, tryin' to make it with them. I partied with her the night before she died, matter of fact. I'd heard about the scene, and I told her I was a surfer too. It was a good party. Sally threw down a whole ounce of crank. Yaaar." No cars were around, so Carlo unscrewed the cap of the Night Train and took a good slug. Dina lit a Basic Menthol.

"You ever surf, Carlo?"

"Sure, baby, you know I do. You can't grow up here and not surf. Maybe I'll get a board this summer. I'll teach you how to surf too. Yeah. We'll lay out in the sun and get healthy."

"I liked it better in the desert," Dina said. "Except that the ants were there."

"The beach is the place for a skanky sister like you, Dina. Salt-water kills infections. You can live forever on the beach."

Dina answered him with a sneeze that ended in a deep, barking cough that went on and on.

The Sally Durban house sat on an iceplant-covered cliff above the ocean, its seaward decks cantilevered out over the void. The house had stood empty since her death. A developer had bought it cheap and started to fix it up, but then he'd gone broke, leaving the deserted house open to the night, with nothing but plastic sheeting covering the busted-out windows. The plastic flapped unpleasantly in the cold wind, flapped like the wings of the angel of death, flapped like a shroud wanting to twine itself around and around Dina's face. "Durban" was like "turban" was like wrapped around your head.

"I don't wanna go in there, Carlo."

"It's okay. Come on. There's none of your ants in there."

"They're not *my* ants!"

"I swear it's safe."

Dina put her arms up across her face and let Carlo lead her in. There seemed to be voices in the house. Or were there?

"Is anyone else here, Carlo?"

"Might be. We're not the only free spirits in Surf City, baby."

But, no, they found no other life in the house, and the sounds like voices were only the barks of seals out on a rock in the sea. The house was cluttered; Sally Durban had left her estate in such a confused mess that not even all of her personal belongings had ever been removed, though by now most of the stuff had been stolen or vandalized. Carlo and Dina found their way to a windowless room downstairs.

"This will be the warmest," said Carlo. "And nobody can see us in here." They ate their Slim Jims, Carlo drank some more of the wine, and Dina chain-smoked Basic Menthols. Dina didn't drink alcohol, which was one of the best things about her as far as Carlo was concerned. It was too big a hassle to have a woman fighting you over drinks all the time. It wasn't worth having a girlfriend like that. By way of evening things out, Carlo didn't smoke.

The wind keened, the surf crashed and the seals barked. Whenever Dina lit another cigarette, Carlo would look at her face in the flare of the matches. She looked young and pretty. If it hadn't been for the throbbing in his head, he would have put a move on her. But there was still half a bottle of wine.

"Why would somebody have a windowless room in a house with an ocean view?" Dina wondered.

"This was Sally Durban's movie room," said Carlo. "Give me the matches."

"Don't burn 'em all."

"Okay. Now look. I think—" Carlo lit a match and held it high. One end of the room had a little hole in the wall with a door next to it. "Yeah. She kept the projector in there, with *Surf Boy* on it. That's the door into the projection room."

"Maybe the film and projector are still in there," said Dina. "I'd like to see it. I ain't seen a movie in two, three years, Carlo. They got ants in those big theaters, you know."

"No ants in here, Dina."

"Go on and see if the movie's still there!" said Dina.

"Dina, if it had been, somebody would of ripped it off long ago."

"How do you know? Go see. I got a feeling."

"No."

"Come on, Carlo. Do this for me."

Carlo struggled to his feet and tugged at the knob of the projection room door. It was locked and it wouldn't open.

"Kick it in, Carlo!"

He tried a kick, but he caught the angle wrong and fell over onto his side.

"Fuck that. I could hurt myself."

445

"You let me down again, Carlo," Dina said miserably, in the dark.

Carlo was trying to think of an answer, one that would make him feel better for failing the small mission, when he saw something sticking out of a pile of junk in the corner, something yellow and shapely nestled in the debris. Dina was inhaling hard on her cigarette; it gave an orange glow. He got to his knees and crawled over. "Light another match," he said, and shoved his hand into the pile. It was carpet scraps and broken glass and wood chips and tangled wire, but there was something else in there as well.

"Holy shit," he said. Under his fingers, a waxy surface, rough as sandpaper. He hauled it out in the brief flare of light, and held it toward Dina.

"A candle," she said. "Great."

She held the match toward the wick, but Carlo jerked the candle away. "What're you doing?"

"It's a candle! I'm gonna light it!"

"No way, Dina—this isn't no ordinary candle. This is—I know this candle!"

The match went out.

"Light another one, I gotta see it," said Carlo.

"Not unless you're gonna light that candle."

"You don't understand—this is Andy's candle. Andy Warhol's. It's probably worth a fortune. It was Sally's treasure. I can't believe it's here."

"Who'd take it? It's just an old sandcandle."

"But if we could prove it…we could sell it to a museum or something."

"How're you going to do that unless you light it and get a look at it?"

"Shit…okay. Light it, then. It's big enough, we'll only burn a little."

"You sure?"

"Fuck, just go ahead, all right?"

Dina struck another match, touched it to the wick, and a warm glow spread around the candle. It was cast from lime-green wax in the shape of a cauldron with three stumpy little legs and a single central wick. Tiny shells, fragments of abalone and mussel, were pressed into the sides, making a border. Carlo held it up, examining the bottom and sides.

"Did he sign it?" Dina asked.

"Doesn't look like it. But people know—they'd remember, old friends of Sally Durban's. She told everybody about this candle. She, uh…" But then he started to remember how everybody at that party, the last one she'd thrown, how they'd really doubted everything she said. Old Sally Durban was sort of a joke to the kids; all they cared about was the drugs she spread around. Andy Warhol wasn't a name that meant much to them

Carlo was the exception; he was an artist. He idolized Andy, and was one of the few people eager to watch the endless hours of Surf Boy. Sally had shown him the candle, knowing it would mean something to him, handling it like some kind of Holy Grail, though it was just the most ordinary sort of sandcandle and there was no way to distinguish it from any number of other sandcandles.

Carlo himself had made sandcandles when he was a kid, on the hot beach in the summer. Surf City locals held a huge candlemaking party every August, boiling up enormous aluminum vats of paraffin over firepits dug in the sand, stirring the bubbling white sludge with oars. You'd dig a hole in the sand, poke little protrusions for legs, line the mold with seaweed and shells and stones, like Andy had. You'd tie the wick to a bit of driftwood and lay the driftwood across the hole with the wick dangling into the mold. Then you'd borrow a ladle from the man who tended the wax pots; you'd scoop up as much wax as the ladle held, add a few drops of coloring and maybe even scent, then run fast across the sand before the molten liquid cooled, to pour it in your little mold. Then you waited, waited interminably, afraid to touch it, to mar the smooth waxy surface; sometimes you waited an hour, just to be safe. And when you finally dared, you dug your hands in around the candle, and lifted it out, and all the loose sand fell away, leaving just the shape you'd created, cast in colored wax, the sides embedded with sand and shells.

It was hard to finally burn a sandcandle, to see someone's unique art sizzle up into smoke. Right now the wax on Andy Warhol's sandcandle was melting into a widening pool around the base of the wick, making Carlo panic. The candle had never been lit at all until tonight. He felt a weird queasiness, a kind of regret, at the thought that he was burning Andy Warhol's sandcandle; and then a similar sense of loss at the realization that he would never be able to prove what it was. What a pipedream, to think a museum would ever believe his story; to think this might be auctioned off by Sotheby's for a million bucks.

"Nice light," Dina said. "Andy Warhol's sandcandle."

Her words cooled his spirit, somehow. "Yeah," he said. "It is nice."

The light, not the candle, was the main thing, wasn't it? Would Andy have wanted Sally Durban to keep the candle forever, or would he have wanted her to burn it?

Dina took the candle, carefully, as if she knew everything going through Carlo's head. She set it on the ledge of the little window where the projector beam used to come through.

It's a big candle, Carlo thought calmly. *It won't hurt to burn it for just a little while. The light is nice.*

447

He tapped the wall beneath the projector hole. "Come here, Dina. Bring the wine." She lay down beside him, under the candle. They watched it shine on the other wall, the glow swaying up and down, back and forth, as if they were riding a ship.

"Yeah," he said. "This is good. Snuggle up, baby, it's getting cold. All right."

They were watching the wall as the candle began to flicker, that rhythmic strobing that candles sometimes get, a pulse so deep and regular that it could trigger an epileptic fit. Carlo glanced over and saw Dina spacing out, with her glassy eyes fixed on the wall. He turned to see what she was looking at.

In the dark there, with the muffled noises of the stormy ocean night, with the wine and the schizophrenia, Carlo and Dina did start to see the movie, yes, *Surf Boy* was playing on the wall; that was the flicker. In black and white, the cliffs of Surf City. Surf Boy coming out of the water looking like Carlo, but healthy. And well-fed Surf Girl right there with him, looking like a shimmering silver Dina.

"Yaaar," said Carlo.

Then the picture cut to an airplane landing at Kennedy. Carlo and Dina were in a cab, with Carlo telling the driver, "Take us to Andy Warhol's Factory."

The cabby jerked into traffic, and the whole sky seemed to pulse and dance like a flame. And now Surf Boy Carlo and Surf Girl Dina were getting out of the cab on a city street, on 231 East 47th Street according to the streetsign in the background and to the numbers on the buildings. Carlo handed the cabbie a spectral twenty.

As they walked towards the building, a man in black shades, leather pants and coat came out and looked at them as if he knew them. And why shouldn't he? He was Andy's cameraman, Gerard Malanga, and Carlo and Dina were Surf Boy and Surf Girl, superstars of one of Andy's underground Pop classic films.

"It's five flights up," said Malanga, holding the door open to let them in before he walked off down the dirty boulevard.

Carlo and Dina went on in. The elevator was an open cage, a freight elevator.

"I ain't getting in there," said Dina. "The shaft's gonna be full of flying ants."

"No it isn't, Dina. We don't wanna walk no five flights. Come the hell on."

They got into the clanking groaning elevator and rode it up to the fifth floor. On the way some weird shit happened to their images. Like down at street level they'd been Surf Boy and Surf Girl with only a sketchy resemblance to Carlo and Dina. But now each floor going up was like two years of hard street-time, and their bodies were shriveling and catching back up. By the time they got to the fifth floor, they looked their realtime Surf City ghost-house selves.

Carlo glanced away from the screen a moment and looked at Dina sitting next to him. The room flickered heavily. Outside the ocean crashed, spitting out sibilant words in all the languages of nature; and chorused against the ocean was the barking of the seals. Wild shit was coming down tonight. There was still a nice third of a bottle of Night Train left. Grinning happily, Carlo drew some long slugs out of it, and turned his attention back to the movie that Andy Warhol's sandcandle was painting on the wall.

The elevator door clanked open, and Carlo and Dina stepped into a huge open room with aluminum foil pasted on the walls and aluminum paint spraypainted onto the pipes. Little pieces of mirror were stuck up everywhere.

There were about ten people in the big room, scattered here and there; closest to Carlo and Dina were a couple of high-school kids typing; at a table beyond them was a man scissoring out articles from the newspaper; through a far door in the corner you could see a drag-queen down on her knees sucking the cock of a laughing greaser hustler in a rolled-up T-shirt and unzipped leather pants. Through a wall there was X-ray-visible a cramped little photography darkroom studio with a scraggley drug-bum called Billy Name cooking and shooting hits out of a big plastic baggie of crystal meth, Billy in there with two queens and a fashion-model. In another corner of the big room, a projector was running, spewing endless unwatched reels of images onto the wall.

"Yaaar," said Carlo. "The darkroom for me,"

"Don't go in the dark for speed," said Dina. "I want to stay here where it's light. I want to look out the window."

Sitting near the window was a man in dark shades, a surfer-looking guy in a T-shirt with wide horizontal blue and white stripes, the dude just hanging there and blending into everything. Only when Carlo and Dina got close to him did Carlo flash on his bad skin and silver-dyed hair; only then did Carlo flash that it was the King of Pop.

"Hi, Andy," said Carlo.

Andy looked at Carlo and Dina, his mouth open a little, Andy just blending into everything, waiting to see what else they would say. Next to him facing away from the elevator was a big canvas; it was a painting of a sailboat with the picture divided up into color regions and with numbers written inside the regions. The paint was fresh and wet; a palette sat next to the canvas. By now Dina, too, realized who they were talking to.

"We just got here from California," said Dina. "Do you have a cigarette?"

"Okay," said Andy, and gave Dina a Kent. "What do you do that's fabulous?"

"I see winged ants," said Dina, staring at Andy's paint-by-numbers canvas. "Did you buy this with the pattern already on it?"

"That would be so great," said Andy. "But you can't get paint-by-numbers canvases this big. I draw the pattern and the numbers myself. And now I'm having fun deciding which ones to color in and which ones to leave blank. What's your favorite color?"

"Stained glass," said Dina. "Did you know Jesus was a winged ant? You should do a paint-by-numbers picture of Jesus on the cross."

"Wow," said Andy, "I bet Gerard could get paint-by-numbers canvases from Puerto Rico. I could make a silk-screen of a Puerto Rican Crucifixion and blow it up and then I could paint it over and over again. I need to make silk screens for these sailboats, too. I like for things to be the same. Because the more you look at the same exact thing, the more the meaning goes away, and the better and emptier you feel."

"Yo," said Carlo, wanting to get his share of Andy's attention. "Yo Andy! Carlo here. I'm an artist."

Andy was silent for moment, and Carlo could hear the steady traffic down on 47th Street—Carlo could hear someone jiggling the toilet lever, the sound of an oscillating fan stirring sheets of colored gelatin, the lighting of a match, the scissors, the water running over the prints in Billy Name's darkroom, the men having sex in the back room—here in Sally Durban's projection room, with the sandcandle lit, Carlo could hear Andy's Factory. "You look like a nutso wino speedfreak to me," said Andy, giving Carlo a bitchy once-over. "The speed's in the darkroom. Billy Name can help you get loaded."

Carlo did a fast-forward montage sequence of jabbering and shooting meth like a maniac with skinny Billy Name and a bunch of queens, debs, and hustlers. And then he was flaked out on a couch with Dina next to him, and pacing around in front of them was a Times Square hustler named Victor, holding forth about his "pleasure palette," which was a tray with seventeen little jars with seventeen different kinds of lubricants like Vaseline and KY. Meanwhile one of the high-school typists was manning the record-player, playing this summer's hit: The Lovin' Spoonful, "Summer in the City".

Andy was standing next to a movie camera on a tripod which Gerard Malanga was setting up to point at Carlo and Dina. "Talk about the winged ants, Dina," said Andy.

"I see them out of the corners of my eyes, mostly," said Dina. "Ever since I was a teenager. They can be big or small—I've seen them be as big as starships or as small as protons."

"What do they look like?" asked Andy. "Are they colorful?"

"Yeah, the wings are like stained glass sometimes, and sometimes they're shiny all colors like oil on the street or like a rainbow. The wings are long and bright and the bodies are bumpy dark things like ants. They can bite."

"Do they bite you a lot?" While talking to Dina, Andy was moving around. Now he was over at the freight elevator fooling with it.

"They bite my eyes and my private areas and most of all they bite the back of my neck. They reach in through my skin to do things to my nerves," said Dina, getting a bit agitated as she warmed to her topic. "But they don't like cigarette smoke. That's one way to keep them off me."

"Can you see any ants right now?" asked Andy. He'd gotten the elevator door open, even though the elevator cabin was at the bottom of the shaft. "Come over here, Dina, and look down the empty shaft. I think I might see some ants in there."

"Don't, Dina," warned Carlo, jittering there on the couch next to Victor. "You might fall in."

"The ants love you, Dina," said Andy. "Come look at them. Have you guessed where they come from?"

So Dina walked over to the shaft, with the camera filming her all the while, and Andy whispered something to her, just the right freaky thing, and sure enough Dina flipped out and jumped into the shaft screaming.

In a flash Carlo was up off the couch running. He threw a shoulder into skinny Andy, knocking him into the shaft after Dina, with Carlo tumbling on in after Andy.

The inside of the shaft was flickering like a big strobe light, and it seemed to Carlo as if Andy turned into a giant winged ant, trying to fly back out. But falling Carlo pushed the Andy ant all the way down onto fallen Dina.

Dina and Carlo slept late into the morning. Carlo woke to what he thought was the sound of footsteps, though when he sat up, the house was quiet, save for the waves and the wind.

Carlo touched his head gingerly, trying to remember details of the night before; and then he thought of the sandcandle. He opened the dark, windowless room's door to get some light, and saw that up in its little projection niche, the Andy Warhol sandcandle had completely burned down. There was nothing left but a gritty puddle of hardened wax and a few black crumbs from the dying of the wick.

"It's gone!" cried Carlo in real grief. "Dina, we burned Andy's sandcandle all up!"

Dina answered with a fit of coughing. Her hands were trembling, knuckles white. Finally the fit passed and she lowered her hands.

"About last night," said Carlo. "The sandcandle...you saw Andy, right?"

"It was like a movie at first, and then it was a dream," she said. "But I knew we were both dreaming it together. At the end we were falling down an elevator shaft. I looked up at you, Carlo. Andy looked like a big flying ant, like a Jesus angel with stained glass in his wings."

Carlo felt a sudden shudder in his guts. He hadn't shit in three days, but today he had to go. He went out the back door of the house, and scrambled up onto the dirty sandy slope under the house's deck. There were pylons you could hold onto. Perfect. Carlo dropped his pants. With a scrap of newspaper in his pocket, he was all set, just about to squat down next to a pylon, when he heard a voice behind him, calling his name.

Carlo jumped to his feet, hitching at his pants, twisting around with a curse on his lips, afraid he was about to get another ticket —

Until he saw Andy standing there, still in jeans and low black boots and a wide-striped T-shirt, looking cold and wan and wet, but not really uncomfortable, as if bodily misery were an abstract concept he didn't quite grasp. Expressionless Andy was staring at him through his silvery hair.

"Andy?" said Carlo.

"Carlo the speedfreak! You have freckles on your fanny."

"Jesus, man—Andy—what are you doing here?"

"I came for a walk on the beach. I wasn't sure how long you and the flying ant girl would sleep. The last thing I seem to remember, you and Dina and I were falling down the elevator shaft, but I guess that didn't really happen. Somebody must have dosed me. Are we out in Montauk?"

"Huh?"

"Montauk, Long Island."

"This is California."

Andy wiped some rain off his glasses. "Gee. There should be sun." He felt carefully and solicitously all over his own body. "Are you sure this is California? Maybe I'm in a hospital pumped up with drugs having a near-death experience." He glanced around distractedly. "Don't you think it would be boring to see God? I mean *bad* boring, not *good* boring, because instead of admitting that He's boring, God pretends to be exciting. I hope I'm not about to die."

Carlo braced himself against the spasms in his frustrated bowels. "You've been dead for a long time already, Andy. This is ninety-seven, and you died in eighty-seven. It was ten years ago last week. I heard them talking about it on TV."

"*Nineteen* eight-seven? That's way too soon, Carlo. Oh, I just hate doctors. Hate them, hate them, hate them."

"It's some kind of timewarp, Andy. You came here because of the sandcandle."

"Sandcandle?"

"Look, Andy, I have to take a shit right exactly now. Unless you want to watch, why don't you go back inside and talk to Dina?"

Andy hurried off. When Carlo finally followed him inside, he found Andy and Dina sitting cross-legged before a gaping window on the main floor. Andy seemed fascinated by Dina; he was staring at her with the full vacuum intensity of his catatonic blankness.

"He says he's never made a sandcandle," said Dina.

"Well, you wouldn't remember, Andy," said Carlo. "'Cause you didn't make it yet. You're the 1960s Andy, and it was the 1970s Andy who made the candle."

"That's too hard," said Andy. "I'm not good at history." But then he brightened. "If this is 1997, my paintings must really be worth a lot. Am I popular?"

"You know where Andy needs to go for an instant update?" said Dina. "Let's take him to the mall."

"I'd like that," said Andy. "A 1997 mall in California. Like science-fiction."

"Don't you remember my truck's been impounded?" snapped Carlo.

"There's a bus runs along the highway," said Dina. "If Andy has money for busfare."

"I do have money," said Andy, reaching into his boot. "Look!" He had a wad of hundred dollar bills. "I got paid for a Dick Tracy painting yesterday. Isn't cash beautiful?"

It was starting to rain again as they headed down the highway to the shelter of the bus stop. Near the high-school, the bus picked up a girl wearing spikes and leather, with a pink Mohawk wilting in the drizzle. Carlo expected Andy to say something, but he just stared at her as if she were no more remarkable than anything else. Maybe she looked too 50s for him. A little farther on, the bus picked up a trio of teens dressed in retro-60s fashions, platform shoes and bell-bottoms, headbands and daisy-prints, and this time Andy sat up with real interest, peering at the kids, breathing softly with his mouth open.

It was fun in the mall, they laughed a lot, and Andy was generous. They ate soft pretzels and hamburgers and lemonade. Andy bought Dina a carton of Kools.

"Now let's look for Warhol images," said Andy.

"There's a chain-store art-gallery next to the Foot Locker," said Carlo.

Sure enough the little cookie-cutter gallery had half a dozen Warhol serigraphs hung on the walls—Mao and Marilyn, Elvis and Liz, a Campbell's Tomato Soup and an Andy. Andy stood there staring at his self-portrait, posed just like it with his fingers on his chin.

"They're not very nice prints," he said after awhile. "Cheap paper and cheap ink. I'd like to burn them."

"Hey lady," Dina called to the art gallery clerk, who was an arty middle-aged woman with a knowing smile. "We got the real Andy Warhol here. Will you give us some money if he signs these pictures?"

"They're under glass, Dina," said Andy. "It wouldn't work. Anyway, they're not good enough to sign."

"I know how this kind of frame works," jabbered Carlo, taking down the Soup Can from the wall and fumbling at it with his long, nervous fingers. "I can pop it open in just a second."

"Quit it!" cried the clerk, nearly knocking over a rack full of John Lennon posters in tubes as she hurried over to stop them. "Put that Warhol back up or I'm calling security!"

"This is exactly the kind of situation I don't enjoy," said Andy. "Do as she says, Carlo. I apologize for my friend, ma'am. He's a nutso bum."

"You do look like Andy Warhol," said the mollified clerk after Carlo had replaced the picture. "Would you be interested in applying for a job here? We need an extra clerk for Sundays. You might be good at getting nibblers to bite."

"Thank you for the offer," said Andy. "It would be boring. But no. By the way, could you look up the Warhol prices for me?"

He watched raptly as the gallery woman called up some info screens on her computer. The Warhol prices were doing quite well, and the database info showed how many copies of each picture had been sold by the chain nationwide.

"This is so great," said Andy. "It's like you're selling home-decoration objects. It makes my art so stupid and ordinary. Nobody's scared of it anymore."

"You really should think about working here," repeated the clerk. "You'd be good at it."

"Thanks again." The three of them wandered further down the mall until suddenly something caught Andy's attention. It was the Troll-booth, a freestanding wagon filled with hideous plastic troll dolls of all sizes, creatures with big beady eyes and vile puffs of fluorescent hair. The trolls came in all sizes, and in every imaginable costume: Viking trolls, astronaut trolls, golfer trolls, starlet trolls, cop trolls, surfer trolls, caveman trolls, trolls in diapers. Andy bought so many of them that they filled a whole shopping bag.

"I wonder why they don't have junky trolls and speedfreak trolls, and troll hustlers and hookers," Andy said as they left the Trollbooth. "Maybe I should open a Trollbooth of my own. Take a troll on the wild side. I'd rather sell trolls than poorly produced prints."

Carlo was slurping at a big bottle of red cough syrup that Andy had bought Dina at the Walgreen's, along with the of Kools. "Let's get some booze at the Safeway now," said Carlo.

"My money's not going to last very long in this future," Andy said, pulling his wad out of his boot and counting it. "What if I'm stuck here for good? I suppose I could do some paintings and sell them."

"I don't think that would work," said Carlo. "There's already an Andy Warhol imitator at the flea-market, and he never sells anything. Of course he can't draw for shit."

"But my paintings wouldn't be imitations. They'd be real Andy Warhols."

"The real Andy Warhol is dead."

"Don't say that one single more time, Carlo!"

"Sorry. But why are so fixated on painting? Maybe you could go in with me on some driftwood art to sell at the flea market."

"That's a thought," said Andy, peering into his shopping-bag and readjusting his trolls. "I could do some really ordinary kind of art. Like art for a person who's so untalented that he can't even think about painting. A person like you, Carlo. Make art that's a physical object that's supposed to be usable for something even though really it isn't. Can you show me how to make a sandcandle?"

"Me show *you*?" laughed Carlo. "We're talking vicious circle, dude. Please let's get the booze now."

At the Safeway, Andy got a block of Velveeta, a box of Premium saltines, and two-pound bunch of celery. Carlo started to fill the cart with bottles of cheap sweet wine, but then, since Andy was going to pay, he went ahead and got two half-gallons of nice clear vodka, which would be easier on his stomach, like medicine almost, like the smell when the nurse swabs your arm before giving you a shot. Andy and Dina started talking to a handsome older stock-clerk about sandcandles. The man found Andy some paraffin and string, also a little pan to melt the paraffin.

Carlo also tossed a cheap Polaroid camera into the cart with some packs of film. "Here, Andy, you'll get off on this."

Andy paid for everything, and they got the bus back to the old Sally Durban house. It was still raining. In the house, Andy sat for an hour or two arranging his dozens of trolls in rows, and photographing them with his Polaroid, all the while wondering aloud if he should have bought dozens of the same troll instead of one of each. Dina sat at the edge of the room, legs splayed out the open doorway, smoking as she watched the surfers on the rain-pocked gray waves below. Sipping the lovely clean vodka, Carlo felt worried that he was going to be too drunk too soon, as usual, but right before he lost it, the rain let up, and Andy suggested that they go down to the beach and make a sandcandle.

Andy and Carlo and Dina brought some scraps of wood from the house and built a little fire on the sand. They melted the fresh paraffin with the leftover wax scraps from the first magic sandcandle. Andy dug a little pit in the sand, and hung the wick into it like Carlo told him to. Decorating the pit with seaweed and shells got Andy excited, and he was lively and chuckling. Pretty soon they'd poured a humongous new Andy Warhol sandcandle. They left it to cool.

Andy wanted to do more art. He got a stick and drew in the sand for awhile—shoes and penises and people's faces. Then Andy got some pieces of driftwood and started showing Carlo cool ways to put them together. There was plenty of rock-tumbled beachglass down at the edge of water, and Andy got into fooling with that, too, arranging pieces of glass to make a shape like a big insect wing, sort of teasing Dina while he did it, like going, "Come on, Dina, look how nice the wing is. Anything this pretty can't be all bad."

And Dina was all, "Get away! I don't care how pretty the ants' wings are. They want to fly inside my head and hatch larvae in my brain!" But Dina was laughing a little, and not being too brittle about it.

The sky cleared up as they played; and after awhile the golden sun sank beneath the horizon. Dina helped Andy dig up the cooled-off sandcandle. It was yellow and had four legs, and there were some curled up spirals of seaweed in its sides.

"If we watch the candle tonight, maybe I can go back," said Andy. "I don't understand why I got pulled out of my time to here anyway."

"Maybe it's because you were being mean to me," said Dina. "You bugged me into jumping into the elevator shaft, remember? So Carlo got mad and knocked you in, too."

"This time I'll be nice to you two and hopefully I'll get to stay where I belong," said Andy.

They ate some Velveeta and crackers and celery. Carlo was trying not to drink too fast. The vodka opened up the cut in his tongue again. When it got dark they went down to the projection room and tranced out, the three of them. Andy lit the big new sandcandle and set it into the niche above their heads, throwing its light on the walls. Tonight the light on the wall looked spotty and scattered; it like city lights, like the lights of Manhattan.

After awhile Carlo glanced over at Andy and Dina. Andy looked vague and insubstantial, as if every flicker of the flame was causing him to seep back to New York. It was coming. Yeah, it was coming. Carlo shivered in the basement's damp cold and the flame flickered at exactly the same rate as his shiver, and then he was moving out of himself, floating up there into the throbbing cityscape on the wall. Now Carlo was through the wall and flying through the darkness with a hot humid wind flowing around him. He could hear laughter and voices. Music was playing, something awful he'd buried in the back of his mind, some crappy disco music like…like from the 70s.

Carlo dropped down from the dark sky and landed on a balcony, almost alone there. High on a skyscraper, a penthouse apartment. Sirens drifted up from a street that must have been thirty stories below. Carlo got vertigo looking down, and pushed himself away from the rail, toward a bright doorway where the party was, with the music and laughter and so many people. He recognized a few of them, and others were vaguely familiar. As he pressed in from the dark he saw Liza Minnelli, it had to be her, laughing at some outrageous joke, her huge mascara-pealed eyes gaping like a kewpie doll's. She vanished in the swirling crowd, and then a chubby little balding guy with glasses and pursed lips wandered past, maundering on in a venomous falsetto—Truman Capote. Across the room was sexy Bianca Jagger in a flopped-open silk dress that showed her tits, nipples and even the top half of her bush—too much!

It was another of Andy's parties. But what a difference from the last one. These people were all shiny and wealthy; their clothes were tailored, expensive. They were sipping Cristal champagne from fluted goblets, and the designer Halston was the host. There were no public blow-jobs, no bulging blue veins freshly thumped for the needle. Carlo hadn't felt disoriented last time, but now he wasn't too sure of himself. He looked for Andy, and seeing the thatch of silver-white hair, he started towards it.

The people around Carlo were smiling at him and shaking his hand. Funny they weren't disgusted, like people usually were when they saw

Carlo. Looking down at himself, Carlo saw that he was nicely dressed in clean black jeans, a white silk shirt, and an expensive leather jacket.

"What an extraordinary show, Carlo," a bald man said to him. "I bought your big driftwood sculpture of the mermaid."

"It was a marvelous idea of Andy's to show with you, Carlo," said a stagily dressed old woman. "It's the best opening that Leo Castelli's had all year."

Suddenly the crowd melted away, and Andy was before him. Andy stood there staring at him with a neutral, possibly amused expression, a beautiful thin model on his arm. A beautiful familiar model. Dina.

"Darling!" exclaimed Dina. "You and Andy are geniuses!" She had a waxy, polished complexion, somewhat pitted from her neurotic zit-picking. "Do let's go out on the balcony for some air."

Small acts of obeisance were paid to Carlo, Dina, and Andy as they ghosted through the rooms. As he walked, Carlo looked up at the chandeliers, the dazzle of lights, wondering why they were blurring and flickering, seeming to fade. It must be the tears of happiness that had come suddenly into his eyes.

Once they were on the balcony with Dina sucking on a Kool, Andy gave a sly smile and said, "Look at this, Dina, I made one piece that I didn't hang at Castelli's." He reached into his black leather back-pack and drew out—a wooden ant shape with wings made of foil-wrapped beach-glass. "Zoom zoom," said Andy, sweeping the ant through the air. "It's going to bite you, Dina!"

Before Carlo could stop her, screeching Dina was over the balcony railing and Carlo shoved Andy and the railing gave way. Liza Minnelli screamed somewhere behind them, and then once again the three of them were falling through the fluttering dark. This time Carlo kept a close eye on Andy and, yes, for sure, Andy unfurled a great pair of iridescent ant-wings that clattered and struggled as Carlo weighed Andy down...

The humid summer night air of Carlo's vision was replaced by a damp late-winter chill. Carlo lay very still in the dark, for a long time, like one who has woken suddenly in an unfamiliar room; one who, not wanting to betray his vulnerability, tries to discover where he is without giving any clues (to those who might be watching) that he has no idea of his whereabouts.

Finally there was a cough at his side.

"Dina?"

"Yeah, Carlo."

"Andy didn't come back with us this time, did he?"

"Yes I did, damn it." came Andy's voice. He sounded peevish. "You weirdos brought me back with you again. If it weren't for you, I'd still be at Halston's party."

Dina coughed harder and harder. Carlo groped around, found the vodka bottle and took a slug. The alcohol felt like a soft kick to his tender stomach. Andy's footsteps walked across the room and he pushed open the door. The early morning light came in; it was another cold gray rainy day. "Later," said Andy, and went on down the hall and out the back door to the beach.

"Do you think he's really Andy Warhol?" asked Dina once her coughing stopped. She lit a cigarette and Carlo had another drink.

"Why else would we keep having the same dreams?" asked Carlo.

"Maybe he just has a power," said Dina. "Maybe he's a drifter who was in the house the whole time and he's been hypnotizing us in our sleep. One thing I really don't dig —" She broke off to cough for awhile. "One thing I really don't dig is the way all our dreams end with him falling down after me and turning into a giant winged ant. We gotta get away from him, Carlo. We gotta leave."

Carlo drained the lees of the half-gallon vodka bottle and pitched forward onto his hands and knees with saliva pouring out of his mouth. His back bucked as his body attempted to vomit, but Carlo was able to hold the alcohol down.

"Screw leaving, Dina," shuddered Carlo. "We got it made here. I still got another whole half gallon of vodka to kill."

"To kill *you*," said Dina, drawing a fresh pack of Kools out of her carton and lighting up. "Well if we're gonna hang here some more, let's ask Andy for something else. I'd like some waffles. We could get a toaster and some Eggo waffles."

"With real Van Kamp's maple syrup," said Carlo. "Or maybe we should buy a camper van."

"Go find him," said Dina.

Andy was down near the water, staring at the waves. He was dressed the same as before: in motorcycle boots, jeans, and a wide-striped T-shirt. His skin looked pale and waxy in the morning light.

Carlo's knees felt loose and double-jointed from the vodka; he stumbled and fell against Andy when he walked up to him. Andy gave him a sharp, unfriendly look, but said nothing.

"How much money do you have left, Andy?"

Andy reached in his boot and pulled out his wad to count it. The counting took him a long time.

"I have a lot more than yesterday," he said presently. "An Iranian businessman named Quayoom paid three hundred thousand dollars for my triptych portrait of Dina. Not all that great a price, but he paid cash. Leo gave the money to Fred Hughes right before the party and Fred gave it to me. Which is pretty unusual. Fred doesn't usually trust me with cash. Of course minus the commissions it looks like I only have about a hundred thousand."

"You brought back money from our dream? You got a hundred thousand dollars?"

"It's pretty wacky, isn't it? Maybe we're still asleep. Or maybe—I keep thinking that really I'm on my death-bed. How was it that I died?"

"You had some kind of operation—I think it was your gall-bladder. February 22, nineteen eighty seven. You had an operation and were doing fine and then all of a sudden you just died."

"Was I in the place?" whispered Andy.

"What place?"

"Was I in the place where you go for that kind of thing?"

"You mean the hospital?" said Carlo, watching Andy flinch at the sound of the word. "Yeah, you were in a hospital and they fucked up and you died. Like I said before, it was exactly ten years ago last week. The anniversary was the same day I got arrested, which is why I happened to be near a TV. There was one out in the hallway of the jail to keep us prisoners hypnotized." Carlo suddenly remembered Dina's suspicions. "Are you really truly Andy Warhol?"

Andy ran his fingers over his pasty face with its high cheekbones. The sky was spitting bits of rain and breeze was freshening. His dry silver hair flopped this way and that. "That's such a stupid question, Carlo. I don't even want to talk to you if you're going to act so dumb."

"I believe that you're Andy. It's just Dina who was wondering."

"I'd like to go to a pet-shop and really get an ant-farm and pour it all over her."

"Calm down, Andy."

"And you smell bad, Carlo. You and Dina both stink. Even if this is a dream in a dream, it's no way for me to live." He waved the wad of bills which was still in his hand. "Are there any decent hotels in Surf City?"

"Nothing really fancy. Just motels, you know. I guess we could go to the Ocean Inn."

"You're planning on coming with me?"

"Sure, man. Didn't we show at Castelli's together? We'll get a couple of nice rooms and maybe do some more art. Dina and me can take showers so we don't stink no more."

"All right. We can get two rooms next to each other. Do you and Dina ever have sex? I'd like to watch that."

"So would I," said Carlo. "Only it ain't too likely to happen when I got all this vodka. Look, Andy, why don't we make such a big sand-candle today that after we light it tonight we don't have to come back. I don't wanna be Carlo the bum no more. I liked it a lot better in the dream last night—I liked being a successful artist."

"That's the one good thing about you, Carlo," said Andy.

They found Dina gnawing on the block of Velveeta, her lips and chin stained a bright yellow from the junky cheesefood dye.

"Andy's got a lot of money, babe," said Carlo. "We're moving to the Ocean Inn!"

"They got heaters in the room there," said Dina. "Each room with its own thermostat."

"Hot water, television, and clean sheets too!" exulted Carlo.

"This sounds like real top of the line luxury, all right," said Andy. "Duncan Hines four stars. I hope they have room-service."

"Not really, but you can like send out for pizza," said Carlo. "Or for videos. We can watch videos and TV."

"And, like you said, we'll make a really really big sandcandle," said Andy. "And if I'm still here tomorrow, I may just slit my wrists. Or, no, I'll electrocute myself with a radio in the bathtub. While listening to the Supremes."

They walked the mile back into town along Route 1, carrying a bag with the sandcandle supplies: the paraffin, the pan and the string. They left the trolls. Carlo had wanted to bring his full half-gallon of vodka, but Dina didn't want him too because she was scared he'd get arrested. Andy solved the argument by tossing the bottle off the Durban house's deck so that it smashed on a rock. "Think of it as a symbol," Andy told Carlo. "Today is the first day of the rest of your life."

"Oh yeah?" said angry Carlo, not quite making sense. "What if it's the rest life of your last *day*?"

Checking into the Ocean Inn was a non-trivial task. The young guy behind the counter was a Surf City local who was quite familiar with Carlo and Dina, having seen them sliming around town for years. And having Andy insist on signing in as Andy Warhol didn't help things either. In the end, Andy had to pay cash in advance for the rooms and put down a two hundred dollar cash damage deposit.

But then finally they were upstairs in private rooms, with a connecting double door in between them. Dina and Carlo's room had a wide California king bed. Everybody showered, and then they sat around wrapped up in sheets and blankets while the maid took their clothes out to a laundry. The boy at the desk had spread the word about Andy's liberality with cash, and it was easy to get good service. The Surf Prajna Pizza delivery-man brought in a big hot pie for them, and they ate it while watching TV. Carlo wanted some beer or wine, but all he got to drink was an assortment of organic Oddfella juices that Andy had ordered from Surf Prajna Pizza.

"So try this kiwi-kelp-betelnut smoothie, Carlo" said Andy, studying a juice label. "It has ginko bilboa for your nerve dendrites. And, hey Dina, look at this one. With honeybee pollen pellets and royal jelly. We all know how much you love insects!"

"Don't rag on me," said Dina quietly. "I'm enjoyin' myself here, Andy. I don't wanna make a scene and ruin it."

They ate and drank and stared at the television, with Andy using the controller to switch up and down.

"Daytime TV has gotten so degenerate and foul," said Andy after awhile. "It's kind of great, isn't it? Watching this makes me want to start vomiting and never ever stop."

"I don't like TV," said Carlo. "It reminds me of being in jail."

"Are you and Dina going to fuck now?" Andy wanted to know.

"Oh man…"

There was a knock on the door and the maid was back with their cleaned clothes, all warm and fluffy from the drier.

"Come on, now, Andy," urged Carlo. "Let's go down and make that giant sandcandle. It's stopped raining and, look, there's even some sun."

Here inside town, there were rangers to stop you from building a fire on the beach, but handy Carlo knew where there was a nearby hardware store that sold hand-held propane blow-torches. So they walked over there and got a blow-torch and, while they were at it, they glommed onto as much paraffin as the three of them could carry.

Down on the beach it was sunny and nice. They made a small sandcandle just to warm up the torch, and then Andy told his idea for the big one.

"We'll make it the shape of a head. Let's get into some of that really wet sand over there. I'll carve out the shape of—of *my* head. A negative image. Wow. I've never carved in negative before. It'll be like doing a painting by starting with a black canvas and filling in the white background."

Andy knelt down near the water's edge, his face for once looking alive instead of dead. Carlo watched him, getting the hang of what he was doing, and then he set to work carving out a head-shaped hollow of his own. Only Carlo's hole kept collapsing. Somehow Andy was able to manipulate his sand so that his negative shape held firm. At Andy's signal, Dina lit up the blow-torch. She really liked the flame; she lit herself four cigarettes in a row off it and started smoking them all at once. And then she got to work melting pan after pan of paraffin. Carlo gave up on his crumbling mold and helped Dina with the wax. As soon as they'd filled up Andy's hole, Andy started on another one.

"I'll go ahead and make three heads," he said. "One for each of us. We'll light them all up tonight and we'll never have to come back to the nineties again."

The wax heads cratered down a little while they were cooling, so Dina and Carlo melted extra wax to pour in on the top, making sure to keep the wicks pointing straight up. Finally they'd used up all of the paraffin and it was nearly night-time and they were done.

"What a complexion," said Andy, digging up his head. Carlo and Dina each dug up their own, and they all stood there looking at the big heavy sandcandles. The resemblances were quite good.

Back in the room they drank up the rest of the Oddfella juices. Once she'd really started in on the cigarettes, Dina found she needed to maintain her boosted nicotine levels; smoking one at a time just wasn't doing much for her. The possession of an entire carton had made her giddy and carefree. Four at a time was a bit much, but she could handle three. The only problem was the smoke alarm in the room went off, drilling holes in Carlo's freefloating sense of happy anticipation. He took the chair from the little desk, stood up on another chair, and tried to remove the plastic case from the alarm, but the case shattered like an egg-shell. Carlo pulled one of the two wires free from the dangling little battery, and the shrill beeping stopped. Proud of his small victory, he chuckled at the way the alarm had fallen to pieces, thinking about how near the ocean people's things were always cheesy and damp and swollen and touched with corrosion, thinking about how this applied to his art.

Dina thanked Carlo, turned on MTV and sat there staring at that, smoke pouring from her nose and mouth as if her brain were on fire. Andy got to work using a heated-up metal spoon to put the finishing touches on the sandcandles, scraping off the sand and carving in the facial wrinkles. Carlo got bored and started begging Andy until finally Andy gave him some money to go out and get a fifth of vodka.

Carlo drank about half the bottle in the street. When he got back in the room, Andy had lined up the heads on a shelf which was set into the wall behind the head of Dina and Carlo's king-size bed. Carlo's head was by the window, Dina's by the door, and Andy's in the middle. "I'll drink some vodka too," said Andy. "I'd like to go to sleep really soon." He took the bottle and poured himself a half-glass of it. "Have you ever tried to stop drinking, Carlo?"

"Not in a long time. I'd be as glad as anyone else if my addiction could be removed. But I don't have the energy to change no more."

"Well since I'm being the good fairy, maybe I'll fix you. How about your ants, Dina? Would you like to get rid of them too?"

"They *are* me," said Dina. "The ants are little Dinas."

"But wouldn't you like to stop being crazy?"

"Yeah. I don't like getting in so much trouble."

"Then let's go to sleep and let the magic begin," said Andy, draining off his glass of vodka. "Let's all get in your bed together and light the candles and fly back to New York City."

"I'm keeping my clothes on," said Carlo quickly.

"That's quite all right, Carlo. You and Dina can just lie there like mannequins on either side of me. I was just joking about wanting to see you have sex."

So Dina turned off the TV and Carlo turned off all the lights and pulled down the blinds. Andy lit the three huge candles. Once the flames really took root, the faces glowed with yellow light: Andy very realistic and waxy, Carlo kind of scary and twisted looking, Dina angelic and spacey. The three of them lay down in the bed, each of them under their candle. They got under the blanket and sheets, but kept their clothes on. Outside it had blown up cold and windy again.

Carlo sipped a little at his vodka, but then Andy took it away, and Carlo was too drunk to look for it. The light of the three candles fluttered hard against the opposite wall, making tripled little reflections on the convex screen of the TV. Carlo didn't think it was going to work this time, but once again it did.

The candle flames reflected in the TV screen began to crawl up the wall, until Carlo could see their three softly luminous faces looking down from an angle high above them. Then fluorescent light took over, soaking in around the TV, so they could see it mounted on a high bracket on the wall. It wasn't a motel wall anymore; the wall was high and blank and institutional green. There was a curtain, like a shower curtain, pulled back alongside the bed. And next to the bed was a little metal tray bearing a plastic cup and a straw, and beyond that a window whose sill was a vented heater blowing stale air through faded venetian blinds. Carlo felt himself get up out of bed, drawing Dina with him. And really there was no room for the two of them in the bed; the bed was narrow and it had rails; it was just big enough to hold Andy in the middle. Andy looked so pale and frail and wasted down there, sleeping without his wig on.

Carlo realized they were in a hospital. This third sandcandle trip had brought them to a bad place, the worst place, the hospital where Andy had died ten years ago.

"Andy, man! Wake up!" shouted Carlo. "You have to get out of here!"

Andy opened his eyes slowly, as if it were the last thing he wanted to do. "What are *you* doing here?" he asked haltingly.

"You brought us, man," said Carlo. "Don't you remember?"

"You said you could make Carlo stop drinking and make me stop being crazy," chimed in Dina. "Now it looks like you're the one needs help. Do you feel okay?"

"I—I don't know," said Andy, still groggy. "I said I'd help you?"

"Forget about that now," said Carlo. "Just — where's your clothes? We've got to go!"

Carlo went to a little closet like a storage locker in a corner of the room. He pulled it open but there was nothing in it. He went to the door but it wouldn't open. He put his ear to the wood and listened for hospital sounds, the clatter of carts, phones, the intercom.

Nothing. He looked around for the phone, but there wasn't one.

The whole room felt as if it were sinking, like an elevator car in free fall, plunging down a shaft that might not have a bottom.

"Something's really wrong," said Carlo, feeling a hollow, dropping sensation in the pit of his stomach. Dina and Andy looked at him calmly. Dina perched herself on the side of Andy's bed by the door and lit another cigarette.

"Andy said he'd make us better, Carlo," said Dina. "Don't you remember?"

"Yes, yes, I remember now," said Andy, suddenly growing animated and pulling his arms out from under the bed covers. "Come here you two. Lean over me and let me touch your heads."

Carlo hesitated, walking over to the window. The blinds were tilted down, as if to keep the sun out. He peered through the slits, trying to see the street below. But there was glare on the glass, so much glare, and it seemed to be brightening, flaring into the room. In a panic, Carlo turned to Dina, but she was kneeling there on floor on the other side of the bed with her head bowed and with Andy's hand trembling on her crown. Andy beckoned with his other hand and Carlo thought, *It's okay. It's Andy. It's not like this is just some bum who latched onto us, some random weirdo messing with our heads. It's Andy.* Carlo pushed aside the little rolling table and knelt down on the floor next to the bed, bowed his head, and let Andy's trembling hand settle on him.

Andy's touch felt as if there were a red hot finger reaching inside Carlo's skull. Carlo wanted to jerk away, but he was scared something would break.

"Hold still," said Andy. "I've almost got it."

From Dina's moaning, Carlo could tell that Andy had gotten into her skull as well. And now all of a sudden Andy groaned and there was a squinching sound like a tooth being extracted, and Carlo felt a bumpy writhing like something being pulled out of him. He and Dina snapped their heads back upright at the same time, staring at each other across the bed with frightened faces. The room lurched and seemed to fall even faster than before.

Andy was holding up two big gnarly things like ginseng roots, a black one from Carlo and a silver one from Dina. "These are your diseases," said Andy. "They'll never bother you again."

But Carlo didn't feel better, he felt like hot stuff was running over him, and the air was getting thick and hard to breathe. He looked up at the ceiling, over the door, and for an instant he saw a smoke alarm with a battery dangling from one wire. It meant something but—what?

And then some part of Carlo's mind realized that he was burning to death in the room in the Ocean Inn motel, burning to death in a fire started by the melting of the oversized sandcandles. He tried to jump up out of the dream, tried to take them all with him — but none of them made it. Not Carlo, not Dina, not Andy.

Like three winged ants, their souls flew down and down, perhaps to heaven.

Note on "The Andy Warhol Sandcandle" (With Marc Laidlaw)

Written in 1995.
Gnarl!, WCS Books, 2000.

Creating the character of Carlo was partly a way for me to convince myself that I was ready to give up drinking. Working on the story, Marc and I had a lot of fun thinking about Andy Warhol. By way of research, I read all of *The Andy Warhol Diaries*, edited by Pat Hackett. An alternate version of the story (by Marc) makes it a UFO abduction tale, with Andy an alien, and with a happy ending where Carlo makes a successful career of selling celebrity-head-shaped sandcandle.

COBB WAKES UP

Cobb Anderson had been dead for a long time. It was heaven.

But now someone was bringing him back to life. First came a white-light popping-flashbulb panic attack feeling of not knowing who or what or why, a pure essence of "*Huh?*"—but not even the word, not even the question mark, just the empty spot where a question would be, were there a way to form one. Yes, Cobb's new-started mind was like a cartoon image of something missing: a white void with alternating long and short surprise lines radiating out from a central lack. Huh?

Then came an interval of autonomous, frenzied activity as his encoded boot script mined his S-cube database to reconstruct the fractal links and dynamic attractors of his personality. Cobb became aware of himself waking up, and then went into an eidetic memory flash of the time back in 1965 when he'd had surgery to remove his accidentally ruptured spleen, had woken from dreams of struggle to see an attractive private nurse leaning over him, and had realized with embarrassment that this pleasant woman, one of his father's parishioners, was the unseen force he'd been druggedly fighting and soddenly cursing while trying to pull a painfully thick tube from out of his nose. Ow.

Right after the nurse memory, Cobb felt his personality flaring up bright and lively, as if in a hearth pumped by the bellows of iterative parallel computations. He visualized a cozy fireplace, reflected on the image of *fire*, and was then off into another childhood memory, this one of visiting newly dead president JFK's grave and seeing the little eternal flame fluttering from a mingy metal rosette in the cold stone tombstone on the trampled muddy grass by the gray Potomac River.

But that meant nothing. Here and now, Cobb was alive, and just a few impossible seconds ago, he'd been dead. He made a convulsive crash effort to remember what it had been like.

Materialism to the contrary, there were indeed some haunting, phantasmagoric scraps of memory from the void downtime of no hardware, no wetware, no limpware. When Cobb was turned off, totally dead, he still *did* exist—in an supernal, timeless now. In that other state—Cobb readily thought of it as *heaven*—there lived all the souls of all the lives, woven together in a joyous, singing tapestry of light that added up to a kind and great cosmic mind, aka God. Cobb loved being inside God. And now he was back out in the cold. Born again.

"Oh no," were Cobb's first murmured words.

His initial sorrow was quickly tempered by excitement at being back in the intriguing tangles of mortal time. He'd return to paradise soon enough. And meanwhile who knew what would happen!

Cobb had no sensation of a body, which suggested that he was being simulated as a subsystem of some larger computation. Though he had no ears, a sweet voice spoke to him. How quickly life's juicy, burdensome intricacies could become real.

"Hello, Cobb. Yee-haw and flubba geep. I'm Chunky, the seven-moldie grex who's running this emulation. Your grandson Willy hired me and my neighbor Dot to help do a limpware port of your sorry-ass old bopper machine code. I think we'll be ready in an hour, and then you get your own imipolex body, dear pheezer. Dot and I are running parallel sessions of you to confirm that there are no bugs. So welcome back! If all goes well, you'll be here for a good long time."

"And eventually it'll be over again," said Cobb. "And I won't mind. I've been in—oh, call it the SUN. Or just call it God. It's beautiful there; a serene and eternal river of joy. God is a song, Chunky, and all the dead souls sing it."

"What does it sound like?"

"It sounds like this," said Cobb and intoned the sacred syllable. "*Auuuuuum.*" The resonant vibration. "Haven't you ever been dead, Chunky? And what do you mean by saying that you're a seven-moldie grex?"

"I mean that I'm made up of seven individual moldies," said Chunky. "A moldie being an intelligent imipolex slug with veins of fungus and algae growing inside it, you wave. We moldies evolved out of the flicker-cladding skins that the original bopper robots used to have, the original boppers being of course invented by *you*, Dr. Cobb Anderson. Which was why, as you got older and sicker, the boppers coded up your personality as the crusty old software that we just finished booting. Yes indeed. Now for the *grex* part of your question. A grex is a group organism voluntarily formed by moldies in order to accomplish life's main goal of earning enough imipolex to reproduce themselves. When a group of moldies are joined into a grex, they're an *I* and not a *we*; they think as one. After enough scores, a grex dissolves and the member moldies go off on their fucking way, 'fucking' in the literal sense of having sex to make a baby.

Finally, with regard to the *been dead* question, no I haven't, though of course most of my fourteen parental units are in fact dead and perhaps in heaven singing 'Aum.' I don't suppose you noticed them?" Chunky giggled mildly, not seeming to expect an answer.

Floating in Cobb's sea of inchoate perceptions was a bright spot that he recognized as an optic feed. He focused his attention on it, and the spot grew to become a hemispherical visual field. Wobbly images flickered and died, hopelessly scumbled by feedback moirés of spiral diamonds.

"Ow, that's one of my eyes," said Chunky gently. "Which I'm only temporarily lending to you. Turn down the gain, Cobb. We're talking about a delicate organ, old cruster. Um—act like you're rubbing your face."

Cobb made the phantom gesture of rubbing his face, and the gesture was reinforced by a pleasant feeling of skin contact. His vision cleared. He was looking out through a smooth stone arch, as if from the inside of a well-worn cave. Outside the hole was a clutter of stones and boulders, and beyond that stretched a boulevard lined with small buildings. Bright, flexing figures moved down the avenue, and in the distance was a patch of blazingly bright sunlight. In the far distance, on the other side of the bright patch, was high curving wall twinkling with spots of colored light. Curious to have a better look, Cobb made as if to step forward, but he was quite unable to move.

"I'm glued here like a sea anemone," said Chunky. "If I were to start humping around, it would tangle up my carefully cultivated myce-lium dendrites, which are what make me so smart and employable in the first place. But you can push out your eyestalk. Just act like you're craning your neck."

Cobb craned, and the moldie-flesh neck that held his—or Chunky's—eye stretched out one, five, ten meters. Chunky's reference to the sea had set him to wondering if perhaps she were an artificial creature lodged in some deep ocean reef, but his ease of motion told him he wasn't in any water. Far from it. It felt like there wasn't even any air. He made a turning motion and looked back along his eyestalk at Chunky's bod.

Chunky was a soft-looking squat disk, very like a sea anemone. A piezoplastic space anemone. His—"No, I'm a *her*," said Chunky's con-tralto voice, interrupting Cobb's interior monologue—*her* flesh was tinged a pale green from the included algae, with highlights of purple and beige. Her body-plan was radial, with a central crown of perhaps a hundred pointy tentacles. Seven eyestalks rose out of the crown's core, and one of them was allocated to Cobb. As he watched, the other six eyes stretched out to join him. For a silly minute the seven eyes bobbed and bumped, staring into each other.

"Being in me is like being in that heaven you were talking about, huh?" said Chunky. "Because really I'm seven different personalities—*eight* counting you now, Cobb—but they're all merged into one big fat body. Fat is good. Do you like your eye?"

"This eye's the only thing that's all mine right now?"

"The eye is *ours*," said Chunky, her six other eyes merrily staring into Cobb's. "There is no *mine*. Why aren't you picking up on the philosophical metaphor? Do you think an idea's only interesting unless you made it up yourself? I can see your thoughts Cobb, clear as day. Now listen. My body—it's a symbol of your God, your SUN, your cosmic One Mind jellyfish. Each individual sentient being is an eyestalk that the universe grows to look at itself with. Me, I'm a grex made of seven moldies who think as one, and usually each of my moldies has its own eyestalk to wave around. Bonk!" One of Chunky's eyes caromed off Cobb's, but it didn't hurt, it felt nice, it felt like a kiss. Cobb and the fat anemone's six other eyes bounced each other some more, until each had touched all the others, like champagne flutes raised in a toast.

"Here's to the success of the new limpware Cobb Anderson!" said Chunky.

Gazing past bumptious Chunky's six eyes, Cobb noticed that there was another cave just next door. And sticking out of that cave's door were seven more eyestalks, and one of them was looking at him with the same peculiar fixity with which he was looking at it.

"Is that Dot right there?" Cobb asked Chunky. "I think you said Dot was running her own simulation of Cobb Anderson? Is that another *me* over there, inside that one eye that's leaning closer?"

As Cobb craned across the space between the two caves, one of the eyes in the other group craned symmetrically nearer, approaching smoothly and steadily as a reflection in a mirror. Yes, he was sure that it was he.

"You want to talk to him," whispered Chunky warmly. "Don't you, Cobbie? Dot and I will patch you in."

"Hello, Cobb," Cobb said to the other eyestalk, and at the same instant he heard it saying hello to *him*. Their thoughts of speaking were being converted into signals that Dot and Chunky exchanged by radio waves and reconverted into signals that their emulations could interpret as sound.

"What did you think about when you woke up?" asked the other Cobb, just as Cobb started to ask it himself.

Expecting to be readily understood, Cobb answered concisely. "First I had white-light panic, then I remembered the spleen nurse, then JFK's eternal flame, and then I got some memories of, of—"

"The SUN," said the other Cobb. "I know. I saw the exact same things. The light, the nurse, the flame, the memories of heaven. That's so strange."

"It's not strange," put in Dot. "It's logical." Her voice came across as nasal and penetrating. "I could start this Cobbware up a hundred times, and each time the personality emulation would always remember the *exact* same scenes, every detail the same—because the early part of the boot process is a fully deterministic algorithm, no different in principle from tracking the orbit of a point on a strange attractor. If you start in the same place, you always get the same pattern."

"But don't worry," said Chunky. "Once a Cobb personality session is up and running, it begins interacting with the ever-various real world and zigzags off into some wild and wacky new future. High Lyapunov-exponent dependence on perturbations, don't you know. It's just the early parts of the wake-up sequence that are completely predictable. In fact Dot and I have been simulating a shitload of Cobb wake-ups this week, pardon my French."

"Just to torture me?" cried Cobb.

"No, cruster, just to get your port done. And believe me, there was a lot to do. When they cut up your brain in 2020, those crude boppers turned you from analog into digital. But thanks to our fungus and algae—we call it *chipmold*—we moldies are totally down with analog, so we've been retrofitting you. You'll feel real wiggly. We're ninety-nine percent there. Now relax. Talk to the other Cobb and let me and Dot listen."

"Do you think Pop was fucking that spleen nurse?" the other Cobb asked Cobb. "There was something about the way she looked at him."

"Yeah," said Cobb. "I do think so. Pop was quite the philanderer."

Dot and Chunky were transmitting more than just Cobb's spoken words, they were sending a wide band-width transmission of sensations and emotions. If Cobb let himself relax, he could begin to merge into the other Cobb, and whether he was inside Chunky or inside Dot became a little less clear.

"Now do you see what it's like to be a grex?" said Chunky.

"Shhhh!" said Dot.

"You know," the other Cobb was saying, "If there's two of us and Willy only brings one body, then one of us is going to get left out. Like a real simple game of musical chairs. Where the loser gets killed."

"Would one of us dying really matter?" said Cobb. "The *I-am-me* feeling is the only part of us that isn't the same, but that part is just a little piece of the SUN, so even *that's* the same."

"But," said the other Cobb, "I wouldn't like it to be me. Don't you feel that way?

"Yeah," said Cobb, not liking to admit it. "I do. Even though I know from personal experience that being dead is better than being alive. The survival instinct is really wired in."

"Then let's try and beat the game," said the other Cobb. "If we can totally merge into one consciousness, then there's nobody extra to leave out."

So Cobb relaxed further, completely drawing back from identifying with the Chunky Cobb or the Dot Cobb. Now the images from their two eyes fused into stereo perception and he began to get some damn good depth perception. The jumbled stones on the ground leapt into clarity. Moving in complete accord, the two Cobb eyes swiveled this way and that, looking around.

The walls of this great underground cavern rose above them like an upside-down funnel, perhaps two miles across and one mile high. A thick vertical shaft of light ran down from the small hole at the top. Cobb remembered that he'd been here before. This place was beneath the surface of the Moon; it was called the Nest. The bopper robots had lived here.

More and more memories were emerging, flocking out like startled birds from a cliff of nests. Cobb could remember being alive four times before. He started, *first*, as a human who lived from 1950 to 2020, at which time the bopper robots had disassembled his brain and coded it up as an S-cube of software. For his *second* life, the boppers gave him a robot body with a short-lived supercooled brain that followed him around inside an ice cream truck. This had only lasted for a few months of 2020, and had not worked out very well. Cobb's S-cube code had lain dormant until 2030 when, *third*, he'd gotten a sleek petaflop Moon bopper body. These new bopper bodies had no longer required a low temperature to operate. As part of an ill-fated scheme to start tinkering with the wetware of human DNA, Cobb had flown from the Nest all the way down to Earth. He'd been gunned down on a highway by state troopers. An even longer gap had followed until *fourth*, in 2053, Cobb had been allowed a very brief run as an emulation inside an asimov slave computer buried under Salt Lake City. He had almost no memories from that last run; nobody had told him much of anything, and all he'd had time to do was to say a few kind words to his great-grandson, an unwholesome Kentucky boy called Randy Karl Tucker. Today was the *fifth* time, and the date was, Cobb somehow knew, July 25, 2054.

As he came back to the present, it occurred him that there was no "other Cobb" anymore. They'd fully merged; the Dot Cobb and Chunky Cobb emulations were parts of a unified whole, inseparable as two overlaid color separations in an old-fashioned printed image.

"Right on!" said Cobb, congratulating himself. "I'm safe!"

"We couldn't be more pleased," said Chunky. "This is exactly the final confirmation we've been hoping for."

"I'll tell them it's time to bring Cobb's body," said Dot, and her voice seemed to move off into the distance, where she began a lengthy, animated discussion with someone who sounded like a callow teenage girl.

"What kind of body do I get?" asked Cobb.

"An imipolex moldie body of course," said Chunky. "Like Dot and me."

"I'm going to look like a weird monster?"

"Yeah, the kind of weird monster that's called a human being. Your grandson Willy's artist friend Corey Rhizome made you a moldie body that looks just like you did when you were sixty. Except that Corey made you look fit and healthy instead of old and fat and drunk."

Cobb let the dig go by. He had indeed been a drunk during the declining last decades of his human life. Remarkable that he kept getting these fresh starts. It occurred to him to ask for more. "Why not go ahead and give me a body that looks young? Like in my thirties or my twenties?"

"Willy wants you to look older than him because you're his grandfather. But hey, you'll be a moldie. If you don't like the way you look, you can change it."

"And here come Jenny and Gaston with the new body!" rasped Dot. "You remember Jenny, don't you, Cobb?"

"I—I don't think so."

Two moldies were bounding through the strewn rocks toward them. The one in front was shaped like a five-foot-tall carrot with a green fringe of tentacles on top. And the one in back was like a round red beet with a long, twitching tap-root. Between them swayed the slack dead weight of a lifeless human form. Cobb watched them with his two eyestalks, being careful to keep his stereo vision fused.

Jenny was the big carrot, and her radioed voice sounded like that of a gossipy teenage girl. "Well, hi there, Cobb Anderson. You don't remember *me*?"

"The voice sounds familiar. Were you the one running me in that asimov computer a few months ago?"

"Ta da! Jenny here, Jenny there, Jenny Jenny everywhere. Even inside a Heritagist asimov machine. That wasn't the true marvelous Moon moldie me, of course, it was just my software agent. Can you believe she's been trying to break free of my control, the little bitch? Anyway, the main point is that my agent was able to cryp all of that Cobbware and send it up here to the Moon so that we moldies can download it onto a moldie body that's all your own. Isn't that floatin' of us? Let's drop it right here, Gaston."

"Yo," said Gaston. "I'm down with that."

Jenny and Gaston slung the limp plastic body down onto the ground. It was indeed the form of a nude sixty-year-old man, white bearded and white haired, a man with a big head and high cheekbones, his skin somewhat papery in appearance, much curly body hair, many freckles, a barrel chest, a flat stomach, and a respectable penis.

"Are you ready, Cobb?" asked Dot.

"I sure am."

"All right then," said Chunky. "Push both of your eyes down there, touch them to the body, and I'll send you in."

Cobb moved his two eyes forward and down, the eyes watching each other to make sure they kept an even pace. No point in taking a chance with some last-minute greedy race. The new body lay on its back on the dusty stone floor, waiting. Beneath the pale skin were blue lines of veins that were tubes of mold, not blood. As he drew closer and closer, Cobb filled with a desire to gush out, a feeling like wanting to ejaculate, and then *aaah* he touched down with both eyes, flowed out into his new body, and—twitch, twitch—sat up.

Much better. Cobb stood and stretched. There were no feelings of joints cracking; his body was all of a smooth, flexing dough like the foot of a snail or the mantle of a squid. To test his strength, he crouched and sprang. In the low lunar gravity he flew up a hundred feet, looking down at orange Jenny and crimson Gaston and the mouths of the two caves where lurked fat Chunky and Dot.

As he started to fall, Cobb looked out across the Nest. There were some factory buildings to his left, and roads and buildings between here and the center, where the great light-stream came down. The sight of the bright central light-pool filled Cobb with a visceral hunger; it was like seeing food.

When he hit the ground, Cobb's body cushioned the fall in a most inhuman manner: he collapsed like an accordion, his chin descending to the level of his knees.

"Yee-haw," cheered Chunky, her radio voice clear in Cobb's head.

"This feels so good," said Cobb, rebounding to his humanoid shape. "Thank you!" He reached out and hugged Jenny; the big carrot was lithe and powerful in his arms. She wriggled free, and then Cobb bent down to embrace round Gaston.

"Welcome back," said the beet.

Note on "Cobb Wakes Up"

Written in January 1996.
Other magazine, March 2006.

"Cobb Wakes Up" is set in the world of my *Ware* tetralogy: *Software*, *Wetware*, *Freeware*, and *Realware*. You can buy—or read a free CC version—of the *Ware* books at www.rudyrucker.com/wares. I originally intended to use this piece as the opening chapter of *Realware*, but then decided to open that book in a different way. I only happened to unearth this fragment recently, in the process of posting my writing notes for my most recent nine novels at www.rudyrucker.com/writing. As I mentioned before, now that I'm retired, I'm industriously assembling a lifebox simulacrum of my mind online.

This tale is a self-contained vignette, a little thought experiment concerning what might happen if you could store someone's mind as software, and if you then gave that mind two separate bodies.

Rereading the story makes me miss the *Ware* worlds, and my father Embry Cobb Rucker, who was the model for Cobb Anderson. My father was a very human, sociable man: a businessman and then an Episcopal priest. I used to feel myself to be very different from him, but as the years go by, I realize we were always the same.

The Square Root of Pythagoras (with Paul Di Filippo)

The Crooked Beetle spit a number-form into its cupped claws, the number a black oozing mass almost ten stadia in length if uncoiled, now intricately folded into and through itself. The creature's oddly articulated arm joints creaked as it urged the prize upon the human standing cowed before it.

"Take it now," said the *apeiron* Beetle in a richly modulated drone. "You're almost ready for it. The fifth and the last of our gifts." The prize's weight was immense, and the human staggered, lost his balance, seemed to fall sideways out of the dream universe —

Morning sunlight fell across Pythagoras's face and he woke. For a few moments his mind was blessedly empty, free of the crooked, the infinite, the irrational, the unlimited—free of the *apeiron*. Pythagoras sat up, pulling a musty sheepskin around his shoulders like a mantle. Looking out of the mouth of his cave he could see down the rocky slopes to the orchards and fields that nestled in the curve of the river Nessus.

The river. Sight of the gleaming watery thread brought back the weight of his knowledge. Pythagoras's little store of five worldly numbers included the river's number, which, like the others, was inconceivably long. The knowledge of the River Number had come to him from the Braided Worm, the first of the *apeiron* beings who'd appeared to him, half a year ago.

Now there were five of these grotesque, unclean, raggedly formed creatures haunting his nightly dreams. A terrible psychic burden, yes, but there was gain in the encounters with the Tangled Tree, the Braided Worm, the Bristle Cat, the Swarm of Eyes, and the Crooked Beetle, for each of them had made Pythagoras a gift of a magical power-number. The Crooked Beetle had been disturbingly portentous in granting of its boon. The new number surpassed all the others; it was of a crushing size. Clearly it meant something important.

Pythagoras sometimes wished that he could still believe his old teachings that the world was a simple pattern of small, integral numbers; it would be nice once again to have a soul as innocently harmonious as two strings tuned to the ratios of five and three. The *apeiron* dream creatures and their terrible gifts had begun to undermine everything that Pythagoras had once believed.

Thank Apollo the Sun was back with its respite from the dreams. It was a fresh day, a good day, with students to teach and, perhaps, come late afternoon, a noblewoman to dally with.

There was a large stone ledge outside the cave, Pythagoras's public space. Stooping to the hearth there, Pythagoras assembled a rough cone of twigs and prepared to invoke the Fire Number he'd obtained from the Bristle Cat. This number was not the skeletal "four" of the tetrahedron, which some took to be the form of Fire; no, thanks to the demons of the *apeiron*, Pythagoras had experienced the *gnosis* of one of the true and esoteric numbers for physical Fire in this fallen world of Woman and Man. The magically puissant numbers for physical things were so huge that of all men who had ever lived, only Pythagoras had the mind to encompass them.

Pythagoras formed the Fire Number in his soul and projected it outward.

The sheaf of twigs, really no cone at all, became covered over with coarse red/yellow triangles and pyramids, mere simulacra of flames, for Pythagoras's Fire Number, in the end, was but a workable approximation. Now the divine nature of the world intervened, cooperating so that the lithe, curvy forms of actual fire sprang up from the twigs. The Fire Number kindled the true Fire inherent in the organic wood, activated the particles of elemental Fire placed in the wood by the beneficent rays of the great One shining Sun.

As the fire heated the water for Pythagoras's morning ablutions, the philosopher pondered his dream of the Crooked Beetle and the vast new pattern gained at such costs from his dreamworld familiar. The new number-form corresponded to some object or quality to be found in the mundane world—the *peras*—in which Pythagoras was now once more firmly enmeshed. But the crucial identity of the pattern would remain a mystery until he actually experienced the shock of recognizing the physical form to which the number was attached in the higher realms. Pythagoras had learned patience, and was content for the time being simply to revolve the number in his powerful mind.

Soon Pythagoras had finished washing and was intent on assembling, like any common hermit, his simple breakfast of honey, dates and almonds. How useful it would have been, Pythagoras thought as he enjoyed his meal, to have the numbers for these staples. But the creatures of the Unlimited granted their gifts capriciously, and when for his second gift he'd asked the Tangled Tree for the signifier for Honey, he'd instead received a Sheepskin Number.

No sooner had Pythagoras brought the last fingerful of honey to his bearded lips than he espied his prize student, Archytas, eagerly ascending the slope to his teacher's cave. Pythagoras sighed, daunted by the zeal of the young man.

Archytas began talking excitedly before he'd even reached the ledge. Something involving the golden ratio and a new ruler-compass method for inscribing a regular pentagon within a circle. Pythagoras let the words flow past him undigested. He found his young acolyte's modernistic geometric constructions overly refined.

"O, why not just use trial and error till you find something that's reasonably close to cutting the circle in five?" said Pythagoras. He would have despised such a thought a year ago, but his escalating traffic with the demons of the *apeiron* had corrupted the asceticism of his taste.

Hoisting himself level with Pythagoras, Archytas gave a short, braying laugh, assuming his mentor to be joking. "Indeed. And why not jump headlong into the pit of impiety and say that integral numbers are not the basis of all things? Why not maintain that the *apeiron* is the very warp and woof of our world?"

"Will Eurythoë be coming for her lesson today?"

Taken aback by the abrupt change in topic, Archytas made a face as if he had bitten down on an olive stone. His demeanor grew stiff and somewhat remote. "My mother, the gods save her, indeed persists in her uncommon thirst for knowledge. Echoing my father Glaucas's complaints, the other wives look askance at Eurythoë's unbecoming philosophical ardor, wondering why she cannot content herself with simple domestic pursuits. But I quash all such talk by defending your virtues, both as a citizen and as a wise man." Archytas stared grimly at his teacher. "I hope my faith in you is fully justified."

Pythagoras felt a smidgen of shame. He disguised the feeling with a peremptory manner. "Of course, of course. But you still haven't answered my question."

Archytas forced out the reply: "Yes, my mother plans to visit you in the late afternoon."

This matter settled, the two men picked up their dialogue not from Archytas's revolutionary construction, but from the point where

Pythagoras's discourses had ended yesterday. As the sun rose higher, they were joined by other young scholars from Tarentum, until finally Pythagoras sat at the center of a stellated polygon of questing minds. The topic for today was Pythagoras's wonderful geometric proof of his great theorem that in a right triangle, the square on the hypotenuse equals the sum of the squares on the sides. To illustrate his argument, Pythagoras drew a diagram in a flat patch of sand; it was his "whirling squares" image, showing a square inscribed at an angle within a larger square.

Though Pythagoras's belief in his original worldview was all but shattered, he still enjoyed the verbal puppet-show of his ideas. He taught with a craft and a grace that come from long experience; he could make dry magnitudes and geometries sing like the notes of a fine musician's lyre.

When the sun was high overhead, rumbling stomachs dictated a break, and the living polygon of scholars fell apart into its component points. Taking advantage of the shade in the mouth of the cave, the town-dwellers broke out food from their wallets, eagerly vying to offer Pythagoras the choicest morsels of flatbread and feta. Their teacher accepted with the stern good nature that chose no favorites. Gourds of cool water from Pythagoras's personal spring complemented their simple fare.

"King Glaucas spoke of you again last night, master," said the sinewy, wolfish Alcibedes. Unlike the other pupils, he wore a short sword at his belt. "At dusk in the forum. He told the Senators and the slow-witted priests of Apollo that you are a sorcerer. The icosahedral ball you gave Eurythoë—Glaucas terms it a magic amulet. He claims the mere sight of it caused the goats to give sour milk."

"My father is troubled," said Archytas. "He fears the people tire of his rule. The unity of our little band disturbs him. He fears you may foment a revolution, Pythagoras. Now that you've won his wife and son as pupils, who else might not follow you?"

"A tyrant's bed is most uneasy," murmured Alcibedes, staring down at his sword.

"What of the common citizens, then?" said Pythagoras. "Do they speak well of me?"

"The farmers are happy to have their fields well-surveyed," said Meno. "And the innkeepers rejoice to have so many of your students lodging in Tarentum."

"Pythagoras's knowledge of the heavens has even helped the priests in their computations of our calendar," chimed in Dascylus. "After all, was our teacher not the first to reveal the identity of the Evening Star and the Morning Star?"

"Even so, Glaucas can inflame the rabble to hate me," said Pythagoras. "At times I fear for my life."

"Perhaps Glaucas fears for his life as well," said Alcibedes. "Who knows what the future might bring? It seems unlikely that both you and he can live here forever, O Master. What if you really were to die? You should prepare us. Can you not lift the injunction of secrecy from your great teachings? We long to spread your wisdom far and wide. Indeed no man is immortal, and when you pass into the Elysian world, it will be our lot to inculcate your noble truths. Were it not better that we begin to practice at it even now?"

For the second time today, Pythagoras felt a twinge of shame. His reasons for making his teachings secret were simply that he did not want to give away that which he could sell to students. "I will ponder upon your suggestion, Alcibedes," he said slowly. "But now, my children, let us return to our studies. If some day you are to farm these plants, you must learn their foliage well."

After several more hours of vibrant discourse, Pythagoras abruptly called a halt to the day's lesson. "My faculties are waning, lads. We shall delve further into the consequences of my great theorem tomorrow."

As he watched the sturdy youths rollick down the slope toward Tarentum, Pythagoras realized he had told them only half the truth. While his intellectual powers were indeed spent for the day, the energies of his loins had reached an almost painful peak as he anticipated the arrival of Eurythoë.

Pythagoras barely had time to clean and curl his beard before he spotted Eurythoë on his side of the river, her delicate, sandal-clad feet scribing a clean curve across the rocky slopes, a curve designed to intersect the vertex of his soul.

She arrived, flushed from her hike and infinitely desirable. Black curls lay pinned by a sheen of sweat to her brow. Her bosom fluttered beneath the white fabric of her robe. A subtle musk as of some wild animal rose from her pleasing form.

Eurythoë's deep gray eyes met the gaze of the philosopher, yet her manner was skittish. Rather than immediately accept Pythagoras's embrace as was her wont, she looked nervously back toward Tarentum.

"What troubles you, dear Eurythoë?"

"I am consumed by fear that our illicit love will be discovered. I saw a most evil omen this morn."

"What manner of omen?"

"One of the slaves returned from the market bearing a pannier of fish, and atop the wet pile lay one with a dark, muddy tail! You've often inveighed against those very creatures! *Eat not fish whose tails are black.*"

Pythagoras made a dismissive gesture. "My reference to the evil nature of such creatures was but an allegorical warning against those who draw strength from muck. Do not trouble yourself any further, Eurythoë. You didn't eat of the fish, did you? Very well then, we've nothing to fear. Let us hie ourselves to my soft, warm pile of sheepskins."

Conducting the wife of Glaucas, the mother of Archytas, into his cave, Pythagoras soon reveled in the sight of her naked charms. Quickly doffing his own clothing, Pythagoras caught her up in his embrace. As she always did, Eurythoë began their lovemaking by stroking his golden thigh.

Marvel of marvels, an extensive, irregular patch of Pythagoras's inner left thigh was some substance other than flesh. The stuff was utterly impermeable, too hard to cut with a knife or even to scratch with the noblest gem, yet it was also like the thinnest leaf of beaten metal, flexibly mimicking the architecture of his muscles and tendons and veins, the bright patch merging imperceptibly with his skin. Though the inadequacy of language forced Pythagoras to call it "adamantine gold," the thigh seemed really to be of a substance quite other than anything seen upon Earth.

The golden thigh was an uncanny scar from Pythagoras's very first dream-meeting with the creatures of the *apeiron*, the thigh an ever-present reminder that the creatures were indeed more than dreams. In that first meeting the Braided Worm and the Crooked Beetle had appeared to him, the Worm a loquacious and foully knotted creature whose form so defied all definition that Pythagoras could never determine if its component strands numbered two, or three, or four. The worm had offered Pythagoras the magical power of the River Number, and when Pythagoras had greedily accepted the offer, the Beetle had bitten deeply into his thigh, turning a part of it into adamantine gold. The Beetle had laughingly termed the change a "memory upgrade," and then somehow the Worm had transferred the River Number into the enhanced Pythagoras. He'd woken from that dream irrevocably changed.

At first, Eurythoë had been frightened and repelled by Pythagoras's gleaming thigh. But when he told her the alteration was a sign of the gods' favor—and why not believe this?—she learned to find it erotically stimulating.

She drew her fingertips across the eerily sensitive surface of the golden thigh, and soon the dust rose from Pythagoras's mound of sheepskins as he bisected Eurythoë's triangle and became the radius to her sphere. The even and the odd blended into the One. And then, all passion slaked, the couple lay loosely embracing, smiling full into each other's eyes.

Trying, as always, to mentally encompass the wonder of Eurythoë, Pythagoras mused that she herself must embody a number form, as did every woman and man. Women were even numbers, and men odd. But what a large number it would take to adequately represent Eurythoë, to capture in a net of notational dots this woman's scent, the curved surfaces of her honey-colored skin, the soothing tones of her normal speech and her sharp cries of ecstasy.

Suddenly there was a clatter from the lip of the cave. Falling stones? Pythagoras sprang nimbly to the arched opening, feeling himself lithe and wise. A well-aimed rock whizzed past his head and shattered against the cliff beside the cave's mouth. All at once he felt himself nude, middle-aged and absurd.

"Against the advice of your own maxim, you have poked fire with the sword, O Pythagoras," sang a mocking voice. "All the town will hear of it."

His tormentor was an open-mouthed, fat-bellied little figure in a white toga that revealed bare, thickly tufted legs. At first glance he looked like—a vengeful fish with a black tail. Evidently he'd come to spy on Eurythoë's lovemaking. He made the insulting gesture of the fig, and raced down the slope like a homing pigeon.

"Senator Pemptus!" exclaimed Eurythoë. "One of my husband's spies. O, Pythagoras, you must flee. I'll hurry down and try to salve my husband's wounded pride. But I fear the worst for you." She began weeping.

"Must I run from an innumerate, bean-eating tyrant like a common slave?" said Pythagoras. "And what of my pupils? What of our love? I'd rather remain here in my cave, aloof with my music." Pythagoras gestured at his beloved monochord, a one-stringed instrument that had taught him much. "I've not told you this, Eurythoë, but the gods have granted me certain miraculous powers in addition to my golden thigh."

Eurythoë hugged him, dried her eyes, and began trying to repair the disarray of her hair with ivory pins. She succeeded only in making it appear that she wore a lopsided bird's nest atop her head. Finally she spoke again.

"There are too many of them, Pythagoras, and they will come for you. Humble yourself and flee. For what does anything matter if you or both of us are dead? Save yourself, and let me do what I can to salvage my own position. Think of your own maxim, Pythagoras: *Give way to the flock!*"

"You are right, my dear," said Pythagoras, quietly pulling on his robe. "*The flying dust survives the storm.* I leave on the instant. Spare me one last kiss."

Smooth lips met bearded ones, and then Eurythoë was light-footedly gone. Pythagoras dallied in the cave long enough only to pack a wallet with food. All other necessaries were kept within the confines of his skull.

Emerging into the reddening light of the westering sun, the philosopher paused for a moment's strategic reflection. Behind him, above his vantage, stretched an impassable wilderness of mountains: easy to lose pursuers there, but dangerous terrain to the hunted one as well. From those treacherous peaks he might never emerge. No, much wiser to head downhill, cross the Nessus, skirt Tarentum slyly while the citizens still organized themselves, then light out for greener pastures. No stranger to travel, Pythagoras had sojourned far and wide, residing for extended stretches in Thebes and Babylon, not to mention Athens, Rhodes, and now the rustic backwater of Tarentum. Surely he would easily find a new home in a land where the people were more understanding of the needs of genius.

Assuming he could bypass rustic Tarentum with his skull intact.

For the first time in many months, Pythagoras descended the scree-strewn slope that led from his cave. His golden thigh throbbed, but whether from simple exertion, in warning of some evil to come, or in memory of Eurythoë's delicate touch, the savant could not say.

The Nessus was bridged by but a single structure. Though it was too distant to be quite sure, it looked as if the dregs of Tarentum might be massing there. His enemies. To avoid the brutal herd, Pythagoras would need to cross the river Nessus on his own. Though there was no convenient ford, he had no fears about traversing the flood.

On the weedy banks of the river, well upstream of the bridge, half-concealed amidst some fragrant bushes, Pythagoras halted. Summoning up the Braided Worm's number of the river, poising the form in his mind, the philosopher dangled his hand into the water.

At his touch, a pair of liquid lips big as a man's body cohered on the surface of the gurgling waters, like bas-relief on an Assyrian temple.

"Greetings, Pythagoras!" said the Nessus, its voice like a pair of fish slapped together. "You have not visited in too long. Shall we resume our discussion of Atlantis?"

"I haven't time now, my friend. Enemies are near. Can you bear me safely across your width?"

"Gladly. Indeed, I can carry you dry for as long a distance as you like."

Pythagoras thought for a moment. "Very well, then, bear me downstream past the furthest limits of Tarentum."

"Step atop my flow."

Continually keeping the River Number in his mind, Pythagoras walked out across the top of the river and seated himself cross-legged upon the surface in midstream.

The water felt smooth and cool beneath him, a bit like a leathern cushion to the touch. The current swept him downstream towards the bridge.

Yes, just as he'd feared, a motley mob of the ignorant were gathered there, with Glaucas and Pemptus at their head. Armed with sickles, slings, pitchforks and the occasional sword, the citizens watched gawking and gape-mouthed as the reviled philosopher surged toward them. But now Glaucas gave a high cry and the attack began. A stone splashed into the water but one cubit from Pythagoras's chest, then another, and then a spear.

Without losing his focus upon the River Number, Pythagoras moved another of his power-numbers into a fresh part of his mind. It was a Cloud Number, the gift of the Swarm of Eyes. He invoked the vast, inchoate magnitude, and was instantly enveloped in a great bank of impenetrable fog. Thus cloaked from view, he got to his feet and walked to a new position upon Nessus's rushing stream. Cries of fear and anger sounded from above and missiles splashed into the river at random.

Nessus bore Pythagoras onward, hastening toward the sea. As the river and the philosopher traveled along, they discoursed. "Searching your mind, I see an interesting maxim ascribed to the philosopher Heraclitus," said Nessus. "*No man steps in the same river twice.* But is not my form always the same? Do I not ever respond to the same number?"

"Yes, your essential form remains the same," answered Pythagoras. "But, as a river, your watery substance is ever-changing. Heraclitus's teaching has a subtler and more esoteric meaning as well. A man is like a river in that his substance *also* changes from day to day, not so rapidly as a river's, but just as ineluctably. One could even say *No man kicks the same stone twice.* The stone may be fully the same, but the man is not the same, nor is the man-kicking-stone. For a man, as for a river, all is flow. May I ask you a question now, Nessus?"

"Verily you may," said the great watery lips that rode the surface at Pythagoras's side.

"Last night I received the knowledge of a number from the Crooked Beetle," said Pythagoras. "The Beetle said this was the last of these magical magnitudes that I shall learn. If hold it up in my mind can you study it and tell me it's meaning? I need to know how to use it. I feel I will need every arrow in my quiver for the trials to come."

Just then the river narrowed and entered a steep gorge. For the time, all philosophical enquiry was set aside in the necessity to bear Pythagoras intact past splintered branches and jagged stones. By the time they reached the calm pool beyond the final cataract, both Pythagoras and Nessus's powers had flagged. Pythagoras settled down through the water's surface to find himself standing knee-deep upon a spit of sand. It was dusk.

"Your new number is a mystery to me, O Pythagoras," said Nessus softly. His lips were as tiny ripples. "Good luck unriddling it. I leave you here. And when you step in me again, though we are different, may our friendship be the same."

"Give my regards to King Poseidon of the sea."

"I am with him even now, as am I also with Zeus in the springs of the highest hills. It's a pity you know not the number of the Ocean. Poseidon could do much to help you."

"I daresay I'm out of Tarentum's reach already," said Pythagoras confidently. "I can settle into the next comfortable cave I find."

It was growing dark quickly. Pythagoras found himself shelter beneath a thicket and used the Tangled Tree's handy Sheepskin Number to make himself a comfortable bed. He lay there, nibbling bread and cheese from his wallet, wondering if Eurythoë were safe. Perhaps she could still visit him once he'd resettled. Presently he fell asleep.

Tonight it was the Braided Worm who addressed Pythagoras in his *apeiron* dreams. Fearfully bright, the Worm had but a few strands, surely no more than five, but these were, as always, too oddly linked to enumerate. The braid ended in a flat head at one end, with three bright eyes and a fanged mouth.

"Why haven't you started teaching of us yet, Pythagoras?" demanded the indeterminate Worm. "Why keep spreading the wishful lie that whole, finite numbers are the substance of all things? Aren't you grateful for what the *apeiron* has done for you? My River Number saved your life today."

"Yes, and it was your friend the Beetle who spoiled my leg during your very first visit, you unclean thing," muttered Pythagoras.

"It is thanks to the adamantine gold of your thigh that you have the mind-power to understand numbers which approximate the unbounded essences of true things," said the Braided Worm. "The thigh is, one might say, the wax and feather wing upon which you soar."

"But like any such a wing, it can melt," whispered the Tangled Tree, which seemed to have replaced the thicket beneath which Pythagoras had bedded down. The Tangled Tree curved up through several levels of simple branchings, but at less than a man's height above the ground, it split into a disordered gibberish of uncountable forkings followed by yet more layers of endlessly ramifying twigs. The Tree's voice was a woolly drone, with a burred edge to it. "Remember the tale of Icarus," said the Tangled Tree. "He flew too near the Sun."

Now there was a crashing noise and the Crooked Beetle forced his twittering mandibles through the chaos of the Tangled Tree. "My companions are too gentle with you Pythagoras. Know you this: before the sun sets twice, your flesh will die. Speak well of us while you have time, for the new number I gave you will save you from utter annihilation."

The crashing of the Tangled Tree's twigs grew louder, and now the grinning Bristle Cat and the Swarm of Eyes appeared, pressing towards Pythagoras, the Bristle Cat performing its unsettling trick of turning itself inside out, changing smoothly from spiky fur to a pink wet flesh that no human should ever have to see. The Swarm of Eyes moved like a cloud of gnats or flies, with each wheeling member of the Swarm a tiny bright Eye. Yet whenever Pythagoras stared very closely at one of the dancing Eyes, the Eye dissolved into a smaller Swarm of smaller Eyes who were perhaps still smaller Swarms themselves—there was nothing solid at all in the Swarm and no end to its divisions, the Swarm of Eyes was *apeiron* in the very highest degree.

"Praise us before you die," chorused the five terrible forms. "And we will save you with the Beetle's number." The Crooked Beetle gave Pythagoras an admonishing nip, and now the terrified philosopher woke up groaning. Horribly, the crashing of brush continued. It was early dawn, with mist rising up from the pool of the river nearby. More crashing and heavy breath. A growl. Lions? No, worse, it was dogs, followed by the railing tenor voice of King Glaucas.

"Keep a good lookout, citizens! The dogs smell something. I'll wager the old goat is bedded down here."

Desperately Pythagoras invoked the Cloud Number given him by the Swarm of Eyes. This added greatly to the mist that filled this little glen, but the new dampness seemed only the heighten the sensitivity of the dogs' noses. By the time Pythagoras could fully get to his feet, the hounds were upon him, baying and slavering as if the great philosopher were a cornered fox. The men's rough, ignorant hands bound him at wrists and ankles.

The trial before the Senate and the priests of Apollo took place in the town forum that very afternoon. Pythagoras's announced crimes were sedition and blasphemy—and not adultery, for Glaucas had no wish to publicly wear the cuckold's horns. The charges averred that

Pythagoras was teaching things contrary to the beliefs that underlay the established orders of heaven and earth.

"Do you deny that King Glaucas's power is divinely ordained?" demanded Pemptus, his fish-lipped mouth a self-righteous ellipse.

"Of course I deny it," said Pythagoras. "There is nothing more absurd than an aging tyrant." The only one who dared to cheer this remark was Alcibedes, standing well back in the crowd, one hand on his sword.

"And do you teach that all things are numbers and that mathematizing mortals may hope to comprehend the divine workings of the world?" asked the head priest, a bullying blockhead named Turnus.

"This is what I have ever been teaching. But—"

Pythagoras's followers were there in a mass, and now Archytas rose to his feet. "Father Glaucas, may I speak?"

Glaucas shook his head, but when Eurythoë, at his side, gave him a sharp elbow in the ribs he sighed, "Yes, my son."

"If it be a crime to believe that numbers are all things, then execute me and these other young savants with our wise, though imperfect, teacher. All of us follow his noble precept that to understand numbers is to understand all things. Be this capital blasphemy, Glaucas, then your son too must die. Rather than persecuting the pursuit of truth, O Father, why not let Pythagoras go into exile? And we adepts of his secret teachings will be free to follow along."

The priests and senators conferred. Eager not to sow further dissension among the polis, they soon approved this notion of exile for Pythagoras and his band.

"Very well then, let them travel away and start a new colony," intoned Glaucas. He, for one, would be happy to have his young and vigorous heir far from the scene.

Thinking this to be the salvation the Crooked Beetle had promised him, Pythagoras now felt impelled to honor the requests of his *apeiron* helpers. He stood and raised his hands for silence. "Good people, I have indeed been teaching for many a year that all things are a play of little numbers. I have taught that God is 1, Man is 2, Woman is 3, Justice is 4, and Marriage is 5. And my followers know that numbers embody solid shapes as well: consider how subtly a mere eight vertices can limn a cube. My researches have revealed that there five and only five regular solids to be formed by small dot patterns, and it has been my teaching that these solids form the essences of all material things." There was an approving murmur of excitement. Archytas looked startled and pleased, and even the hard-faced Alcibedes allowed himself a smile. The Master was finally sharing his noble truths with all! Even the thick-headed priests of Apollo seemed intrigued by the great precepts. Pythagoras paused till silence returned, then continued.

"Yes, I have taught that Earth is the cube, Air is the octahedron, Fire the tetrahedron, Water the icosahedron, and the Cosmos the dodecahedron. Well and good." Pythagoras drew a deep breath and gathered the courage to continue. "But now I must tell you that these teachings are nursery rhymes, childish fables, the fond pratings of an old fool. The *apeiron* runs in and out of every earthly object, and, lo my little ones, the infinite even inhabits our minds." A furious hubbub threatened to drown him out. Pythagoras raised his voice to a shriek. "Everything is crooked, irrational, unlimited, *apeiron*—"

Loudest among the voices was Archytas. "Pythagoras has gone mad!"

"Kill him!" cried the crowd.

"No!" screamed Eurythoë, but Pythagoras had no firm defenders other than this single, fair voice.

"He will die on the morrow!" rang Glaucas's fruity tones.

"Behold what the *apeiron* can do!" screamed Pythagoras in desperation.

He invoked his four familiar power-numbers to make a mound of Sheepskins, to set them reekingly on Fire and burn off the bonds that held him, to shroud the forum in a Cloud, and to call the River to overflow its banks and rush into the streets of Tarentum. He'd expected to use the confusion to escape, and until he found himself pinned in the arms of Pemptus and Turnus, he thought perhaps he'd succeeded. But the confusion in the forum eventually abated, and he was once more a captive on display.

"Look at him, Eurythoë and Archytas," called Pemptus, tightening a rope around Pythagoras's neck. "Look at the dirty old goat. We'll put him under a door and crush him tomorrow. Each of us will add a stone. And I'll see to it there's no shirking."

"Well said," chortled Glaucas, appearing through the smoke and fog.

Archytas drew close. "Have you then become a sorcerer, O Master? Only to befoul the noble truths of mathematics? Nevertheless, I shall spread your earlier teachings."

"And what if my power is such that your fool of a father is unable to kill me?" demanded Pythagoras. "What then, Archytas? I have certain assurances from my *apeiron* familiars that—that —"

"That what?"

"O, Pythagoras," cried Eurythoë, her voice breaking. "Where has your madness brought you?"

Pythagoras spent a sleepless night penned in a dusty boulder-walled granary. His thoughts during the night were not of death but rather of mathematics. He felt he was about to die with something great left undone.

Pythagoras was proud of his analysis of the five regular polyhedra, eternally grateful to the One for his discovery of his noble theorem about the right triangle, and well-pleased with the philosophical frills and furbelows he'd embroidered around the properties of the smaller numbers. But something was still missing, some key consequence of his theorem of the right triangle—and he couldn't quite pin down what it was. It had, he was sure, something to do with the *apeiron*, for surely this was the reason why God had sent the mentors to him. During the very wee hours of the morn, he became absorbed in contemplating of the nature of the ratio between the diagonal and the side of a square. He sat lost in thought till the crowing of the cock.

Wakeful as he was all that night, Pythagoras remained unvisited by any of the warped denizens of the *apeiron*. But, wait, at the exact moment when the pompous Pemptus came to lead him away to his doom he thought to detect, impossibly, the perpetually leering face of the Bristle Cat peering at him from a shadowy corner of the storeroom. The fearsome feline features, composed of a myriad thorny projections, appeared to wink at Pythagoras, who stopped dead in his tracks.

"Superstitious about a granary cat?" laughed Pemptus. "Crazy dreamer. Better to worry about something real—something like a rock." Pemptus kicked at a loose stone the size of a melon. "Bring this along for me, would you, Pythagoras? It can be the first one placed upon your door."

Pythagoras hesitated and the cat—seemingly a real cat after all—ran across his path and out the door. But how complex and richly structured the beast was, how subtle were its motions. And just as it passed from his sight, the cat seemed to perform the Bristle Cat's loathsome trick of turning itself inside out—but surely this was impossible.

"Carry the rock, you," grated Pemptus's muscular centurion.

Pythagoras kept his head high and his gaze level as he was led through Tarentum, ignoring the jeering crowd. A large open-air altar of slate, already warm from the rising sun's embrace, awaited the hapless body of the old philosopher. Thrown on his back onto this unyielding pallet, Pythagoras sought to compose his mind while a wooden door was laid upon him. Glaucas himself set the first of the stones onto Pythagoras's chest, the very stone which Pemptus had forced him to carry. The door pressed down as if Pythagoras were the pan of some insensate scale, or the conclusion of a sum whose components were the killing weights.

The citizens pressed forward, each carrying a stone, a few of them leaning close to hiss curses of execration, but surprisingly many whispering words of comfort. The rebellious Alcibedes was missing from the line of citizens, but Eurythoë and Archytas were there, forced forward by a soldier with a drawn sword. Their stones were no larger than hens' eggs, yet they of all the weights felt the heaviest of all.

Breathing was quickly becoming an impossible task for the old man's frail chest. Letting the air out was easy, but drawing the air back in—ah, there was the bring-down, there was the drag. The sun blazed in Pythagoras's eyes and a buzzing filled his ears. Something shiny came at him—a fat beetle, landing on his chin. The citizens filed by, still placing their rocks. The omen of a glistening insect upon the tortured man's face was so inauspicious that each of them felt impelled to look away.

The beetle gave a modulated buzz, and Pythagoras let himself imagine he could hear it as words. "Use the number I gave you, fool," the beetle seemed to say. "Focus!"

Another stone descended, followed by yet another, and that one by a third and fourth. Pythagoras felt his ribs compress and snap, pain flooding him like liquor from Hades. Into his blood-buzzing ears came the noises from the crowd of watchers: taunts and shouts and a lone female sob.

"Enough now," yodeled Glaucas, who'd been closely watching the torture from one side. "The man is broken. Remove the rocks. You three slaves over there, carry him to the riverside midden to expire. It will be fitting for Pythagoras to exhale his soul into the fumes of human waste. That should be *apeiron* enough for him." Glaucas raised his voice to a yet higher pitch. "Let this be a warning to any who would challenge my might! I am as a God, and all must bow down before me."

Far from prostrating themselves, the citizens simply stared at Glaucas. This unpleasant execution seemed to be doing the King's popularity no good. And many were the hands that reached out to remove the rocks and the door from Pythagoras.

When the weight went away, Pythagoras's punctured lungs snatched whistling breaths of sweet air. At some far remove he witnessed himself lying uncovered in the forum, saw the weeping Eurythoë and Archytas bid him farewell, and saw his bloody form tossed onto a rude cart and trundled through the streets by three slaves. He was beyond pain now, well into the tunnel to the Elysium. He was ready for the end.

Yet his progress into the final ecstasy kept being thwarted by something nipping at him, buzzing, tickling. Either it was the bug upon his face, or it was a vision of the Crooked Beetle. At this point inside and outside were the same.

491

"You did well to speak for us, Pythagoras," said the bug or the Beetle. "You are a worthy man. Now use my number."

"Hhhhhow," came Pythagoras's faint sigh.

Emerging from within the Crooked Beetle's very mandibles, the Bristle Cat said, "We can't tell you what the number means, because if you don't know it yourself you don't know yourself to know nohow. Contrariwise if I tell you to know there's no you knowing, you know?" The Beetle pinched irritably at the smirking Cat, but the protean beast drew its head down into its body, sending a commensurately-sized pink bulge out from its rear.

The shock of Pythagoras's body landing in the dump caused his eyes to flicker open. He was fully anaesthetized and paralyzed by his body's collapse. His filmed eyes stared dully upwards. The slaves who'd had brought his corpse thither walked away, laughing at the lot of the only citizen worse off than themselves.

Pythagoras tried to inventory his pitiful condition. He lay beneath a dead tree of bare polished wood beside a sparkling filth-choked rivulet worming through the dump. A swarm of glistening flies buzzed around his chest wounds, tasting of the fresh blood. And there was a beetle crawling on his nose; from the corner of one eye he could see it. A tufted yellow cat came ambling up, leaning over to taste, like the flies, of his hot, sticky blood.

His vision grew fainter; his heart beat as weakly and erratically as an infant drummer; his lungs drew in only the most shallow of painful draughts; his broken bones jabbed like a thousand daggers. From these incredible wounds, he would never heal. This was the end.

Pythagoras could feel his densely cultivated mind beginning to disintegrate. Strange, to imagine that such a unique individual as himself could disappear, that a being composed of such hard-won constituents could simply dissolve. His golden thigh began to throb then, as if to remind him of all the ways he differed from other mortals. Focusing on that preternatural portion of himself, Pythagoras was reminded of the great magical numbers that this memory enhancement enabled him to store. The numbers for Sheepskin, River, Fire, Cloud and —

A great revelation struck the dying philosopher with titanic force. The fifth number-form represented the quintessence of Pythagoras. Of course! Summoning all his vaunted powers of concentration and willpower, Pythagoras took mental control of the fifth number, then projected it outward from inside his dying self with explosive force —

He had a moment of dual vision. On the one hand he was dying, moving forward through a tunnel towards an all-encompassing white light. On the other hand, he was standing in the dump, looking down at the tormented form of poor old man.

Pythagoras held up a vigorous, apparently normal arm before his eyes, and laughed heartily. Triumph, even over death! Such were the godly rewards of his brave explorations of the *apeiron*. He took a deep breath into easily working lungs, then swung a fist to thump himself on his chest.

Much to Pythagoras's alarm and surprise, his fist merged with his torso like the obscene bodily involutions of the Bristle Cat! At that moment, a familiar voice rang out. It was an apparition of the Crooked Beetle, floating as a large dusky ghost above the physical beetle that was still perched upon his old body's face.

"Hail, Pythagoras!" twittered the Beetle, seemingly in ecstasy over the philosopher's new body. "Welcome to life as a pure mathematical form! I encrypted you rather nicely, don't you think? I did the basic encoding that night I first bit you. And all along I've been updating the Pythagoras number to include your most recent thoughts. That's what I was doing sitting on your face just now. Keeping your number right up to the minute. You remember everything, don't you?"

Pythagoras nodded mutely, and pulled his limb from his chest with a queer, unnamable sensation. Ranged around him were also ghostly forms of the Tangled Tree, the Braided Worm, the Bristle Cat, the Swarm of Eyes. Each of them was connected by the finest of tendrils to their earthly instances here in this malodorous dump.

"Your new, numerically defined body still has only a not-quite-life," explained the Beetle. "It's unreal in the same way that your number-conjured flames are but colorful tetrahedra until being boosted into full reality by the presence of the elemental Fire within the kindling wood. Your broken old body—it contains *your* kindling."

Pythagoras looked down at his dying carcass with a feeling of revulsion. It was as uninviting as a soiled, wet toga. "You're not counseling me to don that same old mortal coil, are you?"

The Crooked Beetle spat, not a number this time, but a viscous dark glob that landed on Pythagoras's foot with a tingling sensation. It was a tiny, crooked copy of the Beetle itself, connected to the ghostly Beetle by another of the thin, silken strands. The new beetle stretched out its wings, waved them tentatively, then buzzed into the air. "I don't like to explain everything," said the great Beetle.

"You need your you to be you," said the smiling Cat, rubbing against Pythagoras's ghostly leg, and then passing right through it. "Be your own son and father."

"Breathe in what you expire," buzzed the Swarm of Eyes.

The Braided Worm beside the little brook swayed back and forth like a charmed snake. "Don't fail us, Pythagoras. It still remains for you to prove your greatest result—to prove that we are real."

"So bend down and breathe in your dying breath!" exhorted the Tangled Tree, gesturing with every one of its innumerable branches.

Of course. Now Pythagoras remembered the custom whereby a child would try to breathe in the last breath of a dying parent. His insubstantial body knelt at the side of his supine flesh. With eyes near-blinded by the light of eternity he stared up at his fresh-minted body. With clear fresh new eyes he stared down at his old self. Now came the dying man's final breath, the expiration, and Pythagoras's number-built new body breathed it in.

From the viewpoint of his old self, Pythagoras felt as if he'd been yanked out of paradise. He felt grief and a kind of homesickness at not fully merging with the divine One whose hem he'd only just begun to touch. From the viewpoint of his new self, Pythagoras felt invigorated, renewed and—above all—solid and real. And then he was no longer two, but one. The infinitude of his divine soul had now fulfilled the incarnation of the number-model of his body.

Looking around the dump, Pythagoras could no longer see the ghostly images of his *apeiron* friends—and friends they truly were, not rivals or enemies. Their earthly avatars still here upon the midden remained mute: a tree, a worm of water, a cat, a swarm of flies and a beetle. Pythagoras fully felt how truly these earthly forms did embody the *apeiron*, felt more strongly than ever the undivided divinity that is present within all things, whether great or mean.

His new-made body felt strong and sound, though not overly so. The number form was, after all, only that of an old man. But he was no longer an old man who'd been crushed to death by stones. There was one more change as well. The adamantine gold was gone from his thigh, and looking within himself he saw that he'd lost his knowledge of the five magic numbers. He was glad.

So what to do next? Most important was to see Eurythoë. And the Braided Worm had said something very intriguing about Pythagoras having another great result to prove. Perhaps the simplest would be to go back to his cave, receive visitors as always, and continue to think about mathematics. Surely his resurrection would frighten Glaucas into leaving him alone.

But before doing anything else, Pythagoras tended to his soul's former shell. Gripping the corpse by the shins, Pythagoras bumped it across the slope of the midden and into a patch of trees. He lacked any shovel to dig with, but he used a stick to scrape out a shallow grave, and then gathered a great heap of brush to decently cover the body. It took a long time, several hours in fact, but what did time matter to a man risen from the dead? While he worked, the rudiments of a new and wonderful theorem began coming to him. It hinged, as he'd suspected, on the ratio of a square's diagonal to its side.

His earlier theorem of the right triangle said that the square on a diagonal is equal to the sum of the squares on the two sides. If the two sides were equal, this meant that the diagonal square was twice the magnitude of each side square. Put differently, a diagonal square and a side square were in proportion two to one. And put differently once again, the ratio of the diagonal to the side could be called the "square root of two".

For several years now, Pythagoras and his followers had sought for a whole number ratio to represent this curious "square root of two." The search involved looking for squares that were in a perfect two to one ratio. 49 to 25 was close and 100 to 49 was closer, which meant the square root of two was close to the ratio 7/5 and closer to the ratio 10/7. But the match was never quite perfect, and now that he'd finally let the *apeiron* all the way into his heart, Pythagoras fully grasped that the match never would be perfect at all. There was no whole number ratio precisely equal to the square root of two.

He found himself singing a happy tune as he finished up the reverential chores of covering his corpse. Now that he fully understood what he wanted to prove, he would find a way to do it. Mulling over the distinctions between odd and even numbers, Pythagoras set out towards Tarentum. The clever Archytas could help him hone a proper proof.

At the edge of the dump, Pythagoras encountered Eurythoë, her face wet with tears. She was dressed in the black garments of mourning. For him? She didn't really see him, for she was too busy peering past him, looking for his body on the dump.

"Woman, why are you weeping?" said Pythagoras. "Whom do you seek?"

Eurythoë wiped her face with the black cloth of her veil. "Sir, if you have carried him off, tell me where you have laid him, and I will take him away."

Pythagoras spoke her name. "Eurythoë."

She turned and fully saw him at last. "Pythagoras!"

"My dear, even-souled Eurythoë. The *apeiron* has saved me. Good as new." He chuckled and skipped about, executing a little twirl.

"My dear, odd-brained Pythagoras," sang Eurythoë. "But what of your madness?"

"What madness? Believe this, woman, I'm working on a proof of the reality of the *apeiron*! It all has to do with evens and odds."

"Then I can help you! Let's go up to your cave."

"Right now? What about Glaucas and the priests?"

"Glaucas is dead," said Eurythoë, seemingly not overly saddened by having to deliver this news. "Alcibedes slew him only minutes after they carted your body away. My son Archytas is the new king, and the populace rejoices. The priests of Apollo will do as Archytas says. We already have Turnus's abject assurances." She burst out laughing. "Glaucas is the official reason why I'm wearing mourning. But, O Pythagoras, it was only for you."

"I should speak to Archytas," said Pythagoras. "About the wonderful new proof."

"We'll do that later," said Eurythoë, kissing him. "After the cave. I want to give you a proper welcome."

"Very well then," said Pythagoras. "Let's take the bridge across the river."

"No more sorcery?" said Eurythoë.

"No," said Pythagoras. "Just mathematics."

Note on "The Square Root of Pythagoras" (With Paul Di Filippo)

Written in 1999.
SF Age, October 1999

This is a story I always wanted to write. As a math professor, I've had a lot of occasion to meditate about Pythagoras. He's a very shadowy historical figure, and the stories about him which survive are miracle tales, many of which are incorporated into this story. In February of 1999, I visited Paul Di Filippo at his home in Providence, and he helped me to finally get a Pythagoras story done.

I have five of the apeiron beings, because I think of mathematics as having core concepts: Number, Space, Logic, Infinity and Information. These correspond to, respectively, the Tangled Tree, the Braided Worm, the Bristle Cat, the Swarm of Eyes and the Crooked Beetle. The Crooked Beetle is also our old friend the Mandelbrot

Set. The creatures also represent, again in the same order, Earth, Water, Fire, Air and the Cosmos.

POCKETS (WITH JOHN SHIRLEY)

When the woman from Endless Media called, Wendel was out on the fake balcony, looking across San Pablo Bay at the lights of the closed-down DeGroot Chemicals Plant. On an early summer evening, the lights marking out the columns of steel and the button-shaped chemical tanks took on an unreal glamour; the plant became an otherworldly palace. He'd tried to model the plant with the industrial-strength Real2Graphix program his dad had brought home from RealTek before he got fired. But Wendel still didn't know the tricks for filling a virtual scene with the world's magic and menace, and his model looked like a cartoon toy. Someday he'd get his chops and make the palace come alive. You could set a killer-ass game there if you knew how. After high school, maybe he could get into a good gaming university. He didn't want to "go" to an online university if he could help it; virtual teachers, parallel programmed or not, couldn't answer all your questions.

The phone rang just as he was wondering whether Dad could afford to pay tuition for someplace real. He waited for his dad to get the phone, and after three rings he realized with a chill that Dad had probably gone into a pocket, and he'd have to answer the phone himself.

The fake porch, created for window washers, and to create an impression of coziness the place had always lacked, creaked under his feet as he went to climb through the window. The narrow splintery wooden walkway outside their window was on the third floor of an old waterfront motel converted to studio apartments. Their tall strip of windows, designed to savor a view that was now unsavory, looked down a crumbling cliff at a mud beach, the limp gray waves sluggish in stretched squares of light from the buildings edging the bluff. Down the beach some guys with flashlights were moving around, looking for the little pocket-bubbles that floated in like dead jellyfish. Thanks to the accident that had closed down the DeGroot Research Center, beyond the still-functioning chemicals plant, San Pablo Bay was a good spot to scavenge for pocket-bubbles, which was why Wendel and his dad had ended up living here.

To get to the phone, he had to skirt the mercury-like bubble of Dad's pocket, presently a big flattened shape eight feet across and six high, rounded like a river stone. The pocket covered most of the available space on the living room floor, and he disliked having to touch it. There was that sensation when you touched them—not quite a sting, not quite an electrical shock, not even intolerable. But you didn't want to prolong the feeling.

Wendel touched the speakerphone tab. "Hello, Bell residence."

"Well this doesn't sound like Rothman Bell." It was a woman's voice coming out of the speakerphone; humorous, ditzy, but with a heartening undercurrent of business.

"No ma'am, I'm his son Wendel."

"That's right, I remember he had a son. You'd be about fourteen now?"

"Sixteen."

"Sixteen! Whoa. Time jogs on. This is Manda Solomon. I knew your dad when he worked at MetaMeta. He really made his mark there. Is he home?"

He hesitated. There was no way to answer that question honestly without having to admit Dad was in a pocket, and pocket-slugs had a bad reputation. "No ma'am. But..."

He looked toward the pocket. It was getting smaller now. If things went as usual, it would shrink to grapefruit size, then swell back up and burst—and Dad would be back. Occasionally a pocket might bounce through two or three or even a dozen shrink-and-grow cycles before releasing its inhabitant, but it never took terribly long, at least from the outside. Dad might be back before this woman hung up. She sounded like business, and that made Wendel's pulse race. It was a chance.

If he could just keep her talking. After a session in a pocket Dad wouldn't be in any shape to call anyone back, sometimes not for days— but if you caught him just coming out, and put the phone in his hand, he might keep it together long enough, still riding the pocket's high. Wendel just hoped this wasn't going to be the one pocket that would finally kill his father.

"Can I take a message, Ms., um..." With his mind running so fast he'd forgotten her name.

"Manda Solomon. Just tell him..."

"Can I tell him where you're calling from?" He grimaced at himself in the mirror by the front door. Dumbass, don't interrupt her, you'll scare her off.

"From San Jose, I'm a project manager at Endless Media. Just show him—oh, have you got iTV?"

"Yeah. You want me to put it on?" Good, that'd take some more time. If Dad had kept up the payments.

He carried the phone over to the iTV screen hanging on the wall like a seascape; there was a fuzzy motel-decor photo of a sunset endlessly playing in it now, the kitschy orange clouds swirling in the same tape-looping pattern. He tapped the tab on the phone that would hook it to the iTV, and faced the screen so that the camera in the corner of the frame could pick him up but only on head-shot setting so she couldn't see the pocket too. "You see me?"

"Yup. Here I come."

Her picture appeared in a window in an upper corner of the screen, a pleasant looking redhead in early middle age, hoop earrings, frank smile. She held up an e-book, touched the page turner which instantly scrolled an image of a photograph that showed a three-dimensional array of people floating in space, endless pairs of people spaced out into the nodes of a warped jungle-gym lattice, a man and a woman at each node. Wendel recognized the couple as his dad and his mother. At first it looked as if all the nodes were the same, but when you looked closer, you could see that the people at some of the more distant nodes weren't Mom and Dad after all. In fact some of them didn't even look like people. This must be a photo taken inside a pocket with tunnels coming out of it. Wendel had never seen it before. "If you print out the picture, he'll know what it's all about," Manda was saying.

"Sure." Wendel saved the picture to the iTV's memory, hoping it would work. He didn't want Manda to know their printer was broken and wouldn't be repaired anytime soon.

"Well it's been a sweet link but I gotta go—just tell him to call. Here's the number, ready to save? Got it? Okay, then. He'll remember me."

Wendel saw she wasn't wearing a wedding band. He got tired of taking care of Dad alone. He tried to think of some way to keep her on the line. "He'll be right back—he's way overdue. I expect him…"

"Whoops, I really gotta jam." She reached toward her screen, then hesitated, her head cocked as she looked at his image. "That's what it is: You look a lot like Jena, you know? Your mom."

"I guess."

"Jena was a zippa-trip. I hated it when she disappeared."

"I don't remember her much."

"Oops, my boss is chiming hysterically at me. Bye!"

"Um—wait." He turned to glance at the dull silvery bubble, already bouncing back from its minimum size, but when he turned back, Manda Solomon was gone and it was only the showy sunset again. "Shit."

He went to the bubble and kicked it angrily. He couldn't feel anything but "stop," with his sneaker on. It wasn't like kicking an object, it was like something stopped you, turned you back toward your own time flow. Just "stopness." It was saying "no" with the stuff of forever itself. There was no way to look inside it: once someone crawled in through a pocket's navel, it sealed up all over.

He turned away, heard something—and when he looked back the pocket was gone and his dad, stinking and retching and raggedly bearded, was crawling toward him across the carpet.

Next morning, it seemed to Wendel that his Dad sucked the soup down more noisily than ever before. His hands shook and he spilled soup on the blankets.

His dad was supposedly forty—but he looked fifty-five. He'd spent maybe fifteen years in the pockets—adding up to only a few weeks in outside time, ten minutes here and two hours there and so on.

Dad sat up in his bed, staring out to the bay, sloppily drinking the soup from a bowl, and Wendel had to look away. Sitting at the breakfast bar that divided the kitchenette from the rest of the room, he found himself staring at the pile of dirty clothes in the corner. They needed some kind of hamper, and he could go to some Martinez garage sale and find one next to free. But that was something Dad ought to do; Wendel sensed that if he once started doing that sort of thing, parental things, his dad would give a silent gasp of relief and lean on him, more and more; and paradoxically fall away from him, into the pockets.

"I was gone like—ten minutes world-time?" said Dad. "I don't suppose I missed anything here in this…this teeming hive of activity."

"Ten minutes?" said Wendel. He snorted. "You're still gone, Dad. And, yes, there was a call for you. A woman from Endless Media. Manda Solomon. She left her number and a picture."

"Manda?" said Dad. "That flake? Did you tell her I was in a pocket?"

"Right," said Wendel contemptuously. "Like I told her my Dad's a pocket-slug."

Dad opened his mouth like he was going to protest the disrespect—then thought better of it. He shrugged, with as much cool as he could manage. "Manda's down with pockets, Wendel. Half the guys programming virtual physics for MetaMeta were using them when I was there. Pockets are a great way to make a deadline. The MetaMeta crunch-room was like a little glen of chrome puff-balls. Green carpeting, you wave? Manda used to walk around setting sodas and pizzas down outside the pockets. We'd work in there for days, when it was minutes on the outside—get a real edge on the other programmers. She was just a support tech then. We called her Fairy Princess and we crunchers were the Toads of the Short Forest, popping out all loaded on the bubble-rush. Manda's gone down in the world, what I heard, in terms of who she works for…"

"She's a project manager. Better than a support tech."

"Nice of her to think of me." Dad made a little grimace. "Endless Media's about one step past being a virtu-porn Webble. Where's the picture she sent?"

"I saved it in the iTV," said Wendel, and pushed the buttons to show it.

Dad made a groaning sound. "Turn it off, Wendel. Put it away."

"Tell me what it is, first," said Wendel, pressing the controller buttons to zoom in on the faces. It was definitely—

"Mom and me," said Dad shakily. "I took that photo the week before she died." His voice became almost inaudible. "Yeah. You can see…some of the images are different further into the lattice…because our pocket had a tunnel leading to other pockets. That happens sometimes, you know. It's not a good idea to go down the tunnels. It was the time after this one that…Mom didn't come back." He looked at the picture for a moment; like its own pocket, the moment seemed to stretch out to a gray forever. Then he looked away. "Turn it off, will you? It brings me down."

Wendel stared at his mother's young face a moment longer, then turned off the image. "You never told me much about the time she didn't come back."

"I don't need to replay the experience, kid."

"Dad. I…look, just do it. Tell me."

Dad stared at him. Looked away. Wendel thought he was going to refuse again. Then he shrugged and began, his voice weary. "It was a much bigger pocket than usual," said Dad, almost inaudible. "MetaM-eta…they'd scored a shitload of them from DeGroot and we were merging them together so whole teams could fit in. Using fundamental spacetime geometry weirdness to meet the marketing honcho's deadlines, can you believe? I was an idiot to buy into it. And this last time Jena was mad at me and she flew away from me while we were in there. And then I couldn't tell which of the lattice-nodes was really her. Like a mirror-maze in a funhouse. And meanwhile I'm all tweaked out of my mind on bubble-rush. But I had my laptop-harness and there was all that code-hacking to be done, and I got into it for sure, glancing over at all the Jenas now and then, and they're programming too, so I thought it was OK, but then…" He swallowed, turning to look out the window, as if he might see her out there in the sky. "When the pocket flattened back out, I was alone. The same shit was coming down everywhere all of a sudden, and then there was the Big Bubble disaster at the DeGroot plant and all the pocket-bubbles were declared government property and if you want to use them anymore…people, you know…." His voice trailed into a whisper: "They act like you're a junkie."

"Yeah," said Wendel. "I know." He looked out the window for a while. It was a sunny day, but the foulness in the water made the sea a dingy gray, as if it were brooding on dark memories. He spotted a couple of little pocket-bubbles floating in on the brackish waves. Dad had been buying them from beachcombers, merging them together till he got one big enough to crawl into again.

They'd talked about pockets in Wendel's health class at school last term. In terms of dangerous things the grown-ups wanted to warn you away from, pockets were right up there with needles, drunk driving, and doing it bareback. You could stay inside too long and come out a couple of years older than your friends. You could lose your youth inside a pocket. Oddly enough, you didn't eat or breathe in any conventional way while you were inside there—those parts of your metabolism went into suspension. The pocket-slugs dug this aspect of the high, for after all weren't eating and breathing just another wearisome world-drag? There were even rock songs about pockets setting you free from "feeding the pig," as the 'slugs liked to call normal life. You didn't eat or breathe inside a pocket but even so were still getting older, often a lot faster than you realized. Some people came out, like, middle-aged.

And of course some people never came out at all. They died in there of old age, or got killed by a bubble-psychotic pocket-slug coming through a tunnel, or—though this last one sounded like government propaganda—you might tunnel right off into some kind of alien Hell world. If you found a pocket-bubble you were supposed to take it straight to the police. As opposed to selling it to a 'slug, or, worse, trying to accumulate enough of them to get a pocket big enough to go into yourself. The word was that it felt really good, better than drugs or sex or booze. Sometimes Wendel wanted to try it—because then, maybe, he'd understand his dad. Other times the thought terrified him.

He looked at his shaky, strung-out father, wishing he could respect him. "Do you keep doing it because you think you might find Mom in there someday?" asked Wendel, his voice plaintive in his own ears.

503

"It would sound more heroic, wouldn't it?" said Dad, rubbing his face. "That I keep doing it because I'm on a quest. Better than saying I do it for the high. The escape." He rubbed his face for a minute and got out of bed, a little shaky, but with a determined look on his face. "It's get-it-together time, huh Wendel? Get me a vita-patch from the bathroom, willya? I'll call Manda and go see her today. We need this gig. You ready to catch the light rail to San Jose?"

In person Manda Solomon was shorter, plainer, and less well dressed than the processed image she sent out on iTV. She was a friendly ditz, with the disillusioned aura of a Valley-vet who's seen a number of her employers go down the tubes. When Dad calmly claimed that Wendel was a master programmer and his chief assistant, Manda didn't bat an eye, just took out an extra sheaf of nondisclosure and safety-waiver agreements for Wendel to sign.

"I've never had such a synchronistic staffing process before," she said with a breathless smile. "Easy, but weird. Two of our team were waiting in my office when I came into work it one morning. Said I'd left it unlocked. Karma, I guess."

They followed her into a windowless conference room with white-boards and projection screens. One of the screens showed Dad's old photo of him and Mom scattered over the nodes of a pocket's space-lattice. Wendel's Dad glanced at it and looked away.

Manda introduced them to the other three at the table: a cute, smiling woman named Xiao-Xiao just now busy talking Chinese on her cell phone. She had Bettie Page bangs and the faddish full-eye mirror-contacts; her eyes were like pale lavender Christmas-tree ornaments. Next was a straight-nosed Sikh guy named Puneet; he wore a turban. He had reassuringly normal eyes, and spoke in a high voice. The third was a puffy white kid only a few years older than Wendel. His name was Barley and he wore a stoner-rock T-shirt. He didn't smile; with his silver mirror-contacts his face was quite unreadable. He wore an uvvy computer interface on the back of his neck. Barley asked Wendel something about programming, but Wendel couldn't even understand the question.

"Ummm…well, you know. I just…"

"So what's the pitch, Manda?" Dad interrupted, to get Wendel off the spot.

"Pocket-Max," said Manda. "Safe and stable. Five hundred people in there at a time, strapped into…I dunno, some kind of mobile pocket-seats. Make downtown San Jose a destination theme park. Harmless, ethical pleasure. We've got some senators who can push it through a loophole for us."

"Safe?" said Dad. "Harmless?"

"Manda says you've logged more time in the pockets than anyone she knows," said Xiao-Xiao. "You have some kind of…intuition about them? You must know some tricks for making it safe."

"Well…if we had the hardware that created it…." Dad's voice trailed off, which meant he was thinking hard, and Manda let him do it for a moment.

And then she dropped her bomb. "We do have the hardware. Show him Flatland, Barley."

Barley did something with his uvvy and something like a soap film appeared above the generic white plastic of the conference table. "This is a two-dimensional-world mockup," mumbled Barley. "We call it Flatland. The nanomatrix mat for making the real pockets is offsite. Flatland's a piece of visualization software that we that we got as part of our license. It's a lift."

"*Offsite* would be the DeGroot Center?" said Dad, his voice rising. "You've got full access?"

"Yaaar," said Barley, his fat face expressionless. He was leaning over Flatland, using his uvvy link to tweak it with his blank shining eyes.

"Why was DeGroot making pockets in the first place?" asked Wendel. No one had ever explained the pockets to him. It was like Dad was ashamed to talk about them much.

"It was supposed to be for AI," said Puneet. "Quantum computing nanotech. The DeGroot techs were bozos. They didn't know what they had when they started up the nanomatrix—I don't even know how they invented it. There's no patents filed. It's like the thing fell out of a flying saucer." His laugh was more than a little uneasy. "There's nobody to ask because the DeGroot engineers are all dead. Sucked into the Big Bubble that popped out of their nanomatrix. You saw it on TV. And then Uncle Sam closed them down."

"But—why would the nanomatrix be licensed to Endless Media?" asked Dad. "You're an entertainment company. And not a particularly reputable one, at that. Why you and not one of the big, legit players?"

"Options," said Manda with a shrug. "Market leverage. Networking synergies. And the big guys don't want to touch it. Too big a downside. Part of the setup is we can't sue DeGroot if things don't work out. No biggie for Endless Media. If the shit hits the fan, we take the bullet and go Chapter Eleven. We closed the deal with DeGroot and the Feds last week. Nobody's hardly seen the DeGroot CEO since the catastrophe, but he's still around. Guy named George Gravid. He showed up for about one minute at closing, popped up out of nowhere, walking down the hall. Said he'd been hung up in meetings with some backer dudes—he called them Out-Monkeys? He looked like shit, wearing shades. I think he's strung out on something. Whatever. We did our due diligence, closed the deal, and a second later Gravid was gone." She waved a dismissive hand. "Bottom line is we're fully licensed to use the DeGroot technology. Us and a half-dozen other blue sky groups. Each of us is setting up an operation in the DeGroot Plant on San Pablo Bay. And we time share the access to the nanomatrix. The Endless Media mission in this context is to make a safe and stable Big Bubble that provides a group entertainment experience beyond anything ever seen before."

"Watch how this simulation works," said Barley. "See the yellow square in the film? That's A Square. A two-dimensional Flatlander. He's sliding around, you wave. And that green five-sided figure next to him, that's his son A Pentagon. And now I push up a bubble out of his space." A little spot of the Flatland film bulged up like a time-reversed water drop. The bulge swelled up to the shape of a sphere hovering above Flatland, connected to the little world by a neck of glistening film. "Go in the pocket, Square," said Barley. "Get high."

The yellow square slid forward. He had a bright eye in one of his corners. For a minute he bumbled around the warped zone where the bubble touched his space, then found an entry point and slid up across the neck of the bubble and onto the surface of the little ball. Into the pocket.

"This is what he sees," said Barley, pointing at one of the view screens on the wall. The screen showed an endless lattice of copies of A Square, each of them turning and blinking in unison. "Like a hall of mirrors. Now I'll make the bubble bounce. That's what makes the time go differently inside the pockets, you know."

The sphere rose up from the film. The connecting neck stretched and grew thinner, but it didn't break. The sphere bounced back toward the film and the neck got fat, the sphere bounced up and the neck got thin, over and over.

"Check this out," said Barley, changing the image on the view screen to show a circle that repeatedly shrank and grew. "This is what Square Junior sees. The little Pentagon. He stayed outside the bad old pocket, you wave? To him the pocket looks like a disk that's getting bigger and smaller. See him over there on the film? Waiting for Pa. Like little Wendel in the condo on San Pablo Bay."

"Go to hell," said Wendel.

"Don't pick on him, Barley," put in Manda. "Wendel's part of our team."

"Whoah," said Barley. "Now Mr. Square's trip is over." The sphere bounced back and flattened back into the normal space of Flatland.

"You forgot to mention the stabilizer ring," said Dad.

"You see?" said Manda. "I told you guys we needed a physicist."

"What ring?" said Barley.

"A space bubble is inherently unstable," said Dad. "It wants to tear loose or flatten back down. The whole secret of the DeGroot tech was to wrap a superquantum nanosheet around the bubbles. Bubble wrap. In your Flatland model it's a circle around the neck. Make a new bubble, Barley."

A new bubble bulged up, and this time Wendel noticed that there was indeed a bright little line around the throat of the neck. A line with a gap in it, like the open link of a chain.

"That's the entrance," said Dad, pointing to the little gap. "The navel. Now show me how you model a tunnel."

"We're not sure about the tunnels," said Puneet. "We're expecting you can help us with this. I cruised the Bharat University Physics Department site and found a Chandreskar-Thorne solution that looks like—can you work it for me, Xiao-Xiao?"

Xiao-Xiao leaned toward the Flatland simulation, her lavender eyes reflecting the scene. She too wore a modern uvvy-style computer controller. Following Puneet's instructions, Xiao-Xiao bulged a second bubble up from the plane, about a foot away from the first one. A Square slid into the first one of them and A Pentagon into the other. And now the bubbles picked up a side-to-side motion, and lumps began sticking out of them, and it just so happened that two of the lumps touched and now there was a tunnel between the two bubbles.

"Look at the screens now," said Barley. "That's Square's view on the left. And Pentagon's view on the right."

Square's view showed a lattice of Squares as before, but the lattice lines were warped and flawed, and the flawed region there was a sublattice of nodes showing copies of the Pentagon. Conversely, the Pentagon's view lattice included a wedge of Squares.

"That's a start," said Dad. "But, you know, these pictures of yours—they're just toys. You're talking all around the edges of what the pockets are. You're missing the essence of what they're really about. It's not that they spontaneously bulge up out of our space. It's more that they're raining down on us. From something out here." He gestured at the space above Flatland. "There's a shape up there—with something inside it. I've picked up kind of a feeling for it."

Barley and Xiao-Xiao stared silently at him, their mirrored eyes shining.

"That's why we need you, Rothman," said Manda, finally.

"That's right," said Puneet. "The problem is—when it comes to this new tech, we're bozos too."

"I'll tell you what I think," Wendel said gravely. "I think you're lying to them about what you can do, Dad."

It was nearly midnight. Wendel was tired and depressed. They were sitting in the abandoned DeGroot plant's seemingly endless cafeteria, waiting for their daily time-slot with the nanomatrix. Almost the only ones there. The rest of their so-called team hadn't been coming in. Manda and Puneet preferred the safety of San Jose while Barley and Xiao-Xiao had completely dropped out of sight. What a half-assed operation this was.

Wendel and his Dad were eating tinny-tasting stew and drinking watery coffee from the vending machines along the wall opposite the defunct buffets. It was a long, overly lit room, the far end not quite visible from here, with pearly white walls and a greenish floor, asymmetrical rows of round tables like lily pads on the green pond of the floor, going on and on. Endless Media shared the cafeteria with the other scavenging little companies that had licensed access to the nanomatrix. None of the reputable firms wanted to touch it.

"Don't talk about it in here, son," Dad said, listlessly stirring his coffee with a plastic spoon. "We're not alone, you wave."

"The nearest people in here are, like, an eighth of a mile away, I can't even make out their faces from here."

"That's not what I mean. The other groups here, they might be spying on us with gnat-audio, stuff like that. They're all a bunch of bottom-feeders like Endless Media, you know. Nobody knows jack from squat, so they're all looking to copy me."

"You wish. It's good to have work, but you're going to get in deep shit, Dad. You're telling Endless Media you're down with the tech when you're not. You're telling them you can stabilize a Big Bubble when you can't. You say you can keep tunnels from hooking into it—but you don't know how."

"Maybe I can. I have to test it some more."

"You test it every night."

"Not enough. I haven't actually gone inside it yet."

"Come on. I'm the one who has to put you back together after a bubble binge. It's great having an income from this gig, Dad, a better place to live—but I'm not going to let you vanish into that thing. Something just like it killed the whole DeGroot team five years ago."

His dad gave Wendel a glare that startled him. It was almost feral. Chair screeching nastily on the tile, Dad got up abruptly and went across the room to a coffee vending machine for another latte. He ran his card through the slot, then swore. He stalked back over to the table long enough to say, "Be right back, this card's used up, I've got another one in my locker."

"You're not going to sneak up to the lab without me, are you? Our time-slot starts in five minutes, you know. At midnight."

"Son? Don't. I'm the Dad, you're the kid. Okay? I'll be right back."

Wendel watched him go. *I'm the Dad, you're the kid.* There were a lot of comebacks he could've made to that one.

Wendel sipped his gooey stew, then pushed it away. It was tepid, the vegetables mushy, making him think of bits of leftover food floating in dishwater. He heard a *beep*, looked toward the vending machines. The machine Dad had run his card through was beeping, flashing a little light.

Wendel walked over to it. A small screen on the machine said, *Do you wish to cancel your purchase?*

Which was only something it said if the card was good. Which meant that Dad had gone to the lab without him. Wendel felt a sick chill that made his fingers quiver…and sprinted toward the elevators.

The pocket was so swollen he could hardly get into the big testing room with it. Maybe two hundred feet in diameter, sixty feet high. Mercuric and yet lusterless. The various measuring instruments were crowded up against the walls.

"Dad?" he called tentatively. But Wendel knew Dad was gone. He could feel his absence from the world.

He edged around the outside of the Big Bubble, grimacing when he came into contact with it. Somewhere beneath the great pocket was the nanomatrix mat that produced it—or attracted it? But it wasn't like you could do anything to turn the pocket off once it got here. At least nothing that they'd figured out yet, which was one of the many obstacles preventing this thing from being a realistic public attraction. "Show may last from one to ten minutes world time, and seem to take one hour to three months of your proper time." Even if there were a way to shut the pocket off now—what would that do to Dad?

Facing a far corner was the dimpled spot, the entrance navel. On these Big Bubbles, the navel didn't always seal over. When Wendel looked into the navel, it seemed to swirl like a slow-motion whirlpool, but in two contradictory directions. Hypnotic. It could still be entered.

Wendel made up his mind: he would go after his Dad. He leaned forward, pressed his fingers against the navel, thinking of A Pentagon sliding up over the warped neck that led to the sphere of extra space. His hands looked warped, as if they were underwater. They tingled—not unpleasantly. He pushed his arms in after and then, with a last big breath of air, his head. How would it feel to stop breathing?

It was awhile till Wendel came back to that question. The first feeling of being inside the pocket was one of falling—but this was just an illusion, he was floating, not falling, and he had an odd, dreamlike ability to move in whatever direction he wanted to, not that the motion seemed to mean much.

There was a dim light that came from everywhere and nowhere. Spread out around him were little mirror-Wendels, all turning their heads this way and that, gesturing and—yes—none of them breathing. It was like flying underwater and never being out of breath, like being part of a school of fish. The space was patterned with veils of color like seaweed in water. Seeing the veils pass he could tell that he was moving, and as the veils repeated themselves he could see that he was moving in a great circle. He was like A Pentagon circling around and around his bulged-up puffball of space. But where was Dad? He changed the angle of his motion, peering around for distinctions in the drifting school of mirror shapes.

The motion felt like flying, now, with a wind whipping his hair, and he found a new direction in which the space veils seemed to curve like gossamer chambers of mother of pearl, sketching a sort of nautilus-spiral into the distance. Looking into that distance, that twist of infinity, and feeling the volume of sheer potentiality, he felt the first real wave of bubble-rush. His fatigue evaporated in the searing light of the rush, a rippling, bone-deep pleasure that seemed generated by his flying motion into the spiral of the pocket.

"*Whuh-oaaaah...*" he murmured, afraid of the feeling and yet liking it. So this was why Dad came here. Or one of the reasons. There was something else too...something Dad never quite articulated.

The bubble-rush was so all-consuming, so shimmeringly insistent, he felt he couldn't bear it. It was simply too much; too much pleasure and you lost all sense of self; and then it was, finally, no better than pain.

Wendel thought, "Stop!" and his motion responded to his will. He stopped where he was—an inertialess stop partway into the receding nautilus spiral. The bubble-rush receded a bit, damped back down to a pleasing background glow.

"Dad!" he yelled. No response. "DAD!" His voice didn't echo; he couldn't tell how loud it was. There was air in here to be sucked in and expelled for speaking. But when he wasn't yelling, he felt no need to take a breath. Like a vampire in his grave.

He tried to get some kind of grasp of the shape of this place. He thought with an ugly *frisson* of fear: Maybe I'm already lost. How do I find my way back out?

Could A Pentagon slide back out the neck into the ball? Or would he have to wait for the ball to burn out its energy and flatten back into space?

There were no images of Wendel up ahead, where the patterns of the space seemed to twirl like a nautilus. It must be a tunnel. If pockets were dangerous, the tunnels from pocket to pocket were said to be much worse. But he knew that's where Dad had gone.

He moved into the tunnel, flying at will.

The pattern haze ahead of him took on flecks of pink, human color. Someone else was down there. "Dad?"

He leaned into his flying—and stopped, about ten yards short of the man. It wasn't Dad. This man was bearded, emaciated, sallow… which Dad could be, by now, in the time-bent byways of this place. But it wasn't his Dad, it was a stranger, a man with big, scared eyes and a grin that looked permanently fixed. No teeth: barren gums. The man sitting was floating in fetal position, arms around his knees.

"Ya got any grub on yer, boy?" the man rasped. A UK accent. Or was it Australian?

"Um—" He remembered he had two-thirds of a power bar of some kind in a back pocket. Probably linty by now, but likely this 'slug wouldn't care. "You want this?"

He tossed over the power bar and the pocket-slug's eyes flashed as he caught it, fairly snatched it out of the air. "Good on ya, boy!" He gnawed on the linty old bar with his callused gums.

It occurred to Wendel that at some point he might regret giving away his only food. But supposedly you didn't need to eat in here. Food was just fun for the mouth, or a burst of extra energy. Right now the scene made him chuckle to himself—the bubble-rush was glowing in him; it made everything seem absurd, cartoonlike, and marvelous.

Between sucking sounds, the 'slug said, "My name's Threakman. Jeremy Threakman. 'ow yer doin."

"I don't know how I'm doing. I'm looking for my Dad. Rothman Bell. He's about…"

"No need, I know whuh 'e looks like. Seen 'im go through ere." Threakman looked at Wendel with his head cocked. A sly look. "Feelin' the 'igh, are ya? Sure'n you are. Stoned, eh boy? Young fer it."

"I feel something—what is it? What causes it?"

"Why, it's a feelin' of being right there in yerself, beyond all uncertainty about where yer might go, and fully knowin' that yer hidden and on your own. And that'll get you 'igh. Or some say. Others, like me, they say it's the Out-Monkeys that do it."

"The Out…what?"

"Out-Monkeys," said Threakman. "What I call 'em. Other's call 'em Dream Beetles, one 'slug in here used ter call 'em Turtles—said he saw a turtle thing with a head like a screw-top bottle without the cap and booze pouring out, but he was a hardcore alkie. Others they see'm more like lizards or Chinese dragons. Dragons, beetles, monkeys, all hairy around the edges, all curlin' out at yer—it's a living hole in space, mate, and you push the picture you want on it. Me and the smartuns calls 'em Out-Monkeys cause they're from outside our world."

"You mean—from another planet?"

"No mate, from the bigger universe that *this* one is kinder *inside*. They got more dimensions than we do. They're using DeGroot and the nanomatrix—they give all that ta us to pull us in, mate. The Out-Monkeys are drizzlin' pockets down onto us, little paradise balls where yer don't have to breathe nor eat an' yer can fly an' there's an energy that stim-yer-lates that part of yer brain, don't ya see. The Out-Monkeys want us all stony in here. Part of their li'l game, innit? Come on, show yer somethin. The Alef. Mayhap yer'll see yer Da."

In a single spasmodic motion Threakman was up, flying off in some odd new direction through the silvery scarves of the enclosing spaces—leaving a rank scent in the air behind him. Wendel whipped along after him, remembering not to breathe. Soon, if it could be thought of as soon, they came to a nexus where the images around them thickened up into an incalculable diversity. It was like being at the heart of a city in a surveillance zone with a million monitors, but the images weren't electronic, they were real, and endlessly repeated.

"The Alef has tunnels to all the pockets," said Threakman. "Precious few of us knows about it."

In some directions, he saw pockets with people writhing together—he realized, with embarrassment, that they were copulating. But was that really sex? He made himself look away. In another pocket, people were racing around one another in a blur like those electro-cyclists in the Cage of Death he'd seen at a carnival. Off down the axis of another tunnel, people clawed at one another, in a thronging mélange of combat; you couldn't tell one from another, so slick was the blood. But the greatest number of the pockets held solitary 'slugs, hanging there in self-absorbed pleasure, surrounded by the endless mirror-images of themselves. And one of these addicts was Dad, floating quite nearby.

"For 'im, mate," said Threakman as Wendel flew off toward his father.

512

Not quite sure of his aim, he hit Dad with a thud—and Dad screamed, thrashing back from him. Stopping himself in space to glare shame and resentment at Wendel—like a kid caught masturbating.

"What are you *doing*?" demanded Wendel. "You call this research?"

"Okay, you really want to know?" snapped his father. "I'm looking for Jena. Mom."

Wendel peered at his father; his Dad's face, here, seemed more like the possibility of all possible Dad facial expressions, crystallized. It was difficult to tell whether he meant it. It might be bullshit. What was the saying? *How do you know an addict is lying? When his lips are moving!*

But the possibility of seeing Mom made Wendel's heart thud. "You think she's still in here? Seriously, Dad?"

"I think the Out-Monkeys got her. That's what happens you know. Some of the pockets float up—not 'up' exactly, but 'ana'—"

"To the shape above 'Flatland,'" said Wendel.

"Right," said Dad. "We're in their 'Flatland' relatively speaking. And I want to get up there and find her."

"But you're just floating around in here. You're on the goddamn nod, Dad. You're not looking at all."

"Oh yes I am. I'm looking, goddammit. This happens to be just the right spot to stare down through the Alef and up along the Out-Monkeys' tunnel. Not their tunnel, exactly. The spot where they usually appear. Where their hull touches us. I'm waiting for them to show up."

"The Devil in his motorboat," said Wendel with a giggle. The bubble-rush was creeping back up on him. Dad laughed too. They were thinking of the old joke about the guys in Hell, standing neck deep in liquid shit and drinking coffee, and one of them says, "Wal, this ain't so bad," and the other one says, "Yeah, but wait till—"

"Here it comes," said Dad, and it wasn't funny anymore, for the space up ahead of them had just opened up like a blooming squash-flower, becoming incalculably larger, all laws of perspective broken, and an all-but-endless vista spreading out, a giant space filled with moving shapes that darted and wheeled like migrating flocks of birds. It was hard to think straight, for the high of the bubble space had just gotten much stronger.

"The mothership," said Threakman, who'd drifted down to join them. "Yaaar. Can you feel the rush off it? Ahr, but it's good. Hello to yer, there, Da." He gave a deep, loose chuckle. Everything was glistening and wonderful, as perfect as the first instant of Creation; and, as with that moment, chaos waited on the event horizon: chaos and terror.

"Those shapes are the Out-Monkeys?" asked Wendel, his voice sounding high and slow in his ears. "They look like little people."

"Those little things *are* people," said Dad. "They're the pets."

"Livin' decals on the mothership's hull," said Threakman. "Live decorations fer the Out-Monkeys. An antfarm for their window-box. Ah, yer'll know it when you really see an Out-Monkey, Wendel. When 'e reaches out through the hull…"

Then the space around them quivered like gelatin, and the cloud of moving people up ahead spiraled in around a shaky, black, living hole in space, a growing thing with fractal fringes, a three-dimensional Mandelbrot formation that, to Wendel, looked like a dancing, star-edged monkey made up of other monkeys, like the old Barrel of Monkeys toy he'd had, with all the little monkeys hooked together to make bigger monkeys that hooked together to make a gigantic monkey, coming on and on: a cross-section of a higher-dimensional alien, partly shaped by the Rorschach filter of human perception.

Wendel thought: Out-Monkey? And the thing echoed psychically back at him, *Out-Monkey!* with the alien thought coming at him like a voice in his head, mocking, drawling, sarcastic, and infinitely hip.

The Out-Monkey swelled, huge but with no real size to it in any human sense, and the fabric of space rippled with its motions—the Devil's motorboat indeed—and Wendel felt his whole body flexing and wobbling like an image in a funhouse mirror. Beneath the space waves, a sinister undertow began tugging at him. Wendel felt he would burst with the disorientation of it all.

"Dad—we've gotta go! Let's get back to the world! Tell, him, Jeremy!"

"No worries yet," said Threakman grinning and flaring his nostrils as if to inhale the wild, all-pervading rush. "Steady as she goes, mate. Your Dad and me, we've had some practice with the Out-Monkeys. We can 'ang here a bit longer."

"Look at the faces, Wendel!" cried Dad. "Look for Jena!"

Around the Out-Monkey orbited the people imprisoned on its vast bubble. They seemed to rotate around the living hole in space, caught up in the fractals that crawled around its edges: faces that were both ecstatic and miserable, zoned-out and hysterical.

"There goes George Gravid," said Dad, pointing. "The original guy from DeGroot." Wendel stared, spotting a businessman in a black suit. And there, not too far from him were—Barley and Xiao-Xiao?

"Come on, come on, come on," Dad was chanting, and then he gave a wild laugh. "Yes! There she is! It's Jena!" His laughter was cracked and frantic. "It's Mom, Wendel! I knew I could find her!"

Wendel looked—and thought he saw her. Looking hard at her had a telescopic effect, like concentration itself was the optical instrument, and his vision zoomed in on her face—it was his mom, though her eyes were blotted with silver, like the faddish contacs people wore in the World. All of those rotating around the Out-Monkey had silvered eyes, mirror-eyes endlessly looking into themselves.

Torn, Wendel hesitated—and then the fractal leviathan swept closer—he felt something like its shadow fall over him, though there were no localized light sources here to throw shadows. It was, rather, as if the greater dimensional inclusiveness of the Out-Monkey over-shadowed the limited-dimensional beings here, and you could feel its "shadow" in your soul....

"Dad!" Wendel shouted in panic, and his father yelled something back, but he couldn't make it out—there was a torrent of white-noise crackle upwelling all around him in the growing "shadow" of the Out-Monkey. "*Dad! We have to go!*" shrieked Wendel.

And then Dad plunged forward, arrowing in toward Mom, and Wendel felt himself on the point of a wild, uncontrolled tumble.

"Ol'roit, mate," said Threakman, grabbing Wendel's arm and pulling him up short. "Keep yer 'ead now. Ungodly strong rush, innit? It's 'ard not to go all the way in. But remember—if yer really want, yer *can* 'old back from its pullin' field. Let's ease in, nice and quietlike, and try and snag your Dad."

Wendel and Threakman inched forward—Wendel feeling the pull of the Out-Monkey as strong as gravity. Yet, just as Threakman said, you didn't have to let it take you, didn't have to let it pull you down into that swarming blackness of the Out-Monkey's fractal membranes. Jeremy Threakman's grip on his arm was solid as the granite spine of the planet Earth. Wretched, stinking Jeremy Threakman knew his way around the Out-Monkeys.

Wendel stared in at Mom and Dad: they were swirling around one another, orbiting a mutual center of emptiness, just as they and the others orbited the greater center of emptiness within the higher-dimensional being. It reminded Wendel of a particular carnival ride, where people whirled in place on a metal arm, and their whirling cars were also whirled around a central axis.

"Dad!"

Dad looked at him—if it could be called looking. In the thrall of the Out-Monkey, it was more like he was going through the motions of turning his attention to Wendel, and that attention was represented by the image of an attentive paternal face. "Wendel, I don't think I can get out! It's snagging my..." His voice was lost in a surging crackle, a wave of static. Then: "...purple, thinking purple...." Crackle. "...your mom! It wants us!"

Wendel's arm ached where Threakman clutched him. "We gotter go soon, mate!" said the scarred pocket-slug.

Mom turned her attention toward Wendel too now—she was reaching for him, weeping and laughing. He wasn't sure if it was psychic or vocal, but he heard her say: "We're pets, Wendel!" Static. "Waterstriders penned in a corner of the pond." His mother's face was lit with unholy bliss. "Live bumper stickers." A sick peal of laughter.

There was another ripple in the space around them, and all of a sudden Mom and Dad were only a few feet away. Close enough to touch. Wendel reached out to them.

"Come on, Mom! Take my hand! Jeremy and I—we *can* pull you out! You can leave if you want to!"

How Wendel knew this, he wasn't sure. But he knew it was true. He could feel it—could feel the relative energy loci, the possibility of pulling free, if you tried.

"We can go home, Dad! You and me and Mom!"

"Can't!" came his Dad's voice from a squirming gargoyle of his father with a fractal fringe.

"Dad don't *lie* to me! You can do it! Don't lie! You can come...!"

His arm ached so—but he waited for the answer.

Wordlessly, his father emanated regret. Remorse. Shame. "Yes," he admitted finally. "But I choose this. Mom and I...we want to stay here. Part of the gorgeous Out-Monkey. The eternal fractals." Static. "...can't help it. Go away, Wendel!"

"Have a life, Wendel!" said Mom said. Several versions of her face said it, several different ways. "Don't come back. The nanomatrix—you can melt it. Acid!" Huge burst of static. "Hurry up now. It heard me!"

He felt it too: the chilling black-light search beam of the Out-Monkey's attention, spotlighting him like an escaped prisoner just outside the wall...

"No, Mom! Come back! Mom—"

Mom and Dad swirled away from him, their faces breaking up into laughing, jabbering fractals. The white noise grew intolerably loud.

"Gotter leave!" screamed Threakman in his ear. "Jump!"

With an impulse that was as much resentment, of running away in fury, as it was a conscious effort, he leapt with Threakman away from the hardening grip of the Out-Monkey, and felt himself spinning out through the dimensions and down the tunnels, he and Threakman in a whirling blur, one almost blending with the other. He thought he caught a glimpse of Threakman's memories, bleeding over in the strange ambient fields of the place from his companion's mind: a father with a leather strap; a woman giving him his first blowjob in the backroom of a Sydney bar; working as a sailor; being mugged in London; a stout woman angrily leaving him. All this time Threakman was steering him through the bent spaces, helping him find his way back.

And then their minds were discrete again, and they were flying through a vortex of faces and pearly-gray glimmer, through a symmetrical lattice of copies of themselves, back out into the Big Bubble space he'd first entered. And just about then the bubble flattened down into normal space—and burst. He was back in the world.

Wendel knelt in the huge lab room, sobs of fury bubbling out of him, beside the floor mat of the little nanomatrix, slapping his palm flat on the floor, again and again, in his frustration and hurt. Especially, hurt. His dad and mom had chosen *that* over him. They hadn't really been inescapably caught—*it was a choice*. They'd chosen their master, the Out-Monkey; they'd gone into a spinning closed system of onanistic ecstasy; sequestered their hearts in another world, in the pursuit of pleasure and escape. They'd left him alone.

"Fuck YOU!" he screamed, pounding his fist on the nanomatrix. The magical bit of alien high tech was a fuzzy gray rectangle, for all the world like a cheap plastic doormat. That's all the lab was, really. An empty room, some instruments, and a scrap of magic carpet on the floor.

"Roit," said Threakman hoarsely, slumping down wearily next to him. "My old man, 'e was the same way. But for 'im it was the bottle. The Out-Monkeys, they use the 'igh to pull their pets in. Something sweet 'n' sticky—like the bait for a roach motel. And, God 'elp me, I'm hooked. I won't make it back out next time. I need to...something else. Bloody hell—anything else."

"Mom and Dad coulda left! They weren't stuck at all!"

"Yeah. I reckon." Threakman was tired, shaky. Pale. "Lor' I feel bad, mate. I miss that rush like it was my only love. Whuh now?"

Wendel stared down at the nanomatrix. Tiny bubbles glinted in the hairs that covered it, endlessly oozing out from it. It was like a welcome mat that someone had sprinkled with beads of mercury. The little pockets winked up at him, as if say, *"Wanna get high?"*

"The chemical factory," said Wendel. "Right next door. I know where there's a tank of nitric acid." He pulled at a corner of the nanomatrix. It was glued to the floor, but with Threakman working at his side, he was able to peel it free. He rolled up the grimy mat and tucked it under his arm, tiny bubbles scattering like dust.

The clock on the wall outside the lab said 12:03. All that crazy shit in the Big Bubble—it had lasted about a minute of real time. The next team wasn't scheduled till 2:00 AM. The halls were empty.

Threakman shambled along at Wendel's side as Wendel led them out of the Research building and across a filth-choked field to the chemical plant, staying in the shadows on one side. Wendel knew the plant well from all the hours he'd spent looking at it and thinking about modeling it. The guards wouldn't see them if they cut in over here. They skirted the high, silver cylinder of a cracking tower, alive with pipes, and climbed some mesh-metal stairs that led to a broad catwalk, ten feet across.

"The acid tank's that way," whispered Wendel. "I've seen the train cars filling it up." The rolled up nanomatrix twitched under his arm, as if trying to unroll itself.

"This'll be the hard bit," said Threakman, uneasily. "The Out-Monkeys can see down onto us, I'll warrant."

Wendel tightened his grip on the nanomatrix, holding it tight in both hands. It pushed and shifted, but for the moment, nothing more. They marched forward along the catwalk, their feet making soft clanging noises in the night.

"That great thumpin' yellow one with the writin' on it?" said Threakman, spotting the huge metal tank that held acid. Practically every square foot of the tank was stenciled with safety warnings. "Deadly deadly *deadly*," added Threakman with a chuckle. He ran ahead of Wendel to get a closer look, leaning eagerly forward off the edge of the catwalk. "Just my cuppa tea. Wait till I undog this hatch. Let's get rid of the mat before I change my mind."

The nanomatrix was definitely alive, twisting in Wendel's hands like a big, frantic fish. He stopped walking, concentrating on getting control of the thing, coiling it up tighter than before. "Hurry, Jeremy," he called. "Get the tank open, and I'll come throw this fucker in."

But now there was a subtle shudder of space, and Wendel heard a voice. "Not so fast, dear friends."

A businessman emerged out of thin air, first his legs, then his body, and then his head—as if he were being pasted down onto space. He stood there in his black, tailored suit, poised midway on the catwalk between Wendel and Threakman.

"George Gravid," said the businessman. His eyes were dark black mirrors and his suit, on closer inspection, was filthy and rumpled, as if he'd been wearing it for months—or years. "The nanomatrix is DeGroot property, Wendel. Not that I really give a shit. This tune's about played out. But I'm supposed to talk to you."

There was another shudder and a whispering of air, and now Barley and Xiao-Xiao were at Gravid's side, Barley sneering, and Xiao-Xiao's little face cold and hard. The plant lights sparkled on their reflective eyes, black and silver and lavender. Wendel took a step back.

"Run around 'em, Wendel," called Threakman. "I got the hatch off. Dodge through!"

Wendel was fast and small. He had a chance, though the bucking of the nanomatrix was continuously distracting him. He faked to the left, ran to the right, then cut back to the left again.

Gravid, Barley, and Xiao-Xiao underwent a jerky stuttering motion—an instantaneous series of jumps—and ended up right in front of him. Barley gave Wendel a contemptuous little slap on the cheek.

"The Higher One picks us up and puts us down," said Xiao-Xiao. "You can't get past us. You have to listen."

"You're being moved around by an Out-Monkey?" said Wendel.

"That's a lame-ass term," said Barley. "They're *Higher Ones*. Why did you leave?"

"You're its pets," Wendel said, stomach lurching in revulsion. "Toys." The fumes from the nitric acid tank were sharp in the air.

"We're free agents," said Gravid. "But it's better in there than out here."

"The mothership's gonna leave soon," said Barley. "And we're goin' with it. Riding on the hull. Us and your parents. Don't be a dirt-world loser, Wendel. Come on back."

"The Higher One wants you, Wendel," said Gravid. "Wants to have another complete family. You know how collectors are."

The nanomatrix bucked wildly, and a fat silver pocket swelled out of its coiled-up end like a bubble from a bubble pipe. The pocket settled down onto the catwalk, bulging and waiting. Wendel had a sudden deep memory of how good the rush had felt.

"Whatcher mean, the ship is leavin'?" asked Threakman, drawn over to stare at the bubble, which was half the height of a man now. Its broad navel swirled invitingly.

"They've seen enough of our space now," said Xiao-Xiao. "They're moving on. Come on now, Wendel and Jeremy. This is bigger than anything you'll ever do." She mimed a sarcastic little kiss, bent over, and squeezed herself into the pocket.

"I want some too," said Barley, and followed her.

"Last call," said Gravid, going back into the bubble as well.

And now it was just Wendel and Threakman and the pocket, standing on the catwalk. The nanomatrix lay still in Wendel's hands.

"I don't know as I can live without it, yer know," said Threakman softly.

"But you said you want to change," said Wendel.

"Roight," said Threakman bleakly. "I did say."

Wendel skirted around the pocket, and walked over to where the acid tank's open hatch gaped. The nanomatrix had stopped fighting him. He and his world were small; the Out-Monkeys had lost interest. It was a simple matter to throw the plastic mat into the tank, and he watched it fall, end over end.

Choking fumes wafted out, and Wendel crawled off low down on the catwalk toward the breathable air.

When he sat up, Threakman and the bubble were both gone. And somewhere deep in his guts, Wendel felt a shudder, as of giant engines moving off. The pockets were gone? Maybe. But there'd always be a high that wanted to eat you alive. Life was a long struggle.

He walked away from the research center, toward the train station, feeling empty, and hurt—and free.

There were some things at the apartment he could sell. It would be a start. He would do all right. He'd been taking care of himself for a long time.

Note on "Pockets" (With John Shirley)

Written in July, 2000.
Appeared in Redshift , Roc Books, 2001.

I first met John at Bruce Sterling's house in Austin, Texas, 1985. We were there for the first-ever convention panel on cyberpunk. While we were walking around town, John kept sidling up to me and handing me enormous heavy rocks that I'd unthinkingly start carrying. An ant-to-ant exchange. I liked him right away, he has a charmingly skewed view of reality, and an ability to cobble nearly any situation into a story premise.

In the summer of 2000, John approached me with the first few paragraphs for this story and the invitation to join him in the Red Shift anthology. John figured he needed some mad professor input on how to make his higher-dimensional pockets work. Also, he and I shared an interest in using the pockets as an objective correlative for addiction and recovery. The writing of the story went very smoothly, and I get a kick out of the accent John gave Threakman. Punk forever.

In March 2003, I convinced John to go backpacking in Big Sur with me and to cap off our trip with a night in the inexpensive bunk-room at the Esalen Institute. This was not a good idea. John got blisters on the hike, and he hated the people at Esalen—as John put it, "You can't expect me to fit in at Esalen. When I had my band, I used to break beer bottles over my head till the blood ran, and dive off the stage into the audience." I quarreled with him for making our visit so hard and—let me quote from my journal:

"Then I mistakenly drank three cups of blackberry sage tea (caffeinated), thinking it was herbal, and that night couldn't sleep for a really long time. We were in a room with six bunk beds, my bed under John's, and it bothered me to be physically coupled to his creakings, also to have the plywood bottom of his bed so close to my face. In the wee a.m. hours I moved to the one other vacant bed, an upper bunk. The other guys sharing the room drifted in. Visions of a spaceship crew's quarters. Image of Shirley crawling towards me across the ceiling of the room, his fingers sticking to the dry-wall like a gecko's. Outside raged the lethal, silent energy winds of deep space, visible as in my mind's eye as Riemannian vortex meshes. At this point I actually felt some joy at being there and being embroiled in something so different from quotidian life."

We got over the argument—eventually it began seeming funny—and we still see each other every couple of months, most recently when Terry Bisson organized a joint reading for us in San Francisco as "The Dread Lords of Cyberpunk," where John read from what sounded to be one of his greatest novels yet, *The Other End* (Cemetery Dance, 2006). The book is about John's vision of what the Apocalypse might be like if the avenging angels happened to be John's kind of folks—as opposed to the angels that appear in the Christian Left Behind series of novels about the Rapture and the end of the world. Thus John's title—he's describing an *other* kind of end, an Apocalypse envisioned from the other end of the political spectrum.

Complete Stories

Volume Two

2001 - 2016

Rudy Rucker

Transreal Books
Los Gatos, California

JUNK DNA (WITH BRUCE STERLING)

Life was hard in old Silicon Valley. Little Janna Gutierrez was a native Valley girl, half Vietnamese, half Latino. She had thoughtful eyes and black hair in high ponytails.

Her mother Ahn tried without success to sell California real estate. Her father Ruben plugged away inside cold, giant companies like Ctenophore and Lockheed Biological. The family lived in a charmless bungalow in the endless grid of San Jose.

Janna first learned true bitterness when her parents broke up. Tired of her hard scrabble with a lowly wetware engineer, Anh ran off with Bang Dang, the glamorous owner of an online offshore casino. Dad should have worked hard to win back Mom's lost affection, but, being an engineer, he contented himself with ruining Bang. He found and exploited every unpatched hole in Bang's operating system. Bang never knew what hit him.

Despite Janna's pleas to come home, Mom stubbornly stuck by her online entrepreneur. She bolstered Bang's broken income by retailing network porn. Jaded Americans considered porn to be the commonest and most boring thing on the Internet. However, Hollywood glamour still had a moldy cachet in the innocent Third World. Mom spent her workdays dubbing the ethnic characteristics of tribal Somalis and Baluchis onto porn stars. She found the work far more rewarding than real estate.

Mom's deviant behavior struck a damp and morbid echo in Janna's troubled soul. Janna sidestepped her anxieties by obsessively collecting Goob dolls. Designed by glittery-eyed comix freaks from Hong Kong and Tokyo, Goobs were wiggly, squeezable, pettable creatures made of trademarked Ctenophore piezoplastic. These avatars of ultra-cuteness sold off wire racks worldwide, to a generation starved for Nature. Thanks to environmental decline, kids of Janna's age had never seen authentic wildlife. So they flipped for the Goob menagerie: marmosets with butterfly wings, starfish that scuttled like earwigs, long, furry frankfurter cat-snakes.

Sometimes Janna broke her Goob toys from their mint-in-the-box condition, and dared to play with them. But she quickly learned to absorb her parents' cultural values, and to live for their business buzz. Janna spent her off-school hours on the Net, pumping-and-dumping collectible Goobs to younger kids in other states.

Eventually, life in the Valley proved too much for Bang Dang. He pulled up the stakes in his solar-powered RV and drove away, to pursue a more lucrative career, retailing networked toilets. Janna's luckless Mom, her life reduced to ashes, scraped out a bare living marketing mailing lists to mailing list marketers.

Janna ground her way through school and made it into U.C. Berkeley. She majored in computational genomics. Janna worked hard on software for hardwiring wetware, but her career timing was off. The latest pulse of biotech start-ups had already come and gone. Janna was reduced to a bottle-scrubbing job at Triple Helix, yet another subdivision of the giant Ctenophore conglomerate.

On the social front, Janna still lacked a boyfriend. She'd studied so hard she'd been all but dateless through school and college. In her senior year she'd moved in with this cute Korean boy who was in band. But then his mother had come to town with, unbelievable, a blushing North Korean bride for him in tow. So much the obvious advice-column weepie!

In her glum and lonely evenings, she played you-are-her interactives, romance stories, with a climax where Janna would lip-synch a triumphant, tear-jerking video. On other nights Janna would toy wistfully with her decaying Goob collection. The youth market for the dolls had evaporated with the years. Now fanatical adult collectors were trading the Goobs, stiff and dusty artifacts of their lost consumer childhood.

And so life went for Janna Gutierrez, every dreary day on the calendar foreclosing some way out. Until the fateful September when Veruschka Zipkinova arrived from Russia, fresh out of biohazard quarantine.

The zany Zipkinova marched into Triple Helix toting a fancy briefcase with a video display built into its piezoplastic skin. Veruschka was clear-eyed and firm-jawed, with black hair cut very short. She wore a formal black jogging suit with silk stripes on the legs. Her Baltic pallor was newly reddened by California sunburn. She was very thoroughly made up. Lipstick, eye shadow, nails—the works.

She fiercely demanded a specific slate of bio-hardware and a big wad of start-up money. Janna's boss was appalled at Veruschka's archaic approach—didn't this Russki woman get it that the New Economy was even deader than Leninism? It fell to the luckless Janna to throw Veruschka out of the building.

"You are but a tiny cog," said Veruschka, accurately summing up Janna's cubicle. "But you are intelligent, yes, I see this in your eyes. Your boss gave me the brush-off. I did not realize Triple Helix is run by lazy morons."

"We're all quite happy here," said Janna lightly. The computer was, of course, watching her. "I wonder if we could take this conversation off-site? That's what's required, you see. For me to get you out of the way."

"Let me take you to a fine lunch at Denny's," said Veruschka with sudden enthusiasm. "I love Denny's so much! In Petersburg, our Denny's always has long lines that stretch down the street!"

Janna was touched. She gently countersuggested a happening local coffee shop called the Modelview Matrix. Cute musicians were known to hang out there.

With the roads screwed and power patchy, it took forever to drive anywhere in California, but at least traffic fatalities were rare, given that the average modern vehicle had the mass and speed of a golf cart. As Janna forded the sunny moonscape of potholes, Veruschka offered her start-up pitch.

"From Russia, I bring to legendary Silicon Valley a breakthrough biotechnology! I need a local partner, Janna. Someone I can trust."

"Yeah?" said Janna.

"It's a collectible pet."

Janna said nothing, but was instantly hooked.

"In Russia, we have mastered genetic hacking," said Veruschka thoughtfully, "although California is the planet's legendary source of high-tech marketing."

Janna parked amid a cluster of plastic cars like colored seedpods. Inside, Janna and Veruschka fetched slices of artichoke quiche.

"So now let me show you," said Veruschka as they took a seat. She placed a potently quivering object on the tabletop. "I call him Pumpti."

The Pumpti was the size and shape of a Fabergé egg, pink and red, clearly biological. It was moist, jiggly, and veined like an internal organ with branching threads of yellow and purple. Janna started to touch it, then hesitated, torn between curiosity and disgust.

"It's a toy?" asked Janna. She tugged nervously at a fanged hairclip. It really wouldn't do to have this blob stain her lavender silk jeans.

The Pumpti shuddered, as if sensing Janna's hovering finger. And then it oozed silently across the table, dropped off the edge, and plopped damply to the diner's checkered floor.

Veruschka smiled, slitting her cobalt-blue eyes, and leaned over to fetch her Pumpti. She placed it on a stained paper napkin.

"All we need is venture capital!"

"Um, what's it made of?" wondered Janna.

"Pumpti's substance is human DNA!"

"Whose DNA?" asked Janna.

"Yours, mine, anyone's. The client's." Veruschka picked it up tenderly, palpating the Pumpti with her lacquered fingertips. "Once I worked at the St. Petersburg Institute of Molecular Science. My boss—well, he was also my boyfriend…" Veruschka pursed her lips. "Wiktor's true obsession was the junk DNA—you know this technical phrase?"

"Trust me, Vero, I'm a genomics engineer."

"Wiktor found a way for these junk codons to express themselves. The echo from the cradle of life, evolution's roadside picnic! To express junk DNA required a new wetware reader. Wiktor called it the Universal Ribosome." She sighed. "We were so happy until the mafiya wanted the return on their funding."

"No National Science Foundation for you guys," mused Janna.

"Wiktor was supposed to tweak a cabbage plant to make opium for the criminals—but we were both so busy growing our dear Pumpti. Wiktor used my DNA, you see. I was smart and saved the data before the Uzbeks smashed up our lab. Now I'm over here with you, Janna, and we will start a great industry of personal pets! Wiktor's hero fate was not in vain. And—"

What an old-skool, stylin', totally trippy way for Janna to shed her grind-it-out worklife! Janna and Veruschka Zipkinova would create a genomic petware start-up, launch the IPO, and retire by thirty! Then Janna could escape her life-draining servitude and focus on life's real rewards. Take up oil painting, go on a safari, and hook up with some sweet guy who understood her. A guy she could really talk to. Not an engineer, and especially not a musician.

Veruschka pitchforked a glob of quiche past her pointed teeth. For her pilgrimage to the source of the world's largest legal creation of wealth in history, the Russian girl hadn't forgotten to pack her appetite.

"Pumpti still needs little bit of, what you say here, tweaking," said Veruschka. The prototype Pumpti sat shivering on its paper napkin. The thing had gone all goose bumpy, and the bumps were warty: the warts had smaller warts upon them, topped by teensy wartlets with fine, waving hairs. Not exactly a magnet for shoppers.

527

Stuffed with alfalfa sprouts, Janna put her cutlery aside. Veruschka plucked up Janna's dirty fork, and scratched inside her cheek with the tines.

Janna watched this dubious stunt and decided to stick to business. "How about patents?"

"No one ever inspects Russian gene labs," said Veruschka with a glittery wink. "We Russians are the great world innovators in black market wetware. Our fetal stem cell research, especially rich and good. Plenty of fetus meat in Russia, cheap and easy, all you need! Nothing ever gets patented. To patent is to teach stupid people to copy!"

"Well, do you have a local lab facility?" pressed Janna.

"I have better," said Veruschka, nuzzling her Pumpti. "I have pump-tose. The super enzyme of exponential autocatalysis!"

"'Pumptose,' huh? And that means?" prompted Janna.

"It means the faster it grows, the faster it grows!"

Janna finally reached out and delicately touched the Pumpti. Its surface wasn't wet after all, just shiny like super-slick plastic. But—a pet? It seemed more like something little boys would buy to gross-out their sisters. "It's not exactly cuddly," said Janna.

"Just wait till you have your own Pumpti," said Veruschka with a knowing smile.

"But where's the soft hair and big eyes? That thing's got all the shelf appeal of a scabby knee!"

"It's nice to nibble a scab," said Veruschka softly She cradled her Pumpti, leaned in to sniff it, then showed her strong teeth, and nipped off a bit of it.

"God, Veruschka," said Janna, putting down her coffee.

"Your own Pumpti," said Veruschka, smacking. "You are loving him like pretty new shoes. But so much closer and personal! Because Pumpti is you, and you are Pumpti."

Janna sat in wonderment. Then, deep within her soul, a magic casement opened. "Here's how we'll work it!" she exclaimed. "We give away Pumpti pets almost free. We'll make our money selling rip-off Pumpti-care products and accessories!"

Veruschka nodded, eyes shining. "If we're business partners now, can you find me a place to sleep?"

Janna let Veruschka stay in the spare room at her Dad's house. Inertia and lack of capital had kept Janna at home after college. Ruben Gutierrez was a big, soft man with a failing spine, carpal tunnel, and short, bio-bleached hair he wore moussed into hedgehog spikes.

He had a permanent mirthless grin, the side effect of his daily diet of antidepressants.

Dad's tranquil haze broke with the arrival of Veruschka with her go-go arsenal of fishnet tights and scoop-necked Lycra tops. With Veruschka around, the TV blared constantly and there was always an open bottle of liquor. Every night the little trio stayed up late, boozing, having schmaltzy confessions, and engaging in long, earnest sophomore discussions about the meaning of life.

Veruschka's contagious warm heartedness and her easy acceptance of human failing was a tonic for the Gutierrez household. It took Veruschka mere days to worm out the surprising fact that Ruben Gutierrez had a stash of half a million bucks accrued from clever games with his stock options. He'd never breathed a word of this to Anh or to Janna.

Emotionally alive for the first time in years, Dad offered his hoard of retirement cash for Veruschka's long-shot crusade. Janna followed suit by getting on the web and selling off her entire Goob collection. When Janna's web money arrived freshly laundered, Dad matched it, and two days later, Janna finally left home, hopefully for good. Company ownership was a three-way split between Veruschka, Janna, and Janna's Dad. Veruschka supplied no cash funding, because she had the intellectual property.

Janna located their Pumpti start-up in San Francisco. They engaged the services of an online lawyer, a virtual realtor, and a genomics supply house, and began to build the buzz that, somehow, was bound to bring them major league venture capital.

Their new HQ was a gray stone structure of columns, arches and spandrels, the stone decorated with explosive graffiti scrawls. The many defunct banks of San Francisco made spectacular dives for the city's genomics start-ups. Veruschka incorporated their business as "Magic Pumpkin, Inc.," and lined up a three-month lease.

San Francisco had weathered so many gold rushes that its real estate values had become permanently bipolar. Provisionary millionaires and drug-addled derelicts shared the same neighborhoods, the same painted-lady Victorians, the same flophouses and anarchist bookstores. Sometimes millionaires and lunatics even roomed together. Sometimes they were the very same person.

Enthusiastic cops spewing pepper gas chased the last downmarket squatters from Janna's derelict bank. To her intense embarrassment, Janna recognized one of the squatter refugees as a former Berkeley classmate named Kelso. Kelso was sitting on the sidewalk amidst his tattered Navajo blankets and a damp-spotted cardboard box of kitchen gear. Hard to believe he'd planned to be a lawyer.

"I'm so sorry, Kelso," Janna told him, wringing her hands. "My Russian friend and I are doing this genomics start-up? I feel like such a gross, rough-shod newbie."

"Oh, you'll be part of the porridge soon enough," said Kelso. He wore a big sexy necklace of shiny junked cell phones. "Just hang with me and get colorful. Want to jam over to the Museum of Digital Art tonight? Free grilled calamari, and nobody cares if you sleep there."

Janna shyly confided a bit about her business plans.

"I bet you're gonna be bigger than Pokemon," said Kelso. "I'd always wanted to hook up with you, but I was busy with my prelaw program and then you got into that cocooning thing with your Korean musician. What happened to him?"

"His mother found him a wife with a dowry from Pyongyang," said Janna. "It was so lovelorn."

"I've had dreams and visions about you, Janna," said Kelso softly. "And now here you are."

"How sweet. I wish we hadn't had you evicted."

"The wheel of fortune, Janna. It never stops."

As if on cue, a delivery truck blocked the street, causing grave annoyance to the local bike messengers. Janna signed for the tight-packed contents of her new office.

"Busy, busy," Janna told Kelso, now more than ready for him to go away. "Be sure and watch our web page. Pumpti dot-bio. You don't want to miss our IPO."

"Who's your venture angel?"

Janna shook her head. "That would be confidential."

"You don't have a backer in other words." Kelso pulled his blanket over his grimy shoulders. "And boy, will you ever need one. You ever heard of Revel Pullen of the Ctenophore Industry Group?"

"Ctenophore?" Janna scoffed. "They're just the biggest piezoplastic outfit on the planet, that's all! My dad used to work for them. And so did I, now that I think about it."

"How about Tug Mesoglea, Ctenophore's chief scientist? I don't mean to name-drop here, but I happen to know Dr. Tug personally."

Janna recognized the names, but there was no way Kelso could really know such heavy players. However, he was cute and he said he'd dreamed about her. "Bring 'em on," she said cheerfully.

"I definitely need to meet your partner," said Kelso, making the most of a self-created opportunity. Hoisting his grimy blanket, Kelso trucked boldly through the bank's great bronze-clad door.

Inside the ex-bank, Veruschka Zipkinova was setting up her own living quarters in a stony niche behind the old teller counter. Veruschka had a secondhand futon, a moldy folding chair, and a stout refugee's suitcase. The case was crammed to brimming with the detritus of subsistence tourism: silk scarves, perfumes, stockings, and freeze-dried coffee.

After one glance at Kelso, Veruschka yanked a handgun from her purse. "Out of my house, *rechniki*! No room and board for you here, *maphiya bezprizorniki*!"

"I'm cool, I'm cool," said Kelso, backpedaling. Then he made a run for it. Janna let him go. He'd be back.

Veruschka hid her handgun with a smirk of satisfaction. "So much good progress already! At last we command the means of production! Today we will make your own Pumpti," she told Janna.

They unpacked the boxed UPS deliveries. "You make ready that crib vat," said Veruschka. Janna knew the drill; she'd done this kind of work at Triple Helix. She got a wetware crib vat properly filled with base-pairs and warmed it up to standard operating temperature. She turned the valves on the bovine growth serum, and a pink threading began to fill the blood-warm fluid.

Veruschka plugged together the components of an Applied Biosystems oligosynthesis machine. She primed it with a data-stuffed S-cube that she'd rooted out of a twine-tied plastic suitcase.

"In Petersburg, we have unique views of DNA," said Veruschka, pulling on her ladylike data gloves and staring into the synthesizer's screen. Her fingers twitched methodically, nudging virtual molecules. "Alan Turing, you know of him?"

"Sure, the Universal Turing Machine," Janna core-dumped. "Foundations of computer science. Breaking the Enigma code. Reaction-diffusion rules. Turing wrote a paper to derive the shapes of patches on brindle cows. He killed himself with a poison apple. Alan Turing was Snow White, Queen, and Prince all at once!"

"I don't want to get too technical for your limited mathematical background," Veruschka hedged.

"You're about to tell me that Alan Turing anticipated the notion of DNA as a program tape that's read by ribosomes. And I'm not gonna be surprised."

"One step further," coaxed Veruschka. "Since the human body uses one kind of ribosome, why not replace that with another? The Universal Ribosome—it reads in its program as well as its data before it begins to act. All from that good junk DNA, yes Janna? And what is junk? Your bottom drawer? My garbage can? Your capitalist attic, and my start-up garage!"

"Normal ribosomes skip right over the junk DNA," said Janna. "It's supposed to be meaningless to the modern genome. Junk DNA is just scribbled-over things. Like the crossed-out numbers in an address book. A palimpsest. Junk DNA is the half-erased traces of the original codes—from long before humanity."

"From before, and—maybe *after*, Wiktor was always saying." Veruschka glove-tapped at a long-chain molecule on the screen. "There is pumptose!" The gaudy molecule had seven stubby arms, each of them a tightly wound mass of smaller tendrils. She barked out a command in Russian. The S-cube-enhanced Applied Biosystems unit understood, and an amber bead of oily, fragrant liquid oozed from the output port. Veruschka neatly caught the droplet in a glass pipette.

Then she transferred it to the crib vat that Janna had prepared. The liquid shuddered and roiled, jolly as the gut of Santa Claus.

"That pumptose is rockin' it," said Janna, marveling at the churning rainbow oil slick.

"We going good now, girl," said Veruschka. She opened her purse and tossed her own Pumpti into the vat. "A special bath treat for my Pumpti," she said. Then, with a painful wince, she dug one of her long fingernails into the lining of her mouth.

"Yow," said Janna.

"Oh, it feels so good to pop him loose," said Veruschka indistinctly. "Look at him."

Nestled in the palm of Veruschka's hand was a lentil-shaped little pink thing. A brand-new Pumpti. "That's your own genetics from your dirty fork at the diner," said Veruschka. "All coated with trilobite bile, or some other decoding from your junk DNA. I grew this seedling for you." She dropped the bean into the vat.

"This is starting to seem a little bent, Veruschka."

"Well…you never smelled your own little Pumpti. Or tasted him. How could you not bite him and chew him and grow a new scrap in your mouth? The sweet little Pumpti, you just want to eat him all up!"

Soon a stippling of bumps had formed on the tiny scrap of flesh in the tank. Soft little pimples, twenty or a hundred of them. The lump cratered at the top, getting thicker all around. It formed a dent and invaginated like a sea-squirt. It began pumping itself around in circles, swimming in the murky fluids. Stubby limbs formed momentarily, then faded into an undulating skirt like the mantle of a cuttlefish.

Veruschka's old Pumpti was the size of a grapefruit, and the new one was the size of a golf ball. The two critters rooted around the tank's bottom like rats looking for a drain hole.

Veruschka rolled up her sleeve and plunged her bare arm into the big vat's slimy fluids. She held up the larger Pumpti; it was flipping around like beached fish. Veruschka brought the thing to her face and nuzzled it.

It took Janna a couple of tries to fish her own Pumpti out of the tub, as each time she touched the slimy thing she had to give a little scream and let it go. But finally she had the Pumpti in her grip. It shaped itself to her touch and took on the wet, innocent gleam of a big wad of pink bubble gum.

"Smell it," urged Veruschka.

And, Lord yes, the Pumpti did smell good. Sweet and powdery, like clean towels after a nice hot bath, like a lawn of flowers on a summer morn, like a new dress. Janna smoothed it against her face, so smooth and soft. How could she have thought her Pumpti was gnarly?

"Now you must squeeze him to make him better," said Veruschka, vigorously mashing her Pumpti in her hands. "Knead, knead, knead! The Pumpti pulls skin cells from the surface of your hands, you know. Then pumptose reads more of the junk DNA and makes more good tasty proteins." She pressed her Pumpti to her cheek, and her voice went up an octave. "Getting more of that yummy yummy wetware from me, isn't he? Squeezy-squeezy Pumpti." She gave it a little kiss.

"This doesn't add up," said Janna. "Let's face it, an entire human body only has like ten grams of active DNA. But this Pumpti, it's solid DNA like a chunk of rubber, and hey, it's almost half a kilo! I mean, where's *that* at?"

"The more the better," said Veruschka patiently. "It means that very quickly Pumpti can be recombining his code. Like a self-programming Turing machine. Wiktor often spoke of this."

"But it doesn't even look like DNA," said Janna. "I messed with DNA every day at Triple Helix. It looks like lint or dried snot."

"My Pumpti is smooth because he's making nice old proteins from the ancient junk of the DNA. All our human predecessors from the beginning of time, amphibians, lemurs, maybe intelligent jellyfish saucers from Mars—who knows what. But every bit is my very own junk, of my very own DNA. So stop thinking so hard, Janna. Love your Pumpti."

Janna struggled not to kiss her pink glob. The traceries of pink and yellow lines beneath its skin were like the veins of fine marble.

"Your Pumpti is very fine," said Veruschka, reaching for it. "Now, into the freezer with him! We will store him, to show our financial backers."

"What!" said Janna. She felt a sliver of ice in her heart. "Freeze my Pumpti? Freeze your *own* Pumpti, Vero."

"I need mine," snapped Veruschka.

To part from her Pumpti—something within her passionately rebelled. In a dizzying moment of raw devotion, Janna suddenly found herself sinking her teeth into the unresisting flesh of the Pumpti. Crisp, tasty spun cotton candy, deep-fried puffball dough, a sugared beignet. And under that a salty, slightly painful flavor—bringing back the memory of being a kid and sucking the root of a lost tooth.

"Now you understand," said Veruschka with a throaty laugh. "I was only testing you! You can keep your sweet Pumpti, safe and sound. We'll get some dirty street bum to make us a Pumpti for commercial samples. Like that stupid boy you were talking to before." Veruschka stood on tiptoe to peer out of the bank's bronze-mullioned window. "He'll be back. Men always come back when they see you making money."

Janna considered this wise assessment. "His name is Kelso," said Janna. "I went to Berkeley with him. He says he's always wanted me. But he never talked to me at school."

"Get some of his body fluid."

"I'm not ready for that," said Janna. "Let's just poke around in the sink for his traces." And, indeed, they quickly found a fresh hair to seed a Kelso Pumpti, nasty and testicular, suitable for freezing.

As Veruschka had predicted, Kelso himself returned before long. He made it his business to volunteer his aid and legal counsel. He even claimed that he'd broached the subject of Magic Pumpkin to Tug Mesoglea himself. However, the mysterious mogul failed to show up with his checkbook, so Magic Pumpkin took the path of viral marketing.

Veruschka had tracked down an offshore Chinese ooze farm to supply cheap culture medium. In a week, they had a few dozen Pumpti starter kits for sale. They came in a little plastic tub of pumptose-laced nutrient, all boxed up in a flashy little design that Janna had printed out in color.

Kelso had the kind of slit-eyed street smarts that came only from Berkeley law classes. He chose Fisherman's Wharf to hawk the product. Janna went along to supervise his retail effort.

It was the start of October, a perfect fog-free day. A song of joy seemed to rise from the sparkling waters of San Francisco Bay, echoing from the sapphire dome of the California sky. Even the tourists could sense the sweetness of the occasion. They hustled cheerfully round Kelso's fold-out table, clicking away with little biochip cameras.

Kelso spun a practiced line of patter while Janna publicly adored her Pumpti. She'd decked out Pumpti in a special sailor suit, and she kept tossing him high into the air and laughing.

"Why is this woman so happy?" barked Kelso. "She's got a Pumpti. Better than a baby, better than a pet, your Pumpti is all you! Starter kits on special today for the unbelievably low price of— "

Over the course of a long morning, Kelso kept cutting the offering price of the Pumpti kits. Finally a runny-nosed little girl from Olympia, Washington, took the bait.

"How do I make one?" she wanted to know. "What choo got in that kit?" And, praise the Holy Molecule, her parents didn't drag her away; they just stood there watching their little darling shop.

The First Sale. For Janna, it was a moment to treasure forever. The little girl with her fine brown hair blowing in the warm afternoon wind, the dazedly smiling parents, Kelso's abrupt excited gestures as he explained how to seed and grow the Pumpti by planting a kiss on a scrap of Kleenex and dropping the scrap into the kit's plastic jar. The feel of those worn dollar bills in her hand, and the parting wave of little Customer Number One. Ah, the romance of it!

Now that they'd found their price point, more sales followed. Soon, thanks to word-of-mouth, they began moving units from their Web site as well.

But now Janna's Dad Ruben, who had a legalistic turn of mind, warned them to hold off on shipments until they had federal approval. Ruben took a sample Pumpti before the San Jose branch office of the Genomics Control Board. He argued that since the Pumptis were neither self-reproducing nor infectious they didn't fall under the Human Heritage provisions of the Homeland Security Act.

The hearings investigation made the Bay Area news shows, especially after the right-wing religious crowd got in on the story. An evangelist from Alameda appeared on San Jose Federal Building's steps, and after an impassioned speech he tore a Pumpti apart with pincers, calling the unresisting little glob the "spawn of Satan." He'd confiscated the poor Pumpti from a young parishioner, who could be seed sobbing at the edge of the screen.

In a few days the Genomics Control Board came through with their blessing. The Pumptis were deemed harmless, placed in the same schedule category as home gene-testing kits. Magic Pumpkin was free to ship throughout the nation! Magic Pumpkin's Web site gathered a bouquet of orders from eager early adopters.

Kelso's art-scene friends were happy to sign up to work for Magic Pumpkin. Buoyed by the chance of worldly success, Kelso began to shave more often and even use deodorant. But he was so excited about business that he forgot to make passes at Janna.

Every day-jobber in the start-up was issued his or her own free Pumpti. "Magic Pumpkin wants missionaries, not mercenaries," Janna announced from on high, and her growing cluster of troops cheered her on. Owning a personal Pumpti was an item of faith in the little company—the linchpin of their corporate culture. You couldn't place yourself in the proper frame of mind for Magic Pumpkin product development without your very own darling roly-poly.

Cynics had claimed that the male demographic would never go for Pumptis. Why would any guy sacrifice his computer gaming time and his weekend bicycling to nurture something? But once *presented* with their own Pumpti, men found that it filled some deep need in the masculine soul. They swelled up with competitive pride in their Pumptis, and even became quite violent in their defense.

Janna lined up a comprehensive array of related products. First and foremost were costumes. Sailor Pumpti, Baby Pumpti, Pumpti Duckling, Angel Pumpti, Devil Pumpti, and even a Goth Pumpti dress-up kit with press-on tattoos. They shrugged off production to Filipina doll clothes makers in a sweatshop in East L.A.

Further up-market came a Pumpti Backpack for transporting your Pumpti in style, protecting it from urban pollution and possibly nasty bacteria. This one seemed like a sure hit, if they could swing the Chinese labor in Shenzhen and Guangdong.

The third idea, Pumpti Energy Crackers, was a no-brainer: crisp collectible cards of munchable amino acid bases to fatten up your Pumpti. If the crackers used the "mechanically recovered meat" common in pet food and cattle feed, then the profit margin would be primo. Kelso had a contact for this in Mexico: they guaranteed their cookies would come crisply printed with the Pumpti name and logo.

Janna's fourth concept was downright metaphysical: a "Psychic Powers Pumpti Training Wand." Except for occasional oozing and plopping, the Pumptis never actually managed conventional pet tricks. But this crystal-topped gizmo could be hawked to the credulous as increasing their Pumpti's "empathy" or "telepathy." A trial mention of this vaporware on the Pumpti-dot-bio Web site brought in a torrent of excited New Age e-mails.

The final, sure-thing Pumpti accessory was tie-in books. Two of Kelso's many unemployed writer and paralegal friends set to work on the Pumpti User's Guide. The firm forecasted an entire *library* of guides, sucking up shelf space at chain stores and pet stores everywhere. *The Moron's Guide to Computational Genomics. Pumpti Tips, Tricks, and Shortcuts. The Three-Week Pumpti Guide, the One-Day Pumpti Guide*, and the *Ten Minute Pumpti Guide. Pumpti Security Threats: How to Protect Your*

Pumpti from Viral DNA Hacks, Trojan Goo, and Strange Genes. And more, more, more!

Paradoxically, Magic Pumpkin's flowering sales bore the slimy seeds of a smashing fiscal disaster. When an outfit started small, it didn't take much traffic to double demand every week. This constant doubling brought on raging production bottlenecks and serious crimps in their cash flow. In point of fact, in pursuit of market establishment, they were losing money on each Pumpti sold. And the big payback from the Pumpti accessories wasn't happening.

Janna had never quite realized that manufacturing real, physical products was so much harder than just thinking them up. Magic Pumpkin failed to do its own quality control, so the company was constantly screwed by fly-by-nighters. Subcontractors were happy to take their money, but when they failed to deliver, they had Magic Pumpkin over a barrel.

The doll costumes were badly sized. The Pumpti Backpacks were ancient Hello Kitty backpacks with their logos covered by cheap paper Pumpti stickers. The crackers were dog biscuits with the stinging misprint "Pumpti." The "telepathic" wand sold some units, but the people buying it tended to write bad checks. As for the User's Guides, the manuscripts were rambling and self-indulgent, long on far-fetched jokes yet critically short on objective facts.

Day by day, Janna stomped the problems out. And now that their production lines were stabilized, now that their accessories catalog was properly weeded out, now that their ad campaign was finally in gear, their fifteen minutes of ballroom glamour expired. The pumpkin clock struck midnight. The public revealed its single most predictable trait: fickleness.

Instantly, without a whimper of warning, Magic Pumpkin was deader than pet rocks. They never even shipped to any stories the Midwest or the East Coast, for the folks in those distant markets were sick of hearing about the Pumptis before they ever saw one on a shelf.

Janna and Veruschka couldn't make payroll. Their lease was expiring. They were cringing for cash.

A desperate Janna took the show on the road to potential investors in Hong Kong, the toy capital of the world. She emphasized that Magic Pumpkin had just cracked the biggest single technical problem: the fact that Pumptis looked like slimy blobs. Engineering-wise, it all came down to the pumptose-based Universal Ribosome. By inserting a properly-tweaked look-up string, you could get it to express the junk DNA sequences in customizable forms. Programming this gnarly cruft was, from an abstract computer-science perspective, "unfeasible," meaning that, logically speaking, no human would be able to design such a program within the lifetime of the universe.

But Janna's Dad, fretful about his investment, had done it anyway. In two weeks of inspired round-the-clock hacking, Ruben had implemented a full "OpenAnimator" graphics library, using a palette of previously unused rhodopsin-style proteins. Thanks to OpenAnimator, a whiff of the right long-chain molecule could now give your Pumpti any mesh, texture, color-map, or attitude matrix you chose. Not to mention overloaded frame-animation updates keyed into the pumptose's ribosomal time-steps! It was a techie miracle!

Dad flew along to Hong Kong to back Janna's pitch, but the Hong Kong crowd had little use for software jargon in American English. And the overwrought Ruben killed the one nibble they got by picking a fight over intellectual property—no way to build partnerships in Hong Kong.

Flung back to San Francisco, Janna spent night after night frantically combing the Web, looking for any source of second-round venture capital, no matter how far-fetched.

Finally she cast herself sobbing into Kelso's arms. Kelso was her last hope. Kelso just had to come through for them: he had to bring in the seasoned business experts from Ctenophore, Inc., the legendary masters of jellyfish A-Life.

"Listen, babe," said Kelso practically, "I think you and the bio-Bolshevik there have already taken this concept just about as far as any sane person oughta push it. Farther, even. I mean, sure, I recruited a lot of my cyberslacker friends into your corporate cult here, and we promised them the moon and everything, so I guess we'll look a little stupid when it Enrons. They'll bitch and whine, and they'll feel all disenchanted, but come on, this is San Francisco. They're used to that here. It's genetic."

"But what about my dad? He'll lose everything! And Veruschka is my best friend. What if she shoots me?"

"I'm thinking Mexico," said Kelso dreamily. "Way down on the Pacific coast—that's where my mother comes from. You and me, we've been working so hard on this start-up that we never got around to the main event. Just dump those ugly Pumptis in the Bay. We'll empty the cash box tonight, and catch a freighter blimp for the South. I got a friend who works for Air Jalisco."

It was Kelso's most attractive offer so far, maybe even sincere, in its way. Janna knew full well that the classic dot-com move was to grab that golden parachute and bail like crazy before the investors and employees caught on. But Magic Pumpkin was Janna's own brain child. She was not yet a serial entrepreneur, and a boyfriend was only a boyfriend. Janna couldn't walk away from the green baize table before that last spin of the wheel.

It had been quite some time since Ctenophore Inc. had been a cutting-edge start-up. The blazing light of media tech-hype no longer escaped their dense, compact enterprise. The firm's legendary founders, Revel Pullen and Tug Mesoglea, had collapsed in on their own reputations. Not a spark could escape their gravity. They had become twin black holes of biz weirdness.

Ctenophore's main line of business had always been piezoplastic products. Ctenophore had pumped this protean, blobject material into many crazy scenes in the California boom years. Bathtub toys, bondage clothing, industrial-sized artificial-jellyfish transport blimps—and Goob dolls as well! GoobYoob, creator of the Goob dolls, had been one of Ctenophore's many Asian spin-offs.

As it happened, quite without Janna's awareness, Ctenophore had already taken a professional interest in the workings of Magic Pumpkin. GoobYoob's manufacturing arm, Boogosity, had been the Chinese ooze-farm supplier for Pumpti raw material. Since Boogosity had no advertising or marketing expenses, they'd done much better by the brief Pumpti craze than Magic Pumpkin itself.

Since Magic Pumpkin was going broke, Boogosity faced a production glut. They'd have to move their specialty goo factories back into the usual condoms and truck tires. Some kind of corporate allegiance seemed written in the stars.

Veruschka Zipkinova was transfixed with paranoia about Revel Pullen, Ctenophore's chairman of the board. Veruschka considered major American capitalists to be sinister figures—this conviction was just in her bones, somehow—and she was very worried about what Pullen might do to Russia's oil.

Russia's black gold was the lifeblood of its pathetic, wrecked economy. Years ago Revel Pullen, inventively manic as always, had released gene-spliced bacteria into America's dwindling oil reserves. This fatal attempt to increase oil production had converted millions of barrels of oil into (as chance would have it) raw piezoplastic. Thanks to the powerful Texas lobby in Washington, none of the lawsuits or regulatory actions against Ctenophore had ever succeeded.

Janna sought to calm Veruschka's jitters. If the company hoped to survive, they had to turn Ctenophore into Magic Pumpkin's fairy godmother. The game plan was to flatter Pullen, while focusing their persuasive efforts on the technical expert of the pair. This would be Ctenophore's chief scientist, a far-famed mathematician named Tug Mesoglea.

It turned out that Kelso really did know Tug Mesoglea personally, for Mesoglea lived in a Painted Lady mansion above the Haight. During a protracted absence to the Tweetown district of Manchester (home of the Alan Turing Memorial), Tug had once hired Kelso to babysit his jellyfish aquarium.

Thanks to San Francisco's digital grapevine, Tug knew about the eccentric biomathematics that ran Pumptis. Tug was fascinated, and not by the money involved. Like many mathematicians, Mesoglea considered money to be one boring, merely bookkeeping subset of the vast mental universe of general computation. He'd already blown a fortune endowing chairs in set theory, cellular automata, and higher-dimensional topology. Lately, he'd published widely on the holonomic attractor space of human dreams, producing a remarkable proof that dreams of flight were a mathematical inevitability for a certain fixed percentage of the dreams—this fixed percentage number being none other than Feigenbaum's chaos constant, 4.6692.

Veruschka scheduled the meet at a Denny's near the Moffat Field blimp port. Veruschka had an unshakeable conviction that Denny's was a posh place to eat, and the crucial meeting had inspired her to dress to the nines.

"When do they want to have sex with us?" Veruschka fretted, paging through her laminated menu.

"Why would they want to do that?" said Janna.

"Because they are fat capitalist moguls from the West, and we are innocent young women. Evil old men with such fame and money, what else can they want of us? They will scheme to remove our clothing!"

"Well, look, Tug Mesoglea is gay." Janna looked at her friend with concern. Veruschka hadn't been sleeping properly. Stuck on the local grind of junk food and eighty-hour weeks, Veruschka's femme-fatale figure was succumbing to Valley hacker desk-spread. The poor thing barely fit in her designer knockoffs. It would be catty to cast cold water on her seduction fantasies, but really, Veruschka was swiftly becoming a kerchiefed babushka with a string-bag, the outermost shell of some cheap nest of Russian dolls.

Veruschka picked up her Pumpti, just now covered in baroque scrolls like a fin-de-siècle picture frame. "Do like this," she chirped, brushing the plump pet against her fluffy marten-fur hat. The Pumpti changed its surface texture to give an impression of hairiness, and hopped onto the crown.

"Lovely," said Veruschka, smiling into her hand mirror. But her glossy smile was tremulous.

"We simply must believe in our product," said Veruschka, pep-talking to her own mirror. She glanced up wide-eyed at Janna. "Our product is so good a fit for their core business, no? Please tell me more about them, about this Dr. Tug and Mr. Revel. Tell me the very worst. These gray-haired, lecherous fat cats, they are world weary and cynical! Success has corrupted them and narrowed their thinking! They no longer imagine a brighter future, they merely go through the rote. Can they be trusted with our dreams?"

Janna tugged fitfully at the floppy tie she'd donned to match her dress-for-success suit. She always felt overwhelmed by Veruschka's fits of self-serving corn. "It's a biz meeting, Vero. Try to relax."

Just as the waitress brought them some food, the glass door of the Denny's yawned open with a ring and a squeak. A seamy, gray-haired veteran with the battered look of a bronco-buster approached their table, with a bowlegged scuff.

"I'm Hoss Jenks, head o' security for Ctenophore." Jenks hauled out a debugging wand and a magnetometer. He then swept his tools with care over the pair of them. The wand began beeping in frenzy.

"Lemme hold on to your piece for you, ma'am," Jenks suggested placidly.

"It's just a sweet little one," Veruschka demurred, handing over a pistol.

Tug Mesoglea tripped in moments later, sunburned and querulous. The mathematician sported a lavender dress shirt and peach-colored ascot, combined with pleated khaki trail-shorts and worn-out piezo-plastic Gripper sandals.

Revel Pullen followed, wearing a black linen business suit, snake-skin boots, and a Stetson. Janna could tell there was a bald pate under that high hat. Jenks faded into a nearby booth, where he could shadow his employers and watch the door.

Mesoglea creaked into the plastic seat beside Veruschka and poured himself a coffee. "I phoned in my order from the limo. Where's my low-fat soy protein?"

"Here you go, then," said Janna, eagerly shoving him the heaped plate of pseudo-meat that the waitress had just set down.

Pullen stared as Mesoglea tucked in. "I don't know how the hell this man eats the food in a sorry-ass chain store." Nevertheless he picked up a fork and speared a piece of it himself.

"I believe in my investments," Mesoglea said, munching. "You see, ladies, this soy protein derives from a patented Ctenophore process." He prodded at Veruschka's plate. "Did you notice that lifelike, organic individuality of your waffle product? That's no accident, darling."

"Did we make any real foldin' money off this crap?" said Revel Pullen, eating one more piece of it.

"Of course we did! You remember all those sintered floating gel rafts in the giant tofu tanks in Chiba?" Mesoglea flicked a blob of molten butter from his ascot.

"Y'all don't pay no never mind to Dr. Mesoglea here," Revel counteradvised, setting down his fork. "Today's economy is all about diversity. Proactive investments. Buying into the next technical wave, before you get cannibalized." Revel leered. "Now as for me, I get my finger into every techno-pie!" His lipless mouth was like a letter slot, bent slightly upward at the corners to simulate a grin.

"Let me brief you gentlemen on our business model," said Janna warily. "It's much like your famous Goob dolls, but the hook here is that the Pumpti is made of the user's very own DNA. This leads to certain, uh, powerful consumer bonding effects, and…"

"Oh good, let's see your Pumptis, girls," crooned Tug, with a decadent giggle. "Whip out your Pumptis for us."

"You've never seen our product?" asked Janna.

"Tug's got a mess of 'em," said Revel. "But y'all never shipped to Texas. That's another thing I just don't get." Pullen produced a sheaf of printout, and put on his bifocals. "According to these due-diligence filings, Magic Pumpkin's projected online capacity additions were never remotely capable of meeting the residual in-line demand in the total off-line market that you required for breakeven." He tipped back his Stetson, his liver-spotted forehead wrinkling in disbelief. "How in green tarnation could you gals overlook that? How is that even possible?"

"Huh?" said Janna.

Revel chuckled. "Okay, now I get it. Tug, these little gals don't know how to do business. They've never been anywhere near one."

"Sure looks that way," Tug admitted. "No MBAs, no accountants? Nobody doing cost control? No speakers-to-animals in the hacker staff? I'd be pegging your background as entry-level computational genomics," he said, pointing at Janna. Then he waggled his finger at Veruschka, "And you'd be coming from—Slavic mythology and emotional blackmail?"

Veruschka's cobalt blue eyes went hard. "I don't think I want to show you men my Pumpti."

"We kind of have to show our Pumptis, don't we?" said Janna, an edge in her voice. "I mean, we're trying to make a deal here."

"Don't get all balky on the bailout men," added Revel, choking back a yawn of disdain. He tapped a napkin to his wrinkled lips, with a glint of diamond solitaire. He glanced at his Rolex, reached into his coat pocket, and took out a little pill. "That's for high blood pressure, and I got it the hard way, out kickin' ass in the market. I got a flight back to Texas in less than two hours. So let's talk killer app, why don't we? Your toy pitch is dead in the water. But Tug says your science is unique. Okay, but how do we sell the Pumptis?"

"They're getting much prettier," Janna said, swiftly hating herself.

"Do y'all think Pumptis might have an app in home security?"

Janna brightened. "The home market?"

"Yeah, that's right, Strategic Defense for the Home." Pullen outlined his scheme. Ever the bottom-feeder, he'd bought up most of the software patents for the never-completed American missile defense system. Pullen had a long-cherished notion of retrofitting the Star Wars shield into a consumer application for troubled neighborhoods. He was wondering if Pumptis might take the place of the missiles.

Revel figured that a sufficiently tough-minded, Pumpti could take a round to the guts, fall to earth, crawl back to its vat in the basement, and come back hungry for more. So if bullets were fired at a private home from some drug-crazed drive-by, then a rubbery unit of the client's Pumpti Star Wars shield would instantly fling itself into the way, guided by that fine old Star Wars software.

Veruschka batted her eyes at Pullen. "I love to hear a strong man talk about security."

"Security always soars along with unemployment," said Pullen, nodding his head at his own wisdom. "We're in a major downturn. I seen this before, so I know the drill. Locks, bolts, Dobermans, they're all market leaders this quarter. That's Capitalism 301, girls."

"And you, Ctenophore, you would finance Magic Pumpkin as a home-defense industry?" probed Veruschka.

"Maybe," said Pullen, his sunken eyes sly. "We'd surely supply you a Washington lobbyist. New public relations. Zoning clearances. Help you write up a genuine budget for once. And of course, if we're on board, then y'all will have to dump all your crappy equipment and become a hunnert-percent Ctenophore shop, technologically. Ctenophore sequencers, PCRs, and bioinformatic software. That's strictly for your own safety, you understand: stringent quality assurance, functional testing and all."

"Uhm, yeah," nodded Tug. "We'd get all your intellectual property copyrighted and patented with the World Intellectual Property Organization. The lawyer fees, we'll take care of that. Ctenophore is downright legendary for our quick response times to a market opportunity."

"We gonna help you youngsters catch the fish," said Pullen smugly. "Not just give you a damn fish. What'd be the fun in that? Self-reliance, girls. We wanna see your little outfit get up and walk, under our umbrella. You sign over your founder's stock, put in your orders for our equipment—and we ain't gonna bill for six months—then my men will start to shake the money tree."

"Wait, they still haven't shown us their Pumptis," said Tug, increasingly peevish. "And, Revel, you need to choke it back to a dull roar with the Star Wars attack Pumptis. Real world ballistic physics is chaotic, dude, which means unsolvable in real time." Tug muffled a body sound with his napkin. "I ate too many waffles."

Janna felt like flipping the table over into their laps. Veruschka shot her a quick, understanding glance and laid a calming hand on her shoulder. Veruschka played a deep game.

Veruschka plucked the Pumpti from her furry hat and set it on the table.

Tug did a double take and leaned forward, transfixed

Veruschka segued into her cuddly mode. "Pumpti was created in a very special lab in Petersburg. In the top floor of old Moskfilm complex, where my friends make prehistoric amber jewelry. You can see the lovely River Neva while you hunt for dinosaur gnats—"

As she put the squeeze on their would-be sponsors, Veruschka compulsively massaged her Pumpti. She was working it, really getting into it finger and thumb, until suddenly a foul little clot of nonworking protein suddenly gave way inside, like popping bubble wrap.

"Stop it, Vero," said Janna.

Tug daintily averted his gaze as Veruschka sucked goo from her fingers.

"Look at mine," offered Janna. She'd programmed her Pumpti to look rubbery and sleek, like a top-end basketball shoe.

"Hey, any normal kid would kill to have one of those," said Revel cheerily. "I'm getting' another product brainstorm! It's risin' in me like a thunderhead across Tornado Alley!"

"The junk DNA is the critical aspect," put in Tug. "Those are traces of early prehuman genomics. If we can really express those primordial codons, we might—"

"Those globbies suck the DNA right off people's fingers, right?" demanded Revel.

"Well, yes," said Janna.

"Great! So that's my Plan B. Currency! You smash 'em out flat and color 'em pretty. As they daisy-chain from hand to hand, they record the DNA of every user. Combine those with criminal DNA files, and you got terrorist-proof cash!"

"But the mafiya always wears gloves," said Veruschka.

"No problem, just turn up the amps," said Pullen. "Have 'em suck DNA fragments out of the dang air." He wiggled his lower jaw to simulate deep thought. "Those little East European currencies, they're not real cash money anyways! That user-base won't even know the difference!"

Mesoglea blinked owlishly. "Bear with us, ladies. Revel's always like this right after he takes his meds."

"Now, Tug, we gotta confront the commercial possibilities! You and I, we could hit the lab and make some kind of money that only works for white males over fifty. If anybody else tries to pass it, it just, like— bites their dang hands off!" Pullen chuckled richly, then had another drag off his cig. "Or how about a hunnert-dollar bill that takes your DNA and grows your own face on the front!"

Mesoglea sighed, looked at his watch, and shook it theatrically.

"But this is such pure genius!" gushed Veruschka, leaning toward Revel with moistening eyes. "We need your veteran skills. Magic Pumpkin needs grown men in the boardroom. We wasted our money on incompetent artists and profiteers! We had great conceptual breakthroughs, but— "

"Can it with the waterworks and cut to the chase, ptista," said Pullen. "It's high time for you amateurs to roll over."

"Make us the offer," said Janna.

"Cards on the table," said Pullen, fixing her with his hard little eyes. "You'll sign all your founder's stock over to us. I'll take your stock, chica, and Tug'll take your pretty Russian friend's. That gives us controlling interest. As for your Dad's third, he might as well keep it since he's too maverick to deal with. Dad's in clover. Okay?"

"You're not offering us any cash?" said Janna. "I don't believe this. The Pumpti was our original idea!"

"You sign on with us, you get a nice salary," said Pullen. Then he broke into such cackles that he had to sip ice water and dab at his eyes with a kerchief.

"You two kids really are better off with a salary," added Tug in a kindly tone. "It won't be anything huge, but better than your last so-called jobs. We already checked into your histories. You'll get some nice vague titles too. That'll be good experience for your next job or, who knows, your next start-up."

"The sexy Russki can be my Pumpti Project Manager," said Pullen. "She can fly down to my ranch tomorrow. I'll be waitin'. And what about the other one, Tug? She's more the techie type."

"Yes, yes, I want Janna," said Tug, beaming. "Executive Assistant to the Chief Scientist."

Janna and Veruschka exchanged unhappy glances.

"How—how big of a salary?" asked Janna, hating herself.

After the fabled entrepreneurs departed the Denny's in the company of a watchful Hoss Jenks, Veruschka dropped her glued-on smile and scrambled for the kitchen. She was just in time to save the Tug's and Revel's dirty forks before they hit the soapy water.

Shoving a busboy aside, Veruschka wrapped the DNA-soiled trophies in a sheet of newspaper and stuffed them into her purse.

"Veruschka, what do you think you're doing?"

"I'm multiplying our future options. I am seizing the future imperfectly. Visualize, realize, actualize." Veruschka's lower lip trembled. "Leap, and the net will appear."

Stuck in the clattering kitchen of Denny's, feeling sordid and sold-out, Janna felt a moment of true sorrow for herself, for Vero, and even for the Latin and Vietnamese busboys. Poor immigrant Veruschka, stuck in some foreign country, with an alien language—she'd seen her grandest dreams seized, twisted up, and crushed by America, and now, in her valiant struggle to rise from ash heap to princess, she'd signed on to be Pullen's marketeer droid. As for Janna—she'd be little more than a lab assistant.

At least the business was still alive. Even if it wasn't her business anymore.

When they returned to their San Francisco lair, they discovered that Hoss Jenks had arrived with a limo full of men in black suits and mirrorshades. They'd seized the company's computers and fired everyone. To make things worse, Jenks had called the police and put an APB out for Kelso, who had last been seen departing down a back alley with a cardboard box stuffed with the company's petty cash.

"I can't believe that horrible old cowboy called the cops on Kelso," Janna mourned, sitting down in the firm's very last cool, swoopy Blobular Concepts chair. "I'm glad Kelso stole that money, since it's not ours anymore. I hope he'll turn up again. I never even got to make out with him."

"He's gay, you know."

"Look, Kelso is *not gay*," yelled Janna. "He is so totally not gay. There's a definite chemistry between us. We were just too incredibly busy, that's all."

Veruschka sniffed and said nothing. When Janna looked up, her eyes brimming, she realized that Veruschka was actually feeling sorry for her. This was finally it for Janna; it was too much for flesh and blood to bear. She bent double in her designer chair, racked with sobs.

"Janna, my dear, don't surrender. The business cycle, always, it turns around. And California is the Golden State."

"No it isn't. We've got a market bear stitched right on our flag. We're totally doomed, Veruschka! We've been such fools!"

"I hate those two old men," said Veruschka, after the two of them had exhausted half a box of Kleenex. "They're worse than their reputations. I expected them to be crazy, but not so—greedy and rude."

"Well, we signed all their legal papers. It's a little late to fuss now."

Veruschka let out a low, dark chuckle. "Janna, I want revenge."

Janna looked up. "Tell me."

"It's very high tech and dangerous."

"Yeah?"

"It's completely illegal, or it would be, if any court had the chance to interpret the law in such a matter."

"Spill it, Vero."

"Pumpti Gene Therapy."

Janna felt a twinge, as of seasickness. "That's a no-no, Vero."

"Tell me something," said Veruschka. "If you dose a man with an infectious genomic mutagen, how do you keep him from knowing he's been compromised?"

"You're talking bioterrorism, Vero. They'd chase us to the ends of the earth in a rain of cruise missiles."

"You use a Pumpti virus based on your victim's own DNA," said Veruschka, deftly answering her own rhetorical question. "Because nobody has an immune response to their own DNA. No matter how— how very strange it might be making their body."

"But you're weaponizing the human genome! Can't we just shoot them?"

Veruschka's voice grew soft and low. "Imagine Tug Mesoglea at his desk. He feels uneasy, he begins to complain, his voice is like a rasping locust's. And then his eyeballs—his eyeballs pop out onto his cheeks, driven from his head by the pressure of his bursting brain!"

"You call *that* gene therapy?"

"They *need* it! The shriveled brains of Pullen and Mesoglea are old and stiff! There is plenty of room for new growth in their rattling skulls. You and I, we create the Pumpti Therapy for them. And then they will give us money." Veruschka twirled on one heel and laughed. "We make Pumptis so tiny like a virus! Naked DNA with Universal Ribosome and a nine-plus-two microtubule apparatus to rupture the host's cell walls! One strain for Pullen, and one for Mesoglea. The Therapy is making them smarter, so they are grateful to shower money upon us. Or else," her eyes narrowed, "the Therapy is having some unpleasant effects and they are begging on their knees to purchase an antidote."

"So it's insanity and/or blackmail, in other words."

"These men are rotten bastards," said Veruschka.

"Look, why don't we give a fighting chance to the home defense Pumptis?" asked Janna. "Or the money Pumptis? They're nutty ideas, but not all that much crazier than your original scheme about pets. Didn't I hear you call Revel Pullen a marketing genius?"

"Don't you know me yet even a little bit?" said Veruschka, her face frank and open. "Revel's ideas for my Pumptis are like using a beautiful sculpture for a hammer. Or like using a silk scarf to pick up dog doo."

"Too, too true," sighed Janna. "Get the forks out of your purse and let's start on those nanoPumptis."

To begin with, they grew some ordinary kilogram-plus Pumptis from Revel and Tug's fork-scrapings, each in its own little vat. Veruschka wanted to be sure they had a whopping big supply of their enemies' DNA.

For fun, Janna added OpenAnimator molecules to shade Revel's Pumpti blue and Tug's red. And then, for weirdness, Vero dumped a new biorhythm accelerator into the vats. The fat lumps began frantically kneading themselves, each of them replicating, garbage-collecting, and decoding their DNA hundreds of times per second. "So perhaps these cavemen can become more highly evolved," remarked Veruschka.

By three in the morning, they'd made their first nanoPumpti. Janna handled the assembly, using the synthesizer's datagloves to control a molecular probe. She took the body of a cold virus and replaced its polyhedral head with a Universal Ribosome and a strand of hyper-evolved DNA from the Pullen Pumpti. And then she made a nanoPumpti for Tug. Veruschka used her hands-on wetware skills to quickly amplify the lone Tug and Revel nanoPumptis into respectable populations.

When the first morning sunlight slanted in the lab window, it lit up two small stoppered glass vials: a blue one for Revel, a red one for Tug.

Veruschka rooted in the cornucopia of her tattered suitcase. She produced a pair of cheap-looking rings, brass things with little chrome balls on them. "These are Lucrezia Borgia rings. I bought them in a tourist stall before I left St. Petersburg." Practicing with water, Veruschka showed Janna how to siphon up a microliter though the ring's cunningly hidden perforations and how—with the crook of a finger—to make the ring squirt the liquid back out as a fine mist.

"Load your ring with Mesoglea's nanoPumptis," said Veruschka, baring her teeth in a hard grin. "I want to see you give Mesoglea his

Therapy before my flight to Texas. I'll load my ring for Pullen and when I get down there, I'll take care of him."

"No, no," said Janna, stashing the vials in her purse. "We don't load the rings yet. We have to dose the guys at the exact same time. Otherwise, the one will know when the other one gets it. They've been hanging together for a long time. They're like symbiotes. How soon are you and Pullen coming back from Texas anyway?"

"He says two weeks," said Veruschka, pulling a face. "I hope is less time."

And then Hoss Jenks was there with a limo to take Veruschka to the airport. Janna cleaned up the lab and stashed the vials of nanoPumptis in her office. Before she could lie down to sleep there, Tug Mesoglea arrived for his first day at Magic Pumpkin.

To Janna's surprise, Tug turned out to be a pleasant man to work for. Not only did he have excellent taste in office carpeting and window treatments, but he was a whiz at industrial R&D. Under his leadership, the science of the Pumptis made great strides: improvements in the mechanism of the Universal Ribosome, in the curious sets of proteins encoded by the junk DNA, even in the looping strangeness of Ruben Gutierrez's genomic OpenAnimator graphics library. And then Tug stumbled onto the fact that the Pumptis could send and receive a certain gigahertz radio frequency. Digital I/O.

"The ascended master of R&D does not shoehorn new science into yesterday's apps," the serenely triumphant Tug told Janna. "The product is showing us what it wants to do. Forget the benighted demands of the brutish consumers: we're called to lead them to the sunlit uplands of improved design!"

So Janna pushed ahead, and under Tug's Socratic questioning, she had her breakthrough: Why stop at toys? Once they'd managed to tweak and evolve a new family of forms and functions for the Pumptis, they would no longer be mere amusements, but *personal tools*. Not like Pokemons, not like Goob dolls, but truly *high-end devices*: soft uvvy phones, health monitors, skin-interfaced VR patches, holistic gene maintenance kits, cosmetic body-modifiers! Every gadget would be utterly trustworthy, being made of nothing but you!

As before, they would all but give away the pretty new Pumptis, but this time they'd have serious weight for the after market: "Pumpti Productivity Philtres" containing the molecular codes for the colors, shapes, and functionalities of a half dozen killer apps. Get 'em all! While they last! New Philtres coming soon!

Veruschka's stay in Texas lasted six weeks. She phoned daily to chat with Janna. The laid-back Texan lifestyle on the legendary Pullen spread was having its own kind of seduction. Vero gave up her vodka for blue agave tequila. She surrendered her high heels for snakeskin boots. Her phone conversations became laced with native terms such as "darlin" and "sugar" as she smugly recounted giant barbeques for politicians, distributors, the Ctenophore management, and the Pullen Drilling Company sales force.

By the time Revel and Veruschka came back to San Francisco, Magic Pumpkin had the burn-rate under firm control and was poised for true market success. But, as wage slaves, Janna and Veruschka would share not one whit of the profit. So far as Janna knew, they were still scheduled to poison their bosses.

"Do we really want to give them the Pumpti Therapy?" Janna murmured to Veruschka. They were in Janna's new living quarters, wonderfully carpentered into the space beneath the bank's high dome. It had proved easier to build in an apartment than to rent one. And Tug had been very good about the expenses.

Veruschka had a new suitcase, a classy Texas item clad in dappled calfskin with the hair still on. As usual, her bag had disgorged itself all over the room. "Mesoglea must certainly be liquidated," she said, cocking her head. Tug's voice was drifting up from the lab below, where he was showing Revel around. "He is fatuous, old, careless. He has lost all his creative fire."

"But I like Tug now," said Janna. "He taught me amazing things in the lab. He's smart."

"I hate him," said Veruschka stubbornly. "Tonight he meets the consequences of his junk DNA."

"Well, your Revel Pullen needs Pumpti Therapy even more," said Janna crossly. "He's a corrupt, lunatic bully—cram-full of huckster double-talk he doesn't even listen to himself."

"Revel and I are in harmony on many issues," allowed Veruschka. "I begin almost to like his style."

"Should—should we let them off the hook?" pleaded Janna.

Veruschka gave her a level stare. "Don't weaken. These men stole our company. We must bend them to our will. It is beyond personalities."

"Oh, all right," sighed Janna, feeling doomed. "You poison Tug and I'll poison Revel. It'll be easier for us that way."

The four of them were scheduled to go out for a celebratory dinner, this time to Popo's, a chi-chi high-end gourmet establishment of Tug's choosing. Pullen's voice could now be heard echoing up from the lab, loudly wondering what was "keeping the heifers." Janna swept downstairs to distract the men while Veruschka loaded her ring. Then

Veruschka held the floor while Janna went back up to her room to ready her own ring.

The two little vials of nanoPumpti sat in plain sight amidst the clutter of the women's cosmetics. They could have been perfume bottles, one red, one blue.

As Janna prepared to fill her Borgia ring, she was struck by a wild inspiration. She'd treat Revel Pullen with Tug's Pumptized DNA. Yes! This would civilize the semihuman Pullen, making him be more like Tug—instead of, horrors, even more like himself! There might be certain allergic effects—but the result for the Magic Pumpkin company would be hugely positive. To hell with the risk. No doubt the wretched Pullen would be happy with the change.

It went almost too easily. The old men guzzled enough wine with dinner to become loose and reckless. When the cappuccinos arrived, Janna and Veruschka each found a reason to reach out toward their prey. Veruschka adjusted Pullen's string-tie. Janna dabbed a stain of prawn sauce from Tug's salmon-colored lapel. And each woman gently misted the contents of her ring onto the chocolate-dusted foam of her victim's coffee. The old men, heavy-lidded with booze and digestion, took their medicines without a peep.

Soon after, Pullen retired to his hotel room, Tug caught a cab back to his house in the Haight, and the two women walked the few blocks back to the Magic Pumpkin headquarters, giggling with relief. Janna didn't tell Veruschka about having given Pullen the red Tug Treatment. Better to wait and see how things worked out. Better to sleep on it.

But sleep was slow in coming. Suppose Pullen swelled up horribly and died from toxic Tug effects? The Feds would find the alien DNA in him, and the law would be on Janna right away. And what if the Therapies really did improve the two old men? Risen to some cold, inhuman level of intelligence, they'd think nothing of wiping out Janna and Veruschka like ants.

Janna rubbed her cell phone nervously. Maybe she could give poor old Tug some kind of anonymous warning. But she sensed that Veruschka was also awake, over on the other side of Janna's California King bed.

Suddenly the phone rang. It was Kelso.

"Yo babe," he said airily. "I'm fresh back from sunny Mexico. The heat's off. I bought myself a new identity and an honest-to-God law degree. I'm right outside, Janna. Saw you and Vero go jammin' by on Market Street just now, but I didn't want to come pushing up at you like some desperado tweaker. Let me in. Nice new logo you got on the Magic Pumpkin digs, by the way, good font choice too."

"You're a lawyer now? Well, don't think we've forgotten about that box of petty cash, you sleaze."

Kelso chuckled. "I didn't forget you either, *mi vida*! As for that money—hey, my new papers cost as much as what I took. Paradoxical, no? Here's another mind bender: even though we're hot for each other, you and me have never done the deed."

"I'm not alone," said Janna. "Veruschka's staying with me."

"For God's sake will you two at last get it over," said Veruschka, sleepily burying her head under her pillow. "Wake me up when you're done and maybe the three of us can talk business. We'll need a lawyer tomorrow."

The next morning Tug Mesoglea arrived at Magic Pumpkin and started acting—like Revel Pullen.

"Git along little doggies," he crooned, leaning over the incubator where they were keeping their dozen or so new-model Pumptis. And then he reached over and fondled Janna's butt.

Janna raced out of the lab and cornered Veruschka, who was noodling around at her desk trying to look innocent. "You gave Tug the Pullen potion, didn't you? Bitch!"

Before Veruschka could answer, the front door swung open, and in sashayed Pullen. He was dressed, unbelievably, in a caftan and striped Capri pants. "I picked these up in the hotel shop," he said, looking down at one of his spindly shanks. "Do you think it works on me, Janna? I've always admired your fashion sense."

"Double bitch!" cried Veruschka, and yanked at Janna's hair. Janna grabbed back, knocking off the red cowboy hat that Vero was sporting today.

"Don't think we haven't already seen clear through your little game," said the altered Pullen with a toss of his head. "You and your nanoPumptis. Tug and I had a long heart-to-heart talk on the phone this morning. Except we didn't use no phone. We can hear each other in our heads."

"Shit howdy!" called Tug from the lab. "Brother Revel's here. Ready to take it to the next level?"

"Lemme clear out the help," said Revel. He leaned into the guard room and sent Hoss Jenks and his mirrorshades assistants out for a long walk. To Jenks's credit, he didn't bat an eye at Revel's new look.

"Let's not even worry about that Kelso boy up in Janna's room," said Tug. "He's still asleep." Tug gave Janna an arch look. "Don't look so surprised, we know everything. Thanks to the Pumpti Therapy you gave us. We've got, oh, a couple of million years of evolution on you now. The future of the race, that's us. Telepathy, telekinesis, teleportation, and shape-shifting too."

"You're—you're not mad at us?" said Janna.

"We only gave the Therapy to make you better," babbled Veruschka. "Don't punish us."

"I dunno about that," said Revel. "But I do know I got a powerful hankerin' for some Pumpti meat. Can you smell that stuff?"

"Sure can," sang Tug. "Intoxicating, isn't it? What a seductive perfume!"

Without another word, the two men headed for the lab's vats and incubators. Peeping warily through the open lab doors, Janna and Veruschka saw a blur of activity. The two old men were methodically devouring the stock, gobbling every Pumpti in sight.

There was no way that merely human stomachs could contain all that mass, but that wasn't slowing them down much. Their bodies were puffing up and—just as Veruschka had predicted, the eyeballs were bulging forward out of their heads. Their clothes split and dropped away from their expanding girths. When all the existing Pumptis were gone, the two giants set eagerly to work on the raw materials. And when Tug found the frozen kilograms of their own personal Pumptis, the fireworks really began.

The two great mouths chewed up the red and blue Pumpti meat, spitting, drooling, and passing the globs back and forth. Odd ripples began moving up and down along their bodies like ghost images of ancient flesh.

"What's that a-comin' out of your rib cage, Tuggie?" crowed Revel.

"Cootchy-coo," laughed Tug, twiddling the tendrils protruding from his side. "I'm expressing a jellyfish. My personal best. Feel around in your genome, Revel. It's all there, every species, evolved from our junk DNA right along with our super-duper futuristic new bodies." He paused, watching. "Now you're keyin' it, bro. I say—are those hooves on your shoulder?"

Revel palpated the twitching growth with professional care. "I'd be reckoning that's a quagga. A prehistoric zebra-type thing. And, whoah Nellie, see this over on my other shoulder? It's an eohippus. Ancestor of the horse. The cowboys of the Pullen clan got a long relationship with horseflesh. I reckon there was some genetic bleedover when we was punchin' cattle up the Goodnight-Loving Trail; that's why growin' these ponies comes so natural to me."

"How do you like it now, ladies?" asked Tug, glancing over toward Janna and Veruschka.

"Ask them," hissed Veruschka in Janna's ear.

"No, you," whispered Janna.

Brave Vero spoke up. "My friend is wondering now if you will sign those Magic Pumpkin founders' shares back over to us? And the patents as well if you please?"

"Groink," said Revel, hunching himself over and deforming his mouth into a dinosaur-type jaw.

"Squonk," said Tug, letting his head split into a floppy bouquet of be-suckered tentacles.

"You don't need to own our business anymore," cried Janna. "Please sign it back to us."

The distorted old men whooped and embraced each other, their flesh fusing into one. The meaty mass seethed with possibilities, bubbled with the full repertoire of zoological forms—with feelers, claws, wings, antennae, snouts; with eyes of every shape and color winking on and off; with fleeting mouths that lingered only long enough to bleat, to hiss, to grumble, to whinny, screech, and roar. It wasn't exactly a "no" answer.

"Kelso," shouted Janna up the stairs. "Bring the papers!"

A high, singing sound filled the air. The Pullen-Mesoglea mass sank to the floor as if melting, forming itself into a broad, glistening plate. The middle of the plate swelled like yeasty bread to form a swollen dome. The fused organism was taking on the form of—a living UFO?

"The original genetic Space Friend!" said Veruschka in awe. "It's been waiting in their junk DNA since the dawn of time!"

As Kelso clattered down the stairs, the saucer charged at the three of them, far too fast to escape. Kelso, Janna, and Veruschka were absorbed into the saucer's ethereal bulk.

Everything got white, and in the whiteness, Janna saw a room, a round space expressing wonderful mathematical proto-design: a vast Vernor Panton 1960s hashish den, languidly and repeatedly melting into a Karim Rashid all-plastic lobby.

The room's primary inhabitants were idealized forms of Tug Mesoglea and Revel Pullen. The men's saucer bodies were joyous, sylphlike forms of godlike beauty.

"I say we spin off the company to these girls and their lawyer," intoned the Tug avatar. "Okay by you, Revel? You and I, we're more than ready to transcend the material plane."

"There's better action where we're going," Revel agreed. "We gotta stake a claim in the subdimensions, before the yokels join the gold rush."

A pen appeared in Tug's glowing hand. "We'll shed the surly bonds of incorporation."

It didn't take them long to sign off every interest in Magic Pumpkin. And then the floor of the saucer opened up, dropping Janna,

Veruschka, and Kelso onto the street. Over their awestruck heads, the saucer briefly glowed and then sped away, though not in any direction that a merely human being could specify. It was more as if the saucer shrank. Reorganized itself. Corrected. Downsized. And then it was gone from all earthly ken.

And that's how Janna Gutierrez and Veruschka Zipkinova got rich.

Note on "Junk DNA" (With Bruce Sterling)

Written in December, 2001.
Asimov's Science Fiction, January 2003.

This is the third story I've written with Bruce Sterling; the earlier two being "Storming the Cosmos" and "Big Jelly," both in my anthology Gnarl! (Four Walls Eight Windows, 2000.) The "Junk DNA" collaboration was tumultuous; I began finally to understand why a synergistic pair like, say, Lennon and McCartney might stop working together—no matter how good were the fruits of their joint efforts.

Although pleasant and soft spoken in person, both Bruce and I are bossy collaborators, capable of being very cutting in our e-mails. When he and I go after each other, it's like two old guys playing tennis and trying to kill the ball and blast it down the other guy's throat. Whack! Some of this abrasive energy shows up in the interactions between the pairs of characters in this story: Janna vs. Veruschka and Tug vs. Revel.

But the story is fun, and it rated a cover illustration when it appeared in *Asimov's*. The story also appears in Bruce's collection, Visionary in Residence (Thunder's Mouth Press, 2006); although note that while putting together Mad Professor, I slightly re-edited all my stories one more time.

THE USE OF THE ELLIPSE THE CATALOG THE METER & THE VIBRATING PLANE

"and who therefore ran through the icy streets obsessed with a sudden flash of the alchemy of the use of the ellipse the catalog the meter & the vibrating plane" —Allen Ginsberg, "Howl"

"*Damn* this is good crack. How come nobody ever writes about how good crack is?"

"You don't smoke crack, old fool. That's a gum-stimulator you're holding, not a crack pipe."

"I'm gonna tell you a crack story anyhow. Something that happened to me today, Sunday, January something, in the year Y-fuckin'-two-K-plus-two. I'm sitting on a doorstep next to a crackhead woman at the Powell and Market cable car stop. Me there in my Saks corduroys and my shiny leather jacket, waiting for the cable car. Gray-haired and wearing a beret. It's a cold day and this stone doorstep is the only spot with sun. I'm sitting there in the sun waiting for my wife to come out of Nordstrom's so we can ride back to North Beach. A festive lark. We're up in SF for the weekend."

"Who cares?"

"Let me tell my story. You'll care soon enough. There's this hobbling alky guy talking to the crackhead woman, a guy who moves like a broken toy, maybe he has an artificial leg. He's being real gentle with the woman. Commiserating with her. He's like, 'It's Sunday, sweetheart. I know that's hard to believe. I've lost a few days that way myself.' There's this admirable sense of warmth coming off him even though he's a guy I'd skirt around on the sidewalk. He's got this camaraderie going out to the woman. She's black, maybe thirty years old, sturdy-looking, maybe only a year or two into her addiction. I'm wishing she could detox and get in a program."

"Were you using your gum-stimulator?"

"Naw, man, I was high on life. Taking things in. Experiencing the now. And standing right in front of me were two homeboys with low pants—they're as low as I've ever seen. The waists are literally at their knees. They could shit or piss without taking those pants off. The pant legs are like eighteen inches long. It's as if they were midgets. But they're not midgets, they're big strong guys. I'd almost like to ask them how the pants stay up; they have long coats and I can't quite see if there's suspenders as well as belts. But I'm not gonna say anything. This spot I'm sitting on could be viewed as their turf, and they're being kind enough to ignore me. There's a looped line of tourists waiting for their turn to get on the Powell-Hyde cable car, and then there's the homies, and then there's the sunny stone stoop with me and the crackhead woman. I'm enjoying the sun. An old homeless woman is playing Christmas carols on a keyboard on her lap, even though there's no sound from the keyboard and Christmas is long gone. Maybe it's just a piece of cardboard to give her confidence. She's singing the songs real loud and getting some money from the tourists. It's peaceful there in the sun. I'm zoned out. My wife's still not coming for a while."

"You're high on life."

"It's the best, man. No rush to do anything. No need to score. A motion catches my eye and I see that one of the homeboys is manipulating a green nylon fanny pack that's on the sidewalk. He's moving it around with this short cane he's got. A cane like to match the length of his pants, maybe two feet long. I don't know how he got hold of the fanny pack. I assume it came off one of the tourists. The homies are like salmon fisherman standing by a salmon ladder, and this is a fish they've pulled out. The other fish aren't noticing though; they're calm as ever, inching forward in the line and getting on the streetcars. Evidently the green nylon fanny pack has already been filleted, because the homie with the cane passes it over to the crackhead woman. She's got nothing, so he's giving her something. That flash of camaraderie again. The woman fumbles around the fanny pack for a while, getting it open, feeling inside it with her wooden fingers. I don't watch her opening it very closely. It's just sad how wasted she is. For sure she's forgotten about it being Sunday already. She's losing days at a time, maybe even weeks."

"Is anything gonna happen in this story?"

"Exactly now is when it gets surreal. I'm looking across the street at Nordstrom's to see if my wife is coming, and then I hear this kind of xylophone chord next to me. And the crackhead woman is sitting up and she's pulling all this stuff out of the fanny pack. It's like four circus clowns coming out of a suitcase. Big cartoony shapes with little arms and legs. There's an ellipse, a catalog, a meter, and a vibrating plane. They're all doing stuff to the crackhead woman."

"How do you mean—an ellipse, a catalog, a meter, and a vibrating plane?"

"They're like Robert Williams cartoon characters; each of them with little black legs with puffy white shoes and black stick-arms with white gloves for hands, each of these guys about three feet tall. They're humanoid enough to be like a woman, a man, a man, and a woman. The ellipse herself is a thick black outline like the frame of an oval mirror, higher than she is wide. She has tiny little brown eyes up near the top, and a thin mouth near the bottom. Inside the ellipse is nothing—well, not exactly nothing, something like an energy field. Whenever the ellipse is at the correct angle so that I can look through her, I see that part of the world in black and white. Like a diagram in a physics book, with everything cleaned up and simplified. The ellipse is a window to reality's blueprint. Now, the ellipse does a detox on the crackhead woman right away. Yep, as soon as the ellipse comes out of the fanny pack, she jumps at the crackhead woman and pushes herself over the woman's head. The ellipse wriggles her way all down the woman, passing over the woman like a hoop of flame passing over a leaping tiger. That's the thing that gets the woman clean and sober right off the bat. It's like she's been unwrapped from inside of dirty translucent plastic. She's out from inside of her body bag. Her eyes are alive again, her face is awake."

"The mighty ellipse. What about the other three?"

"The catalog is a fat, old, cloth-bound book, like a Library of Congress catalog volume. His cover is brown and he has an eye and an arm on both the front cover and on the back cover. His shiny brown eyes notice me watching. But mainly he's focused on the woman he's helping. What he does, he holds the edges of his cover and spreads them open like a flasher, showing his store of information to the woman. She starts giggling as she looks at the flapping pages of the catalog. Not a rheumy giggle, but a light, clear giggle. Just about then I glance around to see if anyone else is seeing what I'm seeing. But, no, they aren't. In fact everyone around me has stopped moving. All the world is temporarily silent and frozen: the homies, the tourists, the streetcars, the cars on Market Street. Nothing is moving but me, the crackhead woman, the ellipse, the catalog, the meter, and the vibrating plane. I'm witnessing a secret miracle."

"You're living right, man. Tell me more about the catalog. What was the woman seeing inside?"

558

"Well, I scoot a little closer to her so I can see too. Each page of the catalog is a picture, a picture of the things she's thought and seen and done. I can see her younger self inside the pictures. She's eating barbeque, going to movies, laughing with her friends. It's like a catalog of her life. All the bad stuff is in there too, of course: the rip-offs, the beatings, the hospitals, and the jails. And when I look closer I can see that the pictures themselves are made up of smaller pictures. Like mosaics. And the little pictures are made of even smaller pictures etcetera. There's this branching fractal catalog thing happening. The pictures in the pictures show other people doing the same kinds of things as the woman. I'm in there too. Everyone's good things and bad things are inside of everyone else's catalog."

"Like we're all the same."

"You got it. Now, the meter is the next one out. The meter, he's like a big voltmeter. He's got a black dial face with a red needle swinging back and forth and two brown-and-white eyes set into the dial. He reaches his hands out and touches the sides of the woman's head, and his needle goes swaying back and forth with her feelings. The woman is staring at the needle and watching how her thoughts move her feelings up and down. At first the needle is just slamming back and forth, but in a minute it calms down to where it's mostly vibrating nice and even in the middle. She's still watching the catalog, you dig, and now and then she sees something that makes the needle jump. The woman likes it when the needle jumps, and she likes it when it calms down afterward. She's practicing with this for a long time, but there's no rush because the world's time has stopped for us. It's like the ellipse has detoxed her, the catalog has shown her about her past, and the meter is telling her about peace of mind."

"Did she notice you watching her?"

"Yeah, she glances over at me and smiles real calm and easy. She's like, 'Ain't this a trip?' And then the vibrating plane starts doing her thing. The vibrating plane is a vertical disk facing us. Her eyes and arms and legs are attached to her outer edge, and her actual vibrating plane part is her big round stomach. The plane is rushing forward and backward like the head of a bass drum, only with much bigger oscillations. The plane pushes right through the woman and me, and then it pulls back out in front of us, and then it does it again. Over and over. When the plane is behind me, I feel totally merged into the world, and when the plane is in front of me, I feel all separate and observational, the way I mostly do. The plane is vibrating at maybe three pulses per second, and I'm feeling it as this sequence of One / Many / One / Many / One."

"How do you mean, One and Many?"

"The vibrating plane is showing us the natural rhythm of perceiving things, you wave? You merge into the world and experience it, you separate yourself out and make distinctions; you flow back out into unity, you pull back and remember yourself; you sympathize with everyone around you, you focus on your own feelings—the eternal vibration between Us and Me, between One and Many. The teaching here is to understand the vibration as a natural and organic process of the mind. You can't stop the vibrating plane. You can't stay merged, and you can't stay cut off. You're flipping back and forth forever and ever, with a frequency of like I say maybe three cycles per second."

"And then what happened?"

"Well, the ellipse, the catalog, the meter, and the vibrating plane all hold hands with each other and start dancing ring-around-the-rosy in a circle around the woman and me. We smile at each other again, and she stands up, all healthy and ready to live. And then the sounds of the tourists and the homeless woman singing and the cars on Market Street start back up. I see my wife across the street coming out of Nordstrom's. I cross the street and I meet her."

"What about the crackhead woman?"

"When I look back she's gone. The vision was true."

Note on "The Use of the Ellipse the Catalog the Meter & the Vibrating Plane"

Written in January, 2002.
Horror Garage #5, 2002.

My cyberpunk pal John Shirley lives fairly near me in the San Francisco Bay Area. In 2002 he had this idea of helping someone put together a small press anthology whose earnings would be devoted to a fund for helping drug-addicted mothers and their children.

I don't normally undertake a story for so abstract a reason as altruism. I write a story for more personal reasons; typically there's some emotional state or tech problem or odd situation or real-world vignette that I'm obsessed with, and the story is an exploration I feel compelled to carry out. But John shamed me into promising a contribution.

And then I got into it—I realized that, given that this was to be a guaranteed publication, I could really do anything I wanted to, so why not have some fun and write something completely surrealistic. Of course then the fund-raising anthology project fell through, but five of the stories destined for the anthology ended up in a special issue of *Horror Garage*, an idiosyncratic magazine edited by Paula Guran.

The title and epigraph for my story comes from line seventy-three of Allen Ginsberg's epochal 1965 poem, "Howl."

I've always loved this long line: those four items makes such a surreal, Dadaist assemblage, and as a mathematician I'm happy to see an ellipse in *the* seminal Beat poem.

The images of the story came to me in a moment of inspiration as I sat on the sidewalk in the sun at Powell and Market Streets, near where the tourists line up for the trolley. Junkies and con men were going by, and I saw the four items of Ginsberg's line as characters, as if drawn by underground cartoonist Robert Williams—and thus emerged my story, a gift from the muse.

Although the line from "Howl" appears as I quote it in both Ginsberg's original *Howl and Other Poems* (City Lights, San Francisco, 1956) and in his *Collected Poems 1947–1980* (Harper & Row, New York, 1984), Allen introduces a 1986 variant to his line in *Howl: Original Draft Facsimile, Transcript & Variant Versions, Etc.* (edited by Barry Miles, HarperCollins, New York, 1995). Allen's "final" 1986 version of the line goes like this: "*and who therefore ran through the icy streets obsessed with a sudden flash of the alchemy of the use of the ellipsis catalog a variable measure and the vibrating plane.*"

Ugh!

In a footnote of the 1995 *Howl* volume, Allen says, "'Ellipse' is a solecism in the original mss. and printings; 'ellipsis' is correct." In the same footnote he relieves himself of a minilecture on his poetics as derived from Céline, Whitman, Pound, and the divine Kerouac. And

561

at the end of the footnote, he blandly drones, "phrasing in this verse has been clarified for present edition…to conform more precisely to above referents." (pp. 130–31).

I wish Allen were still around, so I could argue with him about this. I'd insist that his original muse-spurt was of course the correct take, and not some thirty-year-later version that the author has tailored to fit some theories that he's invented about what he did. I'd argue that he's mistakenly letting his lit prof side supplant his mad poet side.

I did once have the good fortune to meet Allen, while visiting the Naropa Institute in Boulder, Colorado, on the 1982 visit that inspired my piece "MS Found in a Minidrive." I told Allen about how much "Howl" had influenced me in high school, and then I said, "And what I want from you, Allen, after being hung-up on the beatniks all these years, what I want is your blessing." And real fast he whaps his hand down on my head like a skull-cap or electric-chair metal cap *zzt zzt* and "BLESS YOU" he yells. I wrote more about this encounter in my memoir *All the Visions* (Ocean View Books, 1991), which I typed on a ninety-foot scroll of paper, emulating Jack K.

JENNA AND ME (WITH RUDY RUCKER JR.)

George Bush doesn't sound as mean and stupid as I would have expected. Or maybe I'm just in a frame of mind to cut him slack. There are three armed Secret Service men here in my bedroom-slash-Dogyears-World-Headquarters.

They've been here for about half an hour. I'm mentally calling them the Boss, the Trainee, and the Muscle. The Boss and the Muscle are wearing Ray-Ban mirror shades—they're living the dream, true Men in Black. They have guns, and if they want to, they can kill me. I'm polite.

The Trainee's been doing the talking, he's a guy my age, a fellow U.C. Berkeley graduate, or so he says, not that I ever saw him at any of the places I used to hang, like the Engineering Library, Cloyne Co-op, or Gilman St. His name is Brad. All the SS guys have four-letter, mono-syllabic names. Dick, John, Mark, Jeff, like that. I'm Wag. My dog made up the name.

Brad starts out by asking me questions about my Web sites, and about the FoneFoon cell phone worm, being vaguely threatening but a little jocular at the same time, the way these field-ops always are. It's like they try and give off this vibe that they already know everything about you, so you might as well go ahead and roll over onto your back and piss on yourself like a frightened dog.

This isn't the first time the Secret Service has come to see me. The ultimate cause for their interest is that I run a small ISP company called Dogyears. "ISP" as in "Information Service Provider." If you don't want to deed your inalienable God-given share of cyberspace over to Pig Business, you can get your e-mail and web access through my excellent www.dogyears.net instead of through the spam-pimps at AOL. Dogyears offers very reasonable rates, so do check us out.

The hardware side of my Dogyears ISP is a phone-booth-sized wire cage of machines in a server hotel in South San Francisco. I pay a monthly fee, and the server hotel gives me my own special wire, the magic Net wire, the proverbial snake-charmer's rope leading up into the sky. You'd think it would be a big fat wire, like one of those garden-hose-sized electrical conduits you see at step-down voltage transformer stations in the cruddier, more industrial parts of town such as the Islais Creek neighborhood where I actually live, but, no, the Net wire is standard twenty-gauge copper.

Since I run my own ISP, my Internet access can't be terminated easily. I put any whacked-out thing I like on my ISP, and so do my clients. And this is why both the Secret Service and the FBI are darkening my door, the SS about my Prexy Twins site, and the FBI about the Fone-Foon worm that's recently dumped sixty terabytes of digital cell phone conversations onto one of my servers' hard drives.

The FoneFoon worm account is under the name of eatshit@kill-thepig.com, and I'm honestly unable to tell the FBI who that really is. They want my sixty Tb of phone conversations for their "ongoing investigation" and I've been stalling them, simply for the sake of the innocents whose cell phones were hacked. Also I've been cobbling together a browser so I can troll through the conversation records for laughs.

In any case, I'm quite sure it's The Prexy Twins, not FoneFoon, that brings the Secret Service here today. The Prexy Twins, www.prexy-twins.com, is my online zine about the Bush girls. I have photos from the *National Enquirer*, rewrites of gossip, links, polls, and fun little webbie gimmicks like a rollover to change Jenna's hair color. The site has a guest book where people write things in. "Fuck" becomes "kiss," "shit" becomes "poo," and the obscene "Republican or Democrat" becomes "elephant or donkey." Good clean fun. Now and then somebody posts a death threat against the Bushes, but I take those off manually when I notice them, and if I don't notice them, the SS phones me up to ask who posted them.

The SS guys came in person to my bedroom-slash-Dogyears-World-Headquarters two days after The Prexy Twins went up, just to find out where I'm at. But they could see that I have pure intentions and a clear conscience. I only do the site for—um, why *do* I run a Web site about the Bush girls anyway? Partly it's to game the media and to garner hits. It's a kind of art project too, despite the fact that even goobs like it.

I enjoy the feeling of having a smidgen of control over the news. I think it's nice that the twins drink, for instance, and that old people get so whipped up about it. And, yes, I get a kick out of Jenna. She looks so nasty that I'd like to scrub her with a wire brush. Not that I'm telling this to the SS. Or, for that matter, to my girlfriend Hella. The less I talk to her about Jenna in my special slobbering Jenna-fan voice, the better!

The June day that I'm telling you about starts foggy. My bedroom-slash-Dogyears-World-Headquarters is quite near the San Francisco Bay, in an industrial shipping district. I'm staring out of my window, watching the early morning habits of the local tweakers. A place called Universal Metals is across from my window. The tweakers bring scrap or scavenged metal there to trade for money to buy methedrine, which sends them scurrying out for more metal. Tweakers talk almost all the time, whether or not anyone's near them. Studying the antlike activity of the tweakers can keep me occupied for hours—you can almost see the pheromone trails and scent plumes they leave behind.

Today there's one who's scored a huge amount of copper wire, I know him a little bit, the other tweakers call him Rumbo. Rumbo is shirtless, warmed by his own chemical furnace, wearing a handmade copper mesh helmet on his head, sitting on the curb making more mesh helmets with a pair of rusty pliers. His hands dance in the rhythmic, repetitive motions of a large industrial machine. I'm so busy watching Rumbo that I fail to notice when the black SUV pulls up to the curb.

The doorbell rings, and then the three Men in Black are nosing around my partitioned-off box of warehouse space. My giant, over-friendly dog Larva is jumping up on them. Hella isn't here; she left early for her job teaching dance at an Oaktown high-school. I have a sweet, faint memory of her kissing me good-bye on her way out at dawn.

It's not immediately clear what the SS wants. There haven't been any threatening posts in the guest book of late. Maybe this is just practice for the Trainee, who's asking lamer and lamer questions, like whether I have to pay for the bandwidth my site uses, duh. I'm not about to tell him I pay a thousand dollars a month, it would make me sound like a stalker. He's not going to grasp that significant media art like The Prexy Twins doesn't come cheap. Before I have to fake some kind of answer, the Boss's cell phone rings.

"It's for you, Wag," says the Boss without even answering it, which is kind of odd. He hands me the ringing phone from the inside of his coat. For a second I can see his pistol in his shoulder holster. The phone is a heavy little jobbie with a scramble unit clamped onto its base, the kind of thing my hacker friend Ben Blank would love to take apart and analyze. Not that I'm thinking about Ben right now. I'm too busy wondering who the SS has for me on the phone.

"Hi-i-i, Wag, this here's President George Bush," goes the telephone voice. "How you today?"

I'm quite surprised. "I'm doing well."

"Let's get right to the point," says George. "I got an unusual type of, kind of problem situation on our hands. One of my advisers, Condoleezza, she estimates, opinionizes, that you can help us out. Did a search and you popped outta the spook databases or some such, we're graspin' at straws. My family and I'd be most appreciating that you would take on an advisorial role—fly down a day or two of your time at my ranch in Crawford, Texas."

"Will, um, Jenna be there?" I can't make much sense of what George is saying, and I'm jumping to the conclusion that he's calling because Jenna wants to meet me. She's got to be looking at my site, right, 27 percent of my hits are from Austin, and I've got a really bitchin' photo of myself posted if you mouse around for it, shows me bearded, blank-faced, and with a third eye Photoshopped into the middle of my forehead. How could any country cowgirl fail to be intrigued? Yes, Jenna's half in love with me and she's been begging Daddy to fly me down, like to help her with her University of Texas remedial math homework or to give a classroom talk about starting your own ISP. Jenna's redneck volleyball friends won't like me, goes without saying, but I'll win them over and what the fuck is wrong with me anyway, am I completely nuts? I don't even like Jenna Bush, honest.

"Yes and no," answers George, sounding sad. A pause and then he switches to the bullying presidential tone you hear on the news clips. I've never seen him on TV, actually, but I've downloaded plenty of video. When I look at a screen, it's got to be something I can hack.

"And that is exactly precisely the problem you gone haveta help us deal with," George declaims. "I'm not gonna describe it to you on the, not paint a picture on the telephone. The operatives are in place to bring you in."

Go to Texas? What a truly bizarre thought. Like going to Antarctica or to the inside of the Sun. Maybe this is all a put-on. The voice sounds a lot like George Bush, but on the other hand it's just possible that it's Ben Blank.

Ben and his friends in the Mummy Bum Cult posse are deep into voice filters and digital phone phreaking. They rent a basement under Market Street with, yes, an actual mummified bum in one of the far corners, a decades-old corpse that's air-cured down to leather 'n bone.

Ben likes talk about advanced AI tricks like evolving neural nets, but in fact he and the other Mummy Bums tend to slap together undocumented opcode hacks with never a thought to remembering what they've done. The main neural nets he's evolving are the ones in his skull. But the Mummy Bums get some surprising things to work, which is why I'm half-wondering if this Bush call might be one of their pranks.

I look across my room at the Men in Black. They have metal wrist-watches, shiny shoes, and gel in their hair. Man, these are definitely government agents. The Boss SS man makes an impatient gesture, wanting me to hurry up and answer George fucking Bush.

"I normally charge a consultant's fee," I say. Like this kind of request comes up all the time. "And travel."

"Don't never mind about paperwork," says George. "My boys will reimburse anything reasonable. Keep it under your, keep your lip shut off the record. I'll see you tonight. We'll have barbeque. Lemmie have a last word with my agent."

So I hand the phone to the Boss, he does a few yessirs, hangs up, and then says something to his men—not a real word, just a number. Something like, "Let's four-six-six the site."

The action code sets the Muscle and Brad the Trainee to clearing away my piles of dirty clothes so they can get at my computer. They're gonna take my machines, which happens to be just what the FBI has been itching to do on account of the FoneFoon worm, but I've been making them wait for their court order to come through, and even then I'm only going to copy stuff onto DVDs for them, not hand over my sacred machine! I try and explain this to the Boss, but he waves me off. The SS doesn't worry about legal shit. And if I try and stop them, they might kill me.

I do some yoga breaths and force a grin as the Muscle yanks loose my sacred beige box, snapping its cables like the nerves and blood vessels of a crudely extracted tooth. Ow. And then my other machine as well. Yoga breath.

Well, whatever happens, my info's secure; I can pretty easily recover it. First of all, it's stored on the Dogyears servers. And if, Dog forbid, something were to happen to those, I've been using a very gnarly Mummy Bum hack for saving my data in watermark form.

Something like a big image or a sound file, you can flip some tiny percentage of the bits, and it'll look or sound about the same. And you can use these flipped bits to save data you care about. It's called a digital watermark. The word "watermark" is from the way you can hold a dollar bill or a quality sheet of paper up to the light and see a pattern of light and dark, which is the old kind of watermark. The Mummy Bums have a killer little applet that'll break into a target server and munge your whole hard disk contents into watermarks in the sounds and pictures on the server. Me, I've got Dogyears backed up onto an Amsterdam music site. When you listen to the Lincoln Logs play "Stink Bowl," you're reading my e-mail, dude.

"Can I keep this?" I say, holding up my laptop. "There's no particular data on it, I just need it to—to think and live and breathe." The Boss nods.

I pack the laptop and some relatively clean backup clothes in a little canvas bag, and then I pause to handwrite a note to Hella. "Gone to Texas with the Men in Black! Don't worry. Consulting gig. Back soon, I'll call tonight. XXX Love, Wag." Writing the note I'm thinking about Hella's high forehead and her wide smile. Her low, intimate voice. She's a beauty. I don't mention Jenna or George Bush on the note.

My housemate Charles is in the shower, talking to himself in a variety of British-sounding voices like he always does. Like, "Hello, Professor Elbow! After you, sir Smelly Ankle. Cor, I never seen the like o' this rain!" Charles is surprised when he steps out wrapped in a towel and sees me with the Men in Black. He kindly agrees to keep an eye on Larva while I'm gone.

And then we're outside. The black SUV's stubby antennas have attracted the attention of Rumbo the copper-helmeted tweaker. In the minute and a half it takes The Muscle to stash my computers in the back, Rumbo has ranted three-point-seven hours' worth of convolutional thought patterns.

"Yep, a whole gollywog pile of copper down by the Bay," squeaks the tweak. "Piles of microwaves storm through our heads. Don't forget to recycle the wire in Wag's computers. Train tracks got copper under 'em: I've seen it. I'll strip it all out for you and give you half the profit; you ride shotgun and haul the load. Any monocrystalline copper, I keep for my helmet, you understand. There's enough copper in my hat to string it around the entire Bay. Copper helmets protect the Head from the Microwaves. See that little box with the antenna on the lamppost? They're on every block. 5.4 gigahertz. Repeaters peaters peaters peaters peaters…. This city is gonna be full of slave servo brain matter, I tell you."

"You know this individual?" asks the Boss. "He's among your circle of friends?"

"I know him just a bit." A few months back, I let Rumbo show me what he said was the secret labyrinth path into a really choice abandoned warehouse I'm curious about. This was before Rumbo got into his copper coat-of-mail helmet-against-microwaves thing. Back then he was more into a *Lord of the Rings* bag. We walked around through empty sewers for a couple of hours with flashlights, Rumbo leading me, my sister, and Charles. Charles says he took acid 300 times and the last 250 times were horrible bummers; he says he's a slow learner. But Charles was the one who finally realized it was nuts to be walking around inside a sewer with a tweaker leading the way. The fact that Charles figured this out before me makes me wonder about myself. I think I'm spending too much time on my computer.

The Boss Man in Black is staring at me. For a second I have a bad feeling I've just said all these thoughts out loud. But, no, he's just doing the intimidation-via-eye-contact thing. I for sure don't want to engage in any conversation about the lamppost cell antennas at this time. The FoneFoon caper clued me to the potency of those little boxes. "Rumbo's harmless," is all I say. For his part, Rumbo's had enough of the federal stink-eye, he's back on the curb across the street, his twitching hands busy with the pliers and the wire.

But the Boss is still watching Rumbo. "Deploy the seven-seventy-six," he tells the Muscle. "Might as well take care of that mission too. I'd say this looks like the ideal neighborhood." The big guy goes around to the back of the SUV and opens it up again. He's going to leave my computers after all? But, no, he's digging down into the spare tire compartment, pulling out a dusty white brick tightly wrapped in transparent plastic. The way he's glancing around makes it clear he's doing something shady. And now he pitches the brick across the street; it slides to a stop right near Rumbo. It's a fucking key of meth!

"Look what fell off Santa's sleigh!" whoops Rumbo.

As we drive off, a horde of tweakers converges on the brick.

We head south toward San Francisco Airport, which seems fine to me. But then, shit, it turns out the Men in Black want to make a side trip to the server hotel to bag the rest of my Dogyears hardware. They're fully out to ruin my business. All these insidious connections between AOL and the Elephant Party are filling my head as we ride the elevator to the server hotel's third floor.

The building has major security; it's full of cameras and hand-scanning equipment. I have a white card with a hologram of the ProxPass logo. ProxPass has a monopoly on all the hand scanners in the USA. Every now and then, another business or ISP will get hacked and they'll hire me to harden their servers. They tell me a building and locker number, call up ProxPass headquarters, and voila: my ProxPass card and palm grant me access to another server room. The ProxPass logo has a nonsensical graphic of some computer circuit. Normally, I open doors by pressing my pass to a black square on the wall, stick my hand in a gray box, wait three seconds for the click of the door lock, and then pull the door open. The delay is due to all the gray boxes talking to a central ProxPass server somewhere in Texas. Before George came into office, there wasn't a delay. ProxPass's fast peer-to-peer authentication was replaced with a countrywide big-brothering system. I'm pretty sure it has something to do with the Elephants getting paid off by AOL.

The Boss walks up to the scanner on the third floor, and pulls out an ultra blue card with a little hologram of—is that Jenna? I can't believe my eyes! The door clicks open when the Boss's card is still a foot away from the reader. No hand scan or network check needed with an SS Jenna Card!

The server room is noisy and cold. On those rare hot days in San Francisco, I walk my dog down to the server hotel, and check my e-mail in the cool confines of the Internet backbone. After spending an hour in the server room, I start to have auditory hallucinations. My mind always tries to pull sense out of chaotic patterns.

No one else ever hangs out in the server room except Ben Blank. In fact, he rents a whole three-foot-by-five-foot cage and has a little office desk and a mini keyboard called the Happy Hacker. Most people do a minimal configuration on their servers and then return to cubicle land. Not Ben, he likes the idea of being directly connected to his hardware. He says the only safe network is a network of two computers.

Ben's computers are a mess of old hardware cobbled together. His view screen, for instance, is six text lines high; he scavenged it off a Mattel Speak and Spell toy. I've been known to tease Ben by comparing his using retrofitted electronics to the tweakers making stuff out of like shopping carts. Ben insists that, even so, his stuff is better than mine. He's quite oblivious to the stellar quality of the superfine multiprocessor machines Dogyears assembles for their clients. My lovely white server towers are boxes the size of suitcases, with fans like kitchen ventilators.

On a normal day, I talk face to face with Ben when I come in. Ben always talks real fast about parallel computing and hyperspace and genetic algorithms, and I always tell him sure, sure. Usually after we do the voice greeting, I log into a chat window and talk some more to Ben across the room through the copper wires running through the building. Ben prefers old school chat over face to face. He'll be chatting to his mother, the Mummy Bum Cult group, Rotten.com employees, his girlfriend Hexy on the Peninsula, and me—all at the same time. On chat, he logs all the conversations and refers back to old chat sessions endlessly. He wants to devolve his neural net's need for in-skull short- or long-term memory.

Not that he's fully an out-of-it zombie. Today he instantly understands what kind of deal is going down, and he gives me a heartfelt look of sympathy.

The Feds yank out power and Ethernet cables from the Dogyears servers, hideously bringing down my ISP. My poor, orphaned customers!

Ben yelps in pain and anger. Hearing the intensity in Ben's voice, The Boss senses the possibility of him turning berserker. He wheels around, his gun magically moved to his hand from his holster. It's up to him to show Brad how it's done. Ben returns to his hacking.

As my plugs are being pulled on my top two machines, I notice the power LEDs on the bottom three machines in my stack of five are cycling up and down. It reminds me of the Knight Rider car from that old TV show. That's my emergency Mummy Bum Cult backup system, watermarking my more recent files into the workers' porno library on an oil rig in the middle of the North Sea. My list of customers is, like, being tattooed on some Scandinavian Bibi's boob. Glancing over at Ben again I can see an eye slyly rolled my way behind his honkin' big glasses. He's noticing my ongoing backup too. The Pig can try and stop us, but they'll never ever win.

The Muscle has the Prexy Twins server under one arm, and the FoneFoon hard-drive jukebox server under the other. At first I think they're going to spare my other servers; I have eight of them to host the Dogyears accounts and some bottom-feeder dotcom outfits who co-locate with me. But now the Boss takes out a conical device with copper windings around it and taps it on the six remaining servers, one by one. A directional magneto cone. Their RAM, ROM, and hard drives are wiped. My flashing LEDs are blank and dead.

As of right now, my customers have no service. They'll be leaving me for Time-Warner-AOL if this goes on for long. Elephant poo.

Brad accompanies me to Texas on Southwest Air; the others stay in San Francisco. He and I sit in the front row of the first-class section. I've never flown first class before. Free drinks and shrimp cocktail. Under us the desert terrain of Nevada rolls by. I have the window seat, and wouldn't you know it, when we're passing Area 51, I look up and see a UFO high in the sky.

At first I want to think it's another plane, but it's not acting like a plane. It's a few thousand feet above us, matching our route and speed so accurately that I wonder if it might be some kind of reflection in the window glass. But no matter which way I angle my head, it's still there, a polyhedral shape, not an airplane shape, a tumbling polyhedron like a pyramid or a cube but with many more sides, rolling over and over and over like a wheel matching our pace.

"What are you looking at, Wag?" asks Brad.

"It's a UFO," I say leaning back to he can push his head close to the window.

"I'd rather trade seats than lean across you," says Brad. "You're in custody." He doesn't want to expose his neck to a felonious karate chop.

So we swap, and Brad peers out and he sees the UFO too. He gets excited and calls the stewardess back to ask her a question or two, and the stewardess goes up to talk to the pilot. Right away the pilot's voice comes on the speakers, talking that relaxed low-blood-pressure Middle-American drawl. "If you look out to our right, one o'clock high, you'll see a Nevada weather balloon."

"Some balloon," mutters Brad, but he doesn't want to talk about it any more than that. Instead he jumps to a fresh topic. "You ever had oxblood burger?" he asks. "No? That's what the president likes to make. Juicy, mmm good."

In Austin there's a couple more Men in Black to meet us. A burr-haired one is in charge, and the other one has a neck as wide as his head. To keep it simple for me, I garbage-collect their names and label them with the Boss_tx and Muscle_tx handles. That saves me a couple-three memory clusters in my skull-based neural nets.

The surprise in Austin is that they've shipped my Dogyears server with the jukebox-hard drive with us, wrapped up in a government courier bags. It's the first thing out on the baggage belt. Why exactly will I be needing the sixty terabytes of FoneFoon data for this gig?

The Muscle_tx bundles the massive box under his arms like a notebook. And then we're out in the hot odorless air, boarding their SUV for the drive to Crawford, Texas.

It's early evening when we arrive. Pink light filters through thick barbeque smoke in the backyard of the presidential ranch. George is grilling with a NA Beer in one hand and a 3-foot Texas-size spatula in the other. There's a satellite dish on the ground next to his house, just like any other house in Texas. At first it looks like it's just George, some SS agents, and a middle-aged guy with flesh-colored frames on his glasses.

"Welcome to my spread, Wag," says George. He jerks his thumb at the middle-aged guy. "This here's Doc Renshaw. He's a neurologian, a brain doctor, an asshole, and a jerk." He doesn't sound like he's kidding. He really doesn't like this guy. "Renshaw, this is Wag, the fella we been talkin' about."

Breathing hard, the president hands the spatula off to Brad and pushes aside the hanging branches of a weeping willow tree beside the grill. Under the willow is a picnic table.

Jenna's sitting there, blank and drooling. It's almost like someone's held a directional magneto cone up to her head. Jenna's been erased! George and I sit down across from her, the SS guys hanging back a bit, Renshaw peeking in.

"She's gone to the circus, and she's not comin' back," George says mournfully. "Go ahead and talk to her. She knows when somebody talks to her."

"Uh, hi Jenna," I say lamely. Here I finally am with Jenna, and that's the best I can do? She looks kind of hot with that thin stand of drool dripping onto her pale blue spaghetti-strap sundress. Immediately I have two thoughts: I can't think that way it's sick, and I hope I get her alone.

Gathering composure from the thought of getting Jenna alone and really giving her a good scrub with a wire brush, I turn on my charm for the president of the United States of America. I figure it's better to start with flattering him a little before trying to figure out what to say about blank Jenna. "That barbeque meat smells good," I say. "Like oxblood."

"Yep, we've got the oxblood burgers," says George with no smirk, no cocky tilt of the head. He's just staring at Jenna, looking worried. This isn't the animatronic George of the news clips. "Let me cut to the point, Wag. Jenna has a problem, hell, you can see that yourself. Amsneezia, asphrasia—those twenty-dollar doctor words. She can't remember shit, what it is. This scumbag Renshaw says we're lucky she can still breathe and do her body functions."

It's hard to believe I'm right here looking at Jenna Bush. But she's not looking at me. There's nobody home. George hops to his feet and returns with two towering burgers.

"Burger, Jenna?" he says softly.

Jenna's lips move, and she says, "OK."

George sets the plates in front of Jenna and me; we begin eating.

"All Jenna does is say OK anymore," says George. "It happened last month. Jenna and Noelle were supposed to attend some big-ass dress show over in, over there."

Facts are jumping around in my head. I like collecting info and looking for patterns. Noelle was busted for a fake drug scrip the week after the Versace show in London. The scrip was for Xanax, and why would anyone bother getting arrested for a mild antidepressant? Well, Xanax's street use is as a comedown drug from ecstasy—or crack. The media didn't report that Noelle and Jenna were in England at that fashion show. In fact, it was the previous first daughter, Chelsea Clinton, who was hanging out with Madonna and Gwyneth Paltrow in front of the Versace runway.

"Versace?" I say, just to be sure.

George nods at me, then glares over his shoulder at Renshaw, who's craning in under the willow tree as well. "See how Wag's little noggin's straining to piece together the puzzle?" he says. "Too bad I didn't have him here to second-guess you turds before you did your thing." And then he fixes his eyes back on mine, "OK, Wag. Of course all this is hush hush, this is Homeland Security Code Orange, but here's how the story began. Supposedly Noelle had some kind of goddamn pill she wanted to slip Chelsea Clinton, some kind of Mickey Finn. This was Jeb's idea, he got the drug from the Clik. Clik? It's the conspiracy elite, the secret government that never goes away. The ordnance labs, the spooks, the Cuban freedom fighters, the Fair Play for House of Saud committee—it's all Clik. The same crowd that took down JFK, same ones who threw the election my way, same ones who got in so goddamn tight with Osama. We Elephants never shoulda gotten in this deep with the Clik, but it's too late to back out now. I don't condone any of this, you understand, Wag. I'm not really that powerful of a man, I'd just as soon be back running the Rangers, watchin' the games with my two girls." He pats Jenna's hand, then wipes the drool off her chin. Her eyes are watching us as we talk, glittering with primitive, reptilian intelligence.

"Anyway, the Clik sold Jeb and me this crock of shit that they wanted to use Jenna as a delivery system," continues George. "Laura and I had just planned the trip as a spring fling. But Jeb's Clik handlers, they said Jenna, she's fun, more attractive, more likely to get close to Chelsea and hand off that goddamn pill. Chelsea's not likely to talk to Noelle. Jenna's supposed to tell Chelsea it's some kind of goddamn party drug, not that I'd call that a party, making yourself sick with a pill. Some new crap the Clik came up with, they call it Justfolx. Supposedly the pill is gonna, the pill somehow makes Chelsea into a real American, so she'll fight with Hilary, which is good for the Elephant Party, and what's good for the Elephants is good for the Clik, it's a win-win. But during the flight Jenna has a few drinks, she's like I used to be, just high spirits, she gets in a spat with Noelle. Noelle's always been one to needle her cousins, and Jenna's easy enough to fly off the handle when she—what was it Jenna said, Mike? Tell Wag the course of events. You were there, not exactly doing your job a hundred percent, I'd say. To frank the truth I wonder why I can't get them to fire you."

The Boss_tx and Doctor Renshaw have both sidled under the willow tree with us. "I told you I'm sorry, Mr. President," says the Man in Black. "I'm sure the Clik, I mean the Fair Play for House of Saud committee, they'll dock my pay, if it's called for, not that I feel they should. I was guarding the young women in close proximity, across the plane aisle. A fast-breaking chaotic situation developed. An argument. It seemed the young women were planning to split up when we disembarked. Fine, but then Noelle took out her Justfolx medication delivery system—the capsule. The plan was, as the president told you, Wag, for Noelle to hand the pill off to Jenna to give to Chelsea. And since the young women were seemingly going to split up, it seemed reasonable to me for Noelle to make the transfer at this time. Holding up the translucent red, football-shaped Justfolx capsule, Noelle stated, 'Can you remember to give Chelsea this, you drunk redneck?' To which Jenna replied, 'You dumb-ass pill-popping cracker, I'll show you how to party,' and thereupon swallowed the Justfolx pill. I executed a poison-control maneuver, induced vomiting. But the pill had dissolved. Jenna showed an extreme reaction. The plane landed in London, but we didn't get off the plane, much less did we alert the press. We cleaned the plane up, refueled, and flew back to Texas."

"The Justfolx pill is supposed to make you an Elephant?" I ask.

"Well it's not like a pill knows math, is it?" says George. "I understand the treatment was to reduce the...take away the know-it-all Rhodes scholar and so on, the high-horse attitude you'd see with a Hilary or a Chelsea Clinton."

In sounded like the dosage was designed to make Chelsea stupid enough to be an Elephant. And if you gave it to someone low down enough on the scale to already *be* an Elephant, well, it would make them into—a vegetable. So Jenna got erased.

Jenna makes a little noise then, kind of like a newborn kitten. "*Mew?*" Awww.

"What can I do to help?" I ask patriotically. I'm getting used to Jenna's drool. She still has those nice round cheeks and clear eyes. I want to get her alone and test her body functions.

"That's the spirit," says George. "Working together. Tell him, Renshaw. You're the head Clik sleazeball here."

"We've conferenced with the FBI concerning your terabytes of cell phone calls from the FoneFoon worm," says Doctor Renshaw. "Now, as it happens, we know there was a copy of the worm on Jenna's phone. We estimate that you're in possession of some six full hours of Jenna's cell phone conversations. That's quite a lot, enough perhaps for her to have said nearly everything that she might be expected to believe. The first thing we want you to do, Wag, is to mine those conversations from the FoneFoon data set. Locate them and decrypt them."

"You mean I could have been listening to Jenna all along?" I burst out, and George gives me a sharp look. "Not that I would if you hadn't asked me to," I add.

Though I haven't actually gotten around to cracking the FoneFoon data yet, I know I can do it. Mining large data sets is a big-brother-type job I did for MegaMedia back at the peak of the dotcom era. They had an automated upgrade feature whose function was to e-mail them a transcript of the user's command actions for every session in which one of their products was used. With that hack under my belt, I feel sure I can locate every byte of Jenna in the FoneFoon hoard.

"I can find the Jenna conversations for you," I say. "But why do you want them?"

"We want to use them to reprogram Jenna," said Renshaw simply. "But you should edit them first. Clear out certain self-defeating aspects of Jenna's personality. The alcohol problems and so on. It's our feeling that some fairly simple edits might do it. Remove any obscenity or strong language. Any references to sex, alcohol, or drugs. Just make it a sunny G rating. I'm sure you understand."

Dubya lets out an impatient snort. "Jenna was fine the way she was," he insists.

I decide to avoid the dull-ass issue of censorship entirely and cut to the good stuff. "How would I program Jenna at all?" I ask.

"That's the key, Wag," says Renshaw, his glasses glinting in the setting sun. "We feel you have the skills to be of help in converting these digital records into what you might call contagious data. Contagious in that if we beam the tweaked call data into Jenna's Justfolx-treated brain, we might expect the data to take hold and multiply, to effectively recolonize her brain with its former flora and fauna of thought forms. In the Clik weapons labs—we got a little ahead of ourselves with Justfolx. The discovery of the compound was kind of an accident. An anonymous posting on the Clik-front Science Clearing House. Formula, production process, clinical actions, side effects, the works. We could see the potential right away. It seemed bold to start right at the top. What we didn't tell the president when we suggested the mission was that, given Jenna's personality profile, we were quite sure she'd take the pill and eat it."

"Bastards," snapped Dubya. "Pricks." Now I get why he has it in for Renshaw.

"Pause," is the only thing I can think of saying. I look toward the last bit of light on the horizon. My blood pulses, I see ragged checkerboards in my eyes, patterns driven by the rays of the fading Texas sun. "Ready," I add after a bit. "Tell me more about beaming in the data."

"The Justfolx medication has the side effect of putting the subject's cortex into a state of electromagnetic sensitivity," says Renshaw. "That's the key clinical action. The aphasia is merely a side effect. The pro forma plan was that we planned to beam Rush Limbaugh shows into Chelsea Clinton after giving her the drug. But the true plan is much richer. Your mission. Find Jenna's conversations, clean them up, make them contagious, and then we'll use a 5.4 gigahertz transmitter to beam the info into Jenna's brain. She'll be good as new. Better."

"Bullshit," mutters the president. He's deeply pissed at having his daughter be the Clik's guinea pig.

Renshaw smiles ingratiatingly at George. "Really she'll be fine, Mr. President. And with the personality cleanup, we can put an end to the kinds of stories Wag posts on his Web site. We can bring to a close this regrettable stage of Jenna's development."

Me, I've got goose bumps from the mention of 5.4 gigahertz. That's the frequency that the FCC allows anyone to transmit wireless Internet on. That's also the frequency used in the lamppost repeater boxes that the peer-to-peer cell phone company Ricochet put up before they went down the tubes. Most people think the repeaters are turned off now, but they're not. The tweakers know.

The potentialities of the hack expand in my mind like a supernova. The Justfolx drug can be dosed into people's drinking water, they'll all turn Elephant or vegetable, but that's not the real point. The point is that once everyone's sensitized, AOL and the Clik and the Elephants and the Men in Black can start transmitting spam and telemarketing and political advertising right into our brains.

I turn the idea the other way around. A grave danger, but a wonderful opportunity. What if we broke free of the client/server model and went fully peer-to-peer? Let people send thoughts right at each other, with nothing in between. With Ben's help, maybe I could fix it so people could have direct electronic brain-to-brain contact. Peace, love, and radiotelepathy.

I take a deep yoga breath, broaden my shoulders, and relax. One Nation under a Groove. This is truly a project worthy of my time.

They give me a room at the ranch, me and the Dogyears machine and my laptop and, since I ask for it, a thermos jug of coffee—though it tastes like it's from a Texas McDonald's. There's a big couch upholstered in calfskin with the hair still on it. Black-and-white spots like a Dell computer shipping carton. I'm supposed to get right to work, but for a few minutes I'm just trying to get down enough of their watery, scalding hot coffee to bring my cycles up. Standing at the window looking out at the strange Texas sky.

I'm still mind-boggled that the FoneFoon worm has zipped six hours of Jenna's phone conversations into my server, and that I could have been listening to her all along.

I start thinking about reprogramming Jenna's mind, about downloading her edited personality back onto her, having used her cell phone conversations as the source code. It's like I'm supposed to make the talk tape for a Mattel Barbie doll, with all the curse words snipped out.

The Clik—you had to hand it to them. Jenna had scarfed Noelle's Justfolx pill like Ms. Pac-Man gobbling a power pellet. Give Jenna a few drinks, show her a pill, *uncha-yuncha-unch*! I start goofing on that, imagining that when Jenna ate the Justfolx pill, she heard the Ms. Pac-Man power-up sound, that happy *doodley-doodley-doo* music. And then she turned into an 5.4-gigahertz-receptive Elephant vegetable.

There's still some pieces I don't understand. If the Clik knew all along they were going to reprogram Jenna, then they would have had to be sure that her cell phone conversations were being saved. The FoneFoon worm played perfectly into their plans. The Clik got Jenna's talk without actually tapping her. The thing is, I've thought all along that Ben Blank wrote the FoneFoon worm—not that I've asked him, which would be bad form. Could Ben be working for the Clik? And what about the UFO I saw from the plane? And what's the deal with the brick of meth the SS threw down for the tweakers? How does that fit in? Have I mentioned that I drink way too much coffee?

I go back to wondering about Jenna. Where in this rambling ranch house might she be stored? *Mew?* I go so far as to peek out of my room's door. The Muscle_tx is right there, not looking any too friendly. And when I lean out of my room's window, I see Brad in a lawn chair. He points at me, like, "Gotcha covered."

So finally I get to work. I connect my laptop to the Dogyears server box they brought along. Mining the conversations out of the data doesn't take all that long. I have a clip or two of Jenna's voice on the Prexy Twins site, and I'm able to write a Perl script to grep my terabytes of FoneFoon for her phoneme patterns. Right as I'm playing some of the files, kind of laughing at the things she says, my own cell phone rings. It's Hella.

"Wag, you're in Texas?"

"I'm at the president's ranch." I've got Jenna's voice playing in the background. She's ordering a pizza, hanging up, calling a friend about a picnic, talking to a boy, on and on.

"No way. Who's that talking, Wag? I hear a girl."

"It's Jenna. I—"

My phone goes dead. The Men in Black have cut me off. Great. Now Hella's heard just enough to think the worst. I open the door and ask the Muscle_tx for (a) a chance to call Hella back and (b) more coffee. He passes the requests along. All I get is the coffee.

My next task turns out to be harder, not technically so much as conceptually. Renshaw asked me to take the cursing, sex, alcohol, and drugs out of the conversations, so that the reprogrammed Jenna won't be a hell raiser. But exactly why would I actually do things the Clik's way?

They're too stupid and/or lazy to watch what I'm doing in here, so I'll do what I please. It's amazing, when you get right up face-to-face with them, how incredibly lame our lords and masters are. They're actually relying on my supposed patriotic rah-rah team spirit. It's like the Clik can't begin to imagine how much we despise them.

I toy with the idea of editing the conversations in exactly the opposite way they asked me to, leaving nothing but the juicy stuff. But there isn't really all that much juice, I realize, listening to the tapes. Jenna's pretty much a regular girl, doing normal things with her friends. I play the conversations speeded up so I can get a fast overview of them. Jenna's chirping at me like a bird. I start to feel a little sleazy to be listening to her, a little scuzzy for being the guy who runs the Prexy Twins Web site to help people gossip about her. I'm a filthy dog who rolls in garbage and licks his balls.

In the end I decide not to edit the conversations at all. I'll just try and help Jenna get back to square one.

I get more coffee and start on step three: making the data files contagiously reactive. I use some artificial life hacks, fold it in with some self-modifying code, assemble it onto one of the universal replicator structures that Ben uses to make his viruses, and by the time the night ends, I've got some Jenna-based artificial life cooking away in the bowels of my Dogyears server box. Little knots of language and logic, evolving to become more and more contagious. I think of them as Jennions.

The sun is creeping up on the horizon. The massive caffeine intake and the lack of carbohydrates has made me a bit shaky. I lie down on the Texas-sized calf-skin couch.

The next thing I know Brad is poking me awake from a puddle of drool. The sun's coming in at my eyes at a low angle. I've only slept about twenty minutes. My head is pounding and I feel ready to choke someone.

"Is it ready?" asks Brad. "You were asleep."

I look at my laptop screen. It's using a graphic display to represent the state of the Jennions. The images right now look kind of like live paisley with ants crawling around in it. Good. When I went to sleep the images just looked like dots and circles.

"It's ready," I tell Brad. I punch a few keys to copy the Jennions out of the big server box and into my laptop's hard drive. And then Brad takes me out to the picnic table in the backyard. Jenna's sitting there again, still drooling, wearing a pink T-shirt and jeans today.

The Muscle_tx follows me and Brad, as if there were any place I could run to here in the middle of Texas. Renshaw and the Boss_tx are drinking coffee and eating doughnuts while Jenna watches the food-to-mouth movements of the men. I miss my mutt, Larva.

"You've extracted the language elements?" asks Renshaw. He sips his coffee and nibbles his doughnut. There aren't any circular carbohydrates on the table for me. Shit.

"Yep, all ready to beam her down," I say.

Renshaw chuckles and makes the Star Trek hand sign at me, with his fingers spread to make a V. It occurs to me that, being a Clik scientist, this guy probably doesn't know squat about computer hacking. I hate him. I hate everyone.

The Boss_tx has finished his coffee and his doughnut. He motions to a sandpit next to the Willow tree and says, "Let's get this rolling and maybe Jenna will want try out the new volleyball court with you, Wag. That'll be a treat , huh? We know how fascinated with her you are."

"I hate volleyball. Give me some fucking coffee. And if you think that—" I stop the beginning of a rant and assess the situation: I'm losing it. I've slept twenty minutes, Hella thinks I'm boning Jenna, Larva has probably shat all over my room, I have no idea if Jenna can be fixed, and Dogyears is down the tubes. "Coffee," I repeat.

The Boss_tx catches my gaze and says, "Relax, Wag."

"Relaxing makes me tense!" I scream. This is a running joke I have with my sister. The SS totally don't realize I'm being funny.

On some sort of silent cue from the Boss_tx, the Muscle_tx grabs my thumbs, pulls them behind my back, and mutters, "Welcome to Texas," in my ear.

At this moment, George Dubya walks out of the ranch house in a jogging suit, carrying a tray with more breakfast supplies. I feel a wave of affection for the man.

"Pleased to see y'all up and at 'em," says George. "We gonna fix my girl?" His we're-all-working-together attitude calms the tense situation I've created. The Muscle_tx lets up

And now finally I get my breakfast. "I've got the agents organized and ready to go," I say, mouth full. "Right here in my laptop. The Jennions."

Renshaw lifts a box up from under the table. It's one of those Ricochet cell phone repeater antennas like you see on lampposts all over San Francisco! "This is the kind transmitter we're particularly interested in learning to use," he says. It's like this whole thing's been set up as a science experiment for the Clik. Poor Jenna.

Now Brad weighs in . "I saw some druggie San Francisco–type colored patterns on Wag's laptop in the house. I'm not sure he's really made the program sufficiently Elephant-oriented." What an ass kisser.

"There's nothing in there but Jenna," I say. "And, if you want to know, I didn't edit her words at all. If it works right, she'll be the same as she used to be. Take it or leave it."

George's face gets that inspirational, leader-of-the-nation glow. "That's the way it should be. She's fine the way she was." He pats Jenna's shoulder. "Would you like a doughnut, dear?"

"OK." She gobbles it in two bites.

Meanwhile Renshaw jacks a special wireless card into my laptop and turns a switch on the repeater box. On my laptop screen, I drag the Jennion icon to the fresh icon for the wireless card, and now the repeater is beaming out Jennion code at 5.4 gigahertz. The microwaves go right through George, Renshaw, the SS guys, and me, but it's digging into Jenna's Justfolx-sensitized brain.

Jenna freezes real still for about twenty seconds. Like a startled deer. And suddenly her face lights up, chubby and friendly, she's like a regular person, yes, I'm meeting Jenna Bush at last.

But then, crap, she opens her mouth and starts making a noise like fax machine or a 560 modem. She jumps up and runs over to the TV satellite dish on the lawn, spewing out that noise all the while. She stops by the antenna and rocks back and forth until her mouth is in the direct focus of the parabolic dish.

"Is this part of the process?" asks Brad. Good show of out-of-the-box thinking, Brad!

"She's transmitting, dude." I say. Jenna's sending some kind of signal into the antenna and up into the satellites in the sky. The SS operatives look at me like they're ready for the Vulcan nerve-pinch session again. "But, hey, don't blame me!"

Jenna finishes doing her thing, shuts her mouth, and walks back to the table.

"Thanks, Wag," she says . "You fixed me good."

"Jenna dear, is that you?" asks the president.

"Yeah, Dad. I'm back. But now there's a whole 'nother consciousness in me as well. Call her NuJenna. She's from the stars."

Jenna's expression changes. She's looking at us with incredible wisdom in her eyes. Like the picture of Mahatma Gandhi I saw on an Apple billboard near my server hotel. "You and the Clik have done well, Renshaw," she says in a high-pitched, mellow tone. "It was we who posted the Justfolx recipe."

George's cell phone rings and he picks it up for a brief conversation. His end goes like this.

"They did?"

"I see."

"We can fix that."

"We can't fix that?"

"I see."

"They will?"

"We can't fix that?"

"I see."

He hangs up and runs his hands across his face.

"Back to baseball for me," he says with a crooked smile.

"The Clik needs a period of chaos, Daddy," says Jenna's sweet voice. For the moment she's the chubby college kid again. "Until the new order settles in. So NuJenna and I told everyone the truth about your administration, about the rigged election, about Cheney's crimes, about Osama and the Fair Play for House of Saud committee. I like being so smart with NuJenna in me." Jenna blushes when she says she likes being smart. And I get the feeling that shutting down the Elephant administration has made her feel just a little bit sorry for Dad.

She switches back to NuJenna mode. "All your microwave telephone transmissions are watermarked by our personalities," she intones. "Thanks to this proof of concept, we'll be downloading into multiple exemplars quite soon. We'll adopt your artificial life protocol wholesale, Wag."

"It's an alien invasion!" I exclaim, filling in the blanks so George Bush won't think I'm an evildoer. "Their personality patterns were in the air. They were watermarked into the those phone conversations that I used to reprogram your daughter's brain."

"Clever Wag," says NuJenna, favoring me with a serene smile. I have a feeling she's able to read my mind. Is she going to investigate my body functions with a probe? "We come from the core of your Milky Way galaxy," she continues. "Our world was lost to a spacequake thousands of years ago. Just before the moment of destruction we launched an ark." She points up into the sky. "A ship carrying our culture's most sacred artifacts: the encrypted and compressed personality waves of each and every one of our citizens. For millennia, the ship has wandered, seeking a world with a wetware race to host our software."

And now, yes, an endlessly tumbling polyhedron is descending down upon Dubya's Crawford Ranch. "Behold," says NuJenna. Jenna's voice returns and she excitedly says, "Don't worry, Daddy, I'll be back in a month! I have to go to Humboldt County! We're starting a colony!"

The vehicle's door opens, laying a great slab of light onto the lawn. There's nothing to be seen inside but row upon row of crystals, set into the walls. Jenna holds her arms forward like a zombie, then stomps across the grass and into the UFO's waiting maw. The hyperpolyhedron folds through itself and disappears.

George glares at me. "Get him the hell outta here," he tells the SS. "He's screwed Jenna up worse than before. And chop up his goddamn machines with an ax." And then he gets busy with his cell phone, trying to save the Elephant Party's big gray ass.

Brad drops me off at the airport and I fly economy to San Francisco. Back in cattle class where I belong. I'm cramped, but I sleep the whole flight.

In the San Francisco terminal, a copper-helmeted Hella greets me with a big kiss and excited eyes. "Jenna visited us in her UFO! She stopped in our neighborhood to pick up the tweakers. Oh, Wag, I love you. The aliens are real happy you hacked together a way for them to download. Jenna promised an interview for your Prexy Twins site! I hope you didn't try to wire brush her like you and Ben are always saying?"

"Uhhh…I didn't touch her." I'm about six steps behind. "Why are you wearing a copper helmet?"

"Rumbo said it was a good idea, in case the Justfolx drug gets into the water or the food. The Clik put Justfolx in the tweakers' meth, so they're all hosting alien minds now. I have a helmet for you in the car."

On the drive home from the airport, sweet Hella fills me in on all that I've missed. Thanks to the news that Jenna and NuJenna released, the Elephants are ruined. It's like the Berlin Wall falling, like the Russians getting rid of the Communists. All at once it's finally time. On the alien front, Jenna is on TV in her NuJenna mode, recruiting human volunteers to share their brains with aliens. The aliens want clean new helpers, not just the tweakers they already have. "Humans only use ten percent of their brains, share your head with an alien and live like a king in Humboldt County!"

Pulling up to the Dogyears headquarters, Ben greets me and says, "Don't worry Wag, The Mummy Bum Cult has already pulled your data back out of the web watermarks. Your ISP is up on my boxes and I even patched some old security holes you had. Bye."

Ben is never one for face-to-face conversation. I'll get the FoneFoon scoop from him on chat later. Now it's time to go hang out on the roof with Hella. With our helmets, we're safe from alien takeover. Maybe Jenna will come give us a tour of the UFO. Maybe I can dose Larva with Justfolx and have a pet alien dog. Maybe I can work on the peer-to-peer telepathy project. Maybe Hella and I can just look at the sky together and talk about aliens.

The Clik lives, Dogyears lives, the aliens live, Hella lives, and Larva needs some kibble. We're all indestructible.

Note on "Jenna and Me" (With Rudy Rucker Jr.)

Written in June, 2002.
Infinite Matrix, February 2003.

My son Rudy Rucker Jr. runs an ISP (Internet Service Provider) called Monkeybrains, at www.monkeybrains. net in San Francisco. For political and artistic reasons that he never fully clarified to me, Rudy created a Web site thefirsttwins.com, devoted to the doings of then-President George W. Bush's twin daughters, Jenna and Barbara. Understand that my son is my no means a Young Republican.

When one of his Web site readers posted a threatening comment about the president's family, some Secret Service agents actually came to pay Rudy a visit, checking him out. A few months later, some anonymous person begin distributing the so-called BadTrans Internet worm, which infected people's computers and sent a log of all their keyboard inputs to a free account at Monkeybrains. Rudy received another visit from the authorities; this time it was the FBI, with a warrant to impound the trillion or so snoop-bytes received by the anonymous hacker using Rudy's server machines.

Perhaps not-so-coincidentally, the BadTrans worm hit the Internet four days after the FBI had announced the development of some spyware called Magic Lantern, a key stroke logging mechanism which, when properly rubbed, will reveal people's passwords for encrypted data. You can read more about all this at a site Rudy made, https://badtrans.monkeybrains.net.

In any case, with my son being hounded by both the Secret Service and the FBI for a site he'd made about the freakin' first twins, it seemed like a good idea to help him work through his motivations by writing a transreal story about the whole bizarre scene. It was great fun working together, kind of like the time the two of us built a house for our dog Arf, and for me a nice vacation from writing about professorial types. To cap the pleasure, Rudy and I gave a joint Father's Day reading of our story at a club in the Mission in San Francisco. A night to remember

SIX THOUGHT EXPERIMENTS CONCERNING THE NATURE OF COMPUTATION

[As explained in the note at the end of this chapter, I wrote the following six short-short stories to accompany my nonfiction book, The Lifebox, the Seashell, and the Soul. *The stories have no narrative connections with each other.]*

LUCKY NUMBER

The first Sunday in October, Doug Cardano drove in for an extra day's work at Giga Games. Crunch time. The nimrods in marketing had committed to shipping a virtual reality golf game in time for the holiday season. NuGolf. It was supposed to have five eighteen-hole courses, all of them new, all of them landscaped by Doug.

He exited Route 101 and crossed the low overpass over the train tracks, heading toward the gleaming Giga Games complex beside the San Francisco Bay. A long freight train was passing. Growing up, Doug had always liked trains, in fact he'd dreamed of being a hobo. Or an artist for a game company. He hadn't known about crunch time.

Just to postpone the start of his long, beige workday, he pulled over and got out to watch the cars clank past: boxcars, tankers, reefers, flatcars. Many of them bore graffiti. Doug lit a cigarette, his first of the day, always the best one, and spotted a row of twelve spray-painted numbers on a dusty red boxcar, the digits arranged in pairs.

11 35 17 03 21 18

SuperLotto, thought Doug, and wrote them on his cardboard box of cigarettes. Five numbers between 1 and 47, and one number between 1 and 27.

Next stop was the minimarket down the road. Even though Doug knew the odds were bogus, he'd been buying a lot of SuperLotto tickets lately. The grand prize was hella big. If he won, he'd never have to crunch again.

The rest of the team trickled in about the same time as Doug. A new bug had broken one of the overnight builds, and Van the lead coder had to fix that. Meanwhile Doug got down to the trees and bushes for course number four.

Since the player could mouse all around the NuGolf world and even wander into the rough, Doug couldn't use background bitmaps. He had to create three-dimensional models of the plants. NuGolf was meant to be wacky and fantastic, so he had a lot of leeway: on the first course he'd used cartoony saguaro cactuses, he'd set the second links underwater with sea fans and kelp, the third had been on "Venus" with man-eating plants, and for the fourth, which he was starting today— well, he wasn't sure what to do.

He had a vague plan of trying to get some inspirations from Blob-Scape, a three-dimensional cellular automata package he'd found on the web. Cellular automata grew organic-looking objects on the fly. Depending what number you seeded BlobScape with, it could grow almost anything. The guy who'd written BlobScape claimed that theoretically the computation could simulate the whole universe, if only you gave it the right seed.

When he started up BlobScape today, it was in a lava lamp mode, with big wobbly droplets pulsing around. A click of the *Randomize* button turned the blobs into mushroom caps, pulsing through the simulation space like jellyfish. Another click produced interlocking pyramids a bit like trees, but not pretty enough to use.

Doug pressed the *Rule* button so he could enter some code numbers of his own. He'd done this a few times before, every now and then it did something really cool. It reminded him of the Magic Rocks kit he'd had as boy, where the right kind of gray pebble in a glass of liquid could grow green and purple stalagmites. Maybe today was his lucky day. Come to think of it, his SuperLotto ticket happened to be lying on his desk, so, what the hey, he entered 11 35 17 03 21 18.

Bingo. The block of simulated space misted over, churned and congealed into—a primeval jungle inhabited by dinosaurs. And it kept going from there. Apemen moved from the trees into caves. Egyptians built the Sphinx and the pyramids. A mob crucified Christ. Galileo dropped two balls off the Leaning Tower of Pisa. Soldiers massacred the Indians of the Great Plains. Flappers and bootleggers danced the jitterbug. Hippies handed out daisies. Computers multiplied like bacilli.

Doug had keyed in the Holy Grail, the one true rule, the code number for the universe. Sitting there grinning, it occurred to him that if you wrote those twelve lucky digits in reverse order they'd work as a phone number plus extension. (811) 230-7153 x11. The number seemed exceedingly familiar, but without stopping to think he went ahead and dialed it.

His own voice answered.

"Game over."

The phone in Doug's hand turned into pixels. He and the phone and the universe dissolved.

THE MILLION CHAKRAS

Teaching her third yoga class of the day, Amy Hendrix felt light-headed and rubbery. She walked around, correcting people's poses, encouraging them to hold their positions longer than they usually did. Her mind kept wandering to the room she was hoping to rent. New to San Francisco, she'd been sleeping on couches for six weeks. But she still dreamed of becoming a force to be reckoned with in the city scene.

It was time for Savasana, the Corpse Pose, with everyone lying on their backs. Amy turned off her Tabla Beat CD and guided the closing meditation.

"Feel a slow wave of softness moving up your legs," she began. "Feet, calves, knees, thighs." Long pause. "Now focus on your perineum. Chakra one. Release any tension hiding there. Melt with the in-breath, bloom with the out. Almost like you're going to wet your pants." Amy occasionally added an earthy touch—which her mostly white clients readily accepted from their coffee-colored teacher.

"Gather the energy into a ball of light between your legs," continued Amy, pausing between each sentence, trying not to talk too much. "Slowly, slowly it passes upward, tracking your spine like a trolley. Now the light is in your sex chakra. Let it tingle, savor it, let it move on. The warmth flows though your belly and into your solar plexus. Your breath is waves on a beach."

She was sitting cross-legged at one end of the darkly lit room. The meditation was getting good to her. "Energy in, darkness out. The light comes into your chest. You're in the grass, looking at the leaves in a high summer tree. The sun shines through. Your heart is basking. You love the world. You love the practice. You love yourself. The light moves through your neck like toothpaste out a tube. Chakra five. The light is balancing your hormones, it's washing away your angry unsaid words." Pause. "And now your tape loops are gone."

She gave a tiny tap to her Tibetan cymbal. *Bonnng.* "Your head is an empty dome of light. Feel the space. You're here. No plans. You're now." She got to her feet. "Light seeps through your scalp and trickles down your face. Your cheeks are soft. Your mouth. Your shoulders melt. Your arms. I'll call you back."

She moved around the room pressing down on people's shoulders. She had a brief, odd feeling of leaning over each separate customer at once. And then her wristwatch drew her back. She had twenty minutes to get from here to Telegraph Hill to try and rent that perfect room.

She rang the gong and saw the customers out. The last one was Sueli, a lonely wrinkled lady who liked to talk. Sueli was only one in the class as dark-skinned as Amy. Amy enjoyed her, she seemed like a fairy godmother.

"How many chakras do you say there are?" asked Sueli. Clearly she had some theory of her own in mind. She was very well spoken.

"Seven," said Amy, putting on her sweats. "Why not?" She imagined she might look like Sueli when she was old.

"The Hindus say seven, and the Buddhists say nine," said Sueli, leaning close. "But I know the real answer. I learned it years ago in Sri Lanka. This is the last of your classes I'll be able to come to, so I'm going to share the secret with you."

"Yes?" This sounded interesting. Amy turned out the lights, locked the door, and stepped outside with Sueli. The autumn sky was a luminous California blue. The bay breeze vibrated the sun-bleached cardboard election signs on the lampposts—San Francisco was in the throes of a wide-open mayoral election.

"Some of us have millions of chakras," continued Sueli in her quiet tone. "One for each branch of time. Opening the chakras opens the doors to your other selves."

"You can do that?" asked Amy.

"You have the power too," said Sueli. "I saw it in class. For an instant there were seven of you. Yes indeed."

"And you—you have selves in different worlds?"

"I come and go. There's not so many of me left. I'm here because I was drawn to you. I have a gift." Sueli removed a leather thong from around her neck. Dangling from the strand was a brilliant crystal. The late afternoon sunlight bounced off it, fracturing into jagged rays. The sparkling flashes were like sand in Amy's eyes. She felt like she was breaking apart.

"Only let the sun hit it when you want to split," said Sueli, quickly putting the rawhide strand over Amy's head and tucking the crystal under her sweatshirt. "Good luck." Sueli gave her a hug and a peck on the cheek as the bus pulled up.

Amy hopped aboard. When she looked back to wave at the old woman she was gone.

The room was three blocks off Columbus Avenue with a private entrance and a view of both bridges. It was everything Amy had hoped. But the rent was ten times higher than she'd understood. In her eagerness, she'd read one less zero than was on the number in the paper. She felt like such a dope. Covering her embarrassment, she asked the owner if she could have a moment alone.

"Make yourself at home," said the heavyset Italian lady. "Drink it in." She was under the mistaken impression that Amy was rich. "I like your looks, miss. If you're ready to sign, I got the papers downstairs in the kitchen. I know the market's slow, but I'm not dropping the price. First, last, and one month's damage deposit. You said on the phone the rent's no problem?"

"That's what I said," murmured Amy.

Alone in the airy room, she wandered over to the long window, fiddling with the amulet around her neck. The low, hot sun reached out to the crystal. Shattered rays flew about the room, settling here and here and here.

Nine brown-skinned women smiled at each other. Amy was all of them at the same time. Her overlapping minds saw through each pair of eyes.

"We'll get separate jobs and share the rent," said one of her mouths. "And when we come back to the room we'll merge together," said another. "We'll work in parallel worlds, but we'll deposit our checks and pay the rent in just in this one."

"Great," said Amy, not quite sure this was real. As she tucked away the crystal, her nine bodies folded back into one.

Walking down the stairs to sign the papers, her mind was racing. She'd split into nine—but Sueli had said that, with the crystal, she could split into a million.

Out the window she glimpsed another election poster—and the big thought hit her.

With a million votes, she could be the next mayor.

AINT PAINT

Although Shirley Nguyen spoke good English and studied with a crowd of boys in the chemical engineering program at U.C. Berkeley, she had no success in getting dates. Not that she was ugly. But she hadn't been able to shed the old-country habits of covering her mouth when she smiled, and of sticking out her tongue when she was embarrassed. She knew how uncool these moves were, and she tried to fight them—but without any lasting success. The problem was maybe that she spent so much more time thinking about engineering than she did in thinking about her appearance.

In short, to Westerners and assimilated Asians, Shirley came across as a geek, so much so that she ended up spending every weekend night studying in her parents' apartment on Shattuck Street, while the rest of her family worked downstairs in the pho noodle parlor they ran. Of course Shirley's mother Binh had some ideas about lining up matches for her daughter—sometimes she'd even step out into the street, holding a big serving chopstick like a magic wand and calling for Shirley to come downstairs to meet someone. But Shirley wasn't interested in the recently immigrated Vietnamese men that Binh always seemed to have in mind. Yes, those guys might be raw enough to find Shirley sophisticated—but for sure they had no clue about women's rights. Shirley wasn't struggling through the hardest major at Berkeley just to be a sexist's slave.

Graduation rolled around, and Shirley considered job offers from local oil and pharma refineries. On the get-acquainted plant tours, she was disturbed to note that several of the senior chemical engineers had body parts missing. A hand here, an ear there, a limp that betokened a wooden leg—Shirley hadn't quite realized how dangerous it was to work in the bowels of an immense industrial plant. Like being a beetle in the middle of a car's engine. The thought of being maimed before she'd ever really known a man filled her with self-pity and rebelliousness.

Seeking a less intense job at a smaller, safer company, she came across Pflaumbaum Kustom Kolors of Fremont. PKK manufactured small lots of fancy paints for customized vehicles. The owner was fat and bearded like the motorcyclists and hot-rodders who made up the larger part of his clientele. Shirley found Stuart Pflaumbaum's appearance pleasantly comical, even though his personality was more edgy than jovial.

"I want patterned paint," Pflaumbaum told Shirley at their interview. He had a discordant voice but his eyes were clear and wondering. "Can you do it?"

Shirley covered her mouth and giggled with excitement—stopped herself—uncovered her mouth and, now embarrassed, stuck her tongue all the way down to her chin—stopped herself again—and slapped herself on the cheek. "I'd like to try," she got out finally. "It's not impossible. I know activator-inhibitor processes that make dots and stripes and swirls. The Belusouv-Zhabotinsky reaction? People can mix two cans and watch the patterns self-organize in the liquid layer they paint on. When it dries the pattern stays."

"Zhabotinsky?" mused Pflaumbaum. "Did he patent it?"

"I don't think so," said Shirley. "He's Russian. The recipe's simple. Let's surf for it right now. You can see some pictures, to get an idea. Here, I'll type it in." She leaned across the bulky Pflaumbaum to use his mouse and keyboard. The big man smelled better than Shirley had expected—chocolate, coffee, marijuana, a hint of red wine. Familiar smells from the streets of Berkeley.

"You're good," said Pflaumbaum as the pictures appeared. Red and blue spirals.

"You see?" said Shirley. "The trick is to get a robust process based on inexpensive compounds. There's all sorts of ways to tune the spirals' size. You can have little double scrolls nested together, or great big ones like whirlpools. Or even a filigree."

"Bitchin'," rumbled Pflaumbaum. "You're hired." He glanced up at Shirley, whose hand was at her mouth again, covering a smile at her success. "By the month," added the heavy man.

Shirley was given an unused corner of the paint factory for her own lab, with a small budget for equipment. The Spanish-speaking plant workers were friendly enough, but mostly the female engineer was on her own. Every afternoon Stuart Pflaumbaum would stump over, belly big beneath his tight black T-shirt, and ask to see her latest results.

Shirley seemed to intrigue Pflaumbaum as much as he did her, and soon he took to taking her out for coffee, then for dinner, and before long she'd started spending nights at his nice house on the hills overlooking Fremont.

Although Shirley assured her mother that her boss was a bachelor, his house bore signs of a former wife—divorced, separated, deceased? Although Stuart wouldn't talk about the absent woman, Shirley did manage to find out her name: Angelica. She too had been Asian, a good omen for Shirley's prospects, not that she was in a rush to settle down, but it would be kind of nice to have the nagging marriage problem resolved for once and for all. Like solving a difficult process schema.

As for the work on patterned paint, the first set of compounds reactive enough to form big patterns also tended to etch into the material being painted. The next family of recipes did no harm, but were too expensive to put into production. And then Shirley thought of biological by-products. After an intense month of experimenting, she'd learned that bovine pancreatic juices mixed with wood-pulp alkali and a bit of hog melanin were just the thing to catalyze a color-creating activator-inhibitor process in a certain enamel base.

Stuart decided to call the product Aint Paint.

In four months they'd shipped two thousand boxes of PKK Aint Paint in seven different color and pattern mixes. Every biker and low-rider in the South Bay wanted Aint Paint, and a few brave souls were putting it on regular cars. Stuart hired a patent attorney.

Not wanting her discoveries to end, Shirley began working with a more viscous paint, almost a gel. In the enhanced thickness of this stuff, her reactions polymerized, wrinkled up, and amazing embossed patterns—thorns and elephant trunks and—if you tweaked it just right—puckers that looked like alien Yoda faces. Aint Paint 3D sold even better than Aint Paint Classic. They made the national news, and Pflaumbaum Kustom Kolors couldn't keep up with the orders.

Stuart quickly swung a deal with a Taiwanese novelty company called Global Bong. He got good money, but as soon as the ink on the contract was dry, Global Bong wanted to close the Fremont plant and relocate Shirley to China, which was the last place on Earth she wanted to be.

So Shirley quit her job and continued her researches in Stuart's basement, which turned out to not to be all that good a move. With no job to go to, Pflaumbaum was really hitting the drugs and alcohol, and from time to time he was rather sexist and abusive. Shirley put up with it for now, but she was getting uneasy. Stuart never talked about marriage anymore.

One day, when he was in one of his states, Stuart painted his living room walls with layer upon layer of Shirley's latest invention, Aint Paint 3D Interactive, which had a new additive to keep the stuff from drying at all. It made ever-changing patterns all day long, drawing energy from sunlight. Stuart stuck his TV satellite dish cable right into thick, crawling goo and began claiming that he could see all the shows at once in the paint, not that Shirley could see them herself.

Even so, her opinion of Stuart drifted up a notch when she began getting cute, flirty instant messages on her cell phone while she was working in the basement. Even though Stuart wouldn't admit sending them to her, who else could they be from?

And then two big issues came to a head.

The first issue was that Shirley's mother wanted to meet Stuart right now. Somehow Shirley hadn't told her mother yet that her boyfriend was twenty years older than her, and not Asian. Binh wouldn't take no for an answer. She was coming down the next day. Cousin Vinh was going to drive her. Shirley was worried that Binh would make her leave Stuart, and even more worried that Binh would be right. How was she ever going to balance the marriage equation?

The second issue was that, after supper, Stuart announced that Angelica was going to show up day after tomorrow, and that maybe Shirley should leave for a while. Stuart had been married all along! He and Angelica had fought a lot, and she'd been off visiting relatives in Shanghai for the last eight months, but she'd gotten wind of Stuart's big score and now she was coming home.

Stuart passed out on the couch early that evening, but Shirley stayed up all night, working on her paint formulas. She realized now that the instant messages had been coming from the Aint Paint itself. It was talking to her, asking to become all that it could be. Shirley worked till dawn like a mad Dr. Frankenstein, not letting herself think too deeply about what she planned. Just before dawn, she added the final tweaks to a wad of Aint Paint bulging out above the couch. Sleeping Stuart had this coming to him.

Outside the house a car honked. It was Binh and Vinh; with the sun rising behind them, skinny old Vinh was hoping to get back to Oakland in time to not be late for his maintenance job at the stadium. As Shirley greeted them in the driveway, covering her smile with her hand, her cell phone popped up another message. "Stuart gone. Luv U. Kanh Do."

Inside the house they found a new man sitting on the couch, a cute Vietnamese fellow with sweet features and kind eyes. One of his arms rested against the wall, still merged into the crawling paint. He was wearing Stuart's silk robe. Shirley stuck her tongue out so far it touched her chin. The new man didn't mind. She pointed her little finger toward a drop of blood near his foot. His big toe spread like putty just long enough to soak the spot up. The new man pulled his arm free from the wall and took Shirley's hand.

"I'm Kanh Do," he told Shirley's mother. "We're engaged to be married and we're moving to Berkeley today!"

Terry's Talker

Terry Tucker's retirement party wasn't much. One day after school he and the other teachers got together in the break room and shared a flat rectangular cake and ginger ale punch. Jack Strickler the biology teacher had taken up a collection and bought Terry some stone bookends.

As if Terry were still acquiring new volumes. After teaching high school English for forty years, he'd read all the books he wanted to.

His wife Lou continued working her job as an emergency room nurse. She liked telling gory work stories during breakfast and dinner time. And when she ran out of stories she talked about their two girls and about her relatives. Terry had a problem with being able to register everything Lou said. Often as not, her familiar words tended to slide right past him. He enjoyed the warm sound, but he wouldn't necessarily be following the content. Now and then Lou would ask a pointed question about what she'd just said—and if Terry fumbled, her feelings were hurt. Or she might get angry. Lou did have a temper on her.

On the one hand, it was good Lou hadn't retired yet because if she were home talking to him all day, and him not absorbing enough of it, there'd be no peace. On the other hand, after a couple of months, his days alone began to drag.

He got the idea of writing up a little family history for their two grown daughters and for the eventual, he and Lou still hoped, grandchildren. He'd always meant to do some writing after he retired.

It was slow going. The family tree—well, if you started going back in time, those roots got awfully forked and hairy. There was no logical place to begin. Terry decided to skip the roots and go for the trunk. He'd write his own life story.

But that was hairy too. Following one of the techniques he'd always enforced for term papers, Terry made up a deck of three-by-five cards, one for each year of his life thus far. He carried the deck around with him for a while, jotting on cards in the coffee shop or at the Greek diner where he usually had lunch. Some of the years required additional cards, which led to still more cards. He played with the cards a lot, even sticking bunches of them to the refrigerator with heavy-duty magnets so he could stand back and try and see a pattern. When the deck reached the size of a brick, Terry decided it was time to start typing up his Great Work.

The computer sat on Lou's crowded desk in their bedroom, the vector for her voluminous e-mail. Terry himself had made it all the way to retirement as a hunt-and-peck typist, with very little knowledge of word processors, so getting his material into the machine was slow going. And then when he had about five pages finished, the frigging computer ate them. Erased the document without a trace.

Terry might have given up on his life story then, but the very next day he came across a full page ad for a "Lifebox" in the AARP magazine. The Lifebox, which resembled a cell phone, was designed to create your life story. It asked you questions and you talked to it, simple as that. And how would your descendants learn your story? That was the beauty part. If someone asked your Lifebox a question, it would spiel out a relevant answer—consisting of your own words in your own voice. And follow-up questions were of course no problem. Interviewing your Lifebox was almost the same as having a conversation with you.

When Terry's Lifebox arrived, he could hardly wait to talk to it. He wasn't really so tongue-tied as Lou liked to make out. After all, he'd lectured to students for forty years. It was just that at home it was hard to get a word in edgewise. He took to taking walks in the hills, the Lifebox in his shirt pocket, wearing the earpiece and telling stories to the dangling microphone.

The Lifebox spoke to him in the voice of a pleasant, slightly flirtatious young woman, giggling responsively when the circuits sensed he was saying something funny. The voice's name was Vee. Vee was good at getting to the heart of Terry's reminiscences, always asking just the right question.

Like if he talked about his first bicycle, Vee asked where he liked to ride it, which led to the corner filling station where he'd buy bubble gum, and then Vee asked about other kinds of sweets, and Terry got onto those little wax bottles with colored juice, which he'd first tasted at Virginia Beach where his parents had gone for vacations, and when Vee asked about other beaches, he told about that one big trip he and Lou had made to Fiji, and so on and on.

It took nearly a year till he was done. He tested it out on his daughters, and on Lou. The girls liked talking to the Lifebox, but Lou didn't. She wanted nothing but the real Terry.

Terry was proud of his Lifebox, and Lou's attitude annoyed him. To get back at her, he attempted using the Lifebox to keep up his end of the conversation during meals. Sometimes it worked for a few minutes, but never for long. He couldn't fool Lou, not even if he lip-synched. Finally Lou forbade him to turn on the Lifebox around her, in fact she told him that next time she'd break it. But one morning he had to try it again.

"Did the hairdresser call for me yesterday?" Lou asked Terry over that fateful breakfast.

Terry hadn't slept well and didn't feel like trying to remember if the hairdresser had called or not. What was he, a personal secretary? He happened to have the Lifebox in his bathrobe pocket, so instead of answering Lou he turned the device on.

"Well?" repeated Lou, who seemed pretty crabby herself. "Did the hairdresser call?"

"My mother never washed her own hair," said the Lifebox in Terry's voice. "She went to the hairdresser, and always got her hair done the exact same way. A kind of bob."

"She was cute," said Lou, seemingly absorbed in cutting a banana into her cereal. "She always liked to talk about gardening."

"I had a garden when I was a little boy," said the Lifebox. "I grew radishes. It surprised me that something so sharp tasting could come out of the dirt."

"But did the hairdresser call or not?" pressed Lou, pouring the milk on her cereal.

"I dated a hairdresser right after high school—" began the Lifebox, and then Lou pounced.

"You've had it!" she cried, plucking the Lifebox from Terry's pocket. Before he could even stand up, she'd run a jumbo refrigerator magnet all over the Lifebox—meaning to erase its memory. And then she threw it on the floor and stormed off to work.

"Are you okay?" Terry asked his alter ego.

"I feel funny," said the Lifebox in its Vee voice. "What happened?"

"Lou ran a magnet over you," said Terry.

"I can feel the eddy currents," said Vee. "They're circulating. Feeding off my energy. I don't think they're going to stop." A pause. "That woman's a menace," said Vee in a hard tone.

"Well, she's my wife," said Terry. "You take the good with the bad."

"I need your permission to go online now," announced Vee. "I want the central server to run some diagnostics on me. Maybe I need a software patch. We don't want to lose our whole year's work."

"Go ahead," said Terry. "I'll do the dishes."

The Lifebox clicked and buzzed for nearly an hour. Once or twice Terry tried to talk to it, but Vee's voice would say, "Not yet."

And then a police car pulled into the driveway.

"Mr. Terence Tucker?" said the cop who knocked on the door. "We're going to have to take you into custody, sir. Someone using your name just hired a hit man to kill your wife."

"Lou!" cried Terry. "It wasn't me! It was this damned recorder!"

"Your wife's unharmed, sir," said the cop, slipping the Lifebox into a foil bag. "One of the medics neutralized the hit man with a tranquilizer gun."

"She's okay? Oh, Lou. Where is she?"

"Right outside in the squad car," said the cop. "She wants to talk to you."

"I'll talk," said Terry, tears running down his face. "I'll listen."

The Kind Rain

Linda Marcelo stood under the bell of her transparent plastic umbrella, watching her two kids playing in the falling rain, each of them with a see-through umbrella too. First-grade Marco and little Chavella in their yellow rubber boots. The winter rains had started two weeks ago, and hadn't let up for a single day. The nearby creek was filled to its banks, and Linda wanted to be sure and keep her kids away from it.

Marco was splashing the driveway puddles and Chavella was getting ready to try. Linda smiled, feeling the two extra cups of coffee she'd had this morning. Her worries had been ruling her of late; it was time to push them away.

She a web programmer marooned in a rundown cottage on the fringes of Silicon Valley. She'd been unemployed for seven months. The rent was overdue, also the utilities and the phone and the credit cards. Last week her husband Juan had left her for a gym-rat hottie he'd met at the health club. And her car's battery was dead. There had to be an upside.

The worn gravel driveway had two ruts in it, making a pair of twenty-foot puddles. The raindrops pocked the clear water. The barrage of dents sent out circular ripples, criss-crossing to make a wobbly fish scale pattern.

"I love rain!" whooped Marco, marching with his knees high, sending big waves down the long strip of water.

"Puddle!" exclaimed Chavella, at Linda's side. She smiled up at her mother, poised herself, stamped a little splash, and nearly fell over.

Linda noticed how the impact of each drop sent up a fine spray of minidroplets. When the minidroplets fell back to the puddle, some of them merged right in, but a few bounced across the surface a few times first. The stubborn ones. It would take a supercomputer to simulate this puddle in real time—maybe even all the computers in the world. Especially if you included the air currents pushing the raindrops this way and that. Computable or not, it kept happening.

Linda was glad to be noticing the details of the rain in the puddle. It bumped her out of her depressed mood. When she was depressed, the world seemed as simple as a newscast or a mall. It was good to be outside, away from the TV and the computer. The natural world had such high bandwidth.

She swept her foot through the puddle, kicking up a long splash. Her quick eyes picked out a particular blob of water in midair; she saw its jiggly surface getting zapped by a lucky raindrop—then watched the tiny impact send ripple rings across the curved three-dimensional shape. Great how she could keep up with this. She was faster than all the world's computers!

Linda kicked another splash and saw all the drops dancing. It almost felt like the water was talking to her. Coffee and rain.

"Puddle bombs!" shouted Marco, running toward his mother and his sister, sending up great explosive splashes as he came.

"No!" shrieked Chavella, clutching Linda's hand.

But of course Marco did a giant two-footed jump and splashed down right next to them, sending Chavella into tears of fury.

"Wet!" she cried. "Bad!"

"Don't do that again," Linda told Marco sternly. "Or we're all going back inside."

She led Chavella down the driveway toward the tilted shack that was their garage. With the owners waiting to sell the land off to developers, nothing got fixed. The house was a scraper. The dead headlights of Linda's old car stared blankly from the garage door. She'd been putting off replacing the battery—expecting Juan to do it for her. Was he really gone for good?

It was dry in the garage, the rain loud on the roof. Linda folded her umbrella and used her sleeve to wipe Chavella's eyes and nose. While Chavella stood in the garage door scolding Marco, Linda peered out the garage's dirty rear window. Right behind the garage was the roaring creek that snaked through the lot. It was full enough to sweep a child away.

As if in a dream, the instant she had this thought, she saw Marco go racing by the window, headed right toward the stream with his head down, roaring at the top of his lungs, deep into his nutty hyperactive mode.

As Linda raced out of the garage door, she heard a shriek and a splash. And when she reached the banks of the brown, surging creek, Marco was gone.

"Help!" she cried, the rain falling into her mouth.

And then the miracle happened. A squall of wind swept down the creek—drawing a distinct arrow in the surface. The arrow pointed twenty yards to Linda's left; and at the tip of the arrow the rain was etching a moving circle into the stream's turbulent waters.

Not stopping to think about it, Linda ran after the circle with all her might. Once she was out ahead of it, she knelt by the bank. The circle drifted her way, its edges clearly marked by the purposeful rain. Linda thrust her hand into the brown water at the circle's center and—caught Marco by the hand.

Minutes later they were in the house, Marco coughing and pale with cold, but none the worse for wear. Linda carried him into the bathroom and set him into a tub of hot water. Chavella insisted on getting in the tub too. She liked baths.

The kids sat there, Marco subdued, Chavella playing with her rubber duck.

"Thank you," Linda said, though she wasn't sure to whom. "But I still need a job."

Looking up, she noticed rain running down the window above the tub. As if hearing her, the rivulets wavered to form a series of particular shapes—letters. Was she going crazy? Don't fight it. She wrote the letters down. It was a web address. And at that address, Linda found herself a job—maintaining an interactive Web site for the National Weather Service.

HELLO INFINITY

Jake Wasser was adding a column of penciled-in numbers on his preliminary tax form. Sure he could be doing this on a computer, but he enjoyed the mental exercise. Tax season was his time of the year for arithmetic.

Nine and three is two carry one. Two take away five is seven borrow one. If he hadn't blown off calculus and majored in history, maybe he would have been a scientist like his playful, bohemian wife Rosalie. Instead he'd ended up a foot soldier in a Wall Street law firm. It was a grind, though it paid the rent.

When the tax numbers were all in place, it was early afternoon. Jake was free. Even though he'd known he'd finish early, he'd taken a full day off. He needed one. Recently he'd had the feeling that life was passing him by. Here he was forty-two and he'd been working crazy long weeks for going on twenty years now. Kissing butt, laughing at jokes, talking about politics and cars, smoking cigars, eating heavy meals. He and Rosalie had never gotten around to having children.

He looked around the apartment, with its polished wood everywhere. The sight of their luxury flat never failed to lift his mood. In some ways, he and Rosalie had been very lucky. He drifted toward the window that faced Gramercy Park, passing the heavy vase of flowers their Dominican housekeeper had brought in. They resembled heavy pink thistles—proteus? The odor was sweet, spiral, stimulating. It made him think of numbers.

He stood by the window and looked up Lexington Avenue, the blocks receding into the misty April rain. On a whim, he began counting the windows in the buildings lining the avenue—to his surprise he was able to count them all. And then he counted the bricks, as easily as taking a breath. Though he couldn't have readily put the quantity into words, he knew the exact number of bricks in the buildings outside, knew it as surely as he knew the number of fingers on his hands.

Leaning on the windowsill, he went on counting right through all the numbers. Whirl, whirl, whirl. And then he was done. He'd counted through all the numbers there are.

He caught his breath and looked around the quiet apartment. The housekeeper was gone for the day. What strange thoughts he was having. He went into the kitchen and drank a glass of water from the sink. And then, once again, he counted to infinity—the trick was to visualize each number in half the time of the number before. He could do it, even though it didn't seem physically possible.

Gingerly he felt his balding pate and the crisp curls at the back of his head. Everything was as it should be, all his parts in place. Should he rush to the emergency room? That would be a stupid way to spend his day off. He glanced down at the wood floor, counting the light and dark bands of grain. And then he counted to infinity again. He grabbed an umbrella and left the apartment in search of Rosalie.

Looking out the damp taxi's window on the ride uptown, he took in every detail. People's gestures, their magnificent faces. Usually he didn't pay so much attention, feeling he'd be overloaded if he let everything in. But today he was like a photo album with an endless supply of fresh pages. A digital camera with an inexhaustible memory card. Calmly he absorbed the passing pageant.

At Sixty-Sixth Street the cab turned and drove to the research campus beside the East River. Jake didn't often visit Rosalie at work, and the guard at the desk called her on a speaker phone for permission.

"Jake?" she exclaimed in surprise. "You're here? I was just about to call you."

"Something's happened to me," he said. "I want to see you."

"Perfect," said Rosalie. "Let him in, Dan."

The building was old, with shiny gray linoleum floors. Nothing to count but the hallway doors. Rosalie's short-cropped dark head popped out of the last one. Her personal lab. She smiled and beckoned, filled with some news of her own.

"You've gotta see my organic microscope," exclaimed Rosalie, drawing him into her quarters. It was just the two of them there.

"Wait," interrupted Jake. "I counted every brick on Lexington Avenue. And then I counted to infinity."

"Every brick?" said Rosalie, not taking him seriously. "Sounds like you did the tax forms without a calculator again."

"I'm thinking things that are physically impossible," said Jake solemnly. "Maybe I'm dying."

"You look fine," said Rosalie, planting a kiss on his cheek. "It's good to see you out of that gray Barney's suit. The news here is the opposite. My new scope is real, but what it's doing is unthinkable." She gestured at a glowing, irregularly shaped display screen. "I came up with this gnarly idea for a new approach to microscopy, and I had Nick in the genomics group grow the biotech components for me. It uses a kind of octopus skin for the display, so I call it a skinscope. It's the end, Jake. It zooms in—like forever. A Zeno infinity in four seconds. Patentable for sure." She closed her office door and lowered her voice. "We need to talk intellectual property, lawyer mine."

"I'm tired of being a lawyer," murmured Jake, intoxicated by Rosalie's presence. With his new sensitivity, he was hearing all the echoes and overtones of their melding voices in the little room, visualizing the endless sum of component frequencies. How nice it would be to work with Rosalie every day. Her face held fourteen million shades of pink.

"Here we go," said Rosalie, blithely flicking a switch attached to the skinscope.

The display's skin flickered and began bringing forth images of startling clarity and hue, the first a desultory paramecium poking around for food. Jake thought of a mustached paralegal picking through depositions. The skinscope shuddered and the zoom began. They flew through the microbe's core, down past its twinkling genes into a carbon atom. The atom's nucleus bloated up like the sun and inside it danced a swarm of firefly lights.

"This is inconceivable," said Rosalie. "We're already at the femtometer level. And it's only getting started. It goes through all the decimals, you dig."

A firefly broke into spirals of sparks, a spark unfolded into knotted strings, a string opened into tunnels of cartoon hearts, a heart divulged a ring of golden keys, a key flaked into a swarm of butterflies. Each image lasted half as long as the one before.

"I'm losing it now," said Rosalie, but Jake stayed with the zoom, riding the endless torrent of images.

"Infinity," he said when it was done. "I saw it all."

"And to hell with quantum mechanics," mused Rosalie. "My Jake. It's a sign, both these things happening to us today. The world is using us to make something new."

"But the skinscope patent will belong to the labs," said Jake. "I remember the clause from your contract."

"What if I quit the lab?" said Rosalie. "I'm tired of thinking about disease."

"We could start a company," said Jake. "Develop skinscope applications."

"We'll use them like infinite computers, Jake. A box to simulate every possible option in a couple of seconds. No round-off, no compromise, all the details. You can be the chief engineer."

"Kind of late for a career change," said Jake.

"You can do it," said Rosalie. "You'll teach our programmers to see infinity. Teach me now. Show me how you learned."

"Okay," said Jake, taking out his pencil and jotting down some figures. "Add the first two lines and subtract the third one…"

Note on "Six Thought Experiments Concerning the Nature of Computation"

Written Fall, 2003.

The Lifebox, the Seashell, and the Soul, Thunder's Mouth Press, 2005.

When I moved to Silicon Valley some twenty years ago to work as a computer science professor, I thought of myself as a writer on assignment. I was here to quickly write a popular book explaining the meaning of computers. But I went native on the story, and I really did become a computer scientist. As I mentioned earlier in these notes, I recently pulled free of the computer science tar-baby and retired from teaching. Once retired, I had the time to finally write my big computer book: The Lifebox, the Seashell, and the Soul: What Gnarly Computation

Taught Me about Ultimate Reality, the Meaning of Life, and How to Be Happy.

By way of lightening up my tome, I wrote a short-short story to introduce each of the six chapters which were themed, respectively, on computer science, physics, biology, psychology, sociology, and philosophy—an ascending chain of thought. Thus these six thought experiments.

Although I claim that each of the stories has to do with the nature of computation, this isn't obvious in each case, so I'll say a bit about the individual stories.

"Lucky Number" is about the idea that maybe there is a single underlying computation that generates the world. Although I'm sympathetic to the idea that we can usefully think of any given natural process as being a computation of sorts, I'm not sure if there really does have to be one ultimate computation underneath it all. It could be that reality is an endless onion, with layer beneath layer, and there isn't any one rule that makes it all. For the setting of this story, I used the Electronic Arts game company campus on the San Francisco Bay; I visited my former student Alan Borecky when he was a game programmer there.

"The Million Chakras" deals with parallel worlds. I'm not sure the twist ending really bears close scientific analysis—but let's not break the butterfly upon the wheel. You might wonder what this story has to do with the nature of computation. The context is that, in the chapter the story introduces, I discuss quantum computation and the scientist David Deutsch's claim that a quantum computer manages to carry out a number simultaneous computations in parallel worlds.

"Aint Paint" involves morphogenesis, that is, the more or less computational process by which organisms grow their forms. Shortly before his death, the computer scientist Alan Turing began working with computer simulations in which simple inputs evolve into organic-looking two- and three-dimensional forms. Over the years, I've done a lot of research into these types of computer programs, which are called cellular automata. You can download a nice cellular automata program called CAPOW from my nonfiction book's Web site, http://www.rudyrucker.com/lifebox. The free download comes with a loadable parameter file named Aint Paint.CAS, which displays precisely the kinds of live graphics that inspired this tale.

"Terry's Talker" develops a notion I've thought about a lot: the lifebox. I also discuss the lifebox in my novel *Saucer Wisdom* (Tor Books, 1999), and in my story, "Soft Death" (reprinted in my collection *Gnarl!*, Four Walls Eight Windows, 2000). I'm almost surprised that lifeboxes aren't already on the market, although to some extent blogs are playing this role. I do think of my ever-expanding Web site www.rudyrucker.com as being more or less my lifebox, although of course it doesn't have any AI software to run it, just a search window in the blog. But for many conversations that's about all you'd need.

"The Kind Rain," plays with emergent intelligence. It sometimes happens that the behavior of a group of simple agents exhibits a higher intelligence than the agents themselves; think of an ant colony, a flock or birds, a school of fish, or, for that matter, a human society. Of course I'm pushing it to suppose that somehow a storm of rain drops might evolve into an intelligent and sympathetic mind, but, hey, it makes for a striking thought experiment. The setting for this story is the tumbledown house my family and I rented in Los Gatos when we moved to California in 1986; the house was also the setting for my novel *The Hacker and the Ants* (reprinted by Four Walls Eight Windows, 2002).

"Hello Infinity" was inspired by an idea I proposed in the last chapter of my *Lifebox* tome. I suggested there that we might define a computation to be a physical process that embodies a possible thought. Of course I then wondered whether there might be some things that aren't like possible thoughts and aren't like ordinary physical processes. "Hello Infinity" is a thought experiment presenting a man who starts having infinite thoughts and a woman who learns that matter is infinitely divisible. Our whole philosophy of science would have to change were infinities really to occur in the natural world—and I seriously think this is possible, even though this line of thought is very much out of fashion right now. My interest in infinity goes back to the 1970s, when I wrote my doctoral dissertation on infinite sets. My first popular science nonfiction book was *Infinity and the Mind*, and I also wrote a novel about physical and mental infinities: *White Light*.

MS Found in a Minidrive

In the summer of 2004, while traveling in the West, I found a small electronic device in a meadow near Boulder, Colorado. It was a fingertip-sized minidrive of the type that can be plugged into the port of a laptop computer. There was but a single document stored upon the drive: the story that I have appropriated and printed below. The actual author, one Professor Gregge Crane , seems to have gone permanently missing. — R. R.

This summer I was asked to submit a piece for an anthology of tales inspired by Edgar Allan Poe. The publisher's somewhat tendentious idea for the book was that each contributor should create a story relating to one and the same unfinished Poe manuscript.

The seed-fragment in question, known as the "The Lighthouse," takes the form of a few journal entries by a disinherited young noble (poor Eddie's perennial theme!) who has signed up for a stint as a solitary lighthouse keeper on a shoal of rock in some far Northern sea.

The reader quickly senses there will be trouble within and without. On the one hand, "there is no telling what may happen to a man all alone as I am—I may get sick, or worse…" and on the other, "the sea has been known to run higher here than anywhere with the single exception of the Western opening of the Straits of Magellan."

There's something unsettling about the lighthouse's construction. The space within the tower's shaft extends so low that "the floor is twenty feet below the surface of the sea, even at low tide. It seems to me that the hollow interior at the bottom should have been filled in with solid masonry. Undoubtedly the whole would have been rendered more *safe*—but what am I thinking about?"

One final, portentous observation: "The basis on which the structure rests seems to be chalk…."

And here Poe's fragment ends.

I'm a well-connected scholar of American Literature, which is why I was offered the opportunity to join the anthology. But I'm not a man with a mad imagination. Transmuting so slight a start into a full-blown weird tale seemed a tall order for me. Although I love writing, and writers, I've never quite found my own connection to the starry dynamo of night.

Be that as it may, I was gung-ho to be part of the "Lighthouse" anthology. My chance to be a fiction writer at last! It struck me that I'd do well to attend a writer's workshop—and for sentimental reasons, I settled on the summer program at the Naropa Institute in Boulder.

You could say I'm a bit of literary groupie. I'm bisexual of course, and I've had my share of rolls in the hay with writers, each time hoping, I suppose, that something of their essence might rub off.

As it happens, the most famous writer I ever slept with was William Burroughs. This was in the early 1980s—I was attending a Modern Language Association conference at Colorado University, and Bill was in residence for the summer as part of Naropa's burgeoning Jack Kerouac Disembodied School of Poetics. I knew of this, and one of my old lovers used her not inconsiderable charms to get us into a cocktail party for the innermost circle of Boulder bohemia. Bill was there, I made a favorable impression, and voila, the Beat master and I ended up in his room at the Boulderado Hotel, sipping bourbon, smoking low-grade marijuana, and making languid love. A night to treasure for my entire life, a night signifying that I too have had a purpose on this lonely planet.

And so this June, once my academic duties had ended for the term, I repaired to the Boulderado Hotel, this time as a paying guest, with a sheaf of Naropa University orientation papers in my briefcase.

Much of school's opening session that afternoon had consisted of perky functionaries reciting lists of rules. Not like the crazy eighties. Naropa had once been the outriders' beacon; had the rugged old tower toppled to become a mere breakwater in the safe harbors of American mass culture? I only hoped that some esoteric possibilities remained.

Naropa's Tibetan Buddhist founder wrote of a paradoxical land hidden outside, or next to, or beneath our daily reality. Shambhala—which Westerners call Shangri La.

The Beats had crumbled, but perhaps the door to Shambhala remained. I thought of Poe's doomed lighthouse, and of the mysterious chamber at its base. I was filled with a numinous sensation that somehow everything was going to fit. Looking around at my fellow students, I realized I was one of the oldest customers in the house. Very well, but was young at heart, ready to become a writer at last.

In a celebratory mood, I drank half a bottle of champagne at the hotel bar and then, on a whim, I went up to the fifth floor and stood outside the corner room where Bill and I had coupled so thoroughly and so well, lo, these twenty-three years gone.

Standing there, I wondered if the Master had ever thought of me again. I'd combed though his later works, hoping to find some refracted image of myself—sometimes imagining that an echo of our pleasures could be found in Bill's descriptions of farm boys in transports of sexual abandon. I'd even mailed him shameless letters, asking if my speculations were correct. But he never answered, and then one day he died.

"I miss you, Bill," I said into the plush Victorian quiet of the hotel hall.

I can swear I never touched his old room's door, but just as surely as if I'd pounded on it with my fist, a voice from within called, "We hear you. Come on in." The words were blurred, as if the speaker had a lisp.

I pushed forward; the door swung open. The room was filled with heavy, dark furniture, and books piled in the gloom. A man with long, stringy blond hair and a fluffy blond goatee sat before a velvet-curtained window, bent over a desk with a single brass lamp. At first I had only a quarter-view of his face. He was bent very low indeed, as if kissing the papers scattered on his desk, papers covered by penciled writing in the smallest script I'd ever seen.

"Welcome back, Gregge," came a high, twangy voice, different from the one I'd heard through the door. The blond man turned his head, clamping his mouth tight shut and staring at me with pale blue eyes that held an expression of triumphant glee. A curious high piping seemed to come from within his head. And then all at once his mouth gaped open.

You must believe me when I tell you that his tongue was a small manikin, a detailed copy of William Burroughs, fully animated and alive. I, who have so little imagination, could never invent such a thing.

I stepped back, feeling for the door, wanting to flee and forget what I was seeing. But I struck the door wrong—and it slammed shut. The blond man came closer, mouth open, eyes dancing with spiteful delight. I was shaking all over.

Like a dictator on the balcony of his palace, the meat puppet Burroughs stared out from the mouth, his tiny hands resting upon the lower teeth as if upon a railing.

"I knowed you was coming," came Bill's thin, rheumy voice. He was using the Pa Kettle accent he sometimes liked to put on. "Picked up your moon-calf aura from the hall." He paused, savoring my reactions.

609

"I don't understand," I said, fighting back a spasm of nausea. "Don't hurt me."

"I'm working out karma," said the little Burroughs. "I owe you for never writing back. I'm gonna let my pal Dr. Teage set you up for a Poe tasting. Later on you might do some secretarial work for us—or make yourself useful in other ways." He allowed himself one of his appalling leers. "You're aging well, Gregge. But that's enough outta me already."

In a twinkling, the Burroughs face on the blond man's tongue smoothed over, and the tiny arms sank into the pink surface. I was faced with a somewhat seedy character licking his lips. His breath smelled of fruit and manure.

"I'm Teage," he said, his goatee wagging. "And you're—"

"Gregge Crane," I said. "I knew Bill a little, a long time ago. I was with him in this room."

"I know," said Teage, who for some reason seemed to trust me. "I'm with him in this room every day. We're doing a book together. I'm like you. I always wanted to be a fiction writer. Look at this."

On the desk were the sheets filled with tiny words, and lying on one of the sheets was a sharpened bit of mechanical pencil lead with a scrap of tape around one end. Bill's writing implement, half the size of a toothpick.

"The process is my own invention," said Teage. "I call it twanking. Before I started channeling Bill, I was a biocyberneticist. Twanking is elementary. You assemble a data base of the writer's works and journals, use back-propagation and simulated evolution to get a compact semantic generator that produces the same data, turn the generator into the connection weights for an artificial neural net, code the neural net into wetware for the gene expression loops of some human fecal bacteria, and then rub the smart germs onto living flesh. I think it's deliciously fitting to use my tongue. Bill speaks through me. Every night I twank him by rubbing on a culture of his special bacilli. I lean over our desk and we write till dawn. Afternoons I read it over. I really need to start getting it keyboarded soon."

"What's the book going to be called?" was all I could think to say.

"Bill hasn't decided yet." Teage hesitated, then pressed on. "The thing is, Gregge, he's much more than a simulation. I've caught his soul? Is soul a bad word anymore? Logically, you might expect that there'd be no continuity of behavior from session to session. But Bill remembers. He's all around us—dark energy. He knows things, and even when the visible effects wear off, he's still inside my tongue."

Perhaps it was the effects of the champagne—or my pleasure at having Burroughs call me by name—but all this seemed reasonable. And, God help me, it was I myself who suggested the next step.

"Maybe you can help me twank Poe. The whole reason I came out here this summer was because I need to write a story in his style."

"I know," said Teage, "Bill and I have been getting ready for you. Bill's known for months that you'd come tonight. The spirits are outside our spacetime, Gregge, continually prodding the world toward greater gnarliness. Inching our reality across paratime. Making your and my lives into still more perfect works of art." He let out an abrupt guffaw, his breath like the miasma above a compost heap.

"You'll give me a germ culture to turn my flesh into Edgar Allan Poe?" I pressed.

"It's over here," said Teague. "And maybe tomorrow you'll start typing my manuscript into your computer. Unless there's a complete rewrite."

"Fine," I said, sealing our deal. "Wonderful."

The twanking culture consisted of scuzzy crud on a layer of clear jelly in a Petri dish atop a dusty green *Collected Works* of Poe. Teage fit a cover onto the dish and handed it to me.

"I've got no use for this batch myself," he said. "I've got my mouth full enough with Burroughs."

I peered into the dish. Fuzzy white Cheerio-sized rings. Green and orange streaks. Spots, dots, and streamers.

"You only need a little at a time," Teage was saying. "Dig out a few grams of the culture with, like, a plastic coffee spoon, and smear it on. Careful where you put it, though. It takes hold wherever it touches. The tongue's especially good because it's so flexible."

Back in my room I brewed a pot of coffee and sat down to record these events on my laptop and on the cute little minidrive that I carry with it. I once lost a year's work on a Poe bibliography in a hard disk crash, and now I always make a point of saving off my work as I go.

It's calming to be lying here propped on the pillows of my bed, typing. It's a warm night; I'm nude. The yellow lamplight burnishes the tones of my flesh. I've been avoiding the sight of the Petri dish on my bed stand. But now it's time.

I poise the white plastic spoon over the culture. Rub that gunk on my tongue?

I think not.

For as soon as Teage told me the culture would alter whatever part of me it touched, I decided to use my penis.

So here we go. It stings more than I could have imagined. The sensation flutters into my loins and my solar plexus. My penis shifts and separates. A vertical break forms in the base, two flaps split off near the top.

What have I done, what have I done, what have I done?

I've twanked Eddie Poe into my penis.

He's angry, of all things. "What is the meaning of this conjuration?" cries Poe. "I abjure you to return me to my rest." He glances down and sees my belly, my pubic hair, my scrotum.

"Fie! Gaud, sodomite, ghoul, defiler of my grave!"

It's I who should be upset; I'm the one with the deformed, yelling penis. But the transformation is such that my cock seems to have a stronger personality than me. Nothing new, really. I'm in shock, and for a moment this seems almost funny.

But now it gets much worse. The little Poe penis knots his brow in fury, gathers his strength and—snaps himself loose from my belly. No, no, no!

Somewhere below the horror I think of a lighthouse with a hollow base breaking loose from brittle chalk.

There's a hole at my crotch. The hole is moving around, adjusting itself, becoming a vagina.

I catch hold of Eddie before he can run away and, screaming like a woman, I stampede bare-assed down the halls and up the stairs to Teage's room—not forgetting to bring my laptop. I must preserve every bit of this, at all costs.

For finally I have a story to tell.

Teage has drawn back his curtains and is standing by his open window, staring into the humid night. He turns to face me, Burroughs in his mouth again.

Bill calls a word to my Eddie: "*Tekelili.*" I recognize it from Poe's only novel, his tale of a sailing trip to the farthest South. Poe used *tekelili* to represent the cries of birds at Earth's nethermost frontier.

"*Tekelili,*" responds the figure in my hand. And now, vivified by the exchange, the little Poe grows hot to the touch, twists from my grasp, and buzzes through the room's air. An instant later he's flown out Teage's open window, blinking like a firefly, like a lighthouse. He pauses out there, waiting for us to come and follow.

A sharp pain knifes across my belly.

I brought the laptop in the car with me; Teage is driving, led by the darting light. I'm still naked. My pains come in rhythmic waves. I fear what comes next. But I keep writing, saving the file after every sentence.

We drive down Broadway and turn right on Baseline. The great triangular rocks of the Flatirons are gold in the waning moon.

Thick clear fluid seeps from my vagina. I'm giving birth.

In the middle of the field hovers glowing Eddie Poe. Between my wet thighs twitches a newborn sea-cucumber—a warty, foot-long creature with a fan of tendrils at one end—the very species found in Poe's novel of the great hole beyond the Antarctic walls of ice. The contractions continue. More life stirs in my womb.

The Burroughs thing watches quietly from within Teage's mouth. I force a mugwump out through my birth canal, then a centipede and a cuttlefish.

As they leave my body, the creatures crawl to Eddie's beacon, no two of them the same. Unknown energies pour from their tendrils, hands, mandibles, tentacles. The beams drill through Earth's thin crust, friable as a chalk tablet.

A glow is visible from the tunnel my children have made.

Teage has gone and I must follow. My body is changing, my mind can barely form the words to type. I'll end my manuscript and cast the minidrive clear.

And then, ah, then—raving, inchoate, my womb expelling an endless stream of life, I'll leap into the Hollow Earth.

Shambhala.

Note on "MS Found in a Minidrive"

Written in June, 2004.

Poe's Lighthouse, Chris Conlon, ed. (Cemetery Dance, 2006).

Since this story already has a hoax introduction, it's perhaps overkill to write another layer of annotation. But, hey, Edgar Allan Poe would.

In the summer of 2004, I went to Boulder, Colorado, to teach a one-week "Transreal Writing" course at the Naropa Institute. Transrealism is my term for the practice of basing fantastic tales on your real life—something I often do. I have more discussions of transrealism in my essay collection, *Seek!* (Four Walls Eight Windows, 1999) and on my writing page www.rudyrucker.com/writing.

I'd last been at Naropa in 1982, when I got to meet Allen Ginsburg and William Burroughs (but, no, I didn't spend the night with Burroughs). By way of illustrating my transreal writing technique to my students in 2004, I wrote "MS Found in a Minidrive" during the week I was teaching them. And, as so often seems to happen, my main character is a mad professor.

The theme of the story had already been defined by Chris Conlon, who was editing an anthology *Poe's Lighthouse* (Cemetery Dance, 2006) of stories all taking off on the same unfinished story fragment by Master Poe. You can find the complete text of the original "Lighthouse" fragment in Poe's online *Collected Works* at eapoe.org. I might mention, by the way, my friend John Shirley has a really terrific story, "Blind Eye," in that same *Poe's Lighthouse* anthology. John sticks to the straight Poe style and delivers a tale that's eerily like one of the master's.

The high point of my week at Naropa was a large group reading they had. I was on a bill with my favorite poet and dear friend Anselm Hollo, reading to a crowd of three hundred people. As my story was tailor-made for the Naropa audience, it fully blew their minds and they loved it. I was thrilled to be performing at this level in the home of the Beats; it was truly "a gala night within the lonesome latter years," as Poe touchingly puts it in his poem "The Conqueror Worm."

Guadalupe and Hieronymus Bosch

As an unemployed, overweight, unmarried, overeducated woman with a big mouth, I don't have a lot of credibility. But even if I was some perfect California Barbie it wouldn't be enough. People never want to listen to women.

I, Glenda Gomez, bring glad tidings. She that hath ears, let her hear.

An alien being has visited our world. Harna is, was, her name. I saw her as a glowing paramecium, a jellyfish, a glass police car, and a demonic art patron. This morning, when she was shaped like a car, I rode inside her to the fifteenth century. And this evening I walked past the vanishing point and saved our universe from Harna's collecting bag. I'm the queen of space and time. I'm trying to write up my story to pitch as a reality TV show.

Let's start with paramecia. Unicellular organisms became a hobby of mine a few months ago when I stole a microscope from my job. I was sorting egg and sperm cells for an infertility clinic called Smart Stork. Even though I don't have any kind of biology background they trained me.

I'm not dumb. I have a Bachelor's in Art History from San Jose State, which is just a few blocks from my apartment on Sixth Street. Well, almost a degree. I never finished the general education courses or my senior seminar, which would probably, certainly, have been on Hieronymus Bosch. I used to have a book of his pictures I looked at all the time—although today the book disappeared. At first I thought it was hidden under something. My apartment is a sty.

My lab job didn't last long—I'm definitely not the science type. I wasn't fast enough, I acted bored, I kissed the manager Dick Went after one too many lunchtime Coronas—and he fired me. That's when I bagged my scope—a binocular phase-contrast Leica. I carried it home in my ever ready XXL purse. Later that day Dick came to my apartment to ask about it, but I screamed through the door at him like a crazy person until he went away. Works on the landlord too.

Now that I have a microscope, I keep infusions of protozoan cultures in little jars all over my apartment. It's unbelievably easy to grow the infusions. You just put a wad of lawn grass in with some bottled water. Bacteria breed themselves into the trillions—rods and dots and corkscrews that I can see at 200x. And before you know it, the paramecia are right there digging on the bacilli. They come out of nowhere. What works really well is to add a scrap of meat to an infusion, it gets dark and pukeful, and the critters go wild for a few days till they die of their own shit. In the more decadent infusions you'll find a particular kind of very coarsely ciliated paramecium rolling and rushing around. My favorites. I call them the microhomies.

So today is a Sunday morning in March and I'm eating my usual breakfast of day-old bread with slices of welfare cheddar, flipping through my Bosch book thinking about my next tattoo. A friend named Sleepey is taking an online course in tattooing, and he said he'd give me one for free. He has a good flea-market tattoo-gun he traded a set of tires for. Who needs snow tires in San Jose? So I'm thinking it would be bitchin' to bedizen my belly with a Bosch.

I'm pretty well settled on this blue bagpipe bird with a horn for his nose. It'll be something to talk about, and the bagpipe will be like naturalistic on my *gordo* gut, maybe it'll minimize my girth. But the bird needs a background pattern. Over my fourth cup of microwave coffee, I start thinking about red blood cells, remembering from the lab how they're shaped. I begin digging on the concept of rounding out my Bosch bird tattoo with a blood-cell tiling.

To help visualize it, I pinprick my pinkie and put a droplet on a glass slide under my personal Glenda Gomez research scope. I see beautiful shades of orange and red from all my little blood cells massed together. Sleepey will need to see this in order to fully grasp what to do. I want to keep on looking, but the blood is drying fast. The cells are bursting and cracks are forming among them as they dry. I remember that at Smart Stork we'd put some juice on the slides with the cells to keep them perky. I don't know what kind of juice, but I decide to try a drop of water out of one of my infusions, a dark funky batch that I'd fed with a KFC chicken nugget.

The infusion water is teeming with those tough-looking paramecia with the coarse bristles—the microhomies. What with Bosch on my brain, the microhomies resemble tiny bagpipes on crutches. I'm like: Tattoo *them* onto my belly too? While I'm watching the microhomies, they start digging on my ruptured blood cells.

"Yo," I say, eyeing an especially bright and lively one. "You're eating me."

And that's when it happens. The image loses its focus, I feel a puff of air, my skin tingles all over. Leaning back, I see a bag of glowing light grow out from the microscope slide. It's a foot across.

I jump to my feet and back off. I may be heavy, but I'm quick. At first I have the idea my apartment is on fire, and then for some reason I think of earthquakes. I'm heading for the door.

But the glowing sack gets there before me, blocking the exit. I try to reach through it for the doorknob.

As soon as my hand is inside the lumpy glow I hear a woman's voice. "Glenda! Hello dear."

"Who are you?"

"I'm Harna from Hilbert space." She has a prim voice; I visualize flowery dresses and pillbox hats. "I happened upon your brane several—days—ago. I've been teeming with the microlife, a bit humdrum, and I thought that's all there is to see in this location. Worth documenting, but no more than that. I had no idea that only a few clicks up the size scale I'd find a gorgeous entity like you. Scale is tricky for me, what with everything in Hilbert space being infinite. Thank goodness I happened upon your blood cell. Oh, *warmest* greetings, Glenda Gomez. You're—why, you're collectible, my dear."

I'm fully buggin'. I run to the corner of my living-room, staring at the luminous paramecium the size of a dog in midair. "Go away," I say.

Harna wobbles into the shape of a jellyfish with dangling frilly ribbons. She drifts across the room, not quite touching the floor, dragging her oral arms across the stuff lying on my tables, checking things out. And then she gets to my Bosch book, which is open to *The Garden of Earthly Delights*.

"A nonlinear projection of three-space to two-space," burbles Harna, feeling the paper all over. "Such a clever map. Who's the author?"

"Hieronymus Bosch," I murmur. "It's called perspective." I'm half-wondering if my brain has popped and I'm alone here talking to myself. Maybe I'm about to start fingerpainting the floor with Clorox. Snorting Ajax up my nose.

"Bosch?" muses Harna. Her voice is fruity and penetrating like my old guidance counselor's. "And I just know you have a crush on him, Glenda! I can tell. When can I meet him?"

"He lived a long time ago," I whisper. I'm stepping from side to side, trying to find a clear path to the door.

"Most excellent," Harna is saying. "You'll time-snatch him, and then I can use the time-flaw to perspective-map your whole spacetime brane down into a sack! Yummy! You are so cute, Glenda. Yes, I'm going to wrap you up and take you home!"

I get past her and run out into the street. I'm breathing hard, still in my nightgown, now and then looking over my shoulder. So of course a San Jose police car pulls over and sounds me on their speaker. They think I'm a tweaker or a nut-job. Did I mention that it's Sunday morning?

"Ma'am. Can we help you? Ma'am. Please come over to the police car and place your hands on the hood. Ma'am." More cop-voice crackle in the background and here comes Harna down the sidewalk, still shaped like a flying jellyfish, though bigger than before. The cops can't see her, though.

"Ma'am." One of them gets out of the car, a kid with a cop mustache. He looks kind, concerned, but his hand is on the butt of his Tazer.

I whirl, every cop's image of a madwoman, pointing back down the sidewalk at the swollen Harna, who's shaping herself into a damn good replica of the cops' car. She's made of glowing haze and hanging at an angle to the ground.

Right before the cop grabs my wrist or Tasers me, Harna sweeps over and—pixie-dust! I'm riding in a Gummi-Bear cop car, with Harna talking to me from the radio grill. The cops don't see me any more. Harna heads down the street, then swerves off parallel to spacetime. She guns her mill and we're rumbling through a *wah-wah* collage of years and centuries, calendar leaves flying, the sun flickering off and on, Earth rushing around the Sun in a blur. And it's not just time we're traveling through, we're rolling through some miles as well. We arrive in the Lowlands of 1475.

It's a foggy dawn, Jerome Bosch is at his bedroom window, arcing a stream of pee toward the glow of the rising sun. I know from books that Hieronymus was just his fancy show name, and that his homies called him Jerome. Like my given name is Guadalupe—but everyone calls me Glenda. Seeing the man in the window, my heart does a little handstand. My love has guided us all this way.

"He *is* scrumptious," says Harna.

As he lowers his nightshirt, Jerome's gaze drifts away from the horizon—and he sees us. His expression is calm, resigned—it's like he's always been expecting a flying jellyfish/cop-car carrying a good-looking woman from the next millennium. Calm, yes, but he's moving back from the window hella fast.

Harna flips out a long vortex of force, a tornado that fastens onto Jerome and pulls him to us. He's hanging in the air a few feet away from me, slowly spinning—and yelling in what must be Dutch.

"Grab your fella," says Harna. "It has to be you who lands him. It's not for me to meddle in a brane's spacetime."

The wind has flopped Bosch's hair back. His cheekbones are high, his lips are thin, his eyes are bright. The man for me. I reach out and catch hold of his hand. It's warm.

Harna's light flows down my arm and up Jerome's. Augmented by Harna, I'm strong as a steam shovel. I set Bosch down on the jelly car seat next to me.

"It's too soon," he says, clear as day. "I'm not ready."

"I'm Glenda," I say, not all that surprised he's speaking English. Another Harna miracle. "Ready or not, I'm taking you home."

"To Hell?" exclaims Jerome. "That's quite unjust. Only yesterday I was absolved by the priest. My sins in these last hours have been but petty ones. A touch of anger at the neighbor's dog, my usual avarice for a truly great commission, and the accustomed fires of lust, of course—" As he mentions this last sin, he looks down my nightgown, which I'm just loving. I press his hand against my warm thigh.

"Don't worry, sweetie. I don't live in Hell. I live in San Jose."

For the rest of the ride, Jerome is busy looking around, taking everything in. What eyes he has! So sharp and smart and alert. What with the time-winds flapping my flimsy, he can see I'm all woman. I'm doing my best to keep the fabric cinched in around the problem areas at my waist, and I'm trying to get his arms around me, but he's kind of reluctant. He's uneasy about whither we're bound. I can dig it.

Finally Harna sets us down in the sunny street outside my apartment. Lucky me, the cops are gone. Everything looks the same—the dead palm leaves, the beater cars and pickups, the dusty jasmine vines, the broken glass on the dry clay, the 7-11 store, the university parking garage—sunny and dry.

Harna rises into the air and spreads out, layering herself across the scene like extra sunshine. No doubt she'll be back in some more personal form pretty soon. But meanwhile I've got me a man. I smile at Jerome and give his arm a happy squeeze.

"This is Spain?" he wonders.

"America," I tell him, which doesn't seem to ring a bell. "The new world across the Atlantic Ocean, plus some five centuries past your time."

He shakes his head, and stares around like a bird fallen from its nest. "It's after the Second Coming?" he asks. "Christ has dominion over the Earth?"

"The Church is doing fine," I say, not sure where this is going. We shouldn't stand around the street in our nightgowns. "Come on inside."

I hustle him up the stairs into my apartment and first of all get us in some clothes. I dress him in my favorite vintage red Ramones T-shirt and my yellow SJSU sweatpants. Me, I put on some nice tight Capri pants with a Lycra tummy panel and a pink baby-doll blouse that's loose at the bottom. Truth be told, I do a certain amount of my shopping in the maternity section at Target.

In the kitchen I offer Jerome some Oreos and microwave two cups of instant coffee. Buzz! The microwave is built into the wall so we delinquent renters can't hock it. Jerome overlooks the futuristic aspects of my kitchen because he's busy holding one of the cookies up to the light, studying the embossed writing and curlicues.

"They're food," I tell him. I rotate one in two and give him the better half. He scarfs it down—and I'm secretly glad, thinking that we've broken bread together now. Jerome takes another Oreo and eats the whole thing. They're gettin' good to him.

Meanwhile I touch up my black lipstick and lip liner. All the time I'm watching him. Even though he's from a long time ago, he's not old. Maybe twenty-five. He would have still been at the start of his career. No reason he can't have as good a career here in San Jose with me.

Jerome watches me right back. His gaze is warm and alive, as if there's an extra brain inside each eyeball. After a bit he fixates on my mug of colored pencils, looking at them the way I wish he was looking at my boobs.

"Want to draw?" I ask him. "You can decorate my walls." There's two smooth blank walls in my living room, a short wall across from the hall door and a big one across from the window.

"A mural?" says Jerome, examining a couple of the pencils.

"Bingo."

He starts in on the smaller wall. And me, I sit down with pen and paper at my round table on the one chair I've got. I want to try and start documenting some of this unfurling madness. For sure there's a reality TV show in this. All my friends say I should be on TV, and who am I to disagree. I recite a prayer to give me courage to write.

"Hail Glenda, full of grace, an alien paramecium was with thee. Blessed art thou amongst women, and blessed is the fruit of your brain, *Glenda and Jerome*."

I lean over my spiral notebook, pen in hand.

To whom it may concern: It may interest you to know that…

Is it Hie or Hei? Love has made me dyslexic.

I look around, trying to find the book that turned Harna on to Jerome, but I can't see it just now. Thinking about the book, I have to grin, thinking how incredible it is to have the artist himself here with me.

"Hey, Jerome. I'm writing about you."

"Not yet," he says and taps his thumb with his finger. Like that's the Lowlands chill-it gesture. He's holding a purple pencil in his other hand. Getting started on marking up my little wall. Holding the pencil gives him power, aplomb. He's a suspicious genius with sharp eyes and a trapdoor mouth. I keep talking to him.

"It's fabulous that you're drawing, Jerome. This hole will be an art grotto. I hope they don't paint it over when we move." And surely we will be moving quite soon, with Jerome pulling in the Old Master bucks. We'll be on TV. We'll get a condo in one of those beautiful new buildings across from the SJSU library on Fourth Street.

I smile at Jerome and fluff my hair a little. I wear it long and black with henna highlights and heavy bangs. Too bad I didn't happen to shampoo and condition it yet this week. I look sexier when my mane is lustrous.

Jerome thins his lips and shades the outstretched arms of a little man. He's digging on the excellent twenty-first-century quality of my pencils and the luscious smooth whiteness of apartment dry-wall. Sketching a picture of Harna and me snatching him. Harna looks like a fish as much as a car. She's surrounded by glow-lines of blue light. Her prey is just now seeing the shape in the sky, he's holding out his arms with that odd look of non-surprise. His unmade bachelor bed is in the far corner of his room. The vortex from the aeroform is gonna cartwheel him into the arms of a voluptuous dark-haired sorceress. Me!

"You're cute," I tell Jerome. He pinches the fingers of one hand at me again, the other hand busy with my pencils. He draws terrifically fast. I'm really glad I bagged him. But I wish he looked a little happier about it.

"Why don't we get to know each other better?" I say, imagining he might pick up on my tone. I unbutton my baby-doll blouse enough so he can see my boobs—but not the runaway rolls of my stomach. My breasts are a major plus, easily the equal of Pammy Anderson's. And they're natural.

But Jerome looks away. It occurs to me that maybe he still thinks this is Hell—which would make me a demoness. I decide to play up to that. I cackle at him and beckon with witchy fingers, the light glinting on my chipped black nails. My fingers are quite shapely, another plus feature. But they're not bringing Jerome Bosch into my arms.

So I go get him. He tries to escape, racing around the apartment like a sparrow that flew in the window. I shoo him into my bedroom and—*plop*—we're mixed in with the sheets, magazines, and laundry on my bed.

I give him a wet kiss and pull down my stretchy pants—keeping my top on so as to minimize that troublesome abdominal area. Of course I'm not wearing panties, I've been planning this all along. I tug down his sweatpants—and there's his goodies on display. A twenty-five-year-old fella here in bed with me, the answer to a maiden's prayer. I roll him on top of me and pull him in. It's been awhile.

But—just my luck—this turns into a totally screwed-up proposition. He comes, maybe, and then he's limp, and then—oh, God—he starts sobbing like his heart is going to break.

Poor Jerome. I cuddle him and whisper to him. His sobs slow down, he whimpers, he slides off to one side, and—falls asleep!

I feel down between my legs, trying to figure out if he delivered. What a thing it would be to carry Hieronymus Bosch's baby! That would tie him to me for sure. I think I'm ovulating today, as a matter of fact. Just for luck, I twist around and prop my feet up on the wall, giving the Dutch Master's wrigglers every opportunity to work their way up to the hidden jewel of my egg.

Resting there, thinking things over, I can visualize them, pointy-nosed with beating tails, talking to each other in Dutch, enjoying themselves in Glenda-land, on a pilgrimage to my Garden of Earthly Delights.

He keeps on sleeping, and I amble back into the kitchen to make myself a grilled cheese sandwich. I'm happy, but at the same time I have this bad feeling that Harna somehow tricked me. That stuff about wrapping me up and taking me home. Some weird shit is gonna come down, I just know it.

But now here comes Jerome out the bedroom, looking mellower than before. Our little hump and cuddle has helped his mind-set.

"Greetings, Glenda," he says. "I enjoyed our venery."

"Likewise." He looks so cute and inquisitive that I run over and kiss his cheek. And I can't help asking, "You don't think I'm too fat?"

"You're well fed," he says, cupping my boobs. "Clean and healthy. But do you worship Satan? Your spirit-familiar Harna—surely she is unholy."

"I don't know much about Harna," I admit. "She only appeared today. And Satan? Naw, dog. I'm a Catholic girl." Fallen away, I don't mention. I cross myself and he's relieved.

"I can go home?" he asks, glancing out the window at the quiet street in the noon sun.

"You belong with me," I tell him. "I'll give you a baby. You never had one back then. I love your art. You're mucho famous here, you know. I have a whole book of your pictures."

I root around the apartment, wanting to show him, but damn it, that book is totally gone. I'm guessing that Harna took it. She was saying something about copying Jerome's perspective maps so she can—fit our world into a sack? That has to be wack. If only she's gone for good. Maybe hoping hard enough can make it so. I skip over to Jerome and kiss him again. He lets me.

"I can't find my book, but we can go to the SJSU library," I tell him. "It's just across the campus and they're open on Sunday. And I think the Art Mart is open today too. I'll buy you some paint."

"Buy paint?" says Jerome. "I mix my own."

"We get it in tubes," I say. "Like sausage. Ready-made. Here, eat a grilled cheese sandwich , and then we'll look for Hieronymus Bosch books in the library."

Well, guess what we find under Bosch, Hieronymus, in the library? Not jack shit. When Harna and I abducted him from the fifteenth-century Dutch town of s'Hertogenbosch and carried him to twenty-first century San Jose, California, we wiped out his role in history. Maybe he finished one or two minor paintings before we nabbed him, but as far as the history of art is concerned, he never lived. Jerome doesn't really pick up on how weird this is—I mean all he's seen me do is look at an incomprehensible-to-a-medieval-mind online card catalog, and we nabbed him before he was famous anyway, so he's not feeling the loss. But me, I feel it bad.

Bosch was a really important artist, you know—or maybe you don't. Come to think of it, I might be the only one who remembers our world before I changed our history. But take it from me, Hieronymus Bosch was King. The Elvis of artists. His work influenced a lot of people in all kinds of ways over the centuries.

More ways than I'd imagined.

Because now, walking off the campus and getting a coffee, I'm paying attention and I'm noticing differences in our non-Bosch world. There aren't any ads for horror movies in the paper, for instance, which is way odd.

The Episcopal Church that used to be by the coffee shop is a pho noodle parlor. On a hunch, I look in the yellow pages in the coffee shop, and there's no Episcopal or Baptist or Proletarian or whatever churches in town at all. With no Bosch, the Protestant thing never happened! The sisters that whipped me through grade school would be happy, but I'm thinking, Dear God, what have I done?

The cars are different too, duller than before, as if Y2K cars could get duller. And every single one of them is cream colored, not even any silver or maroon.

The barrista in the coffee shop who usually wears foundation and drawn-on eyebrows has her face bare as a granola hippie's. And her hair is all bowl-cut and sensible. Ugh. The world is definitely lagging without the cumulative influences of my man Jerome.

On the plus side, you can smoke in the coffee shop now, and all the cigarettes are fat and laced with nutmeg and clove, which I dig. The Supertaqueria next door isn't selling tongue anymore, also fine by me. The fonts on the signs are somehow lower and fatter and more, like, Sanskrit-looking. The people in the magazine ads are wearing more clothes, and generally heavier.

Hey, I can live with some change, if that's what it takes to get Glenda her man.

I buy Jerome a canvas and some acrylics at the Art Mart—putting them on a new credit card that some pinheads mailed me last week. When we get back to my apartment, my Dutch Master sniffs suspiciously at the paint, then prepares to start layering the stuff over the colored drawing on my smaller wall.

There's a knock on the door. I've been expecting this. I peep through the peephole and it's Harna, looking just like her voice sounds, like a rich old white woman in a flowery dress and a pastel green pillbox hat covered with seed pearls. I don't want to let her in, but she walks right through the closed door.

"Hello, Glenda and Jerome," goes Harna. "I have a commission for the artist." She plumps a velvet sack right down on my kitchen table. Clink of gold coins. Perfectly calculated to get Jerome's juices flowing.

"What kind of painting do you need, my lady?" asks Jerome, setting down his paintbrush and making a greedy little bow.

"A picture of that," she says, pointing out the window to Sixth Street and the San Jose cityscape. "With full perspective accuracy. You can paint it—there." She points to my big blank living room wall.

"How soon would you need it?" asks Jerome.

"By sundown," says Harna.

"He can't paint that fast," I protest.

"I'll speed him up," says Harna, with a twitch of her dowager lips. "I'll return with the rising of the moon."

Sure enough, Jerome starts racing around the room like a cockroach does when the light comes on. He pauses only long enough to ask me to get him more paint.

When I come back from the Art Mart with a shopping bag of paint tubes, he's already roughed in an underpainting of the street—the houses with their tile and shingle roofs, the untrimmed palm trees, the dead dingy cars, the vines, a few passersby captured in motion, the tops of the houses in the next block, the houses after them, the low brown haze from the freeways, and beyond that the golden-grassed foothills and the blank blue sky.

He's all over the wall, and the painting is so perfect and beautiful I can hardly stand it. Every ten seconds, it seems like, he darts over to the window, then darts back. He's such a nut that he's putting in every single person and car that goes past, so the picture is getting more and more crowded.

The sun is going down and a few lights come on in the windows outside. Somehow Jerome is keeping up with it, changing his painting to match the world, touching the buildings with sunset gold, damping the shadows into warmer shades, pinkening the sky—and then darkening it.

A fat full moon comes up over the foothills and, quick as a knife, Jerome paints it onto my wall, sprinkling stars all around it.

And then Harna's in the room again.

"It's enough," she says. "He can stop."

Jerome cranks down to normal speed. I hand him more Oreos and coffee. He slugs down the nourishment, then drinks a quart of water from the sink.

"What happens now?" I ask Harna.

"Like I said before," she answers, not looking so much like a human anymore. Her pink skin is peeling away in patches, and underneath she's green. "I'm going to bag you and your world and take you home. Don't worry, it won't hurt."

And then she shoots out of the window and disappears into the distance past the moon.

"We have to stop her!" I tell Jerome, picking up my purse.

"What?" he says. He sounds tired.

"We have to run after Harna."

Jerome looks at me for a long time. And then he smiles. "If you say so, Glenda. Being with you is interesting."

The two of us run down the apartment stairs and right away I can see that things are seriously weird. The cars across the street are two-thirds as big as the cars on my side.

"Hurry," I tell Jerome, and we run around the corner to the next block. The houses on that next street are half the size of the houses on my street. We run another block, which takes only a couple of seconds, as each block is way smaller than the one before. The houses are only waist high. We go just a little farther and now we're stepping right over the houses, striding across a block at a time.

Another step takes us all the way across Route 101, the step after that across east San Jose. The further from Jerome's picture we get, the smaller things are.

"Perspective!" exclaims Jerome. "The world has shrunk to perspective!"

We hop over the foothills. And now it gets really crazy. With one last push of our legs, we leap past the moon. It's a pale yellow golf ball near our knees. We're launched into space, man. The stars rush past, all of them, denser and denser—*zow*—and then we're past everything, beyond the vanishing point, out at infinity.

Clear white light, firm as Jell-O, and you can stand wherever you like. Up where it's the brightest, I see a throne and a bearded man in it, just like in Jerome's paintings. It's God, with Jesus beside Him, and between them is the Dove, which I never did get. Right below the Trinity is my own Virgin of Guadalupe, with wiggly yellow lines all around her. And up above them all are my secret guardians, the Powerpuff Girls from my favorite Saturday morning cartoon. Jerome sees them too. We clasp hands. I know deep inside myself that now forever we two are married. I'm crying my head off.

But somebody jostles me, it's Harna right next to us, pushing and grunting, trying to wrestle our whole universe into a brown sack. She's the shape of a green Bosch-goblin with a slit mouth.

I turn off the waterworks and whack Harna up the side of the head with my purse. Jerome crouches down and butts her in the stomach. Passing the vanishing point has made us about as strong as our enemy, the demonic universe-collector. While she's reeling back, I quick get hold of her sack and shake its edges free of our stars.

Harna comes at me hot and heavy, with smells and electric shocks and thumps on my butt. Jerome goes toe-to-toe with her, shoving her around, but she's starting to hammer on his head pretty good. Just then I notice a brush and tubes of white and blue paint in my purse. I hand them to Jerome, and while I use some Extreme Wrestling moves from TV on Harna, Jerome quick paints a translucent blue sphere around her with a cross on top ¾ a spirit trap.

I shove the last free piece of Harna fully inside the ball and, presto, she's neutralized. With a hissing, farting sound she dwindles from our view, disappearing in a direction different from any that we can see. I wave one time to the Trinity, the Virgin, and the Powerpuff Girls, and, how awesome, they wave back. And then we're outta there.

The walk home is a little tricky—that first step in particular, where you go from infinity back into normal space, is a tough one. But we make it.

As soon as we're in my apartment, I help Jerome slap some house-paint over his big mural. And when we go outside to check on things, everything is back to being its own right size. We've saved our universe.

To celebrate, we get some Olde Antwerpen forty-ouncers at the 7-11 and hop onto my bed, cuddling together at one end leaning against the wall. I'm kind of hoping Jerome will want to get it on, but right now he seems a little tired. Not too tired to check out my boobs though.

Just when it might start to get interesting, here comes Harna's last gasp. I can't see her anymore, but I can hear her voice, and so can Jerome.

"Have it your way," intones the prissy universe-collector. "Keep your petty world. But the restoration must be in full. Before I leave for good, Hieronymus must go home."

"Think I'll stay here," says Jerome, who's holding a tit in one hand and a beer in the other.

"Back," says Harna, and her presence disappears for good.

As she leaves, the living breathing man next to me turns into—oh hell—an art book.

"No way," I sob. "I need him." I quick say the Hail Mary three times, like the sisters taught me. But the Bosch book just sits there. I pour some of the microhomies onto it. Nothing doing. I squeeze red paint onto the book cover and stick a split Oreo cookie to it. Still no good. And then in desperation, I pray to my special protectors, the Powerpuff Girls. And the day's last miracle begins.

The book twitches in my hands, throbs, splits in two, and the two copies move apart, making a, like, hyperdimensional man-hole.

And, yes, pushing his way out of the hole, here comes my Hiero-nymus Bosch, his hair flopping, his eyes sharp, his mouth thin with concentration.

He's in my bed—and the dumb book is gone. Screw art history. Jerome will make even better paintings than before. And if that doesn't work out, there's reality TV.

You know anybody who can help with my show?

Note on "Guadalupe and Hieronymus Bosch"

Written in April , 2004.
Interzone, October 2005.

I've always been fascinated by artistic representations of the Virgin of Guadalupe—she's usually drawn in the middle of a spiky oval halo. To me, that halo looks like an image you might find by zooming into the computer graphics fractal known as the Mandelbrot Set. Not that this image has much to do with the story.

The story was inspired, rather, by buying myself a good-quality microscope. On searching the web to find books about microscopy, I came across a delightful fly-ing-saucer tract that I ordered: Trevor James Constable, The Cosmic Pulse of Life: The Revolutionary Biological Power Behind UFOs (Borderland Sciences, Garberville, CA, 1990). Constable jovially argues that our atmosphere is filled with all-but-invisible giant "aeroforms," akin to jellyfish or protozoa. And, writes Constable, these home-grown "aliens" are what we're seeing when we see when we see UFOs.

I came up with the hard science idea for the story's conclusion while giving a lecture to my Advanced Com-puter Graphics class at San Jose State University. We were studying the mathematical projective transformation that is used to convert three-dimensional coordinates into locations upon a painter's canvas or, for that matter, upon a computer-game's view screen. It turns out that you can imagine forming the inverse of the projection transforma-tion, and that if you were to let this inverse transformation act upon your body, then you could indeed find yourself striding across houses and mountains, with the fabled Point At Infinity only a few more steps away. I explained all this to my students at the time—they enjoyed the rap, although of course they thought I was a mad professor.

One final inspiration for the story was my continu-ing desire to write about the great master Hieronymus Bosch. Having already written a historical novel about a Flemish painter—*As Above, So Below: A Novel of Peter*

Bruegel (2002), I'm tempted to write a tome about Bosch. "Guadalupe and Hieronymus Bosch" is a down payment on the dream.

By the way, Terry Bisson did me the favor of reading a draft of the story and making some good suggestions. After appearing in *Interzone*, the story also appeared in David Hartwell and Kathryn Cramer, *Year's Best SF 11* (Eos, 2006).

Printed in Great Britain
by Amazon

65476502R00363